THE YEAR'S BEST

Fantasy & Horror

Also Edited by Ellen Datlow

Blood Is Not Enough

A Whisper of Blood

Endangered Species

The Dark

With Terri Windling

THE ADULT FAIRY TALE SERIES

Snow White, Blood Red

Black Thorn, White Rose

Ruby Slippers, Golden Tears

Black Swan, White Raven

Silver Birch, Blood Moon

Black Heart, Ivory Bones

A Wolf at the Door

Sirens

The Green Man

The Year's Best Fantasy and Horror:
First through Sixteenth Annual Collections

Edited by Ellen Datlow and Kelly Link & Gavin J. Grant

The Year's Best Fantasy and Horror:
Eighteenth Annual Collection

Also by Kelly Link

Stranger Things Happen (collection)

Magic for Beginners (collection)

Trampoline (editor)

THE YEAR'S BEST

Fantasy & Horror

NINETEENTH ANNUAL COLLECTION

Edited by

Ellen Datlow and

Kelly Link & Gavin J. Grant

St. Martin's Griffin ✇ New York

www.stmartins.com

Summation Fantasy: 2005 copyright © 2006 by Kelly Link and Gavin J. Grant
Summation Horror: 2005 copyright © 2006 by Ellen Datlow
Fantasy and Horror in the Media: 2005 copyright © 2006 by Edward Bryant
Graphic Novels: 2005 copyright © 2006 by Charles Vess
Anime and Manga: 2005 copyright © by 2006 Joan D. Vinge
Music of the Fantastic: 2005 copyright © 2006 by Charles de Lint

ISBN-13: 978-0-312-35614-9 (pbk)
ISBN-10: 0-312-35614-5
ISBN-13: 978-0-312-35615-6 (hc)
ISBN-10: 0-312-35615-3

First Edition: August 2006

10 9 8 7 6 5 4 3 2 1

For Holly Link and Ross Grant

Contents

Acknowledgments

Thanks to the editors, publishers, publicists, authors, artists, and readers who sent us review material and suggestions, but most especially thanks to Terri Windling, Ellen Datlow, Jim Frenkel, Charles Brown and *Locus*, *Rain Taxi*, and *Publishers Weekly*.

We were grateful for the generous assistance of the following people: Diane Kelly, Jim Cambias, Deb Tomaselli, Jonathan Strahan, Elizabeth LaVelle, Mark & Cindy Ziesing and their essential catalog, Sean Melican, and interns Jedediah Berry and Gwyneth Merner.

Any omissions or mistakes are always, of course, our own.

Because we can only select from what we see, please submit or recommend published fantasy material to the address on this page: www.lcrw.net/yearsbest/

—G.G. & K.D.L.

Thanks to Harlan Ellison, William Smith, Stefan Dziemianowicz. Special thanks to Jim Frenkel, our hard-working packager, and his assistant, Melissa Faliveno, and interns Kevin Bennett, Bethany Billman, Emma Phillips, and Alan Rubsam.

And always, a very special thanks to Tom Canty for his unflagging visual imagination. Finally, thanks to my co-editors, Kelly Link and Gavin Grant.

I'd like to acknowledge the following magazines and catalogs for invaluable information and descriptions of material I was unable to obtain: *Locus*, *All Hallows*, *Publishers Weekly*, *Washington Post Book World* Web site, *The New York Times Book Review*, *Hellnotes*, *Darkecho*, *Prism* (the quarterly journal of Fantasy given with membership to the British Fantasy Society), and *All Hallows*. I'd also like to thank all the magazine editors who made sure I saw their magazines during the year and the publishers who got me review copies in a timely manner.

—E.D.

Thanks to our editors and contributors, and to my assistant, Melissa Faliveno, for this, her inaugural anthology, and our interns, Kevin Bennett, Bethany Billman, Emma Parry Phillips, Alan Rubsam, Merrill Hill, and Brianna Pintens. Thanks also to those who provided information for obituaries: *Locus*, Steven Silver, *Chronicle, the Guardian*, imdb.pro.

And very special thanks to my wife, Joan D. Vinge, for putting up with another Year's Best in a very difficult year.

Each year we do our best to correct old errors, and we know we'll make new ones.

—J.F.

Summation 2005: Fantasy

Kelly Link and Gavin J. Grant

Welcome to the summation of the year in fantasy for the nineteenth annual edition of *The Year's Best Fantasy and Horror*.

2005 was a very strong year for novels and collections, although there did not seem to be as many anthologies to recommend this year. Despite that, we found more than enough stories to fill our half of the Year's Best twice over.

We have again put this summary on a diet, in order to leave more space for fiction. But there are still a library's worth of good books out there that we will attempt to sum up in a small space.

Looking toward the future of the field, we were excited to learn about AboutSF (www.aboutsf.com), a "project of the University of Kansas, the Science Fiction and Fantasy Writers of America, and the Science Fiction Research Association, with generous support from Tor Books and several individual donors." AboutSF will eventually host a speakers' bureau, literature donations, and curriculum resources, as well as coordinating volunteer efforts. Also of interest, the Clarion Writers' Workshop became a nonprofit foundation. (Kelly is on the board). There are now a variety of genre-friendly workshops available to beginning writers, including Clarion West, in Seattle; Clarion South, in Australia; Odyssey, in New Hampshire; Viable Paradise, on Martha's Vineyard; and the Science Fiction Writers Workshop at the University of Kansas. Online there are Critters and the Online Writing Workshop, as well as a host of other workshops. Looking even further into the future, in 2005 the fourth annual ALPHA Science Fiction, Fantasy, and Horror Workshop for Young Writers (ages 14–19) was held in conjunction with the Confluence convention in Pittsburgh.

Each year we see more young adult fantasy, much of which should appeal to older readers. This year, as well, we saw an explosion in small press—oftentimes print-on-demand—anthologies. While there is excellent work showcased in some of these anthologies, we wonder if, in many of these efforts, there is any time or energy left over for marketing and distribution, after the work of editing and publishing. Unfortunately, marketing and distribution are crucial if readers are to find these books.

How people read books is, perhaps, at last beginning to shift. We don't yet have electronic books which offer the advantages that printed books do: affordability, portability, ease of use; nevertheless, e-books are slowly rising in popularity and usage.

In recent years, writers including John Scalzi, Cory Doctorow, and Charles Stross have offered their books online for free under the Creative Commons Copyright. This year, fantasy author Lawrence Watt-Evans experimented with alternative publishing strategies. As his series, "Legends of Ethshar" (eight novels so far) does not currently have a traditional publisher, Watt-Evans asked his readers to directly support his writing. Between April and October he received sufficient donations to publish the first draft of a new novel, *The Spriggan Mirror*, online. A revised version will be published this year, online at sonandfoe.com, and in print by FoxAcre Press. Young-adult fantasy author Diane Duane is now engaged in a similar project and we expect that in a couple of years this style of publication may become, if not popular, then at least not uncommon. Poet and short-story writer Bruce Holland Rogers offers a weekly short-story subscription by e-mail. If you enjoy an author's work, take a look online to see whether he or she keeps a blog, a livejournal account, or a Web site of some kind. You'll probably turn up something interesting.

Online access to book content continues to be a contentious issue as writers and publishers take up positions on Google.com's Book Search and Amazon.com's Search Inside feature. We can't help feeling that readers' access to scarce or out-of-print books is a good idea, especially when libraries are currently downsizing their collections. No online library will ever replace an actual library, but fortunately this isn't an either/or proposition.

Resources

Once again we recommend *Locus* magazine, Mark R. Kelly's *Locus Online*, and the *Locus Awards Database* (www.locusmag.com) for up-to-the-minute news, reviews, and more on the field. We recommend catalogs from both DreamHaven Books and Mark Ziesing Books, and Borderlands Books offers an excellent email newsletter. *The Speculative Literature Foundation* (www.speculativeliterature.org) has become an enormously useful site for readers and writers; the SLF administers the Fountain Award, an annual speculative short story prize. (See the Awards section for the 2005 winner and honorable mentions.) *Rain Taxi Review of Books* can be counted on for unusual and rewarding recommendations. *Books to Watch Out For* (www.btwof.com) is a new resource comprised of three subscription-based monthly e-mail newsletters (lesbian, gay, and women's books). All three include a healthy dollop of fantasy titles. *Prism*, the newsletter of the British Fantasy Society offers insight into the U.K. publishing scene. *Chronicle* offers reviews and news, although its schedule is irregular. Other recommended online resources include (and are obviously not limited to): *Ansible, The Alien Online, Green Man Review, the Internet Review of Science Fiction, New York Review of Science Fiction, Newpages, Revolution SF, Rambles, SF Site, Emerald City, Speculations,* and *Tangent*.

Disclosure: We are the editors and publishers of Small Beer Press, and the zine *Lady Churchill's Rosebud Wristlet*.

Favorite Books of 2005

Twentieth-Century Ghosts by Joe Hill (PS Publishing), was Kelly's favorite book this year. In fact, we haven't talked to a single reader who didn't love *Twentieth-Century Ghosts*. In this debut collection, which demonstrates a tremendous range, Hill tackles almost every mode available to a writer: ghost stories, horror, fantasy, historical, and contemporary realism, as well as one or two stories much more difficult to categorize or describe. "My Father's Mask" is reprinted within.

Lydia Millet's *Oh Pure and Radiant Heart* (Soft Skull Press) is an immersive modern fantasy of reincarnation, religious infatuation, and nuclear power. Three scientists, all of whom worked on the atom bomb, reappear in 2004; they latch onto a young couple (a gardener and a librarian). A cult of personality quickly builds around the scientists and just as quickly grows out of control. Millet's book offers darkly brilliant insights into characters both historical and fictional, as well as our societal fascination with power and those who wield it.

Luis Alberto Urrea worked on his second novel, *The Hummingbird's Daughter* (Little, Brown), for over a decade. It's a lyrical and substantial historical novel based on the story of Urrea's ancestress, Teresita, a woman whose inexplicable healing powers wreak political and personal havoc in prerevolutionary Mexico. This is a novel to luxuriate in and was one of Gavin's favorite books of the year.

Marvin Kaye put together an anthology of novellas, *The Fair Folk* (Science Fiction Book Club), including Kim Newman's "The Gypsies in the Wood," reprinted here. If we had more space we would have reprinted Patricia A. McKillip's "The Kelpie," as well. Megan Lindholm, and Jane Yolen and Midori Snyder also contributed strong stories, making this the best all-original short-fiction anthology we read this year.

Our other favorite anthology was a poetry anthology, *Chance of a Ghost: An Anthology of Contemporary Ghost Poems* (Helicon Nine) edited by Gloria Vando and Philip Miller, from which Willa Schneberg's poem within is taken. Over 150 poets contributed. *Chance of a Ghost* is strongly recommended to anyone who has an interest in poetry of the fantastic. (We also recommend Sean Wallace's new magazine, *Jabberwocky*. See Magazines.)

Paul Park's *A Princess of Roumania* (Tor) is the first in a series about a contemporary teenaged girl, Miranda, who lives an ordinary life in New England, only to discover her real history is actually very different from what she has always believed. The world, Miranda, and her friends undergo a series of startling transformations; Miranda must evade enemies and discover allies, both of whom are equally mysterious to her. Beautifully written, with a richly detailed setting, sympathetic characters, and a really fascinating villainess; fans of Joyce Ballou Gregorian's Tredana trilogy ought to enjoy *A Princess of Roumania*.

Patricia A. McKillip's long-overdue collection, *Harrowing the Dragon* (Ace), gathers together fifteen stories published between 1982 and 1999. World Fantasy Award–winner McKillip is better known for her elegant high-fantasy novels, but this collection of traditional and contemporary fantasy demonstrates that she is a master of the short-story form as well. Her novel, *Od Magic*, is also recommended.

Helen Oyeyemi's debut novel, *The Icarus Girl* (Doubleday), is the story of a young girl whose family returns, for a summer, to Nigeria. In Nigeria, and later, when she goes home to the United Kingdom, she makes an unsettling friendship with a prickly girl named TillyTilly whose motives and origin are obscure and whom no one else can see. There are a number of collisions here between Nigerian and British culture, between the secrets which adults and children keep from each other. Oyeyemi's prose, and her depiction of childhood are both haunting.

Caitlín R. Kiernan's *To Charles Fort, with Love* (Subterranean Press) is a lovely and evocative collection of dark fantasy and fantasy-tinged horror. As a writer, Kiernan has been compared to Lovecraft and Bradbury, but her work stands on its own. "La Peu Verte," which is original to the collection, is a small masterpiece. Highly

recommended, and one of Kelly's favorite collections of the year. With interior illustrations by Richard Kirk.

Cory Doctorow's *Someone Comes to Town, Someone Leaves Town* (Tor) is funny
and fantastic—equal parts horror novel and magic realism, fairytale and tech man-
ual on do-it-yourself free, metropolitan wireless Internet. The novel centers on Alan,
whose father was a mountain. His mother was a washing machine, and this kind of
surreal recombination is typical of the delights within Doctorow's book, which,
thankfully, never devolves into whimsy. The wonderful sense of strangeness and the
characters—Alan, squatters, a neighbor who routinely amputates her own wings,
outsiders all—who populate Doctorow's first fantasy novel, made this one of Kelly's
favorite novels this year.

Julia Slavin's first novel pokes fun at politics, entertainment, and politics-as-
entertainment in a near-future U.S.A. Like many of the books on the list this year,
Carnivore Diet (Norton) is difficult to sum up—there is the pleasure of Slavin's sly
caricatures, nimble prose, and the plot, which involves the urban and suburban pre-
dations of a mythical, carnivorous beast. Absurd, bold, and painfully on-target,
Slavin's fiction belongs on the shelf beside Vonnegut, George Saunders, and Carol
Emshwiller. Slavin is also the author of the often-surreal collection, *The Woman
Who Cut Off Her Leg at the Maidstone Club and Other Stories*.

Haruki Murakami's might-as-well-be-trademarked blend of the surreal, the metaphysical, the philosophical, and the pop-cultural makes *Kafka on the Shore* (Knopf)
a satisfying if slippery book. One of the most high-profile fantastic novels of the year,
it offers a man who talks to cats (and collects their souls), ghosts, veterans of WWII,
and a runaway boy whose name is Kafka. Murakami's prose is so lucid, so deft that
even the most grotesque incidents have a certain dreamlike and anaesthetized texture.

Holly Black and Tony DiTerlizzi's *Arthur Spiderwick's Field Guide to the Fantastical World Around You* (Simon & Schuster) is the kind of coffee-table book that
makes *having* a coffee table seem like a good idea. Beautifully packaged, lavishly illustrated, and crammed with bits of faerie lore and mythological arcana, this project
looks as if Audubon and Lady Gregory had collaborated on a book of fantastical
creatures. Black's text and DiTerlizzi's art will appeal to both children and adult fans
of fantasy.

Salvador Plascencia's debut novel *The People of Paper* (McSweeney's) upsets
every sensible boundary or division between reader, author, and book-as-object.
Even the imaginative layout suggests the fantastic and the odd. *The People of Paper*
begins with an act of origami surgery, performed on a cat, whose organs are successfully replaced with paper constructions. It only gets stranger from there, as Plascencia and his characters tell a story; stop, and tell it again. Visually arresting cutouts in
the pages signal word gaps and loss as the story progresses—the characters are at war
with their author, but in the end, it is the reader, presented with this beautiful and
inventive novel, who wins.

Neil Gaiman's *Anansi Boys* (Morrow) is something of a change of pace, after his
bestseller, *American Gods*. Fat Charlie discovers that his recently deceased father
was somewhat larger than life, as well as the existence of a twin brother, Spider.
There are some lovely screwball scenes in *Anansi Boys*, and there are also some
rather dark bits involving a serial killer, which make this novel something rather
more unusual than most novels about dysfunctional trickster-god families. Along the
way, Gaiman retells traditional Anansi stories. Of note: British comic Lenny Henry
reads the audiobook edition.

Elizabeth Knox's *The Rainbow Opera* (Faber) is the first of The Dreamhunter Duet series (*Dreamhunter* in Australia). In this novel, which is being marketed as young adult, the children of famous dreamhunters, cousins Laura and Rose are expected to follow the family trade and learn to enter a territory known as The Place. Dreamhunters bring dreams back to our world from The Place, for entertainment as well as for more sinister purposes. Knox (*The Vintner's Luck*) has long been one of our favorite authors, and her latest novel will appeal to adults as well as younger readers. Knox is a compelling storyteller, and there is a strong political undercurrent to her work. Readers should be advised that *The Rainbow Opera* ends on something of a cliffhanger.

An Edgar Award–winner and well received by fantasy readers, Jeffrey Ford's *The Girl in the Glass* (Dark Alley) ought to become his breakout book. It's a lovely romp—a ghost story and also a mystery, complete with bloodcurdling murders, chatty oddball characters, and a glass room full of butterflies—which ends up being, at heart, about the kinds of families that we choose for ourselves. Set in the 1930s on Long Island, Ford's narrative introduces con artists, genetics, seances, a ghost, and the Ku Klux Klan into what is nevertheless a compact, accessible, lyrical, coming-of-age novel.

Traditional and Epic Fantasy

The highly anticipated fourth volume in George R.R. Martin's Song of Ice and Fire series, *A Feast for Crows* (Bantam Spectra) is a doorstopper of a book. It's also only half the novel that Martin was planning to write. Fans of epic fantasy should begin at the beginning of Martin's series, not here, but Martin's strengths—three-dimensional characters, intrigue, gritty battle scenes, fantasy in which magic and worldly power have consequences and weight—are on display here as usual. M. John Harrison's *Viriconium* (Bantam Spectra) collects Harrison's classic tales of the imagined eponymous city. Harrison is a master prose stylist, and readers are strongly encouraged to pick up a copy. Lois McMaster Bujold's *The Hallowed Hunt* (Eos) is the third novel of her award-winning Chalion series. While these novels can stand on their own, we don't recommend starting here. Tor published two volumes of Steven Erikson's epic ten-novel Malazan Book of the Fallen cycle, *Deadhouse Gates* and *Memories of Ice*, catching up with Erikson's U.K. publisher. Night Shade Books also reprinted two Erikson titles, *The Healthy Dead* and *Blood Follows*. Ian Cameron Esslemont, who helped Erikson create the Malazan world, published a Malazan companion novella, *Night of Knives* (PS). PS Publishing also published Erikson's novella *Fishin' with Grandma Matchie*. Lisa Goldstein's second book as Isobel Glass, *The Divided Crown* (Tor), is set fifteen years after *Daughter of Exile* (although you don't have to read the first to enjoy the second). We recommend it to fans of epic fantasy. Michael Moorcock's *The White Wolf's Son* (Warner) continues the saga of Elric. *Shaman's Crossing* (Eos) is the first in the Soldier Son trilogy from Robin Hobb. Hobb's are deep, political, humanist fantasies which we highly recommend. Charles Stross's *The Hidden Family* (Tor) is the second episode in The Merchant Families series.

Also of note: Hope Mirlees's classic British pastoral fantasy of faery, *Lud-in-the-Mist* (Cold Spring), is back in print once more, with an introduction by Neil Gaiman. Children's author Ellen Steiber has now published a novel for adults, *A Rumor of Gems* (Tor), centered around magic-infused jewelry. Glen Cook began a new series, The Instrumentalities of the Night, with *The Tyranny of Night*; Del Rey's

Robert E. Howard reprint series is engaged in reprinting the earlier illustrated Wandering Star limited editions. This year saw *Bran Mak Morn: The Last King, The Conquering Sword of Conan* (illustrated by Gregory Manchess), and *The Coming of Conan the Cimmerian* (illustrated by Mark Schultz), which will please readers to whom these stories have long been unavailable. Holly Lisle's *Talyn* (Tor) is a thoughtful look at what happens to a society long at war when peace is forced upon them. *Mists of Everness* (Tor) by John C. Wright is an Arthurian-infused (and almost every other myth or legend you might think of) sequel to *The Last Guardian of Everness*. Wright's second book of the year, *Orphans of Chaos* (Tor), is the first in a new series, Chronicles of Chaos, about five students in a boarding school. Neither the teenagers nor the school are what they seem, and although the novel might have appealed to a younger audience, there are tinges of S&M which render it adult reading. Storm Constantine completed Michael Moorcock's unfinished tale of the multiverse, *Silverheart* (Pyr). Cecilia Dart-Thornton embarked on a new series, The Crowthistle Chronicles, with *The Iron Tree* (Tor), while fans of Jacqueline Carey should look for the second novel in her The Sundering series, *Godslayer* (Tor).

Small Beer Press reprinted Naomi Mitchison's classic fantasy *Travel Light*.

Contemporary and Urban Fantasy

John Crowley's *Lord Byron's Novel: The Evening Land* (Morrow) braids together Byron's missing novel; notations on the novel by Ada Lovelace, Byron's mathematician daughter; and the e-mail correspondence of a contemporary researcher who has reasons to be interested in both Ada and her father. The reader has the pleasure of reading not only Crowley, but Byron-as-written-by-Crowley. Highly recommended.

In Lisa Tuttle's dark fantasy *The Mysteries* (Bantam), Ian Kennedy investigates a series of seemingly supernatural disappearances. Tuttle deserves a far wider audience, and this is a particularly fine atmospheric novel, which draws on stories of the sidhe and Celtic folklore. We recommend this.

Graham Joyce's *The Limits of Enchantment* (Atria) takes place in England during the 1960s, and concerns the clash between folk medicine (and magic) and rationality. Fern is the adopted daughter of a healer whose work is cast into doubt when one of her patients dies. Joyce is the author of a number of gorgeously written recent novels in which the real world and the fantastic are handled sympathetically, deftly, plausibly. Set in the years of Graham's own childhood, the autobiographical elements lend the novel a warmth of characterization and setting.

Paul Witcover's *Tumbling After* (Eos) is, like many of the books we saw this year, a hybrid work—in this case, a fantasy and science fiction novel set in a world that evokes both a Dungeons & Dragons–style game, and the 1970s. The narratives lead toward an ambiguous and somewhat dark end. Jonathan Carroll's *Glass Soup* (Tor), is, as always for Carroll, an evocatively named, contemporary fantasy of the sort that nobody else could have written. It's also a follow-up to the novel *White Apples*, and as usual, Carroll's strengths are on display here: situations that are nightmarish or dreamlike and yet somehow true to life; characters who, when they talk, manage to read like the best conversation you've ever eavesdropped on. Someone really ought to film one of Carroll's novels or better yet, make a television series from them. *Snake Agent* (Night Shade) looks to be the first in a new science fiction/fantasy crossover series for British author Liz Williams. Inspector Chen is the eponymous hero who has to break a "ghost smuggling" ring as well as keep a plague from breaking out. In a change of pace from her usual novels, Jane Lindskold's beautifully written *Child of a Rainless Year* (Tor) is the impressionistic and engrossing tale of a young artist, Mira, who comes back to the house of her childhood in New Mexico, a house with many mirrors and mysteries. Full of color, both local and otherwise: we recommend it to both mainstream and fantasy readers. Marjorie M. Liu's debut novel, *Tiger Eye* (Love Spell), is a paranormal romance of shapeshifters in China. James A. Hetley's *Dragon's Eye* (Ace) is a fast-paced story of magic users and smugglers in Maine. Steve Cash's *The Meq* (Del Rey) is the first in a series which will center on American secret histories. In Orson Scott Card's *Magic Street* (Del Rey) a war between the king and queen of fairies bleeds into present day Los Angeles. Also of note: Carrie Vaughn's strongly recommended anthropological/chick lit/dark fantasy comedy about a radio show host who also runs with a pack of werewolves, *Kitty in the Midnight Hour* (Warner Aspect); Bryn Llewellyn's urban noir, *The Rat and the Serpent* (Prime); Michael Bergey's amusing tale of trickster-figure Coyote reborn in present-day Seattle, *New Coyote* (Five Star).

Historical, Alternate History, and Arthurian Fantasy

Gregory Feeley's *Arabian Wine* (Temporary Culture) expands the novella of the same title, originally published in *Asimov's*. Feeley is always an interesting writer, and this alternate history, the story of the introduction of coffee and steam engines to Venice at the start of the seventeenth century, is intelligent and engagingly written. *Arabian Wine* is the second book from Henry Wessel's Temporary Culture press (named after his extinct zine) and this is a handsome-looking book as well as a good one.

Jeffrey Ford's *The Cosmology of the Wider World* (PS) recounts the story of Belius the minotaur who has retreated to finish his book, *The Cosmology*, as well as a philosophical treatise on one's place in the world. Ford is a master of detailed, emotionally complex and highly surreal fiction, and we recommend this novella.

Although Alexander C. Irvine's *The Narrows* (Del Rey) is best described as an alternate historical thriller, the heart of the book is in the note-perfect characterization of Jared Cleaves, a blue-collar worker in Henry Ford's golem factory in World War II–era Detroit, and in the details of the factory work. Irvine's golems are somber, magically mass-manufactured figures, and Irvine seamlessly welds together actual history, conspiracy theories, riots, and African American and Jewish folklore. Highly recommended.

Rick Bowes's *From the Files of the Time Rangers* (Golden Gryphon) is in the same vein as Kage Baker's Company fiction, blending mythology with science fiction, and centered on strongly appealing characters. This is a heart-of-genre mosaic novel, incorporating stories Bowes published in *F&SF*, on SCI FICTION and elsewhere. Highly recommended.

Political speechwriter and novelist Mark Helprin's massive satirical novel, *Freddy and Fredericka* (Penguin), takes some entertaining political potshots at the English monarchy, royal families, and the media. Helprin's humor won't be for everyone, but there is an enjoyable secret/alternate history that runs through the novel. Ian R. MacLeod's *The House of Storms* (Ace) continues his beguiling sequence of alternate English historical steampunk fantasies (following *The Light Ages*). MacLeod's second novel of last year, *The Summer Isles* (Aio Publishing), is also an alternate history of England in the 1930s, wherein Great Britain has lost World War I and turned to fascism. This is the first title from Aio, a new press. We wish them luck and encourage readers to seek out MacLeod's work. Mary Gentle's *A Sundial in a Grave: 1610*

(Perennial) is a somewhat revised edition of the British book of the same name, concerning a secret history of science, astrology, and religion in seventeenth century England. Judith Tarr's hugely enjoyable second historical fantasy about William the Conqueror, his descendants, and the clash between Saxon Christianity and British magic, is *King's Blood* (Roc). Also of note: Luis Alberto Urrea's *The Hummingbird's Daughter* (Little, Brown); Penelope Lively's anti-memoir *Making It Up* (Viking) in which she imagines how her own life might have gone differently; Gwyneth Jones's excellent fourth novel in the "Bold as Love" sequence, *Band of Gypsies* (Gollancz), which features rock stars, political demagogues, and an Arthurian underpinning; Cecilia Holland's third ninth-century tale, *The Serpent Dreamer* (Forge); Barbara Hambly's second Egyptian-flavored novel, *Circle of the Moon* (Warner Aspect); Diana Gabaldon's sixth Outlander novel, *A Breath of Snow and Ashes* (Delacorte); Paul Kearney's unsentimental first novel in The Sea Beggars trilogy, *The Mark of Ran* (Bantam Spectra); Manda Scott's third novel of four in the Boudica series, *Dreaming the Hound* (Delacorte); and Alan Massie's *Arthur the King* (Carroll and Graf).

Humorous Fantasy

In Terry Pratchett's latest Discworld novel *Thud!* (HarperCollins), we get a fantasy novel about chess, race relations (especially between dwarves and trolls), and demagoguery. Pratchett seems ever more interested in how and why a society goes to war, and in the ways in which war narratives are used by politicians and others for public and private gain. Very few writers can handle this material as deftly as Pratchett. Reading the Discworld novels is always a bit like eating a delicious and expertly prepared souffle and discovering that somehow, in the process, you've learned something useful about life. Delicious *and* filling *and* nutritious. Peter Cannon's *The Lovecraft Chronicles* (Mythos Books) is either a work of deep scholarship or a hilarious mock autobiography of H.P. Lovecraft. Either way, it's enjoyable. And informative! Complicated and full of genre in-jokes, Steve Aylett's novel *Lint* (Thunder's Mouth) is a biography of invented pulp science-fiction-and-fantasy writer Jeff Lint.

Fantasy in the Mainstream

Susan Cokal's historical novel, *Breath and Bones*, is a voluptuous, Angela Carter–like, first-person, historical novel in which a consumptive artist's model travels from Denmark to the American west in search of a pre-Raphaelite painter. Kelly enjoyed this book a great deal; astute readers will appreciate how Cokal structures her novel around the fairytales of Hans Christian Andersen. Strictly speaking, there's no fantasy element, and yet this novel has the feel of a bawdy fairytale.

Gregory Maguire's revisionary novel of Oz, *Wicked,* is now an award-winning and much-loved Broadway musical. *Son of a Witch* (ReganBooks) is the beautifully written sequel which picks up with the story of both Oz, and Elphaba's son, Liir. Compulsively readable, thanks to Maguire's elegant prose and insights into character, and the nature of fantastic literature, this novel can stand comfortably on its own, although we recommend starting with the wonderful *Wicked*.

Highly recommended, Hilary Mantel's *Beyond Black* (Holt) is a darkly brilliant novel of both life and the afterlife. Peter Sís illustrates Jorge Luis Borges's *The Book of Imaginary Beings* (Viking, translated by Andrew Hurley). Walter Moers's illustrated fable *The 13½ Lives of Captain Bluebear* (Overlook, translated by John

Brownjohn) is told by the eponymous bear at the halfway point of his twenty-seven-lived life. George Saunders offers an enjoyable and surreal political fable, *The Brief and Frightening Reign of Phil* (Riverhead), which feels equally inspired by Dr. Seuss, Franz Kafka, and Edwin A. Abbott's *Flatland*. In his captivating debut, *Tokyo Canceled* (Black Cat) Rana Dasgupta takes a page from Boccaccio's *The Decameron* and *The Arabian Nights*, telling the stories of thirteen passengers whose plane has been grounded because of bad weather. *John Crow's Devil* by Marlon James (Akashic) draws on the Jamaican spirit world and postcolonial angst to tell the story of a struggle for the soul of a Jamaican village. Ghosts, religion, prying neighbors and dueling preachers make for a spirited (no pun intended), sensual, satisfying debut novel. *The Whale Caller* (FSG), Zakes Mda's fifth novel, is about a man in Hermanus, South Africa, who can communicate with whales but who, despite the depth of his feelings, can never do anything more. Mda uses the whales (and the town drunk!) to write about frustrated love, love across barriers, and the compromises that love insists upon. Jeffrey Lewis's sequel to *Meritocracy*, *The Conference of the Birds* (Other), speculates about what people would do after the death of their god. Two novels set in lighthouses which are worlds apart: Jeanette Winterson's fable *Lighthousekeeping* (Harcourt), and *Cold Skin* (FSG) by Albert Sánchez Piñol. We recommend *Lighthousekeeping*, although fans of darker fare may appreciate *Cold Skin*.

First Novels

Vellum: The Book of All Hours (Macmillan, U.K.) is the first novel in Hal Duncan's sprawling fantasy/science fiction series. Duncan reworks creation myths, legends, plays, and poetry into a postmodern mythology of his own creation. The book is centered on the Vellum, which includes all possible worlds, and Duncan channels multiple plot strands and archetypal characters caught up in a war between Heaven and Hell; Duncan's prose is dense and allusive, but far from impenetrable. This is ambitious, genre-expanding work which ought to find a wide readership.

Judith Berman's *Bear Daughter* (Ace) is the story of Cloud, a changeling girl who threatens the reign of the immortal Lord Stink. Berman was trained as an anthropologist, and *Bear Daughter* draws on Native American myths. It has the shape of a fairytale; Berman's writing is earthy, matter of fact, and yet also quite beautiful. This is a coming-of-age novel of transformation and magic which ought to find an audience of both younger and older readers. Highly recommended.

Fly by Night (Macmillan) by Frances Hardinge is an inventive young adult novel in which an orphan girl and her bad-tempered goose become involved in revolution and political upheaval. Like Joan Aiken's Dido Twite series, this debut takes place in a somewhat-altered Britain, and like the work of Joan Aiken, this novel ought to charm anyone who is fond of books, cantankerous birds, or plucky young orphans. Recommended to both younger and older readers.

Sarah Monette's *Melusine* (Ace) is the first novel of a four-book series; it's packed with baroque courtly politics, magic, and complicated gender and sexual dynamics. Like writers Dorothy Dunnett and Ellen Kushner, Monette has a flair for prose, for intrigue, and for writing tortured characters who end up wielding power against their own will.

In Charles Coleman Finlay's debut novel, *The Prodigal Troll* (Pyr) Maggot, or Claye, who has been brought up by trolls, must search for his place in the world. His somewhat episodic (and quixotic) quest is an opportunity for Finlay to showcase his considerable worldbuilding skills. Finlay is a gifted short-story writer and an equally gifted novelist.

Zahrah the Windseeker by Nnedi Okarafor-Mbachu (Houghton Mifflin) is a young-adult crossover novel of African-sourced science fiction/fantasy, which recounts the coming-of-age story of a young girl who must discover how to use her powers.

In Dean Bakopoulis's literary novel, *Please Don't Come Back from the Moon* (Harcourt), a number of fathers disappear. The children left behind believe their fathers have gone to the moon. Bakopoulis never explores what this means, nor the mechanism; instead he follows the lives of the chronically depressed Michael and his friends as they deal with their loss.

Tim Pratt's gonzo Western fantasy, *The Strange Adventures of Rangergirl* (Bantam Spectra) is an inventive coffeeshop-of-horrors novel in which Marzi, a comics artist and barista, must use her art to battle her own creations and save California. Pratt is a short story writer whose "Hart and Boot" was reprinted last year in *Best American Short Stories*; this is a promising and energetic debut novel.

Adam Stemple digs into his own experience as a musician for his debut fantasy novel *Singer of Souls* (Tor). This is a gritty story of music, addiction, and the faery realm, with a likeable Zelazny-esque antihero.

Also of note: Cherie Priest's extremely enjoyable contemporary gothic *Four and Twenty Blackbirds* (Tor), which leaves plenty of room for a sequel; Brandon Sanderson's stand-alone tale of a country where the magic has failed, *Elantris* (Tor); Maria V. Snyder's romantic fantasy *Poison Study* (Luna); an expanded edition of Jeff VanderMeer's cross-genre *Veniss Underground* (Bantam Spectra) which included four extra stories set in the world of the novel; *Spotted Lily* (Prime) by promising Australian writer Anna Tambour, a playful, Rabelaisian, deal-with-the-devil story.

Poetry

Again, we recommend the anthology *Chance of a Ghost: An Anthology of Contemporary Ghost Poems* (Helicon Nine). We enjoyed Kelly Everding's poetry chapbook *Strappado for the Devil* (Etherdome). Her poem "Omens" is reprinted in this anthology. Catherynne M. Valente's *Oracles: A Pilgrimage* (Prime) was hypnotic, sardonic, and knowing. Jeannine Hall Gailey's *Female Comic Book Superheroes* (Pudding House Publications) is a collection of funny and opinionated spins and retellings of the eponymous heroes and their complicated lives. Anne Sheldon's *The Adventures of the Faithful Counselor* (Aqueduct) is a retelling of the epic of Inanna based on Diane Wolkstein and Samuel Noah Kramer's *Inanna, Queen of Heaven* (Harper & Row) from the point of view of Ninshubur, the faithful counselor.

The Science Fiction Poetry Association and Dark Regions Press publish *The Rhysling Anthology* each year to encourage readers to read speculative fiction poetry, to join the association, and to vote for the award. There were three issues of *The Magazine of Speculative Poetry*, which is perhaps the most wide-ranging of the poetry-specific zines. Sean Wallace's new magazine, *Jabberwocky*, is highly recommended to anyone who is curious about poetry which uses fantasy or slipstream tropes. It included work by Sonya Taaffe, Theodora Goss, Catherynne M. Valente, Jane Yolen, and others. Other magazines: *Jubilat*, *Dreams and Nightmares*, *Star*Line: The Journal of the Science Fiction Poetry Association*, *Mythic Delirium*, and many of the literary journals noted in the magazine section. Also of note: from Ireland, John W. Sexton's *Vortex* (Doghouse).

More from Elsewhere

Fans of short story master Andy Duncan will want to look for *Alabama Curiosities: Quirky Characters, Roadside Oddities, and Other Offbeat Stuff* (Globe Pequot). Although this is a nonfiction travel book, it's also—perhaps unsurprisingly, given the author—a page-turner; there are enough monsters, ghosts, aliens, and stories in here to satisfy any genre reader. And Duncan's prose goes down like neat whiskey. Highly recommended to anyone who's ever stopped on a road trip to visit a large ball of string. Also recommended to travelers who've so far managed to resist roadside attractions of dubious merit: you won't find them so easy to resist, next time around.

Mecca 1 Mettle is the debut title from indie press Payseur & Schmidt. Illustrated by Tim Kirk, it's a strange, boundary-enlarging collection of fiction from Thomas M. Disch as well as pastiches from others. Accompanied by a CD with music by BlöödHag as well as X's for Eyes, and Thomas M. Disch.

Although the stories are mostly science fiction, readers of this anthology will want to look out for Night Shade Press's reprints of Manly Wade Wellman's *Strangers on the Heights* (ESP and cults) and *Giants from Eternity* (meteorites and a plague).

C.J. Henderson, an author who has previously worked within the Cthulhu Mythos, expands the career of H.P. Lovecraft's detective from "The Call of Cthulhu" by seven stories (or cases), in *The Tales of Inspector LeGrasse* (Mythos Books).

Children's/Teen/Young Adult Fantasy

In addition to Elizabeth Knox's *The Rainbow Opera*, Frances Hardinge's *Fly by Night*, and *Zahrah the Windseeker* by Nnedi Okarafor-Mbachu, we recommend the following books.

Carol Emshwiller's *Mister Boots* (Viking) is a spare and magical novel which encompasses childhood, the Great Depression, and the multitude of identities each person contains. Bobbie is a girl dressed as a boy; Mr. Boots is a horse who is also a man. When Bobbie's mother dies, her stage-magician father returns to look after, and use, his daughters. Emshwiller writes beautifully of the West and childhood. Highly recommended.

Valiant (Simon & Schuster), is Holly Black's follow-up to her excellent debut novel *Tithe*. Like her first young-adult novel, it's a fast-paced and enormously enjoyable novel about the interaction of the mortal world and the fairy world. There's an unlikely but wonderful love story in here, and an irresistible setting: New York City's subways, including abandoned stations and tunnels where young runaways establish a den. Highly recommended to readers both young and old.

The late Joan Aiken's last Wolves of Willoughby Chase novel is *The Witch of Clatteringshaws* (Delacorte). As usual, it rattles along at high pace as Dido Twite attempts to help her friend, Simon, get out of a job he hates: being King of England. We recommend beginning with Aiken's first Dido Twite novel, *The Wolves of Willoughby Chase*, rather than here. Aiken is a much beloved writer, and if you haven't tried her alternate histories, well, fortunately they're still in print.

A Certain Slant of Light (Houghton Mifflin), by Laura Whitcomb, is a gentle, lovely fantasy about a young woman who, since her death, has clung to the living. The novel moves between a contemporary high school setting and the narrator's past; the resolution is both romantic and satisfying.

Jean Thesman's *Singer* (Viking), based on the Irish folktale "The Children of Lir," follows the struggle between Gwenore and her mother, Rhiannon, a witch with an unquenchable thirst for power. In Thesman's medieval England, not all women are trapped in secondary roles, but neither does she pretend that life was easy. *Singer* is an enjoyable, multifaceted novel that may encourage readers to read more deeply into the history of the fantastic.

Justine Larbalestier's debut novel *Magic or Madness* (Razorbill) is the first of a lively bicontinental trilogy in which Reason Cansino must come to terms with a family legacy of magic, insanity, and early death. The characters here are engaging, and Larbalestier, an Australian who spends some of each year in the States, builds the narrative around a door which allows Reason to tumble from summery Australia into wintery New York City. This is a page turner, and it ends on something of a cliffhanger. Readers (adults as well as young adults) will be glad to know that the sequel is already out.

Touching Darkness (Eos) is the middle novel in Scott Westerfeld's Midnighters trilogy about the five teenagers in Bixby, Oklahoma, to whom the twenty-fifth hour of each day belongs. This is an inventive and enjoyable series where the interactions of the misfit characters are as enjoyable as the vigorous plot. Westerfeld also published a stand-alone, New York–based, vampire novel, *Peeps* (Razorbill), in which there are interchapter nonfictional digressions on various real-life parasites. Not for the weak of stomach, but a good book for anyone who likes vampires, cats, or is at all interested in food-chain dynamics.

The first volume in M.T. Anderson's Thrilling Tales series is *Whales on Stilts* (Harcourt). This hilarious and deadpan children's adventure novel is replete with amazing devices, last-minute escapes, clever children and nefarious villains. Recommended for reading aloud.

Diana Wynne Jones's *Conrad's Fate* (Greenwillow) is an entertaining new entry in the Chrestomanci novels. Readers may wish that the story had gone on a bit longer, but perhaps Conrad will show up again in a later book, and in any case, as always, Jones presents us with likeable characters, believable magic, and a compelling story which captures something of the messiness of real life. This was a good year for Jones's fans, who got to see acclaimed animator Hayao Miyazaki's film adaptation of *Howl's Moving Castle*.

In Susan Vaught's *Stormwitch* (Bloomsbury) a naïve young woman warrior from Haiti goes to live with her grandmother in early 1960s Mississippi. Horrified by the way in which black Americans are forced to live, she still comes to find a community which includes her grandmother, and friends.

In the eighth book in Diane Duane's Young Wizards series, *Wizards at War* (Harcourt), a dark force takes magic and the knowledge of magic away from all adults, leaving the children to defend the world against alien invaders. Duane's novels are popular with readers of all ages.

In *Quicksilver* (Knopf) Stephanie Spinner retells the story of Hermes, the messenger of the gods. With its maps and glossary of characters this book is a handy primer for those who haven't read *D'Aulaires' Book of Greek Myths* for a while. (Meanwhile *D'Aulaires' Book of Norse Myths* was reprinted by New York Review Children's Collection with a new preface by Michael Chabon.) Also in the pantheon: *The Lightning Thief* (Miramax/Hyperion) by Rick Riordan, where Percy, part-Greek god, has to stop a family fight—in Olympus.

Bruce Coville's comical *Thor's Wedding Day* (Harcourt) about Thor dressing up as a bride to regain his stolen hammer is based on what Coville calls the only truly funny myth he knows, the Norse myth Thrymskvitha.

The Water Mirror by Kai Meyer (McElderry, translated from the German by Elizabeth D. Crawford) is the successful first book in the Dark Reflections trilogy. Set around the start of the twentieth century, magic is real, Hell has been located inside the Earth by a National Geographic expedition, and an Egyptian Pharaoh is trying to take over the world. Much fun ensues.

Also noted: Judith Berman's Bear Daughter (Acc). Once again, bookshop owners and readers met up at midnight of the release date to celebrate the sixth book in J. K. Rowling's bestselling series, Harry Potter and the Half-Blood Prince (Scholastic). We suspect you may have heard of these books. The books get longer, but, alas, the end is in sight. This latest was an enjoyable addition to the series. Sharon Shinn's The Truth-Teller's Tale (Viking), a sequel to The Safe-Keeper's Secret, is the coming-of-age story of two sisters: one cannot tell a lie; the other cannot reveal any secrets she is told. Philip Pullman's The Scarecrow and His Servant (Knopf) is the story of an orphan and a scarecrow fighting corruption. Young readers get the pick of T.C. Boyle's stories in The Human Fly and Other Stories (Viking); Sally Gardner's I, Coriander (Dial) is a historical fantasy of a girl who finds that to save herself she also has to save fairyland. Gabrielle Zevin's Elsewhere (FSG) is a joy-filled post-life tale where the dead age backward to zero when they are once more taken back to Earth; TWOC (PS) stands for "Taking Without Owner's Consent" and is Graham Joyce's first young adult novel, a coming-of-age story full of ghosts, guilt, and the promise of redemption. Patricia Santos Marcantonio's Red Ridin' in the Hood (FSG), illustrated by Renato Alarcão, is a series of middle-reader fairy tale retellings. 47 (Little, Brown) is bestselling author Walter Mosley's first young adult novel and tells the story of a slave who is rescued by a man from another time; L.M. Boston's final Green Knowe novel, The Stones of Green Knowe (Harcourt) in which Roger, son of a Norman lord, meets the later occupants of the house; Paul Bajora's debut, The Printer's Devil (Little, Brown) plays with the fantastic (and sometimes with its own printing) in nineteenth-century London; Garth Nix's thrillingly bad week continued in The Keys to the Kingdom: Drowned Wednesday (Scholastic) and the title novella of Nix's Across the Wall: A Tale of the Abhorsen and Other Stories (Eos) will please fans of the beautiful, dark fantasy Abhorsen trilogy; Livi Michael's The Whispering Road (Putnam) is a slow-in-places road story about tramps, ghosts, and a gang of orphans; Irish author O.R. Melling's Chronicles of Faerie are already successful in Canada and elsewhere, the first volume, The Hunter's Moon (Amulet), introduces a pair of cousins who make the mistake of sleeping in a fairy ring; Adam Stemple coauthored a second novel this year, Pay the Piper: A Rock 'n' Roll Fairy Tale with Jane Yolen (Starscape); Libba Bray's dark fantasy of boarding schools, Rebel Angels (Delacorte); Shannon Hale's well-received Princess Academy (Bloomsbury) was enjoyable for its world building and its stubborn heroine; Nina Bernstein's Magic by the Book (FSG) is a tale of travels in a magical book perfect for younger readers; two very popular illustrated gift books Fairyopolos (Frederick Warne) by Cicely Mary Barker and Wizardology (Candlewick) edited by Dugald A. Steer; Cornelia Funke's follow-up to Inkheart, Inkspell (Chicken House) plays on books within books and will be particularly enjoyed by bibliophiles; we hear good things about Canadian writer Kenneth Oppel's second airship novel, Skybreaker (Eos); T.A. Barron's Shadows on the Stars, second in the Great Tale of Avalon series (Philomel); Mary Hoffman continued her fantasy series with Stravaganza: City of Flowers (Bloomsbury); Victoria Hanley, The

Light of the Oracle (David Fickling Books); Alice Hoffman, *The Foretelling* (Little, Brown); *New Yorker* writer Adam Gopnik's Paris-based *The King in the Window* (Miramax) reads quite young; Dan Greenburg and Scott M. Fischer produced two books in a new series, The Secrets of Dripping Fang, *The Onts* and *Treachery and Betrayal at Jolly Days* (Harcourt).

Single-Author Story Collections

This was another strong year for short story collections. Highlights included books by Joe Hill, Caitlín R. Kiernan, and Patricia A. McKillip, as well as the following authors.

Carol Emshwiller's *I Live with You* (Tachyon) is a collection of recent work (including two new stories) as well as her Guest of Honor speech from Wiscon. In the last few years, Emshwiller has written a number of stories dealing with various aspects of war, as well as stories about flight. This year Emshwiller also published the young adult novel, *Mr. Boots*, and received a Life Achievement World Fantasy Award. Highly recommended.

China Miéville's debut collection, *Looking for Jake* (Del Rey), contains stories ranging from post-apocalyptic tales to suburban ghost stories to political satire to a comic (drawn by artist Liam Sharp). The best stories here are perhaps also the darkest, but Miéville's short work deserves to be recognized for the risks it takes, and for those unfamiliar with his novels, this collection will provide an enticing entry point.

Howard Waldrop's *Heart of Whiteness* (Subterranean Press) collects short stories from 1995 to 2002. Waldrop's alternate history and fantasy stories are without peer; happily this collection includes afterwords for each story from the author. The title story takes Christopher Marlowe, Marlowe from *Heart of Darkness*, and Raymond Chandler's Marlowe the detective, and combines them into one dazzlingly strange journey of discovery.

Aimee Bender's second collection, *Willful Creatures* (Doubleday), contains fifteen stories, many of which are surreal or fantastic in one way or another. Standouts include a story about a boy born with keys for fingers, and "End of the Line," in which a man buys a miniature man as a pet, only to torture him. Beautifully written, these stories have the feel, the strangeness, and the small, sharp cruelties of fairy tales.

Nice Big American Baby (Knopf) is Judy Budnitz's second collection. It includes the marvelous story, "Where We Come From" as well as other work that has a fantastic slant. Budnitz is a political satirist with a humanist bent; these are stories about captive salesmen, girls with webbed feet, and pregnant women who delay giving birth until they have made it into the promised land. Highly recommended.

Robert Coover's *A Child Again* (McSweeney's) is a bawdy, bloody, enjoyably politically incorrect collection of retold fairy tales which includes "The Last One," reprinted here. The book, itself a beautiful object, also contains three "Puzzle Pages" and a story, to be shuffled and read in any order, printed on a set of cards bound to the back of the book.

In the Palace of Repose (Prime) is Holly Phillips's debut collection. Unusually, it contains mostly original work; Phillips has a distinctly original and mature voice, and this was one of the most exciting discoveries of the year. Standouts in the collection were the title story, in which a godking discovers that his guards have grown careless and his palace/prison can no longer contain him, and "A Woman's Bones," in which, again, something supernatural and powerful threatens to escape. But even the slightest of the stories here were evocative, imaginative, and beautifully told. We look forward to future stories from Phillips.

Scott Thomas's collection of linked stories, *Westermead* (Raw Dog Screaming), was one of the happy surprises of the year. It's an odd but heady book reminiscent of the pastoral novels of Thomas Hardy, with perhaps a touch of M.R. James. *Westermead* is also available in a limited edition.

Terry Bisson's third collection, *Greetings* (Tachyon), is full of his dry wit and of-the-moment cultural commentary. It includes "Almost Home," which was reprinted in the seventeenth volume of this anthology, and nine more wonders, both science fiction and fantasy.

Gregory Frost's debut collection, *Attack of the Jazz Giants and Other Stories* (Golden Gryphon) is long overdue. It contains most of Frost's short fiction and showcases the wide range of his interests and skills. The stories are a mix of dark fantasy, magic realism, horror, science fiction, and humor. Highlights include "Madonna of the Maquiladora" and "The Girlfriends of Dorian Gray."

Kit Reed's latest collection, *Dogs of Truth: New and Uncollected Stories* (Tor), mixes science fiction, horror, and dark fantasy. It includes "Perpetua" and the lovely, haunting "Visiting the Dead" among other recent favorites.

Doan Le's *The Cemetery of Chua Village and Other Stories* (Curbstone Press, translated by Rosemary Nguyen) was an unexpected delight, as we were unfamiliar with this Vietnamese author who has also published poetry and novels, as well as other short story collections. This is a collection of subtle and gently satirical work of which the title story is the standout.

Charles Coleman Finley's debut collection *Wild Things* (Subterranean Press), collects stories of heroic fantasy, science fiction, and fare more humorous or surreal. Finley has become a mainstay of *F&SF*, and like that other *F&SF* mainstay, Robert Reed, his work shows tremendous range, in genre, in style, and in voice.

Tim Powers fans who missed *Night Moves and Other Stories* (Subterranean) can catch up with what is basically an expanded edition, *Strange Itineraries* (Tachyon), collecting almost all of Powers's short stories so far—including three written with James Blaylock. Powers's stories, like his longer work, are haunted by ghosts and conspiracies. Highly recommended.

Paul Di Filippo's *The Emperor of Gondwanaland and Other Stories* (Thunder's Mouth) collects tales from all strands of Di Filippo's genre explorations, including at least one fairy tale ("Puss in Boots") retold as space opera.

Mary Frances Zambreno's debut collection, *Invisible Pleasures*, is also the first collection from publisher American Fantasy. There are four original stories in this mostly fantasy collection.

Brian Aldiss's *Cultural Breaks* (Tachyon) was published to coincide with his eightieth birthday. It includes three new short stories and stories ranging from 1968 to 2005.

Psychologist Lauren Slater's first fiction collection *Blue Beyond Blue: Extraordinary Tales for Ordinary Dilemmas* (Norton) is a series of reworked fairy tales in which Slater attempts to reach the hidden truths within the tales in a process she dubs "narrative psychotherapy."

Lucius Shepard's *Eternity and Other Stories* (Thunder's Mouth) is a fine collection for newer or for occasional readers: the contents replicate some material from other recent collections.

Also of note: *The Man Who Lost the Sea: Volume X: The Complete Stories of*

Theodore Sturgeon is the final entry in North Atlantic's ambitious reprint series. Lucy Sussex's second collection, *A Tour Guide in Utopia* (MirrorDanse Editions), is a recommended collection of dark fantasy from Australia. *H.P. Lovecraft: Tales* (Library of America) means that Lovecraft's tales will find (and disturb) an entirely new audience; Gene Wolfe's *Starwater Strains* (Tor) is a collection of mostly science fiction but is a welcome companion volume to his recent fantasy collection, *Innocents Aboard*. Ash-Tree Press put out a very nice omnibus edition of John Buchan's short fiction, *The Watcher by the Threshold*; *The Grinding House* (CSFG) is Australian writer Kaaron Warren's dark debut collection. Warren's fiction will appeal to readers of Joe Hill and Poppy Brite. James Van Pelt's *The Last of the O-Forms* (Fairwood Press) is a mixed-genre collection which includes a few nicely old-fashioned fantasy stories. The inimitable Forrest Aguirre debuts with experimental collection *Fugue XXIX* (Raw Dog Screaming); Andrew Hook *Beyond the Blue Horizon* (Crowswing). Michael Jasper's *Gunning for the Buddha* (Prime) leans toward horror, but is a first collection with a number of promising stories; *Off the Map* (Two Cranes Press) contains four stories (one new) written and illustrated by Daniel Wallace, author of the cult novel *Big Fish*.

Small Beer Press published two collections in 2005: Maureen F. McHugh's debut collection, *Mothers & Other Monsters* and Kelly Link's second collection, *Magic for Beginners*, illustrated by Shelley Jackson. *Mothers & Other Monsters* was a finalist for the Story Prize.

Anthologies

The Dedalus Book of Finnish Fantasy (Dedalus) was an unexpected treat. Edited by Tiptree-winning author Johanna Sinisalo and translated by David Hackston, we recommend this for those readers looking for slightly uncommon fare. We selected Pentti Holappa's "Boman" for this anthology, and there is an impressively thorough sampling of authors, genres, and styles included here. Highly recommended.

McSweeney's latest literacy fundraiser is a nominally young adult, profusely illustrated anthology, *Noisy Outlaws, Unfriendly Blobs, and Some Other Things . . . : That Aren't as Scary, Maybe, Depending on How You Feel About Lost Lands, Stray Cellphones, . . . Quite Finish, So Maybe You Could Help Us Out*. It featured stories by Neil Gaiman, Jonathan Safran Foer, George Saunders, Kelly Link, and others.

The fifth *Polyphony* (Wheatland Press) anthology is, again, a generously proportioned grab bag of genres, with a slight bias toward slipstream. Under editors Deborah Layne and Jay Lake, this series continues to introduce newer writers of interest, as well as featuring more familiar names; stories from Paul O. Miles, Robert Freeman Wexler, Leslie What, and Sarah Totten were particularly good.

Tesseracts Nine: New Canadian Speculative Fiction (Edge), edited by Nalo Hopkinson and Geoff Ryman, is a strong cross-genre anthology with an essay by each of the editors. Yves Menard's "Principles of Animal Eugenetics" and poetry by Sandra Kasturi were the highlights for us.

Nova Scotia: New Scottish Speculative Fiction (Crescent Books), edited by Neil Williamson and Andrew J. Wilson, is another vigorous country-specific anthology, which showcases a mix of styles and genres, from historical fantasy to space opera and everything in between. We particularly enjoyed the stories by Jane Yolen and Andrew C. Ferguson.

A couple of years ago we reprinted Dean Francis Alfar's story "L'Aquilone du Estrellas (The Kite of Stars)" from *Strange Horizons* in this anthology series. Alfar inaugurates a new anthology series himself with the first volume of *Philippine Speculative Fiction* (Kestrel). This is a rich and vivid assortment of stories. It includes strong work by Nikki Alfar, Francezka C. Kwe, and Vincent Michael Simbulan.

Rabid Transit: Menagerie (Velocity Press), edited by Christopher Barzak, Alan De Niro, and Kristin Livdahl, is an annual anthology of quality writing that tends toward the peculiar. Dean Francis Alfar and Rudi Dornemann's stories were of particular note.

The Nine Muses (Wheatland Press), edited by Forrest Aguirre and Deborah Layne, explores the eponymous muses from Greek mythology. Sarah Totten's story was the standout, while Elizabeth Hand's introductory essay on muses was lovely (and inspiring).

The Book of Voices (Flame Books), edited by Michael Butscher, is a fundraiser in support of Sierra Leone PEN and includes "The Boatman's Holiday" by Jeffrey Ford, reprinted herein.

We saw many more anthologies from small presses this year. While some would have been improved by better editing or design, others, including *Northwest Passages: A Cascadian Anthology* (Fandom Press), edited by Cris DiMarco, are well worth picking up. This book included Marly Youmans's story from *Argosy*, reprinted herein, "An Incident at Agate Beach," as well as good stories by Ruth Nestvold and Jacques L. Condor.

The number of yearly reprint anthologies continues to rise. Among the *Best of the Year* anthologies available were: *Year's Best Australian Science Fiction & Fantasy: Volume 1*, edited by Bill Congreve and Michelle Marquardt (MirrorDanse; Prime), *Fantasy: The Best of 2004* (ibooks), edited by Karen Haber and Jonathan Strahan; *Best Short Novels 2005* (SFBC), edited by Jonathan Strahan; and *Year's Best Fantasy 5*, edited by David G. Hartwell and Kathryn Cramer (Eos).

Also of note: *The Elastic Book of Numbers* (Elastic Press), edited by Allen Ashley, an all-original multigenre collection themed around numbers; Douglas Anderson's *Seekers of Dreams* (Cold Spring Press), mostly reprints but one new Tolkien-influenced story; *Tel: Stories* (Wheatland Press), edited by Jay Lake, reprints Greer Gilman's "Jack Daw's Pack" and other, original experimental work by Tim Pratt, Jeff VanderMeer, Sonya Taafe, Anil Menon, Gregory Feeley, and others. *Daikaiju! Giant Monster Tales* (Agog! Press), edited by Robert Hood and Robin Pen, contains a couple of giant monster tales that live up to the great cover art by Eggleton. This seemed liked a fun project. *Lords of Swords* (Pitch Black Books), edited by Daniel E. Blackston; *Time for Bedlam: A Collection of Cautionary Tales* (Saltboy Bookmakers), edited by Ian Donnell Arbuckle, is the first book from a new print-on-demand mini-press; *Young Warriors: Stories of Strength* (Random House), edited by Tamora Pierce and Josepha Sherman, includes good stories by Holly Black, Janis Ian, and Margaret Mahy; *Fantastical Visions III* (Fantasist Enterprises), edited by W.H. Horner, Christina Stitt, and C. Nathan Dadek, includes enjoyable stories by Sarah Totten and others; *Emerald Eye: The Best Irish Imaginative Fiction* (Aeon), edited by Frank Ludlow and Roelof Goudriaan, is a strong anthology of all reprints; *The Devil in Brisbane* (Prime), edited by Zoran Živković, is a themed anthology (the title will tell you the subject matter) which includes good stories by Australian writers K.J. Bishop, Grace Dugan, and Kim Westwood; *Adventure* (Monkeybrain Books) is a recently launched annual anthology of new pulp fiction; *Circles in the Hair*, edited by the members of the eponymous writers' group; *Triskaideka: Thirteen Tales from Midwest Authors* (Cave Hollow), edited by R.M. Kinder, Georgia R. Nagel, and James Henry Taylor; *Coney Island Wonder Stories* (Wildside), edited by

Robert J. Howe and John Ordover is a fun reprint anthology; *Spirits Unwrapped*, edited by Daniel Braum, entertained on the theme of mummies; two POD charity anthologies, *Southern Comfort* (proceeds to the Red Cross) and *Animal Magnetism* (proceeds to Noah's Wish), edited by S.A. Parham and W. Olivia Race.

Magazines and Journals

When SciFi Channel canceled Ellen Datlow's online magazine, *SCI FICTION*, fans of the genre lost their best free regular read. Four times a month, Datlow published one original, and, in addition, also regularly republished classic genre stories; stories from *SCI FICTION* have consistently won major genre awards. Datlow published outstanding work by established writers such as Lucius Shepard, Elizabeth Hand, Howard Waldrop, Jeffrey Ford, Pat Murphy, and Kit Reed, and also introduced its readership to promising newer writers, including Catherine Morrison, M.K. Hobson, and Sean Klein. Readers can still access *SCI FICTION's* online archive. Writer David Schwartz set up a blog at edsfproject.blogspot.com which encouraged writers to write appreciations of the roughly 320 stories Datlow published on *SCI FICTION. The Magazine of Fantasy & Science Fiction* had a great year: two stories from the December issue are included here and a number of stories were on our long list. *Realms of Fantasy* had a strong year, once again, with a couple of lovely Richard Parks stories, as well as stories by newer writers like Amy Beth Forbes, Joe Murphy, and Graham Edwards, among others. *Asimov's* remit is still mostly science fiction under editor Sheila Williams. Stories by Kage Baker and Nisi Shawl were among the very enjoyable fantasies.

A new annual magazine that we highly encourage readers to subscribe to (or perhaps your library can) is *Fairy Tale Review*. 2005's issue, The Blue Issue, was an excellent introduction, including art by Kiki Smith, and fiction by Aimee Bender, and Stacey Richter, whose fractured fairy tale, "A Case Study of Emergency Room Procedure and Risk Management by Hospital Staff Members in the Urban Facility," is reprinted here. *Subterranean* is a new magazine from Subterranean Press that steers toward darker fantasies and often features work by authors associated with the press, such as Caitlín R. Kiernan. The two issues from 2005 were compelling; it's heartening to see a new magazine carefully and thoughtfully put together. *Fantasy Magazine* also got off to a solid start. The first issue was distributed to the members of the World Fantasy Convention. Printed on newsprint, it should appear on newsstands and bookshops four times in 2006. It featured work from Prime Books authors and others, including Tim Pratt, Holly Phillips, and Jeffrey Ford. We were happy to see the return of *The Women's Review of Books. Shimmer* is a good-looking new zine with strong ambitions. *Oddfellow*, a humorous magazine, included Wendy Norris's enchanting "Tales of Persephone."

On newsstands, *The New Yorker* offered haunting stories by Lorrie Moore, Karen Russell, and George Saunders. *Harper's* included surreal fiction from George Saunders and Margaret Atwood. *Ninth Letter* is consistently the most beautiful magazine we see each year. Brian Tierney's "A Child Born with Wings" was the best of the few genre-inflected stories. *Conjunctions* always has a handful of fantasy-tinged stories and this year included weird and wonderful work from Karen Russell and Brian Evenson, as well as the story "Kronia" by Elizabeth Hand, which you can find within these pages. *McSweeney's* got out four quarterly issues this year; they included remarkable stories from Judy Budnitz and Steven Millhauser among others. Online, they published a good variety of short fiction which ought to appeal to genre readers, including Stephany Aulenback's "Grim Stories" and "More Grim Stories" and Mike Richardson-Bryan's "Klingon Fairy Tales." *Virginia Quarterly Review* had a great year—we selected Isabel Allende's story and Jennifer Chang's poem for reprint—and received six National Magazine Award nominations. *Marvels & Tales: Journal of Fairy-Tale Studies* produced two issues including one on "Reframing the Early French Fairy Tale." *Glimmer Train* published a subtle and lovely fantasy by Bruce McAllister—although they have repeatedly told us they do not publish genre fiction of any description. Literary journals which featured fiction or poetry of interest to genre readers included *One Story*, *The Land-Grant College Review*, *Tin House*, *The Columbia Review*, *The Georgia Review*, *Black Warrior Review*, *The Kenyon Review*, and *Prairie Schooner*, *The Harvard Review*, *The Paris Review*, *StoryQuarterly*, *The MacGuffin*, *Cicada*, and *Agni*.

With the disappearance of *SCI FICTION*, *Strange Horizons*, under the editorship of Susan Marie Groppi, is now the top venue for online speculative fiction readers. Their remit is broad and the magazine offers free weekly fiction, frequently by up-and-coming writers, as well as poetry, and nonfiction columns by Matthew Cheney, Debbie Notkin, and others. Notable stories this year came from Leah Bobet, Deborah Coates, Meghan McCarron, and John Schoffstall. New magazines just coming online include Orson Scott Card's *Intergalactic Medicine Show* and Jim Baen's *Universe*. There were many impressive, mostly religiously themed stories at *Aeon SF*. *Ideomancer* moved to a quarterly schedule and maintained its standards of generally high quality fiction which ranged from slipstream to sf&f. *Fortean Bureau*, *Ideomancer*, *Abyss and Apex*, and *ChiZine* are the first places to look online for up-and-coming writers. (Note: we have recently heard that *Fortean Bureau*, which was run by Jeremy Tolbert and others, will be shutting down. That is a shame, as from its start, it was an excellent and nicely designed source for strong genre fiction.) *Lone Star Stories* had an excellent year with memorable stories by Samantha Henderson and others. *Revolution SF* is mostly sf, but put up enjoyable work by Danny Adams. *Lenox Avenue* published five issues, and announced they were closing. They published engaging work, including stories by Adam Browne and Steve Nagy and will be missed. Eileen Gunn's *Infinite Matrix* remains mostly closed, although there are occasional flickers of life. In 2005, they published a lovely, dark fantasy by Patrick O'Leary, "The Witch's Hand."

British stalwart *Interzone* had a strong year—hitting its 20th anniversary and 200th issue. It is very much science fiction–oriented, but published strong fantasy stories by David Ira Cleary and John Aegard. *The Third Alternative*'s publication schedule suffered as *Interzone* was brought into the TTA Press stable. Disconcertingly, editor Andy Cox renamed *The 3rd Alternative*. It's now *Black Static*. We look forward to reading more work by writers like Doug Lain and Matthew Francis in upcoming issues, whatever the name. We saw one issue of PS Publishing's *Postscripts*, which still tends toward sf and horror. Highlights included Joe Hill's gentle, nongenre, zombie-extras story, "Bobby Conroy Comes Back from the Dead." We saw one massive triple issue of Australian magazine *Aurealis*, and also enjoyed one issue each of *Borderlands*, *Orb*, and *Fables & Reflections*—all of which are also from Australia. *Andromeda Spaceways Inflight Magazine* consistently includes one or two strong stories in its six yearly issues, although the layout sometimes renders the contents difficult to read. Canadian magazine *On Spec* had a good year, revitalized by new managing editor, Diane Walton.

The first issue of pocket-sized magazine *Jabberwocky* featured many authors familiar to readers of Prime Books: Sonya Taaffe, Holly Phillips, Vera Nazarian, Catherynne M. Valente, Yoon Ha Lee, Theodora Goss, Anna Tambour. We particularly enjoyed work by Catherynne M. Valente, Ainsley Dicks, and JoSelle Vanderhooft. *Paradox*, the magazine of historical and speculative fiction decreased to two issues a year, both of which were good. There were two almost-book-like issues of *Black Gate*, which offers enjoyable stories of heroic fantasy. *Tale of the Unanticipated* officially shifted to an annual anthology. There was one issue (the 99th!) of *Space and Time*. Sadly, their 100th issue will also be their last. The second issue of *The Dogtown Review*, from writers David J. Schwartz and Keith Demanche, included an energetic and surreal tale by Michael Samerdyke. *Argosy* managed to produce one issue (Marly Youmans's story is reprinted here), although it seems increasingly unlikely that there will be many more. *Talebones* continues (ten years down the line!) very nicely with their particular mix of horror and dark-fantasy fiction and poetry, and a respectably thorough review section. *Zahir* gets better with each issue. This year there were good stories stories by William Alexander and Sonya Taafe, among others.

In the micropresses, Tim Pratt and Heather Shaw produced one excellent issue of *Flytrap* with good, odd stories from Theodora Goss and Jeffrey Ford, and lots of smaller pieces of interest. Christopher Rowe and Gwenda Bond also published one issue of their beautifully produced, themed-issue zine, *Say . . . (Say . . . have you heard this one?)*, shifting to an annual production schedule. Janni Lee Simner's "Practical Villainy" was most enjoyable. John Klima's *Electric Velocipede* tends more toward sf, but he made space for solid fantasy stories by Hal Duncan, among others. William Smith's third annual issue of the zine *Trunk Stories* is lovely, with equal attention paid to art, design, and quirky, dark fiction. The highlight was Carole Lanham's wonderful vampire story, "The Good Part." *Sybil's Garage* is a newer, well-designed, mostly sf zine. *Not One of Us* is another stalwart of the zine scene. Editor John Benson produced his regular two issues and annual one-off, this year entitled *Clarity*. *Dark Horizons* comes from the British Fantasy Society. There was one issue of the quirky, enjoyable, anonymously-authored *Nemonymous*, now known as *Nemo Book*.

Small Beer Press published three issues of *Lady Churchill's Rosebud Wristlet* with stories by Karen Russell, John Kessel, and Deborah Roggie, among others.

The following titles appeared with regularity and all include good work: *Weird Tales*, *Space and Time*, *Leading Edge*, *Full Unit Hookup*, *Harpur Palate*, *Scheherazade*, and *Premonitions*.

Amazing died (again) after two issues (and a third online). It would be nice if it came back. The second issue of Thom Davidsohn and Alex Irvine's *Journal of Pulse-Pounding Narratives* was, sadly, also the final. Stories by Tim Pratt and Jim Cambias, and especially Jeffrey Ford's "Giant Land" stood out. Edgewood Press's *Alchemy* promises one more issue before disappearing.

Also of note: we didn't see a great many original chapbooks this year, but we did enjoy Steve Rasnic Tem's *The World Recalled* (Wormhole Books), copiously illustrated by writer/poet/artist Tem.

Art

"Spectrum: The Exhibition" was an spectacularly packed exhibit at the museum of American Illustration at the Society of Illustrators in New York City; it included two hundred or so pieces of art selected from the first eleven *Spectrum* anthologies. *Spectrum 12: The Best in Contemporary Fantastic Art* (Underwood) edited by Cathy and Arnie Fenner is a lovingly produced celebration of fantastic art and works both as a contact directory for artists as well as a handy summation of the field today. Audrey Niffenegger's success led to Abrams reprinting her thirteen-years-in-the-making handmade art book *The Three Incestuous Sisters*. Art dominates text with page after page of reproductions of her beautiful, idiosyncratic, handcut aquatint illustrations. Well worth picking up.

Leonora Carrington: Surrealism, Alchemy, and Art (Lund Humphries/Ashgate) by Susan L. Aberth is a richly illustrated, although at times somewhat workmanlike introduction to the life and work of this fascinating artist. Although light on the latter half of Carrington's life, the chapters that describe her youth and early adulthood are captivating: Carrington's "induction" into the Surrealist movement, her time in an insane asylum, marriage and subsequent emigration to Mexico, and her relationship with Remedios Varos.

Both of us greatly enjoyed Emily Flake's mini-collection of surreal, loopy, and inspired comics, *Lulu Eightball* (Atomic Books). Highly recommended.

Readers can explore Max Ernst's art and his life in two new books from Yale University Press, Robert McNab's *Ghost Ships: A Surrealist Love Triangle* and *Max Ernst: A Retrospective*. Adrian Woodhouse's *Beresford Egan* (Tartarus Press) is an expensive, beautiful, limited edition which celebrates the centenary of the art deco and bohemian artist's birth. Clive Barker's *Visions of Heaven and Hell* (Rizzoli) collects more than 300 pieces of Barker's richly colored work as well as his black-and-white art. The beautiful monsters in 2004's *Monstruo: The Art of Carlos Huante* now have a companion volume, *Mas Creaturas: Monstruo Addendum* (Design Studio). Australian artist Robert Ingpen's illustrations are collected and annotated in *Pictures Telling Stories: The Art of Robert Ingpen* (Penguin). Rob Alexander's *Welcome to My Worlds: The Art of Rob Alexander* (Paper Tiger) collects the haunting paintings of an artist most often associated with traditional fantasy. Robert Williams's *Through Prehensile Eyes* (Last Gasp) is a very up-to-the-minute cycling and recycling of modern and retro art themes ranging from biker culture to quantum mechanics. Tom Kidd's cheerful notes accompany 150 illustrations selected from his twenty-five years of work in *Kiddography: The Art of Tom Kidd* (Paper Tiger).

See also: Holly Black and Tony DiTerlizzi's *Arthur Spiderwick's Field Guide to the Fantastical World Around You* (Simon & Schuster).

Picture Books

Iassen Ghiuselev's lavish illustrations bring John Ruskin's 1889 fable *The King of the Golden River* (Simply Read) to life in a beautiful edition which includes information on Ruskin for those discovering him for the first time.

Virginia Hamilton's famous folktale, *The People Could Fly* (Knopf), which has been available for years in the collection of the same name, is now a breathtaking picture book illustrated by Leo and Diane Dillon.

Judy Sierra's *The Gruesome Guide to World Monsters* (Candlewick), illustrated by Henrik Drescher, is a guide to monsters from folktales around the world and will provide hours of reading for parents and children alike.

Judy Allen's heavily illustrated *Fantasy Encyclopedia* (Kingfisher) is a handy reference book.

Amy Lowry Toole's light and fanciful illustrations complement her successful relocation (to China) and retelling of Hans Christian Andersen's *The Pea Blossom* (Holiday House).

Chris Riddell's lively illustrations will please young readers of this edition of Jonathan Swift's *Gulliver* (Candlewick); older readers will be disappointed by the abridged text.

General Nonfiction

Soundings: Reviews 1992–1996 (Beccon) is the first collection of *Locus* reviewer Gary K. Wolfe's reviews and year-end summaries. Wolfe is a generous and thoughtful reviewer of wide-ranging interests, and reading these reviews makes for pleasurable browsing. It will also make you want to take certain books down off your shelf and read them again.

About Writing (Wesleyan) is an indispensable collection of Samuel R. Delany's essays, letters, and lectures on writing. Both Delany's prose and ideas on writing are lucid, vigorous, and usefully provocative. Highly recommended to both writers and readers.

Michael Bishop's *A Reverie for Mister Ray* (PS) is an impressive collection including seventy or so essays by Bishop on the speculative field.

Voices of Vision: Creators of Science Fiction and Fantasy Speak, by Jayme Lynn Blaschke (Bison), features interviews with Samuel R. Delany, Patricia Anthony, and many others.

David King's *Finding Atlantis* (Harmony) is the story of Olaf Rudbeck and his 1679 claim that Atlantis was located north of Sweden, and he would prove it. Which is what he attempted to do for thirty years.

Jess Nevins's *The Encyclopedia of Fantastic Victoriana* (MonkeyBrain) is a hefty tome which covers the fantastic literature of the nineteenth century. Writers like Wells and Verne have entries, as do Russian newspaper serial novels, *Boy Heroes*, *Lunatics, Monkeys, Martians*, and *Mummies*. Highly recommended. There is an introduction by Michael Moorcock as well.

Sam Weller's *The Bradbury Chronicles* (Morrow) is a light pop-culture take on the life of the acclaimed short-story writer who has introduced many to genre fiction.

In the updated edition of *Divine Invasions: A Life of Philip K. Dick* (Carroll & Graf) Dick's official biographer Lawrence Sutin takes a shot at telling Dick's life story; he also provides a useful overview of Dick's career for readers and fans.

Horror: Another Hundred Best Books (Caroll & Graf) edited by Stephen Jones & Kim Newman is an excellent bedside companion for readers of dark fantasy and horror.

Small Beer Press published Kate Wilhelm's memoir-cum-book on writing, *Storyteller: Writing Lessons and More from 27 Years of the Clarion Writers' Workshop*.

Also noted but not seen: *Transformations: The Story of the Science Fiction Magazines from 1950 to 1970*, Mike Ashley (Liverpool); *Anatomy of Wonder: A Critical Guide to Science Fiction*, 5th edition, Neil Barron (Libraries Unlimited); *Supernatural Literature of the World: An Encyclopedia*, S.T. Joshi & Stefan R. Dziemianowicz, eds. (Greenwood); *Latin American Science Fiction Writers: An A-to-Z Guide*, Darrell B. Lockhart, ed. (Greenwood); *Fantasy Literature for Children and Young Adults*: Fifth Edition, Ruth Nadelman Lynn (Libraries Unlimited); *Historical Dictionary of Fantasy Literature*, Brian Stableford (Scarecrow); *The Greenwood Encyclopedia of Science Fiction and Fantasy: Themes, Works, and Wonders*, Gary Westfahl, ed. (Greenwood); *and Science Fiction Quotations*, Gary Westfahl, ed. (Yale).

Myth, Folklore, and Fairy Tales

One of the biggest and most ambitious publishing projects of the year was Canongate's series, The Myths, which will be simultaneously published throughout the world in a host of languages. One hundred books are promised in the series (so we'll be reading them for years to come!) of which three were published in 2005. The first title, religious scholar and bestseller Karen Armstrong's *A Short History of Myth*, is a nonfiction survey of myth building. *The Penelopiad: The Myth of Penelope and Odysseus* by Margaret Atwood is much livelier. Penelope, not particularly patiently waiting for Odysseus's return, has to outwit her suitors. The interruptions of the twelve maids, hanged for conspiring with her suitors, adds weight to this slim book. In *Weight: The Myth of Atlas and Heracles*, by British fabulist Jeanette Winterson, Heracles takes on Atlas's task, holding up the world for a day—and then has to persuade Atlas to take back the weight again. These three make for an intriguing beginning to a long series which will set both fantasy readers' and book collectors' hearts on fire.

In *Spinning Straw into Gold: What Fairy Tales Reveal About the Transformations in a Woman's Life* (Random House) Joan Gould considers the effect and the ubiquity of fairy tale caricatures and archetypes on women's lives. Gould's book deals with the stories underlying many of the most popular fictions of our time from *Jane Eyre* to the Harry Potter series.

The Robber with a Witch's Head; More Stories from the Great Treasury of Sicilian Folk and Fairy Tales Collected by Laura Gonzenbach (Routledge) is the second volume translated and introduced by the apparently indefatigable Jack Zipes. The first volume, *Beautiful Angiola*, was outstanding, and this offering is also highly recommended.

Patrick Atangan, *Silk Tapestry and Other Chinese Folktales: Songs of Our Ancestors, Vol 2* (NBM) is part of a series retelling Asian folktales. Artist and writer Atangan focuses on China in this volume, retelling the title story and two others.

Marvels & Tales reported that UNESCO accepted the Brothers Grimm's annotated reference copies of their *Kinder und Häusmarchen* (Children's and Household Tales) into their Memory of the World Registry. Meanwhile, Valerie Paradiz's fascinating *Clever Maids: The Secret History of The Grimm Fairy Tales* (Basic Books) explores the source of many of the Brothers Grimm tales—their sister, Lotte, and a circle of women friends. *Clever Maids* is a biographical examination of the sometimes straitened circumstances of the Grimm family. For a taste of Wilhelm and Jacob Grimm's original unexpurgated tales, Maria Tatar introduces a dark, entertaining, and sometimes gruesome selection in *Grimm's Grimmest* (Chronicle, illustrated by Tracy Arah Dockray). This is a beautifully put together collection but is definitely not for squeamish children—or, more likely, squeamish adults!

Tiina Nunnally's new translation of thirty of Hans Christian Andersen's *Fairy Tales* (Viking) strips away everything but the essence of the storyteller's stories. This wonderful collection features an introduction by Andersen's biographer Jackie Wullschlager and is illustrated throughout with Andersen's own amazingly skilled paper cutouts. Jens Andersen's (no relation) biography, *Hans Christian Andersen* (Overlook), also translated by Tiina Nunnally, is a satisfying companion to *Fairy Tales*. H.C. Andersen was a child prodigy who, as an adult, despite his success, was a particularly fragile creative soul, frequently neurotic and needy. Jens Andersen's extensive research shows through on every absorbing page. Both books are recommended.

The Gaelic Otherworld: John Gregorson Campbell's Superstitions of The Highlands and Islands of Scotland and Witchcraft and Second Sight in The Highlands and Islands (Birlinn Publishers) includes notes and an introduction by Ronald Black. In the 1850s and 1860s, Campbell traveled the Highlands and islands of Scotland, collecting word-of-mouth stories of fairies, ghosts, witches, superstitions, and more. He was known for the authenticity of these accounts. This anthology reprints Campbell's two rare collections of folklore in one volume. Highly recommended.

From the Land of Sheba: Yemeni Folk Tales (Interlink) is a wonderful—if slim—collection of twenty-four tales translated by Kamal Ali al-Hegri, and retold by Carolyn Han. It includes an appealing story on how coffee from the town of Al-Mokha became so popular.

Don't Know Much About Mythology: Everything You Need to Know About the Greatest Stories in Human History but Never Learned (HarperCollins) by Kenneth C. Davis is a comprehensive and inclusive exploration of various world mythologies.

Terri Windling and company's Endicott Studio online (endicottstudio.com) is one of the best resources for work on myth. Terri (among others) also writes a column for *Realms of Fantasy*, which covers folklore, mythology, and fairytales. Also of note: an annual convention, Mythic Journeys, which explores the place of myth in everyday life.

See also: Suzanne Weyn's *The Night Dance* (Simon Pulse) which retells "The Twelve Dancing Princesses." *The Barefoot Book of Fairy Tales* (Barefoot) by Malachy Doyle and illustrated by Nicoletta Ceccoli, retells a dozen folktales from around the world. See also: Jean Thesman's *Singer* (Viking) and Stephanie Spinner's *Quicksilver* (Knopf) in the young adult section, and Judith Berman's *Bear Daughter* (Ace) in first novels; Anne Sheldon's *The Adventures of the Faithful Counselor* (Aqueduct) in poetry.

Awards

The 31st annual World Fantasy Convention was held in Madison, WI. Graham Joyce, Robert Weinberg, Terri Windling, and Kinuko Y. Craft were the guests of honor. The following awards were given out: Life Achievement: Carol Emshwiller and Tom Doherty; Novel: *Jonathan Strange & Mr Norrell*, Susanna Clarke (Bloomsbury); Novella: "The Growlimb," Michael Shea (*F&SF*, 1/2004); Short Story: "Singing My Sister Down," Margo Lanagan (*Black Juice*); Anthology: *Acquainted with The Night*, ed. Barbara & Christopher Roden (Ash-Tree Press) and *Dark Matter: Reading The Bones*, ed. Sheree R. Thomas (Warner Aspect); Collection: *Black Juice*, Margo Lanagan (Allen & Unwin Australia); Artist: John Picacio; Special Award, Professional: S.T. Joshi (for scholarship); Special Award, Non-Professional: Robert Morgan (for Sarob Press).

The James Tiptree, Jr. Memorial Award for genre fiction that expands or explores our understanding of gender was awarded to Joe Haldeman for *Camouflage* and Johanna Sinisalo for *Not Before Sundown*. The award was presented at Gaylaxicon in Cambridge, MA. The judges also provided an additional short list of books that they found worthy of note: *Little Black Book of Stories*, A.S. Byatt (Vintage International); *Love's Body, Dancing in Time*, L. Timmel Duchamp (Aqueduct); "All of Us Can Almost . . .", Carol Emshwiller (*SCI FICTION*); *Sea of Trolls*, Nancy Farmer (Scholastic); *Stable Strategies and Others*, Eileen Gunn (Tachyon); *Life*, Gwyneth Jones (Aqueduct); "Kissing Frogs," Jaye Lawrence (Fantasy & Science Fiction, May 2004).

The second annual Fountain Award went to Jeffrey Ford's "The Annals of Eelin-Ok" (*The Faery Reel*). Honorable mentions: "Cold Fires" by M. Rickert (*Fantasy & Science Fiction*, October/November); "The Faery Handbag" by Kelly Link (*The Faery Reel*); "The Golden Age of Fire Escapes" by John Aegard (*Rabid Transit: Petting Zoo*); "The Immortal Feet" by Katharine Haake (*One Story*); "The Lethe Man" by David J. Schwartz (*Say . . .*); "Music Lessons" by Douglas Lain (*Lady Churchill's Rosebud Wristlet*); "Retrospective" by Sonya Taaffe (*Not One of Us*); "Things Penguins Do" by Katherin Nolte (*Fence*); "The Wolf at the Door" by Rebecca Curtis (*StoryQuarterly*); "Zavtra aptBaZ" by Liz Williams (*Scheherazade*).

The International Association for the Fantastic's William L. Crawford Fantasy Award went to Steph Swainston for *The Year of Our War* (Eos) and the IAFA Distinguished Scholarship Award to Damien Broderick. At Mythcon the Mythopoeic Award winners were: Adult Literature: Susanna Clarke, *Jonathan Strange & Mr Norrell* (Bloomsbury); Children's Literature: Terry Pratchett, *A Hat Full of Sky* (HarperCollins); Scholarship Award in Inklings Studies: Janet Brennan Croft, *War and the Works of J. R. R. Tolkien* (Greenwood Press); Scholarship Award in General Myth and Fantasy Studies: Stephen Thomas Knight, *Robin Hood: A Mythic Biography* (Cornell University Press 2003). The Science Fiction Poetry Association 2005 Rhysling Awards were awarded at Readercon: Short poem: "No Ruined Lunar City," Greg Beatty (*Abyss & Apex*, October '04); Long poem, "Soul Searching," Tim Pratt (*Strange Horizons* July 12, '04).

We never have enough space in which to include all the stories we've particularly loved. Here are a few more we encourage you to seek out.

Kage Baker, "Two Old Women," *Asimov's*, February
Judy Budnitz, "Where We Come From," *Nice Big American Baby*
Carol Emshwiller, "I Live with You," *F&SF*, March
Samantha Henderson, "Manuscript Found Written in the Paw Prints of a Stoat," *Lone Star Stories*, 8
Joe Hill, "Pop Art," *Twentieth-Century Ghosts* (PS Publishing)
Caitlín R. Kiernan, "La Peu Verte," *To Charles Fort, With Love*
Yves Meynard, "Principles of Animal Eugenics," *Tesseracts Nine*
Patrick O'Leary, "The Witch's Hand," *The Infinite Matrix*
Holly Philips, "In the Palace of Repose," *In the Palace of Repose*
Karen Russell, "Haunting Olivia," *The New Yorker*, June 13 & 20
Sarah Totten, "The Teasewater Fire," *The Nine Muses*
Catherynne M. Valente, "Mother is a Machine," *Jabberwocky*, 1
JoSelle Vanderhooft, "Helen," *Jabberwocky*, 1
Satu Waltari, "The Monster," *Dedalus Book of Finish Fantasy*
Jane Yolen, "A Knot of Toads,"*Nova Scotia*

We keep a small Web page for this anthology series at www.lcrw.net/yearsbest and we encourage recommendations by email of published works for consideration in next year's volume. However, please check the Summation and Honorable Mention list to see the types of material we are already reading. Thank you and we hope you enjoy the following stories as much as we did.

—*Kelly Link & Gavin J. Grant*
Northampton, MA

Summation 2005: Horror

Ellen Datlow

2005 was another good year for short horror fiction. There were more magazines, anthologies, and single-author collections publishing at least some horror than ever before. If I had more than my allotted 125,000 words, I would have included three novellas: Laird Barron's "The Imago Sequence," Joe Hill's "Voluntary Committal," and Kim Newman's "The Serial Murders."

Six of the stories I chose were from collections, seven from anthologies (one, an anthology that was published on the cusp of 2004–5 and which has already been lauded during 2005), one from a chapbook created specifically for a mini-book tour, and eight (including the two poems) from magazines.

Generally, as in the past, I'm still finding that most of the best horror stories are being published in mixed-genre magazines, anthologies, and collections, so if you're a real connoisseur of horror don't confine yourself to those media that proclaim horror because you're missing out on most of the best work.

Awards

The Bram Stoker Awards for Achievement in Horror are given by the Horror Writers Association. The full membership may recommend in all categories but only active members can vote on the final ballot. The awards for material appearing during 2004 were presented Saturday, June 25, 2005 in Los Angeles, CA during the Stoker weekend.

2005 Winners for Superior Achievement:

Novel: *In the Night Room* by Peter Straub (Random House); First Novel: (Tie) *Covenant* by John Everson (Delirium Books) and *Stained* by Lee Thomas (Wildside Press); Long Fiction: *The Turtle Boy* by Kealan-Patrick Burke (Necessary Evil Press); Short Fiction: "Nimitseahpah" by Nancy Etchemendy (*The Magazine of Fantasy & Science Fiction*); Fiction Collection: *Fearful Symmetries* by Thomas F. Monteleone (Cemetery Dance Publications); Anthology: *The Year's Best Fantasy and Horror: Seventeenth Annual Collection*, edited by Ellen Datlow and Kelly Link & Gavin J. Grant (St. Martin's Press); Nonfiction: *Hellnotes* edited by Judi Rohrig; Illustrated Narrative: *Heaven's Devils* by Jai Nitz (Image Comics); Screenplay: (Tie) *Eternal*

Sunshine of the Spotless Mind by Charlie Kaufman, Michel Gondry and Pierre Bismuth and *Shaun of the Dead* by Simon Pegg and Edgar Wright; Work for Young Readers: (Tie) *Abarat: Days of Magic, Nights of War* by Clive Barker (HarperCollins) and *Oddest Yet* by Steve Burt (Burt Creations); Poetry Collection: *The Women at the Funeral* by Corrine De Winter (Space & Time); Alternative Forms: *The Devil's Wine* (Poetry Anthology) edited by Tom Piccirilli (Cemetery Dance Publications); Lifetime Achievement Award: Michael Moorcock.

The International Horror Guild awards recognize outstanding achievements in the field of horror and dark fantasy. The 2004 awards were presented at the World Fantasy Convention in Madison, WI, Thursday, November 3, 2005.

Nominations are derived from recommendations made by the public and the judges' knowledge of the field. Edward Bryant, Stefan R. Dziemianowicz, Ann Kennedy, and Hank Wagner adjudicate.

Gahan Wilson was named the recipient of the Living Legend Award.

Recipients of the 2004 Award:

Novel: *The Overnight* by Ramsey Campbell (2004: PS Publishing, U.K.; 2005: Tor, U.S.); First Novel: *The Ghost Writer* by John Harwood (Harcourt, US; Jonathan Cape UK); Long Fiction: *Viator* by Lucius Shepard (Night Shade); Mid-Length Fiction: "Flat Diane" by Daniel Abraham (*The Magazine of Fantasy & Science Fiction*, Oct./Nov. 04); Short Fiction: "A Pace of Change" by Don Tumasonis (*Acquainted With the Night*); Collection: *The Wavering Knife* by Brian Evenson (Fiction Collective Two); Anthology: *Acquainted With the Night*, edited by Barbara Roden and Christopher Roden (Ash-Tree Press); Nonfiction: *A Serious Life* by D.M. Mitchell (Savoy, U.K.); Art (Tie): Darrel Anderson and Rick Berry; Film: *Shaun of the Dead* directed by Edgar Wright; written by Simon Pegg and Edgar Wright; Television: *Lost* created by J.J. Abrams and Damon Lindelof (ABC); Illustrated Narrative: *The Bug Boy* by Hideshi Hino (DH Publishing, Japan); Periodical: *The 3rd Alternative*, Andy Cox, Editor/TTA Press, Publisher.

Notable Novels of 2005

I rarely have time to read novels, so there are only a few about which I say more than a few words. But if one judges the health of a field by the *number* of novels published, there seem to be no fewer horror novels published than in previous years. However, a good chunk of them are now published as mainstream fiction.

Glass Soup by Jonathan Carroll (Tor) is a follow-up to *White Apples*, and continues to explore life after death as God—a Polar Bear named Bob—and Chaos—in the person of an evil sexual predator named John Flannery—battle over Anjo, the unborn child of Vincent Ettrich and Isabelle Neukor. Dark and imaginative, as is all of Carroll's work (notice—I am Carroll's editor at Tor).

Harry Potter and the Half-Blood Prince by J.K. Rowling (Bloomsbury) is darker than the earlier books as the teenage Potter outgrows his whininess and he and his friends fall in love, Professor Dumbledore takes on Harry's advanced education, and bad things happen to good people.

Bangkok Tattoo by John Burdett (Alfred A. Knopf) the follow-up to *Bangkok 8*, again takes place mostly in the seedy districts of Bangkok. A devout Buddhist Thai policeman investigates the gruesome mutilation murder of a CIA agent. The book is described as "giddy" by *The New York Times* and it is. Manic, ironic, with entertaining side trips into Thai culture and everyday life.

Beyond Black by Hilary Mantel (Henry Holt) is a very British novel about a genuine psychic who takes on a newly divorced woman as her assistant and their increasingly abrasive relationship. The psychic's "spiritual guide" is a drunken vulgar sot who plays nasty tricks on her and her psychic friends. The book is leisurely and witty and its matter-of-fact treatment of what lies beyond the veil is absorbing.

The Colorado Kid by Stephen King (Hard Case Crime) is a short novel that is as much about the nature of mysteries as it is about a specific mystery. It's also about the growing camaraderie between a young aspiring journalist interning on a small island off Maine and the pair of old newspapermen who tell her about a twenty-five-year-old unsolved mystery. Some readers will find the book exasperating with its drawing out of the tale, but I enjoyed it.

The Spirit Box by Stephen Gallagher (Subterranean Press) is an excellent thriller about a scientist's pursuit of a young woman who has swallowed an experimental drug that seems to break down the boundary between the natural and supernatural realms.

Cold Skin by Albert Sánchez Piñol, translated from the Catalan by Cheryl Leah Morgan (Farrar, Straus and Giroux) is a short novel about a young man assigned as weatherman on a supposedly uninhabited island. He encounters a dour and hostile German inhabiting the lighthouse and fighting off a scourge of indigenous humanoids. The relationship between the two men, a female native, and the rest of the "monsters" shifts over time and the book interestingly explores ideas of the alien and of sexuality. However, the ending does not satisfy.

The Girl in the Glass by Jeffrey Ford (HarperCollins/ Dark Alley) is a dark mystery about a group of fake spiritualists who ply their dubious wares among the rich of New York during the Great Depression. The master scammer Thomas Schell finds his rationalism challenged when he sees the image of a young girl pleading for help during one of his seances. The colorful cast of characters, the impeccable historical detail, and the fast-moving plot makes for an excellent ride. The book won the Edgar Award.

Valley of Bones by Michael Gruber (William Morrow), the absorbing follow-up to *Tropic of Night,* is about the murder of a Sudanese oilman. The prime suspect is a possibly delusional woman who claims to commune with saints. The novel switches between Afro-Cuban Miami Detective Jimmy Paz's investigation into the murder, his budding romance with a hypochondriac psychologist, a brief history of the Society of Nursing Sisters of the Blood of Christ, and the suspect's "confessions"—how she developed from an abused child, drug dealer, and hooker into a soldier in a religious order dedicated to serving the wounded in war torn countries.

Also noted:

The Bitten by L. A. Banks (St. Martin's Press), *The Forbidden* by L. A. Banks (St. Martin's), *The Demonologist* by Michael Laimo (Leisure), *Fiend* by Jemiah Jefferson (Leisure), *Rabid Growth* by James A. Moore (Leisure), *Time Hunter: Echoes* by Iain McLaughlin and Claire Bartlett (Telos), *The Book of Renfield* by Tim Lucas (Touchstone), *Doctor Jekyll & Mr. Hyde* by Amarantha Knight (Circlet), *The Beloved* by J.F. Gonzalez (Midnight Library), *Haunted* by Kelley Armstrong (Bantam), *November Mourns* by Tom Piccirilli (Bantam), *Perfect Nightmare* by John Saul (Ballantine), *States of Grace* by Chelsea Quinn Yarbro (Tor), *Grave Intent* by Deborah LeBlanc (Leisure), *Fear Me* by Stephen Laws (Leisure), *The Tower* by Simon Clark (Leisure), *Identity* by Steve Vance (Leisure), *Predators Prayers* by

Philip Caro (Leisure), *Poison* by Chris Wooding (Orchard Books), *Sign of the Raven* by Julie Hearn (Atheneum Books for Young Readers), *Multiple Wounds* by Alan Russell (Leisure), *Manitou Blood* by Graham Masterton (Leisure), *Lethal Dose* by Jeff Buick (Leisure), *Lord Loss* by Darren Shan (Little, Brown), *Ghost of Albion: Accursed* by Amber Benson and Christopher Golden (Del Rey), *Sweet Miss Honeywell's Revenge* by Kathryn Reiss (Harcourt), *Nobody True* by James Herbert (Tor), *The Witch's Boy* by Michael Gruber (Harper Tempest), *Undead and Unreturnable* by Mary Janice Davidson (Berkley Sensation), *Everybody Scream!* By Jeffrey Thomas (Raw Dog Screaming Press), *The Loch* by Steve Alten (Tsunami Press), *Grave Sight* by Charlaine Harris (Berkley Prime Crime), *Blood-Angel* by Justine Musk (Roc), *Flashback* by Gary Braver (Forge), *The Backwoods* by Edward Lee (Leisure and Cemetery Dance, the latter in a limited edition), *The Reckoning* by Sarah Pinborough (Leisure), *Into the Fire* by Richard Laymon (Leisure), *Joplin's Ghost* by Tananarive Due (Atria), *The Narrows* by Alexander C. Irvine (Del Rey), *Follow* by A.J. Matthews (Rick Hautala) (Jove), *Courting Midnight* by Emma Holly (Berkley Sensation), *The Town That Forgot How to Breathe* by Kenneth J. Harvey (St. Martin's), *Fledgling* by Octavia E. Butler (Seven Stories Press), *Dispatch* by Bentley Little (Signet), *Berserk* by Tim Lebbon (Necessary Evil limited edition), *Cold Blooded* by Robert J. Randisi (Leisure), *In the Name of the Vampire* by Mary Ann Mitchell (Leisure), *In Golden Blood* by Stephen Woodworth (Dell), *The Mad Cook of Pymatuning* by Christopher Lehmann-Haupt (Simon & Schuster), *Fetish* by Tara Moss (Leisure), *Mistress of the Dark* by Sèphera Girón (Leisure), *Terminal* by Brian Keene (Bantam Spectra), a heavily revised and expanded version of the novella of the same title, *The Abandoned* by Douglas Clegg (Leisure), *The Preserve* by Patrick Lestewka (Necro Publications), *Bad Magic* by Stephen Zielinski (Tor), *Underground* by Craig Spector (Tor), *The Wandering Jew's Daughter* by Paul Féval translated by Brian Stableford (Black Coat Press), a novella originally published in French in 1878, *Gil's All Fright Diner* by A. Lee Martinez (Tor), *Woman* by Richard Matheson (Gauntlet Press), *Infernal Devices* by Philip Reeve (Scholastic, U.K.), *The Devil's Footsteps* by E.E. Richardson (The Bodley Head, U.K.), *Velocity* by Dean R. Koontz (Bantam), *Thin Line Between* by M.A.C. Petty (Cold Spring Press), *Come Dance with Me* by Russell Hoban (Bloomsbury), *Never Let Me Go* by Kazuo Ishiguro (Alfred A. Knopf), *Innocent Blood* by Graham Masterton (Severn House, U.K.), *The Hollow: Horseman* by Christopher Golden and Ford Lytle Gilmore (Penguin/Razorbill), *Ashes* by H.R. Howland (Berkley), *Smoke and Mirrors* by Tanya Huff (DAW), *The Historian* by Elizabeth Kostova (Little, Brown), *Within the Shadows* by Brandon Massey (Kensington/Dafina), *Twisted Branch* by Chris Blaine (Berkley), *Keepers* by Gary A. Braunbeck (Leisure), *Bloodline* by Kate Cary (Razorbill), *The Vampire Files: Song in the Dark* by P.N. Elrod (Ace), *In Shadows* by Chandler McGrew (Dell), *Already Dead* by Charlie Huston (Del Rey), *Like Death* by Tim Wagoner (Leisure), *The Home* by Scott Nicholson (Pinnacle Books), *In the Rain With the Dead* by Mark West (Pendragon Press, U.K.), *Laughing Boy* by Bradley Denton (Subterranean), *Last Burn in Hell* by John Edward Lawson (Raw Dog Screaming), *Blood of Angels* by Michael Marshall (Jove), *Desolation* by Tim Lebbon (Leisure), *The Boy Who Couldn't Die* by William Sleator (Harry N. Abrams/Amulet Books), *The Vampyricon: The Priest of Blood* by Douglas Clegg (Ace), *Hive* by Tin Curran (Elder Sign Press), *To Kingdom Come* by Will Thomas (Touchstone), *Autumn Castle* by Kim Wilkins (Warner Aspect), *Broken Angel* by Brian Knight (Delirium), *Kiss the Goat* by Brian Stableford (Prime), *The Dark De-*

stroyer by John Glasby (Sarob Press), *Play Dead* by Michael A. Arnzen (Raw Dog Screaming Press), *The Hides* by Patrick Kealan Burke (Cemetery Dance), *Siren Promised* a first novel by Alan M. Clark and Jeremy Robert Johnson (Bloodletting Press)—the book is illustrated throughout by Clark, *Nowhere Near an Angel* by Mark Morris (PS) in two signed limited hardcover editions, with introduction by Stephen Gallagher, *City of the Dead* by Brian Keene (Leisure)—also in a limited hardcover edition in two states, with jacket art by Alan M. Clark (Delirium), *Night's Kiss* by Amanda Ashley (Zebra), *The Good, the Bad, and the Undead* by Kim Harrison (HarperTorch), *Seize the Night* by Sherrilyn Kenyon (St. Martin's), *Sex, Lies, and Vampires* by Katie MacAlister (Dorchester/Love Spell), *Unspeakable* by Graham Masterton (Pocket Star), *Steel Ghosts* by Michael Paine (Berkley), *Phantom Nights* by John Farris (Tor), *Ghosts of Eden* by T.M. Gray (Gale Group/Five Star), *Flesh Gothic* by Edward Lee (Leisure), *Tales from the Dark Side: Blood on the Snow* by Tim Bowler (Hodder Children's Books, U.K.), *The Wereling: Prey* by Stephen Cole (Bloomsbury, U.K.), *Darkroom* by Graham Masterton (Severn House, U.K.), *The Falls of Death* by Christopher Nicole (Severn House, U.K.), *Wildwood Road* by Christopher Golden (Bantam Spectra), *Hex and the City* by Simon R. Green (Ace), *A Stroke of Midnight* by Laurell K. Hamilton (Ballantine), *Incubus* by Nick Gifford (Penguin/Puffin, U.K.), *Bloody Harvest* by Richard Kunzmann (Macmillan, UK), *Dark Moon Rising* by James M. Thompson (Kensington/Pinnacle), *Moon's Web* by C.T. Adams and Cathy Clamp (Tor), *Bite Club* by Hal Bodner (Alyson), *Dark Whispers* by Chris Blaine (Berkley), *Night Life* by Ray Garton (Subterranean), the sequel to *Live Girls*, *The Drive-In: The Bus Tour* by Joe R. Lansdale (Subterranean), the third volume in the series, *Last Girl Dancing* by Holly Lisle (Onyx), *Heretic* by Joe Nassise (Pocket), *Lone Wolf* by Edo van Belkom (Tundra), *The Black Angel* by John Connolly (Hodder & Stoughton, U.K.), *Twisted Souls* by Shaun Hutson (Time Warner, U.K.), *Drowned Night* by Chris Blaine (Berkley), *Personal Demons* by Gregory Lamberson (Broken Umbrella Press), *What Rough Beast* by H.R. Knight (Leisure), *Dead Beat* by Jim Butcher (Roc), *Lunar Park* by Bret Easton Ellis (Knopf), *Creepers* by David Morrell (CDS Books), *Infernal* by F. Paul Wilson (Forge), *King Kong* by Edgar Wallace, Merian C. Cooper, and Delos W. Lovelace (Underwood Books), an illustrated reprint of the 1932 Grosset & Dunlap book, which was adapted from the screenplay but not the finished film, *Merian C. Cooper's King Kong* by Joe DeVito and Brad Strickland (St. Martin's Griffin), a rewrite of the 1932 novel with some black & white illustrations by Joe DeVito, *Monster* by Frank Peretti (Westbow Press), *Disconnection* by Erin Samilogu (Medallion Press), *The Book of Spirits* by James Reese (William Morrow), *The War of the Worlds* by H.G. Wells (The Modern Library Classics), a new edition in trade paperback with an introduction by Arthur C. Clarke, *Succulent Prey* by Wrath James White (Bloodletting Press), *The Last Motel* by Brett McBean (Biting Dog Publications), *Lake Mountain* by Steve Gerlach (Bloodletting), *The Cleansing* by Shane Ryan Staley (Bloodletting), *Dark Tales of Time and Space* by Sean Wright (Crowswing Books, U.K.), *Limits of Enchantment* by Graham Joyce (Atria), *Twilight* by Stephanie Meyer (Little, Brown), *Tyrannosaur Canyon* by Douglas Preston (Forge), *Peeps* by Scott Westerfeld (Razorbill), *The Healer* by Michael Blumlein (Pyr), *Night of Knives* by Ian Cameron Esslemont (PS), *The Mysteries* by Lisa Tuttle (Bantam), *Rancor* by James McCann (Simply Read Books), *Secret Stories* by Ramsey Campbell (PS) in a signed, limited hardcover edition in two states, with an introduction by Jeremy Dyson and jacket art by David Kendall, and *Voodoo Season* by Jewel Parker Rhodes (Atria).

xlvi ·•· Summation 2005: Horror

Anthologies

There were fewer original horror anthologies published by the larger publishers in 2005, but the small press continued to take up the slack as far as quantity.

Don't Turn Out the Light, edited by Stephen Jones (PS), has more originals in it than earlier volumes in this nontheme series and they are all quite impressive, particularly those by Roberta Lannes, Mark Samuels, and Jay Russell (the latter two reprinted herein). Highly recommended.

Acquainted With the Night, edited by Christopher Roden (Ash-Tree Press, Canada), the publisher's first simultaneous hardcover and trade paperback edition, is an excellent all-original, nontheme anthology. The mix is a good one, and all the stories were quite readable but if I'm forced to choose favorites they would be those by Barbara Roden, Joel Lane, and Steve Duffy. Roden's is reprinted herein. The excellent jacket art is by Jason Van Hollander.

Weird Shadows over Innsmouth edited by Stephen Jones (Fedogan & Bremer) is an excellent, mostly original anthology of stories inspired by Lovecraft's mythos of a degraded race of deep sea creatures. The variety of stories is noteworthy; my favorites among the originals are those by Michael Marshall Smith, Caitlín R. Kiernan, Paul McAuley, Kim Newman, Richard A. Lupoff, and a novella by Brian Lumley. The book is wonderfully illustrated in black and white by Randy Broecker, Les Edwards, Alan Servoss, and Bob Eggleton, who also painted the cover art.

Darkness Rising 2005 edited by L.H. Maynard and M.P.N Sims (Prime), is a nontheme horror anthology. There are notable stories by Steve Duffy, Peter Tennant, and some other, newer writers.

Bernie Herrmann's Manic Sextet edited by Gary Fry (Gray Friar Press, U.K.) is a strong original nontheme anthology of six novelettes. Adam L.G. Nevill, Gary McMahon, Paul Finch, Simon Strantzas, Rhys Hughes, and Donald Pulker all contribute well-told and varied pieces of dark fiction. The cover art on this trade paperback is by Ben Baldwin, and Mike O'Driscoll provides a brief preface.

Poe's Progeny, edited by Gary Fry (Gray Friar), a solid, all-original anthology of stories inspired by classic dark fiction, has a number of notable stories, including those by Richard Gavin, Joel Lane, Tim Lebbon, Mike O'Driscoll, Nicholas Royle, Stephen Volk, Conrad Williams, Adam L.G. Nevill, Greg Beatty, Chico Kidd, John Llewellyn Probert, Ramsey Campbell, Donald R. Burleson, and Simon Clark. Michael Marshall Smith provides an introduction. Adam L.G. Nevill's story is reprinted herein.

Taverns of the Dead, edited by Kealan Patrick Burke (Cemetery Dance), mixed new and reprinted tales of horror relating to bars. There are good original contributions by Chaz Brenchley, Tom Piccirilli, P.D. Cacek, Jack Cady, Nicholas Royle, Ramsey Campbell, Roberta Lannes, Thomas Monteleone, David Morrell, Melanie Tem, and Chet Williamson. The Cady is reprinted here.

Horrors Beyond: Tales of Terrifying Realities, edited by William Jones (Elder Signs Press) is an anthology of eighteen stories, most originals, infused with Lovecraftian themes. There are notable stories by William Mitchell, Gerard Houarner, and Tim Curran.

Corpse Blossoms, edited by Julia and R.J. Sevin (Creeping Hemlock Press) has twenty-four original, nontheme horror stories, and is the press's first publication. The trade edition is attractive, with simple but classy cover art and design by publisher/editor R.J. Sevin and interior decorations by co/publisher/editor Julia Sevin. Included are brief afterwords by the editors on each story and author bios. There are notable stories by Gary A. Braunbeck, Ramsey Campbell, Michael Canfield, Brian Freeman, Bentley Little, Tom Piccirilli, Eric Shapiro, Darren Speegle, Steve Rasnic Tem, Steve Vernon, and Kealan Patrick Burke.

Dark Notes From NJ, edited by Harrison Howe (GSHW Press) features fourteen new stories by members of Garden State Horror Writers. The theme is "dark tales inspired by songs of New Jersey musicians." There is a foreword by Brian Keene, and notes by each author about his or her inspiration. Also, profiles of each of the musicians whose songs provided inspiration. The most striking stories were by William Mingin, Mary SanGiovanni, and Neil Morris.

Fourbodings: A Quartet of Uneasy Tales, edited by Peter Crowther, has novellas by Simon Clark, Tim Lebbon, Mark Morris, and Terry Lamsley (Cemetery Dance). While well-written, interesting, and creepy, all four novellas could have used some trimming to increase their impact.

Lost on the Darkside, edited by John Pelan (Roc) is the newest in this nontheme series. Notable stories by Ramsey Campbell, Michael Laimo, David Niall Wilson, Gerard Houarner, Mark Samuels, and Jeffrey Thomas. I was disappointed to note that there were no bios of the contributors nor an introduction by the editor.

Night Voices, Night Journeys: Lairs of the Hidden Gods, Volume 1 and *Inverted Kingdom: Lairs of the Hidden Gods, Volume 2*, both edited by Asamatsu Ken (Kurodahan Press, Japan), are oddities. A Japanese anthology, translated into English, of Lovecraftian horror stories. The translations are smooth and very much in the vernacular, and the stories are literate, well crafted, and quite enjoyable. Included in Volume 1 is a list of Cthulhu Mythos manga and a bibliography of works by Japanese authors, related to H.P. Lovecraft and the Cthulhu Mythos. In Volume 2 there's an essay on the Cthulhu Mythos in gaming. Robert M. Price provides introductions to both volumes and the editor provides forewords. The cover art on each book is an accurate reflection of the Lovecraftian and Japanese sensibilities of the anthologies.

Dark Delicacies edited by Del Howison and Jeff Gelb (Carroll & Graf) is a nontheme anthology of twenty new stories, most by authors who have signed at the Dark Delicacies bookstore owned by Del and Sue Howison. Some of the more notable stories are by Nancy Holder, Clive Barker, Steve Niles, Lisa Morton, and David J. Schow.

Outsiders, edited by Nancy Holder and Nancy Kilpatrick (Roc), is a mix of twenty-two original horror and fantasy stories concerning the theme of the outsider/misfit. Overall, the book isn't as disturbing as I would like, but there are good stories by Elizabeth Massie, David J. Schow, Steve Rasnic Tem, Joe R. Lansdale, Léa Silhol, and Melanie Tem.

Phantoms at the Phil, edited by John Smith (Side Real Press/ Northern Gothic, U.K.), is a slim volume of three ghost stories originally told for Christmas at the Literary & Philosophical Society of Newcastle upon Tyne. The stories are by Sean O'Brien, Gail-Nina Anderson, and Chaz Brenchley. This limited edition is the second from the small press.

The Blackest Death Volume II, edited by The Staff of Black Death (Black Death Press) has twenty-four original stories. There's nothing wrong with the lineup, but very few of the stories stand out. The two that do are by Marc Paoletti and Christopher Fulbright.

Thicker than Water (Tigress Press) has nine vampire stories, all but one published for the first time, by promising newcomers Cullen Bunn, Mark Worthen, J.P. Edwards, and Curtis Hoffmeister.

Cold Flesh, edited by Paul Fry (Hellbound Books Publishing) has twenty-five gruesome, disgusting flesh-eating-zombie stories, few with more than a skeleton plot to throw some gore onto. The one story that stood above the rest was by Robert Morrish.

Wicked Karnival Halloween Horrors, edited by Tom Moran and Billie Moran (Sideshow Press), has thirty-three, mostly original tales about Halloween. The book is illustrated by James Helkowski and Tom Moran.

Kolchak: The Night Stalker Chronicles, edited by Joe Gentile, Garrett J. Anderson, and Lori Gentile (Moonstone). Twenty-six contemporary stories featuring the character from the 1970s television show. Each story has a full page illustration.

Revenant, edited by Armand Rosamilia (Carnifex Press) has five horror stories by relative newcomers.

Tales Out of Dunwich, edited by Robert M. Price (Hippocampus Press) has reprints by Nancy A. Collins, Jack Williamson, and Richard A. Lupoff, and seven original stories, including a good one by Eddy C. Bertin.

The Evil Entwines (revised edition) by John B. Ford & Guests (Rainfall Books/BJM Press) is an expanded version of Ford's collaborations with F. Paul Wilson, John Pelan, Tim Lebbon, Thomas Ligotti, Ramsey Campbell, and several others. Paul Kane wrote the introduction.

H.P. Lovecraft's Favorite Weird Tales, edited by Douglas A. Anderson (Cold Spring Press) has eighteen of Lovecraft's favorites, including stories by Arthur Machen and A. Merritt.

Bare Bone, edited by Kevin L. Donihe, formerly a magazine, is now published by Raw Dog Screaming Press as a semiannual anthology. It comes as an attractive, trade paperback. In 2005 there was notable fiction and poetry by Gary Fry, Charlee Jacob, Chris Ringler, Jeff Somers, Robert Dunbar, Mark Patrick Lynch, and C.S. Fuqua.

Darkness Rising: The Rolling Darkness Review 2005 (Earthling Publications) is an entertaining anthology featuring several writers who organized a mini-tour for themselves. This chapbook was sold during the tour, and has original stories by Peter Atkins, Glen Hirshberg, Michael Blumlein, Robert Morrish, and Robert Masello, plus a reprint by Nancy Holder. Hirshberg's "American Morons" is reprinted herein.

Teddy Bear Cannibal Massacre, edited by Tim Lieder (Dybbuk Press) has eleven original horror stories by mostly new writers.

Potter's Field, edited by Cathy Buburuz (Sam's Dot Publishing) has twelve stories (two reprints) about unmarked graves. The best original is by Gary McMahon. The chapbook is illustrated by Marcia A. Borell and the cover art is by Lis Anselmi.

Bone Ballet, edited by John Weagly (Iguana Publications), is a chapbook of seven stories using bones as their motif.

The Dead Cat Poet Cabal by Gerard Houarner [and the Poet Cabal] (Bedlam Press) presents another batch of poetry and bits of prose in the Dead Cat series by Tom Piccirilli, Linda Addison, Rain Graves, Darrell Schweitzer, and thirteen others. The cover art is by GAK.

Chimeraworld #2, edited by Mike Philbin (Chimeracana Books), has some really brutal stories in it, many filled with mutilation and blood and other bodily fluids.

There are good stories by Steve Lockley and Paul Lewis, Dustin La Valley, William D. Carl, and Quentin S. Crisp.

Deathgrip: It Came from the Cinema, edited by Horns (Hellbound Books), is a book of stories "inspired" by various horror movie tropes. Unfortunately, most of the stories are uninspired, with a couple of notable exceptions by Kevin James Miller and Daniel Kayson.

Shadow Box, edited by Shane Jiraiya Cummings and Angela Challis (Brimstone Press), is a CD-Rom of flash horror fiction by Australian, American, and Canadian writers. It's an attractive package with appropriate sound effects and art by coeditor Cummings. All profits will be donated to Mission Australia and the Australian Horror Writers Association. The best pieces of fiction are by Shei Tanner and Shane Jiraiya Cummings.

Horror Between the Sheets, edited by Michael Amorel, Oliver Baer, and Benjamin X. Wretland (Two Backed Books), is a selection of twenty-three stories from *Cthulhu Sex* Magazine. It includes stories by Mark McLaughlin, Brian Knight, and others.

The Best of Borderlands, compiled by Elizabeth Monteleone (Borderlands Press), culls fifty stories from the five volumes of the non-theme anthology series.

Fear of the Unknown, the Harrow Anthology, edited by Kfir Luzatto and Monica O'Rourke (Echelon Press) has thirteen stories, five reprints, and eight originals. All are interesting. Chelsea Quinn Yarbro wrote the introduction. The book is intended to benefit Bone Cancer International. Each story has skillful and attractive spot-illustrations by GAK and other artists.

Bite, ed. by Anonymous (Jove), is an original anthology of five vampire romance stories by Laurell K. Hamilton, Charlaine Harris, and three other writers.

The Campfire Collection: Thrilling, Chilling Tales of Alien Encounters, edited by Gina Hyams (Chronicle), has thirteen horror reprints by Stephen King, Philip K. Dick, and others.

Late Victorian Gothic Tales, edited by Roger Luckhurst (Oxford University Press), has twelve gothic stories by Vernon Lee, Henry James, Sir Arthur Conan Doyle, and others. The editor provides an extensive introduction and notes.

The Mammoth Book of New Horror 16, edited by Stephen Jones (Robinson, U.K./ Carroll & Graf), with twenty-one stories, only overlaps with two stories from *YBFH #18*. Jones writes an extensive summary of the year in horror and with Kim Newman writes a Necrology.

Mixed-Genre Anthologies

Fourth Planet From the Sun: Tales of Mars from The Magazine of Fantasy & Science Fiction, edited by Gordon Van Gelder (Thunder's Mouth), includes darker stories by Alfred Coppel and Philip K. Dick. *Book of Voices* edited by Michael Butscher (Flame Books, U.K.) aims to raise funds for, and awareness of, the work of Sierra Leone PEN. The only real horror story is the excellent "Boatman's Holiday" by Jeffrey Ford, reprinted herein. But there is also interesting work by Tanith Lee and Catherynne M. Valente. *Transgressions*, edited by Ed McBain (Forge), is a terrific, all-original collection of crime novellas by some of the best in the field. The best and darkest stories are by Joyce Carol Oates, John Farris, and Stephen King. *No Longer Dreams*, edited by Danielle Ackley-McPhail, L. Jagi Lamplighter, Lee Hillman, and Jeff Lyman (Lite Circle), is a showcase for the mostly new writers belonging to an internet newsgroup and has sf/f/h reprints and originals. *TEL: Stories*, edited by Jay Lake (Wheatland Press), is an interesting original anthology (with two reprints) of mostly experimental mixed-genre fiction. Not all the stories/vignettes are successful, but there are enough effective darker stories to appeal to the horror reader, including those by Sonya Taaffe, Toiya Kristen Finley, Timalyne Frazier, and Tim Pratt. *Brooklyn Noir 2: The Classics*, edited by Tim McLoughlin (Akashic Books), has excerpts and reprints by writers ranging from H.P. Lovecraft and Thomas Wolfe and Irwin Shaw to Jonathan Lethem, Hubert Selby, Jr., Lawrence Block, and Colson Whitehead. *Emerald Eye: The Best Irish Imaginative Fiction*, edited by Frank Ludlow and Roelof Goudriaan (Aeon Press, Ireland), is a showcase for Irish fantasy and dark fantasy and includes reprints by Anne McCaffrey, William Trevor, Bob Shaw, James White, Mike O'Driscoll, and others. *Daikaiju!*, edited by Robin Hood and Robin Pen (agog! Press, Australia), will be disappointing to those looking for scary stories about the formidable Godzilla because the stories just aren't horrific. They are, however, for the most part entertaining. *Circles in the Hair* (CITH) was published by a New York City writing workshop that includes Linda D. Addison, Gerard Houarner, Keith R.A. DeCandido, and others. The notable horror stories are by Tim Hatcher, Natalia Lincoln, M.P. Melnis, and Robert Emmett Murphy Jr. *All Hell Breaking Loose*, edited by Martin H. Greenberg (DAW), is an entertaining, mostly fantasy anthology of sixteen original stories. The few notable horror stories in the book are by David Niall Wilson, Ed Gorman, Tom Piccirilli, and Sarah A. Hoyt. *The Elastic Book of Numbers*, edited by Allen Ashley (Elastic Press, U.K.), has the ingenious theme of stories about numbers. The twenty-one stories are a mixed bag with the best dark stories by Marion Arnott, Toiya Kristen Finley, Sam Hayes, Charles Lambert, Mark Patrick Lynch, Donald Pulker, E. Sedia, Joy Marchand, and Neil Williamson. *Tales of the Unanticipated*, formerly a magazine but newly dubbed "The Anthology of *TOTU* Ink," is edited by Eric M. Heideman. Its twenty-sixth "issue" was thicker than usual. There were a couple of notable dark stories by Martha A. Hood and Patricia Russo, and a notable poem by Mike Allen. *In the Shadow of Evil*, edited by Martin H. Greenberg and John Helfers (DAW) is based on the premise that evil is the default and good doesn't necessarily triumph. This is certainly a theme that provides fertile ground for horror, yet none of the stories are particularly horrific. *Tesseracts Nine*, edited by Nalo Hopkinson and Geoff Ryman (Edge Science Fiction, Canada), spotlights twenty-three science fiction and fantasy (with the occasional horror tinge) stories and poems written by Canadians. *Tempting Disaster*, edited by John Edward Lawson (Two Backed), has twenty-four stories and vignettes, all but seven original, about forbidden pleasures. Although a few of the stories are dark, the best is by Simon Logan. *Requiem for the Radioactive Monkeys*, edited by John Weagly (Iguana Publications), features eight stories using the image of radioactive monkeys. A couple of the tales are dark. *Nova Scotia: New Scottish Speculative Fiction*, edited by Neil Williamson and Andrew J. Wilson (Mercat Press, U.K.), is an excellent showcase of twenty-one fantasy, science fiction, and horror stories by writers such as Ken MacLeod, Hal Duncan, Jane Yolen, Marion Arnott, John Grant, and Charles Stross. There are very good dark stories by Marion Arnott, Jane Yolen, Deborah J. Miller, and Stefan Pearson. *Ghosts at the Coast: The Best of Ghost Story Weekend Volume 2*, edited by Dianna Rodgers (TripleTree Publishing) showcases twenty-five stories written during an annual weekend event during which the assignment is to write a ghost story. Although only a few of the stories have real scares, there are good ones by Jeremy Robert Johnson and Eric M. Witchey. *Spirits Unwrapped*, edited by Daniel

Braum (Lotus Bubble), has four stories about mummies. Illustrations and cover art is by Élena Nazzaro. *Blood Surrender*, edited by Cecelia Tan (Blue Moon) has fifteen erotic vampire stories, most original, few horrific. *Murder, Mystery, Madness, Magic, and Mayhem II Triskaideka*, edited by R.M, Kinder, Georgia R. Nagel, and James Henry Taylor (Cave Hollow Press), has thirteen stories chosen from submissions to the publisher's short fiction contest. *The Year's Best Australian Science Fiction & Fantasy*, edited by Bill Congreve and Michelle Marquart (Prime), has eleven stories of science fiction, fantasy, and horror by writers including Terry Dowling, Cat Sparks, Rjurik Davidson, and others, plus a brief overview of the fantastic fiction publishing market in Australia. Also a recommended list of Australian publications. *Seekers of Dreams: Masterpieces of Fantasy*, edited by Douglas A. Anderson (Cold Spring Press), has twenty-stories of light and dark fantasy, including stories by Lord Dunsany, Jonathan Carroll, Andy Duncan, Thomas Ligotti, Robert Holdstock, and others.

Collections

Hotel Midnight by Simon Clark (Robert Hale, U.K.), the author's third collection of stories, contains ten reprints (one is the British Fantasy Award-winning "Goblin City Lights") and two effective, original novellas.

Never Seen by Waking Eyes by Stephen Dedman (infrapress) is this talented Australian storyteller's second collection, and it includes twenty-four horror stories, plus one new one.

Twentieth-Century Ghosts by Joe Hill (PS) is one of the best collections of the year. Hill is a relative newcomer who consistently creates creepy, very disturbing stories. His is the most important horror debut in short fiction since Glen Hirshberg. The book won the William L. Crawford Award for best first fantasy book, the first time a collection has ever won the award. "My Father's Mask" is reprinted herein.

Haunted by Chuck Palahniuk (Doubleday) "a novel of stories," is a collection with some wraparound and interstitial material, presumably to make the book more palatable to those readers who eschew the short story. The stories are dark, mordant, some are very funny, and they're always entertaining. One of them, "Hot Potting" is reprinted herein. "Guts" was in our eighteenth annual collection.

Home Before Dark: The Collected Cedar Hill Stories, Volume 2 (Earthling Publications) is the excellent follow-up to Braunbeck's 2003 collection, set in the fictional town of Cedar Hill, Ohio, the scene of much of the author's short fiction. There is some short additional material but only one new piece of fiction, a novella, which is quite good. Jacket and interior art is by Deena Holland. Available in two limited editions.

Hornets and Others by Al Sarrantonio (Cemetery Dance) is the author's second collection. It contains two original stories and the original novella "Hornets," the first story of the Orangefield cycle. The fourteen other pieces were originally published between 1981 and 2004.

The Silence Between the Screams by Lucy Taylor (Overlook Connection), has four original stories and a reprint of the novella "Spree" by a writer whose fiction often has been raunchy and powerful but who mostly seems to have dropped out of the horror field. Unfortunately, for some reason her new collection (delayed from 2004) barely made a blip on the radar.

The Complete Symphonies of Adolf Hitler & Other Strange Stories by Reggie

Oliver (The Haunted River, U.K.) is the author's second collection, with sixteen stories, most published for the first time. Oliver continues to produce excellent traditional supernatural tales, as he successfully did with his first collection, *The Dreams of Cardinal Vittorini & Other Strange Stories.* "Among the Tombs" is reprinted herein.

The Shadow at the Bottom of the World by Thomas Ligotti (S&S/Cold Spring Press) includes sixteen reprints culled by Ligotti and Douglas A. Anderson from previous collections, meant as an introductory sampler of the author's work. With a foreword by Anderson.

Terrors by Richard A. Lupoff (Elder Signs Press) contains sixteen entertaining pastiches of pulp's classic writers. Three of the stories were first published in 2005. With an introduction by Fred Chappell and an afterword by the author, describing the inspiration for each story.

Death Sentences: Tales of Punishment and Revenge by Matthew Warner (Undaunted Press) has five stories, two published for the first time. Gary A. Braunbeck provides an introduction. The illustrations are by Deena Warner.

Dark Duets by Michael McCarty and his Band (Wildside) has fifteen original collaborations with writers such as P.D. Cacek, Mark McLaughlin, Jeffrey Thomas, and twelve others.

The Night People by Michael Reaves (Babbage Press) is the author's first collection, with twelve stories and novellas written over the past thirty years, when not focusing on novels and television scripts. He's a talented storyteller whose short fiction is always entertaining. Marc Scott Zicree provides a foreword and Steve Perry provides an afterword. And there are introductions to each story, explaining its inspiration.

The Tales of Inspector Legrasse by H.P. Lovecraft and C.J. Henderson (Mythos Books) reprints Lovecraft's "The Call of Cthulhu," the story that introduced Inspector Legrasse, and showcases six new stories by Henderson featuring the inspector. A good bet for anyone looking for well-crafted Lovecraftian horror.

Slime After Slime by Mark McLaughlin (Delirium) reprints a selection of stories from the author's 2003 *Once Upon a Slime* and adds six original stories. McLaughlin has carved out a very specific niche in horror by specializing in humorous tales making disgusting use of various bodily fluids.

Pocket Full of Loose Razorblades by John Edward Lawson (Afterbirth Books) has eleven dark surreal stories, three original to the collection. The striking cover art is by Bob Siddoway.

Lovecraft Tales by H.P. Lovecraft. Lovecraft finally gets some respect in this handsome volume of twenty-two stories from the Library of America series. The stories are arranged in approximate chronological order of composition, and all but one are taken from the S.T. Joshi–edited texts. Peter Straub provides notes and there is a chronology of Lovecraft's life and writings.

Conference With the Dead by Terry Lamsley (Night Shade) reprints this modern classic originally published by Ash-Tree, but which fell out of print. This new edition has ten stories. The limited edition has one previously unpublished bonus story. Introduction by Ramsey Campbell.

Ghost Dance by Tony Richards (Sarob Press) has eight haunting stories and novellas, two original to the collection. Graham Joyce has written an introduction to the first novella (one of the originals). The cover art is by Paul Lowe.

Angel Dust Apocalypse by Jeremy Robert Johnson (Eraserhead Press) has eighteen stories and vignettes, ten original to the collection. Cover art is by Morten Bak.

Borderlands published two mini-collections in their ongoing limited edition series: *A Little Magenta Book of Mean Stories* by Elizabeth Massie has seven stories, one original and *A Little White Book of Lies* by David B. Silva has five reprints.

Evil, Death, Destruction and Horror by Rafael E. Cariaga (Outskirts Press, Inc.) has eight stories by a new writer.

Wicked Odd by Steve Burt (Burt Creations) is the third in the author's series of young adult horror collections. This volume has six original stories.

Black Dust & Other Tales of Interrupted Childhood by Graham Joyce (Beccon Publications, U.K.) reprints three stories, with an introduction by Mark Chadbourn and commentary about the stories by Jeff VanderMeer, Zoran Živković, Jeffrey Ford, and Joyce. The cover illustration is by Tony Baker. The book was conceived of and put together by Bob Wardzinski and his students at Westwood St. Thomas's School, U.K. in order to benefit the students at the Nqabakazulu Secondary School near Durban in South Africa.

Invasion of the Road Weenies by David Lubar (Starscape) has thirty-five original dark morality tales aimed at kids. They're entertaining and often creepy.

Richard Matheson: Collected Stories, Volume Three, edited by Stanley Wiater (Edge/Gauntlet Press), is an expanded trade paperback version of the 1989 Dream/Press hardcover limited edition. It has eighty-six stories with tributes to Matheson by Stephen King, the late Robert Bloch, Ray Bradbury, and other admirers. There's also an introduction by the author.

The House of Cthulhu by Brian Lumley (Tor) is a reprint of the British edition published by Headline in 1991. It collects ten Lovecraftian horror stories originally published between 1973 and 1988.

The Occult Detective by Robert Weinberg (Twilight Tales) has seven entertaining stories about hard-boiled psychic detective Sidney Taine. The one original is about Sidney's sister Sydney—first female detective in 1930s New York City. Introduction by Stefan Dziemianowicz.

Body Counting by David Whitman (Delirium) is the fourth book in the Exclusives series—books ordered in advance to determine the print run, but limited to one hundred copies. There are twelve stories in Whitman's first solo collection, four of them appearing for the first time. The title story is funny/macabre. Jacket art is by Dave Kendall.

The Lovecraft Chronicles by Peter Cannon (Mythos Books) was published in 2004, but I missed it. It's an episodic alternate history in the form of a memoir, chronicling in three sections how Lovecraft was discovered and published by a mainstream publisher; a trip to England where he met Arthur Machen; and of his life back in Providence and his death in 1960.

Just a Little More Than Strange by D.S. Dollman (Echelon Press) has thirty supernatural stories.

The Book of a Thousand Sins by Wrath James White (Two Backed) contains fifteen graphically violent stories about murder and mayhem. If you like Edward Lee's extreme fiction, you might enjoy this. Good cover art by Mike Bohatch.

Call to the Hunt by Steven E. Wedel (Scrybe Press) has twelve stories about werewolves, three original to the collection. Kelly Armstrong provides an introduction.

Beastie and Other Horrific Tales by Armand Rosamilia (Carnifex Press) is a chapbook with six short stories by a new writer.

Raw Dog Screaming published *Spider Pie* by Alyssa Sturgill, with twenty-four short-shorts of humorous, surreal horror, most of them original. The book has interesting cover art by Kris Kuksi and a title page collage by Cake Earthhead. They also published *The Unauthorized Woman* by Efrem Emerson, with sixteen brief stories, six previously published.

The Terror and Other Tales by Arthur Machen (Chaosium Press) has thirteen stories and an essay on "The Literature of Occultism." This is volume three of *The Best Weird Tales of Arthur Machen*, edited by and with an introduction by S.T. Joshi.

Adrift on the Haunted Seas: The Best Short Stories of William Hope Hodgson (Cold Spring Press) has seventeen stories and four poems. Edited and with an introduction by Douglas A. Anderson.

Silver Lake Publishing brought out several collections I didn't see, including *Rumors of the Grotesque*, twenty-three stories by Steven Lee Climer; *Terrible Thrills*, twenty-five stories by C. Dennis Moore; and *Two Die Four*, four stories by Tim Curran and Tim Johnson.

Count Magnus and Other Ghost Stories by M.R. James (Penguin Classics) contains fifteen stories edited by and with an introduction and notes by S.T. Joshi. Also included are two essays and prefaces by James originally published in his classic collections *Ghost Stories of an Antiquary* and *More Ghost Stories of an Antiquary*.

Subterranean published collections including: *The Fear Planet and Other Unusual Destinations: The Reader's Bloch, Volume One* by Robert Bloch, edited by Stefan R. Dziemianowicz, bringing together twenty-one stories from the author's pulp days, many never before reprinted. *The Girl in the Basement and Other Stories* by Ray Garton (from 2004) includes the short novel of the title, a long novella about an exorcism, and four original short stories. It was produced as a super limited, that is, only enough copies were produced to fill orders from specialty dealers, with an additional one hundred copies produced for Subterranean to sell direct. *To Charles Fort, With Love* by Caitlín R. Kiernan is the author's third collection of short fiction and contains twelve of her more recent stories, including the marvelous "Onion," published in an earlier volume of this anthology. The book has one haunting original story. Each piece has an afterword by Kiernan, and there's an afterword by Ramsey Campbell. The beautiful, disturbing cover art is by Ryan Obermeyer. *Mr. Fox and Other Feral Tales* by Norman Partridge includes the seven stories from the Bram Stoker Award-winning collection plus eleven early tales, an excerpt from an unpublished zombie novel, an introduction, afterword, and extensive story notes by the author covering the business as well as the creative side of writing. *Zombie Jam* by David J. Schow showcases four of the author's zombie stories. Included is Schow's classic "Jerry's Kids Meet Wormboy" in a longer version than was originally published. Schow's introduction discusses how most contemporary zombie literature has been inspired by movies, particularly the ground-breaking George Romero zombie series. There's also an afterword about how the Romero zombies have even infiltrated popular consciousness. The book has terrific illustrations by Bernie Wrightson. *The Hour Before Dawn and Two Other Stories From Newford* by Charles de Lint has three stories, one original, and is the first book to be illustrated by the author, with a full black-and-white illustration for each story. De Lint also illustrated the dust jacket.

Sarob Press, out of the United Kingdom, published *Ghosts and Family Legends* by Catherine Crowe, volume seven of Richard Dalby's "Mistresses of the Macabre" series. Mrs. Catherine Crowe (1790–1872) became the first great literary authority on the supernatural with her bestselling and influential work *The Night Side of Na-*

ture, or *Ghosts and Ghost Seers* (1848). Jacket Art by Paul Lowe. Also *Solar Pons: The Final Cases* by Basil Copper, which presents five Solar Pons novels in the author's preferred and definitive versions. Each novella appeared in the early 1970s in much altered form—so much so that the author now disowns them. Cover art by Les Edwards.

Ash-Tree brought out *Sea Mist*, by E.F. Benson, edited by Jack Adrian, the fifth and final volume of "Collected Spook Stories." The stories are arranged in chronological order of their original publication and cover the period between 1927 and Benson's death in 1940. Jacket art is by Douglas Walters. *Mr Justice Harbottle and Others* is the third and final volume in Ash-Tree's series reprinting J. Sheridan Le Fanu's supernatural fiction, covering the period between 1870 and the author's death in 1873. Edited and with an introduction by Jim Rockhill. Jacket art by Douglas Walters. *More Tales of the Uneasy* by Violet Hunt with an introduction by John Pelan, the second and final volume of this series of Hunt's supernatural fiction. The book contains four stories originally published in book form in 1925, with Hunt's preface. Jacket art is by Jason Van Hollander. *The Watcher by the Threshold* by John Buchan collects his weird and supernatural tales in one volume for the first time, arranging them chronologically. Introduction by Kenneth Hillier, the secretary of the John Buchan Society. Jacket art is by Keith Minnion.

Stranger and Other American Tales, from The Works of Robert E. Howard series, edited by Steven Tompkins (University of Nebraska Press/Bison Books), includes the title Conan novella along with a dozen other tales.

Moon of Skulls: The Weird Works of Robert E. Howard, Volume 2 by Robert E. Howard (Wildside) has five stories and four poems, all but one originally published in *Weird Tales* from 1929 to 1930.

Bonechillers: 13 Twisted Tales of Terror by D.W. Cropper (Llewellyn) is a young adult collection of thirteen horror stories.

The House of Sounds by M.P. Shiel (Hippocampus Press) is a collection of seven stories, and the novel *The Purple Cloud* in its original 1901 version. It's part of the Lovecraft Library Series edited and with an introduction by S.T. Joshi.

Shadows of Death by H.P. Lovecraft (Ballantine/Del Rey) has sixteen stories and four fragments by Lovecraft. Introduction by Harlan Ellison.

Mixed-Genre Collections

As the Crow Flies by Dave Hutchinson (BeWrite Books, U.K.—2004) is this underrated British writer's fifth collection. The fifteen short stories are varied and imaginative, showcasing Hutchinson's equal ease with science fiction, fantasy, and the darker realms. Almost half of the stories appear for the first time. "The Pavement Artist" is reprinted herein. *Looking for Jake* by China Miéville (Del Rey) is the author's first collection and has at least one gem that I took for an earlier volume of this anthology. The book includes *The Tain*, originally published in the U.K. as a stand-alone novella. There are three new stories; one "The Ball Room," (reprinted herein), is a terrific collaboration with Emma Bircham and Max Schaefer. There's also a graphic novel done with artist Liam Sharp. Miéville's work blends science fiction, fantasy, and horror—usually quite successfully. *Strange Itineraries* by Tim Powers (Tachyon Publications) has nine stories, three of them collaborations with James P. Blaylock. *In the Palace of Repose*, by Holly Phillips (Prime), this promising author's first collection, includes nine mostly fantasy and dark fantasy stories and a couple that edge over into horror. Seven of the stories are original to the collection. *The Grinding House*, by Kaaron Warren (CSFG Publishing, Australia) is an excellent debut collection by one of several new voices in Australian literature. Most of the sixteen reprints were originally published in small press and/or Australian markets in the decade preceding 2004. There are four original stories. *Magic for Beginners*, Kelly Link's second collection (Small Beer Press) demonstrates her growing maturity as a writer, collecting such masterpieces of complexity as "Lull" and "The Hortlak" and the charm of "The Faery Handbag." The limited edition comes with a deck of cards illustrated with artwork by Shelley Jackson from the book. *Specimen Days* by Michael Cunningham (Farrar, Straus and Giroux) is a wonderful collection of three novellas written in three different genres: ghost story, mystery, and science fiction, taking place in the past, the present, and the future with some overlapping characters. The first is about a young boy whose older brother dies in an industrial accident; the second is about terrorists using children to blow up seemingly random people. The last is about an artificial human who longs to confront his maker. *Two-Handed Engine* by Henry Kuttner and C.L. Moore (Centipede Press) is a very expensive limited edition of three hundred copies. In it are thirty-seven stories by the long-time collaborators. *Cultural Breaks* by Brian Aldiss (Tachyon Publications) has twelve stories, three original, with an introduction by Andy Duncan. *The English Soil Society* by Tim Nickels (Elastic Press, U.K.) is the author's first collection of twenty-one stories, some of them dark. PS Publishing has produced a set of Ray Bradbury titles in three limited states: *S is for Space*, a handsome revised and illustrated collection of sixteen stories (despite the jacket copy saying there are twenty-two) by a master short story writer who has always slipped among the genres. The classic cover art is by Joe Mugraini. Sir Arthur C. Clarke provides a foreword and Tim Powers contributes an introduction. *R is for Rocket*, has seventeen classics, including "The Fog Horn," and "A Sound of Thunder." The foreword is by Ray Harryhausen and the introduction is by Michael Marshall Smith. Both books are illustrated throughout (with art from the stories' original appearances in the pulps) by various artists. The most limited edition of one hundred copies includes a third volume called *Forever and the Earth*: *Yesterday and Tomorrow Tales*. *The Life to Come* by Tim Lees (Elastic) is this talented author's first collection, reprinting stories from *The 3rd Alternative*, *Crimewave*, and *Midnight Street*, and with five new stories. The striking cover art is by Richard Marchand and was designed by Dean Harkness. *Harrowing the Dragon* by Patricia A. McKillip (Ace) collects fifteen fantasy and dark fantasy stories by the author, most originally published in anthologies. *Eternity and Other Stories* by Lucius Shepard (Thunder's Mouth) has seven stories, a few of them reprinted from *Trujillo*, Shepard's massive 2004 collection. *The Traveling Tide* by Rosaleen Love (Aqueduct Press) is part of the "Conversation Pieces" series from the publisher. The author is an Australian who often writes on feminist themes in fiction and nonfiction. There are seven stories in the chapbook, two original. *The Minotaur in Pamplona Books I and II*, edited by Neil Ayres (D-Press), was created to thank the Spanish animal welfare society ADDA, "instrumental in the ban of the 'sport' of bullfighting in Barcelona." Each chapbook has four stories and poems (the first volume has three and a poem by Brian W. Aldiss), all original except for the title story by Rhys Hughes. Very good work in here but only a few twinges of horror. *Rust and Bone* by Craig Davidson (Viking, Canada) is an excellent debut mainstream collection with some very dark stories. Which shouldn't surprise too much, as the author writes out-and-out graphic horror under his pseudonym, Patrick Lestewka. *The Old Child and Other stories* by Jenny Erpenbeck translated by Susan Bernofsky (New Directions) introduces a young German author with a novella and four stories, some darkly tinged. *Across the Wall, A Tale of Abhorsen and Other Stories* by Garth Nix (Eos) has twelve short stories (one original) and an original novella set in the world of the author's bestselling fantasy trilogy. At least one of the stories is horror. *The Motion Demon* by Stefan Grabinski translated by Miroslaw Lipinski (Ash-Tree) is the first in a series of Grabinski volumes that will duplicate the original Polish books. Grabinski, known as the Polish Poe, was a dark surrealist whose work has been painstakingly translated and publicized over the years by Lipinski. There are three stories in the current volume published in English for the first time. The wonderful jacket illustration is by Chris Pelletiere. *Singing Innocence and Experience* by Sonya Taaffe (Prime) is the author's first collection of fiction and poetry. Taaffe's work is dreamy, and she skillfully weaves myth into her stories and poems. Of the twenty-three pieces, two stories appear for the first time. *Underground Atlanta* by Gregory Nicoll (Marietta Publishing) the first collection by this versatile writer, includes four new stories and one expanded story. Includes a brief foreword and introductions to each story by the author. *Punktown* by Jeffrey Thomas (Prime) is an expanded edition of the excellent collection originally published in 2000. Some of the stories here were written but not used in that first edition. Some have been written since. One was reprinted by me in an earlier volume of this series. Thomas's world is imaginative, nightmarish, and riveting. Michael Marshall Smith has written an introduction to the new edition. *Shadow Play* by Jeffrey B. Burton (Pocol Press) has twenty stories, half original. *Attack of the Jazz Giants and Other Stories* by Gregory Frost (Golden Gryphon) is a long overdue collection by a talented writer. The fourteen stories (with one original novella) are all very readable, and some are excellent, the illustrations and jacket art by Jason Van Hollander is imaginative and clever, and Karen Joy Fowler supplies a foreword. In addition, the book comes with an illustrated pamphlet containing an interview of Frost by John Kessel, and a bibliography. *Dogs of Truth* by Kit Reed (Tor) has seventeen recent stories by this biting satirist. Her work—covering every genre—is irreverent, clever, and right on the mark with regard to popular culture. A couple of the stories are original to the collection. *Once Upon a Time (she said)* by Jane Yolen (NESFA Press) is a collection of more than eighty stories, poems, and articles in honor of the author's Guest of Honor appearance at Interaction, the 2005 World Science Fiction Convention. Most are reprints, but there are a handful of new poems. Yolen writes for adults, young adults, and children and this book should appeal to all ages. *The Fiction Factory* by Jack Dann et al. (Golden Gryphon) collects most of Dann's collaborations with one or more coauthors: Susan Casper, Gardner Dozois, Michael Swanwick, George Zebrowski, Barry N. Malzberg, Janeen Webb, and Jack C. Haldeman II. The eighteen stories range from the light-hearted fantasy about an unpopular girl's date to the prom and a science fictional story about work in the future, to a horror classic about a vampire in a concentration camp. Each story is introduced by the collaborators who tell (as each remembers it—and they don't always jibe) how the story came to be. A fascinating and entertaining book. *Not in Kansas* by Janet Fox (Dark Regions Press) includes seven stories and twenty poems, reprinted from such magazines as *The Twilight Zone* and *Weird Tales*. Illustrated by Allen Koszowski and with an introduction by A.R. Morlan. *Beyond Each Blue Horizon* by Andrew Hook (Crowswing Books, U.K.) is an excellent second collection by the British author who is also the publisher of Elastic Books. The varied stories are well written, some dark crime stories, others fantasy or science fiction, others mixing the genres. Ten of the twenty-one stories are previously unpublished. The beautiful, strange cover art is by Richard Marchand. *Different Kinds of Dead and Other Tales* by Ed Gorman (Five Star) showcases fifteen sf/f/h suspense stories by the consummate storyteller, written and published over twenty-five years. *The Masque of Mañana* by Robert Sheckley (NESFA Press) was published in honor of Sheckley's appearance as Author Guest of Honor at the 63rd World Science Fiction Convention, Interaction, in Glasgow, Scotland. (Unfortunately, Sheckley was too ill to attend). The book contains forty-one short stories from Robert Sheckley's long career as a deeply compassionate science fiction satirist whose work occasionally turned toward the horrific. David G. Hartwell wrote the introduction. *From the Files of the Time Rangers* by Richard Bowes (Golden Gryphon) can be read as a fix-up novel or a series of short stories—the way they were originally published. I prefer the latter. The stories are a lovely mixed bag of time travel, alternate worlds, gods, and politics. And there's plenty of darkness throughout. Foreword by Kage Baker, afterword by the author, gorgeous jacket art by John Picacio. *I Live With You* by Carol Emshwiller (Tachyon) has twelve stories, two original. Emshwiller's fiction is sardonic, political, sometimes funny, sometimes dark. The cover art is by her late husband, artist and filmmaker Ed Emshwiller. *Gunning for the Buddha* by Michael Jasper (Prime) is the first collection by a talented young writer who creates characters who behave believably in whatever situation they find themselves. John Kessel wrote the introduction. *Tonight, Somewhere in New York* by Cornell Woolrich (Carroll & Graf), collects some of the last stories and an unfinished novel by the author of the works that sired the classic suspense films *Rear Window, The Bride Wore Black,* and *The Night Has A Thousand Eyes*. The book was edited and has an Introduction by Francis M. Nevins, author of the biography *Cornell Woolrich: First You Dream, then You Die. Dead Travel Fast* by Kim Newman (Dinoship) reprints ten imaginative, satirical, sometimes dark, always wonderful stories influenced by the movies, old TV shows, and pulps that the author so loves. He provides an afterword to each story. Although the book is welcome, the production leaves something to be desired: there's no table of contents with page numbers. *The Man Who Lost the Sea* by Theodore Sturgeon (North Atlantic Books) is the tenth volume of The Complete Stories of Theodore Sturgeon, containing thirteen stories written between 1957 and 1960. Series editor Paul Williams includes extensive story notes and quotes by Sturgeon about the stories. Jonathan Lethem provides a foreword. *Live! From Planet Earth* by George Alec Effinger (Golden Gryphon) has twenty-two stories. Although Effinger is better known for his humorous lightweight sf and fantasy, he also wrote dark stories, some included in this collection. Each story has commentary by a writer or editor friend of the late author. *The Beasts of Love* by Steven Utley (Wheatland) has thirty-one stories of sf/f and horror, originally published between 1973 and 1985. Lisa Tuttle wrote the Introduction. *Wild Galaxy* by William F. Nolan (Golden Gryphon) collects nineteen science fiction stories published between 1954 and 2000. Although Nolan is possibly most famous for cowriting the novel *Logan's Run,* over the past twenty years or so he has produced as much horror as science fiction. *My Rose and My Glove: Stories (Real and Surreal)* by Harvey Jacobs (Darkside) has twenty-four stories published between 1963 and 2003 by a master fantasy satirist. Think of him as the male Kit Reed. His fiction is sometimes dark, often funny. Two of the stories are original to the volume.

Publisher John Pelan provides an introduction. *Star Changes* by Clark Ashton Smith edited by Scott Connors and Ron Hilger (Darkside) collects what the editors say is the best of Smith's science fiction, working from the original manuscripts. There is an extensive introductory overview of the author's science fiction. *Eternity Lost* by Clifford D. Simak (Darkside Press) is the first volume of a projected twelve-volume set of Collected Stories. Each volume will have 125,000 words of obscure and well-known work and a guest introduction by a well-known writer in the genre. The whole project is edited by Phil Stephensen-Payne. This first volume, containing twelve stories, is introduced by John Pelan. *Homecalling and Other Stories: The Complete Solo Short SF of Judith Merril* (NESFA Press) has twenty-six stories by the author who is better known as an anthologist. Her first sf/horror story, "Only a Mother," still packs a powerful punch and is one of the best of its kind. Introductions by Elizabeth Carey and Emily Pohl-Weary. *Fear and Other Stories From the Pulps* by Achmed Abdullah (Wildside) has seven exotic, weird adventure and crime stories and novellas by the author—second cousin of Tsar Nicholas II—whose Russian name was Alexander Nicholayevitch Romanoff and whose Muslim name was Achmed Abdullah Nadir Khan el-Durani el-Iddressyeh. Although originally published in the early 1900s, at least some of the stories hold up quite well. *Fugue XXIX* by Forrest Aguirre (Raw Dog Screaming) has twenty-nine mostly surreal, sometimes dark stories. Six are original to the collection. *Little Machines* by Paul McAuley (PS) has seventeen stories by an excellent writer who moves with ease from hard science fiction to alternate histories to sf/horror. Introduction by Greg Bear. The book includes McAuley and Kim Newman's sf/h novelette "Residuals," reprinted in an earlier volume of this series. *Times Like These* by Rachel Ingalls (Graywolf) has nine reprints by a mainstream writer who occasionally dips into dark, even horrific waters. *Greetings and Other Stories* by Terry Bisson (Tachyon Publications) showcases ten recent stories and novellas by a writer who's not afraid of writing about politics, nor of making gentle fun of his own past. As with much of Bisson's work, there's a distinct chill as well as charm running throughout the contents. *Heart of Whiteness* by Howard Waldrop (Subterranean) lays bare the imagination of a writer who takes his research seriously but never forgets to entertain the reader. Waldrop is the master of the secret and alternate history, and this is his first collection since 1998 (I admit to publishing six of the ten stories). Get your Waldrop fix while you can (and look for *Howard Who?*, which is being reprinted by Small Beer Press in 2006). *The Cuckoo's Boys* by Robert Reed (Golden Gryphon) has twelve stories published between 1996 and 2005, plus one original. Some of them deal with the dark side of our bright scientific future. There an extensive afterword by Reed explaining the genesis of each story. *Quicksilver & Shadow* by Charles de Lint (Subterranean) is the second volume (of a projected three) of de Lint's Collected Early Stories. The book is nearly 150,000 words and includes the obscure 20,000–word novella, "Berlin," and the 30,000–word "Death Leaves an Echo." MaryAnne Harris did the jacket illustration. *Westermead* by Scott Thomas (Raw Dog Screaming) is a collection of dark fantasy stories, songs, tale, fables. Illustrations are by the author. *A Tour Guide to Utopia* by Lucy Sussex (MirrorDanse Books, Australia), the author's first collection in fifteen years, has twelve stories, published from the nineties to 2004, including several excellent dark ones. Afterword by the author. *The Crazy Colored Sky and Other Tales* by Kevin James Miller (Silver Lake Publishing) has seventeen stories. *Wild Things* by Charles Coleman Finlay (Subterranean), the author's first collection, has fourteen stories ranging from Arthurian romance to space opera and horror. *We're All in This Together* by Owen King (Bloomsbury) is the debut collection of a quirky literary writer. Although most of the five stories are mainstream, at least a couple are pretty dark. Two (including the title novella) appear for the first time.

The artists who work in the small press toil hard and receive too little credit (not to mention money) and it's important to recognize their good work. The following artists created art that I thought noteworthy during 2005:

Steven Hickman, Allen Koszowski, James Hannah, Reggie Oliver, Adam Noble, Vincent Chong, Andrea Wicklund, Eric Dinyer, Magdalena Zmudzinska, Web Bryant, Peter Ferguson, Kinuko Y. Craft, Michael Komarch, Mark Rich, Camille Kuo, Chris Nurse, Mike Bohatch, Robyn Evans, Glitchwerk, Jesse Speak, Godfrey Blow, Jason Van Hollander, George Barr, Joan Hall, Mark Summers, Bill Sienkiewicz, Peter Loader, Les Peterson, Adam Duncan, Lynette Watters, A.R. Menne, H.E. Fassl, Augie Wiedemann, Cat Spark, Richard Marchand, Russell Dickerson, Beatriz Inglessis, Jesse Young, Dennis McCambridge, John Hoffman, John Picacio, Dave Emrich, Tantra Bensko, Marc Hirshfeld, Kenn Brown, Stefan Olsen, SMS, Edward Noon, Josh Finney, Fahrija Velic, David Gentry, Ben Baldwin, Robert Dunn, Marc B. Adin, Chris Cartwright, Sheridan Morgan, Michael J. King, Marge Simon, Allison Lovelock, Alan Hunter, A.C. Evans, Alex McVey, Richard Bartrop, Steven Gilberts, Colin Foran, Dave Carson, Cathy Buburuz, Stephanie Rodriquez, Eric Asaris, Carole Humphreys, Regina Brewster, Tim Mullens, Marcia A. Borell, Elizabeth Fuller-Nicoll, Deena Warner, Phil Parks, Chad Savage, and Simon Moore.

Magazines, Webzines, and Newsletters

Small press magazines come and go with amazing rapidity, so it's difficult to recommend buying a subscription to those that haven't proven their longevity. But I urge readers to at least buy single issues of those that sound interesting. The following are those I thought the best in 2005.

Some of the most important magazines/webzines are those specializing in news of the field, market reports, and reviews. *Hellnotes*, the e-mail and print newsletter edited by Judi Rohrig, is indispensable for overall information, news, and reviews of the horror field. It also runs interviews and has a weekly bestseller list. *The Gila Queen's Guide to Markets*, edited by Kathryn Ptacek, is an excellent font of information for markets in and outside the horror field. Ralan.com is *the* Web site to go to for market information. Paula Guran's knowledgeable and interesting *Darkecho*, is sent out as an irregular e-mail newsletter. *Locus*, edited by Charles N. Brown and *Locus Online*, edited by Mark Kelly specialize in news about the science fiction and fantasy fields, but include a lot of horror coverage as well. The only major professional venues specializing in reviewing short fiction are *Tangent Online* (www.tangentonline.com), *The Internet Review of Science Fiction* (www.irosf.com/) and *Locus*, but none of them specialize in horror. Rumor has it that *The Fix*, a short-lived magazine that reviewed short fiction and was edited by Andy Cox, is going to be returning in 2006. Here's hoping.

Most magazines have Web sites with subscription information, eliminating the need to include it here. For those magazines that do *not* have a Web site, I have provided that information:

The Horror Fiction Review, edited by Nick C. Cato, is a quarterly fanzine with interviews and reviews of books, the occasional movie, and magazines. In 2005 there were interviews of Bentley Little, Nick Mamatas, Michael Laimo, James A. Moore,

Jeff Strand, and newcomer Bryan Smith, a series of mini-interviews with Elizabeth Massie, Rain Graves, Mary Ann Mitchell, Angeline Hawkes-Craig, Teri A. Jacobs, and Deborah LeBlanc, and coverage of horror conventions.

Wormwood, edited by Mark Valentine, is a biannual journal devoted to discussion of authors, books and themes in the fields of the fantastic, supernatural and decadent in literature. It contains essays, articles, short appreciations, new research and perspectives from new and established writers about acknowledged major authors, less-studied writers, and those who are unjustly neglected. *Wormwood* also features the columns "Camera Obscura," surveying recently published but overlooked books, "Late Reviews," reappraising titles from the past, and Brian Stableford's "Decadent World-View."

Necropsy: The Review of Horror Fiction, edited by June Pulliam, is a Web site with new issues up quarterly. The reviewers cover novels, anthologies, and movies and there's also an art and photo gallery.

Video Watchdog, edited by Tim Lucas, is one of the most exuberant film magazines around, and seems especially gleeful when its reviewers discover variant versions of videos and DVDs. The magazine is invaluable for the connoisseur of trashy, pulp, and horror movies and enjoyable for just about everyone. Some of the special articles appearing during 2005 were Charlie Largent's extensive historical overview of Ray Harryhausen's work, with lots of color and black & white stills and posters, an overview by David J. Schow of John Wyndham's triffids from their original magazine appearance as a series called "Revolt of the Triffids" to books, movies and television series.

Rue Morgue, edited by Rod Gudino, is an entertaining magazine that went from bimonthly to monthly mid-year. It's graphic in its coverage of mayhem and perfect for fans of extreme horror. Although it focuses on movies and video, there's a regular book column, a monthly "classic cut"—one month it discussed Francisco José de Goya, and his dark painting *Saturn Devouring His Children*. In 2005 there were articles about the Shudder Pulps, about a line of collectible Boschian replicas (I knew about them earlier and have most of them, of course), the Mütter Museum, an interview with Takashi Miike about his shattering movie *Audition*, a profile of Thomas Ligotti, an interview with S.T. Joshi about H.P. Lovecraft, and an article about the magnificent surreal/grotesque films of the brothers Quay and Jan Svankmajer.

Fangoria, edited by Anthony Timpone, is the granddaddy of contemporary horror movie magazines. A monthly, it mostly covers Hollywood horror productions rather than the independents and runs regular columns on DVD releases and books. There's a lot of overlap in coverage with *Rue Morgue*, but the content seems a bit thinner and restricted more to big movies. The punning captions are frustrating and annoying, making one cringe.

Scarlet Street, edited by Richard Valley, published two issues in 2005. The magazine is all over the place, covering horror classics, mysteries and film noir, and sometimes other types of movies. It takes a more historical and less grisly view of film and television than *Rue Morgue* or *Fangoria*.

There are very few magazines specializing in horror fiction. Some of the best are mentioned below.

Inhuman, edited by Allen Koszowski, brought out two issues in 2005, with good stories and poems by Michael Laimo, Kealan Patrick Burke, Bruce Boston, and Don D'Ammassa, illustrations by the editor and by Alan M. Clark, a film column, and a DVD column.

Cemetery Dance, edited by Robert Morrish, published three issues in 2005, with good stories by Greg Kishbaugh, Tom Piccirilli, Joel Lane, Scott Nicholson, J.T. Petty, Dominick Cancilla, Adam-Troy Castro, and Michael Cadnum. There were interviews with Robert McCammon, Melanie Tem, Chelsea Quinn Yarbro, Stephen Laws, Sèphera Girón, and with Charles Ardai, the publisher of a new line of noir books, and regular columns by Thomas F. Monteleone, Paula Guran, and John Pelan. There were also plenty of reviews.

Horror Garage, edited by Rich Black, brought out one issue in 2005. In it, there were six original stories plus brief interviews with Shocklines online bookstore proprietor Matt Schwartz and Thomas Ligotti. No reviews in the issue.

Supernatural Tales, edited by David Longhorn, is now an annual. In 2005 the perfect-bound magazine had 194 pages, with excellent stories by Nina Allen, Paul Finch, Barbara Roden, Adam Golaski, John Llewellyn Probert, and Tina Rath.

H. P. Lovecraft's Magazine of Horror, edited by Marvin Kaye, featured Richard Matheson, with an interview, a critical overview of movies made of his fiction, and a rediscovered, unpublished story. I would have liked to have seen an overview of Matheson's fiction as well. The best story in the issue was by newcomer Joe McRennary.

All Hallows, edited by Barbara Roden and Christopher Roden, is published thrice yearly by the Ghost Story Society and is always a good read. 2005 was a very good year for its fiction. There were notable stories by Sue Gedge, Rick Kennett (an extremely short story), Marc Lecard, Elaine Lovitt, Reggie Oliver, Elsa Wallace, Benedict Clibborn, Tim Foley, Mike Solomon, Simon Strantzas, Aaron Albrecht, Bill and Jane Read, Helen Grant, Sarah Lister, Eric Bryan, Michael O'Connor, David Evans Katz, Christopher Harmon, Peter H. Wood, Bob Franklin, Robin Lindy, David Acord, Kay Fletcher, Don Stewart, and Jason A. Zwiker. In addition to fiction, the magazine runs essays, letters, reviews, obituaries, and an update of Web sites of interest.

Dark Horizons, edited by Marie O'Regan, is a bonus for members of The British Fantasy Society. The magazine tries to publish twice a year (although there was only one issue in '05) and the stories and poems are always readable—highly recommended for those interested in traditional supernatural fiction. The British Fantasy Society is open to everyone. Members receive the informative quarterly magazine, *Prism*, edited by Bennett, which has opinionated magazine, book, and movie reviews plus interviews with U.K. writers. Also, Paul Kane and Marie O'Regan edited a 2006 calendar illustrated with excellent dark fantasy art by Mike Bohatch, Russell Dickerson, and others and excerpts from the works of Clive Barker, Ramsey Campbell, John Connolly, Muriel Gray, Poppy Z. Brite, and seven other notable writers. Check the Web site to see if there will be a 2007 calendar. The society organizes Fantasycon, the annual British Fantasy Convention, and its membership votes on the British Fantasy Awards. For information write: The British Fantasy Society, the BFS Secretary, 201 Reddish Road, Stockport SK5 7HR, England. Or check out the Web site at: www.britishfantasysociety.org.uk.

Not One of Us, edited by John Benson, is one of the longer-lived small press magazines specializing in dark stories and poetry. It's generally published twice a year and has notable original work with good black and white illustrations. During 2005 there were good stories and poetry by Sonya Taaffe, Jennifer Rachel Baumer, K.S. Hardy, Patricia J. Esposito, Kevin Donihe, Terry Black, Mark Steensland, and Kristine Ong Muslim. It's worthy of your support.

The Horror Express, edited by Mark Shemmans, published two issues in 2005 and had some good stories and poetry by Tim Lebbon, John Dodds, Graham Masterton, and Lavie Tidhar. It also runs interviews with writers and artists, and movie and book reviews.

Book of Dark Wisdom: The Magazine of Dark Fiction, edited by William Jones is a good looking, thrice yearly magazine specializing in Lovecraftian horror. The quality of the fiction is inconsistent but there were notable stories by Michael Kelly, Tim Curran, Simon Owens, John Shire, J. Michael Straczynski, and Bruce Boston. The magazine has book reviews and other nonfiction: Richard A. Lupoff on writing, and a short essay about influences that inspired Lovecraft to write *At the Mountains of Madness* and in turn, of that works influence on subsequent art and literature. There is also a regular column covering unusual, overlooked, or condemned movies.

Midnight Street, edited by Trevor Denyer, is an excellent British magazine in its second year of publication (having mutated from *Roadworks*), that, although it advertises itself as publishing "horror dark fantasy science fiction slipstream," actually seems to concentrate enough on darker fiction that it belongs in the horror magazine section, rather than mixed-genre. There were very good stories by Tim Lees, Gary Fry, Paul Edwards, Tony Richards, Paul Finch, Nina Allen, Michael Beeman, and Andrew Roberts. The magazine also runs interviews with horror authors. Ralph Robert Moore's story is reprinted herein.

Dark Discoveries, edited by James Beach, came out three times in 2005 and had some very good stories, particularly those by Paul Finch and Jeffrey Thomas. The summer issue had five interviews with horror writers.

Wildside Press purchased DNA Publications' interest in *Weird Tales* ® with Wildside publisher John Betancourt joining the editorial staff of George Scithers and Darrell Schweitzer. Betancourt's note at the front of Issue #337 announced that the venerable magazine would expand by eight pages and would resume its quarterly schedule (something achievable in recent history only in 2003). Two issues were published in 2005. There were poems and stories—originals by Jack Williamson, Fred Chappell, and the first section of a two-parter by William F. Nolan. Also several reprints, a column by Douglas E. Winter, and a letters column.

Strange Tales of Mystery and Terror #9, edited by Robert M. Price, is the second issue of the revived magazine. The original was published during the pulp era of the 1930s and ran for seven issues. The second issue of the new quarterly has original stories and poetry by L. Sprague de Camp, Hugh B. Cave (his last), Ann K. Schwader, and others. The interior illustrations are by George Barr and Stanley C. Sargent. The cover is by Jason Van Hollander (although mistakenly credited to Bob Eggleton).

Pulp lovers should try *Lovecraft's Weird Mysteries*, edited by John Navroth, where they'll discover reprints and originals by Charlee Jacob, Gary Fry, Tim Curran, and others, a classic interview with Robert Bloch and a new one with Kim Harrison, advertisements for magic rocks and for earning a degree in occult sciences through Miskatonic University, and illustrations by Allen Koszowski and others.

Dark Animus, edited by James Cain out of Australia, published two issues, the first on the cusp of 04-05, the second unseen by me. The best stories were by Terry Gates-Grimwood and Paul Melniczek.

Mixed-genre magazines

Many of the best of the current crop of magazines, zines, and websites that publish horror are not strictly horror magazines. Over the past several years *The Magazine of Fantasy & Science Fiction*, *The Third Alternative*, *Crimewave*, and a few others have done a marvelous job of mixing dark and light, sf and fantasy and horror. *The Magazine of Fantasy & Science Fiction*, edited by Gordon Van Gelder, published two wonderful dark pieces by Laird Barron: the novelette "Proboscis" and the novella (mentioned at the top as one of my favorite novellas of the year) "The Imago Sequence," plus excellent dark stories by Albert E. Cowdrey, Marc Laidlaw, Carol Emshwiller, Claudia O'Keefe, Bruce McAllister, David Gerrold, Robert Reed, M. Rickert, and Gene Wolfe. "Proboscis" by Barron and "Twilight States" by Cowdrey are reprinted herein. *SCI FICTION*, the fiction area of SCIFI.COM (edited by me, and discontinued December 2005) published many dark stories among the science fiction and fantasy, including those by David Prill, Kit Reed, M. Rickert, Eric Schaller, Lucius Shepard, Lucy Sussex, Steve Rasnic Tem, Lavie Tidhar, Elizabeth Bear, Richard Bowes, Jeffrey Ford, Gavin J. Grant, Ellen Klages, Kim Newman, and Marc Laidlaw. "Follow Me Light" by Elizabeth Bear is reprinted herein. *The 3rd Alternative*, edited by Andy Cox (and soon to be renamed *Black Static*), had good dark stories by Paul Meloy, Matthew Francis, Elizabeth Bear, Jason Erik Lundberg, Patrick Samphire, Conrad Williams, Cody Goodfellow, Chaz Brenchley, Darren Speegle, and Doug Lain. The Brenchley is reprinted herein. *Crimewave 8: Cold Harbors*, also edited by Andy Cox, generally publishes a fine variety of crime stories, most of them dark. The best in 2005 were by Steve Rasnic Tem, Tom Brennan, Andy Humphrey, Joel Lane, Ron Savage, Stephen Volk, Michelle Scalise, and Darren Speegle. Tom Brennan's story is reprinted herein. *Zahir: Unforgettable Tales*, edited by Sheryl Tempchin, is a simply but attractively produced triennial magazine of sf/f/h. *Electric Velocipede*, edited by John Klima, publishes a good mix of sf/f/h. *Postscripts*, edited by Peter Crowther, published three issues in 2005 and had a good mix of fiction, but was lighter on horror than in 2004. *Realms of Fantasy*, edited by Shawna McCarthy, has the occasional dark fantasy. *Albedo One*, edited by John Kenny, Bob Neilson, David Murphy, and Roelof Goudriaan, is the only Irish mixed-genre magazine that I know of. In addition to its fiction, the magazine ran interviews with Norman Spinrad, Alan Dean Foster, and Clive Barker. It also has book reviews. *On Spec*, edited by Diane L. Walton, is the only major Canadian sf/f/h magazine. It's an attractive, perfect bound quarterly. In 2005 there were good dark stories by Kate Riedel, Paul Bartel, Rob Hunter, Kevin Cockle, Jack Skillingstead, Suzan Tessier and Catherine MacLeod, and a poem by Tony Pi. *Subterranean* is a new quarterly magazine edited by Bill Schafer, publisher of Subterranean Press, who says in his first editorial that publishing and editing a magazine has been his dream almost from the beginning of Subterranean Press. The first issue has a nice mix of fantasy and darker material, including new stories by Norman Partridge, Kealan Patrick Burke, Mark Morris, and Terry Matz, a teleplay by George R.R. Martin based on the Matz story, an excerpt from Joe R. Lansdale's new *Drive-In* novel, a revised reprint by Harlan Ellison, and an interview with Thomas Ligotti. The second issue showcased Caitlín R. Kiernan with an interesting, original dark sf novella and a reprint, plus an interview. Dorman T. Schindler joined the magazine as a book reviewer. *Jab-*

berwocky, edited by Sean Wallace, is a lovely undersized magazine debuting with some very good literary fantasy and dark fantasy by some of the more promising young voices in the field today, in addition to a couple of poems by the more seasoned Jane Yolen and Greer Gilman. Poems by Theodora Goss and Andrew Bonia are reprinted in this volume. In addition, Wallace debuted *Fantasy Magazine* at the World Fantasy Convention, which showcased some dark as well as light fantasy. The best darker stories were by Sarah Brandywine Johnson, Eugie Foster, Simon Logan, and Catherynne M. Valente. There was an interview with Jeffrey Ford, as well as book reviews by Peter Cannon, John Grant, Paula Guran, Douglas E. Winter, and others. The attractive cover art was by Socar Myles. *Nemonymous*, part five, edited by D.F. Lewis, had notable dark stories by Robyn Alezanders, Gary McMahon, Neil Williamson, and Iain Rowan. Other magazines that contained some marginal horror: *Full Unit Hookup*, edited by Mark Rudolph, had one notable dark story co-written by Jay Lake and Scott William Carter; *Say . . . Have You Heard This One?*, edited by Christopher Rowe and Gwenda Bond, had a very good dark story by Craig Laurance Gidney. *Argosy Quarterly*, edited by James A. Owen, had only one issue, with good dark fiction by Steve Rasnic Tem. The Web site *Strange Horizons*, whose fiction is edited by Karen Meisner, Susan Marie Groppi, and Jed Hartman, occasionally publishes dark fiction. In 2005 there were notable stories by Hal Duncan and Merrie Haskell. *Chizine*, edited by Brett Alexander Savory, Paul G. Tremblay, and Michael Kelly, is the fiction section of the Chiaroscuro Web site. In 2005 there were notable dark stories and poems by Bruce Boston, Hannah Wolf Bowen, M.K. Hobson, Charlee Jacob, Jennifer Jerome, Livia Llewellyn, K.Z. Perry, Cat Rambo, and Stephen M. Wilson. *Space and Time*, edited by Gordon Linzner, published one issue in 2005, and had some very good stories and poems by Uncle River, Mike Allen, John Everson, John Rosenman, and Sharon Bailly. *Aurealis* #33/34/35 is a big fat triple issue and the last to be edited by Keith Stevenson. It's long been a staple of mixed-genre fiction from Australia and here's hoping it continues to produce regular and excellent issues under new editors Robert Hoge and Ben Payne. There were notable stories by Peter Barber, Rjurik Davidson, Gregory Hill, Lee Battersby, and Philip Raines and Harvey Welles. *Flytrap*, edited by Heather Shaw and Tim Pratt, tries to come out twice a year but in 2005 made only one issue. It was a good one, with interesting darker fiction by Michael Canfield and Melissa Marr and a smart article on writing professionally by Nick Mamatas. *NFG*, edited by Shar O'Brien, is a Canadian magazine that suspended publication with its sixth issue. It's a shame because there was good fiction in it, including an Aurealis Award-winning story. *Borderlands*, edited by Stephen Dedman, is an Australian magazine of science fiction, fantasy, and horror. There were two issues out in 2005. In addition to the fiction there are a few articles. There were notable horror stories by Jo-Ann Whalley, Kyla Ward, Shane Jiraiya Cummings, and Stephani Campisi. *Trunk Stories #3*, edited by William Smith, had a good horror story by Carole Lanham. *Songs of Innocence (and Experience)*, edited by Michael Pendragon, is always interesting, with a variety of fantasy and dark fantasy prose and poetry. There was good work by Sue Parman, Sybil Bank, Scott Thomas, and by Pendragon himself. Pendragon also edited the excellent *Penny Dreadful: Tales & Poems of Fantastic Terror*, which also has articles and reviews. There was strong work by Elizabeth Howkins, John B. Ford, Nancy A. Henry, Michael Pendragon, and Ann S. Schwader. Out of Australia comes *Andromeda Spaceways Inflight Magazine*, edited by Stuart Barrow. There's an occasional horror story in this one. *Shimmer* is a worthwhile new quarterly mixed-genre magazine edited by Beth Wodzinski. Its Autumn issue had some darker stories in it.

Poetry Collections and Magazines

Dreams and Nightmares, edited by David C. Kopaska-Merkel, has been the premier magazine for dark poetry for almost twenty years and it's still publishing excellent work. There were notable poems by Michael Greenhut, Gary Every, and Sonya Taaffe.

The Magazine of Speculative Poetry, edited by Roger Dutcher, published three issues and is a reliable mixed-genre venue. There was strong, dark poetry by Peg Duthie, Jennifer Crowe, John Borneman & Jaime Lee Moyer, Maureen McQuerry, Sonya Taaffe, Duane Ackerson and Ann K. Schwader.

Mythic Delirium, edited by Mike Allen, brought out two issues in 2005. The best dark poems in them were by Sonya Taaffe, Catherynne M. Valente, Aurelio Rico Lopez III, Constance Cooper and Carma Lynn Park.

*Star*Line*, the Journal of the Science Fiction Poetry Association, is edited by Marge Simon. It publishes six issues a year, and although it specializes in sf and fantasy poetry, there are always at least a few darker poems lurking within. Notable poems in 2005 were penned by Helen Marshall, Melissa Marr, Karen R. Porter, Denise Dumars, Mike Allen and Deborah Cimo.

Poe Little Thing: the Digest of Horrific Poetry, edited by Donna Taylor Burgess, published one issue with ten poems in 2005. My favorite was by Kelli Dunlop.

Prime published several beautiful looking chapbooks of poetry in 2005: Catherynne M. Valente's *Apocrypha*, an excellent collection of passionate and often dark poetry and prose poems, more than half of them published for the first time and *Oracles: A Pilgrimage*, also by Valente, another excellent collection of poetry reprints and originals with a note by the author about her inspiration. Beautiful classical paintings are used for the covers art of both chapbooks. *Disturbing Muses*, by Mike Allen, is an excellent collection showcasing new and reprinted poetry about major artists such as Picasso, O'Keefe, Chagall, Escher, and others. The cover art is by de Chirico. Sonya Taaffe's *Postcards Form the Province of Hyphens* is the author's first full-length collection, containing almost fifty poems and prose pieces, ten published in 2005. Included is her Rhysling Award–winning poem "Matlacihuatl's Gift."

Sam's Dot Publishing brought out simple, nicely designed poetry chapbooks, most with illustrations by 7ARS and Marcia A. Borell: *Inside the Blood Museum* by Karen R. Porter is a very good collection by a poet who is new to me. Most of the twenty poems are original to the collection. *Psychoentropy* by Julie Shiel has sixteen poems, all but one reprints. *Insanity on Ice* by Cathy Buburuz has twenty-one poems, more than half reprints. Marcia A. Borell illustrated most of it and there's one illustration by the poet. *I Don't Know What You're Having* by David C. Kopaska-Merkel, illustrated by Sandy DeLuca, fifteen poems, five new. *EEKU* by Karen L. Newman collects forty of her original horror haikus.

Sineater by Charlee Jacob (Cyber Pulp) is an excellent, all original collection of dark poetry by one of the best dark poets around.

Stigmata Junction by Thomas Wiloch is a reprint of a chapbook that has twenty-six wonderful surreal miniature prose poems. Illustrations by M. W. Anderson and Alicia Burgess.

Poems Bewitched and Haunted edited by John Hollander (Everyman Library Pocket Poets) is the perfect Halloween anthology for those interested in poetry, published as it is in an undersized hardcover edition with dozens of poems about death, ghosts, witches, haunted houses, and other appropriate fare. Some of the poets included are Edgar Allan Poe, Emma Lazarus, John Donne, Robert Graves, Homer, and Emily Dickinson.

Naked Snake Press published *Bloodied Lips* by Justin Josephnek Klör, which has thirty poems, illustrated by the poet and by Swati Lingnurker. *The Horrible* by John Edward Lawson contains thirty-three poems, about a third of them original to the collection.

Seasons: A Series of Poems Based on the Life and Death of Edgar Allan Poe by Daniel Shields (Foothills Publishing) is #44 of the Springfield Chapbook series.

Freakcidents by Michael A. Arnzen (Shocklines Press) has thirty mostly light-hearted rhymes about freaks of every sort and their travails. About half appear for the first time. Cleverly illustrated by GAK.

Etiquette with Your Robot Wife and Thirty More sf/Fantasy/Horror Lists by Bruce Boston (Talisman) with illustrations by Marge Simon reprinted poems—some dark—from various genre magazines.

Life Among the Dream Merchants and Other Phantasies by Kurt Newton (Coscom Entertainment) has thirty-one poems, some very good, and eleven of them appearing for the first time. The cover art by Jeffrey Thomas is nicely surreal. Thomas also contributes an introduction to Newton's work.

There is Something in the Autumn: A Treasury of Autumnal Verse edited by Michael M. Pendragon (Pendragonian Publications) has over eighty short original and reprinted poems by Edgar Allan Poe, John Keats, Nancy Bennett, Wendy Rathbone, David C. Kopaska-Merkel, Denise Dumars, Ann Schwader, and other poets living and dead. Although many of them are not horrific or even dark, there are some well-wrought gems in the entertaining anthology.

Chance of a Ghost, edited by Gloria Vando and Philip Miller (Helicon Nine Editions), is an anthology of contemporary ghost poems, many original. Many are excellent, some are dark, although it's a little surprising to me how often the "ghosts" are used in fantastical and elegiac ways rather than as a horror images. The project benefits the library of The Writers Place, a literary community center in Kansas City.

The Lost Poetry (Three Collections) by William Hope Hodgson, with an introduction by Jane Frank (PS, U.K.) presents three previously unpublished collections of Hodgson's verse, as he arranged them: *Mors Deorum and Other Poems, Through Enchantments and Other Poems on Death*, and *Spume*, which together include forty-three poems never seen before.

The 2005 Rhysling Anthology: The Best Science Fiction, Fantasy, & Horror Poetry of 2004, edited by Drew Morse (Prime), is for the first time available in a well-designed, hardcover edition, with beautiful jacket art by Maxfield Parrish. The book has sixty-one poems, separated into two sections: short and long poems. Suzette Haden Elgin introduces the book by providing the history of the Science Fiction Poetry Association, which she founded in 1978. The paperback version of the book is used by the membership to select the winners.

Nonfiction Books

Profondo Argento by Alan Jones (FAB Press, U.K.); *Monster Kid Memories* by Bob Burns as told to Tom Weaver (Dinoship, Inc) is the memoir of a major fan and collector of monster memorabilia. *Smirk, Sneer and Scream: Great Screen Acting in Horror Cinema* by Mark Clark (McFarland Books); *The Brian Lumley Companion*, edited by Brian Lumley and Stanley Wiater (Tor) has interviews, essays, a bibliography, and photographs; *The Perfect Medium: Photography and the Occult* by Clément Chéroux, Andreas Fischer, Pierre Apraxine, Denis Conguilhem, and Sophie Schmit (Yale University Press) assembles more than 250 photographic images from the Victorian era to the 1960s, each purporting to document an occult phenomenon. From an exhibition at the Metropolitan Museum of Art in New York in late 2005; *Michael Powell: International Perspectives on an English Film-Maker*, edited by Ian Christie and Andrew Moor (British Film Institute), is a collection of essays by critics and scholars about the filmmaker who made the chilling horror film *Peeping Tom*. *Beasts in the Cellar: The Exploitation Film Career of Tony Tenser* by John Hamilton (FAB) is about the British producer of Roman Polanski's *Repulsion, Witchfinder General*, and other horror movies, in addition to nudies and comedies. *Reading Angel: The TV Spin-Off with a Soul*, edited by Stacey Abbott (I.B. Taurus) covers all five seasons of the show, with a complete episode guide and fourteen essays about the show; *The Bradbury Chronicles* by Sam Weller (William Morrow) is a portrait of the great fantasist, much of whose work has been quite dark. *As Timeless as Infinity: The Complete Twilight Zone Scripts of Rod Serling, Volume Two*, edited by Tony Albarella (Gauntlet Press) with notes and appreciations by Carol Serling and Robert McCammon, commentary on each script and interviews with some of the cast and crew. *H. P. Lovecraft: Against the World, Against Life* by Michel Houellebecq, translated from the French by Dorna Khazeni (Believer Books/McSweeney's Press). *Fantasy Fiction: An Introduction* by Lucie Armitt (Continuum) is a critical introduction to fantasy, including essays on such dark science fiction works as *The Time Machine* and *Frankenstein*. *Readings on Stephen King*, edited by Karin S. Coddon (Gale Group/ Greenhaven Press) has thirteen essays, a brief biography, a bibliography, and an index. *Italian Horror Film Directors* by Louis Paul (McFarland) with forewords by Jess Franco and Antonella Fulci, recounts the origins of the genre, celebrating ten auteurs who have contributed to Italian horror, and mentions many others who made noteworthy films. *The Mexican Masked Wrestler and Monster Filmography* by Robert Michael "Bobb" Cotter (McFarland) features some of the oddest cinematic showdowns ever concocted—Mexican masked wrestlers battling monsters, evil geniuses and other ne'er-do-wells. With ninety photographs, bibliography, and index. *Jekyll and Hyde Dramatized: The 1887 Richard Mansfield Script and the Evolution of the Story on Stage*, edited by Martin A. Danahay and Alex Chisholm has the authoritative, collated version of the Mansfield script and charts the evolution of his play through various productions. *Kenneth Strickfaden, Dr. Frankenstein's Electrician* by Harry Goldman with a foreword by Ed Angell, is about the innovative genius of illusionary special effects from silent films to the age of television. *Earth vs. the Sci-Fi Filmmakers 20 Interviews* by Tom Weaver includes interviews with Gene Barry, Merian C. Cooper, Peter Graves, and Arch Hall Jr., among others. Extensively illustrated. *The Life of Arthur Machen* by John Gawsworth (The Friends of

Arthur Machen, Reino de Redonda, Tartarus Press, U.K.) was written during Machen's lifetime, but this is its first publication. Illustrated with photographs of Machen and of Machen's residences. *Supernatural Literature of the World: An Encyclopedia*, edited by S.T. Joshi and Stefan Dziemianowicz (Greenwood), is in three volumes totaling 1556 pages. It has more than fifty contributors and includes roughly one thousand alphabetically arranged entries on special topics and cultural traditions in the genre, covering canonical and contemporary authors. *Shirley Jackson: Essays on the Literary Legacy*, edited by Bernice M. Murphy (McFarland), instead of concentrating on "The Lottery" and *The Haunting of Hill House*, her most famous works, widens the scope of Jackson scholarship by studying such works as *The Road through the Wall* and *We Have Always Lived in the Castle*, and topics ranging from Jackson's domestic fiction to ethics, cosmology, and eschatology. The book also makes newly available some of the most significant Jackson scholarship published in the last two decades. *Horror: Another 100 Best Books*, edited by Stephen Jones and Kim Newman (Carroll & Graf) is a follow-up to the editors' indispensable 1988 volume, *Horror: 100 Best Books*. This time around they include works ranging from Theodore Roszak's novel *Flicker* and David G. Hartwell's massive anthology *The Dark Descent* to Alan Moore and Eddie Campbell's graphic novel *From Hell* and Stephen Sondheim and Hugh Wheeler's musical *Sweeney Todd*. Marvelously entertaining (truth in advertising: I've written an entry for the book). *The Encyclopedia of Vampires, Werewolves, and Other Monsters* by Rosemary Ellen Guiley (Facts on File/Checkmark Books) is a reference guide to supernatural monsters with separate articles on some writers. Bibliography and index. *Clever Maids: The Secret History of the Grimm Fairy Tales* by Valerie Paradiz (Basic Books) is a reference book about the women who provided many of the Grimm's stories. Bibliography and index. *Beating the Devil: The Making of Night of the Demon* by Tony Earnshaw (Tomahawk Press) details the making of the classic movie based on M.R. James's short story "Casting the Runes," directed by Jacques Tourneur. The brief book includes mini-biographies of the actors (and gossip about them). Introductions by Alex Cox and Christopher Fraying. *The World's Worst: A Guide to the Most Disgusting, Hideous, Inept, and Dangerous People, Places, and Things on Earth* by Mark Frauenfelder (Chronicle) is a celebration/indictment of nearly fifty infamous and little-known exemplars of the awful, such as the most disgusting fruit—the durian, the most gruesome bug bite—the brown recluse, etc. *Iron Man: The Cinema of Shinya Tsukamoto* by Tom Mes (FAB) covers the filmmaker's life and each of his eight feature films. Illustrated with hundreds of stills, behind-the-scenes pictures and rare photographs from Tsukamoto's private collection. *The Ring Companion* by Denis Meikle (Titan Books, U.K.) is a comprehensive look at the origins and influence of the movie from the original novels by Koji Suzuki through their film adaptations and remakes. *Mexploitation Cinema: A Critical History Of Mexican Vampire, Wrestler, Ape-man And Similar Films, 1957–1977* by Doyle Greene (McFarland) sets Mexploitation films in their historical and cultural context, showing how they can be seen as important documents in the cultural debate over Mexico's past, present and future. There are stills from the movies throughout, and a selected filmography and bibliography. *A Ghost in My Suitcase: A Guide to Haunted Travel in America* by Michael Whitington (Atriad Press) details ghostly hotspots around America for those who want a different kind of road trip. The author reviews one spot for each of the fifty states and delves into possible explanations for why spirits linger in some spots more regularly than others. In addition to such famous places as The Stanley Hotel in Colorado, which inspired Stephen King's *The Shining*, Whitington includes some little-known spots off the beaten track. *Living Dangerously: The Adventures of Merian C. Cooper, Creator of King Kong* by Mark Cotta Vaz (Villard) is the biography of film pioneer Cooper (1893–1973), producer-director of the original 1933 *King Kong* and chronicles his exploits as a globetrotting explorer, war hero, big game hunger, aviator, and documentary moviemaker pre–*King Kong*. *Shock! Horror!: Astounding Artwork from the Video Nasty Era* by Francis Brewster, Harvey Fenton, and Marc Morris (FAB) combines the three authors' decades of personal experience as collectors with access to original archive material from the pre-1984 time of "video nasties." This period, beginning in 1980—the freewheeling beginning of video—ended when the British Parliament cracked down and passed censorship laws forcing all videos to be approved before being released to the public. *Beautiful Monsters* by David McIntee (Telos, U.K.), the compulsively readable "unofficial and unauthorized guide to the *Alien* and *Predator* films" includes cast and crew details for each movie, bios of major actors, goofs in each film. *The Lure of the Vampire: Gender, Fiction and Fandom from Bram Stoker to Buffy* by Milly Williamson (Wallflower Press, U.K.) pretty much ignores literature and goes straight to the cinema and television arts in its examination of the issue of gender of vampires and vampire fans. The book seems meant more for other scholars than for readers or viewers, or for that matter fans. *American Sideshow: An Encyclopedia of History's Most Wondrous and Curiously Strange Performers* by Marc Hartzman (Jeremy P. Tarcher/Penguin) is a respectful and absorbing history of dozens of sideshow performers to today's new breed, some of whom have created themselves. Illustrated. *The Cult of Alien Gods: H. P. Lovecraft and Extraterrestrial Pop Culture* by Jason Colavito (Prometheus Books) theorizes that von Däniken's ancient astronaut bestseller *Chariots of the Gods* and all the pseudoscientific and crackpot theories sprouting from that bestseller were inspired by Lovecraft's fiction. *Eton and King's* by Montague Rhodes James (Ash-Tree) is the first reprint ever of James's 1925 recollections of his time in the Colleges, and his only autobiographical work. *Weapons of Mass Seduction: Film Reviews and Other Ravings* by Lucius Shepard (Wheatland Press) collects film reviews that mostly appeared first on the *Electric Story* website and in *The Magazine of Fantasy & Science Fiction*. Shepard takes a vicious glee in eviscerating almost every movie he sees, yet his reviews are always entertaining. The downside is that many of the reviews are incredibly self-indulgent, and purposefully blind about the exigencies of being an actress in Hollywood. *More Giants of the Genre: Interviews Conducted by Michael McCarty* (Wildside) has twenty-three interviews with a mixed group of writers, moviemakers, and one husband-and-wife art team. The interviewees include John Carpenter, Harry Turtledove, Laurell K. Hamilton, Harlan Ellison, Terry Brooks, Connie Willis, Joe R. Lansdale, and others. *The Shadow of the Unattained: The Letters of George Sterling and Clark Ashton Smith*, edited by David E. Schultz and S.T. Joshi (Hippocampus Press), presents the complete surviving fifteen year correspondence between the two writers. All of Smith's essays on Sterling, and Sterling's writings on Smith, are gathered in the Appendix. *H.P. Lovecraft: Letters to Rheinhart Kleiner*, edited by S.T. Joshi and David E. Schultz (Hippocampus) prints, for the first time, the complete surviving letters of Lovecraft to Kleiner. They address such wide-ranging subjects as erotic love, racial prejudice, the art of poetry, Lovecraft's boyhood and upbringing, and much else. The volume includes all of Lovecraft's and Kleiner's poems addressed to each other, along with several provocative essays by Kleiner on Lovecraft. *Collected Essays 3: Science by H.P. Lovecraft*, edited by S.T. Joshi (Hippocampus), includes the scientific journals, treatises, and astronomy columns of Lovecraft's early years, and continuing throughout his life, these writings illuminate the author's thought in a unique, and until now, largely unappreciated way. As a bonus, almost two dozen of HPL's hand-lettered star maps are reproduced. *Collected Essays 1. Travel by H.P. Lovecraft*, edited by S.T. Joshi (Hippocampus), collects all HPL's formal travelogues and includes *A Description of the Town of Quebeck, in New France, Lately Added to His Britannick Majesty's Dominions*, which, at 75,000 words, was Lovecraft's longest work. As a bonus, all of Lovecraft's hand-drawn maps and illustrations of the regions he visited are reproduced. *Horror Fiction: An Introduction* by Gina Wisker (Continuum) is a critical introductory guide to literary horror, its development, themes, and major authors. Bibliography, suggested reading, and index. *Blood Relations: Chosen Families in Buffy the Vampire Slayer and Angel*, by Jes Battis (McFarland). *The Films of Fay Wray* by Roy Kinnard and Tony Crnkovich (McFarland). *Embracing the Darkness: Understanding Dark Subcultures* by Corvis Nocturnum (Dark Moon Press) takes a psychological and historical look at the similarities between the subcultures of the Goths, witchcraft, Satanists, BDSM/Fetishists, and vampires, using interviews and conversations with self-proclaimed practitioners. *A Disease Apart: Leprosy in the Modern World* by Tony Gould (St. Martin's) is a cultural and medical history of a disease that has been shrouded in dread and superstition. *The Wandering Soul: Essays and Letters by William Hope Hodgson* edited by Jane Frank and with an introduction by Mike Ashley (PS Publishing and Tartarus Press, U.K.), is available in two limited editions. Much of the previously unpublished or uncollected material is from Sam Moskowitz's "Hodgson Archives." *Cinderella's Sisters: A Revisionist History of Footbinding* by Dorothy Ko (University of California Press), is a refreshing counterpoint to books that treat the practice as merely patriarchal and fetishistic. Ko presents a new picture of footbinding from its beginnings in the tenth century through its demise in the twentieth, combining (as the flap copy says) "methods of literary criticism, material culture studies, and the history of the body and fashion to illustrate how a practice that began as embodied lyricism—as a way to live as the poets imagined—ended up being an exercise in excess and folly."

Chapbooks and Other Small Press Items

Seascape by Jack Ketchum (Shocklines Press) is a moving tale based on a true story about a long-married couple in their twilight years who are both ailing, and the difficult decision they make together. The cover is a stark black and there's an illustration inside by Allen Koszowski. *A Small Room* by Steve Rasnic Tem, is an exceptionally creepy story about a madwoman. The cover art is by Glenn Chadbourne.

Naked Snake Press published *When Darkness Falls* by Steven Lloyd, about an elderly man who tells his grandson a frightening story about his youth—only some of which is true. The truth is much more horrifying. From the Naked Snake anthology series: *Trouble Visions* by Paul Melniczek has three stories about dark futures. Illustrations by Jesse Bunch. *All Prettied Up*, three stories by Elizabeth Blue. *Home in the Rat* by Paul Dracon, three tales of brutal horror—not for the squeamish. The cover art is by Michael King. *Through a Glass Darkly* by Angeline Hawkes-Craig is a horror story about stem-cell research.

The World Recalled by Steve Rasnic Tem (Wormhole Books) is a marvelous rendering of a man's life—backward, from senility to childhood. Tem creates verbal collages to portray wisps of life. He's also a terrific artist, illustrating the chapbook in the style of his favorite artists for children.

Subterranean Press published the novella *Voluntary Committal* by Joe Hill as a chapbook a few months before it came out in the author's collection. As Hill says, he wanted to write a darker type of story, one in which "Alice goes down the rabbit hole and never comes back. The rabbit hole swallows her and spits out the bones." He succeeds—it's one of the best novellas of the year. Also, *Crown of Thorns* by Poppy Z. Brite, an enigmatic tale about a New Orleans medical examiner who discovers a long-dead corpse with a mysterious object in the place where its heart should be. The limited edition chapbook is nicely designed, with illustrations by Mary Fleener.

Bloodletting Press published *Wormwood Nights*, a novella by Charlee Jacob. It takes place at the end of the nineteenth century, a period when absinthe is the sophisticated drink of Parisians, and in London a madman dubbed Jack the Ripper is making headlines. A British crime photographer finds that as he becomes more addicted to "the green fairy," the stranger his photographs of dying and diseased women become. Available in hardcover and paperback signed, limited editions. The cover art is by Caniglia. Also the novellas *The Terminal* by Brian Keene, #2 in the novella series (an expanded edition was published by Leisure, see above), and *Thrust* by Tom Piccirilli, #3 in the novella series of limited editions.

An Occupation of Angels by Lavie Tidhar (Pendragon Press) is a novella in which archangels appear in 1945, heralding a cold war by occupying national monuments worldwide. Fifty years later, a cold-eyed British operative is sent after a missing cryptographer who might hold the key as to who is killing off the angels one by one. A violent, exhilarating spy thriller/fantasy held together by the skin of its teeth by a talented new writer.

It's Only Temporary by Eric Shapiro (Permuted Press) is about the accelerated road trip taken by a young man on the last day of life on Earth. His decision to spend his last minutes with his ex-girlfriend leads him through surreal adventures. The novella is more charming than horrific given the subject matter.

Telos Publishing Ltd. out of the UK published *Another War* by Simon Morden, which starts out with the British army investigating a British manor house that miraculously reappears after disappearing without a trace eighty years earlier. Add a mysterious machine, monsters slipping between dimensions, brave men, and a man who would be a god and you've got the ingredients for an exciting horror adventure yarn. Also, *Valley of Lights* by Stephen Gallagher, reprinting the novel originally published in 1987, adding a prequel novella, the diary of an aborted film version, an interview with the author, introduction by Stephen Laws, and afterword by Gallagher. *Parish Damned* by Lee Thomas is an expansion of the author's vampire novelette originally published as an e-book in 2003. This new version is about 12,000 words longer.

Necessary Evil Press published *Zero* by Michael McBride, an effective science fiction horror novella about a young man who becomes involved with a project to reanimate amputated limbs. With an introduction by Kealan Patrick Burke and cover art by Caniglia. The interior illustrations are by the author. *Pieces of Hate* by Tim Lebbon is the second novella in the Assassin series. A man whose family was slaughtered centuries before seeks revenge and allies himself with bloodthirsty pirates in order to catch his quarry, a half-man/half-demon named Temple. Introduction by Brian Keene and afterword by the author. *In the Midnight Museum* by Gary A. Braunbeck moves into Jonathan Carroll territory with this powerfully told novella about a failed suicide who begins to see fantastical beings and is given instructions as to what he must do to save the world.

Novello Publishers debuted with two good-looking, numbered, limited edition chapbooks: *Two Twisted Nuts*, a pair of humorous horror stories, by Jeff Strand and Nick Cato. Each author introduces his story. Caniglia did the cover illustration. *Right House on the Left* has three humorous stories by Steve Vernon, Mark McLaughlin, and L. L. Soares and an introduction by James A. Moore. The cover illustration is by Mr. Eye.

Delirium published: *My Eyes Are Nailed But Still I See* by David Niall Wilson and Brett Alexander Savory is a gruesome, surreal, disorienting novella about which nothing is certain but that there are two people in a therapist's office: a therapist and a young boy. Dave Kendall did the jacket art. *Vestal*, a novel by Charlee Jacobs, with jacket art by Alan M. Clark, in two states of limited edition hardcovers. *Ship of Dreams*, *Mad Moon of Dreams*, and *Iced in Aran*, books two, three, and four in the Dreamlands series by Brian Lumley, were published in 2005, each in a fifty-two-copy leather-bound limited edition, and each with different full color frontispiece art by Dave Kendall. *Scarecrow Gods*, a novel by Weston Ochse is a signed, limited edition in two states, with jacket art by Alan M. Clark, *Earthworm Gods* by Brian Keene is an expanded version of the story published in the anthology *4×4* four years ago and comes in a signed, limited edition in two states with creepy, nicely realized jacket art by Dave Kendall. *Deep Night* by Greg F. Gifune is a signed and numbered limited edition in two states. The jacket art is by Mike Bohatch. *Descent* by Sandy DeLuca (Delirium) is a limited edition hardcover novel. Jacket art is by Mike Bohatch. *Night of the Daemon* by Harry Shannon is a limited-edition hardcover novel and the final book of his Night trilogy.

The Dark Essentials series focuses on titles that have never before been published in hardcover and includes special original bonus material not found in the original paperbacks. The following titles were published by Delirium in 2005: The reprinted novels *Hush* by Tim Lebbon and Gavin Williams, *Deathgrip* by Brian Hodge, *A Lower Deep* by Tom Piccirilli, and *Prodigal* by Melanie Tem.

Earthling Publications brought out a beautiful new limited hardcover edition of China Miéville's first novel, *King Rat* with excellent interior illustrations by Richard Kirk and an introduction by Clive Barker. Miéville has added an afterword describing his musical inspiration. *Song of Kali* by Dan Simmons is the twentieth anniversary edition of the World Fantasy Award–winning horror novel. The jacket art is by François Baranger. Simmons provides an introduction describing his early writing career and how he came to write the book. *Blood Red* by James A. Moore is the first of Earthling's "Halloween" novels, intended to celebrate the holiday by publishing one out-and-out horror book every October. The jacket art is by Les Edwards. Simon Clark provides an introduction. *Apocalypse Now, Voyager* by Jay Russell (copyright 2004 but not seen until 2005) is a marvelous novella about former child star Marty Burns now turned somewhat reluctant "detective." Burns has already appeared in three novels and two short stories and here he's abducted by a crazy woman who expects him to help resurrect a dead woman. The publisher also brought out three limited edition chapbooks for the World Horror Convention in 2005: *Little Lost Angel* by Erik Tomblin, *After the Elephant Ballet* by Gary A. Braunbeck, and *Blood Tide* by James A. Moore. Also, *Riverside Blues,* a novella chapbook by Erik Tomblin, about a man who still grieves for his beloved wife, who's been missing for fifty years. This is an engrossing and haunting tale of love, grief, and evil.

The Cemetery Dance novella series: *The Eyes of the Carp* by T.M. Wright is a fascinating, subtle tale of madness, about a couple who move into a small house in Maine. *Blue November Storms* by Brian Freeman is an sf/horror story about a group of men who meet up to camp in the woods where twenty years earlier they were faced with human evil, and the unpleasant surprise mother nature has for them. *Walpuski's Typewriter* by Frank Darabont was originally published in the late 80s in the magazine *Midnight Graffiti.* The new edition has interior illustrations by Bernie Wrightson and an introduction by the author. *Retribution, Inc* by Geoff Cooper is about the escalating tensions of a rock band about to get its big break. *Sims, Book Four: Zero* by F. Paul Wilson continues this series of dark, futuristic novellas about genetic engineering and its consequences. *Where's Bobo?* And *Glory Hole* by Ray Garton is a two-story chapbook. "Where's Bobo?" is fast-moving, short, and clever; "Glory Hole" is a real creep-out. Keith Minnion did the artwork. *The Good, the Bad, & the Ugly: Eight Secondary Characters from the Dark Tower Series* by Bev Vincent covers some of the characters deleted from the author's nonfiction work *The Road to the Dark Tower.*

Charnel House published very expensive limited editions of Dean Koontz's novels *Frankenstein* and *Velocity* in two states.

Biting Dog published some nicely designed chapbooks: Also, *Socially Awkward Moments With an Aspiring Lunatic* by Jeff Strand, about a loser who decides that the only way he can become a lunatic is by murdering people. Cover and interior art is by Keith Minnion. *Hard Night* by Brian Eisenthal is a zombie tale, with art by Keith Minnion (not seen).

Gauntlet Press published *The Halloween Tree* by Ray Bradbury, edited by Jon Eller, in a signed limited numbered edition that contains Bradbury's preferred text, the original manuscript (complete with handwritten corrections), and the screenplay Bradbury wrote before he wrote the novel. The front and back covers are Bradbury oil paintings of Halloween trees. The limited lettered edition comes with several extras, including a never-before-published short story, a CD of Bradbury reading a Halloween poem, prints of the back and front cover signed by Bradbury, and a chapbook called *Fragments,* containing fragments of eight unfinished stories by the author, dealing with the Halloween theme. Cover art by Bradbury. *Duel & The Distributor: Stories and Screenplays* by Richard Matheson collects two stories and the scripts made from each (*The Distributor* was never produced). Matheson expert Matthew Bradley provides commentary on both screenplays. Also included in both editions are the illustrations used to promote the theatrical release of *Duel.* Plus an afterword by Matheson and an interview with actor Dennis Weaver, who starred in the Spielberg film. *Unrealized Dreams* by Richard Matheson consists of three screenplays that were never produced. The book was published in an oversized format in signed limited hardcover editions. Edited by Dennis Etchison.

We Now Pause for Station Identification by Gary A. Braunbeck (Endeavor Press) is about a deejay who is alone in his broadcasting booth while the world around him is being taken over by the dead. Cover art by Chad Savage. Also, *The Pumpkin Boy,* a novelette by Al Sarrantonio about another horrific Halloween season in the disaster-plagued town of Orangefield. When a young boy disappears, two local cops—each with his own demons—push themselves to the limit to find him before it's too late. Both stories were published as individual chapbooks.

Dead Letter Press published an expensive series of uniform chapbooks that cover the essential works of the vampire genre. Included in this "Literary Vampire series" are: *The Vampyre: A Tale* by John Polidori, *Classic Vampires Revisited: The Bloody Roots, The Last Lords of Gardonal* by William Gilbert, *Classic Vampires Revisited: Fearful Feasting, The Vampire in Literature* by Reverend Montague Summers, *Classic Vampires Revisited: Dark Sucklings, Carmilla* by Joseph Sheridan Le Fanu, *The House of the Vampire* by George Sylvester Viereck, *Classic Vampires Revisited: A Harvest of Horror*, and *Supernatural Horror in Literature* by H. P. Lovecraft. Each paperback, saddle-bound booklet is limited to 26 lettered copies.

Necro Publications brought out two signed, numbered editions of the expanded, novel-length version of Charlee Jacob's novella, *Dread in the Beast*. Edward Lee provides the introduction. Necro also published two signed and numbered editions of Edward Lee's first children's book, the novel *Monster Lake*. Also published in two limited hardcover editions, *The Pig & The House* by Lee, is a reprint of the novella "The Pig" with a sequel, "The House."

The Decorations is a Christmas story by Ramsey Campbell with engravings by Ladislav Hanka (Alpenhouse Apparitions). It's the first publication of a new imprint from Sutton Hoo Press. The imprint is dedicated to printing the best supernatural and other genre fiction in hand-made letterpress editions. The books are signed by author and artist, and numbered.

Simon Clark: Bibliography of Short Fiction, 1972–2005, compiled by Tony Mileman, was published by Midnight Street, the U.K. magazine, and was given away free with issue #5. Clark introduces the booklet, describing how he got his start in publishing. There is also an introduction by Mileman. Included are photographs of the author and of some of his books.

Art Books and Odds & Ends

Two coffee-table books came out in conjunction with the Dave McKean/Neil Gaiman fantasy film *MirrorMask*. The first is simply called *MirrorMask* (William Morrow), and it's the illustrated film script (storyboards) with stills from the movie and early notes between the two creators. *The Alchemy of MirrorMask* by Dave McKean (Collins/Design) is a gorgeous behind-the-scenes rendition of the movie made by McKean and Neil Gaiman. Profusely illustrated, expertly designed and with commentary by the filmmakers. Also, an introduction by Lisa Henson. This latter book is breathtaking and is by far one of the best illustrated books of the year.

The Plucker by Brom (Stewart, Tabori & Chang) is an extremely dark illustrated novel for children of all ages. Although the story is effective, it's the artwork that shines, showing Brom at his creepy best.

Visions of Heaven and Hell by Clive Barker (Rizzoli not seen) has more than three hundred illustrations, most in color. Barker provides an introduction and text on the inspirations for his art.

This Specterd Isle: A Journey Through Haunted England by Simon Marsden (English Heritage Publications, U.K.) with photographs by Marsden and text by Val Horsler and Susan Kelleher.

The Creeps by D.W. Frydendall (Burnside Publications) compiles black and white pen and ink illustrations done over the past decade for comic books and other media.

The Book of Imaginary Beings by Jorge Luis Borges with illustrations by Peter Sis

(Viking) is a spanking new translation by Andrew Hurley of the 1967 classic bestiary. It's really lovely; the only disappointment is the sparseness of illustrations—it should have been done up right rather than with only twenty-three or so drawings for over one hundred creatures.

Grimm's Grimmest illustrated by Tracy Arah Dockray (Chronicle Books) takes nineteen stories by the Brothers Grimm and puts back in the darker elements. The color and black and white illustrations are in two different styles and nicely enhance the text with gibbets, chopped-off hands, and half-transformed animal-humans. Introduction by fairytale expert Marie Tatar.

Go to Hell: A Heated History of the Underworld by Chuck Crisafulli and Kyra Thompson (Simon Spotlight Entertainment) is a cheeky little book, perfect for light reading when you don't want to get into the heavy theology of hell. Multicultural and scattershot in its coverage, this is meant to be fun and once in a while, even illuminating.

Mrs. Ballard's Parrots by Arne Svenson (Harry N. Abrams) is a joy to behold, from its bright yellow jacket with the photograph of a parrot dressed as a pizza deliveryman—miniature pizza in hand—to its paisley end papers, to its fascinating text by Svenson about how he tracked down the Long Island housewife who dressed up parrots. And of course, the best part is the photographs of the parrots (clothed by Mrs. Ballard, photographed by her husband) dressed up and riding on motorcycles as in *Easy Rider*, as sailors ogling a hula doll, as General Custer, and more.

The Mystery of Eilean Mor by Gary Crew and Jeremy Geddes (Lothian Books) is an eerily told and beautifully illustrated ghost story of a lighthouse on the haunted isle of Eilean Mor in the outer Hebrides.

Vile Verses by Roald Dahl (Viking) is divided into seven sections and illustrated by Lane Smith, William Joyce, Gerald Scarfe, Helen Oxenbury, and other children's illustrators. Although most of the verses are from Dahl's more famous books such as *Charlie and the Chocolate Factory* and *James and the Giant Peach*, there's a handful of more unfamiliar verses.

Dracula Book 1, based on the novel by Bram Stoker (Heavy Metal), is a graphic novel illustrated by Hippolyte. The illustrations are quite good but the text is so abbreviated that the story barely makes sense. So buy it as an art book but not as any kind of faithful telling of the novel itself.

Still Lovers by Elena Dorfman (Channel Photographics) is a coffee-table book of seventy-two photographs of people and their sex dolls. Yes, really. In 1995 a creative young man conceived of a "Real Doll" made of silicon. The dolls became an overnight sensation when Howard Stern was given one for a week and devoted each broadcast to "Celine," describing sex with her as better than with a real woman.

The synthetic women cost around $7,000 and over time, often become more than sex toys, taking the place of real female companionship in their owners' lives—the perfect, nonaging, silent compliant female. There are photographs of the dolls in their component parts and of them "watching" TV with their owners, "eating" meals, etc. It's quite a fantasy world. Horror? Maybe. Depressing? Certainly.

The Dodo and Mauritius Island, Imaginary Encounters by Harri Kallio (Dewi Lewis Publishing, U.K.)—By examining the remains and studying illustrations of dodos, Finnish author/photographer Kallio was able to reconstruct two versions of what the dodo looked like and poses them in their native habitat. The result is an eerie double vision—the viewer knows these are not real landscapes, but it almost doesn't matter. The text describes Kallio's interest in the dodo and includes a brief history of the bird's disastrous encounters with humans, plus numerous eyewitness accounts and photographs of actual remains found around the world. For anyone who ever wanted dodos to still exist.

Pop ink Goth-Icky: A Macabre Menagerie of Morbid Monstrosities by Charles S. Anderson Design Co. with text by Michael J. Nelson (Harry N. Abrams) is a collection of pop-monster images that have been used as cartoon stereotypes for decades. The text isn't as interesting as the art.

Cinema Panopticum by Thomas Ott (Fantagraphics Books) is a wordless visual suite of interconnected tales set in a classic multi-story frame: a young girl attending an old-fashioned carnival slips inside a tent with five coin-operated viewers. Each shows a brief silent film with a dark tale to tell. The black and white scratchboard style illustrations are visually arresting. Ott is Swiss.

Spectrum 12: The Best in Contemporary Fantastic Art, edited by Cathy Fenner and Arnie Fenner (Underwood Books), juried by major fantasy artists, continues to be *the* showcase for the best in genre art—the sheer variety of style and tone and media and subject matter is stunning. Swiss surrealist H.R. Giger was honored as Grand Master and Harlan Ellison profiles the artist. There is also an overview of the field and a necrology. The jury—all artists themselves—convene and decide on Gold and Silver awards in several categories. This is a book for anyone interested in art of the fantastic, whether dark or light.

The Three Incestuous Sisters by Audrey Niffenegger (Harry N. Abrams) is a beautifully designed graphic novel of sibling rivalry, illustrated with aquatints. Jealousy, tragedy, and remorse are the major elements of this dark fairy tale. Niffenegger took fourteen years to create this book, first as a handmade book of ten copies, before she finished, she wrote the bestselling *The Time Traveler's Wife*.

Alpenhouse Apparitions: P.O. Box 1407, Winona, MN 55987-7407. www.sutton hoopress.com/Alpenhouse/index.html

Ash-Tree Press: P.O. Box 1360, Ashcroft, BC V0K 1A0, Canada. www.Ash-Tree.bc.ca/ashtreecurrent.html

Babbage Press: 8939 Canby Avenue, Northridge, CA 91325. www.babbage press.com/

Biting Dog Press: 2150 Northmont Pkwy Suite H, Duluth, Georgia 30096. www.bitingdogpress.com/

Bloodletting Press: 3732 Havenhurst CT, Modesto, CA 95355. www.blood lettingbooks.com

Borderlands Press: P.O. Box 660, Fallston, MD 21407. www.borderland-spress.com

Carnifex Press: Armand Rosamilia, P.O. Box 1686, Ormond Beach, FL 32175. http://carnifexpress.net/

Cemetery Dance Publications: 132-B Industry Lane, Unit #7, Forest Hill, MD 21050. www.cemeterydance.com/

Charnel House: P.O. Box 633, Lynbrook, New York 11563. http://charnel-house.com/

Creeping Hemlock Press: Box 3463, Grapevine, TX, 76099. www.creeping hemlock.com/

Crowswing Books: Trish Cole, P.O. Box 301, King's Lynn, Norfolk PE33 0XW England. www.crowswingbooks.co.uk/

Dark Regions Press: P.O. Box 1264, Colusa, CA, 95932. www.darkregions. com/index.html

Delirium Books: P.O. Box 338, N. Webster, IN 46555. www.delirium books.com

Earthling Publications: P.O. Box 413, Northborough, MA 01532. www.earth lingpub.com

Elastic Press: 85 Gertrude Road, Norwich, Norfolk, NR3 4SG, UK. www.elastic press.com/

Elder Signs Press: P.O. Box 389, Lake Orion, MI 48361-0389. www.elder signspress.com/

Endeavor Press: P.O. Box 4307, Chicago, IL 60680-4307. www.endeavor press.net

Gauntlet Press Publications: 5307 Arroyo St., Colorado Springs, CO 80922. www.gauntletpress.com

Golden Gryphon: 3002 Perkins Road, Urbana, IL 61802. www.goldengryphon. com/

Gray Friar Press: 19, Ruffield Side, Delph Hill, Wyke, Bradford, West Yorkshire, BD12 8DP, United Kingdom. www.grayfriarpress.com/

Hellbound Books: P.O. Box 530585, West Palm Beach, FL 33403. www.hell boundbooks.com/

The Haunted River: Silver Street, Besthorpe, Attleborough, Norfolk NR17 2NY United Kingdom. www.hauntedriver.co.uk/

Hippocampus Press: P.O. Box 641, New York, NY 10156. www.hippocampus press.com

Infrapress: http://www.infrapress.com/ IFD Publishing: P.O. Box 40776, Eugene OR 97404. www.ifdpublishing.com/

Marietta Publishing: P.O. Box 3485, Marietta, GA 30061-3485. www.marietta publishing.com

McFarland & Company: Box 611, Jefferson NC 28640. www.mcfarland pub.com/

Midnight House and Darkside Press: 7713 Sunnyside North, Seattle, WA 98103. www.darksidepress.com

Mythos Books: 351 Lake Ridge Road, Poplar Bluff, MO 63901-2160. www.mythosbooks.com/

Naked Snake Press: 6 Rain Tree Lane, Pawleys Island, SC 29585. www.naked snakepress.com

Necro Publications: P.O. Box 540298, Orlando, FL 32854-0298. www.necro publications.com

Necessary Evil Press: P.O. Box 178, Escanaba, MI 49829. www.necessaryevil press.com

Night Shade Books: 1470 NW Saltzman Road, Portland, OR 97229. www.Night Shadebooks.com

Novello Publishers: Nick Cato, Box 060382, Staten Island NY 10306. www. novellopublishers.com/

Overlook Connection Press: P.O. Box 526, Woodstock, GA 30188. www.over lookconnection.com

Pendragon Press: P.O. Box 12, Maesteg, Mid Glamorgan, South Wales, CF34 0XG, UK. www.pendragonpress.co.uk

Permuted Press: 177 Hillcrest Lane, Mena, AR 71953. www.permuted press.com/

PS Publishing: Grosvenor House 1 New Road, Hornsea, East Yorkshire HU18 1PG. UK www.pspublishing.co.uk/

Raw Dog Screaming: www.rawdogscreaming.com/

Sam's Dot Publishing: Tiree Campbell, P.O. Box 782, Cedar Rapids, Iowa, 52406-0782. www.samsdotpublishing.com/

Sarob Press: Ty Newydd, Four Roads, Kidwelly, Carmarthenshire, SA17 4SF Wales UK. http://home.freeuk.net/sarobpress

Scrybe Press: 15 Cook Street, Massena, NY 13662. www.scrybepress.com

Shocklines Press: www.shocklines.com

Side Real Press: 34 Normanton Terrace, Newcastle Upon Tyne. NE4 6PP, United Kingdom. //www.siderealpress.co.uk/

Silver Lake Publishing: 11 S. Mansfield Rd., Lansdowne, PA 19050. www.silver lakepublishing.com/

Small Beer Press: 176 Prospect Avenue, Northampton, MA 01060. www.lcrw. net/

Subterranean Press: P.O. Box 190106, Burton, MI 48519. www.subterranean press.com/

Tachyon Press: 1459 18th Street #139, San Francisco, CA 94107. www.tachyon publications.com/

Tartarus Press: Coverley House, Carlton, Leyburn, North Yorkshire, DL8 4AY, U.K. http://homepages.pavilion.co.uk/users/tartarus/welcome.htm

Telos Publishing: 61 Elgar Avenue, Tolworth Surrey KT5 9JP. www.telos.co.uk/

Twilight Tales: 2339 N. Commonwealth #4C. Chicago, IL 60614. www .TwilightTales.com

Undaunted Press: www.undauntedpress.com/

Underwood Books: P.O. Box 1919, Nevada City, CA, 95959. www.under woodbooks.com

Wildside Press and Prime Books: 9710 Traville Gateway Dr. #234, Rockville, MD. 20850. www.wildsidepress.com/ and www.primebooks.net/

Wormhole Books: 7719 Stonewall Run, Fort Wayne, IN 46825.

Yard Dog Press: 710 W. Redbud Lane, Alma, AR 72921-7247. www.yarddog press.com

Fantasy and Horror in the Media: 2005

Edward Bryant

The Big Screen

THE WHITE HOUSE MADE ME DO IT?

There's a peculiar conventional wisdom that maintains that horror does better during Republican administrations. It's perhaps a topic awaiting the careful attention of a graduate student with far too much time on his or her hands. But it should be noted that 2005, as George W. Bush started his final term, sported an abundance of horror films. Halloween came early.

New Year's Day was barely stirring from its national hangover when *Darkness*, a reasonable if undistinguished haunted house flick opened its run. Filmed in Spain with Anna Paquin, a couple spooky houses, suggestions of devilish ritual, treacherous family members, and the usual impending apocalypse, the movie was fun to look at, but finally ground down to a mechanically twisty ending. The true horror generated from fine actress Lena Olin struggling to escape from her role as an American mom-in-trouble.

White Noise struggles, largely unsuccessfully, to spin a coherent plot out of a Thomas Alva Edison quote about communicating with the dead. EVP is the high concept here, Electronic Voice Phenomena. In other words, recording the audio and video of communications from the deceased. Think of this as a variation on the Kevin Costner/*Dragonfly* theme. This time it's Michael Keaton who loses his wife in a mysterious accident, and who then is contacted by a dotty widower who has had great success with EVP and now wants to let Keaton know that his dead spouse is on the line. Problem is, not all the dead are benign messengers, and some indeed are hideous crank callers. It's also worth noting that revenant communications seems highly vulnerable to static, pixel dropout and sunspots. Watch this on DVD and you'll never be sure whether you're blinking at deliberate visual effects or simply purchased a defective disk.

Okay, so *Alone in the Dark* is based on the video game from Atari. Is that a bad sign? In this case, very. Be warned, Christian Slater fans, even if you're a lover of gargoyle lizard-creatures.

Hide and Seek, as you might suspect, features good acting by Robert De Niro, the grieving father who moves his young daughter (Dakota Fanning) to a creepy house in upstate New York after the girl finds her mom dead in the family tub. Then Fanning's character meets a new invisible friend named Charlie. As you might guess, Charlie's not a terribly likable entity. John Polson's direction does its job well. The flaw is that there's nothing really new here.

Sam Raimi, a filmic talent for whom I have enormous affection and respect, cannot, alas, bask in much glory over coproducing *The Boogeyman*. It would not be too harsh to suggest at this point that those who cannot manage to tell a coherent story should probably not spend millions on a motion picture. One almost suspects that *The Boogeyman* was made up as it went along. Director Stephen Kay wrestles with a script from three writers. Poor Barry Watson, seemingly cast as a clone of Ashton Kutcher, goes back to the old family house after his mom dies. Fifteen years before, Watson's character saw his somewhat abusive dad beaten to a pulp and disappeared by the malign eponymous creature living in the kid's bedroom closet. Now he's a magazine editor, involved with a truly annoying blonde named Jessica, and ill advised by his childhood shrink to go back home and spend a night in the dreaded home. Things then happen sometimes strikingly, more often arbitrarily, until the poor guy limps into the redemptive morning light of a terminally lame ending. There are fitful bits and pieces of nice film and startling cuts, but finally one is reminded that we already have a pretty good boogeyman film, *A Nightmare on Elm Street*, from which *The Boogeyman* shamelessly borrows some good riffs.

AND THEN THINGS PERKED UP

Constantine seemed a dicey proposition from the git-go, what with DC Comics' sardonic supernatural detective, John Constantine, becoming American rather than British. But then who better to play the flat-affect, totally alienated hero but Keanu Reeves? What results is an intriguing Christian debate over good versus evil. Tilda Swinton's a terrific angel Gabriel, and Peter Stormare does a marvelous turn as Satan. And when you see this supernatural melodrama, wait through the credit crawl for a worthwhile Easter egg.

Kung Fu Hustle is not exactly the most prepossessing title for a film that will appeal to a much wider audience than the Tarantino acolytes and Kung Fu fans who still eat their Asian dishes with a fork. Actor/director/writer Stephen Chow's moderately budgeted action comedy wiped out the box office competition in Asia, wowed 'em at Sundance, and persuaded American critics to start mentioning him in the same breath with Chaplin. It's not hyperbole. Chow, best known at home as a comic, has blended digital effects, frenetic physical comedy, superb Hong Kong wire work (courtesy of fight choreographer Yuen Wo Ping of *The Matrix* and *Crouching Tiger, Hidden Dragon*), and a classic antic spirit into a sort of live-action Warner Bros. cartoon. In China it's called "Mo Lei Tau"—nonsense humor. It's an empowerment fantasy by a grown-up kid who worshiped Bruce Lee movies when he was young and impressionable. If you're a western filmgoer, you might have noticed Chow's *Shaolin Soccer* in 2001. *Kung Fu Hustle* is set in the 1930s in a wretched Hong Kong neighborhood called Pig Sty Alley that is so impoverished it's usually beneath the notice of the vicious Axe Gang. But then, of course things change. Stephen Chow and Lam Tze Chung play two ambitious but not terribly bright young men who are attempting to get into an imagined cushy life of crime by joining the gang. And the gang itself tangles with the decent folk of Pig Sty Alley, some of whom—well, *many* of whom—turn out to be not at all what they first appear. Some are accomplished fighters when they're not working days, making noodles and sewing clothing. And some would seem to be retired celestial figures. A particular high point is the business between vintage Hong Kong film villain Yuen Wah and once-retired stuntwoman Yuen Qui as the bickering, chain-smoking landlords of the crumbling residential block that is Pig Sty Alley. The narrative is nonstop and unexpected surprises abound. The film's energy never flags. And its heart never falters.

Also from the Asian front, check out *Ong-Bak: Thai Warrior*. I'm told director Prachya Sithiamphian wanted to introduce Thai martial arts to the global audience and has done so with a timeworn plot bolstered by superb action. You've never seen anything like the initial full-contact, hyperkinetically violent, giant tree-climbing competition. Onetime stuntman Panom Yeerum, now calling himself Tony Jaa, will remind you of a young Jackie Chan, springing through amazing physical feats without wires or computer graphics.

Imagine an unholy love-child relationship between John Grisham and William Peter Blatty and you've got *The Exorcism of Emily Rose*. Laura Linney is the defense attorney who takes the case of a priest (Tom Wilkinson) whose exorcism of a college coed ends in death. The Catholic horror imagery is familiar enough, but the movie is salvaged by the cast.

BIG STUFF

Batman Begins . . . with a bang. As tired and over-tilled as the cinematic bat-soil may have seemed, Christopher Nolan's rejiggering of the beginning of Batman's career as a crime-fighting superhero works well. As the latest Batman avatar, Christian Bale functions just fine.

2005 finally saw Terry Gilliam's long and frustratingly delayed *The Brothers Grimm* with Heath Ledger and Matt Damon as the brothers in question, magical con men who get caught up in the real thing. The movie's perhaps less quirky than fans of Gilliam are accustomed to. But it still has a striking dollop of grim realism streaked through the fantasy. Not-nice characters are *really* bad. One way to put it is that the film sparks a lot, but never quite kindles.

Finally. It's over. Well, unless a tanned and rested George Lucas decides to execute the long-ago announced *final* trilogy in the *Star Wars* saga.

But if he doesn't, then note that the saga ended with something of a whimper last spring with *Episode III: Revenge of the Sith*. This was the episode in which we saw the seductive dark side finally claim Anakin and the no-nonsense Darth Vader finally rose from the slab, er, lab. There were plenty of good visuals as one would hope, but everything else seemed like something of a strained effort to make the final pieces of the *Star Wars* jigsaw fit into their occasionally ill-fitting holes.

Like clockwork the summer got the fourth Harry Potter chapter, *Harry Potter and the Goblet of Fire*. I liked Mike Newell's directing a bit better than Chris Columbus's in the first two films, but not as well as Alfonso de Cuaron's in the third. Harry, in his fourth year at Hogwarts, is a bit older now, gaining in maturity, still troubled by the mystery of his biological family's murder by the ultimately evil Voldemort, maybe somewhat hornier now that teen hormones are coming into play, and sobered by the increasing darkness of his world.

Steven Spielberg's new version of the H. G. Wells classic, *War of the Worlds*, didn't get a lot of respect. Was it because most of the year's critical spotlight on

Spielberg was narrowly focused on *Munich*? Was it because *War*'s lead, Tom Cruise, spent the release year becoming one of Hollywood's most annoying stars with the whole Katie Holmes/Scientology/Brooke Shields/Oprah sideshow? It's worth noting that *War of the Worlds* was one of 2005's five highest-grossing films.

So was it any good? Absolutely. Spielberg's whole concept and Josh Friedman and David Koepp's script were pleasantly interwoven not only with the H. G. Wells novel, but as well with affectionate connections with the 1953 Byron Haskin production and Orson Welles's earlier notorious radio play. I have to be honest; I would love to see a period version set in England. But taking the Spielberg production on its own terms, it worked pretty darned well. Actually Cruise did fine considering that his role as the deadbeat dad in an extremely dysfunctional New Jersey family was not written even close to a sympathetic anchor. The Martians (or whatever) and their tripod machines were nicely visual, and Tim Robbins added substantially with his apparent walk-in from the original novel. Bookended with classic quotes from H. G. Wells, the movie suitably reminds us to forget about watching the skies—we need to pay closer attention to the earth beneath us.

So who knew when Fox dumped Joss Whedon's westernish sf series *Firefly* after fewer than a dozen episodes that the fans would rise up in wrath and make a considerable noise? They did, and that may be a part of why Universal agreed to front a modestly budgeted feature-length episode for the big screen called *Serenity*. All the original cast was back to crew the tramp spacer of the title, and to square off against both a repressive government and the berserker reavers out on the fringes of known space. There were good bits (the sly references to things like the Earth starship in *Forbidden Planet*) and good lines (particularly the character River's dialog after the pell-mell escape from the reavers early in the film), and plenty of other virtues. The one real problem was that the feature never quite achieved the momentum that the series episodes achieved. I have a bad feeling that the movie worked better for fans of the series than it did for a new audience. But I believe that the feature still made sufficient gross, there may be another *Firefly* in our future.

It wasn't a "big" movie, but it was large in terms of entertainment and provocation. I'm speaking of *CSA: The Confederate States of America*, a faux documentary about a parallel time-stream America in which the Civil War went exceedingly badly for the Yankees. It's not just a matter of eliminating the Emancipation Proclamation. Many things are different in today's world. Sometimes broad, sometimes cuttingly specific, *CSA* performs its job well.

Zathura is nominally a sequel to *Jumanji*, but it stands just fine on its own. Based like its predecessor on a book by the superb children's author and illustrator Chris Van Allsburg, *Zathura* gives us a trio of squabbling siblings left alone by their father for an afternoon. The teenage girl is supposed to be watching, but she falls asleep inside the audio cocoon of her headphones. The two combative sons eventually mess around with a retro mechanical board game squirreled away in the basement. The game, an interplanetary quest, turns out to be all too real and the kids—and their suburban home—are plucked up and sent on a dangerous junket into the wilds of space. Things get complicated when a mysterious astronaut shows up, along with a species of vicious reptilian aliens. Colorful and kinetic, it's a considerable amount of fun. Many of us in the audience might wistfully wonder how long it will take for the tie-in game to be released?

Arguably the best pure fantasy film of the year would have to be *Chronicles of Narnia: the Lion, the Witch, and the Wardrobe*, adapted from the second book in C. S. Lewis's perennial popular novel series. It's a beautiful (literally) all-ages (with no condescension to the kids) version. The four Prevensie children are sent by their mother to the English countryside to escape the German blitz. In the large, echoing home of an elderly eccentric, they find the titular wardrobe in the back of which is a magical entrance to an otherworldly realm in which winter, under the direction of the White Witch (a frostily alien but magnificent Tilda Swinton holds eternal sway). Aslan, the noble lion who represents all that's good and holy has been driven into exile. The unknowing children are the x-factor who have come to Narnia to upset the balance of everything. It's not exactly a secret that writer and theologian Lewis wrote these books as Christian allegory, though he had the good sense and the skillful talent to couch his ideology unobtrusively and almost seamlessly into his characters and story. Still, the studio made some attempt to market this as a very Christian product, almost as this year's *Passion of the Christ*. While that seemed to work at first, it's clear that less piously dedicated viewers also discovered and enjoyed the film. Consider: how could a film fail in which the lion Aslan fills out his messianic metaphor as a Jesus figure who kicks major butt—and is possessed of Jedi wisdom (Liam Neeson voices the role)? Plus it needs to be noted that British character actor Ray Winstone and *Absolutely Fabulous*'s Dawn French play the Beav and his wife.

The long-awaited *King Kong*, one of Peter Jackson's pet projects, was another crowd displeaser that, regardless, was still a top-five grosser of the year. Some audience displeasure may well have been because of that expected question: how can anyone compete with a much-beloved cultural icon, the original romantic thriller about that big, lovable, anthropoid lug who falls in love with Fay Wray after being kidnapped from his idyllic life on Skull Island, and who climbs the Empire State Building in a hopeless effort to elude the rest of the world before being killed by machine gun bullets, gravity—and beauty.

Some audience irritation probably comes from the film's sheer bulk. I hate to sound snippy, but the movie's three hours feel increasingly long when we get into the third act. All the action scenes on Skull Island do go on, and some trimming could have helped. Perhaps Jackson's unapologetic love for the original has had unintended consequences. Jackson fills out everything from the original that was skimped on or even lost. This is an unmoderated love letter to a boy's-own-adventure story that the director must have endlessly filled out in his own mind after he first saw the original. The effects are, of course, spectacular—particularly the exactingly detailed scenes of Manhattan in the 'thirties.

Kong, modeled by Andy Sirkis (as he did with Gollum in the *Lord of the Rings* movies) is personable and convincing. Naomi Watts, playing the role of Ann Darrow made famous by Fay Wray, handles her role with aplomb, and even expands carefully and fruitfully upon the original. Jack Black and Adrian Brody handle their roles capably, but the spotlight, as it should, never really veers away from Ann Darrow and her ape-guy.

NO GHOSTS, VAMPIRES, NOR WEREWOLVES NEED APPLY

Sometimes it's hard to explain why something can walk like a duck, squawk like a duck, swim beautifully like a duck, but just isn't a duck. So here I make the claim that there are works of sterling quality that will appeal to viewers of smart sensibility who love fiction of the fantastic, but these are not fantasies.

David Cronenberg's feature film adaptation of John Wagner and Vince Locke's graphic novel *A History of Violence* is a virtuoso exploration of normal lives strained, warped, and transfigured by violence. Viggo Mortenson is superb as Tom Stall, small-town Indiana diner owner who finds himself in the unwelcome glare of publicity after being obliged to dispatch a pair of urban killers who threaten him, his staff, and his customers. Maria Bello's equally superb as the wife who's a bit confused by her husband's unexpected faculty for mayhem. Ed Harris shines darkly as a vengeful thug who surfaces from a whole different world, claiming that Tom is a onetime killing machine who's forged a new life. And William Hurt got an Oscar nod for his turn as a creepily familial East Coast crime boss. Director Cronenberg is expert at plumbing the unexpected depths of dark souls—and the film works not just for its clever touches and unexpected humor, but also for its adroit exploration of a loving American family forced to examine its own relationships and internal dynamics when stressed by hard moral choices and the minefields sown long before by a deeply and violently buried past.

On UPN, *Veronica Mars* continues to be the smart, sharp, charming avatar of *Buffy* but without the element of the supernatural. Kristen Bell's eponynmous character is a bit like Nancy Drew's great-granddaughter growing up hip in a moneyed suburb of San Diego. Veronica's the daughter of a single-dad PI (a wonderful Enrico Colantoni), and is well aware of the surrounding community's immersion in political chicanery, corporate corruption, murder, rape, sex, and drugs. The characters are all shaded in moral complexity. The crisp dialog and intriguing relationships make the melodramatic plot work. Veronica rocks! The critics love her, Stephen King has proclaimed his love for her in *Entertainment Weekly*, and I would set Kristen Bell in the series pantheon along with Peta Wilson and Sarah Michelle Gellar. But there's that matter of demographics, ratings, and the imminent meltdown of the WB and UPN into a single consolidated network, the CW. Pray for *Veronica Mars*.

ANIMATED? YOU MEAN BACK FROM THE DEAD?

Animation was good to us in 2005.

Tim Burton's Corpse Bride? Absolutely terrific stop-motion tale of a young beau's logistical error falling prey to the law of unintended consequences. Young mortal Victor (the voice of Johnny Depp) finds himself hooked up with the lovely but deceased Corpse Bride (voiced by Helena Bonham Carter), soon discovering that the literally jazzy Land of the Dead is a heck of a lot more lively than his stuffy world back home. The other character voices (Emily Watson, Christopher Lee, Tracey Ullman, Albert Finney, et al.) are terrific, and Danny Elfman's score is perfect. Death has rarely been so romantic—and amusing.

For a parallax view of wedded bliss, there's a return to the fractured fairy tale world of ogres and talking donkeys. *Shrek 2* wasn't nearly so bright or entertaining as its predecessor. But it would still be worth the price of admission for Antonio Banderas buckling his swash as Puss in Boots, cat for hire. The set piece in which Puss, hired by Shrek's disgruntled father-in-law to assassinate the lovable green ogre, foils his own villainy by coughing up a hairball, is unforgettable.

By a hair, I'd have to opine that *Howl's Moving Castle*, based upon the novel by Dianne Wynne Jones, was the most impressive animated feature of the year. From Japanese director Hayao Miyazaki, creator of the unique *Spirited Away*, *Howl's Moving Castle* dazzles with its visual magic.

Madagascar's a big-budget, big-star romp in which a pack of rebellious zoo critters from the Central Park Zoo escape, get cornered and recaptured at Grand Central Station, and then are crated up for shipment to a Kenyan wildlife preserve. One shipwreck later, Alex the lion (Ben Stiller), Marty the zebra (Chris Rock), Melman the giraffe (David Schwimmer), and Gloria the hippo (Jada Pinkett Smith) find themselves marooned in the genuine wild on something of a fantastical Madagascar. Everything goes fine until hungry Alex, starting to recover his dormant predatory nature, starts fantasizing that his friends are prime cuts of meat. But the real scene stealers are the penguins and the lemurs. A gang of hard-beaked penguins provides a *noir*-ish Greek chorus, amusingly enough, but the real showstopper is Sacha Baron Cohen, the bizarre comic cable interviewer Ali G, who plays Julien, the whacked-out king of the lemur tribe. He inhabits his role with marvelously warped zest.

After seducing much of the viewing audience over the years with short animation pieces such as *The Wrong Trousers*, the British animation shop Aardman has moved characters Wallace and Gromit into the feature-length arena with the superbly quirky *Wallace & Gromit: The Curse of the Were-Rabbit*. Wallace, you'll recall, is the cheese-obsessed human. Gromit, in spite of being a dog, is the brains of the operation. Nick Park's claymation creations do justice to the resourceful canine/human investigation team as they first try to protect the local carrot farmers from rabbit depredations, then attempt to solve the mystery of a monstrous creature that is apparently big, hungry, and perhaps unstoppable as it spreads terror among local growers of championship vegetables. It's all a delight.

Hoodwinked is a peculiar independent animation production that adds a *noir* tinge to the *Little Red Riding Hood* legend and borrows its narrative technique from *Rashomon*. Intriguingly, sophisticated computer animation techniques are sometimes used (as with the wolf) to simulate technically cruder claymation and stop motion effects. All in all, it's a lovely confection.

LITTLE GREEN SCREENS

Even if it didn't achieve script brilliance, 2004's *Sky Captain and the World of Tomorrow*'s grand, stylish 1930s-style visuals, all shot against a green screen with live actors and real foreground props, left unforgettable images. 2005 saw more experimentation with virtual sets. The highest-profile production was Robert Rodriguez's amalgamation of three Frank Miller *Sin City* graphic novels. Miller also got a codirecting credit, and there was a drop-in guest-directed sequence from Quentin Tarantino. That all drove the Director's Guild nuts, but that's a story for another time.

Bruce Willis, Mickey Rourke, and a cast of what felt like thousands gave *Sin City* a heavy dose of star power. Occasional dollops of brutal and graphic violence put off some viewers; futuristic and fantastical elements disoriented others. But all in all, for technical reasons and otherwise, *Sin City* is a landmark.

The somewhat softer side of green-screen came in Neil Gaiman and Dave McKean's *MirrorMask*. Shot for a mere $4 million and backed by the Henson Company, it was directed by accomplished comics artist McKean from Gaiman's script. After a teenage girl wishes her mother dead and Mom falls into a coma, the girl is magically transported to a realm where the Queen of Light and the Queen of Darkness (both resembling her mother) battle over her. It's gorgeous but perhaps not escapist enough for some watchers. It's important for the audience to realize and remember this is a real movie concerning genuine issues.

POPCORN WEASELS

I've admitted it publicly before. I *liked* the two *Resident Evil* films. Although a video game is generally a dubious pedigree for a multi-zillion dollar film, every once in a while the bet pays off. And that it did—barely—with *Doom*. Indeed, it's a hopeful sign when the Universal Pictures logo at the beginning incorporates Mars rather than Earth. Things begin promisingly enough when something unseen but awful starts pursuing and slaughtering scientists at a Martian research facility sometime in about fifty years or so. Naturally the Company—isn't there always a Company—is concerned and teleports a rapid response team of tough Marines commanded by the Rock. In the old days, the diverse band of brothers would have included a Jew and a kid from Brooklyn. Nowadays the squad has a fanatical religionist and a sleazy pervert. Unlike the *Alien* movies, *Doom* still hasn't enlisted women into the combat troops. The only female character of note is the estranged sister of one of the soldiers, a red-planet researcher whose main jobs are to preserve corporate secrets and scream with great volume. The movie's mostly about a great deal of stalking through dimly lit tunnels and corridors (in this future, the military appears to have forgotten its night-vision technology), killing and being killed by really ugly humanoid critters that drool, slobber, pounce, and French-kiss like crazy. Turns out they're the next step in evolution, infected with a twenty-fourth pair of chromosomes drawn from ancient inhabitants of Mars. If the chromosomes affect a good soul, the resulting being is stronger, smarter, tougher, and altogether swell. Unfortunately, most human stock has apparently been becoming stronger, smarter, tougher, and even more homicidal than usual. What the audience eventually gets is the same old same old. Tedious? Yes. You want something more interesting? Go back to the *Resident Evil* movies. You want more fun? Rent *Ghosts of Mars*. The height of *Doom*'s wit is to indicate that a good guy with a 24th pair of chromosomes will suddenly evolve into a consummate first-person shooter, thereby confirming what dweebs have always suspected.

Do you like spelunking? You may reconsider your enthusiasm after watching *The Cave*, a dismal and lurid tale of a Romanian cavern system that gobbles up explorers and then spits them back out as mutants. Or something like that. Claustrophobic underground horror probably won't reach its potential until a talented writer and an extraordinary director tackle an adaptation of Jeff Long's classic novel of subterranean terror, *The Descent*.

On the comic-book superhero front, Jennifer Garner as *Elektra* was better than Ben Affleck as *Daredevil* and vastly better than Halle Barry as *Catwoman*. Further, the deponent sayeth naught, in spite of the appeal of tight red leather outfits and some decent fight choreography. I could suggest renting back seasons of *Alias* on DVD.

Now then, what *about* yet another remake, this time a new version of 1953's *House of Wax*? Honestly, does this exploitation flick have anything to recommend itself other than providing an audience-pleasing moment when Paris Hilton's character dies horribly and messily? Well, yes. This isn't a *good* movie, mind you, but it has sufficient script and visual interest to keep you intrigued for the full screening time. Don't worry about the plot. The attractive young folks on their way to a college football game in the American deep south are just a pretext to strand them in one of those strangely unpopulated small rural towns that usually turn out to be the death of most of the cast. This time, the town is centered around a wax museum. The design of the town and its museum is architecturally brilliant. If you watch this on DVD, you may wish simply to turn down the volume and just absorb the visuals.

It's eerie watching Kate Hudson's voodoo melodrama, *Skeleton Key*. Portions were shot in New Orleans not long before Hurricane Katrina. It's like watching a ghost. The movie itself is pleasant enough, but not particularly surprising. Hudson plays a woman hired to come to a remote bayou mansion to be a caretaker for a very sick gentleman. Unfortunately the plot machinations creak as loud as spirits in the night.

SOME DISAPPOINTMENTS

The remake of John Carpenter's low-budget 1976 thriller *Assault on Precinct 13*, even with Ethan Hawke as the besieged officer trying to gain redemption as he fends off an assault team of rogue cops attempting to break into his isolated, soon-to-be-shut-down Detroit precinct building to kill about-to-rat druglord Laurence Fishburne, even with Drea de Matteo, Maria Bello, Brian Dennehy, Ja Rule, John Leguizamo, and Gabriel Byrne (as the chief villain) in the supporting cast, can't save this self-basting turkey. Perhaps the original was too much a product of its time. Even in a blizzard in the wilds of Detroit, the makers of this retread couldn't quite figure out, what with cell phones and the Internet, how to keep our protagonists totally isolated from the rest of the world. Call it a failure of imagination.

To make things worse, there was also a remake of John Carpenter's well-remembered *The Fog*. Tom Welling, Selma Blair, and Maggie Grace starred in a version that explained more to the audience than twenty-six years ago about exactly why a crew of rotting pirates off in the concealing fog are coming ashore in coastal Oregon to take revenge for a slight now lost to history. Twenty-six years ago, at least, *The Fog* had atmosphere. Now the remake just has dank, unpleasant condensation on your glasses.

Here's another test question. In 2005 Charlize Theron starred in both *North Country* and *Aeon Flux*. She got an Oscar nod for one. Hint: for once, the Academy of Motion Picture Arts and Sciences got it right.

The Fantastic Four gave it the old college try. But even with colorful effects and a few slyly tasteless in-jokes (pay attention to the high-tech character evaluation scenes when you watch this on DVD with your finger on the pause button), this comics adaptation didn't make it far beyond the minimal boredom threshold.

The Small Screen

Three years ago, HBO's *Carnivale* was good. In 2005, the second season of Daniel Knauf's Depression-era drama about a hardscrabble traveling carnival, a charismatic radio preacher, and the eternal struggle between light and darkness, was superb. The second set of twelve episodes truly caught fire, though the show continued to be a hard sell to the audience. That's a pity, since *Carnivale* ought to be counted as the poster child for small-screen dark fantasy. The ensemble cast just gets better. Nick Stahl, the young guy with an enigmatic background, finally moves his acting affect from fairly wooden to genuinely tortured. Since it's 1935 now, the similarly mysterious Brother Justin Crow uses the still-unexploited airwaves to increasingly scary hate-mongering rhetoric reminiscent of real history's Father Coughlin, a cleric who makes Rush Limbaugh look like Paula Abdul by comparison. This season's most striking newcomer is John Carroll Lynch as Varlyn Stroud, Brother Justin's new right-hand disciple, a jovial monster sprung from prison to raise literal hell on earth. Clea DuVall, Amy Madigan, Michael Anderson, Adrienne Barbeau, Ralph Waite, Tim DeKay, and the rest of the crew from the first season all get a chance to shine, however darkly. Along with the steadily accelerating story arc (will the Trinity nuclear test signal the End of Days?), the scripts are increasingly packed with genuinely striking set-pieces that range from Nick Stahl's character discovering that his actual kinfolk seem to be drawn equally from the Sawney Beane legend and the family from *Texas Chain-Saw Massacre*, to the imperturbably violent Varlyn Stroud blowing away a pair of Bonnie and Clyde wannabes at a service station—then shooting the witness without hesitation. Daniel Knauf and his crew of actors, writers, and directors have masterfully worked the economic chaos of the Depression, the Apocalyptic landscape of the Dust Bowl, and the uncertain post–World War I new global order into an effective set of metaphors for the good-versus-evil play of *Carnivale*. Maybe the trick for the audience is to experiment until each audience member finds the right individual mouthful. For me, it was taping the whole series and watching it two hours at a time. One hour was too choppy; more than two hours was exhausting. Two hours, in the best sense, just blew me away. Knauf clearly has a third season in mind. HBO, tragically, did not agree.

At least in terms of program inspiration, the Apocalypse notion was big in 2005. Fox debuted *Point Pleasant*, a hideously uneven series which suggested that in our contemporary America, the spawn of Satan would turn out to be a knockout teen (*All My Children*'s Elisabeth Harnois) who drifts ashore at the affluent New Jersey beach town of the title. In Hollywood terms think *The OC* meets *The Omen*. Fortunately for humanity and the plot line, young Ms. Lucifer is, like plenty of other post-pubescent young women, deeply conflicted. Oh, should I annihilate the world and damn all mankind? Or should I go to the dance? The forces of darkness, never eager to allow a fair moral fight, load the dice by dispatching a handsome but evil emissary (Grant Show from *Melrose Place*). It's all pretty silly. The characters can't figure out the significance of three sixes laid out like a Wankel corporate logo on the heroine's eye. Actually the scariest thing about *Point Pleasant* is that a principal of the creative team is Marti Noxon, one of Joss Whedon's producing confederates on *Buffy the Vampire Slayer*.

A step up from *Point Pleasant* (though nowhere as good as *Carnivale*) is the NBC miniseries *Revelations*. You guessed it. Satan and his minions are plotting something nefarious, and it's up to the hipper among the Catholic priesthood to save all the Muslims, Jews, Hindus, nonbelievers, etc. from a terrible doom. I'm not saying it's not an engaging series, but I do note that I kept forgetting to tape the episodes.

For something both respectable and quite enjoyable on broadcast television, the answer was NBC's new series, *Medium*. I admit I had my doubts at first. Okay, here was going to be an episodic melodrama about a crime-consulting psychic in Phoenix, and it was said to be based on, or at least inspired by, the life of real-life professional psychic, Allison Dubois. It only took the pilot episode to hush the skeptics. Created by *Moonlighting*'s Glenn Gordon Caron, writing and acting turned out to be the key to success. Patricia Arquette plays the married mother of three daughters to perfection as a woman coming to terms with her disconcerting mental gifts. Jake Weber is her loving but exceedingly rational scientist husband. The great and effective device of *Medium* is the relationship shared by husband and wife and their kids. It lends a base of stable and affecting reality to the imaginative leaps in the plots. The show depends heavily on the device of beginning-of-the-episode dreams which generally bewilder and often terrify Allison before the unexpected nuances of meaning and unanticipated consequences surface as the hour unfolds. As is so frequently the truth of television series we can both respect and enjoy, it's the people who make the difference.

Nothing succeeds in network programming like cloning, so we have ABC's *The Ghost Whisperer* with Jennifer Love Hewitt. She plays a small-town medium who is newly married and has the challenge of grappling with her ability to jump-start stalled spirits into moving on to their next spiritual evolutionary stage. Call it pleasant but bland.

Ever more big-screen filmmakers continue to dabble in episodic television. Biological brothers and brother screen directors Ridley Scott and Tony Scott are the executive producers of CBS's *Numb3rs*. It's essentially a contemporary police drama, but does keep dipping its toe in slipstream criminal behavior and, more important, doesn't apologize for using science as an integral and imaginative part of crime solving. Rob Morrow plays an L.A.-based FBI agent; David Krumholtz is his somewhat geeky brother, a mathematical genius who sets up sophisticated math models in an effort to figure out where to search for the truck with stolen nuclear materials, where the quirky serial killer will strike next, etc. The nicest thing about *Numb3rs* is that it takes science seriously, and respects both the people who take numbers seriously and those whom numbers baffle. Perhaps the strangest thing about the series is seeing Judd Hirsch in the Fred MacMurray role as the two adult sons' dad. He's a retired city planner who helps the kids out now and again. And then I recall that actors age, as do we all.

Who would have thunk it? Whole pop cultural generations have grown up never lacking new *Star Trek* series. But that ended in 2005. UPN's *Star Trek: Enterprise* wound down to a final, fourth-season black hole with no new successor clearly on the event horizon. True, there was that rumor of *Galactic Championship Poker Series with Quark*, but that seems to be in a permanent parking orbit.

A more lamentable dying was endured by the WB's crackerjack slipstream series about two young brothers growing up in a small American town, *Jack & Bobby*. The catch is, of course, that one of them will become president. And one will die untimely. You might consider this something of a speculative parallel-worlds drama driven by a terrific faux documentary style and fine coming-of-age relationships between brothers and their single mother (Christine Lahti).

While it's not dead yet, it has been announced that the WB's *Charmed* is winding down into its final season of witchery. On the other hand, UPN's *Smallville* has found new breath and is on the upswing. USA Network's *The Dead Zone* has lost some of its considerable steam. So has *The 4400*, the series about all the UFO abductees coming back to Earth one night, only to discover they all now have special powers. *The 4400*, however, will be returning with a new season in 2006.

The powerhouse on the SciFi Channel is still *Battlestar Galactica*, that new and admirable reworking of a long-ago cult bad melodrama. *Battlestar* still succeeds because of its complex background, its diverse cast, and its involving character relationships. This is pretty darned good science fiction, paying real attention to how the universe works even as it pays close allegiance to the bells and whistles of interstellar genocide, spaceships, and cyborg spies.

There was plenty of promise as the fall season started on television. After all, *Lost* came back with new episodes that greatly complicated the lives of our plane crash survivors on the mysterious Pacific island. Last season, some of our heroes had finally blown their way into the mysterious hatch in the rain forest floor. We discovered there was a shaft and part of a metal ladder. This autumn we discovered a mysterious bunker down below, a headquarters for—something; something replete with nostalgically archaic-looking computer equipment. It was like walking into Radio Shack in 1985. But soon to come were the revelations about the experiment that involved saving the world, the meetings with the Others—or at least some of the Others. Or the possibility that there were *other* Others, or even *other* other Others. Not to mention the revelation that there were still survivors from the severed tail of the doomed Oceanic flight, characters who had landed on a distant part of the island. And so it goes. *Lost* will probably never be as fresh as it was at the beginning, but it's still a complicated and involving *X-Files*-ian soap opera.

Autumn saw the debut of *Supernatural* on the WB. Two hunky young men (Jared Padalecki and Jensen Ackles), sons of a known demon hunter, suffer various personal tragedies, are abandoned by their dad, and go out on their own to track down and destroy emissaries of the forces of evil. The guys aren't all that charismatic, but the plots can be fun and are a little fresher for viewers too young to have seen series like *Kolchak: the Night Stalker.*

Speaking of *Kolchak*, the series was briefly revived on ABC as *Night Stalker* with Stuart Townsend as the rebellious news reporter who *knows* there is more out there than dreamed of by Horatio or anyone else. There's also an unconvincing overarching story arc in which Kolchak's wife has been killed by some kind of supernatural entity, a provocative act that sends her husband off on a crusade to find out The Truth. Stuart Townsend has some charisma, but he's definitely not another Darren McGavin, and that's a pity. Even the talented Gabrielle Union, cast as Kolchak's buddy and arch-competitor back at the paper, couldn't save the day.

Plenty of series invaders started to ravage the Earth, but not all with success. In CBS's *Threshold*, multidimensional diamonds in the sky started changing beholders to alien intelligences. Or something. The cast looked like it would carry the day. Carla Cugino played a FEMA executive who knew what she was doing—a bright woman who'd come up with all manner of advance plans for any emergency—including alien invasion of the U.S. She quickly assembles a brilliant team including the likes of Peter Dinklage (star of *The Station Agent*) and Brent Spiner, late of the *Star Trek* universe. Good people all. The series tanked. What seemed to work better with the audience was more relationship-based invasion drama.

Case in point: ABC's *Invasion.* After a massive hurricane devastates a big chunk of Florida, clues start to surface that maybe the storm wasn't a completely natural phenomenon. There were mysterious lights that cascaded into the waters. And now there's something glowing beneath the surfaces of the lakes and rivers. The Everglades seems to be infested with little-glimpsed but lethal new aquatic life. Citizens appear to be getting body-snatched by something alien. What seems to make the melodrama work are the complex interrelationships of two families. The local sheriff married the doctor ex of the local park ranger who remarried the local TV anchorwoman. They've all got children and various shirttail relatives. The sheriff, played by William Fichtner is spectacularly sinister. Is he the first of the subverted human citizens? *Invasion*'s the creation of Shaun Cassidy, the originator of the late and lamented weird series, *American Gothic.*

Surface is a bit less involving than *Invasion*, but it still benefits from having a virtual repertory cast of related characters. It's also got apparently dangerous critters lurking down below the surface, both in the oceans and in our inland waters. A continuing plot thread for this NBC series has been the adoption of an apparent baby alien by a couple of kids—and the revelation that the aliens just might be benevolent, with a wonderful healing power. And so the exploration of our cultural fear of what lurks below the surface of water, and how we'll react to first meeting alien intelligence continues.

Late in the year, the cable provider Showtime provided an intriguing thirteen-episode anthology series called *Masters of Horror.* This was a favorite project from director-writer Mick Garris, known particularly for his adaptations of Stephen King stories. The gimmick with *Masters of Horror* was to adapt real stories by known horror writers, and have them directed by experienced horror directors.

Though, cable being cable, the emphasis tended to be heavy on sex and graphic violence, the results still included material well worth the watching. The series debuted with Don Coscarelli (*Bubba Ho-tep*) directing an adaptation of Joe R. Lansdale's "Incident On and Off a Mountain Road," essentially a "biter bit" story with an extra twist. Bree Turner plays a young woman apparently fleeing an abusive husband when she runs afoul of a small crew of homicidal madmen up in the mountains. The story teaches that apparent victims may sometimes surprise us.

Other directors included John Carpenter, Tobe Hooper, Larry Cohen, John Landis, and even Lucky McGee, creator of the indie Angela Bettis cult body-modification flick, *May*. Contributing writers ranged from Canadian star Dale Bailey to the old gentleman himself, H.P. Lovecraft. Stuart Gordon's adaptation of "The Dreams in the Witch House" may not endear itself to purists.

In any case, *Masters of Horror* was sufficiently successful to warrant a second season; and there is in preparation a *Masters of Science Fiction*.

SMALL SCREENS, SMALL MOVIES

If you want a respectable disaster movie, check out the Discovery Channel's *Pompeii: The Last Day*. It's not Irwin Allen, but that's just fine. This is a docudrama using a fair number of computer-generated effects to depict the Roman coastal resort city's last day in A.D. 79 when Mount Vesuvius stifled it with superheated air and a deep cloak of ash. Jonathan Firth, Jim Carter, Robert Whitelock, Rebecca Clark, and Tim Pigott-Smith star, highlighted by Martin Hodgson as Pliny the Younger, the on-scene observer whose written account remains the accepted account of the cataclysm.

But if you're still nostalgic for the Irwin Allen approach to sturm, drang, and doom, you can go even further with the CBS original movie, *Locusts*. Lucy Lawless stars as a scientist trying to stop the spread of jumbo, really omnivorous super-bugs that are busily eating our crops and stripping the flesh from our bones. Naturally the bad bugs are a genetically engineered phenomenon, but even the avatar of *Xena: Warrior Princess* has a pretty tough time of it. Less than scrupulous researchers have tinkered with the super-locusts to make them unaffected by insecticides. The writing will make your skin itch, though the bugs probably won't.

Here's a trivia question for you: name two network fantasy/sf movies based on work by major sf writers that appeared in the last month of 2005. Okay, we'll skip any false suspense.

First, along about Thanksgiving, CBS presented *Snow Wonder*, based upon the story "Just Like the Ones We Used to Know" by Connie Willis, with Mary Tyler Moore starring. It wasn't a bad film, if you could ignore the fact that the adapter had removed all that nasty chaos theory stuff from the original, and then made sure that anything else smacking of science fiction was expunged.

Second, hard sf writer Wil McCarthy was hired by the SciFi Channel to help bring real sf back into SciFi's world by scripting an original feature film. The result was *Basilisk*, a thriller suffering mightily from going from McCarthy's word processor directly to the focus-group burger grinder. What one can say is that the result was probably the best science fiction movie filmed all year in Bulgaria.

Pandora's Toy Box

Gretel in fishnets while her bro Hansel languishes in a too-small cage suspended from a peppermint cane? Hoo-boy! Not-so-little Miss Muffet is ravished by the spider—or maybe it's she who's ravishing the arachnid! Things are amusingly Grimm indeed in McFarlane's Monsters series 4, *Twisted Fairy Tales*, six action figures drawn from favorite fairy tales and nursery rhymes. Red Riding Hood, Humpty Dumpty, and Peter Pumpkin Eater are all cool, but that Gretel now, she's hot. In its grotesquely askew way, McFarlane Toys has restored much of the unsparing nastiness of the originals.

It's always enlightening to see Asia's contribution when licensing agreements flurry during the summer blockbuster season. *The Revenge of the Sith* distributed 31 *Star Wars* toys through Burger King. These Super-D creations were all perfectly competent (the Jar Jar Binks spitting squirter had a real flair), but BK went the extra parsec by molding the chicken tenders into science-fictional shapes; to wit, stars and what appeared to be road-kill lizards. But my vote for the best *Sith* giveaway were the three colors of illuminated light saber spoons given away inside a variety of Kellogg's cereals.

Burger King also gave away five *Fantastic 4* figures, the titular quartet plus Dr. Doom. The Thing bore a reasonable resemblance to actor Michael Chiklis, and clapped his hands together to make a terrific crashing noise. All he needed was a red velvet fez and a cymbal in each hand to emulate an offbeat organ grinder's monkey. The Invisible Woman figure also struck a retro resonance. Drop Sue Storm into a glass of cold water and she would put *on* her natty blue uniform. Remember the incorrect old days when various female effigies were designed to *remove* their clothing as the payoff?

IT'S A WRAP

Fans of grimmer filmmaking got a thoughtful gift on Christmas Day, 2005. The sequence worked out well. Carve your turkey, then go to see human characters treated like Christmas turkeys. In other words, top of the holiday with *Wolf Creek*. Writer-director Greg McLean's feature debut is tight, edged, and uncompromising. He gives us three attractive young adults, two female and one male, who drive off on holiday into Australia's outback. Their destination is Wolf Creek, a huge meteor crater where watches stop and cars break down. One could argue about strange forces affecting timepieces. There's no mystery about why cars stop running. Our protagonists are "rescued" by Mick (John Jarrett, whom you may recall from *Picnic at Hanging Rock*), a garrulous character who clearly has watched *Crocodile Dundee* too many times for his own good. Before they know it, the tourists have been treated to glasses of drugged rainwater. When they wake up, they're bound—both in duct tape and for a terrible fate. The down-under chainsaw massacre just gets darker and darker. Yes, the victims fight back, but Mick, sociopathically disaffected Viet vet that he apparently is, knows some strikingly nasty ways to immobilize a prisoner. When it comes to horror, this is the real McCoy.

The Don't-Miss Recap for 2005

Battlestar Galactica
Batman Begins
Carnivale
Charlie and the Chocolate Factory
Chronicles of Narnia: the Lion, the Witch and the Wardrobe
Corpse Bride
CSA: the Confederate States of America
A History of Violence
Howl's Moving Castle

Invasion
King Kong
Kung Fu Hustle
Masters of Horror
MirrorMask
Serenity
Unleashed
Veronica Mars
Wallace & Gromit: Curse of the Were-Rabbit
Wolf Creek

TRAILERS

2006 will apparently see no scarcity of popcorn. We will all go out to see *Superman Returns*. And Johnny Depp in that new Keith Richards flick, *Pirates of the Caribbean 2*. The latest James Bond, Daniel Craig, will attempt to teach us new levels of cool in *Casino Royale*. Brett Ratner's *X3* will deluge us in new mutants à la Kelsey Grammer as the Beast. Wolfgang Petersen has directed *Poseidon*, though, alas, without Shelley Winters. Then there will be Ron Howard's version of *The Da Vinci Code* with Tom Hanks, but maybe you don't consider that fantasy—or even fiction at all. And zillions more, both remakes and originals, big-budget and indies.

Graphic Novels: 2005

Charles Vess

Okay, the ocean liner you're on is slowly sinking and you've already filled a good-size bag with all the books and music you want to enjoy during that leisure time you'll have on your own private desert island but there's still some room left over for a few graphic novels.

Here's what I would toss in.

This year brought two new tales from the hand and gently twisted mind of Tony Millionaire: *That Darn Yarn* and *Billy Hazelnuts* (both from Fantagraphics Books). As always, the visual surface that Millionaire applies to his stories creates a strong sense of nostalgia that immediately draws the reader into the narrative. However, once there, the reader is confronted by a playful absurdity and a gloriously warped imagination that brings a fresh and invigorating maturity to his narratives. The first tale takes the form of a traditional children's picture book but with some rather dark twists more suited for the adult mind. The latter story is an epic adventure utilizing all the attributes of the graphic narrative to their best advantage. A practical minded young girl, her would-be boyfriend, a disgruntled poet, and a turnip brought to life by maniacal mice embark on a cosmic voyage to the edge of the universe.

Writer and artist Joann Sfar's *The Rabbi's Cat* (Pantheon) is set in 1930s Algeria where a rabbi's beautiful daughter owns a very opionated cat who, after he swallows an overly talkative parrot, begins to converse with its humans. A difficult, scathingly funny and very adult exchange follows, covering all the philosophical ground from the meaning of existence and man's relationship to god to whom exactly the daughter should be dating. The tale is rendered in a richly detailed but stylized manner reveling in the heady atmosphere of this "lost" world brought to life by Sfar, whose children's books concerning "The Little Vampire" have been enchanting readers for years.

For the better part of ten years Charles Burns has been serializing his emotionally explosive tale, *Black Hole*, and now Pantheon has collected those separate issues into a deluxe hardcover edition. In a small town in the contemporary Pacific northwest coast, a group of teens begins to experience a growing plague of strange mutations to their physical appearance brought on by sexual contact. Some become outwardly repulsive, others manage to hide their newfound deformities beneath their everyday clothes, but once the change has come there is no going back. And someone or something is murdering them one by one. Burns's hypnotically beautiful black and white art is as riveting as his relentless tale of high school angst. He makes his tale all the more metaphorically universal by exploring the horror that all those in high school experience in day to day attempt to fit into a complex society that plays by no rules that they are made aware of.

Writer, artist and designer Jordan Crane has gifted us with his newest work, *The Clouds Above* (Fantagraphics Books). It's an enchanting, whimsical adventure, told one panel per page, of a young elementary school–age youth, a very large cat, and one all-purpose school book and what they do when they miss a day at school. Atop the school building is an old door that opens onto a wooden spiral staircase that leads them up and up and up. Soon after passing a flock of cranky birds they encounter a very lonely cloud monster, angry storm clouds, a stray airplane, and a sky full of those still cranky yellow birds. Crane's clear, simplified drawings and amusing dialog lend these wild adventures a sense of playful absurdity that, at times, reminded me of Kenneth Grahame's *The Wind in the Willows*.

From the late forties till the early 1960s the "good duck" artist, Carl Barks, wrote and drew complex, humorous adventure tales featuring Donald Duck for Dell Comics. While the same character was a star in the animated films from the Disney studio, he remained a fairly one-note punch line throughout his life in the movies. Barks took Donald and developed his own complex storiescape, giving him dramatic situations to react to, and peopling that new landscape with characters from Barks's own fertile imagination. Perhaps the most vivid of these personal creations was the multimillionaire miser Scrooge McDuck, who was always involving Donald in one grand adventure after another, usually in a futile effort to make Scrooge wealthier still. After more than twenty years of such adventures Scrooge McDuck gained a rich and complex history. Here Barks's fan extraordinaire Don Rosa has written and drawn a series of books that pull together all of those disparate tales. He has created his own duck epic by filling in the empty spaces between existing stories. *The Life and Times of Scrooge McDuck* is a loving homage to the work of Barks as well as a rousing and at times hilarious adventure in its own right.

Linda Medley's engaging series *Castle Waiting* (Fantagraphics) was always a complete joy to read, and just as difficult to follow from issue to issue due to her somewhat turbulent attempts at publishing the book. Now she seems to have found herself a comfortable publishing home at Fantagraphics Books, and I hope that we can look forward to many, many more stories from her. Medley has taken characters from familiar fairly tales, dropped in a few of her own original creations, and used them to tell her own stories of what happens after the happily-ever-after ending typical to many of these tales. This edition collects all of Medley's previously published tales under one cover, as well as the never before printed ending to her last series concerning a convent of spectacularly eccentric and bearded nuns. Whimsical, humorous, and wise, they are a delight for young and old alike.

I've spent many paragraphs in previous columns extolling the narrative virtues of Jeff Smith's splendid series, *Bone*, so I won't reiterate those words now. But I did want to alert my readers to the fact that Scholastic Press is now reissuing the series in lovely full-color packages. Two volumes have been produced so far (*Out from Boneville* and *The Great Cow Race*) to great success and another will be in print by the time you read this. Please do seek them out, you will not be disappointed.

Editor/art director Kazu Kibuishi has assembled an amazing group of young graphic narrative artists for the first two volumes of *Flight* (Image). These full color anthologies contain over fifty stories between them and amazingly the quality of both the narratives and the art remain consistent throughout. Most of the new generation of artists represented in these anthologies meet online. It is to Kibuishi's credit that he was able to first recognize the power of their collective vision and then to provide them with such a beautifully produced showcase for the public to see their work is a dream come true for any artist. I would hesitate to pick any standouts among this wealth of art and story but make sure that you check out contributions by Catie Chien, Jacob Magraw-Mickelsen, and Derek Kirk Kim in the first volume and Michael Gagné, Johann Matte, and Jeff Smith in the second. I've been told that Ballantine Books will be publishing future Flight collections, so keep an eye peeled for it. I'm sure; with Kibuishi's firm editorial hand it will be as spectacular as these first two.

By the time you read this column there will be a collected edition of Paul Chadwick's new Concrete adventure, *The Human Dilemma* (Dark Horse). For all its science fictional origins; Concrete is a huge humanoid-shaped rock with a human brain, placed there by aliens who leave without ever explaining the purpose of their experiment, Chadwick's long-running and multi–award winning series always offers challenging ideas presented in a thoughtful manner usually concerning a major dilemma of contemporary society. This time he takes on population control and through his complex cast of characters presents many points of view on this very contentious problem. As big as our planet is, if the population continues to grow at its present pace, we will soon run out of resources to feed, clothe, and house those billions and billions of people. All of this very serious conjecture is wrapped within a tale that shares equal parts humor and pathos. Chadwick's longtime publisher Dark Horse is currently pursuing a publishing program of reprinting all of the earlier adventures of Concrete, and you would do well to purchase all of them. The first of these collections is *Depths*, out now, which presents his earliest tales. There will be more in the months to come.

There are five short stories in Thomas Ott's new collection, *Cinema Panopticum* (Fantagraphics), all lovingly rendered in his detailed black and white scratchboard technique. A young girl wanders into a sideshow attraction at a seedy carny and begins to watch movies. As each film plays for her penny piece, we are given a new story. Cosmic horror, dark humor, and delightful story twists are staples of Ott's imagination and they are given full scope here as is his maturing ability to relate complex stories without using a single word balloon or caption.

Kris Oprisko has adapted Clive Barker's *The Thief of Always* (IDW Publishing) for artist Gabriel Hernandez to illustrate, with spectacularly creepy results. A lonely child is brought to another land and to his delight told that his every wish will be fulfilled. Bit by bit the young man begins to see the terror that lurks in the dark corners of the huge old house that is his new home and the great and awful price he will eventually have to pay in order to have all of his dreams come true. He begins desperately to look for a way out. This sumptuous 144-page color collection also supports an artist's sketchbook of conceptual ideas as well as an informative interview with Clive Barker, which details his creative process in developing the book itself.

Any tale from the hand of artist and writer Mike Mignola is an exciting event but his newest Hellboy tale, *The Island* (Dark Horse) is a stunning, surrealistic graphic narrative that should not be missed. Mignola's bright red demon with his filed horns, cloven hooves, and long tail has always been struggling with a destiny that was given to him at birth; that of the right hand of doom, the very beast of the apocalypse. It is not a path he has chosen to follow, giving himself wholly to an effort to prevent that very destiny. Here, Hellboy is confronted by several potent reminders of his past and portents of his possible future, all of which he faces with a ready fist and a witty, no-nonsense comment or two.

As part of Hellboy's long history he was a member of a top-secret government agency, the Bureau for Paranormal Research and Defense. Because of disagreements with the way it was being run he has long since left the organization, but creator Mike Mignola and writer John Arcudi have developed an interesting cast of new characters and now use them in their own set of adventures in a series of comics, the latest of which are *B.P.R.D.: The Dead* and *The Black Flame* (Dark Horse). Artist Guy Davis visually delivers on the H.P. Lovecraftian premise of these tales. Set in contemporary time they deal with terrors from beyond space, plagues of froglike creatures, and dark worlds better left alone by the likes of you and me. These are enjoyable tales that are, much like Hellboy himself, equal parts superhero bravado and utter cosmic horror.

Well then, the days have been long and its been quite a while since you stepped out of those waves onto this island so you've had time to read and reread all the books you brought with you. Maybe if you got a friendly fellow shipwrecked soul on the island just down the way then he or she could send you a few more graphic novels in a really big glass bottle reserved just for this purpose.

And these are the ones I'd ask for this time.

In my last column I spoke briefly about a new comic book series, *Freaks of the Heartland* (Dark Horse) by writer Steve Niles and painter Greg Ruth. It has now been collected into a hefty trade paperback, and we are all the richer for that. The story concerns a group of teenagers who share a secluded valley in the heartland of America with a band of mutated creatures and the fear-crazed adults who want to hunt those freaks down and kill them. The art by Ruth is full of skillfully executed characters, blissfully evocative shadows and spectacularly brooding landscapes that lend an eerie cast to all the proceedings in Steve Niles's morality tale.

This year marked the debut of a new series *Mouse Guard—Belly of the Beast* (Archaia Studios Press) by a fresh face, David Petersen. This small, square-format, but full-color, comic looks to be the beginning of an enchanting adventure of swashbuckling mice, deep woods, rampaging snakes and a mysterious traitor that needs to be confronted. Delicately drawn and subtly colored, this delightful book has me wishing for more and soon at that.

All four of the previously published adventures of Frank Cammuso's *Max Hamm, Fairy Tale Detective* (Nite Owl Comix are collected here under one cover. As Frank says, "travel with Max through the back alleys and beanstalk jungles of Storybook Land, where the Magic Mirror sometimes gets it wrong and an ever-after isn't always happily lived." I never heard it better told. Dead-on satirical takes on all your favorite and not so favorite fairy tale characters get a reboot that only a true lover of these tales could deliver.

The Dark Horse Book of the Dead (Dark Horse) is the third elegant little book in a series of anthologies edited by Scott Allie. A variety of well-known writers and artists give us sometimes horrific and sometimes hilarious tales that are always a joy to read. Mike Mignola brings us another elegant yet somber Hellboy tale, and writer Evan Dorkin and watercolorist Jill Thompson spin another yarn filled with talking cats and dogs and ghostly goings-on, while Gary Gianni illustrates a ghoulish tale from the pen of Robert E. Howard. All of the stories in this collection are delightful, and I for one look forward to a fourth volume.

Writer and creator Bill Willingham's series *Fables* (DC/Vertigo) continues to be one of the most delightful comic book series being currently produced. His conceit that all the characters from fairy tale and fable have been made homeless by an un-named Adversary and are now settled in a magically created Fabletown nestled in between the mean streets of a very real New York City is refreshing and used to great dramatic effect. A new trade collection, *The Mean Seasons*, has just been released with art by Mark Buckingham, Tony Akins, Steve Leialoha, and Jimmy Palmiott. The battle for Fabletown is over but the current major Snow White is pregnant with multiple, soon-to-be newborns. The father Bigby Wolf has his own immediate con-cerns, and an election for a new major is imminent. Willingham's strong story over-rides any concerns about multiple artists disrupting the eccentric flow of the ever-expanding epic tale he wishes to tell. I would be remiss if I didn't mention that the covers by the always inventive James Jean are an open invitation to sample the delights of this series again and again.

Tree of Love (NBM) is Patrick Atangan's third book in his "Songs of our Ances-tors" series. This time out the tale is set in India where a young prince falls in love with a simple flower seller. Atangan gives us a single artfully drawn and colored im-age per page to echo his seemingly simple tale of the maiden's sudden transforma-tion and disappearance and the prince's long search for his lost love. The simple acts of a grand epic of eternal love.

In my last column I lauded French artist David B's brilliant autobiographical tale *Epileptic*, but now Pantheon Books has gathered all of the previously published pages and almost doubled that page length with new work. It is still a wrenchingly emotional tale of a young man who wants desperately to grow up to be an artist and of his older brother who begins to suffer epilepsy in his teen years. How this condi-tion affects the young artist and his art is the stuff of a profoundly emotional journey for both the artist himself and the reader. Of course every telling mark of David's B's stark black-and-white art is evidence of how his journey has progressed. I cannot rec-ommend this one highly enough.

Writer Robert Rodi has given us the tale of *Loki* (Marvel), which painter Esad Ribic has illustrated with a lush painterly style. Ribic has rendered his notion of Norse Mythology with an exquisite artist's eye, providing a sense of depth and dra-matic grandeur that has seldom been lavished on the superhero milieu. Loki, now Lord of Asgard, has ordered his hated half-brother Thor to be executed. In flashbacks we are shown Loki's version of their common history. Perhaps if we were to believe the trickster god we might agree to this execution. Let us hope that this team is given another chance to bring the mythic struggles of Marvel's Norse gods to life again.

Filmmaker Darren Aronofsky has transformed his screenplay for a soon to be re-leased movie into a script for *The Fountain* (DC/Vertigo) for painter Kent Williams. Williams's moody paintings complement Aronofsky's complex tale of two people whose love is so deep and profound that it follows them through three incarnations and into three different eras. The result is a handsomely produced oversize hard-cover, a suitable showcase for the mature themes and experimental storytelling tech-niques of these two visionaries.

Jenny Finn: Messiah (Boom Studios), written by Mike Mignola and drawn first by Troy Nixey and finished by Farel Dalrymple, is a fine horror tale set in the Lon-don of Victorian England. Down on the docks strange octopus-faced sailors are wreaking havoc among the beer taverns and painted ladies. Beyond the boardrooms of those in power, huge sea monsters are intimate with the leaders of secret societies whose memberships are peopled with relatives of royal blood. It's a fun romp for those who don't expect their stories to be too grounded in historic fact and enjoy all the trappings of the horror genre.

Horus (Ruff Toon) by Johane Matte is a delight to read and a marvel to look at for the sheer beauty of her cartooning skills. Matte's daytime job in an animation studio is evident in the striking character design and the precision that she brings to her comic timing throughout the tale. In ancient Egypt a young woman playing hooky from her chores discovers and subsequently adopts the young god Horus as a pet. Much hilarity and wanton destruction follow in sharp order. An all-ages delight.

Jeff Nicholson's second collection of his engaging series *Colonia: On Into the Great Lands* (AIT/Planet Lar) continues to engage my interest, despite his rather weak drawing skills, with its well-written narrative and sense of spirited playfulness. An alternate history of pirate captains, ancient civilizations, a fountain of youth, several mermaids, and a talking duck, this is a whimsical tale of adventures, discoveries and well rendered characters that engage the heart as well as the mind.

The second volume of Michael Allred's projected adaptation of the entire Book of Mormon into a graphic narrative was released this year, *The Golden Plates* (AAA Pop). This handsome, sixty-four-page full color trade paperback is beautifully drawn but text heavy, taking up the narrative as the ancestors of the Mormons struggle to survive in ancient Egypt. It then follows their perilous voyage across the ocean to the New World and quickly moves forward to the momentous discovery of their sacred texts in 1830 by the founder of modern-day Mormonism, Joseph Smith.

Anyone regularly reading my column here will know that I have a deep affection for the work of Ted Naifeh, especially his young heroine Courtney Crumrin. With *Courtney Crumrin Tales, A Portrait of the Warlock as a Young Man* (Oni Press) Naifeh focuses on the younger days of Courtney's Uncle Aloysius as he begins the long path that will take him to the pinnacle of his mystic powers as a warlock. Elegant yet stylized pen and brush work brings to life a world of magic, spells and deadly dangers. Naifeh's crisp dialog propels this crackling yarn at a lively pace to finally reach a satisfying conclusion. Naifeh has also begun a new series of all-ages adventures of *Polly and The Pirates* (Oni), which I hope will be collected when I next review books for this column.

For the purposes of this column I don't usually take notice of single issues of any comic, but this one is such a treat that I thought I might bend my rule this time. *Lucifer* (DC/Vertigo), the long-running offshoot of Neil Gaiman's popular Sandman series, is written by Mike Carey, and for this special one-off issue he is joined by legendary artist Michael Wm. Kaluta. Kaluta has brought all of his long experience in drawing graphic narratives to full bore on this hilariously macabre tale of wish fulfillment and personal fantasies as the new would-be ruler of Hell engages in a verbal battle of wits with two rather verbose demons. The effort that it might take to find this particular book will be worth it for its crazed humor and excellent drawing.

Later this year Pantheon will be releasing a collected edition of Kim Dietch's *The Stuff of Dreams*, and for that we should all be happy. This strangely endearing story features a compulsive collector, the author himself, whose search for an odd stuffed cat named Waldo, the animated star of many 1930's cartoons, has been a lifelong obsession. When finally found, Waldo is alive and living in retirement, a bitter has-been who berates Gene for spending his entire adult life looking for a worthless bit of memorabilia. And that is only the beginning of this lovely personal odyssey.

Mike Carey's adaptation of Neil Gaiman's novel *Neverwhere* (DC/Vertigo) is meticulously brought to life by artist Glenn Fabry in this new series, which should be collected by the time you read this. The action ranges from the airy rooftops of modern London to the endless gothic world that exists beneath the deepest underground tube station. In this dangerous world filled with vivid characters and sudden violence, our hero Richard must survive, as his life is completely turned upside down.

P. Craig Russell is usually known for work that is classical and coolly elegant, so it is interesting to see how he adapts that aesthetic to tell a tale of that most iconic of pulp heroes, Conan the Barbarian. His adaptation of Robert E. Howard's short story *Conan and the Jewels of Gwahlur* (Dark Horse) is all you would expect from an artist of Russell's caliber: well drawn and well told if a trifle cool emotionally for the sweat streaked-barbarian of pulp legend.

For those of my readers with a high absurdist quotient there is this series from the insanely active mind of Jeff Darrow, *Shaolin Cowboy* (Burlyman Entertainment). Equal part homage to Italian spaghetti westerns, cheap Kung Fu films, the ultra-violent trappings of Quenton Tarantino, and just plain-old-American-been-out-in-the-sun-too-long craziness, this dada-ist western is not for all tastes but it is amazingly well drawn, full of telling detail and exaggerated action. Depending on my mood it is either the most fascinating comic I've ever read or the most ephemeral, but I am captivated enough to be willing to follow it to its own eccentric ending, whatever it may be (Boom Studios).

Audrey Niffenegger's *The Three Incestuous Sisters* (Harry N. Abrams) is the winner of my "not quite in any category" book of the year. This odd book is from the writer of the best-selling prose novel, *The Time Traveler's Wife*, who had long been producing very limited edition art books (at most ten complete copies) combining her quirky art and even more eccentric stories well before she thought to try her hand at works that are all prose. Now, with the success of the novel, her earlier work is being made available to the general public for the first time. This new book is a large-sized, beautifully produced edition with full-page art, reproductions of her initially hand-printed aquatints, each one faced by a small block of text, a short enigmatic and sometimes very droll sentence. Not quite a graphic novel and not quite an illustrated book, it was still very enjoyable indeed.

If you have any trouble locating any of these books through your local bookstore or if you're still on that balmy, sun drenched island and find yourself with yet more time for reading, here are some 'desert island hotlines' that I'm certain could air drop your special needs directly to you.

First you might try calling the official Comic Shop Locator Service at 1-888-266-4226. Those fine folks will assist you in finding a full-service comic shop near you. Then, too, many of these trade collections are carried by the friendly and well-stocked Bud Plant Comic Art (www.budplant.com).

Good luck and happy reading.

Anime and Manga: 2005

Joan D. Vinge

Ahayo, mina-san to otaku-chan—

Loosely translated, that's "Hi, folks and fans—" and . . . *abayo* ('bye), see you later.

This Year's Best summary of 2005's best-in-show manga and anime (Japanese graphic novels and animated movies or TV series) has been cut off at the knees, due to "lawyers, tons (of truck) and money (or its lack)" blocking the road of Destiny.

Yes, that's a lousy pun on an obscure song . . . alas, in the real world it's been a lousy year. (And though this may be the "Language of Shakespeare," the first true novel was written in Japanese; and when it comes to wordplay, Japanese has English beat all hollow.)

"This one," as wandering swordsman Kenshin humbly puts it, hopes to make the passage safely 'round the new year's spiral . . . or find an alternate route to next year's summation. *Sumimasen!* (I am sorry!) is all that I can say to everyone to whom I owe *domos* (thanks), for now: I will make things right as soon as I stop reeling.
THE MI-NUTE WALTZ:

Manga

At least the best manga and anime are still filled with inspiring role models, good laughs and thought-provoking meditations on Fate—always something to keep one looking forward. Lots more of it came out in 2005, and keeps on coming, into 2006.

The true ending of Rurouni Kenshin is unfolding in the manga version of the series right now; the last volume of *Full Metal Panic* came out after only a year's wait; *yokai* (elves or demons), *oni* (usually demons), *ryuu* (dragons), *kyuuketsuki* (vampires), and *chibi* (the cute-yet-strangely-obnoxious "inner child" of characters) abound.

And—hey, readers!—some translations of the actual novels which gave birth to well-known manga and anime (*Slayers*—a comedy series; *Vampire Hunter D*—not one), as well as a few more translated art books, have arrived.

In comics/GNs, *Blade of the Immortal* nears its end—for strong-hearted lovers of beautiful, blood-spattered art—and *Devil's Due* just keeps putting out more terrific, in-color Amerimanga (its new *Udon* line focuses on video game-related stories).

Some venerable magazines and anthologies in the field passed from the scene, or mutated almost beyond recognition (*Animerica*—my first fave; still better "free" than simply "gone"—and its fiction-filled sister, *MangAmerica*). But check out the new *Neo* (British, with all kinds of Japanese entertainment info); or get *Shoujo Beat*, and learn to love strong heroines and droolingly handsome guys, plus all the latest crafts and makeup! (I kid you not, sigh. But it also contains good stories, and informative articles to help you enjoy what you read more.)

Anime

Check out a fistful of cool new movies, like Hayao Miyazaki's latest, *Howl's Moving Castle* and Katsusiro (Akira) Otomo's *Steamboy*. And don't miss classic TV anime series like S.A.C. (the *Ghost in the Shell* TV series, second season), *Samurai Champloo*, and *Inu Yasha*, or sleepers like *Shingu*, and *Kaze no Yojimbo* (based on the classic Kurosawa live-action film, *Yojimbo*). There's still a chance to grab special edition DVD sets of *Trigun*, *Irresponsible Captain Tylor* (uncensored!) and numerous other shows.

But don't overlook the bargain of them all—the new mini-packs of the indomitable *Armored Trooper VOTOMS* series, with extras it never had before . . . though still never enough long-overdue honor, over here. (Central Park Media—the producer—should again be honored for its venerable motto, as well: "World peace through shared popular culture." Who runs that place? Somebody get them to run for President!)

If you've ever, unnervingly, seen the stripes in an image of our country's flag turn to bloodstains—or if you haven't—watch this series. Sure, it's got a haunted hero, a kickass heroine, weirdly loveably sidekicks, action, explosions, romance, politics, and an homage to Marlon Brando in *Apocalypse Now* . . . but this has never been, for me, just another SF/war "adventure." It's an unusually long series by current standards; a fifty-two week series. The series is broken into four story arcs, each reflecting a different type of sf/fantasy genre, as it follows the progress of characters bound together by fate, and also irony. It's like reading a series of novels; the *story*, not the art (which is a couple of decades old—good but not "flashy") is the most significant reason to give it your attention. It takes a long, often-surprising, look into the eyes, the hearts, the minds of a large varied cast, trapped in the crucible of war—where the only gods are hidden puppeteers playing war-and-peace, with their lives as pawns. (Note: You must read subtitles, and look beyond the unfortunate 80s fad of jodhpurs, to see these things; but trust me, this is worth it).

I know I've said this before, and as somebody said before me: "All the best war stories are really anti-war stories." (Oh, and if you've ever asked, "Why me, God?"—this series will give you the answer. Of course that's why they call it fiction.)

Erratum: Before I can move on into the future, I must rectify a shameful error in my past . . . one that appeared in my previous essay. Based on a news article I saw, I reported that Japanese actor Takeshi Kaneshiro, star of numerous films, including *The House of Flying Daggers* and *The Returner,* had died. Kaneshiro-san is in fact alive and well, and undoubtedly at work on another film as you read this. I did not double-check my facts before reporting his death, because of deadline pressure. I apologize and promise that it won't happen again, deadlines be damned.

Sayonara—and *heiwa* (peace), out.

Music of the Fantastic: 2005

Charles de Lint

So much music and so little time to listen to, and talk about, it all. So let's get right to it.

First up, my two favorite releases of the year:

Every country has its creative treasures, sometimes lauded, sometimes unknown to the general populace, but no less talented for that. One of Canada's hidden treasures is a man named Ian Tamblyn.

Tamblyn has been documenting the face of Canada for over twenty years now, painting aural landscapes from coast to coast, illuminating in song the lives and the hearts of the people living in them. But the wild places are especially resonant to him, and his songs of the north, and Algonquin Park, are musical touchstones akin to the paintings of great national visual artists such as Tom Thompson.

Tamblyn is also a collector of sounds. Like an artist using found objects for a visual collage, he has gone out into the wild places to record everything from birdsong to the crack and rumble of icebergs, combining them in the studio with his own instrumentation. The result is a series of highly evocative albums, deeply rooted in their wild environments: *Over My Head*, *Magnetic North*, and *Antarctica*.

But industrial landscapes have distinctive sounds and stories as well. In 2005, Tamblyn released a new instrumental album, *Machine Works*, this time combining his own thoughtful and timeless melodies to the backdrop rhythm and sounds of threshers, windmills, subways, steel mills, trains and highways. Surprisingly, the album finds a tranquil heart at the center of all this man-made "noise," and has a strong, lyrical narrative flow to which the listener will return, time and again.

All of Tamblyn's current catalog can be ordered world-wide at www.tamblyn.com.

She's the darling of Britain (winner of the Brit Award for Best Female Singer, with her album a top seller over Christmas), and much of Europe at the moment, and rightly so, because Scottish singer-songwriter KT Tunstall's *Eye of the Telescope* (Relentless/EMI) was certainly the sleeper of the year.

It took an appearance on *Later . . . with Jools Holland* for her star to rise, but what a performance it was. She used a loop pedal to build up an array of beats and vocal accompaniments that, by the end of the piece, made you think there was a whole band on stage with the diminutive performer.

But she has a cracking good live band as well, and I'd highly recommend you take any opportunity to see her. Some performers are born for the stage, radiating a joyful energy that immediately transforms and entirely engages the audience, and she's certainly one of that select few.

The album seems a bit subdued compared to her live shows, but it's no less enjoyable, and the energy can still be found on tracks like "Black Horse and the Cherry Tree" or "Suddenly I See." The stories she tells are personal, yet universal, and I foresee a terrific future for her.

There's a great and apt description of her on the bio of her Web site: "a sparkling new songwriter with Chinese blood, a Scottish heart, great legwarmers and a cool name—'Well, it's got a bit more attitude than Kate, which just says farmer's daughter to me.'"

Celtic

I'm not one to throw around terms like "supergroup," but when you put together a lineup of Sharon Shannon, Michael McGoldrick, and Frankie Gavin, adding in the formidable talents of up-and-comer Jim Murray on guitar, no other word will do. The musicianship is top-notch, as you might expect, but happily there's no showboating on *Tunes* (The Daisy Label) as can happen when people this talented get together. Instead, the music is played at a tempo to showcase the beauty of the music, in acoustic arrangements that are, if you need a touchstone, somewhat reminiscent of Lúnasa.

God knows I love trad tunes, but there's something particularly invigorating about a whole album of original material that fits so snugly into the tradition that you wouldn't know the difference unless someone told you. *Thomas D'Arcy McGee* (www.mcgeemusic.ca) by Frank Cassidy and James Stephens began as the soundtrack they wrote for a play about the journalist-poet and Father of Canadian Confederation who was assassinated in Ottawa in 1868, but the album grew to encompass other material that they had written in a traditional vein. Masters of the whistle, flute and mandolin (Cassidy) and fiddle and mandolin (Stephens), they are joined by a cast of stellar musicians on this album that is a joy from start to finish.

Also on that album is Greg T. Brown, highly skilled on fiddle, button accordion, guitar, and too many other instruments to list here. Along with Uillean piper Jeremy Keddy, 2005 saw him release *Trees* (Prentice Boy Music), an engaging collection of songs and tunes based on the traditions of Ireland, England, and Newfoundland.

And just to show that they have no spare time at all, Brown and Stephens are also members of Jiig (along with guitarist Ian Clark and singer Ian Robb) who also released their self-titled disc (www.finestkind.ca) this past year. For his work on the CD, Robb won "Best Singer—Traditional" at the 2005 Canadian Folk Music Awards.

Celtic flute music presents a lovely dichotomy. One considers the instrument to be soft and airy, but good trad musicians can call up the same punch with it as others might using a fiddle or pipes. Garry Walsh's *Uncovered* (Ossian) shows off both sides of the coin, but is primarily a CD of great, driving dance music.

Mind you, if it's great Irish-fiddle music you crave, look no further than Liz Carroll's collaboration with guitarist John Doyle, *In Play* (Compass Records). It's the pure drop from start to finish.

Under their band name GiveWay, the four Johnson sisters prove with their sophomore effort *Inspired* (Greentrax) that the infectious and talented performances of their debut album was no fluke.

David Wilkie & Cowboy Celtic save you the trouble of programming a mash-up of jigs & reels and old cowboy tunes with their all-instrumental, 10th anniversary outing on *The Saloon Sessions* (Centerfire Music).

Featuring Scottish fiddler Catriona MacDonald, along with past and present members of bands such as The Peatbog Faeries, Wolfstone, Boys of the Lough, and Tabache, the seven-fiddlers band of Blazin' Fiddles gave us yet another marvelous collection of tunes with *Magnificent Seven* (www.blazin-fiddles.com).

Island cultures tend to be insular, making them places where, even in this day and age, change comes slower. Because of this, Canada's Newfoundland remains a source for some of the purer renditions of songs brought over by Irish and British settlers, as you can find on Pamela Morgan's lovely *Ancestral Songs* (Amber Music). Morgan, for those of you with short memories, was once the voice of Figgy Duff.

Speaking of voices, while April Verch doesn't have the strongest (it's more Nanci Griffith, than, say, Dolores Keane), and she does sing on a couple of tracks of her new CD *Take Me Back* (Rounder), it's her fiddle playing that continues to delight and charm, and that's certainly the case here.

Forget Eliza Carthy's formidable lineage (she's the daughter of Norma Waterson and Martin Carthy), as she's long since come into her own. On *Rough Music* (Topic) she moves away from the original material of her last album *Angilcana* to once again explore the English tradition. Accompanied by the Ratcatchers, this is as good a collection of British traditional music as you're going to get this year.

American roots

Part documentary, part mix-album, part museum exhibit, Tom Russell's *Hotwalker* (Hightone Records) is a fascinating and unapologetic look back at growing up during the Beat era in California, exploring the work of Charles Bukowski, Jack Kerouac, Edward Abbey, and others through their writings, Russell's music and the remembrances of Little Jack Horton, a midway carnie who Russell claims died a few months after recording his parts. (In truth, Horton is all Russell, with his voice speeded up a little in the production process.) This is a brilliant album, one you have to listen to from start to finish instead of picking out cuts—something of an alien concept in this day of the fifteen-second soundbite. But trust me. It's worth it.

Brock Zeman continues to release CDs at an alarming rate—his latest self-titled album with his band the Dirty Hands (www.brockzeman.com) is his third in the past year and a half. But the prolific output is justified when the material is as good as this is. For touchstones, think of a combination of Steve Earle's storytelling ability and Townes Van Zandt's wry humor.

But more doesn't always mean better. Ryan Adams had three releases this year, but only *29* (Lost Highway), the ex-Whiskeytowner's third disc, has the great songs and sound we've come to expect from him.

String band music never sounded so harmoniously good as it does on *She Waits for Night* (Rounder), the newest release from the all-woman band Uncle Earl. This year also saw their banjoist Abigail Washburn release a haunting bare-bones solo release, *Song of the Traveling Daughter* (Nettwerk).

It's hard to say where to file the Duhks newest self-titled release (Sugarhill, 2005) with its mix of Celtic and American tunes, Latin rhythms, old-timey songs, and gospel harmonies. Best just to push the rug aside and make a dance floor in your living room when you put them on.

If you're worried about the state of the world, but don't feel you have a voice to articulate your feelings, James McMurtry is there for you with *Childish Things* (Compadre). The standout track is "We Can't Make It Here", one of the best, hard-eyed looks at the state of the union since Iris Dement's "Wasteland of the Free" (from her 1996 CD *The Way I Should*).

Love Me Like the Roses (www.divinemaggees.com) by the fiddle and guitar duo the Divine Maggees is a punky mix of great songs, playing and harmonies. Think of an Indigo Girls for these contemporary times of ours.

If you were wondering whatever happened to Matthew Ryan, he hasn't disappeared from the recording scene. 2005 saw him in a band setting with Strays Don't Sleep, and their self-titled CD (One Little Indian) fills the gap nicely between his last and his next solo recordings.

More sweet harmonies can be found on the Peasall Sisters' *Home to You* (Dualtone Music Group). You might remember them from their turn in *O Brother Where Art Thou*, but this is much better.

As Broken Social Scene go on to conquer the world, sometime member Jason Collett has released *Idols of Exile* (Arts & Crafts). With his lyrics and phrasing on this disc, he reminds us what a terrific singer and storyteller he is in his own right.

And if Sara Evans's *Real Fine Place* (RCA) isn't enough sweet old country for you, might I recommend you try Shelly Fairchild's debut album *Ride* (Sony)?

There must be something in the Texas water that gives us the unconventional fiction of a Joe Lansdale or a Lewis Shiner, and the dark story songs of musicians such as Ray Wylie Hubbard. With a contemporary crunch, his *Delirium Tremolos* (Philo) mines the vein of storytelling that originated in pioneers of the music such as Hank Williams, Sr.

One of tragedies of North American history is the treatment of the Lakota Sioux, whose Pine Ridge Reservation remains one of the most impoverished zones in the U.S. Marty Stuart tells their story on *Badlands: Ballads of the Lakota* (Superlatone) with respect, heart, and great music.

Latin

With Calexico, and guitarist Charlie Sexton, as house band, the latest CD by Los Super Seven, *Heard it on the X* (Telarc), is a loving tribute to the mix of country, norteño, and R&B that filled the Texas airwaves in the early years of the "X" border radio stations. Featuring vocals by the likes of Ruben Ramos, Joe Ely, Lyle Lovett, and Delbert McClinton, this is great music by any standards.

And speaking of Calexico, they had another collaboration this year, backing up Sam Beam's singing on the album *In the Reins* (Overcoat Recordings), which they then followed up with an extensive Calexico/Iron & Wine tour. Enjoyable as these outings are, I'm eager for them to get back into the studio to do what they do best: their own music. Their new album, *Garden Ruin* (Quarter Stick), will be out as you read this, and you might also be interested in drummer John Convertino's *Ragland* (Sommerweg), a collection of piano and rhythm soundscapes based on a mood that seems to have grown out of his desert roots.

Ry Cooder gives us a tribute as well with *Chávez Ravine* (Nonesuch/Perro Verde), invoking a meditation on the spirit of a lost East L.A. Latino neighborhood that was razed to build Dodger Stadium. With a helping hand from the likes of Flaco Jimenez and Lalo Guerrero, the result is a satisfying blend of conjunto and R&B, corrido and folk music.

A hit on London dance floors early in the year, Tammy Garcia's *Mexico City* EP (www.karmadownload.com) is a heady mix of flamenco vocals, Spanish guitars and bass heavy dancehall beats that will have you up and moving no matter where you happen to be when you hear it.

From the notes of a Portuguese guitar that open the album, to Mariza's astonishing vocal control, *Transparente* (EMI) delights from start to finish. There's a reason she's considered the best new voice in Fado music today, and you only need to listen to this album to understand why.

Shakira gave us a pair of albums this year, the Spanish language *Fijación Oral Vol. 1* and the English *Oral Fixation Vol. 2* (both on Sony). While I still prefer her Spanish singing, I have to admit I'm warming to the English. Whichever you choose, the music and performance remains a treat.

Continuing with the multi-cultural gumbo of their previous albums, Ozomatli's *Live at the Fillmore* (Concord) proves that they've got the chops to make it work just as well when they're away from a studio setting.

The classic trio backup on *Segundo* (WEA Latina), Maria Rita's sophomore release, seems a throwback to the classic recordings of her mother Elis Regina, but while Rita looks to the past, this Brazilian offers us music that's upbeat, jazzy, and cool, and very suited for a contemporary audience.

World

With Bill Bourne in the producer's chair, as well as providing some back up instrumentation and vocals, Eivør Pålsdottir's *Eivør* (12 Tónar) is a lovely, guitar-oriented album of Pålsdottir's original songs, highly accessible even though many of the songs aren't in English. Delicate with a bite.

Stepping away from using music as a tool for palliative care, Ann Mortifee gives us *Into the Heart of the Sangoma* (Bongo Beat), her first album in ten years. It's a musical journey back to her South African homeland to explore the wisdom and visions of the Sangoma, the shaman of the Zulu nation, featuring a mix of theatric and indigenous approaches.

Ry Cooder shows up to play a little guitar and Kawai piano on *In the Heart of the Moon* (Nonesuch), but the show really belongs to Ali Farka Touré and Toumani Diabaté on guitar and the harp-like kora, respectively. This is a gorgeous, reflective album, recorded live in Mali.

It takes a little while to grow on you, but Susheela Raman's *Music for Crocodiles* (EMI) is worth the effort. The songs have a singer-songwriter structure, and many of them are in English this time out, but the musical palette, which includes an Indian string trio, places it firmly in the World music section.

Bedouin Soundclash's *Sounding a Mosaic* (SideOneDummy Records) isn't quite the punk-sounding rave-up you might think from the band's name, but rather an infectious collection of reggae and ska that will have you slow-grooving on the dancefloor.

Mesk Elil (Wrasse) by Souad Massi is a dreamy confection of French chanson, flamenco and various African traditions, all held together by her delicate guitar playing and sensuous voice.

Swedish and Celtic traditions meet in the music of Swåp and their fourth album *Du Da* (Northside) and remind us how closely related the music of those traditions are.

And finally, there's Gogol Bordello with their most recent CD *Gypsy Punks: Underdog World Strike* (SideOneDummy), a mad, bouncing collage of hip hop, punk, and Gypsy music to dance you off into the night.

I always hate ending these columns because I know that they're so incomplete. Inevitably, I'll have forgotten something I really wanted to mention. Sometimes, I just run out of room, or I simply wasn't able to get my hands on a listening copy.

The only redress for that is for you to have a look at some of these Web sites that carry timely reviews and news, and do some exploring on your own:

www.frootsmag.com
www.endicott-studio.com
www.pastemusic.com
www.globalrhythm.net
www.greenmanreview.com
www.rambles.net

Or if you prefer the written page, check out your local newsstand for copies of *Roots* (two issues per year carry fabulous CD samplers), *Global Rhythm* (each issue includes a sampler CD), *Songlines* (also has a CD sampler), *Paste* (with CD sampler; subscribers also get a DVD sampler), *Sing Out!*, *Riddim* (with CD sampler), *No Depression*, and *Dirty Linen*.

While I know there are lots of other great albums out there, I don't have the budget to try everything. But my ears are always open to new sounds. So, if you'd like to bring something to my attention for next year's essay, you can send it to me c/o P.O. Box 9480, Ottawa, ON, Canada K1G 3V2.

Special thanks to Cat Eldridge of Greenman Review, and Ian & James Boyd of Compact Music, for helping to provide music in preparation of this essay.

Obituaries: 2005

James Frenkel

Each year we feel it only appropriate to chronicle the passing of those creative, talented people who contributed in some way to the fantastic arts. Some of the names that follow will be familiar; others may completely unknown to you. Each contributed in his or her own unique way to the shared culture we enjoy.

Andre Norton, 93, wrote more than 130 novels and nearly 100 short stories, and edited numerous anthologies. She was the first woman to win the Life Achievement World Fantasy award and the Nebula Grand Master Award, from the Science Fiction Writers of America. In addition to creating the Witch World, a setting that has been the background for many of her fantastic adventures, she wrote numerous other fantasy novels and shorter works. Miss Norton also was an enormous influence on several generations of young writers, male and female, being especially encouraging to many young writers, engaging in correspondence with them, reading their early works, even collaborating with a number of them. Dozens of successful writers admit to owing a debt to her kindness and generosity in helping them get started.

Considered one of the most important writers of fantasy and science fiction adventure of the twentieth century, she was enormously well read in history and mythology, and she researched her works meticulously. Enormously productive, she never forgot her origins. She had been a librarian, and always loved books as a reader. She also worked, for some years, as a first reader for Gnome Press, an early small press specializing in sf and fantasy.

Will Eisner, 87, was a giant in the world of comics and graphic novels. He created "The Spirit" in 1940, and never really stopped working until he died. He was a great innovator, a champion of the form, and considered by many to be perhaps the single most influential creator in the field during the twentieth century. He received the 1995 Milton Caniff Lifetime Achievement Award and the 1998 Reuben Award as cartoonist of the year from the National Cartoonists Society.

Kelly Freas, 82, was a versatile illustrator who produced sleek, stirring images for science fiction and fantasy books and magazines, and helped shape the image of *Mad Magazine* mascot Alfred E. Neuman. Beginning in the 1950s, he spent seven years as the main cover artist of *Mad*, creating stylishly detailed portraits and helping to make famous Alfred E. Neuman, the freckled, front-tooth-deprived purveyor of the phrase, "What, Me Worry?"

"Kelly Freas created the future in his paintings, sleekly delineating a style that has influenced two generations of designers as the technology became available to make his fantasies real," said Paul Levitz, the current publisher of *Mad*. "And with the impish grin he gave Alfred, he winked and warned us not to take it all too seriously."

With his first wife, Polly, who died a number of years ago, Freas ran the Starblaze imprint of science fiction and fantasy books.

Among his awards, Freas received eleven Hugo awards for his science fiction and fantasy art, five of them awarded in consecutive years.

Jack L. Chalker, 61, was best known for his Well of Souls and Dancing Gods series of novels and frequent columns for *Fantasy Review* and *Pulphouse* magazines. He also founded a small publishing company, The Mirage Press, and was the coauthor of the widely read reference book *The Science-Fantasy Publishers: A Critical and Bibliographic History*.

Humphrey Carpenter, 58, was an English writer, editor, radio broadcaster, and musician who wrote intimate biographies of W. H. Auden, Ezra Pound, J. R. R. Tolkien, Dennis Potter and Spike Milligan, among others. He conducted radio interviews, produced children's theater, wrote trenchant book reviews, and played a variety of instruments. He was best know for his biographies, particularly for his *Tolkien: A Biography*.

Debra Hill, 54, was a pioneering woman in the film industry, not only for her writing, but also for producing films such as *The Dead Zone* (1983) and *Adventures in Babysitting*. She collaborated with John Carpenter on *Halloween*, as well as *The Fog* (1980) and *Escape from New York* (1981). **Robert Wise**, 91, was a director best known for his Oscar winning films *West Side Story* and *The Sound of Music*. Wise also directed the classic *The Day the Earth Stood Still* and the 1963 version of *The Haunting*, as well as many other fine films. In 1941, he worked as a film editor on *Citizen Kane*, and was the last surviving crew member of that film.

Jay Marshall, 85, gained notoriety for his magic performances, appearing 14 times on *The Ed Sullivan Show*. He also wrote a three-volume work for aspiring magicians. **Richard Lupino**, 75, was a TV and stage actor best known for his work on Broadway, and for his appearances on such TV shows as "Alfred Hitchcock Presents." **Sandra Dee**, 62, was an actress best known as Gidget in the film of the same name (1959). Ms. Dee starred in a number of films, some with then-husband Bobby Darin, and some fantastic films, including *The Dunwich Horror* and *Fantasy Island*. **Bob Schiffer**, 88, "Hollywood's Ace of Faces," worked on innumerable films, including *The Wizard of Oz* (1939), *What Ever Happened to Baby Jane?* (1962), *Something Wicked This Way Comes* (1983), and *Splash* (1984). **Nipsey Russell**, 87, was a well-known black stand-up comedian who also acted on tv and in films, most notably in the role of the Tin Man in the 1978 film *The Wiz*. **Richard E. Cunha**, 83, directed 1950's cult horror movies *She Demons*, *Missile to the Moon* and *Frankenstein's Daughter*, among many others. **Richard Eastham**, 89, starred on Broadway with Mary Martin in *South Pacific*. He had a number of roles in movies and television shows including Disney's *That Darn Cat!* and *Wonder Woman*. **Eddie Albert**, 99, stage, film and television actor, received Oscar Nominations for *Roman Holiday* (1953) and *The Heartbreak Kid* (1972). He was probably best known as a lawyer turned farmer, on the tv series *Green Acres*.

Paul Winchell, 82, was a ventriloquist and had his own television show, featuring his creation, the wise-guy "dummy" Jerry Mahoney. He is most famous for voicing the character of Winnie-the-Pooh's friend, Tigger. **John Fiedler**, 80, the film voice of Piglet, in what we believe was merely a coincidence, died in the same week as Winchell. Fiedler played character roles on Broadway and in Hollywood on television and in live action films, as well as in other animated roles. **Anne Bancroft**, 73, won both a Tony and an Oscar for her performances in *The Miracle Worker*. She also won an Emmy. She left an indelible impression as the middle-aged yet seductive Mrs. Robinson in *The Graduate*, starring with Dustin Hoffman. She was married to Mel Brooks and had roles in several of his films. **Moustapha Akkad**, 75, a producer and director, was best known for producing all eight *Halloween* films. **Pat Morita**, 73, played Mr. Miyagi, the mentor to "Daniel-san" in *The Karate Kid*. He began his career as a stand-up comedian and got his first break as Arnold, the restaurant owner on the sitcom *Happy Days*. **Derek Lamb**, 69, was an Academy Award-winning writer, director and producer of animated films. His animated shorts *Special Delivery* (1978) and *Every Child* (1979), both won Oscars for Best Animated Short Film. **Onna White**, 83, received the honorary Oscar at the 1969 Academy Awards for choreographing the year's best picture Oscar winner, *Oliver!* She danced in the Broadway musical *Finian's Rainbow* and choreographed the film version of *The Music Man*. **Howard Morris**, 85, was a character actor during the Golden Age of television. He's best known for his work with Sid Caesar on *Your Show of Shows* from 1950 to 1954, for his memorable role as the manic hillbilly poet Ernest T. Bass on *The Andy Griffith Show*, and for comic turns on the Gary Moore and Carol Burnett shows. **Thrul Ravenscroft**, 91, provided the voice for Kellogg's Tony the Tiger and his signature line "They're Grrrrrreeeeeat!" He also lent his voice on thrill rides at Disneyland, including the Pirates of the Caribbean, Splash Mountain, the Enchanted Tiki Room, and the Haunted Mansion. **Ismail Merchant**, 68, working in collaboration with James Ivory, produced award-winning films including *A Room With a View*, *Howard's End*, *Remains of the Day*, and *Heat and Dust*. **Richard Lewine**, 94, was a television producer and a composer. Among his production credits was the Rodgers and Hammerstein musical created expressly for television, *Cinderella*. **Stephen Elliot**, 86, had a long career as an actor of stage, screen, and television, including roles in Shelley Duvall's *Fairy Tale Theater*. **Mason Adams**, 86, was best known as the warm-hearted managing editor of The Los Angeles Tribune in the television series *Lou Grant*, and received three Emmy nominations for his role. He also starred in many radio shows in the 1940s and 50s, including many roles in tales of the supernatural. **Maria Schell**, 79, who was sometimes called "the blond angel" was named best actress at the Cannes film festival in 1954 and became internationally known for her role as Greushenka in *The Brothers Karamazov*, among many roles. **Marc Lawrence**, 95, had a pockmarked face and brooding mannerisms that made him a natural for roles as tough guys. For more than sixty years, he played the bad guy in dozens of films and television shows. During the Red-scare blacklist days he worked in Europe as an actor and director. **Herbert L. Strock**, 87, directed B-movies like *I Was a Teenage Frankenstein*, *How to Make a Monster*, and *The Crawling Hand*. He also worked on a number of TV series. His creature features included *Blood of Dracula* and *Gog*, shot in 3-D. **Fred S. Fox**, 90, was a comedy writer. He also wrote the 1980 film *Oh God! Book II*, starring George Burns. **Frank Gorshin**, 72, was best known for his role as the Riddler on television's original *Batman*. A masterful impressionist (he did a killer James Cagney), Gorshin also appeared in genre films such as *Twelve Monkeys* and *The Meteor Man*, and guested on television series *Lois & Clark*, *Buck Rogers in the 25th Century*, and

Wonder Woman. **Henry Corden**, 85, was the voice of Fred Flintstone for more than two decades. His first acting role came in the 1947 film *The Secret Life of Walter Mitty*. He also voiced General Urko in *Return to the Planet of the Apes*. **Vincent Schiavelli**, 57, was a character actor who appeared in many films, including *One Flew Over the Cuckoo's Nest*, *Ghost*, and *Batman Returns*, among others. **George P. Cosmatos**, 64, was a director best known for his work on *Rambo: First Blood Part II*, but also directed the horror films *Leviathan* and *Cobra*, among others. **John Mills**, 97, was a British actor who appeared in more than 100 films. He played the title role in *Quatermass* (both the 1978 film and the 1979 television series), and appeared in *Around the World in 80 Days* and in *Frankenstein* (the 1993 television movie). He won the Academy Award for Best Supporting Actor in 1971 for *Ryan's Daughter*, and was knighted in 1976. **Geraldine Fitzgerald**, 91, was an actress of stage and screen who first appeared on screen in 1934. Her one genre film appearance was in *Poltergeist II: The Other Side*. **Don Adams**, 82, became famous when he played Maxwell Smart in the 1960's sitcom *Get Smart*, combining clipped, decisive diction with appalling but hilarious ineptitude. *Get smart* twice won the Emmy for best comedy series, and Mr. Adams won three Emmys for best actor. He was also the voice of Inspector Gadget and Brain.

    Jerry Juhl, 67, was the head writer for Muppets programs including *The Muppet Show* on television and, in some capacity, all the Muppet films, from the first *Muppet Movie* in 1979 to *Muppets from Space* in 1999. He won two Emmy awards for his work on *Sesame Street*. He also won two Writers Guild Awards as head writer of *The Muppet Show* and an Emmy in 1981 for the dance marathon episode featuring Carol Burnett. He worked on *The Cube* in 1969. **Louis Nye**, 92, was best known for playing an unctuous advertising executive in a Steve Allen sendup of Madison Avenue. He was so closely identified with his signature phrase "Heigh-ho, Steverino" that he recorded an album called "Heigh-ho, Madison Avenue," which skewered advertising agencies, market research, and the post–World-War II society made famous by Sloan Wilson's novel *The Man in the Gray Flannel Suit*. He also appeared in a revival of *Charlie's Aunt* that ran in July 1970, and played parts large and small in many television shows. **Margaretta Scott**, 93, appeared in over 50 films, from *Dirty Work* to the television film *The Moth*. She played two parts, Roxana and Rowena, in *Things to Come*, which was scripted by H. G. Wells. **Constance Moore**, 84, was an actress who appeared in comedies, dramas, musicals, westerns, and even the 1939 series *Buck Rogers*. **Ed Kelleher**, 61, was a screenwriter, playwright, and film critic. He wrote *Invasion of the Blood Farmers*, *Shriek of the Mutilated*, *Prime Evil*, *Lurkers*, and *Voodoo Dolls*. He also appeared in *Blood Farmers*, credited as Edouard Dauphin. **Simone Simon**, 93, was a French actress best known for her role in the film *Cat People*. Her career also included its mostly unrelated sequel *The Curse of the Cat People*, and *Mademoiselle Fifi*, the first American film to be shown in France after the invasion at Normandy, among her many other roles. **Teisha "Sadamasa" Arikawa**, 80, created special effects for many films, including the original *Godzilla*. **Thomas Ross "Tommy" Bond**, 79, was known as Jimmy Olsen in two early Superman films, *The Adventures of Superman* and *Atom Man vs. Superman*, and was in the "Our Gang" comedies. **Robert Newmyer**, 49, was an independent-film producer, whose credits include *sex, lies and videotape* and the *Santa Clause* movies. **Virginia Mayo**, 84, was best known for her roles as Danny Kaye's love interest in his MGM films. A star of a number of films including, importantly, *The Secret Life of Walter Mitty*, her blond beauty made her unmistakable. **Philip DeGuere**, 60, was a television writer and producer. His many credits include executive producer on both *Max Headroom* and the revival of *The Twilight Zone*. **John R. Vernon**, 72, was an actor best known for his role as Dean Worner in *Animal House*. His work included voice work as Prince Namor in *The Sub-Mariner* and other Marvel based cartoons. **Ossie Davis**, 87, was an actor of stage, screen and television. He wrote the play *Purlie Victorious*. He was a prominent black actor, active in the Civil Rights movement, and a role model for several generations of younger actors. Married to actress Ruby Dee, he provided the voice in the "A mind is a terrible thing to waste" public service announcement. **Dan O'Herlihy**, 85, was a well-traveled film actor who appeared in *RoboCop* and *RoboCop 2* as the Old Man and played Grig in *The Last Starfighter*. He had the title role in The *Cabinet of Caligari* and played General Black in *Fail-Safe*. **John Raitt**, 88, appeared in only a handful of films, but he created the role of Billy Bigelow in the Broadway production of *Carousel*. **Norman Bird**, 84, was a highly regarded and versatile British character actor who appeared in dozens of films and television shows, including *The Omen III: The Final Conflict*, and *Shadowlands*, a film about the life of C.S. Lewis. In 1978, he provided the voice for Bilbo Baggins in the animated *Lord of the Rings*. **Ed Adlum**, 61, was a screenwriter who wrote *Invasion of the Blood Farmers*, *Prime Evil*, and *Voodoo Dolls*. **Leon Askin**, 97, was an actor perhaps most recognizable as General Burkhalter from *Hogan's Heroes*. He also appeared in *Young Frankenstein*, *Airplane II*, and *Dr. Mabuse*, among many films and television shows. **Lucy Richardson**, 47, worked in the art department for *Star Wars: Episode 1: The Phantom Menace*, *The Princess Bride*, and other films. But her place in pop culture was settled much earlier when she, as a schoolmate of Julian Lennon, provided the inspiration for the Beatles song "Lucy in the Sky with Diamonds." **Michael Billington**, 63, was best known for his role as Col. Paul Foster on the show *UFO*. Often mentioned as a possible James Bond, he appeared in the movie *The Spy Who Loved Me* as Sergei Barsov. **Kevin Hagen**, 77, was an actor best known as Doc Baker on *Little House on the Prairie*. He played multiple roles on *The Time* Tunnel and *Voyage to the Bottom of the Sea*. **Gretchen Franklin**, 94, was an actress who appeared in *Help!*, the 1973 version of *The Three Musketeers*, and *Quatermass* among other productions. **Ed Bishop**, 72, was best known for his role as Ed Straker on the show *UFO*, but also had a bit role in *2001: A Space Odyssey* and appeared in *Battle Beneath the Earth* and *The Mouse on the Moon*. He provided voices for the animated version of *Star Trek*. **Dana Elcar**, 77, best known for his roles on *MacGyver* and *Baa Baa Black Sheep*, he played in many films and television shows. **Robert Clarke**, 85, was a film actor who appeared in many films, including *Midnight Movie Massacre*, *Frankenstein Island*, and *Beyond the Time Barrier*. In 1950, he portrayed D'Artagnan in *The Three Musketeers*, and the following year he had the title role in *Tales of Robin Hood*.

    Lane Smith, 69, was an actor best known for his role as Perry White on the television show *Lois and Clark*. Smith also played the role of reporter Emmett Seaborn in the miniseries *From the Earth to the Moon*. He appeared in both V and *Alien Nation*. Smith made his film debut in 1970 in *Maidstone*. He won an Emmy Award for his portrayal of President Richard Nixon in *Nixon*. **Jonathan Adams**, 74, was a British actor who appeared in *The Rocky Horror Picture Show* as Dr. Everett Von Scott. In 1984, he appeared in a television version of H.G. Wells's *The Invisible Man*, and had a role in the 1987 television series *Star Cops*, among many other credits.

    James Doohan, 85, an actor best known for playing Montgomery Scott on *Star Trek*, did voice work for a variety of cartoons as well. He also appeared on many television shows. **George Wallace**, 88, was an actor. He portrayed Commander Cody in *Radar Men from the Moon*. Four years later, he was a bosun in *Forbidden Planet*. Mostly appearing in Westerns, he did appear in the original television film *The Six Million Dollar Man*, and in *The Bicentennial Man*. **David Jackson**, 71, was a British actor who appeared in *Blood from the Mummy's Tomb* in 1971 and spent the 1978–1979 season on *Blake's 7* playing Olag Gan. He was active in both film and television. **Mel Welles**, 80, appeared in *Abbot and Costello Meet the Mummy* and as a gravedigger in *The Undead*. In 1960, he appeared in the original version of *The Little Shop of Horrors*. He also worked as a writer and director. **Brock Peters**, 78, is best known for his role as Tom Robinson in *To Kill A Mockingbird*, but appeared in numerous genre films and shows, including *Soylent Green*. On *Star Trek: Deep Space Nine*, Peters had a recurring role as Joseph Sisko, Benjamin Sisko's father. He acted in many other films and television shows. **Perry Lafferty**, 86, was a director, and producer, and an actor. He worked almost exclusively in television, in a variety of projects, including three episodes of *The Twilight Zone*.

Bob Denver, 70, was best known for his roles as Maynard G. Krebs on *The Many Loves of Dobie Gillis* and Gilligan on *Gilligan's Island*, he appeared in the genre children's show *Far Out Space Nuts* in the mid-1970s. He also appeared in the made-for-TV movie *The Invisible Woman*, and in other films and tv shows. **William Hootkins**, 57, appeared in many films and television productions including *Raiders of the Lost Ark*, *Batman*, and a wide variety of others. He also provided voice work for the video game "EverQuest II." **Lloyd Bochner**, 81, was a versatile Canadian actor of stage, screen, and television. **Jack Colvin**, 71, was best known for his work as reporter Jack McGee in the 1970s television series *The Incredible Hulk*. Colvin also appeared on *The Six Million Dollar Man* and *The Bionic Woman*, and in various other tv shows and films. **Gregg Hoffman**, 41, was the producer of the *Saw* films as well as *George of the Jungle* 2. **Gilbert Mack**, 92, did voice work. Before that, he had appeared on television and was a vaudevillian and a performer in the Yiddish theater. **Richard Pryor, 65**, was a comedian and actor best known for his stand-up comedy. He was a role model for two generations of black comics. His film work was in comedy films, some of which costarred Gene Wilder. He also appeared in the title role in *The Wiz*. He cowrote Mel Brooks's *Blazing Saddles*. **Michael Vale**, 83, an actor, appeared in *Marathon Man* and other films and tv shows. He was best known for his long-running role as Fred the Baker in a series of commercials for Dunkin' Donuts in which he woke up early announcing "Time to make the donuts." **Michael Pillar**, 57, was best known for his work on *Star Trek*, He was the creator of the short-lived *Legend* as well as a writer for The *Dead Zone*. **Jean Carson**, 80, was an actress in film and television. Perhaps best known for her work as Daphne on *The Andy Griffith Show*, she also was on *The Twilight Zone* and *The Inner Sanctum*, and in films.

Joe Grant, 96, was an animator for Disney. He designed the character of the queen/witch for *Snow White and the Seven Dwarfs* and, in a decades-spanning career, cowrote *Dumbo*, created the concept for *Lady and the Tramp*, and worked on character design for many other animated features, including *Aladdin*, *The Lion King*, and *Mulan*. He was also cowrote the Donald Duck short *Der Fuehrer's Face*. **Joe Ranft**, 45, was a writer, director and voice artist. He worked for Disney and Pixar, beginning with *The Brave Little Toaster*. From the start of his career, he was versatile, providing voices for Heimlich in *A Bug's Life* and Wheezy in *Toy Story 2*. He also did work on animated films for other companies, including *The Nightmare Before Christmas* among others. **Fred Joerger**, 91, was a model maker for Disney.

His best known work is probably Sleeping Beauty's Castle in the middle of Disneyland which was based on his model. He also created models for a number of Disney films.

Magdalena Moujan Otano, 79, wrote a modern SF classic, *Gu Ta Gutarrak [We and Our Own]* (1968), which explores her Basque heritage in a comic tale of time travel. It was censored by Franco's government, who thought it encouraged Basque nationalism. It has been reprinted several times since. **Margaret Hodges**, 94, was an author whose works included illustrated books of familiar stories such as *Merlin and the Making of the King*, *The Wee Christmas*, and *Moses*. Other works include *The Wave*, adapted from Lafcadio Hearn's *Gleanings in Buddha-Fields* and *Saint George and the Dragon: A Golden Legend*, adapted from Spenser's *Faerie Queene*. **John Fowles**, 79, a literary author whose work often involved obsession, is best known for his novels *The Collector*, *The Magus*, and *The French Lieutenant's Woman*, all three of which were adapted for film.

Byron Preiss, 52, was an influential book packager of science fiction and fantasy, as Byron Preiss Visual Publications. Later, he founded the publisher ibooks. One of the first publishers to release books on CD-ROM and as e-books, he also produced various shared world anthologies in the 1980s. His audiobook "The Words of Gandhi," won a Grammy Award in 1985. **Leona Nevler**, 79, was a book editor. She edited *Peyton Place*, which sold more than ten million copies and spawned several movies and a television series. She also handled the work of many prominent writers, among them John Updike, Margaret Atwood, Jane Smiley, P. D. James, Dick Francis, James A. Michener, Jeffrey Archer, Amy Tan, and Fannie Flagg. **Cyril Nelson**, 78, was an editor at E. P. Dutton. He published many seminal books about folk art. **Robert Sheckley**, 77, was a brilliantly original voice in science fiction and fantasy. He wrote dozens of sharply satiric and darkly comic stories in the 1950s and '60s, and was nominated for all the major science fiction and fantasy awards. His story collection, *Untouched by Human Hands*, was filled with gems. His best-known novel was probably *Mindswap*. His story, "The Seventh Victim" was made into the successful film, *The Tenth Victim*. **Michael G. Coney**, 73, was the author of such fantasy novels as *Fang, the Gnome,* and *King of the Scepter'd Isle*. A five-time Aurora Award nominee, he received an Aurora Lifetime Achievement Award in 1987. He was a Nebula finalist for his novelette "Tea and Hamsters" (1995). He also wrote many short stories of fantasy and science fiction. **Josef Nesyadba**, 78, was a prominent Czech author known for his satirical and absurdist writings. His work spanned mystery, fantasy, and science fiction. He was also awarded a Karel Capek award in 1985 and a Ludvick Soucek (the Czech Hugo) Lifetime Achievement Award in 1986. **J.N. Williamson**, 73, was a prolific writer during the horror boom of the '80s, starting with the novel *The Ritual*, and continuing for more than fifteen years. His works included the World Fantasy Award–nominated novella "The Night Seasons," and the "Masques" anthology series. He was accorded a Lifetime Achievement award by the Horror Writers Association. **Evan Hunter**, 78, (born Salvatore A. Lombino) wrote as Evan Hunter, Ed McBain, Kurt Cannon, and Ezra Hannon. Best known for his 87th Precinct procedurals, *The Blackboard Jungle* (1954), and the screenplay for Hitchcock's *The Birds* (1963), he was successful as a writer of mysteries, thrillers, and screenplays. **Chris Bunch**, 61, wrote a number of novels with Allan Cole, including the Sten series. They also collaborated on the Anteros series. Bunch also wrote novels of his own, including the Shadow Warrior books: *The Wind After Time, Hunt the Heavens,* and *The Darkness of God*.

Dan Tsalka, 69, was an early advocate of sf and fantasy in Israel, and wrote articles about the genre in the 1960s. His own genre novels include the YA fantasy *The War Between the Children of the Earth and the Children of the Pit*. **Charles L. Harness**, 89, was a writer whose fiction tended to be science fiction, though some of it was fantasy. His best-known novels were *The Rose* and *The Paradox Men*. **Kenneth Bulmer**, 84, was a prolific writer of science fiction adventure, under his own name and others, most notably Alan Burt Akers. **Howard DeVore**, 80, was a collector and dealer, and a famously generous and friendly person. He compiled *A History of the Hugo, Nebula, and International Fantasy Awards* with Donald Franson. A later revision by DeVore alone was a 1999 Hugo nominee in the Best Related Book category. **Daniel Riche**, 56, was a French magazine and book editor, compiling several "Best of" collections. During the '90s Riche was a screenwriter and story editor for film and television. **Helen Cresswell**, 71, was a children's book author best known for her Lizzie Dripping novels, among others. She received the BAFTA Children's Writer Award and the Phoenix Award for *The Night Watchmen*, and four of her books were runners-up for the Carnegie Medal. **Bruce B. Cassiday**, 84, was a classic pulp writer. He edited *Argosy* from 1954 to 1973 and wrote many novels of various genres: westerns, police thrillers, gothic horror, film and television tie-ins, etc. He wrote Flash Gordon novelizations. With Dieter Wuckel, he co-wrote *The Illustrated History of Science Fiction*. **Geoffrey Palmer**, 92, was a partner in the Compton Bookshop in Islington, England, and in Hermitage Books, which specialized in the works of E.F. Benson. **Raelyn Moore**, 76, was the wife of science fiction author Ward Moore. She herself wrote the novel *What Happened to Emily Goode After the Great Exhibition*, and a nonfiction book about *The Wizard of Oz* in 1974. **Samuel Herbert Post**, 81, was a book editor who, in a diverse career, published various fantasy authors.

Stan Berenstain, 82, was cocreator, with his wife, Jan, of the children's book series The Berenstain Bears, which has sold nearly 300 million books. **Keith Parkinson**, 47, was an artist who had great success in fantasy illustration for books, magazines, calendars and other media, starting with TSR and coming to work for many publishers, game companies, and other purveyors of fantasy entertainment. Some of his artwork has been collected in *Knightsbridge: The Art of Keith Parkinson*, *Spellbound: The Keith Parkinson Sketch Book*, and *Kingsgate: The Art of Keith Parkinson*. Among other awards, he won back-to-back Chesley Awards for best hardcover jacket illustration in 1988 and 1989. **David Sutherland**, 56, was a fantasy artist and art director for TSR. His illustrations include the famed scene of a dragon, a wizard and a bow-flexing knight on the first "D&D" boxed set that brought the game into the mainstream. **Karen Wynn Fonstad**, 59, was a freelance cartographer. She was the author and illustrator of *The Atlas of Middle-Earth*, *The Atlas of Pern*, *The Atlas of the Land*, *The Atlas of the Dragonlance World*, and *The Forgotten Realms Atlas*. **Redmond Simonson**, 62, an artist and graphic designer, he cofounded Simulations Publications, Inc. with Jim Dunnigan to publish their tabletop wargames. He was one of the most influential war-games designers in the business.

Jim Aparo, 72, was considered one of the definitive Batman artists from the mid-1970s. He also did work on Aquaman and the Phantom Stranger. He began working at Charlton in the 1960s, but was brought to DC by Dick Giordano and worked for them for several decades. **Rowland Wilson**, 74, was a cartoonist whose work appeared regularly in *Playboy*, *The Saturday Evening Post*, *Esquire*, and *The New Yorker*. He won a daytime Emmy for his animation on *Schoolhouse Rock!* He also did animation for Disney, working on *The Little Mermaid*, *The Hunchback of Notre Dame*, *Tarzan*, and

Hercules. **Paul Cassidy**, 94, was a comics artist who formalized the S shield on Superman's costume and added it to his cape. **Sam Kweskin**, 81, a comics artist, worked on *Daredevil, Dr. Strange,* and *Sub-Mariner.* He also did advertising art. **Bob White**, 75, was a comics artist best known for his work on Archie Comics, particularly his illustration of Jughead. **Ryan Richard Carriere**, 32, was a comics artist who produced a number of mini-comics and contributed to various small press anthologies. **Bill Fraccio**, 81, a comics illustrator, worked in collaboration with Tony Tallarico, who signed most of their work. In the mid-1960s, Fraccio worked on Charlton's superhero line. Some of their work was published under the name Tony Williamsune. Fraccio also worked for EC, Hillman, and other publishers.

Fritz Richmond, 66, was one of the world's finest players of the jug and washtub bass. He also engineered albums for Jackson Browne, Bonnie Raitt, and others. **John Langstaff**, 84, founded the Christmas Revels, the long-running seasonal pageant of traditional music, dance, and theater that plays in Boston, New York, and other cities around the country. **Willis Hall**, 75, was a British playwright and screenwriter. He wrote children's fantasies for stage and television. His best known work is probably *Billy Liar.* He also wrote musical adaptations of *The Wind in the Willows* and *Peter Pan.*

Jeff Slaten, 49, cowrote *Death Jag* with Albert Ellis and also collaborated with Robert E. Vardeman. He was active in the Society for Creative Anachronism. In the 1970s, he sold some stories to Atlas Comics. **Andy Roberts**, 41, was a rock musician and cartoonist, who created "Frieda's Friends" and helped set up the small press comic convention Caption. Roberts was a songwriter, guitarist and vocalist for the London rock group Linus. **Bernie Zuber**, 72, was an artist, the original vice president of the Mythopoeic Society, and the first editor of *Mythlore.* In 1977, he became the founder and president of the Tolkien Fellowships.

All these people are now gone, but their work remains, part of our cultural heritage, to inspire and entertain us and future generations.

DELIA SHERMAN

Walpurgis Afternoon

Delia Sherman's "Walpurgis Afternoon," first published in The Magazine of
Fantasy & Science Fiction, *is a charming, contemporary, suburban fantasy
in which new neighbors turn out to be eccentric in the best possible ways,
and in which the secrets of gardening are revealed—less surprisingly—to be
more magical than practical. Sherman has published three novels,* The
Porcelain Dove, The Brazen Mirror, *and, with Ellen Kushner,* The Fall of
the Kings. *Her first novel for young adults,* Changeling, *will be published
this year. Sherman makes her home in New York City.*

—K.L. & G.G.

The big thing about the new people moving into the old Pratt place at Number
400 was that they got away with it at all. Our neighborhood is big on historical integrity. The newest house on the block was built in 1910, and you can't
even change the paint scheme on your house without recourse to preserva-
tion committee studies and zoning board hearings. The old Pratt place had generated a tedious number of such hearings over the years—I'd even been to some of the
more recent ones. Old Mrs. Pratt had let it go pretty much to seed, and when she
passed away, there was trouble about clearing the title so it could be sold, and then
it burned down.

Naturally a bunch of developers went after the land—a three-acre property in a
professional neighborhood twenty minutes from downtown is something like a Holy
Grail to developers. But their lawyers couldn't get the title cleared either, and the
end of it was that the old Pratt place never did get built on. By the time Geoff and I
moved next door, the place was an empty lot. The neighborhood kids played Bad
Guys and Good Guys there after school and the neighborhood cats preyed on its
endless supply of mice and voles. I'm not talking eyesore, here; just a big shady plot
of land overgrown with bamboo, rhododendrons, wildly rambling roses, and some
nice old trees, most notably an immensely ancient copper beech big enough to
dwarf any normal-sized house.

It certainly dwarfs ours.

Last spring all that changed overnight. Literally. When Geoff and I turned in, we
lived next door to an empty lot. When we got up, we didn't. I have to tell you, it
came as quite a shock first thing on a Monday morning, and I wasn't even the one
who discovered it. Geoff was.

Geoff's the designated keeper of the window because he insists on sleeping with
it open and I hate getting up into a draft. Actually, I hate getting up, period. It's a

blessing, really, that Geoff can't boil water without burning it, or I'd never be up before ten. As it is, I eke out every second of warm unconsciousness I can while Geoff shuffles across the floor and thunks down the sash and takes his shower. On that particular morning, his shuffle ended not with a thunk, but with a gasp.

"Holy shit," he said.

I sat up in bed and groped for my robe. When we were in grad school, Geoff had quite a mouth on him, but fatherhood and two decades of college teaching have toned him down a lot. These days, he usually keeps his swearing for Supreme Court decisions and departmental politics. "Get up, Evie. You gotta see this."

So I got up and went to the window, and there it was, big as life and twice as natural, a real *Victorian Homes* centerfold, set back from the street and just the right size to balance the copper beech. Red tile roof, golden brown clapboards, miles of scarlet-and-gold gingerbread draped over dozens of eaves, balconies, and dormers. A witch's hat tower, a wrap-around porch, and a massive carriage house. With a cupola on it. Nothing succeeds like excess, I always say.

"Holy shit."

"Watch your mouth, Evie," said Geoff automatically.

I like to think of myself as a fairly sensible woman. I don't imagine things, I face facts, I hadn't gotten hysterical when my fourteen-year-old daughter asked me about birth control. Surely there was some perfectly rational explanation for this phenomenon. All I had to do was think of it.

"It's an hallucination," I said. "Victorian houses don't go up overnight. People do have hallucinations. We're having an hallucination. Q.E.D."

"It's not a hallucination," Geoff said.

Geoff teaches intellectual history at the university and tends to disagree, on principle, with everything everyone says. Someone says the sky is blue, he says it isn't. And then he explains why. "This has none of the earmarks of a hallucination," he went on. "We aren't in a heightened emotional state, not expecting a miracle, not drugged, not part of a mob, not starving, not sense-deprived. Besides, there's a clothesline in the yard with laundry hanging on it. Nobody hallucinates long underwear."

I looked where he was pointing, and sure enough, a pair of scarlet long johns was kicking and waving from an umbrella-shaped drying rack, along with a couple pairs of women's panties, two oxford-cloth shirts hung up by their collars, and a gold-and-black print caftan. There was also what was arguably the most beautifully designed perennial bed I'd ever seen basking in the early morning sun. As I was squinting at the delphiniums, a side door opened and a woman came out with a wicker clothes basket propped on her hip. She was wearing shorts and a T-shirt, had fairish hair pulled back in a bushy tail, and struck me as being a little long in the tooth to be going barefoot and braless.

"Nice legs," said Geoff.

I snapped down the window. "Pull the shades before you get in the shower," I said. "It looks to me like our new neighbors get a nice, clear shot of our bathroom from their third floor."

In our neighborhood, we pride ourselves on minding our own business and not each others'—live and let live, as long as you keep your dog, your kids, and your lawn under control. If you don't, someone calls you or drops you a note, and if that doesn't make you straighten up and fly right, well, you're likely to get a call from the town council about that extension you neglected to get a variance for. Needless to say, the house at Number 400 fell way outside all our usual coping mechanisms. If some contractor had shown up at dawn with bulldozers and two-by-fours, I could have called the police or our councilwoman or someone and got an injunction. How do you get an injunction against a physical impossibility?

The first phone call came at about eight-thirty: Susan Morrison, whose back yard abuts the Pratt place.

"Reality check time," said Susan. "Do we have new neighbors or do we not?"

"Looks like it to me," I said.

Silence. Then she sighed. "Yeah. So. Can Kimmy sit for Jason Friday night?" Typical. If you can't deal with it, pretend it doesn't exist, like when one couple down the street got the bright idea of turning their front lawn into a wildflower meadow. The trouble is, a Victorian mansion is a lot harder to ignore than even the wildest meadow. The phone rang all morning with hysterical calls from women who hadn't spoken to us since Geoff's brief tenure as president of the neighborhood association.

After several fruitless sessions of what's-the-world-coming-to, I turned on the machine and went out to the garden to put in the beans. Planting them in May was pushing it, but I needed the therapy. For me, gardening's the most soothing activity on Earth. When you plant a bean, you get a bean, not an azalea or a cabbage. When you see that bean covered with icky little orange things, you know they're Mexican bean beetle larvae and go for the pyrethrum. Or you do if you're paying attention. It always astonishes me how oblivious even the garden club ladies can be to a plant's needs and preferences.

Sure, there are nasty surprises, like the winter that the mice ate all the Apricot Beauty tulip bulbs. But mostly you know where you are with a garden. If you put the work in, you'll get satisfaction out, which is more than can be said of marriages or careers.

This time though, digging and raking and planting failed to work their usual magic. Every time I glanced up, there was Number 400, serene and comfortable, the shrubs established and the paint chipping just a little around the windows, exactly as if it had been there forever instead of less than twelve hours.

I'm not big on the inexplicable. Fantasy makes me nervous. In fact, fiction makes me nervous. I like facts and plenty of them. That's why I wanted to be a botanist. I wanted to know everything there was to know about how plants worked, why azaleas like acid soil and peonies like wood ash and how you might be able to get them to grow next to each other. I even went to graduate school and took organic chemistry. Then I met Geoff, fell in love, and traded in my Ph.D. for an M-R-S, with a minor in Mommy. None of these events (except possibly falling in love with Geoff) fundamentally shook my allegiance to provable, palpable facts. The house next door was palpable, all right, but it shouldn't have been. By the time Kim got home from school that afternoon, I had a headache from trying to figure out how it got to be there.

Kim is my daughter. She reads fantasy, likes animals a lot more than she likes people, and is a big fan of *Buffy the Vampire Slayer*. Because of Kim, we have two dogs (Spike and Willow), a cockatiel (Frodo), and a lop-eared Belgian rabbit (Big Bad), plus the overflow of semi-wild cats (Balin, Dwalin, Bifur, and Bombur) from the Pratt place, all of which she feeds and looks after with truly astonishing dedication.

Three-thirty on the nose, the screen door slammed and Kim careened into the kitchen with Spike and Willow bouncing ecstatically around her feet. "Whaddya think of the new house, Mom? Who do you think lives there? Do they have pets?"

I laid out her after-school sliced apple and cheese and answered the question I could answer. "There's at least one woman—she was hanging out laundry this morning. No sign of children or pets, but it's early days yet."

"Isn't it just the coolest thing in the universe, Mom? Real magic, right next door. Just like *Buffy*."

"Without the vampires, I hope. Kim, there's no such thing as magic. There's probably a perfectly simple explanation."

"But, *Mom!*"

"But nothing. You need to call Mrs. Morrison. She wants to know if you can sit for Jason on Friday night. And Big Bad's looking shaggy. He needs to be brushed."

That was Monday.

Tuesday morning, our street looked like the Expressway at rush hour. It's a miracle there wasn't an accident. Everybody in town must have driven by, slowing down as they passed Number 400 and craning out the car window. Things quieted down in the middle of the day when everyone was at work, but come 4:30 or so, the joggers started and the walkers and more cars. About 6:00, the police pulled up in front of the house, at which point everyone stopped pretending to be nonchalant and held their breath. Two cops disappeared into the house, came out again a few minutes later, and left without talking to anybody. They were holding cookies and looking bewildered.

The traffic let up on Wednesday. Kim found a kitten (Hermione) in the wildflower garden, and Geoff came home full of the latest in a series of personality conflicts with his department head, which gave everyone something other than Number 400 to talk about over dinner.

Thursday, Lucille Flint baked one of her coffee cakes and went over to do the Welcome Wagon thing.

Lucille's our local Good Neighbor. Someone moves in, has a baby, marries, dies, and there's Lucille, Johnny-on-the-spot with a coffee cake in her hands and the proper Hallmark sentiment on her lips. Lucille has the time for this kind of thing because she doesn't have a regular job. All right, neither do I, but I write a gardener's advice column for the local paper, so I'm not exactly idle. There's the garden, too. Besides, I'm not the kind of person who likes sitting around in other people's kitchens drinking watery instant and hearing the stories of their lives. Lucille is.

Anyway. Thursday morning, I researched the diseases of roses for my column. I'm lucky with roses. Mine never come down with black spot, and the Japanese beetles prefer Susan Morrison's yard to mine. Weeds, however, are not so obliging. When I'd finished Googling "powdery mildew," I went out to tackle the rosebed.

Usually, I don't mind weeding. My mind wanders, my hands get dirty. I can almost feel my plants settling deeper into the soil as I root out the competition. But my rose bed is on the property line between us and the Pratt place. What if the house disappeared again, or someone came out and wanted to chat? I'm not big into chatting. On the other hand, there was shepherd's purse in the rosebed, and shepherd's purse can be a real wild Indian once you let it get established, so I gritted my teeth, grabbed my Cape Cod weeder, and got down to it.

Just as I was starting to relax, I heard footsteps passing on the walk and pushed the rose canes aside just in time to see Lucille Flint climbing the stone steps to Number 400. I watched her ring the doorbell, but I didn't see who answered because I ducked down behind a bushy Gloire de Dijon. If Lucille doesn't care who knows she's a busybody, that's her business. After twenty-five minutes, I'd weeded and cultivated those roses to a fare-thee-well, and was backing out when I heard the screen door, followed by Lucille telling someone how *lovely* their home was, and thanks again for the *scrumptious* pie.

I caught her up under the copper beech.

"Evie dear, you're all out of breath," she said. "My, that's a nasty tear in your shirt."

"Come in, Lucille," I said. "Have a cup of coffee."

She followed me inside without comment, and accepted a cup of microwaved coffee and a slice of date-and-nut cake.

She took a bite, coughed a little, and grabbed for the coffee.

"It is pretty awful, isn't it?" I said apologetically. "I baked it last week for some PTA thing at Kim's school and forgot to take it."

"Never mind. I'm full of cherry pie from next door." She leaned over the stale cake and lowered her voice. "The cherries were *fresh*, Evie."

My mouth dropped open. "Fresh cherries? In May? You're kidding." Lucille nodded, satisfied at my reaction. "Nope. There was a bowl of them on the table, leaves and all. What's more, there was corn on the draining-board. Fresh corn. In the husk. With the silk still on it."

"No!"

"Yes." Lucille sat back and took another sip of coffee. "Mind you, there could be a perfectly ordinary explanation. Ophelia's a horticulturist, after all. Maybe she's got greenhouses out back. Heaven knows there's enough room for several."

I shook my head. "I've never heard of corn growing in a greenhouse."

"And I've never heard of a house appearing in an empty lot overnight," Lucille said tartly. "About that, there's nothing I can tell you. They're not exactly forthcoming, if you know what I mean."

I was impressed. I knew how hard it was to avoid answering Lucille's questions, even about the most personal things. She just kind of picked at you, in the nicest possible way, until you unraveled. It's one of the reasons I didn't hang out with her much.

"So, who are they?"

"Rachel Abrams and Ophelia Canderel. I think they're lesbians. They feel like family together, and you can take it from me, they're not sisters."

Fine. We're a liberal suburb, we can cope with lesbians. "Children?"

Lucille shrugged. "I don't know. There were drawings on the fridge, but no toys."

"Inconclusive evidence," I agreed. "What did you talk about?"

She made a face. "Pie crust. The Perkins's wildflower meadow. They like it. Burney." Burney was Lucille's husband, an unpleasant old fart who disapproved of everything in the world except his equally unpleasant terrier, Homer. "Electricians. They want a fixture put up in the front hall. Then Rachel tried to tell me about her work in artificial intelligence, but I couldn't understand a word she said."

From where I was sitting, I had an excellent view of Number 400's wisteria-covered carriage house with its double doors ajar on an awe-inspiring array of garden tackle. "Artificial intelligence must pay well," I said.

Lucille shrugged. "There has to be family money somewhere. You ought to see the front hall, not to mention the kitchen. It looks like something out of a magazine."

"What are they doing here?"

"That's the forty-thousand-dollar question, isn't it?"

We drained the cold dregs of our coffee, contemplating the mystery of why a horticulturist and an artificial intelligence wonk would choose our quiet, tree-lined suburb to park their house in. It seemed a more solvable mystery than how they'd transported it there in the first place.

Lucille took off to make Burney his noontime franks and beans and I tried to get my column roughed out. But I couldn't settle to my computer, not with that Victorian enigma sitting on the other side of my rose bed. Every once in a while, I'd see a shadow passing behind a window or hear a door bang. I gave up trying to make the disposal of diseased foliage interesting and went out to poke around in the garden. I was elbow-deep in the viburnum, pruning out deadwood, when I heard someone calling. It was a woman, standing on the other side of my roses. She was big, solidly curved, and dressed in bright flowered overalls. Her hair was braided with shiny gold ribbon into dozens of tiny plaits tied off with little metal beads. Her skin was a deep matte brown, like antique mahogany. Despite the overalls, she was astonishingly beautiful.

I dropped the pruning shears. "Damn," I said. "Sorry," I said. "You surprised me." I felt my cheeks heat. The woman smiled at me serenely and beckoned.

I don't like new people and I don't like being put on the spot, but I've got my pride. I picked up my pruning shears, untangled myself from the viburnum, and marched across the lawn to meet my new neighbor. She said her name was Ophelia Canderel, and she'd been admiring my garden. Would I like to see hers?

I certainly would.

If I'd met Ophelia at a party, I'd have been totally tongue-tied. She was beautiful, she was big, and frankly, there just aren't enough people of color in our neighborhood for me to have gotten over my Liberal nervousness around them. This particular woman of color, however, spoke fluent Universal Gardener and her garden was a gardener's garden, full of horticultural experiments and puzzles and stuff to talk about.

Within about three minutes, she was asking my advice about the gnarly brown larvae infesting her bee balm, and I was filling her in on the peculiarities of our local microclimate. By the time we'd inspected every flower and shrub in the front yard, I was more comfortable with her than I was with the local garden club ladies. We were alike, Ophelia and I.

We were discussing the care and feeding of peonies in an acid soil when Ophelia said, "Would you like to see my shrubbery?"

Usually when I hear the word "shrubbery," I think of a semi-formal arrangement of rhodies and azaleas, lilacs and viburnum, with a potentilla perhaps, or a butterfly bush for late summer color. The bed should be deep enough to give everything room to spread and there should be a statue in it, or maybe a sundial. Neat, but not anal—that's what you should aim for in a shrubbery.

Ophelia sure had the not-anal part down pat. The shrubs didn't merely spread, they rioted. And what with the trees and the orchids and the ferns and the vines, I couldn't begin to judge the border's depth. The hibiscus and the bamboo were okay, although I wouldn't have risked them myself. But to plant bougainvillea and poinsettias, coconut palms and frangipani this far north was simply tempting fate. And the statue! I'd never seen anything remotely like it, not outside of a museum, anyway. No head to speak of, breasts like footballs, a belly like a watermelon, and a phallus like an overgrown zucchini, the whole thing weathered with the rains of a thousand years or more.

I glanced at Ophelia. "Impressive," I said.

She turned a critical eye on it. "You don't think it's too much? Rachel says it is, but she's a minimalist. This is my little bit of home, and I love it."

"It's a lot," I admitted. Accuracy prompted me to add, "It suits you."

I still didn't understand how Ophelia had gotten a tropical rainforest to flourish in a temperate climate.

I was trying to find a nice way to ask her about it when she said, "You're a real find, Evie. Rachel's working, or I'd call her to come down. She really wants to meet you."

"Next time," I said, wondering what on Earth I'd find to talk about with a specialist on artificial intelligence. "Um. Does Rachel garden?"

Ophelia laughed. "No way—her talent is not for living things. But I made a garden for her. Would you like to see it?"

I was only dying to, although I couldn't help wondering what kind of exotica I was letting myself in for. A desertscape? Tundra? Curiosity won. "Sure," I said. "Lead on."

We stopped on the way to visit the vegetable garden. It looked fairly ordinary, although the tomatoes were more August than May, and the beans more late June. I didn't see any corn and I didn't see any greenhouses. After a brief sidebar on insecticidal soaps, Ophelia led me behind the carriage house. The unmistakable sound of quacking fell on my ears.

"We aren't zoned for ducks," I said, startled.

"We are," said Ophelia. "Now. How do you like Rachel's garden?"

A prospect of brown reeds with a silvery river meandering through it stretched through where the Morrisons' back yard ought to be, all the way to a boundless expanse of ocean. In the marsh it was April, with a crisp salt wind blowing back from the water and ruffling the brown reeds and the white-flowering shad and the pale green unfurling sweetfern. Mallards splashed and dabbled along the meander. A solitary great egret stood among the reeds, the fringes of its white courting shawl blowing around one black and knobbly leg. As I watched, open-mouthed, the egret unfurled its other leg from its breast feathers, trod at the reeds, and lowered its golden bill to feed.

I got home late. Kim was in the basement with the animals, and the chicken I was planning to make for dinner was still in the freezer. Thanking heaven for modern technology, I defrosted the chicken in the microwave, chopped veggies, seasoned, mixed, and got the whole mess in the oven just as Geoff walked in the door. He wasn't happy about eating forty-five minutes late, but he was mostly over it by bedtime.

That was Thursday.

Friday, I saw Ophelia and Rachel pulling out of their driveway in one of those old cars that has huge fenders and a running board. They returned after lunch, the back seat full of groceries. They and the groceries disappeared through the kitchen door, and there was no further sign of them until late afternoon, when Rachel opened one of the quarter-round windows in the attic and energetically shook the dust out of a small, patterned carpet.

On Saturday, the invitation came.

It stood out among the flyers, book orders, bills, and requests for money that usually came through our mail-slot, a five-by-eight silvery-blue envelope that smelled faintly of sandalwood. It was addressed to The Gordon Family in a precise italic hand.

I opened it and read:

Rachel Esther Abrams and Ophelia Desirée Candarel
Request the Honor of your Presence
At the
Celebration of their Marriage.
Sunday, May 24 at 3 P.M.
There will be refreshments before and after the Ceremony.

I was still staring at it when the doorbell rang. It was Lucille, looking fit to burst, holding an invitation just like mine.

"Come in, Lucille. There's plenty of coffee left."

I don't think I'd ever seen Lucille in such a state. You'd think someone had invited her to parade naked down Main Street at noon.

"Well, write and tell them you can't come," I said. "They're just being neighborly, for Pete's sake. It's not like they can't get married if you're not there."

"I know. It's just. . . . It puts me in a funny position, that's all. Burney's a founding member of Normal Marriage for Normal People. He wouldn't like it at all if he knew I'd been invited to a lesbian wedding."

"So don't tell him. If you want to go, just tell him the new neighbors have invited you to an open house on Sunday, and you know for a fact that we're going to be there."

Lucille smiled. Burney hated Geoff almost as much as Geoff hated Burney.

"It's a thought," she said. "Are you going?"

"I don't see why not. Who knows? I might learn something."

The Sunday of the wedding, I took forever to dress. Kim thought it was funny, but Geoff threatened to bail if I didn't quit fussing. "It's a lesbian wedding, for pity's sake. It's going to be full of middle-aged dykes with ugly haircuts. Nobody's going to care what you look like."

"I care," said Kim. "And I think that jacket is wicked cool."

I'd bought the jacket at a little Indian store in the Square and not worn it since. When I got it away from the Square's atmosphere of collegiate funk it looked, I don't know, too Sixties, too artsy, too bright for a fortysomething suburban matron. It was basically purple, with teal blue and gold and fuchsia flowers all over it and brass buttons shaped like parrots. Shaking my head, I started to unfasten the parrots.

Geoff exploded. "I swear to God, Evie, if you change again, that's it. It's not like I want to go. I've got papers to correct; I don't have time for this"—he glanced at Kim—"nonsense. Either we go or we stay. But we do it now."

Kim touched my arm. "It's *you*, Mom. Come *on*."

So I came on, my jacket flashing neon in the sunlight. By the time we hit the sidewalk, I felt like a tropical floral display; I was ready to bolt home and hide under the bed.

"Great," said Geoff. "Not a car in sight. If we're the only ones here, I'm leaving."

"I don't think that's going to be a problem," I said.

Beyond the copper beech, I saw a colorful crowd milling around as purposefully as bees, bearing chairs and flowers and ribbons. As we came closer, it became clear that Geoff couldn't have been more wrong about the wedding guests. There wasn't an ugly haircut in sight, although there were some pretty startling dye jobs. The dress-code could best be described as eclectic, with a slight bias toward floating fabrics and rich, bright colors. My jacket felt right at home.

Geoff was muttering about not knowing anybody when Lucille appeared, looking festive in Laura Ashley chintz.

"Isn't this fun?" she said, with every sign of sincerity. "I've never met such interesting people. And friendly! They make me feel right at home. Come over here and join the gang."

She dragged us toward the long side yard, which sloped down to a lavishly blooming double-flowering cherry underplanted with peonies. Which shouldn't have been in bloom at the same time as the cherry, but I was getting used to the vagaries of Ophelia's garden. A willowy young person in chartreuse lace claimed Lucille's attention, and they went off together. The three of us stood in a slightly awkward knot at the edge of the crowd, which occasionally threw out a few guests who eddied around us briefly before retreating.

"How are those spells of yours, dear? Any better?" inquired a solicitous voice in my ear, and, "Oh!" when I jumped. "You're not Elvira, are you? Sorry."

Geoff's grip was cutting off the circulation above my elbow. "This was not one of your better ideas, Evie. We're surrounded by weirdoes. Did you see that guy in the skirt? I think we should take Kimmy home."

A tall black man with a flattop and a diamond in his left ear appeared, pried Geoff's hand from my arm, and shook it warmly. "Dr. Gordon? Ophelia told me to be looking out for you. I've read *The Anarchists*, you see, and I can't tell you how much I admired it."

Geoff actually blushed. Before the subject got too painful to talk about, he used to say that for a history of anarchism, his one book had had a remarkably elite readership: three members of the tenure review committee, two reviewers for scholarly journals, and his wife. "Thanks," he said.

Geoff's fan grinned, clearly delighted. "Maybe we can talk at the reception," he said. "Right now, I need to find you a place to sit. They look like they're just about ready to roll."

It was a lovely wedding.

I don't know exactly what I was expecting, but I was mildly surprised to see a rabbi and a wedding canopy. Ophelia was an enormous rose in crimson draperies. Rachel was a calla lily in cream linen. Their heads were tastefully wreathed in oak and ivy leaves. There were the usual prayers and promises and tears; when the rabbi pronounced them married, they kissed and horns sounded a triumphant fanfare.

Kim poked me in the side. "Mom? Who's playing those horns?"

"I don't know. Maybe it's a recording."

"I don't think so," Kim said. "I think it's the tree. Isn't this just about the coolest thing ever?"

We were on our feet again. The chairs had disappeared and people were dancing. A cheerful bearded man grabbed Kim's hand to pull her into the line. Geoff grabbed her and pulled her back.

"*Dad!*" Kim wailed. "I want to dance!"

"I've got a pile of papers to correct before class tomorrow," Geoff said.

"And if I know you, there's some homework you've put off until tonight. We have to go home now."

"We can't leave yet," I objected. "We haven't congratulated the brides."

Geoff's jaw tensed. "So go congratulate them," he said. "Kim and I will wait for you here."

Kim looked mutinous. I gave her the eye. This wasn't the time or the place to object. Like Geoff, Kim had no inhibitions about airing the family linen in public, but I had enough for all three of us.

"Dr. Gordon. There you are." *The Anarchists* fan popped up between us. "I've been looking all over for you. Come have a drink and let me tell you how brilliant you are."

Geoff smiled modestly. "You're being way too generous," he said. "Did you read Peterson's piece in *The Review?*"

"Asshole," said the man dismissively. Geoff slapped him on the back, and a minute later, they were halfway to the house, laughing as if they'd known each other for years. Thank heaven for the male ego.

"Dance?" said Kim.

"Go for it," I said. "I'm going to get some champagne and kiss the brides."

The brides were nowhere to be found. The champagne, a young girl informed me, was in the kitchen. So I entered Number 400 for the first time, coming through the mudroom into a large, oak-paneled hall. To my left a staircase with an ornately carved oak banister rose to an art-glass window. Ahead was a semicircular fireplace with a carved bench on one side and a door that probably led to the kitchen on the other. Between me and the door was an assortment of brightly dressed strangers, talking and laughing.

I edged around them, passing two curtained doors and a bronze statue of Alice and the Red Queen. Puzzle fragments of conversation rose out of the general buzz:

"My pearls? Thank you, my dear, but you know they're only stimulated."

"And *then* it just went 'poof'! A perfectly good frog, and it just went poof!"

". . . and then Tallulah says to the bishop, she says, 'Love your drag, darling, but your *purse* is on fire.' Don't you love it? 'Your *purse* is on fire!'"

The kitchen itself was blessedly empty except for a stout gentleman in a tuxedo, and a striking woman in a peach silk pantsuit, who was tending an array of champagne bottles and a cut-glass bowl full of bright blue punch. Curious, I picked up a cup of punch and sniffed at it. The woman smiled up at me through a caterpillery fringe of false lashes.

"Pure witch's brew," she said in one of those Lauren Bacall come-hither voices I've always envied. "But what can you do? It's the *specialité de la maison.*"

The tuxedoed man laughed. "Don't mind Silver, Mrs. Gordon. He just likes to tease. Ophelia's punch is wonderful."

"Only if you like Ty-dee Bowl," said Silver, tipping a sapphire stream into another cup. "You know, honey, you shouldn't stand around with your mouth open like that. Think of the flies."

Several guests entered in plenty of time to catch this exchange.

Determined to preserve my cool, I took a gulp of the punch. It tasted fruity and made my mouth prickle, and then it hit my stomach like a firecracker. So much for cool. I choked and gasped.

"I tried to warn you," Silver said. "You'd better switch to champagne."

Now I knew Silver was a man, I could see that his hands and wrists were big for the rest of her—him. I could feel my face burning with punch and mortification.

"No, thank you," I said faintly. "Maybe some water?"

The stout man handed me a glass. I sipped gratefully. "You're Ophelia and Rachel's neighbor, aren't you?" he said. "Lovely garden. You must be proud of that asparagus bed."

"I was, until I saw Ophelia's."

"Ooh, listen to the green-eyed monster," Silver cooed. "Don't be jealous, honey. Ophelia's the best. Nobody understands plants like Ophelia."

"I'm not jealous," I said with dignity. "I'm wistful. There's a difference."

Then, just when I thought it couldn't possibly get any worse, Geoff appeared, looking stunningly unprofessorial, with one side of his shirt collar turned up and his dark hair flopped over his eyes.

"Hey, Evie. Who knew a couple of dykes would know how to throw a wedding?"

You'd think after sixteen years of living with Geoff, I'd know whether or not he was an alcoholic. But I don't. He doesn't go on binges, he doesn't get drunk at every party we go to, and I'm pretty sure he doesn't drink on the sly. What I do know is that drinking doesn't make him more fun to be around.

I took his arm. "I'm glad you're enjoying yourself," I said brightly. "Too bad we have to leave."

"Leave? Who said anything about leaving? We just got here."

"Your papers," I said. "Remember?"

"Screw my papers," said Geoff and held out his empty cup to Silver. "This punch is dy-no-mite."

"What about your students?"

"I'll tell 'em I didn't feel like reading their stupid essays. That'll fix their little red wagons. Boring as hell anyway. Fill 'er up, beautiful," he told Silver.

Silver considered him gravely. "Geoff, darling," he said. "A little bird tells me that there's an absolutely delicious argument going on in the smoking room. They'll never forgive you if you don't come play."

Geoff favored Silver with a leer that made me wish I were somewhere else.

"Only if you play too," he said. "What's it about?"

Silver waved a pink-tipped hand. "Something about theoretical versus practical anarchy. Right, Rodney?"

"I believe so," said the stout gentleman agreeably.

A martial gleam rose in Geoff's eye. "Let me at 'em."

Silver's pale eyes turned to me, solemn and concerned. "You don't mind, do you, honey?"

I shrugged. With luck, the smoking-room crowd would be drunk too, and nobody would remember who said what. I just hoped none of the anarchists had a violent temper.

"We'll return him intact," Silver said. "I promise." And they were gone, Silver trailing fragrantly from Geoff's arm.

While I was wondering whether I'd said that thing about the anarchists or only thought it, I felt a tap on my shoulder—the stout gentleman, Rodney.

"Mrs. Gordon, Rachel and Ophelia would like to see you and young Kimberly in the study. If you'll please step this way?"

His manner had shifted from wedding guest to old-fashioned butler. Properly intimidated, I trailed him to the front hall. It was empty now, except for Lucille and the young person in chartreuse lace, who were huddled together on the bench by the fireplace. The young person was talking earnestly and Lucille was listening and nodding and sipping punch. Neither of them paid any attention to us or to the music coming from behind one of the curtained doors. I saw Kim at the foot of the stairs, examining the newel post.

It was well worth examining: a screaming griffin with every feather and every curl beautifully articulated and its head polished smooth and black as ebony. Rodney gave it a brief, seemingly unconscious caress as he started up the steps. When Kim followed suit, I thought I saw the carved eye blink.

I must have made a noise, because Rodney halted his slow ascent and gazed down at me, standing open-mouthed below. "Lovely piece of work, isn't it? We call it the house guardian. A joke, of course."

"Of course," I echoed. "Cute."

It seemed to me that the house had more rooms than it ought to. Through open doors, I glimpsed libraries, salons, parlors, bedrooms. We passed through a stone cloister where discouraged-looking ficuses in tubs shed their leaves on the cracked pavement and into a green-scummed pool. I don't know what shocked me more: the cloister or the state of its plants. Maybe Ophelia's green thumb didn't extend to houseplants.

As far as I could tell, Kim took all this completely in stride. She bounded along like a dog in the woods, peeking in an open door here, pausing to look at a picture there, and pelting Rodney with questions I wouldn't have dreamed of asking, like "Are there kids here?"; "What about pets?"; "How many people live here, anyway?"

"It depends," was Rodney's unvarying answer. "Step this way, please."

Our trek ended in a wall covered by a huge South American tapestry of three women making pots. Rodney pulled the tapestry aside, revealing an iron-banded oak door that would have done a medieval castle proud. "The study," he said, and opened the door on a flight of ladderlike steps rising steeply into the shadows.

His voice and gesture reminded me irresistibly of one of those horror movies in which a laconic butler leads the hapless heroine to a forbidding door and invites her to step inside. I didn't know which of three impulses was stronger: to laugh, to run, or, like the heroine, to forge on and see what happened next.

It's some indication of the state I was in that Kim got by me and through the door before I could stop her.

I don't like feeling helpless and I don't like feeling pressured. I really don't like being tricked, manipulated, and herded. Left to myself, I'd have turned around and taken my chances on finding my way out of the maze of corridors. But I wasn't going to leave without my daughter, so I hitched up my wedding-appropriate long skirt and started up the steps.

The stairs were every bit as steep as they looked. I floundered up gracelessly, emerging into a huge space sparsely furnished with a beat-up rolltop desk, a wing-back chair, and a swan-neck rocker on a threadbare Oriental rug at one end, and some cluttered door-on-sawhorse tables on the other. Ophelia and Rachel, still dressed in their bridal finery, were sitting in the chair and the rocker respectively, holding steaming mugs and talking to Kim, who was incandescent with excitement.

"Oh, there you are," said Ophelia as I stumbled up the last step. "Would you like some tea?"

"No, thank you," I said stiffly. "Kim, I think it's time to go home now."

Kim protested, vigorously. Rachel cast Ophelia an unreadable look.

"It'll be fine, love," Ophelia said soothingly. "Mrs. Gordon's upset, and who could blame her? Evie, I don't believe you've actually met Rachel."

Where I come from, social niceties trump everything. Without actually meaning to, I found I was shaking Rachel's hand and congratulating her on her marriage. Close up, she was a handsome woman, with a decided nose, deep lines around her mouth, and the measuring gaze of a gardener examining an unfamiliar insect on her tomato leaves. I didn't ask her to call me Evie.

Ophelia touched my hand. "Never mind," she said soothingly. "Have some tea. You'll feel better."

Next thing I knew, I was sitting on a chair that hadn't been there a moment before, eating a lemon cookie from a plate I didn't see arrive, and drinking Lapsang Souchong from a cup that appeared when Ophelia reached for it. Just for the record, I didn't feel better at all. I felt as if I'd taken a step that wasn't there, or perhaps failed to take one that was: out of balance, out of place, out of control.

Kim, restless as a cat, was snooping around among the long tables.

"What's with the flying fish?" she asked.

"They're for Rachel's new experiment," said Ophelia. "She thinks she can bring the dead to life again."

"You better let me tell it, Ophie," Rachel said. "I don't want Mrs. Gordon thinking I'm some kind of mad scientist."

In fact, I wasn't thinking at all, except that I was in way over my head.

"I'm working on animating extinct species," Rachel said. "I'm particularly interested in dodoes and passenger pigeons, but eventually, I'd like to work up to bison and maybe woolly mammoths."

"Won't that create ecological problems?" Kim objected. "I mean, they're way big, and we don't know much about their habits or what they ate or anything."

There was a silence while Rachel and Ophelia traded family-joke smiles.

"That's why we need you," Rachel said.

Kim looked as though she'd been given the pony she'd been agitating for since fourth grade. Her jaw dropped. Her eyes sparkled. And I lost it.

"Will somebody please tell me what the hell you're talking about?" I said. "I've been patient. I followed your pal Rodney through more rooms than Versailles and I didn't run screaming, and believe me when I tell you I wanted to. I've drunk your tea and listened to your so-called explanations, and I still don't know what's going on."

Kim turned to me with a look of blank astonishment. "Come on, Mom. I can't believe you don't know that Ophelia and Rachel are witches. It's perfectly obvious."

"We prefer not to use the W word," Rachel said. "Like most labels, it's misleading and inaccurate. We're just people with natural scientific ability who have been trained to ask the right questions."

Ophelia nodded. "We learn to ask the things themselves. They always know. Do you see?"

"No," I said. "All I see is a roomful of junk and a garden that doesn't care what season it is."

"Very well," said Rachel, and rose from her chair. "If you'll just come over here, Mrs. Gordon, I'll try to clear everything up."

At the table of the flying fish, Ophelia arranged us in a semicircle, with Rachel in a teacherly position beside the exhibits. These seemed to be A) the fish; and B) one of those Japanese good-luck cats with one paw curled up by its ear and a bright enameled bib.

"As you know," Rachel said, "my field is artificial intelligence. What that means, essentially, is that I can animate the inanimate. Observe." She caressed the porcelain cat between its ears. For two breaths, nothing happened. Then the cat lowered its paw and stretched itself luxuriously. The light glinted off its bulging sides; its curly red mouth and wide painted eyes were expressionless.

"Sweet," Kim breathed.

"It's not really alive," Rachel said, stroking the cat's shiny back. "It's still porcelain. If it jumps off the table, it'll break."

"Can I pet it?" Kim asked.

"No!" Rachel and I said in firm and perfect unison.

"Why not?"

"Because I'd like you to help me with an experiment." Rachel looked me straight in the eye. "I'm not really comfortable with words," she said. "I prefer demonstrations. What I'm going to do is hold Kim's hand and touch the fish. That's all."

"And what happens then?" Kim asked eagerly.

Rachel smiled at her. "Well, we'll see, won't we? Are you okay with this, Mrs. Gordon?"

It sounded harmless enough, and Kim was already reaching for Rachel's hand. "Go ahead," I said.

Their hands met, palm to palm. Rachel closed her eyes. She frowned in concentration and the atmosphere tightened around us. I yawned to unblock my ears.

Rachel laid her free hand on one of the fish.

It twitched, head jerking galvanically; its wings fanned open and shut.

Kim gave a little grunt, which snapped my attention away from the fish. She was pale and sweating a little.

I started to go to her, but I couldn't. Someone was holding me back.

"It's okay, Evie," Ophelia said soothingly. "Kim's fine, really. Rachel knows what she's doing."

"Kim's pale," I said, calm as the eye of a storm. "She looks like she's going to throw up. She's not fine. Let me go to my daughter, Ophelia, or I swear you'll regret it."

"Believe me, it's not safe for you to touch them right now. You have to trust us."

My Great-Aunt Fanny I'll trust you, I thought, and willed myself to relax in her grip. "Okay," I said shakily. "I believe you. It's just, I wish you'd warned me."

"We wanted to tell you," Ophelia said. "But we were afraid you wouldn't believe us. We were afraid you would think we were a couple of nuts. You see, Kim has the potential to be an important zoologist—if she has the proper training. Rachel's a wonderful teacher, and you can see for yourself how complementary their disciplines are. Working together, they. . . ."

I don't know what she thought Kim and Rachel could accomplish, because the second she was more interested in what she was saying than in holding onto me, I was out of her hands and pulling Kim away from the witch who, as far as I could tell, was draining her dry.

That was the plan, anyway.

As soon as I touched Kim, the room came alive.

It started with the flying fish leaping off the table and buzzing past us on Saran Wrap wings. The porcelain cat thumped down from the table and, far from breaking, twined itself around Kim's ankles, purring hollowly. An iron plied itself over a pile of papers, smoothing out the creases. The teddy bear growled at it and ran to hide behind a toaster.

If that wasn't enough, my jacket burst into bloom.

It's kind of hard to describe what it's like to wear a tropical forest. Damp, for one thing. Bright. Loud. Uncomfortable. Very, very uncomfortable. Overstimulating. There were flowers and parrots screeching (yes, the flowers, too—or maybe that was me). It seemed to go on for a long time, kind of like giving birth. At first, I was overwhelmed by the chaos of growth and sound, unsure whether I was the forest or the forest was me. Slowly I realized that it didn't have to be a chaos, and that if I just pulled myself together, I could make sense of it. That flower went there, for instance, and the teal one went there. That parrot belonged on that vine and every-thing needed to be smaller and stiller and less extravagantly colored. Like that.

Gradually, the forest receded. I was still holding Kim, who promptly bent over and threw up on the floor.

"There," I said hoarsely. "I told you she was going to be sick."

Ophelia picked up Rachel and carried her back to her wingchair. "You be quiet, you," she said over her shoulder. "Heaven knows what you've done to Rachel. I *told* you not to touch them."

Ignoring my own nausea, I supported Kim over to the rocker and deposited her in it. "You might have told me why," I snapped. "I don't know why people can't just ex-plain things instead of making me guess. It's not like I can read minds, you know. Now, are you going to conjure us up a glass of water, or do I have to go find the kitchen?"

Rachel had recovered herself enough to give a shaky laugh. "Hell, you could conjure it yourself, with a little practice. Ophie, darling, calm down. I'm fine."

Ophelia stopped fussing over her wife long enough to snatch a glass of cool mint tea from the air and hand it to me. She wouldn't meet my eyes, and she was scowl-ing. "I told you she was going to be difficult. Of all the damn-fool, pig-headed. . . ."

"Hush, love," Rachel said. "There's no harm done, and now we know just where we stand. I'd rather have a nice cup of tea than listen to you cursing out Mrs. Gor-don for just trying to be a good mother." She turned her head to look at me. "Very impressive, by the way. We knew you had to be like Ophie, because of the garden, but we didn't know the half of it. You've got a kick like a mule, Mrs. Gordon."

I must have been staring at her like one of the flying fish. Here I thought I'd half-killed her, and she was giving me a smile that looked perfectly genuine.

I smiled cautiously in return. "Thank you," I said.

Kim pulled at the sleeve of my jacket. "Hey, Mom, that was awesome. I guess you're a witch, huh?"

I wanted to deny it, but I couldn't. The fact was that the pattern of flowers on my jacket was different and the colors were muted, the flowers more English garden than tropical paradise. There were only three buttons, and they were larks, not par-rots. And I felt different. Clearer? More whole? I don't know—different. Even though I didn't know how the magic worked or how to control it, I couldn't ignore the fact—the palpable, provable fact—that it was there.

"Yeah," I said. "I guess I am."

"Me, too," my daughter said. "What's Dad going to say?"

I thought for a minute. "Nothing, honey. Because we're not going to tell him."

We didn't, either. And we're not going to. There's no useful purpose served by telling people truths they aren't equipped to accept. Geoff's pretty oblivious, anyway. It's true that in the hungover aftermath of Ophelia's blue punch, he announced that he thought the new neighbors might be a bad influence, but he couldn't actually forbid Kim and me to hang out with them because it would look homophobic.

Kim's over at Number 400 most Saturday afternoons, learning how to be a zoolo-gist. She's making good progress. There was an episode with zombie mice I don't like to think about, and a crisis when the porcelain cat broke falling out of a tree. But she's learning patience, control, and discipline, which are all excellent things for a girl of fourteen to learn. She and Rachel have reanimated a pair of passenger pi-geons, but they haven't had any luck in breeding them yet.

Lucille's the biggest surprise. It turns out that all her nosy-parkerism was a case of ingrown witchiness. Now she's studying with Silver, of all people, to be a psychologist. But that's not the surprise. The surprise is that she left Burney and moved into Number 400, where she has a room draped with chintz and a gray cat named Jezebel and is as happy as a clam at high tide.

I'm over there a lot, too, learning to be a horticulturist. Ophelia says I'm a quick study, but I have to learn to trust my instincts. Who knew I had instincts? I thought I was just good at looking things up.

I'm working on my own garden now. I'm the only one who can find it without being invited in. It's an English kind of garden, like the gardens in books I loved as a child. It has a stone wall with a low door in it, a little central lawn, and a perennial border full of foxgloves and Sweet William and Michelmas daisies. Veronica blooms in the cracks of the wall, and periwinkle carpets the beds where old-fashioned fragrant roses nod heavily to every passing breeze. There's a small wilderness of rowan trees, and a neat shrubbery embracing a pond stocked with fish as bright as copper pennies. Among the dusty-smelling boxwood, I've put a statue of a woman holding a basket planted with stonecrop. She's dressed in a jacket incised with flowers and vines and closed with three buttons shaped like parrots. The fourth button sits on her shoulder, clacking its beak companionably and preening its brazen feathers. I'm thinking of adding a duck pond next, or maybe a wilderness for Kim's menagerie.

Witches don't have to worry about zoning laws.

DEBORAH ROGGIE

The Mushroom Duchess

"The Mushroom Duchess" was published in Lady Churchill's Rosebud Wristlet 17. *Roggie is a newer writer, and we suggest that you keep an eye out for her stories, fantasies reminiscent of the work of writers like Ursula K. Le Guin, Lois McMaster Bujold, and Delia Sherman. In the last three years, Roggie's short stories have appeared in magazines and anthologies including* Fantasy: The Best of 2004, Realms of Fantasy, *and* Eidolon. *Roggie lives in New Jersey with her husband and son. She is currently working on a novel.*

—K.L. & G.G.

The Dowager Duchess of Turing had made a lifetime's study of mushrooms. It was an odd occupation, perhaps, for one of her age and station in life; but even Duchesses must have their little hobbies, and fungal botany was hers. Her nurse, many years ago, had piqued her interest in mycology by teaching her what mushroom lore she'd known, and the Duchess supplemented that with field study and close questioning of peasant women, whenever her duties allowed.

Mushrooms are funny things. They can please or poison, cause flying dreams, or wake a sleeping man with a bellyache. One type of mushroom grows as large as a village, spreading stealthily underground until one damp morning, after a heavy storm perhaps, a ring of pale toadstools springs up to mark its boundaries. Some glow, some emit the foulest odors, and some develop so quickly that a patient observer can see them sprout, extend their gray umbrellas to the sun, and disappear, all in a single day.

So, in between hosting formal receptions and supervising the servants, the Duchess studied the most arcane mushrooms she could find. She tracked down one unusually tough, acidic variety of mushroom cap, which, worn internally, prevented conception. And she discovered a rare morel that could impregnate a woman. (Regrettably, she found, the children resulting from such pregnancies were severely impaired.) Her studies turned up species of toadstools that inhibited certain brain functions: speech, for example, or sight. A particular spotted tree-mushroom, when harvested in autumn and used within two days, caused permanent memory loss. A nondescript puffball, dried, powdered, and added to saffron broth, gave the user the power of understanding animals' speech. However, as an unfortunate side effect, the subject lost all ability to communicate with humans.

The Duchess was careful and systematic when testing the properties of various mushrooms. She recorded the age of the specimen, its weight and condition, the dosage administered, the phase of the moon, and the species of her subject. The bulk of her experiments were done on animals, but as they were limited in their ability to communicate their experiences, eventually the Duchess turned to human subjects. In twenty-seven years of tests, she had lost only two maids, a groom, and a stable boy. A scullion or two had gone quite mad, and a footman had committed suicide, but she was quite sure that no one connected her to their unfortunate fates.

She was unaware that in the immediate neighborhood "taking tea with the Duchess" had become synonymous with risky behavior.

Her husband, the Duke of Turing, had had mixed luck. He had lived for quite a number of years after succumbing to an overdose of greenblanket chanterelles; the Duchess told everyone he'd had a stroke, and saw that he had the best of care. He wanted for nothing except health and mobility.

Once he was decently buried, the Dowager Duchess turned to the problem of her son's marriage. Eldred presented no opposition: he quite depended on his mother. It was finding the girl that provided the challenge. In time she found a suitable daughter-in-law who would be decorative and obedient, and who seemed likely to produce an heir. The dowry was negotiated, the bloodlines investigated, the girl inspected, and the contracts signed. Their wedding was splendid, as befit a son and heir of the ducal house of Turing.

But the Duchess was still unsatisfied.

Perhaps no one girl could have appeased her. Eldred seemed happy enough in his animal way. His bride was everything that her parents had advertised.

Yet there was something wrong with Gracinet, of that the Duchess was sure. She puzzled over it as she took her bath, as she ordered new bed hangings, as she fussed over her lap dog. She worried about it while receiving guests and while shortening guest lists afterward. It nagged at her as she sat in her private workroom and sorted and labeled new specimens of dried porcini and ink-caps obtained from foreign markets. And then, as if one of her more troublesome powders had suddenly dissolved because at last the tea was at just the right temperature, the problem became clear.

Gracinet was decidedly bookish, her conversations filled with literary allusions. The Duchess overlooked her quoting Soltari over breakfast. She smiled tolerantly when her daughter-in-law declared that Eldred's manner was right out of *The Voyage of the Sun*.

But during the annual Hunters' Banquet, when Gracinet compared her husband to the mysterious Durial of the *Brinnelid* and Eldred grunted, "Who? Never heard of him," in front of the most cultured people of Turing, the Duchess decided she'd had enough. No wife of Eldred (who had never met a book he liked) must be allowed to put him in so bad a light. Of course the mother of her future grandsons should be intelligent, the Duchess thought, but she should also have the grace not to show it. From that moment the Duchess was convinced that her daughter-in-law must be stopped from asserting her superiority over them all.

"My dear child, you look poorly," said the Duchess to her daughter-in-law some few days later.

"It's just my monthlies, Your Grace," said the girl apologetically. The Duchess smiled and tapped her on the arm.

"I have just the thing. You sit right here and I'll make you a bit of my special tonic."

"Are you sure? I don't want to put you to any trouble."

The Duchess assumed her warmest manner. "Now, Gracinet, my dear, there's no need for you to suffer every month. You're my daughter now, and your health is important to me." And off she bustled, quickly locating the packet she had made up for this occasion, and calling for a maid to heat water for tea.

Gracinet, being new to Turing, saw no reason to excuse herself from having tea with the Duchess. She was uncomfortably aware that her mother-in-law did not like her. Why, she could not fathom; and her husband was no help on that score, for when Gracinet had asked him how she might have displeased the Duchess, he'd said, "Gracious! Don't get on her bad side, whatever you do! That's all I need!"

She was finding this wife business both difficult and rather boring. Her husband had little use for her outside of the bedroom. His mother ran the household and brooked no interference. The Duchess's ladies were older women who loved to gossip and shake their heads over the follies of the young. Noting their mistress's aversion to her daughter-in-law, they followed Gracinet with pitying eyes but did not befriend her. It was unfortunate that she had no little hobby, such as that of her mother-in-law, to amuse her. Gracinet supposed that things would change when she became a mother, and produced children of her own to care for.

In the meantime, she read, embroidered, and offered literary conversation at mealtimes.

The Duchess returned with a steaming cup.

"Drink it up directly, my dear," she said. "Monthly tea is best drunk hot."

Gracinet obediently complied. It was mild-tasting, faintly bitter, with a woodnut flavor. "I'm beginning to feel better already," she murmured as the warmth eased her aching belly and thighs.

"Let's keep this between ourselves, dear," the Duchess said. "This tea is terribly expensive, and I don't want every woman in Turing coming to me for a cup each month."

Gracinet promised. "You're so kind to me," she said.

The Duchess merely stroked her daughter-in-law's forehead and took the empty cup away.

From that point on, Gracinet gratefully drank the monthly tea provided by the Duchess. She suffered no more monthly discomforts: no cramps, or bloating, or exhaustion, or irritability. But it was around this time that she began to feel more isolated than ever. For whatever she said, whatever opinion she offered, she was bound to be either contradicted or ignored.

If Gracinet were to say, "My, it's cool out today," someone would be sure to glare at her and snap, "It's unseasonably warm."

If she said, "Can I help with that?" the reply was invariably, "I doubt it."

If someone's spectacles were missing, and Gracinet said, "I saw them on the hall table," she was simply ignored.

Not only the intimates of the ducal circle responded to her in this way. Servants scorned her and refused her requests. Strangers, even, found whatever Gracinet said to be worthless. The only kindness in her life was that her mother-in-law unfailingly prepared, month-in and month-out, that cup of monthly tea.

As a result, Gracinet grew shy and anxious, saying less and less. She wished she could not mind so much, being dismissed and cut down at every turn. She wished she were brave. She wished that she could shout out a blazing fury of words that could not be ignored. Was there anything she could say that wouldn't be wrong? Any phrase, any formula that was safe?

Eventually silence became her only defense. If she said nothing, she would not be cut down. Tall and pale, Gracinet receded to the background of every gathering. She withdrew from public life. She was terrified of becoming pregnant and raising children who would treat her every utterance as wrong. Her husband installed a mistress at the other end of the house; Gracinet dared not protest.

The Duchess was pleased with the results of her experiment. The bearded toadstool, the active ingredient in her monthly teas, fascinated her with its ability to provoke unpleasant responses to Gracinet's every word. There was a complex mechanism at work here, well worth study. She had never before worked with a mushroom that affected the interaction between a subject and those around her. Despite her foreknowledge, the Duchess saw her own reactions affected. Even when she could see the spectacles on the hall table, she felt a revulsion at hearing the facts stated by Gracinet. It was a relief when the girl began to keep her mouth shut.

True, if the girl never spoke it was impossible to measure the effects of different dosages. But there were other fungi to study. She had recently heard of the tawny ink-cap, which, when well-rotted and tawny no more, yielded an ink that compelled the writer to record only the truth. She longed to test it on her steward, whom she suspected of amassing a small fortune at her expense. She readied a page in her journal to be devoted to the steward's case. Science would not be denied.

For Gracinet, the silent days and months piled one upon the other, adding up to silent years. Over time, she felt insubstantial, corroded by cowardice, worm-eaten by words she dared not express. Even then she found no dignity in keeping silent, for she became a figure of derision—her speechlessness made her an easy target. Some equated her silence with stupidity.

The Duchess made no effort to correct this notion.

Gracinet sought consolation in books. The library became her refuge. When she was quite sure she was alone, she read aloud to hear the sound of her own voice, even if she limited herself to others' words. She found that certain forms of literature lent itself to this kind of treatment. She read aloud Bakinjar's *Sermons*, Linnek's *Letters from Doriven Prison*, and the epic *Tale of the Abbess of Pim*. On her daily solitary walks she whispered the *Blackwater Sonnets*. She gave voice to Soltari's *Ice Comedies* and to the *Tragedies* of Irsan the Younger, trying out different accents on different parts. Anyone overhearing her would conclude that she was quite mad, but the reverse was true: Gracinet was fighting to stay sane.

One hot and humid afternoon while in the library, Gracinet found the obscure book for which she had been looking, and settled on the floor by the bookcase to read. That is why, when they entered the room, the two gentlemen did not see her. She remained as she was, hidden in the shadow of the jutting bookcase, hoping that they would quickly select a book and leave; but, to her horror, one stationed himself on the sofa in the middle of the room while the other roamed about, taking down likely books, flipping the pages, putting them back in the wrong places.

"Are you looking for anything in particular?" said the voice from the sofa.

"Not really. Just something to amuse me while I'm here." He snapped another book closed. Gracinet imagined the cloud of dust that resulted: the library shelves were seldom attended to. Sure enough, the man sneezed.

"Don't you find the people amusing enough?"

"What, His Grace and that lot? Hardly. This is probably the dullest house in Turing."

"Oh, come now," said the voice from the sofa, "it's not all that bad. The Duke's lively enough, once you get him out of the house and away from his mother. Not a bad sort, really."

"I met his mistress. Gives herself airs. I'm surprised he never married."

"Oh, weren't you introduced to the wife? I guess they didn't trot her out for the occasion. Rumor has it she's an idiot. I couldn't tell, myself. They say her family covered it up until after the wedding." Gracinet felt her stomach knot. She knew what was said about her.

"And the old lady stood for it? I shouldn't think she was the kind to allow that sort of thing."

"Ah, the Dowager Duchess must have had her reasons. She always does. Notice how nothing happens around here without her say-so? How the Duke defers to his mother in the least little thing? If the Duchess said 'Marry this stick,' you can bet he'd have done it."

"But why?"

The restless fellow joined his companion on the sofa, who lowered his voice. "The Dowager keeps 'em all in line. The old Duke, too, before he died."

"I don't quite follow your meaning."

"Well, I daren't be more plain. Just, whatever you do, don't have tea with the old lady."

"Are you serious?"

"On my life, I am. There've been some mighty peculiar tea parties in this house. She's famous for them. Notorious is more like it. Tea with unusual ingredients, if you know what I mean. If you're invited to one, make an excuse, invent a dead grandmother, a summons to the king, anything at all, and get out."

"Why has no one put a stop to it?"

"Well, nothing's proven. Perhaps that footman who thought he became a snake after sundown was already going mad. It happens. And that maid with the three bouts of temporary blindness for no known reason? Coincidence. Maybe the story about the two stable boys is just an ugly rumor. But I'd be careful, just the same."

His companion laughed nervously. "Indeed I will."

Gracinet had heard enough. She rose and stepped out from behind the sheltering bookcase, startling the two men on the sofa considerably. They gaped as she swept by them without a word. Whatever would they make of her now? At any rate, she supposed, they were unlikely to stay for dinner.

She had to think. Her feet took her down the hall, down the long staircase, and out onto a familiar garden path, without her conscious mind registering the fact. She had to tease apart the facts, like the matted hair of the Duchess's odious little lap dog. Gracinet had no doubt that the monthly tea did more than ease cramps. What a fool she'd been! The maid, apparently, was not the only one who had been blind. If only she'd listened, if only she'd observed! There were years of *onlys* weighing upon her.

Her retreat, her aloofness, had been her undoing. And she had collaborated in her own silencing. She had hidden; she had cringed.

"It's not me," she said aloud, and realized that she was alone in the shady grove past the kitchen gardens. It was cooler here, and the young trees around her seemed like companions. "It's not me," she told them. "It was her. All along it was her." Gracinet found she was shaking, and tears streaked her face. The trees stood silent and still in the face of her storm. "'Drink it up, dear.' Oh, I could choke her on her own brew!" Grief for the lost years surged up and overwhelmed her; Gracinet sank to the ground and wept.

When the tears had stopped and her face felt like a wrung-out washcloth, she bent to clean the twigs and leaves clinging to her dress, and considered what to do next. I'll pretend to drink the tea, she thought, and see if its effects wear off. But I won't let the Duchess know. It will be better if she thinks I am not a threat. Then perhaps I can find a way to stop her.

She glanced at the house, bright in the sunlight beyond the trees, with its many windows blindly glittering. Oh, yes, thought Gracinet. She must be stopped.

She didn't know just when the feeling began, but the Duchess sensed, somehow, that she was being watched. A footfall in an empty corridor, an open window she was sure she'd latched, an unlocked door. . . . Perhaps it was just age, she thought. Perhaps she was forgetting things. Perhaps there was a mushroom out there that would sharpen memory. She would have to check her notes.

It was an unproductive time for her researches. A recent shipment of rare specimens had been water-damaged—slimy with mold and completely unusable. Her agent had apologized profusely. And her new steward had inexplicably lost the latest shipment. Drat the man! She was surrounded by incompetents. These delays would retard her investigation into a truffle that caused people—even those with the most perfect pitch—to sing off-key. It quite spoiled her temper.

Even her daughter-in-law seemed different, though she was as silent and retiring as ever. But the last time she'd brought Gracinet her monthly tea, she'd noticed an almost imperceptible nod from one of her ladies. Later one of them touched Gracinet on the shoulder when they thought she wasn't looking. And Gracinet had smiled. She wondered briefly if her daughter-in-law was quite as isolated as she'd seemed. But the Duchess shrugged off her misgivings.

One morning soon afterward, she discovered that someone had been in her workroom. The polished brass scales, a gift from her late husband, were out of balance. Her notes, though neatly stacked, were out of order. And, at her feet, a single bearded toadstool lay delicately on the carpet. She picked it up and held it in her cupped palm as if it were the head of a newborn infant; and, examining it, considered her options.

That afternoon, the Dowager Duchess found herself alone in her parlor with Gracinet. While she caught up on some correspondence, she glanced every now and then at the younger woman reading by the window. Her daughter-in-law had changed in some way, although the Duchess could not put a finger on how, exactly. A watchfulness, a sense that she waited for something. Even her posture seemed straighter.

The Duchess approached Gracinet and looked over her shoulder at the book she was reading. It was the *Abbess of Pim*, the scene where the foster-son imagined burning down the abbey.

> ". . . beams burned away, and charred stone
> left monument to bitter days.
> A hundred years of wind and rain
> could not scour this wretched place,"

she read aloud. "I feel that way about this old house sometimes, with all its old memories and misdeeds. What a dreadful thought! Do you ever feel that way?"

"Sometimes," said Gracinet without thinking; then her eyes widened, and she turned to face the Duchess.

Not only had her daughter-in-law spoken, but the Duchess felt no revulsion, no urge to contradict. In that moment the she knew Gracinet had stopped drinking the tea. Her scientist's mind wondered how long it had taken for the effects to wear off, and if there would be any residual symptoms. They stared at each other, each seeing the other clearly for the first time: the pale-haired disciple of science, and the newly determined daughter of literature—each surprised to find the other unmasked at last.

Gracinet tucked her chin toward her chest, like a horse about to throw its weight into pulling a heavy load, and continued the quote:

> "But I and all my sons to come
> through all the days and nights unnumbered
> will remember wrongs done here,
> here in the broken house of Pim,
> though it sink beneath the waves
> and come to rest in dark waters
> the silent home of scuttling crabs . . ."

"Well, then—" the Duchess began, but was interrupted by the entrance of a group of ladies and gentlemen, guests of Duke Eldred, who had come to the parlor to set up a card party. Frustrated, the Duchess was forced to play hostess; Gracinet left unnoticed in the commotion.

As soon as she could manage it, the Duchess took her son aside. "Really, your wife is getting more and more strange," she said. "Her behavior has become highly unsuitable. I must talk to you about her."

"After dinner, mother," said the Duke, pulling out his pocket watch and consulting it.

"But—" He snapped the gold watch case closed so abruptly she jumped.

"Our guests, mother, require my attention, and yours. Now is not the time. Worley, man! Let me introduce you to my mother. . . ." And the Duchess had no choice but to comply with a smile.

The bell rang for dinner. Duke Eldred offered his arm to the Dowager Duchess, and together they led their guests to the dining room. A pair of footmen opened the double doors wide, and the company filed in.

Beneath their startled gazes a riot of mushrooms spilled out of bowls set among the elegant place settings and along the sideboard. They filled crystal glasses, swam in glass compotes, swarmed over silver dishes, overran great platters, tumbled over salad plates and were piled high in a great vase like froth. The elegant dinner service hosted colonies of spotted toadstools and ink-caps of many colors, tiny button mushrooms and the giant termite heap mushroom, puffballs of many sizes, stinkhorns, death caps, and porcini, oyster mushrooms and morels, pink trumpets, white truffles, and black ones, too. The Duchess knew many of them—from the arched earthstar to the bird's nest fungus, the elfin saddle to the slippery jack—as well as she knew the shape of her own hands. They were like cities accumulated by a traveler, marks of where she'd been and the journey yet to come.

"What is the meaning of this—this outrageous display?" said the Duchess in a deep voice that promised terrible consequences and made all there, including her son, flinch.

"It means that it is time you listened to me," said Gracinet.

The Duchess looked up to see her daughter-in-law standing at the far end of the room. The young woman held one of the Duchess's own private journals, and Gracinet opened it and read out loud in a voice that was steady and clear:

"The dosage seems to be key, for when I first administered greenblanket chanterelles to my husband, his stomach rejected them immediately, and he suffered no long term ill effects. But, convincing him that it was the wine that was bad that night, on another occasion I persuaded him to try the dish again; however, I gave him too few; and he merely suffered a fit of apoplexy. I must remember to take into account variations in the weight of the subject when working up the correct dosage. He was of the strongest constitution, and it took careful management to keep him from making a complete recovery. (That, in itself, yielded interesting results, see below.) I finally got the dosage right on the third attempt, some years later."

The Duchess looked about during this recitation, ignoring the shocked and hardening expressions of her guests. She felt distant from them all, as if they were located at the wrong end of a telescope. She noted that the missing shipment of mushrooms must have contributed to the display before her. Well, she mused, she should have demanded a written explanation from this steward, too. She had grown lax. Her glance fell upon a small, covered tureen on the table before her. The Duke, seeing where her attention was fixed, reached forward and removed the lid, to reveal a steaming stew of greenblanket chanterelles. "This is how my father liked them prepared, no?"

The Duchess said nothing.

Her son smashed the lid on the floor so hard it scarred the floorboards before shattering into a thousand porcelain shards. The ladies were protected by their long skirts, but several gentlemen's legs were nicked right through their stockings. "Answer me!"

"Yes," said the Duchess.

The Dowager Duchess of Turing had hoped to contribute her notes and specimens to science, but it was not to be. It fell to Gracinet to oversee the destruction of a lifetime's work: the private museum of mycology, the journals and drawings and fungal powders.

Gracinet glanced through the journals before she consigned them to the flames. There she learned that bitter buttons caused hair to grow in unseemly places, and that oil of ghostgall, if rubbed on the blade of a murder weapon, prevented future hauntings. After a number of such entries, she shuddered and closed the book. It would not do to peer so closely into her mother-in-law's mind. It was time to concentrate on the future. Though the mistress was not yet out of the house, Gracinet had begun to reconcile with her husband. They were reading Soltari's *Ice Comedies* together.

The Dowager Duchess was confined to an upstairs bedroom, and watched day and night. But no one volunteered to share her meals, and no one offered her tea.

Gracinet came to regret her willed ignorance. When they burned the papers and scores of carefully labeled packets of dried mushrooms out by the kitchen garden, two of the gardeners overseeing the bonfire died, and a third became deathly ill from the smoke. He never made a full recovery: ever after he supposed that the bees were plotting against him, and had to give up gardening work altogether. It seemed the Duchess had managed one last experiment after all.

MARLY YOUMANS

An Incident at Agate Beach

We first read Marly Youmans's "An Incident at Agate Beach" in the 2005 anthology Northwest Passages: A Cascadian Odyssey, *although it was origi-nally published in 2005's single issue of the magazine* Argosy. *Youmans's story is magical, eerie, and utterly wonderful. Youmans is the author of a number of novels including the young adult works,* The Wolf Pit, Little Jor-dan, Ingledove, *and* The Curse of the Raven Mocker. *Her short stories have appeared in* Story Quarterly, Southern Humanities Review, *and* SCIFIC-TION, *while her poetry has been published in* Plowshares, Black Warrior Review, The South Carolina Review, *and a collection,* Claire. *She lives with her husband and children in New York State.*

—K.L. & G.G.

Where did you come from?"
  Marsha had jumped when the child materialized at her side, peering over her arm to see what it was she was doing, and she glanced about to look for his parents. But no one leaned from the cliff or climbed slowly down the path; no one was in sight along the beach in either direction, neither strolling along the rock pools nor bent to see what agates and jasper the tide had un-covered.

"What is it?" he asked, not bothering to answer. His eyes moved from the linen in her lap to the sewing basket, the lid thrown open to reveal a tumble of crewel em-broidery thread mixed with silk and cotton floss. The circus gaiety of the contents must have drawn him, for he put his hand out and fingered a hank of purple thread, then ran his fingertips over the cloth tomato, studded with hundreds of pins, many of them a plain stainless steel but others topped with bright, transparent heads.

"It's—"

"Sea urchin?"

"A pincushion," she told him, pulling a redheaded pin from the sawdust to show him.

He took the pin from her and studied it, whispering *ushion, ushion.*" Curious, he tapped the point against his arm.

"Ow!"

"Yes, it's sharp. The pins are to hold the fabric when I hem or appliqué." She saw that the words meant nothing to him. "Look. You see?" She took another sampler from the basket, turning it over to show where she had hemmed half of a side, leav-ing a picket of pins in place.

He seemed fascinated, touching the heads as if he were counting.

"How old are you? You look about seven, I'd say."

"Yes." Though he spoke, all his attention was on the sampler with its motto and vases of flowers and birds. His home-cut hair hung low on his forehead and covered his ears, though he somehow managed to look refined despite its carelessness—it must have been the delicate features and the sharp straight nose. The hair was a pale gold, shifting all together, like a cap. The boy seemed compounded of quickness and light, his fingers darting eagerly across the stitched scene.

"Do you like it?"

"Yes. But there are no fish. There should be fish."

Marsha laughed, folding the cloth and tucking it under the thread.

"It's sad, but very few samplers have fish," she told him. "Now and then you might see a bit of waves and a fish or two. Not often." She wasn't surprised that he wanted fish. Why, seaweed was tied at his waist like a kilt. The pale bladders shone among the dark leaves.

Reaching under the basket, she took out her laptop and showed him some other samplers she had recently completed, along with a project that was still in the planning stage. She had not quite finished copying the stitches onto a grid and making a key as to their colors and types. Her husband had formatted a program for her, so that she could type in the number of threads in warp and weft and the dimensions of the piece and immediately begin work.

"I don't know what it is." The boy patted the unfinished sampler in her lap and added, "I like this one better. It's soft and pretty."

"These are just pictures, you see? You've never seen one of these at school? This is a computer. I store the images of my samplers on it. That's what I do you see—I make museum reproduction kits, and people buy them and make copies of samplers that some little girl stitched a hundred years ago."

"Why?"

"Oh, I don't know. Because they like them, I suppose. For the fun of making."

"Why would you want to *store*?" He appeared to be struggling to follow her words. "That's not how *we* save things."

"What do you mean, *not how we save things*? What do you do with them?"

"Oh, the stones, you know."

"The stones."

"You know, the stones. The ones with the letters on them. We call them *ogil* stones."

"What an imagination you have!"

"You should throw this away." The boy tapped at the metal rim of the computer. "It doesn't belong. But don't toss it in the waves!"

She was amused. "Why not?"

"Because it's not for the sea."

"Well," she said; "I'm not so much on computers. That's my husband's domain. He's a real wizard with programming." And she thought of Jim, somewhere by the shore, searching for agates, as he had done years ago as a child growing up along the coast. She liked seeing him this way, barefoot and away from his desk. Only three months had passed since the day they'd met, and now they were married. His job remained mostly a mystery to her. She had barely seen him at work—two or three times she had watched him rotate figures or objects of white mesh on a blue background. They had appeared rather like the result of a cross between a wire dressmaker's dummy and a three-dimensional drawing of the Earth, showing latitude and longitude like a stiff net holding in an endless sea. Then the next time they had substance and color, and she was disappointed. She had liked them better as enigmatic and blue, glimpses from another world.

"I'm sorry," she said; "I wasn't listening."

"My brother is in love with you." The boy smiled, showing bright nubs of teeth and tiny canines.

"But I'm married," she protested. "He can't be in love with me."

"Well, he is. He told me so. He has been watching you every afternoon, and he loves you."

"I'm on my honeymoon. He can't be in love," Marsha said severely. "And what's your name?"

"Bramble?" He looked hopeful. "You could call me Bramble. Or Ramble. Or Scramble."

She laughed. "All right, Bramble it is, at least for now."

"Good." He gave her a smile of intense sweetness. "And my father is in love with you, no matter what you say."

"Now you're confusing me! You said your *brother* was in love with me. Are they *both* in love?"

"Oh. Well, it's not that. We just don't count us that way—we're just all close and we don't think about those sorts of things. Brother, father, all that. Though he's really my *half* brother." He seemed a little confused about how to explain his meaning. "We're born out of nowhere, right? And so we're all the same."

She lifted her eyebrows. "Okay," she said. "We're the same."

"No, not exactly. Some people are just born knowing. Other people are like you."

"Were you born knowing?"

"Of course."

Every afternoon for three weeks Marsha sewed while Jim poked about the tidal pools or went searching for agates and jasper. Afterward they would wander hand in hand along the shore or swim, and sometimes they would go up to the big bedroom with the plate glass window that framed the sea and the cavernous rock formation (wild when the tide was high) and the beach with its rocks and its animal flowers. They had a keen sense of how rare and precious their time together was, and that it wouldn't come around again—the two of them free to spend the day any way they liked. Both meant to sleep late but neither ever did, as the window had no curtain. Marsha could never get over her feeling of surprise that the sun didn't come up over the edge of the ocean, though the increasing light still managed to wake them at dawn, when they would stir and make love and go back to sleep.

They always intended to do nothing one day, just to stay in bed, but the big swashbuckling sky flung down its swords of light onto the sand and the sea, and they could not stay inside. Jim still had a child's excitement about what he would find and came home from his beachcombing with sacks of treasure—a curve of fossilized dolphin bone, a fossil clam, a bloodstone, opaque jasper in shades of butterscotch, red, brown, and green. He brought black agates, pink ones, occasionally pale blue. The owners of the house had a notebook in which they had recorded the best places to look or dig on or near the beach, and he pored over this homegrown guide, scouring it for clues.

Occasionally Marsha went with him, but she had deadlines to reach on new kits, so usually she sat under an umbrella, detailing the pattern of a sampler on her laptop, or else sewing a reproduction. The few hours apart made them eager to be together again, though it wasn't as if Jim were entirely absent; often she caught sight of him wading in the surf or clambering on the rocks.

Because their access to the beach was a private stairs—the house belonged to Jim's boss and was seldom used by any but his wife and daughters—she didn't see many other people. It wasn't much different from plenty of other nooks along the coast, and the owners called it simply *the agate beach*, though that was the name of a dozen or more near-nameless spots.

Now and then a group of runners would skim by and vanish into mist, and once Marsha had seen a line of karate students punching and blocking their way across the sand, not looking toward her as they moved in unison, each step—right leg, the left, the right—inscribing a crescent on the air. She wondered idly what the name of the move was. A man in a black gi moved swiftly alongside, correcting a stance or the position of an arm. Only he glanced her way and smiled.

The boy came to see her almost every afternoon. Some hours after the karate class had passed, he came and stood before her like a wading bird, one leg up. She kept sewing and didn't look, and he began pivoting, kicking at the air with his raised foot.

"Did you see the teenagers run by? Did you see the yellow belts and the green belts and the brown belts?"

"I don't know what you mean," he said, stopping with his leg still up, the knee bent.

"I thought you must know karate."

"What is *karate*? You mean those people who do this?" He dashed about the sands, kneeing imaginary opponents, striking them with elbow and fist, and ending in the horse stance with a great shout of *Hoah!*

"So you do know karate." She took the fabric she had been working on out of the hoop and tucked the needle with its gold thread into the pincushion. "Bramble, isn't it? I couldn't remember what you wanted to be called."

"Today I would rather be *Eetsch!*" he declared. "But I don't know karate. I just followed them because they were interesting, and I watched when they fought the mist." He came close and leaned against the rock where she was sitting. The faded old tomato caught his attention. Picked up, it sagged against his fingers. "This is so hard and bumpy on top. Soft underneath. But something could grab underneath and tear its guts—"

"What do you mean, *fought the mist*?" Marsha took the cushion from him. It had been her grandmother Josephia's, and she felt a mild attachment to the idea that their hands had touched the same thing, performed the same work.

"They went down by the water, and they did this—" here he flashed about the sand again—"inside a cloud. It was torn to pieces but came back together and won, so they had to go home."

"You have quite an imagination," Marsha observed.

"No," he said, looking puzzled; "I just have eyes that see things."

"So some people have eyes that don't see?"

He didn't appear to think this question worth the answering. Perhaps it was too obvious; perhaps he thought it merely rhetorical.

"The black man asked me to come with them. He chased me, but he couldn't catch me."

"The black man? Do you mean the devil? Oh, I know—the black belt. I thought he looked friendly. What did he say to you?" Marsha tugged at the sampler, straightening the cloth. It had puckered around a large urn from which fantastic flowers sprouted.

"He wanted me for himself. To do his magic. He said I took to it like nobody's business. What did he mean by that?"

She looked at the lithe frame and the feet that seemed never to be still but danced and pattered on the sand.

"He meant that you could be good at karate, that you looked like a natural — somebody who can do it easily by imitation. At least, that's what I suppose he meant. What did you tell him?"

The boy jumped in the air and sank into the horse stance, rocking and grinning at her. "I said *Hoah!* in the deepest voice in the world, deeper than his, so deep that it scared some of the hairs out of his head. Then I shouted *Yah! Yah! Yah!* and *Catch me!* He raced after me, but I lost him in the stones. They were all running after me," he said with satisfaction, "but nobody could catch me. I looked out at them and laughed."

"How? Did you hide?"

"I swam into a rock pool and stirred up the sand so they couldn't see, and I hid in a crack." The silk of his hair swung, as if nodding in agreement with the words.

Marsha wondered if any of his tale was true. Just then he gave a snap punch and another, and began scuttling about comically, still crouched in horse stance.

"Well, you are limber and quick. I don't doubt that he would have wanted to teach you. But you shouldn't hide in the water like that. What if you drowned?"

"You're not calling me *Eetsch*, you know. You should call me *Eetsch*. I'd never drown. I can swim better than you. Better than any of those punch-punch boys. If they had come close, I could've jumped into the sea and swum away from them all, till they gave up and drowned." He put out his chest like a body builder, grinning at her.

"What a little Puck you are," she said, rather charmed by his boastfulness.

"What's that?" He frowned, wrinkling the smooth area between the two gold bows of his eyebrows. Martha felt like touching them, they were so fine and glistening.

"A sort of sprite. A fairy."

"You mean with wings? Oh, I like them."

"Do you know any?" She laughed in sheer pleasure.

"Well, I've *seen* them. You'd have to talk to my brother about those. He knows them — he's met them far out in the ocean, riding on a whale's back."

"Birds, I suppose," she said softly. "So today you are *Eetsch*, and he's your brother again."

"Yes. But I'm really always the same, and he's really all the same." He reached for the pincushion, catching his fingernails on the steel heads.

"Careful with that—"

"And he still loves you. He'll always love you."

"Why?"

"Why love you? I think maybe it's your hair." He crept close and combed his fingers through its ripples. "Looks like gold."

"That's a silly reason."

"Why? Maybe it's not that. You have sea eyes." The boy peered into her face, coming so close that she drew back. "And you sit on the rocks and sew. He likes the songs that you sing . . ."

"Well, he shouldn't. I'm married, and I love my husband, and we'll live a long and happy life together. If all goes well," she added, crossing herself. It seemed bad luck to have said it outloud.

Eetsch's nimble fingers were working with the pins, making a pattern of jags and triangles out of the colored ones, with the steel heads outlining them.

"What's that?"

"A rune, a rune," he caroled.

"What for? How do you know about runes?"

"I don't think there's a word for it." He paused, staring at his handiwork, before squatting to start another shape.

Idly leaning with chin on hand, elbow to knee, she watched him turn the pin-cushion, stabbing the cloth surely and swiftly.

"You're a strange little boy," she said.

This made him laugh. Already the cushion looked like some beaded monstrosity from the Victorians, though perhaps it was too geometrical for that—more like a native product from the Cherokee in the mountains where she had lived until she met Jim.

"It's not like a voodoo doll or something like that, is it? You're not trying to do me some harm? Or what about Jim? Maybe your brother would like Jim to go away?" She slipped down beside him on the sand, in the shadow of the boulder.

Although she had been teasing, he took the question quite seriously.

"No, it's joyful. I just don't know how to say it. You keep the pins the way they are, and everything will turn out all right in the end. The way it should." He didn't look at her; his fingers were too busy. "You see?"

Marsha touched the top of his head; the sunny hair felt hot against her palm. For an instant, he froze. Then he relaxed and went on with his patterns.

"So he wouldn't hurt Jim," she murmured.

"No; why do that if you love him? Besides, he likes Jim." He inspected the pin-cushion as it caught the blaze of afternoon and seemed to ignite in his hands.

"Likes Jim? Have they ever met?"

"No, of course not. But my brother watches out for me, and he sees Jim, too. He helps him with his—his works."

"His works?"

"Yes, my brother puts the pebbles and the big ones, the cobbles, in his path so he can't help but find them. It's a game. He hunts for lovely ones under the water."

"You mean agates and jasper?"

"Yesterday he put out pink agates, and the day before it was blue ones, the kind that you don't see so often. He said that Jim was very pleased."

Marsha gave a little twitch of unrest. It was true; she remembered that he had found blue agates two days back, and he had left pink ones on her pillow only the afternoon before. The coincidence of the thing was queer.

"Did you talk to Jim? How did you know?"

"I told you. My brother told me. I don't talk to Jim. Like I don't talk to the black man."

"Jim wouldn't chase you. He's seen you in the distance."

"I know. I let him see me. Here." He held out the tomato, wrapped in runes. *If they were runes*, Marsha thought, *and not just his play.*

"And what shall I use when I need pins?"

"Oh, there's some left over. I put them on the bottom." So he had, but he couldn't resist the flourish of putting the silver pins into the shape of a star.

Eetsch leaned close to her and made a clicking sound with his tongue.

"What's that for?"

"It's my kiss. I invented it."

Once again she was struck by his smile, which seemed a thing of great purity and sweetness, and on impulse she put her arm around him and pressed him close. Perhaps children were a good idea, she reflected, if they were as bright and nice as this one.

He wriggled out of her grasp and jumped to his feet, laughing at her and showing the sharp little chips of canines—baby teeth, still unshed.

"Should I thank your brother, I wonder?"

The boy shrugged. "It doesn't matter. He did it because of love. Your Jim, what kind of stones does he like best?"

Marsha stared at him, feeling certain that this was a very odd sort of conversation. He drew her gaze and kept it. She would miss him, and the aesthete in her would miss looking at him. Though not conventionally beautiful, the dark eyes and fair hair and the slender, almost sharp features gave her a good deal of satisfaction—the sort of pleasure she might have gotten out of examining a valuable and fascinating sampler, say.

"He likes all the jaspers and agates. But he hasn't found any sagenite, the type with the threads shot through the stone, and I know he would like a good enhydrite. Do you know what that is? The kind with water trapped inside?"

"Sure, I know."

His eyes were no longer on her but on the waves.

"You should go up to your house," he said. "The sea's turning."

At once he sprang away, his shirt ruffling in the wind, and raced into the water. Marsha stood, calling, and witnessed the boy throwing himself into the ocean, under the shadowy lee of a massive rock. Then he was gone, though she raced after him and searched until the tide was waist deep and pouring toward land.

"Marsha!" There was Jim on the cliff steps, with her basket in his hand. "Over here—it's coming in fast."

She knew it was too dangerous to stay. Spars and timbers near the rock pools were floating on the low water. The owners of the house had warned against swimming anywhere but the public beach down the road because a log, riding on a glaze of water, had sometimes killed. Even grown men had been struck and crushed. It wasn't like the beach at Kill Devil Hills where her parents had rented a cottage each summer, where the flags had told them what to watch for—the fluttering red cloth marking rip tides and strong currents.

"This way!" He pointed to a narrow defile between stones where the water was rushing and foaming, and she splashed up from the sea, casting a glance over her shoulder now and then but seeing nothing.

To her relief, the next afternoon the boy was back with a shirtful of sagenites "from my brother," lovely clear and golden stones shot through with needles of air. Marsha and Startle—he had named himself *Startle* for the day—left one on each step of the twisting staircase up to the house, and Jim had been well surprised.

"He'll be stunned," she had told the boy. "Happy."

The newlyweds made love on the boss's king-size bed with the stones all around them on the sheets and pillows. Jim had set them on her naked body and, when she closed her eyes, balanced two ovals on her eyelids.

"I feel like a queen laid out in a Neolithic barrow."

"I'll be a greedy cave man, sacking and pillaging the dead and coming home with treasure."

She arched against him, feeling the stones slide from her skin. The sagenites struck one another with a noise like the clicking of dice.

"My lady of the agates," Jim whispered, reaching for her. He looked exposed and vulnerable without his glasses, like a sea creature out of its shell. His skin was pale, his eyes dark.

The sagenites slipped, momentarily sticking to one and then the other as he pressed against her. When the tide of their lovemaking had broken on the stones and begun to ebb, the smooth shapes lay against her torso, outlining the curve of her side, her waist, the flare of her hip.

"My beauty." Jim took others and outlined her nakedness, then curled beside her with his arm across her breasts and his face nestled in the curve of her neck. She smiled at the strangeness of his fancy and at his delight in the polished forms, which was different but no less than his eagerness for her breasts and thighs. Wasn't it like a boy to pick up stones or sticks?

"Like a man's genitals," she whispered, drawing her hand along the ridgeline of his spine. Was he asleep now, a cobble clasped in one hand like a toy in the hand of a child? "Nothing but a stick and two stones."

As she drifted after him toward sleep, she thought for the first time of how the brother—if there was a brother—had collected the air-needled stones and held them in his hands, so that, if he existed, he had in some sense touched her intimately; or, at least he had reached from one moment in time to another as surely as grandmother Josephia with her much-handled pincushion.

Jim was swimming; she could just detect him, far out, where they had seen the black and white orcas turning leisurely in the sun. Then she glimpsed something in the circle of rocks that the owners had said was named *the devil's porridge bowl* because its contents churned to white at high tide, and she was frightened and called for him to come back, though of course he couldn't hear.

"It was someone—I saw an arm reaching out of the water. But nobody ever surfaced."

She had stayed at the edge of the waves until Jim swam to shore and rose, dripping, from the shallows.

"You saw something. Probably just a trick of the light."

"No, I'm sure. It was a man's arm, and there was something odd . . . bluish, maybe, I'm not sure."

Jim was scrubbing himself with the towel she had brought, his skin becoming rosier by the instant. She hadn't been able to make him understand how afraid she had felt, seeing the arm and hand, knowing that he was out of reach. Perhaps she wasn't even clear on its importance—that instant of seeing the hand.

"Well, if it were a man, he'd probably be blue with cold. It's chilly out there."

"If it *was*," she corrected. *Because it was, it really was*, she thought. "You're not taking me seriously." She dug her bare toes through the sand grains, dredging crystal from below the surface.

"What am I supposed to do? You tell me that you saw an arm in the ocean, and I'm supposed to do something? We could call the Coast Guard, but they'd think we were crazy."

His hair stood up in spikes, and Marsha reached to flatten it with her hand.

"No, not that. You look like a pincushion." She remembered the boy, holding the tomato in his hand. "A sea urchin."

"An urchin that needs a long hot shower," he said. "Brr, I'm going in. You could come along, you know."

"All right. I'll be there in a minute." She had caught sight of a white shirt, fluttering from behind a boulder.

When Jim had climbed halfway up the stairs, the boy came running out to see her. He had a slender spear in one hand, tipped with an arrowhead; he wore a look that she had seen before on his face: excitement, tamped down. Marsha realized that she would miss him when she went away, and that she no longer worried about his parents or where his house might be. He seemed to be well able to take care of himself, and to think that everything that called to his attention was interesting. She liked that about him.

"I saw an arm. In the devil's porridge bowl." She nodded toward the low, jagged walls of the cauldron.

The boy pursed his lips. Perhaps he was busy thinking, perhaps listening. His profile seemed to rest against the light, as if leaning on it for support.

"Where? I mean, exactly."

"You see where there's a jag? Where the rock goes up and there's a curve, with a sort of hole?"

He unbuttoned the shirt, tucking it into a crevice in an upright stone. Then he was naked, all but a necklace she had noticed before—pierced with a hole and ringed by runic shapes—and the long fringe of seaweed hanging from his waist. Skipping into the waves, he quickly waded out, and in an instant he was standing inside the walls of the devil's bowl and reaching up to feel inside the opening she had seen. He waved at her; he was clutching something as he leaped from the cauldron. At other times the hemmed-in surf foamed and was wild, but now the water sloshed gently against the sides.

"From my brother." He put the cobble into her hands. It was a large sagenite, pierced by many shafts.

"It's lovely." She wasn't looking at the stone which was, indeed, remarkable, with traces of blue like clouds, so that its whole aspect bore the air of a picture in a bottle—a cloudy scene with sunlit rain coming down. Instead, she was staring at the spot where she had seen the arm.

"Here." He held up the pendant around his neck, and she grasped the stone's edge, unsure what he wanted of her.

But before he could say another word, she caught a glimpse of something, right through the opening in the center. She made out a man's face rising from the sea. She blinked once, found the head again; then a third time she saw him, looking straight toward them, but when she drew away and stared, she detected nothing, nothing at all. The boy's features were impassive, and he let the necklace fall back to its place. Hardly enough time had elapsed to register the features in memory, but she thought that there was a resemblance and felt—how? The waves could play tricks on a person, she told herself: no reason to be anxious or afraid. And hadn't Jim been swimming out that far, half an hour ago? Perhaps it was a snorkeler who had been floating on the waves and was only occasionally seen.

"What do you call yourself today?"

"I call me King-of-Fishes." He smiled as he stared at the Pacific, peaceful now and dark blue, sparkling in the sun. "That means I'm in charge of all the fishes. But my brother is king over the sea and even the deep gulfs and the creatures of old fire, so he is better than me. Though I am quite good enough," he said proudly.

"And what did you show me just now?" She wasn't sure that he had done so; she wasn't positive of anything except that Jim would be waiting for her at the top of the cliff, and that he would forgive her for not coming to him in the shower when he saw the big sagenite that the boy had put in her hands.

"Did you see something." He spoke softly, walking away from her.

"What is that device around your neck?" She followed, touching him briefly on the hair, where a dazzle of sun rested like a crown.

"Oh that. That's my toy. It's a thing that binds me and heals me and brings me back when I go away. It's my blessing."

He fingered and gave the cord a tug, checking to see if it held secure; his hand reached for the knot at his nape. Afterward he gave the stone a swipe, as if to polish it.

"Sometimes you don't sound a bit like a boy, you little King-of-Fishes."

"But what does that matter? Even when you're an old, old woman, you won't feel any older inside. You won't feel any older than you do today, except for the weight on your breast." He tapped the pendant. "Not this. The dead, I mean, and the things that didn't happen. And mistakes you made."

"Now I know you're not a boy. You're a wise weird thing that's thousands of years old." She drew away from him, teasing him and turning to look back at the ocean and scan the waves for something—a little interruption that was neither whale nor bird nor buoy.

"No, I'm just me. King-of-Fishes." He took her by the hand, and his fingers were cold and a little tacky, as if he had been playing in brine and mud. "Remember what I said at the start. Some are just born knowing. It's easier that way."

At the start of what, she wondered.

"I'll be going home soon." It was surprising how sad saying the words made her feel.

King-of-Fishes leaned against her, his arms chilly against hers, and he made his clicking noise that meant a kiss, and she clicked back at him, pressing her cheek against his. She marveled at how she had become so fond of this boy, when she'd never met his parents and knew almost none of the usual things about him—where he lived or went to school, his favorite movies and games and books. They looked at the water together, and far out a whale breached and showed a flash of black and white, tidy as a domino. *An orca.*

"You'll come back," the boy told her, his voice dreamy. "I promise."

Then he jerked his head up, as if in response to a shrill note—someone close by had whistled.

"Wait, I've got a present for you—"

He darted away between stones, the seaweed flying, and Marsha kept still, her gaze traveling slowly across the surface of the sea but finding nothing to arrest its motion. In only a few minutes he was back again, flushed and smiling.

"This is for him—"

He handed her an enhydrite, cobble-sized. She exclaimed in surprise, holding it up to see the water trapped inside. It had been erratically worn and was smoother on one side than the other.

"My brother told me to give it to your man. Said that he shouldn't go home without one. But I've forgotten his name—"

"Jim. His name is Jim."

"It's hard to remember when the names never change. It's so dull. Don't you ever want to be something besides a *Marsha?*"

"You liked my name because it sounded like marsh, and you like the wet places."

"Yes, but sometimes you could be *Bog* or *Pool.*" He was serious, pressing against her, tilting his head. Its silk clung to her arm.

"A *Puddle*."

"*Rivulet* is nice. I like the sound of it. Or you could be Queen of the Ocean. You *ought* to be Queen of something."

He was absently rubbing the stone that hung from his neck, and when he looked up at her, she thought that his nervous, delicate features were beautiful. Yet she didn't remember finding him so at first. The idea occurred to her that she could take the boy home and adopt him. But it was too soon; she had known Jim for such a short time.

"Maybe Queen of the Sea Slugs."

"Yes."

She was amused to see that his face was serious. He was turning a small bundle in his hands and hardly seemed to notice her words.

"Would you like to live where I do, in a city?"

He pulled away from her, shaking his head.

"I would be crazy," he said; "I would be like that man who fought the sea. *Hoah!*" He scampered toward the waves and jumped in, kicking and whirling and slashing with an imaginary sword. She saw the package fall, striking his leg and tumbling into the shallows. He spun around, feeling the loss, and knelt, groping with his hands. She could hear him crying out, "No, no no, no . . ." and then with a great upward leap he shot from the water, punching the air with his fist.

"I almost lost it," he panted; "My brother would have been very angry. I would have been angry too."

The package was bunched in his hand, its gold cloth poking out in puckers between his fingers.

She knew to wait, that he would show her if he chose. And if she asked and he didn't want to share, King-of-Fishes would be off, the drops flying from his heels.

"It's for you. Open your hands, and I'll give it to you."

She did as he said, seating herself cross-legged on a heap of pebbly crystals and offering her cupped hands. The enhydrite lay before her.

"Now," he told her. "You must keep these for yourself and not give them to the— to Jim. It's very important, because they're meant only for you."

He stared at her. "Well?"

"All right," she agreed. "I won't give them to him or anybody else. I'll keep them for myself, because they're from you, and I'm fond of you and will miss you."

The boy frowned, kicking at the sand.

"It's not exactly from me—that is, my brother gave them to me. For you. And there's one for each of us."

"Your family?"

"That's what you would say, I guess. The ones who are together."

"I suppose that's a family," she told him.

He stood on one foot, thinking. "It's like a school of fish. How they all turn to and fro. We just know the same way—where we are and what's happening and who's going to do something next."

"But you're here with me. You're not with anybody else." She combed her fingers through the fine threads of his hair.

"That's because I'm a boy. The children always have adventures on the beach. That's how it's done. Because they're in between, not a baby and not grown like the sea and the land are when they're together at the shore. Not sea and not earth."

Marsha had entirely forgotten about Jim and the shower. "What stories you tell! I really am going to miss you."

He stamped hard against the sand with his foot, then lifted it up to see the imprint. "You're not holding out your hands anymore."

"Sorry. I forgot."

She cupped them again; obediently she shut her eyes when told to do so. He laid one after another—something smooth and cool—on the shadowlines that separated her fingers. The last he placed on her right palm. Opening her eyes, she looked at the seven enhydrites. In coloring they didn't appear like any she had seen in shops or in Jim's collection, and they were all of similar size and shape, about as long as two of her finger joints. When she held them to the light, they glistened, blue or turquoise with occasional glints of rose and green. No, she had never encountered anything like them.

"Sweet," she said.

He ignored her; perhaps that wasn't enough praise, or perhaps it was just wrong. "This one is me." He pointed with his pinkie finger, indicating the smallest stone. "And this one is my brother." Here he tapped the one that lay on her palm.

"And there are others."

"Of course there are," he said, sounding puzzled that she needed to say so.

"Is one of them your mother?"

"My mother died when I was a baby. I don't remember."

Ah, now we're finding something out, she thought. *So his mother is dead, and maybe the brother acts like a parent. Because his father may be gone or dead as well?*

"If you ever want me and my brother and the rest of us," he said, staring intently and drawing his face so close to hers that his features went out of focus, "you just sow the stones in the ground near the sea."

"You could come and live with us," she suggested, hardly listening, but he gave a jerk of the head in dismissal.

"I would be crazy. I just *told* you, remember? I'd be like that man who tried to kill the sea, remember? And look what happened when I pretended—I lost the stones! I can't live without the sea."

The boy drew back. "You sow them in the earth if you want us. But it has to be by the ocean, or else we'll die. Are you listening to me?" He grasped the thin cloth of her cover-up, gathering it in his hand.

"Yes, but—"

He ran away from her, not even stopping for his shirt, and was lost among the crowd of rocks near the devil's bowl.

"King-of-Fishes," she shouted. "Come back! I'm sorry." But she had to go up the stairs without saying goodbye that afternoon, carrying the cobble and the seven enhydrites, which she wrapped in the strip of gold.

On the last three days she hardly saw him, only spying his figure in the distance. She had finished her projects and now accompanied Jim on his forays in the rocks. Once she saw the boy bounding from steppingstone to steppingstone, and once she saw him perched on the lip of the devil's bowl, staring into the water. Another time she thought that she could make out the shapes of two pale-haired swimmers, far from shore.

Feeling a little disloyal, she had hidden the seven stones in a jewelry case. Jim had been pleased with the enhydrite and wanted to find another. Once when he was asleep she carried the box to the window and scrutinized them closely, noticing lines like the shapes on Josephia's pincushion incised on the surface. A flake of something bright inside the largest one caught her eye. When she held that one up, she detected a thin shard suspended inside the stone's pocket of liquid. It glinted, fluttering in the water like a leaf falling through air.

When Jim was loading the car, she hurried to the beach, hoping to see the boy once more. She looked for him near the stairs and in the hollowed-out boulder where she had once found him sleeping. He must have been watching, but he let her search and call his names and didn't answer until she wandered into the grove of upright stones. He laughed, jumping up to rush at her and throw his arms around her waist.

"Who are you this time?" She leaned and pressed her cheek against his hair.

"I am *Sad*," he told her. "I am sad."

Back in the apartment in the city, the whole episode seemed far away. She put the case on the wardrobe with some other jewelry boxes, and immediately she forgot. The image of the boy in his seaweed skirt and a spear in his hand, the face she had glimpsed as through a keyhole, the hand in the devil's bowl: they appeared like nothing but dreams.

Even her life with her husband became illusory, beginning with the third day of their return. On that date, a truck failed to stop at an intersection and plowed into the driver's side door of her car. His car in the shop for an overdue inspection, Jim had borrowed hers. He was killed only a few blocks from the apartment. Just like that. Simple. *Dead on arrival.* Her car totaled. The death seemed like something that hadn't happened, it came so quickly. Its very abruptness seemed to mitigate against tragedy and to suggest an unreality. Only at the funeral did the loss begin to sink in, though she had an intense desire to get up from the pew and leave the church, to abandon this—this *undertaking*, which was nothing she had ever wanted. His body was cremated, and the ashes placed in a metal tube with a stopper. The cylinder possessed the heft of a costly kaleidoscope, and its sound was a mix of rattles and shifting sands. But there had been nothing to see, neither light nor color: only dark. She hid the blind thing inside a lidded vase.

Strange how Jim's exit from time seemed to distort time. The evenings were long and cavernous and held a multitude of thoughts. Grief seeped in little by little. She bought a television—a device she had always disliked—and let it eat the hours. Marsha sat on the floor in front of the screen, rocking back and forth as she cried, the volume turned up so that no one in the nearby apartments would know.

"I met you three months before we married, and we were at the coast for three weeks, and then we returned and you died on the third day." She gave the vase a shake, as if she could get his attention. "So there were just three months, three weeks, and three days."

At the beginning of her period, she slumped in front of the television with the urn in her arms, crying without making any attempt to stint her tears. She was weeping for their children, who were not and would never come to be, and she was mourning for the body that wanted a baby when it was too late. The image of an enhydrite with a flake of mineral trapped inside came to her mind.

The loss might have been easier if she had not been an only child, born to a mother almost fifty and a father of sixty. Both her parents were now dead. And it might have been better if she had moved to the Carolinas again, but she couldn't make herself do so. She couldn't bear the idea of explaining to everyone she knew what had happened, and hearing how, yes, it was tragic and terrible but that time would heal. For that matter, she didn't want to pack up or get rid of Jim's clothes and the objects in his study. She wore his shirts and bathrobe; a faint fragrance of him lingered in their closet.

Jim's boss always brought her flowers on the seventh day of the month. The two had been best friends since boyhood, and they had gone to Cal Tech together. When small, the pair of them had been called *JimJase*, they were so close. Jason suggested that she go back to the house by the beach of agates and jasper to sprinkle her husband's ashes on the waves. She thanked him but said that she was not ready.

At night she lay in bed, aching for Jim to reach for her or to curl at her back, his breath warm on her neck. Sterile limb, the hand that gripped the tissue was useless, merely her own. No other touch would arrive in the dark, secret and surprising. She often dreamed of seeing him at the shore. He would be wading at the edge of the ocean, picking up jasper and agates, his head down as he examined his finds. She saw that they were nothing like the stones of day; they glowed, and burning needles pierced the sagenites. He would turn but not see her, and the weight of the cobbles looked heavy in his hands. When she pursued him through a labyrinth of upright stones, he only receded into the background until she could not tell him apart from the gray, bent rocks.

She would awake, tears on her face and a terrible pain in her chest, and she would turn on the lamp and stare at the dark windows and at the pale arc lamps in the street.

In time, she had to set his pictures around the house because she began losing his face. She matched the exact shade of his shaggy hair to a hank of Theolian's *bloodroot* floss. His eyes were less easy, and she settled on *wood umber*. Studying his images, she found him slippery and hard to keep. The fashionably ugly glasses got in the way. She wanted to see the exact shape of the line moving from brow to orbit to cheekbone, but it remained elusive. After all, they had had only the three months, three weeks, and three days. *In time*. *After all*. She hated the words; sometimes she thought that she hated language. When she no longer needed it at night, she donated the television to the nearest Goodwill store. A dullness set in, and she found herself still uninterested in needlework projects, though she forced herself to continue.

The worst was when spring came and brought fresh forgetting. Shouldn't April have brought a renewal of desire? But it was impossible to remember a man every minute, every hour. She sat under the fruit trees, sewing a new sampler. The original had been purchased by a private collector, who let her study and measure and take notes in return for a document—accurate description and an assessment of value. The naked man and naked woman were crude but charming. The faded apples on the tree had turned to salmon, as had many of the birds. Petals drifted onto the cloth, and she brushed them away. When she tucked the linen into the basket, her hand grazed the pinheads on Josephia's cushion. Drawing it from the bottom of the basket, she felt surprised all over again by the designs made by the colored and silver pins. She had forgotten—it had been so long since she had needed more than a hoop and a paper of needles.

That night she called Jason and his wife, thanking them for the latest delivery of flowers, left on the mat outside her apartment door. They urged her to use the house again if it wouldn't make her unhappy to be there. Perhaps it would be a help, a resolution, an ending: a something. She would think about it, said that she was not "getting over" Jim but that she seemed to be putting his memory at a little distance, as if their days together had been collected and given a museum space down the hall. That evening she went into his study for the first time in months. Cobbles and pebbles were spread across the library table, dusted with silt. A magnifying glass lay on the blotter of his desk. She took it in her hand, feeling for his grip around the handle. A memory of rolling across sheets littered with sagenites drifted into her mind, and she tried to fix the moment so that it would grow. But the images slid into the shadows and would not stay.

Copies of Jason's sketches for a new game lay scattered in loose sheaves on bookshelves. She inspected one, noticing for the first time that the hero bore a vague resemblance to her husband.

Then, remembering the seven stones, she went to her bedroom and scoured the dresser and chest and wardrobe but found nothing. Only when she looked under and behind the furniture did she find the jewelry case, wedged between the wall and the paneled back of the wardrobe. Unknotting the bundle of gold cloth, she strewed the contents across a pool of lamplight. The fingerlings of stone were lovely. She had forgotten how unusual the color was, almost turquoise in places, with blues and flecks of other colors. Again Marsha felt sure that she had seen nothing like them in Jim's books. The runes were scratched onto the surface and might have been made yesterday, they looked so fresh. Rocks were among the eldest things, but they remained mysteriously youthful. A thousand years from now someone might hold an enhydrous agate in her hand and wonder who had incised it, who had held it, what had become of them—and was the treasure lost only last year or a hundred or more?

They might as well have been elf bolts, flung at her, because they woke a sleeping curiosity and desire. How had she forgotten the boy for so long? She remembered his sharp-cut nose and the darkness of his eyes. How comical he was, wearing a seaweed kilt and a too-big oxford shirt, probably left behind by a tourist. She had seen him bathing naked, diving off the outermost rocks of the devil's bowl. Never had she spied him in mundane dress or looking like an ordinary child in company with his playmates or parents. Once recalled to mind, he became the focus of her thoughts, and she felt eager to see him.

She and Jim's mother, along with Jason and his wife, met at the beach house in June, and they waded out to an island of rock and each tossed a handful of the grit and ash from the cylinder onto the water. Afterward the others lingered for an hour to collect stones, because that seemed right. Roaming along the spits of rock and over black bands of sand and heaps of clear crystal, Marsha had a pleasant sensation that the boy was close by, but after the others departed the feeling drained away. It must have been seeing them at a distance, bending to examine a pebble or toss one into a bag, that made her feel that the day had become familiar—like those lost days when she could spy her husband hunting for treasure, beyond the next pile of shillets or the next curve of the beach.

Although she called for him and looked, she saw no evidence of the child except for his homemade spear, wedged in a crack in the rocks. The shaft was broken, but the stone was still good, bound to its stake with a strip of dried grass.

She felt disappointed and a little worried. He had always been so quick to appear!

When it was time to turn out the lights, she felt afraid and left a lamp burning. She didn't know why or what she feared. The bare-faced moon shone through the glass wall overlooking the sea and lit her empty bed. The evening made so many homely or pleasant figures wear a different aspect. If she were to spy her husband by starlight: what horror. Even seeing the boy tapping on the glass—impossible, as the house jutted from the cliff—would scare her, she felt sure. And if she walked down to the beach at night and saw a pale arm in the surf, or two faces, she would be too trembly and weak to climb the stairs.

———

"You said that I'd come back," she told the handful of enhydrites, "but you didn't say that you wouldn't be here."

Seated close to the edge of the cliff, she surveyed the coast and sea, the pale sands and the black sands, the forest of upright stones, and the devil's bowl. For three days she had searched for the boy, even going so far as to ask at a another house whether they had seen such a figure, dressed in seaweed. Nothing. A heavy silver spoon lay in her lap next to the smooth finger joints of stone. After a while she got up and dug into the soil, prying up low windblown plants she didn't recognize; their roots held crystal, clear or amber, with here and there a jot of red or green jasper. The narrow trench, a few inches long, looked like a model of the grave of some ancient king, heaped with precious jewels. She laid the largest enhydrite in the pit and pressed the plant roots and sand into place. Immediately she felt the impulse to dig it up again but did not. Levering up another clod of sand and roots, she slipped the smallest stone under it. She remembered the year that she had planted tulips upside down and wondered whether there was a right way and wrong way to do this. How close together? She settled on two feet apart—about the width she had used when planting perennials.

"I must be mad to do it," she murmured, patting the last piece of turf.

Looking around, she saw that the soil looked undisturbed, as if she had done nothing, and wished that she had marked the sites. It would be hard to dig up the stones again. Perhaps she would never find them all. But what did it matter? She didn't believe anything would happen—and if not, why were they important? No, it was fine, whether she found them again or not.

The next day she stayed indoors, only once venturing to the beach to watch a rainstorm pelt the standing stones until they were black and glossy. Then she returned to the house and took a shower, the hot water sluicing her back until she was relaxed and sleepy.

She thought of reading a book, but words had lost the meaning for her that they once had held. What was the use of a story? She had been *in* a story of happily-ever-after; then she had fallen out of it, as if the writer had excised her with a flood of ink.

The next day she saw a morning rainbow, and she took the fading vision as a lucky sign. Wind blew away the clouds and rubbed the ocean against its nap, tossing foam. Going to the cliff's edge, she saw that the ground was still saturated, so wet that water had collected in a shallow depression. Although on waking she had decided to dig up the stones, not wanting to lose them, she now planned to wait a day until the ground had dried. That afternoon she walked for miles up the coast, stopping to visit pools of stars and anemones. She came across the black belt, watching his class perform calisthenics, and she paused to examine the faces of the younger boys.

"Excuse me, do you remember—"

He swung around, a wiry, slightly bowlegged man with his hair in a ponytail.

"Do you remember a boy with seaweed—around his waist, I mean—he was very quick and light. He followed you one day and imitated your class."

The man gave a lopsided grin, shaking his head.

"I tried two or three times to catch that one! He used to tease us, but I thought he would have been champion material, with a little training."

"Have you seen him? Recently, I mean."

The class was doing push-ups now, while the surf frolicked to and fro, undermining their grip on land.

"No. I don't think I've seen him since last fall. You know him?"

"He used to come and play and talk to me, when my husband was out of sight. I just hoped nothing had happened to him."

The instructor turned back to his class, perhaps disappointed to hear about her husband. "If you find him, tell him to join my group and be a winner. There's a real spark to that one."

"Perhaps he was afraid of you. He called you *the black man*."

Amused, his eyes flicked to her face.

"Like the devil, you mean? I've got a reputation as a taskmaster, but that's quite a distinction." His hand went to his throat, and she noticed a small Celtic cross and chain between his fingers. "*The black man*. What was the kid's name, anyway?"

"He never had the same one twice. I don't think he ever told me a real name, or certainly not an ordinary one."

"I wouldn't worry about him. He had the look of a kid who can take care of himself. Say, about that husband of yours . . . Are you happy with him?"

This seemed a difficult question, and Marsha puzzled it over in her mind for a second longer than confidence warranted. The ramifications of it seemed more and larger than she would have guessed. Was she content now, with what was left of him—that is, memories of three months, three weeks, three days? Was she capable of living with the Jim that was absence and being at ease, perhaps not now but later? Was he in any way still hers, or still a husband, though separated from her by time? She wondered whether she seemed bereft and abandoned, to make this stranger ask such a question.

"Whenever I have been with Jim," she said at last, "I have been happy." That much she was sure of. The answer was no doubt clouded, but she felt it was the best she could do.

"I guess that's—somehow I thought he might have run off—well, you know where to find me," he said cheerily, jogging away from her and calling for the class to follow.

When she returned to the stairs in the late afternoon, she noticed that the cliff face was marked with long tearstains. Drops plummeted from the lip, and, as she cocked her head to look, one splashed onto her forehead. Checking the top, she noticed that the pool had not shrunk but rather had grown larger. The vegetation was soaked and a brilliant green. Moisture seeped, collecting in rivulets that inched toward the brink.

She supposed that it had rained more than she knew. Inside the house, she curled by the big window overlooking the ocean and stared out. She was hungry but didn't feel like eating. It was restful by the cool glass, with the waves wrinkling the sea's surface and the shadows of the rocks growing long. She took a sampler from the basket but pulled the needle through the fabric only once before letting it drop. The long walk in the sea air had tired her. Like a gradual tide, the night edged in, blurring the line between wakefulness and sleep. In the morning she woke on the floor with her head pillowed on her arm.

Stumbling to the pantry, she took out a sack of coffee. From the kitchen window she could see the moon to the southeast, hanging over North America in a tissue of clouds. As if by magic, the veil turned red, and the crescent glowed a pale, bright sage. She stared, drinking her coffee, until dawn yielded to the daylight. Only then did she rummage in the freezer and find some waffles, eating them fresh out of the toaster with neither butter nor syrup. Without Jim, she no longer had an interest in cooking, so it didn't matter. Nothing inside the house really held her notice; all she wanted was to go outside and wade in the surf and climb the rocks until she became weary.

Barefoot, she stood on the stone doorstep—blue and shaped like a child's drawing of a cloud—and listened to a pattering. The sound, so pleasurable and erratic in its notes, startled her. When she went to look, Marsha found that the water could no longer be thought of as a large puddle. Streamers of liquid splattered against the rock face, blown by the breeze. Peering over, she saw that a stain of considerable size had spread over the sand. All day the pool grew, until it was some yards wide and constantly spilling over the edge of the cliff.

"I wonder," she said aloud, but left the thought unfinished. Although cautious, she ventured close and finally stepped into the shallow circle. The water felt as cold as a mountain spring. "Maybe a coincidence. Could you be coincidence?" she muttered, bending low and combing her hand through the low coastal plants to see if anything had surfaced from the ground. Nothing: nor were there cracks or perforations of any kind. "If you're not a coincidence, what then? Should I feel worried, alarmed? I've done something—what?"

By nightfall, a miasma tinged faintly blue hung over the pool, which was deeper and faster-flowing than before. When she picked her way through its current, Marsha felt streams of bubbles flying against her ankles. Kneeling and then crawling on the drowned plants, she felt her way across the cliff-top.

"Seven. There are seven. Like sand creatures buried by a wave and sending up bubbles." Her voice was muted by the fog that swirled slowly around her. When she moved away, it seemed to settle in columns above the water.

And still she was not afraid. She had no desire to drive off in Jim's little blue sports car with his prescription sunglasses still stuck in the pocket of the visor. Only when the moon rose and the stars came out did she begin to feel uneasy, alone under the zodiac with no one to see or to care what happened to her. Her old friends were three thousand miles away, and only Jason and his wife and perhaps some of Jim's other colleagues knew that she was staying in the beach house—those plus her mother-in-law, who hadn't cared for the daughter so abruptly foisted on her. She didn't go inside, all the same, even when the mist over the pool thickened with dew and streams rushed from the ground and became a torrent, wallowing and then eddying at the base of the cliff until a finger of liquid trickled across the sand and vanished between stones, heading toward the sea. In less than an hour, the waterfall had made a rutted course and now flung itself pell-mell from height to sand to stones, losing itself in the tide. At once, with a *whoosh!* the cliff emptied itself of liquid, the creek twisting in the air like a silver otter with a tail of mist, vanishing between the standing rocks.

Marsha, who had been kneeling on the damp ground, exhilarated by the strangeness and increasing force of the falls, got to feet. Her gaze was on the silvery track, winding across the sand. The water was gone, diving into the sea and hiding itself. The end was as mysterious as the beginning. Going to the site where the pool had formed, she bent and looked closely at the surface in the moonlight. Though the expanse appeared quite undisturbed and felt no more than ordinarily damp to her palm, the seven enhydritic stones were lying close together on top, as if she had never buried them.

She retrieved one after another, tucking them into the pocket of her cover-up, a clingy garment that had been a favorite of Jim's. It recalled the colors of the ocean, an aquamarine with streaks of darker blue and green. The wind tousled her hair and cooled her flushed cheeks. What to do? In the house, she looked at herself in the mirror and turned away, momentarily frightened by the intensity of her own stare—a glittering in the eyes. Out again, she left the door unlocked and slipped slowly down the cliff stairs, her hand on the rail. It wouldn't hurt to go halfway down and see what remained of the waterfall, the stain of its passage glistening by starlight.

The wind toyed with her hair, tickled her skin. The night seemed heartbreakingly lovely, with an edge to its beauty that didn't come from her memory of Jim's loss or from her grief afterward. Just now she seemed to have gone beyond that private sorrow. Motionless in the sky or rocking on the mirror of the sea, the stars drew her thoughts away from self—a mote in the oceans of time and space. Also infinite was the flux of waters that went on forever, wrapping round the globe, and the sadness that was in her like blood and bone seemed for once to be parceled out and shared with the tide and pulse of the sea and the outward-going stars, sailing toward the ever-retreating end of the universe.

A batlike flittering caught at the corner of her vision. She looked toward the upright stones, stabbed onto their flimsy shadows.

"Marsha!"

The boy leaped into a patch of light.

"Come down," he called to her, and she ran down the steps to meet him.

"Thank God! I was afraid you were drowned—"

"Not me! I'm a fish! You remember; I'm a king of the fish. The dolphins love me. They'd never let me drown." He laughed, the pearls of his teeth flashing. Shyly, he put his arm around her waist and smiled up at her.

"You're taller—and where's your seaweed?"

He glanced at the cloth knotted around his waist. The fabric didn't cover much more of him than the seaweed kilt had done, but lacked the impromptu air of his former guise. "I'm older. My brother said that I was too big to dash about the world naked."

"Where have you been?" Marsha touched his cap of hair, silky as ever, and her hand brushed against his jaw. In the moonlight she could see the veins twining blue under his skin.

"Oh, around." He jigged in place, full of the irrepressible joy she remembered.

"I'm glad you came back," she told him.

"Of course. Why wouldn't I? And I knew you wished for me." Here he turned a cartwheel out of sheer excess of spirits. "Besides, my brother wanted to see you again. It's still the same for him as last time. Once we love, we love for keeps."

Marsha watched as he fled through the standing stones, weaving in and out of the light. In a few minutes he returned, skittering across the sands, and took her hand in his own. The fingers had the same slight tackiness that she remembered from before.

"Jim—you know that he died last year, after we went home. Did you know?"

The boy looked at her warily, without smiling. "You know my mother died, didn't you?"

"Yes, you told me. I didn't forget." She wanted to put her arms around him but was shy about it. They felt useless, hanging at her sides.

"Well, that's how I know about your husband. You just told me. I'm sorry, though. He liked the stones. We would have given him better ones this year. My brother said that we should give him some from our—from where we live."

"That would have been nice. He would have liked them." This time she reached for his hand, and he let her take it.

"I wish nobody ever had to die," he said in a low voice. "My mother is the only one that I know who died. And I don't remember her. Why did he?"

"A traffic accident—a truck hit him on the road and killed him."

"I've seen those . . . I knew he hadn't drowned, or the fishes would have told me."

He looked so matter-of-fact in this declaration that she laughed, lacing her fingers with his and letting him tug her across the sand, nearer to the waves that were steadily pouncing closer and closer to shore. She had forgotten how peculiar a little being he was, with his stories about the sea and stones and his ignorance—fancy a child never having held a pincushion! Or perhaps that was twenty-first-century life, with clothes readymade in China and Mexico and Thailand. That must be where all the pin-cushions had gone. She wondered if the boy knew that China existed, and if he would let her teach him the things that he should have learned. She believed he must never have gone to school . . . What she saw after burying the enhydrites was pushed aside now, as if it hadn't occurred at all. The reality of the boy's quick, dancing self overshadowed the past days and made them appear as insubstantial as dreams. Even Jim was merely a shadow, and speaking of him hardly grazed her with sadness.

"You don't believe me! You'll find out—" The boy smiled but not at her, glancing toward the sea.

If she hadn't felt the stones pressing against her hip, she might never have thought of them. But she took out the fingerlings one by one and then spilled the fistful into his hands. He gave another secret smile and tucked them into the waistband of his garment—a short sarong, she thought it might be, if such a thing was worn by boys. The stubby figures were pressed against his skin. No, not figures, she remembered: just stones.

"And I have something for you. Close your eyes." He grasped her hands, pushing them into the shape he wanted. Something hard skimmed her palm, then flopped onto its side.

"Oh—"

It was a cord and pendant, the latter like the one around the boy's neck: that is, transparent, circular, perforated in the center, incised with what he had called runes. Chambers of water were trapped inside, several of them holding minute flakes.

Marsha held the necklace at arm's length, staring at the ocean through the hole. It seemed that she could make out four or five figures in the water, unless they were merely rocks, jutting up from the sea floor. As she moved the stone slowly across her field of vision, she saw something else: the figure of a man, leaning from a jagged perch. She could tell no more from that starlit distance except that he appeared muscular, with fair hair.

"Here, bend down and I'll put it on you."

She didn't give up the pendant for several more moments, staring until she knew that she could learn nothing more.

"Did you see my brother?" He tugged at the string to make sure it was tied well, afterward lifting the pendant to look at the runes.

"I suppose so." She felt a blankness, the sort of bewilderment one feels at the top of a stairs, realizing that the reason for ascending has been left entirely behind. Mar-sha shivered; a breeze had sprung up. She looked back at the steps and the cliff, with its stain that still marked where the waterfall had flung drops against earth. In a few minutes she would go to the house and sleep, and in the morning she would find the boy and ask him to go away with her. She could adopt him; she might even name him after Jim.

The crisp incisions on the hoop of stone pressed their messages against her skin.

"What do these signs mean?"

"It's hard to say. It's like a song. See, here's the sign for *air*, just under the one for *water*. See? *Air* under *water*." He touched each with his fingertip, rubbing lightly.

"This one is a binding or a blessing, see, right next to *heart*. Here's *fish*; here's *woman*. There's healing in it, and reviving, and protection in childbirth. And long life, too."

"That's a lot." She twisted the cord nervously in her fingers. *In the morning. She would go away with the boy in the morning.* "You seem older this year," she said, a little sadly.

"My brother made me learn things. Not just the runes. But I skip off where he can't find me whenever I want. I'm a king too. He can't make me."

"And what do you call yourself? Today, I mean." She remembered the jumble of names, ending in *Sad*. Perhaps he would be happy now.

"Tonight I'm *Merlin*. *Mer*, that's the sea."

"And a merlin is a bird—"

"A falcon who stoops to catch a silver fish!" The boy whirled, his arms lifted into wings and his hands gripping the air like claws.

"Yes, and a wizard who was a seer—"

"I'm a seer too. I see and see and see," he declared, ending with a somersault.

"What do you see? Do you see my future?" She asked but he wouldn't or couldn't tell, so she lifted the pendant to her eye like a monocle. The swimmers bobbing in the waves were gone, but the man was still musing on his rock. Wind lifted his long hair. The skin at his throat and on his chest looked bluish. Maybe that was a trick of the moonlight, though.

"Did I tell you that the black man asked about you? He wanted you to learn karate . . ."

The boy let out a peal of merriment. "He'll never catch me! Not so long as I have legs to run. I would swipe off his head with my sword arm. You hear him talking? *Draw arm, sword arm,* all that, and there's not a blade or scabbard in sight. He's a fool who fights the mist."

Back in the city there would be things that he could learn. Perhaps he could take lessons—he was quick and bright, he would be good in fencing or any of the martial arts. At first he would need a tutor for school.

"I must go inside now," she told him. "But you'll come see me tomorrow, won't you? We can sit and talk all day, and maybe you could come back to the city with me in Jim's car?"

What a rubber face! She suppressed her laugh. He had contracted his brow, squinting at her, and now said only, "traffic accidents," as if that settled the issue.

"Tomorrow, we'll talk about it then," she insisted; "I need to rest."

"But I wanted you to meet my brother," he said. "Look, we're already at the ocean, and he's just right there. Come on." His grasp had a surprising firmness, and she exclaimed as he tugged on her arm.

She stumbled at the edge of the water, going down on one knee. He stopped and waited as she stood up but didn't offer to help.

"A little ways—can't he come here?" She was breathing fast, nervous and—she now admitted it to herself—afraid. A chill flashed over her as she remembered strewing Jim's ashes. His atoms were now the sea's, his death swallowed and spread on the currents.

"What's the matter?" The boy looked at her, frowning.

"I want to go home." She was trembling, not just from the cold. When she lifted the pendant and glanced through it, she saw that the figure had moved from the rock and was chest-high in ocean, moving gently up and down with the rhythm of the waves.

The boy was determined, pulling her in the water, teasing and laughing at her fear, vowing that she would soon see his brother face to face. She had the sensation that they weren't alone, that others were close around them, urging them on, taking her by the hand, pushing against the force of the waves. Along this portion of the coast, the floor dropped away quickly, and soon she felt helpless, riding on the swells, her legs dangling. When she lifted the necklace again, she saw with a shiver that the boy's elder brother was swimming swiftly in their direction. As he came closer, she glimpsed his face, strong-jawed and bold in its contours. In a few more moments, he was close beside her, so that she could only catch glimpses of him through the lens of the stone. These quick angular snapshots frightened her more than ever, because something about him was not right—not just the blue and turquoise flush to the skin but the whole muscularity of him, the too-handsome, chiseled face, and the irises of the eyes that were cool but radiant like two pieces of sagenite set in sockets of stone.

The boy was laughing at his own success. Marsha gripped his shoulder, pinching him tight, as the brother drew her toward him. They each had her by a hand, and for an instant she was drawn against the man and felt the muscular hardness of him along the length of her body. She cried out, and water filled up her mouth with its murmuring.

A jogger in a black gi was leaping through the surf. He heard the sharp note of distress and stopped, staring at the sea.

From the shore, all that could be seen was a slight disturbance in the water, over in an instant. The swells became smooth. Waves kept pushing their freight of sand and weed to the shore, reflecting the upraised sickle of the moon and a harvest of starlight.

REGGIE OLIVER

Among the Tombs

Reggie Oliver has been a professional playwright, actor, and theater director since 1975. Besides being a writer of original plays he is a noted translator of the work of Feydeau. His biography of Stella Gibbons, Out of the Woodshed, *was published by Bloomsbury in 1998. His IHG award nominated volume of ghost stories* The Dreams of Cardinal Vittorini *was published in 2003, and his second collection, entitled* The Complete Symphonies of Adolf Hitler, *was published in 2005. He lives in M.R. James country, near Aldeburgh, Suffolk, England with his wife, the artist and actress, Joanna Dunham.*

"Among the Tombs" was originally published in The Complete Symphonies of Adolf Hitler.

—*E.D.*

I don't think the Church of England will ever take kindly to the idea of sainthood," said the archdeacon. "No. It won't do. It's not in our nature." The archdeacon is one of those people who has decided views about absolutely everything, a useful if exhausting quality.

It was the first night of our annual Diocesan Clergy Retreat at St. Catherine's House. Most of the participants had gone to bed early after supper and Compline, but a few of us had accepted Canon Carey's kind offer of a glass of malt whiskey in the library. It was a cold November evening and a fire had been lit. Low lighting, drawn damask curtains, and a room whose walls were lined from floor to ceiling with faded theology and devotion contributed to an intense, subdued atmosphere.

I suppose whenever fellow professionals get together there will tend to be a mood of conspiracy and competition, and clerics are no exception to the rule. Serious topics are proposed so that individuals can demonstrate their prowess and allegiances. The archdeacon, in any case, does not do small talk.

"But there are people in our tradition whom we do revere as saints," said Bob Mercer, the vicar of Stickley.

"Name them!" said the archdeacon belligerently.

"George Herbert, Edward King of Lincoln . . . What about the martyrs Latimer and Ridley? And Tyndale?"

"Yes, yes. But these are figures from the past. Anyway, ask the average man or woman in the pew what they know about Edward King. I mean that we have no living and popular tradition, no equivalent to Mother Teresa or Padre Pio."

"What about Meriel Deane, who started the Philippians?" said Canon Carey.

A young curate who had just crept in confessed he had never heard of Meriel Deane. I would have said so myself had I been less timid about showing my ignorance. Rather condescendingly the archdeacon enlightened us. Meriel Deane, he said, had founded the Philippian Movement to help the rehabilitation of long-term, recidivist prisoners who had just left jail. They could spend their first six months of freedom at a Philippian House, usually in a remote country spot, supervised by one or two wardens. The regime pursued there was at once austere and easygoing. Inmates could come and go as they liked, and had no work to do apart from minor household chores, but there were regular meals and periods of silence and meditation. People were given space to reflect on their lives. The charity was named after the town of Philippi where St. Paul had been imprisoned. The Philippians were still in existence and doing good work though their founder was now dead.

The Archdeacon concluded his lecture by saying, "I met Meriel Deane on several occasions. The woman was nuts. No doubt a good person in her way, but completely off her head, so not in my view a candidate for sanctification."

"Oh, yes, she was rather disturbed at the end, but she wasn't always like that," said a voice none of us recognized.

The speaker was an elderly priest whom I noticed had been placidly silent all through supper. He wore a cassock rather like a soutane, which put him on the Anglo-Catholic wing of the church, an impression which was confirmed when I heard him being addressed as "Father Humphreys." He must have been past retiring age, a small, stooped man with a wrinkled head, like a not very prepossessing walnut; but, as he spoke, his face gradually assumed character, even a certain charm.

"So you knew her, Father?"

"Very well, for a time. One of her first 'Philippian' houses was in my parish, Saxford in Norfolk."

"And she wasn't potty?"

"She was not potty *then*."

"So when and how did she go potty?" asked the curate. The archdeacon was frowning. He obviously felt that repeated use of the word "potty" was lowering the tone.

"Well," said Father Humphreys, who had sensed the archdeacon's unease and seemed amused by it. "That's not the adjective I would use, but something definitely went wrong. As things do. One wonders why but there is no real answer. Not this side of the grave at any rate." The last sentence was spoken faintly, as if he had forgotten the presence of others and was talking to himself.

"Do you know what exactly 'went wrong,' as you put it?" asked Canon Carey.

"No. Not exactly. But I'll tell you what I know if you like. It would be quite a relief. I've never told anyone before, and it might be good to unbosom."

The rest of us began to settle into armchairs and sofas. A bedtime story! What a treat! That word *unbosom* had marked him out in my mind as an unusual and interesting person. And yet—and I don't think this is merely hindsight—I am sure I felt uneasy, even a little fearful about what Father Humphreys was going to reveal. Despite offers of a more comfortable seat he established himself on a low footstool in front of the fire. In that pose, crouched with his knees almost up to his chin, there was something in his appearance which made one think of a little old goblin out of a book of fairy tales. As he spoke he barely looked at us, but addressed most of his story to the pattern on the threadbare rug at his feet.

Was Meriel Deane a saint? She had saintly qualities certainly, but I tend to think that true saints are less self-conscious about their sanctity, and less disposed to remind you of it. Let us just say that in her eccentric way Meriel was on the side of the angels and leave it at that.

I had been the Rector of Saxford for about five years when she came to our village, and I remember clearly the first time I met her. One's first and last images of a person are often the most vivid. With Meriel, it was the same one: the back of her head. Which was appropriate, I suppose, because she was as distinctive in appearance from the back as from the front.

Every morning I would open the church at seven, say prayers and then go to the rectory for breakfast. In those days—I am talking about 1964—we were less careful about keeping the church under lock and key. I don't know whether any of you know St Winifred's, Saxford? Not very special, but some nice Norman corbels in the porch and a painted rood screen which somehow managed to survive both the Reformation and Cromwell's iconoclasts. One of the panels has a rather lively depiction of St. George and the Dragon on it.

I mention that because one morning in March 1964 when I returned to the church after breakfast I found it to be occupied. A woman was kneeling, very upright, in one of the front pews, directly opposite that painting of St. George and the Dragon. She did not move an inch as I entered. She was wearing a coat and skirt of some loosely knit woolen fabric, rather indeterminate in color, but it was her head which attracted my attention. It was small and neatly shaped; her iron gray hair, obviously long, had been coiled up into an elaborate bun on the back of her head. It reminded me of a sleeping snake.

I don't know what you think is the correct etiquette when you find someone praying in your own church. I tend to sit down quietly in a pew and wait for them to finish. I read a prayer book and tried not to look at her too much, but she did rather fascinate me. She was formidably motionless: evidence of a disciplined, perhaps rather rigid, piety.

After about five minutes she got up, turned round and smiled directly at me.

"You must be Father Humphreys, the rector," she said. "I am most frightfully sorry. I should have come to introduce myself before, but we've just moved in to the Old Tannery in the village and chaos has been reigning supreme. This is positively the first instant I've had to myself. I'm Meriel Deane." She came forward and shook me firmly by the hand.

I rather liked her. I suppose she must have been in her late fifties. She had a handsome, apple-cheeked, sexless face and strangely bright eyes. Her body was tall, spare and without shape; she moved in long, determined strides. She seemed completely unselfconscious, oblivious of the effect she was having on people, like a schoolgirl before her first erotic awakening, but not at all gauche or ungainly. Her voice was an upper class intellectual bleat, like a Girton professor, easily parodied and in itself unattractive, but not offensive in her because she spoke without affectation.

I had vaguely heard of Meriel Deane and the Philippians, but she filled me in on her work. The Old Tannery was her third Philippian House, and she was going to stay to run the place herself for at least a year. By the end of our first meeting I had offered to take Compline for them at the Old Tannery on Friday evenings and had given her a spare key to the church so that she could go in any time she liked and, as she put it, "have a little pray."

I was soon a regular visitor at the Old Tannery. It was a pleasant atmosphere. The furnishing was rather Spartan—very few easy chairs, rush mats on the floors—but it was always warm and clean.

You might think that the village would have objected to an invasion by this strange woman and her gang of ex-convicts, but reaction was very muted. The men who stayed with her were all middle-aged to elderly. One would occasionally see them lumbering about the village, usually in small groups of twos and threes, rarely alone. They bought sweets and tobacco at the local post-office-cum-general-store, but otherwise kept themselves to themselves. They did not go into the pub, having been forbidden it by one of Meriel's few house rules. Otherwise, they had little impact on the community.

I do not remember Meriel's men as individuals. In my memory they all seem to merge into a single generalized portrait. They were big people with simple, troubled faces, and plain, monosyllabic names like Bill and John and Pete. Meriel behaved toward them like a kindly schoolmistress in charge of a class of not particularly bright infants, a treatment to which they responded surprisingly well.

"They are Life's Walking Wounded," Meriel used to say to me. There was something about that phrase, or perhaps the way she said it, that I did not particularly like. It was just a little smug, I thought. That was the one aspect of her which I found mildly objectionable. She could appear rather pleased with herself; but then she had good reason to be.

I say that all these Johns and Bills and Petes were indistinguishable in my mind, but there was one very notable exception. This was a man whom I shall call Harry Mason, and he was distinctive in every way.

He arrived in the summer of that first year, round about July when the air was heavy and hot and green with growth. I noticed him at once because he was one of the few men who always walked alone around our village.

He was maybe a fraction younger than the average run of Meriel's inmates, early forties I should say. He was of average height, but thin with spindly arms and legs. He had a very prominent lower jaw and lip, a near deformity which made him look as if he were permanently and joylessly grinning. This Hapsburg trait, combined with a neat mustache and beard, gave him a striking resemblance to the Emperor Charles V, as portrayed by Titian. Had he cultivated the likeness? It is possible, because, unlike the others at the Old Tannery, he was clearly an educated man.

I never knew what he had been "in for"; I never asked and I doubt if Meriel knew herself. She had a habit of acting as if her charges had no past and only the present mattered.

One Friday evening soon after he had arrived, I conducted Compline as usual at the Old Tannery. These occasions were not in any way solemn or pompous. We all gathered in the main room and seated ourselves in a rough circle. There was no kneeling or anything like that. The men would often follow the service with a prayer book in one hand and a mug of tea in the other, sometimes slurping it noisily during the pauses. But nobody minded and there was a good deal of chatter and laughter when it was all over. Compline is in any case the most simple and beautiful of services.

The Gospel reading for that evening was from Mark Chapter 5: the possessed man called Legion who dwelt among the tombs and whose devils Jesus cast out into the Gadarene swine. It had been in the lectionary for that day, but I remember wishing I had taken thought before and chosen a rather less sinister passage. Meriel read it for us in her clear, high bleat, and it was heard in an unusually intense silence. The customary shuffles and sippings of tea for once were banished.

After it was over normality returned. I was pressed to stay for cocoa and a ginger biscuit, and there was general chat of a not very interesting kind. Meriel was trying to recruit some of the men to go with her in a week's time to an organ recital at a neighboring church. There were few takers, and she was being mildly teased about her enthusiasm for such things. While this was going on I had an opportunity to observe Harry Mason, the new resident to whom Meriel had briefly introduced me before the service.

He was standing by the window, apart from the others, looking on but not participating. I saw one of the other men pass him carrying a tray laden with mugs of cocoa. It seemed to me that that the man made studious efforts to keep as far from Mason as he could. When it was Mason's turn to be provided with a cup of cocoa, the man did not hand it to him directly but put it on an adjacent table where Mason could pick it up.

Mason noticed that I had observed his tiny humiliation. He picked up his mug and saluted me with it before drinking. I returned the compliment.

A little later in the evening I was aware of him threading his way across the room toward me. Again I saw how the others drew away from him as he passed and wondered if it was because they knew what his offense had been.

"Evening, Vicar," he said. "Enjoying your cocoa?" There was a touch of mockery in his voice which took me aback. The other men treated me with a respect that bordered on reverence. I tried not to bridle; there was no reason why he should be deferential, so I smiled and nodded.

Mason paused. He appeared to be searching for something to say to me, then a thought came to him. He put his head on one side and said: "That story we read from the gospels about the man in the cemetery and the pigs." His voice was clear and well produced, in the tenor range, with a slight South London twang.

For a moment I did not know what he meant. It was such an odd way of talking about the story of Legion and the Gadarene swine.

"What about it?"

"Well, let me make it clear, I am personally an atheist, so I have a rather different perspective on these things." He paused again, perhaps to study my reaction to his words. "But if you want my opinion," he went on, "I would say that whoever wrote down that story—"

"St. Mark."

"—whoever—had got it all wrong."

"In what way?"

"Well, for a start, everybody seems to have assumed that this man Legion needed to be healed somehow, *wanted* to be healed. But that was their assumption, wasn't it? I mean, suppose he just liked living that way. Among the tombs and that."

"Cutting himself with stones?"

"Yes. All right. Similar to what some holy men do in your church. Don't they call it mortification? That was his choice."

"It's an interesting point of view," I said, turning away from him. I had had enough of this conversation, but Mason hadn't. He moved uncomfortably close to me.

"You know why everyone wanted him dealt with?" he said.

"No. Why?"

"It says why in the story. It says they had chained him up several times, and he always broke the chains. So he had strength. He had power. And he wouldn't fit in. That's why they wanted to get him. They wanted to destroy his power." By this time, though his voice was not raised, there was something nakedly aggressive about his tone. One of the men close by must have become aware of this because he turned round and said:

"Is this man bothering you, Reverend?"

"No. No," I said. "But I really must be going."

Meriel escorted me to the door. When we were out of earshot of the others, she said: "You've been talking to Harry."

"Yes."

"You mustn't let him bother you."

To anyone else I might have said "he doesn't," but you didn't lie to Meriel. I was silent.

"He's a rather more difficult customer than my average, but we'll soon have him 'clothed and in his right mind,' as they say." It was an odd choice of phrase, though it would have seemed even odder if it had not occurred in the gospel reading for that night. I wondered if Meriel was trying to tell me something about Mason which she had guessed at but was not quite prepared to admit openly.

My walk back to the rectory that night was dominated by thoughts of Harry Mason and Meriel. She had exuded confidence in her work, complacency even. I wondered for the first time whether her confidence was well placed.

The following morning I was on my way to the church when I was waylaid by Mason. It was a disconcerting experience because he suddenly emerged from behind a tombstone in the graveyard. I make no claim to psychic gifts, but I have a strong sense of the presence of other people. Like most of us, for example, I usually know when I am being watched. What shocked me about Mason's appearance was that I had no intimation of his presence until he was there. One moment the churchyard was empty—I was sure of it—the next he was about ten feet away from me standing quite still behind a tombstone and looking at me.

"I apologize if I startled you," he said.

I said: "Not at all," or something equally foolish.

He then embarked on a long and rather rambling apology for what he had said the night before. I am not quite sure what he thought he was apologizing for; except that he seemed to feel that I had been shocked by his unorthodox views. As a matter of fact, I had not. One phrase he used I can remember. He said: "I had no intention of offending the sensibilities of a man of the cloth." It struck me as oddly ponderous, pompous even, and besides, I don't know about you, but I have a peculiar aversion to that phrase "a man of the cloth." Whenever it is used I always feel that there is some sort of sneer behind it.

He talked at great length and I found it extremely difficult to disengage myself from him politely. At one point I thought he was going to follow me into the church, but when I opened the church door he backed away. The next minute he was gone.

It seems rather shaming to have to admit it but when I came out of the church again after about an hour, I felt deeply apprehensive—afraid even—that Mason might be waiting for me among the gravestones. Fortunately he wasn't.

From that day onward I was plagued by Mason's attentions. He never called on me in the rectory or the church, but I am sure that he often contrived apparently accidental meetings: in the village; sometimes when I was walking in the fields, but most often among the tombs in the churchyard. Then he would engage me in conversation. I can't really remember what he said; perhaps I have deliberately blocked it from my mind. Details escape me but I do have a clear impression of always coming away from those meetings the worse for the encounter: distracted, uneasy, drained. But it was not that his talk was wild or evil in any obvious way. Do you know that expressive word *witter*? Well, that describes exactly what he did. He wittered at me. He launched on me a barrage of inconsequential chat about nothing in particular, and, what was worse, he constantly invited my reaction to what he said, so I could never switch off.

I once asked him directly why he needed to talk to me so much. I remember his reply distinctly because it was odd, and, for once, concise.

He said: "I talk to you, Vicar, because I'd rather not talk to myself."

When I saw him walking in the village or in the fields I am ashamed to say I would often hide myself so he wouldn't see me. As a result I was occasionally caught out by my parishioners in undignified positions because I felt a curious compulsion to observe his movements unseen. There was something peculiar about him which struck not only me but others as well.

"There goes that Mr. Mason," the villagers would remark, usually with a slight frown, and their eyes would follow him until he disappeared from view. It was as if, one of them observed to me, it was necessary to "keep an eye" on him.

His walk was odd. He moved quickly, taking long strides with his stick legs, his body bent forward, shoulders slightly hunched. It was as if he were hurrying somewhere with a heavy but invisible weight on his back. Occasionally he would take a quick glance to his left or right, but he never seemed to notice his surroundings much, let alone enjoy them.

I felt I needed to speak to Meriel about him, but what was I to say? That he talked too much? That he had a strange walk? Fortunately, I was relieved of this responsibility by Meriel herself, who came to see me at the rectory. We discussed various churchy affairs. She even canvassed my opinion about a religious controversy which was then raging, but I could tell that something else was on her mind. Her usual stillness—a unique blend of rigidity and serenity—was absent. At last she blurted it out.

"I've never done this before, but I'm going to have to ask him to leave." I asked who she meant, but my question was redundant because I knew she would say it was Mason. "He's upsetting the other men," she said.

"In what way?"

"Nothing violent or insulting. He walks into a room and the atmosphere becomes unsettled. You know me, Rector. I don't judge. It's a necessary principle with me: I have to take people as they are. But there is something wicked about poor Harry."

"You think he's wicked?"

"No. No. I didn't say that. I said there was something wicked *about* him."

She then started talking about Tibbles, the ginger tom who kept down the mouse population at the Old Tannery. Apparently Tibbles would rush headlong out of a room whenever Mason entered it, very unaccustomed behavior for this dignified old bruiser. I thought this was fanciful nonsense, but, all the same, I was very relieved to hear that Mason was going. I felt ashamed at my relief, so I tried to enjoy our conversations when he waylaid me. But he didn't go. And so the summer passed.

One other thing happened that summer which may be of no relevance at all. We had a Summer Fete and Flower show. It was in its way rather well run, not by me, you understand, and used to attract people from miles around. They were very welcome, but it was an invasion, and some of the visitors could be less than considerate, particularly where parking was concerned. There were, of course, fields set aside as car parks, but some found it easier to park in the village with little regard for the convenience of the locals. On this occasion some particularly inconsiderate persons had put their car directly across the little drive which went up one side of the Old Tannery, and it so happened that Meriel had chosen that day to visit a sick friend thirty miles away. For this she needed to use her battered old Morris Oxford, which was in the drive.

The first I knew of it was a furious Meriel bearing down on me as I was judging vegetable marrows in the main marquee. I had never seen Meriel in a temper before. Every aspect of her seemed out of joint. Words poured from her in an incoherent stream; her movements were jerky and uncoordinated. Under other circumstances it might have been comical. She demanded that I make an immediate and stern request over the public address system that the offenders should immediately remove their car. This I did. I escorted Meriel back to the Old Tannery where we discovered that the car had been moved, but evidently not by its owners.

It was a medium-sized saloon car—I cannot remember the make, a Rover perhaps—quite a bulky and heavy thing, but it had been tipped over on its side into a ditch. Two strong men could not have done it, three possibly.

There was a terrible to-do about it. The owners of the car transformed themselves in an instant from offenders into irate injured parties and became particularly indignant when they discovered who the inhabitants of the Old Tannery were. The police were called in and the men interviewed, but the mystery was never resolved. Most of the men had excellent alibis for the time when the deed could have been done. Meriel happened to remark to me much later that the only one who didn't was Mason, and he was the only one she knew had witnessed her rage about the car. But, of course, everyone agreed it would have been quite impossible for one man single-handedly to have overturned a medium-sized saloon car. What made it all the more mysterious was that there had apparently been no witnesses to the incident.

At the end of the summer, I began to wonder why Meriel had not let Mason go, if not altogether, at least to another of her Philippian houses. He had committed no offense, of course, but the atmosphere at the Old Tannery had noticeably deteriorated. There was none of the relaxed warmth that there had been before. My weekly Compline services were held in a stiff reverential silence. Mason was always present, but always apart and aloof. Usually he sat in the window which faced West so that his shadow blocked out the rays of the declining sun.

Eventually I tackled Meriel about it. We were taking a walk together after an early weekday communion at which she had been the only person present. When I pressed her she smiled, as I thought, in an irritatingly superior way.

She said: "You have heard, Rector, of the doctrine of substitution?"

I knew about it theoretically. Certain advanced Anglicans of a mystical persuasion were very keen on it at one time, I remember. The idea is that, like Christ, albeit in a very minor way, you can take on the sins and afflictions of others. In other words, you can not only be the beneficiary of the Passion of Christ, you can also, in a small way, participate in it.

Meriel told me that Mason was suffering from some kind of deep-seated spiritual trauma and that she had been having sessions with him, and also engaging in severe personal mortifications in order to take on some of his burden. When I pressed her for details she became vague and evasive.

Well, I don't know about you, but I have always been somewhat wary of this doctrine of substitution. I think you have to be a very saintly person indeed—or a very arrogant one—to undertake such a task. So which was Meriel? You may think I have prejudged her, but I haven't. I have no way of telling whether she was acting out of vanity and spiritual pride, or a kind of divine and humble recklessness. Or was it a strange mixture of the two?

All I was sure of then—as I am now—was that she was attempting something very dangerous and of dubious practical benefit. I told her so and she disregarded me, as she had every right to do, of course. I was not her spiritual director; that office was filled by the abbot of a local friary of Anglican Franciscans.

For several days after my meeting with Meriel, I did not see Mason. It was the end of summer and the earth was warm. Leaves gave off their last dusty glitter before turning yellow. I wondered whether my unaccustomed feelings of goodwill had anything to do with Mason's absence. As each day passed I began to lose my dread of his sudden appearance in the churchyard. I wondered if he had left altogether as he did not put in an appearance at Compline for two weeks running, but Meriel assured me that he was "still with us."

Then one morning he was there again. This time I knew it the moment I had stepped out of the rectory at six forty-five. It was a pleasant morning as I remember, sunny, but moist with a slight chill in the air.

Though the rectory is adjacent to the church you cannot see it from there. It is hidden by a belt of magnificent and ancient oaks. You walk down the rectory drive past these trees and then, as you come out of the drive, the church is there, embedded in its green graveyard, with its tower of knapped flint tall against the sky. That first sight of St. Winifred's used always to take me by surprise, and often filled me with joy.

On this occasion the joyous expectation was missing. When I reached the end of the drive I looked toward the church. It was the prelude to a hot day. A slight mist was rising from the dew on the grass between the tombs. Behind one of them, and slightly obscured by the haze, stood the figure of a man, rigidly still. Had I not known my own churchyard I might have taken it to be part of some funerary monument. As it was, I knew who was there, and I felt sick.

Of course, I told myself, it was only Mason, and yet the dread of having to pass him on the way into church was very great. I could not understand it. I had never quite felt fear in his presence before: annoyance certainly and unease, but nothing worse. As I came toward him he did not move, but he was staring at me with that mirthless Hapsburg grin on his face.

He was a few feet away from the church path behind a gravestone which leaned at a slight angle away from it. One hand of Mason's was resting on the stone. I noticed how the fingers were reddish pink but the prominent joints and knuckles were white. I felt that I must say something, because to let him speak first would be to show weakness.

I said: "Hello, Harry. How long have you been here?"

He did not seem to notice my question at all, but continued to stare and grin. After a pause, he said: "Do you believe in angels?"

I asked him what he meant by angels. He said: "I mean spirits of the air who fly in and out of you." I said nothing and he seemed to be enjoying my discomfort. When he spoke again, it was in a different tone of voice, higher in pitch, and full of that intense yet understated menace which I had experienced the first time I met him. He said: "Tell Meriel to lay off me. It won't work." Having said this he rolled up his left sleeve. His bare forearm, thin and sinuous, was covered with wiry black hairs through which I could see the livid scars of some half dozen diagonal cuts. They were very evenly spaced; it was a hideously controlled piece of mutilation.

I ran inside the church. I could not help myself. When I came out again after an hour's prayer—I call it prayer, but it was really only a period of agonized mental confusion—he was gone. Later that morning I rang the Old Tannery and asked Meriel to come over to see me.

Once the formalities were dispensed with and she had refused refreshment—a little brusquely, I thought—she dropped into an armchair in my study and anticipated my preamble by saying: "It's about Harry, isn't it?"

When I told her what had happened I could see that the account of my flight into the church had not raised me in her estimation. Her manner toward me changed so that she began to treat me with benign condescension, almost as if I was one of her men at the Old Tannery.

"Oh, I know all about the self-mutilation," she said. "That's been going on for some time now. We've got it down to a reasonable level. The fact that Harry told you to warn me off him is actually a hopeful sign, you know. It means I'm getting through to him."

"But what's wrong with him?" I asked.

"He's possessed, of course!"

It was a shockingly simple answer, but it begged a whole series of further questions. How was he possessed? And by what? I asked them and received the vaguest of answers. I think she was not quite prepared to admit her ignorance. "What matters is how we heal him," she said. I asked her if she was considering exorcism, but she dismissed the option almost contemptuously. She said: "I have been involved in cases where exorcism was used. The effects are very uncertain. I believe there are other means." Then she looked at me with that sudden intuitive gleam that was so characteristic of her. "Now, I know you think I'm being very vain and full of spiritual pride, presuming that I can manage it all by myself, but I'm not, you know. I'm fully aware of the dangers involved and I know I need as much help as I can get. I've got the Franciscans over at the friary all praying away for me like billy-o!"

I smiled, she laughed, the tension eased. "And I want you to pray too!" she said, patting me on the knee, then, for a second, almost caressing it. In that brief space of time I was aware of another Meriel, not the pious, enthusiastic God lover, but a rather lonely, slightly immature woman with sexual and emotional needs like the rest of us. I felt touched, honored even, that she had allowed me to see this side of her. Not that the saintly Meriel which was what most of us saw most of the time, wasn't perfectly real; but she was Legion like the rest of us.

So there was nothing more I could do, except pray and await developments. This is where the story becomes unsatisfactory, because I have very little idea what passed between Meriel and Harry Mason during the following days. I cannot even speculate. I can only tell you what I saw.

For three days after the events I have described I saw neither Meriel nor Mason, then on the Thursday I saw something which I hesitate to tell you. There are certain images which stay fixed in one's mind as memories, but their vividness is no guarantee of veracity. So when I say I saw it, it would be more accurate to say that I have a strong impression of having seen it.

It was late September. I was taking a favorite walk through a little coppice of ash and hazel which bordered some fields which had been harvested a day or two previously. Clouds were high and there was a brisk little wind busying the branches. I happened to glance through the trees and into the field where I saw something moving. It was hard to tell what through the screen of twigs, but I could see that it was a four-footed creature of sorts, and larger than a fox. I could not tell what color it was—darkish brown I think—because I was looking into the sun.

My first thought was that it was one of the Muntjac deer, escaped from some country estate or other, which had just begun to become a pest to the farmers in our neighborhood. But there was something about the posture and the shape of the legs that contradicted this theory. I pushed my way through the thicket to the edge of the field so that I could get an unimpeded view.

Then I saw that it was not an animal of any kind but a man on all fours, his legs slightly bent, his long arms serving as forelegs, so that his whole body was arched and leaning forward. I thought the man would soon stand up and assume a natural posture but he did not. He bounded forward in an ungainly way, but with surprising speed and agility, using all four of his limbs. Moreover the man was naked. The limbs were hairy and scored with red marks and blotches. Something attracted its attention to me and it turned its head in my direction. The face was that of Harry Mason, but the eyes did not have a human expression in them. There was an instant of feral recognition before the creature started to bound away from me at extraordinary speed.

It is hard to describe the horror that filled me. That is perhaps why a part of me is still trying to insist that what I saw was some kind of hallucination.

I ran back to the rectory to ring Meriel and found her equally agitated because Mason had disappeared the night before. When I told her what I had seen—or thought I had seem—she said nothing for a moment, then, with sudden decision, she announced that she would ring the police. Ten minutes later the police rang me to confirm the sighting. I told them that Mason was naked but not that he was on all fours, knowing that this would invite skepticism. ("Are you sure it wasn't an animal you saw, Reverend?") I do not know how assiduously the search was conducted but it was fruitless. The following morning, however, on my way to the church I saw something I did not want to see.

Most of the graves in our churchyard are marked by an upright tombstone, but a few are of the flat topped sarcophagus type, like a rectangular stone box. There was one in particular, of a pale yellow stone, which stood next to the east end of the church and housed members of a long extinguished county family called the Orlebars. It had first been erected in about 1710 and was notable for having carved in low relief on its top a cartouche of the family arms surmounted by a skull and crossed bones, as if predicting the demise of the family. The carving was much worn, but its quality still showed. That is by the by. The point is that though I could barely see it from the church path through the forest of tombstones, it was a notable feature of the place. That morning I noticed that something was different about the Orlebar tomb. Someone was lying down on it.

My heart started to bang inside me. I went to look. The figure that lay there was long and thin, so tall that the head and feet hung over either end at a slight angle. It was the body of a naked man, horribly emaciated and scarred, the limbs and chest covered in coarse dark hairs, sparse but unnaturally long. The open eyes were completely black without whites or irises, and the half open mouth was prognathous, insensately grinning. It was Mason and he was dead.

One evening a few days later, I found myself sitting in Meriel's little study at the Old Tannery. It had been a troublesome time for all of us, so Meriel had decided to sell the Tannery and plant another Philippian House elsewhere. I asked her precisely what had brought about Mason's terrible last journey to the tomb. Meriel was evasive. She was highly strung and in no mood to look at the events clearly or dispassionately. Her conversation kept hopping from subject to subject: the move, the future of the Philippians, the trouble she was having with her teeth. But she did let out a few hints.

The day before I saw Mason in the field she had had what she called "a long session" with him. When she had asked him to unburden and "share" his troubles with her he had been more forthcoming than on previous occasions and at one point had

completely broken down. They had prayed together and it was while they were doing this that something had happened. She would not say what, either because she
was afraid to, or because no words could describe the experience, or because it had
been wiped from her memory. I do not know.

Toward the end of our talk she suddenly said: "The one thing I failed to realize
was that after the thing had come out of him, there was very little of poor Harry left.
I think he died because there was nothing left of him to live, if you see what I mean.
I'm probably burbling, so you must shut me up."

I asked Meriel if she knew anything about Mason's past.

"Virtually nothing. I never ask, as you know. He was an educated man. He told
me he'd once been a teacher; and he implied that he could never go back to teaching. That's all. Something had obviously gone wrong."

Just then we both became aware of a sound. It came from over our heads, and
must have emanated from the room above, but in a curious way it seemed to be in
the room with us.

It was a creaking noise. Something up there was moving rapidly to and fro, not
quite running but traveling fast. The feet were not heavy, they did not thump the old
elm boards above our heads but they made them creak and groan as if oppressed by
the weight which bore down on them. It is a strange thing to talk about a mere pressure on an old piece of wood like this, but it felt clammy and vile, conscious malice
was in every footfall.

Meriel pointed upward and said: "That was Harry Mason's old room." I crossed
myself. Meriel said: "Go in peace" and the sound diminished then ceased altogether.

"It will be back, I'm afraid" said Meriel quite calmly. Then she leaned forward
and said to me: "But it's not Harry, you know." Her usually bright eyes were dull; it
was as if the hope had gone out of them.

A week later Meriel was gone and the Old Tannery was up for sale. In case you
were going to ask, the next occupants experienced nothing unpleasant about the
house, though I had, I must admit, thoroughly blessed the place before their arrival.

I made no effort to keep in touch with Meriel. I'm not quite sure why. It was not
a conscious decision, but I have a feeling that some kind of self-protective instinct
held me back. However, I did see her one last time and it was quite by chance about
twelve years later. I had been asked to address a group of Anglican nuns about something or other—pastoral theology I think it was—because that was what I was teaching at the time at Cuddesdon. Well, this Convent was a small establishment in
Buckinghamshire, part of the Community of the Resurrection. On my arrival I was
shown round the place—one always is—and made to admire its polished floors and
orderliness. All was going well until we entered the chapel, when the nun who was
showing me round muttered a half-suppressed, "Oh!" It was an "Oh!" I recognized;
it said, "if I'd known this was going to happen, I wouldn't have brought you here."

The chapel was lit only by a pair of candles on the altar and a sanctuary lamp. It
was one of those gloomy, over-decorated places, built around 1900 at the height of the
vogue for mystical Anglo-Catholicism. The architecture, by an uninspired follower of
Butterfield, was a neo-Byzantine riot of liver-colored marble columns, alabaster
screens, variegated courses of brick and mosaic panels of biblical scenes: a joyless exuberance. At the ornate brass altar rail knelt a figure that I recognized instantly.

It was the same rigidly upright posture, the same small, neatly shaped head. Her
hair, now white, was coiled up into the familiar bun on the back of her head like a
sleeping snake. It was Meriel. I felt the nun tugging at my sleeve and urging me to
come away. But I resisted, held against her will and mine.

She was the same and yet different. The stillness had gone. The head twitched slightly, as if she were constantly looking from side to side. I wondered if she had Parkinson's disease. I explained to the nun, now very bothered and eager to get away, that I had once known Meriel well. She relaxed a little, explaining that Meriel was having "one of her bad days."

"She harms herself sometimes," she said.

I dismissed the nun, saying that I would like to pray for a while in the chapel. She went reluctantly. I did not go far into the chapel, but knelt in a stall some distance from Meriel.

Something else was wrong. It was as if the air around Meriel was disturbed. There were tiny sounds—whispers, grunts, creaks—all of which emanated from her direction. At the same time the light near her was somehow being broken into little irrational sparks and shadows. It is hard to describe, but it was as if her head were surrounded by a swarm of invisible insects, buzzing, whining, fluttering; the occasional flash of an iridescent wing coruscated weakly in the gloom. I wondered if she would turn and see me, as she had done all those years ago when we first met. She did not, so I said a prayer for her and left the chapel.

That was the last time I saw her, except possibly for the following morning. I had risen early and was taking a walk in the convent's Calvary Garden before morning prayer. The garden, as is customary, adjoins a small burial ground for the nuns. It was one of those damp November mornings when the earth seems entombed in a white fog. There is a special quality to their silences which can be conducive to meditation. I could hear nothing except the faint crackle of my feet along the gravel path, and when I stopped before the stone Calvary in the center of the garden there was perfect stillness. So it could not have been a noise which made me suddenly turn and look in the direction of the cemetery. There, through the mist, I thought I caught a glimpse of a thin white figure standing very upright by one of the nuns' gravestones. It appeared to be naked. I cannot be absolutely certain if it was Meriel, but I think it was, and I think she saw me. When I tried to approach the figure it moved off rapidly into the mist.

Meriel died at the convent a few months later.

There was a pause after Father Humphreys had finished, then Canon Carey asked: "Do you mean she had taken on his—demon, burden—whatever it was?"

"I really couldn't say. That is a possible explanation."

"No, no!" said the archdeacon. "This contradicts the entire doctrine of the Gospels. If you must allow this notion of demons, they can be cast out. Our Lord cast out demons. Why didn't she let herself be exorcised by a properly trained member of the priesthood licensed by the bishop?"

"Perhaps because everyone just thought she was nuts, like you, Archdeacon. Or perhaps she thought she ought to let the entity die with her in case when it was thrown out of her it entered someone else and carried on with its work there. Like the Gadarene swine."

I suddenly noticed that the lights in the room were very dim. Father Humphreys looked at us and smiled, not altogether encouragingly.

"We all carry our own shadows. They run by our side when we are young; they creep behind us when we are old; they sleep with us in the grave. We must learn to live and die with them. We should not try to cut them off, and we should not try to take on anyone else's shadows. Perhaps a real saint could do it, but I'm not sure. A good deed like that never goes unpunished in this world."

JENNIFER CHANG

Obedience, or The Lying Tale

First published in the fall issue of the Virginia Quarterly Review, *Jennifer Chang's "Obedience, or The Lying Tale" is a meditation on fairy tale actions and instructions. Chang is the 2005 Van Lier Fellow in Poetry at the Asian American Writers' Workshop and the 2005 Louis Untermeyer Scholar at Bread Loaf Writers' Conference. Her poems have appeared or are forthcoming in* Barrow Street, Seneca Review, Gulf Coast, Indiana Review, *and other publications. Her poem "Conversation with Owl and Clouds" (from* New England Review) *was selected for* Best New Poets 2005. *She has received fellowships from the MacDowell Colony and the Djerassi Residents Artists Program. She teaches in the creative writing program at Rutgers University and lives in Jersey City with her husband, the poet Aaron Baker.*

—K.L. & G.G.

I will do everything you tell me, Mother.
I will charm three gold hairs
from the demon's head.
I will choke the mouse that gnaws
an apple tree's roots and keep its skin
for a glove. To the wolf, I will be
pretty and kind, and curtsy
his crossing of my path.

The forest, vocal
even in its somber tread, rages.
A slope ends in a pit of foxes
drunk on rotten brambles of berries
and the raccoons ransack
a rabbit's unmasked hole.
What do they find but a winter's heap
of droppings? A stolen nest, the cracked shell

of another creature's child.
I imagine this is the rabbit way
and I will not stray, Mother,
into the forest's thick,
where the trees meet the dark,
though I have known misgivings

of light as a hot hand that flickers
against my neck. The path ends

at a river I must cross. I will wait
for the ferryman
to motion me through. Into the waves,
he etches with his oar
a new story: a silent girl runs away,
a silent girl is never safe.
I will take his oar in my hand. I will learn
the boat's rocking and bring myself back

and forth. To be good
is the hurricane of caution.
I will know indecision's rowing,
the water I lap into my lap
as he shakes his withered head.
Behind me is the forest. Before me
the field, a loose run of grass. I stay
in the river, Mother, I study escape.

GLEN HIRSHBERG

American Morons

Glen Hirshberg's first collection, The Two Sams, *won the International Horror Guild Award, and was selected by* Publishers Weekly *and* Locus *as one of the best books of 2003. Hirshberg is also the author of* The Snowman's Children *and a forthcoming novel,* Sisters of Baikal. *His second collection,* American Morons, *was recently published by Earthling Publications. With Dennis Etchison and Peter Atkins, he cofounded the Rolling Darkness Revue, a traveling ghost story performance troupe that tours the west coast of the United States each October. His fiction has appeared in numerous magazines and anthologies, including* Trampoline, Cemetery Dance, Dark Terrors 6, The Dark, *and multiple appearances in* The Year's Best Fantasy and Horror *and* The Mammoth Book of Best New Horror, *as well as online at the late, lamented* SCI FICTION. *He lives in the Los Angeles area with his wife and children.*

"American Morons" *was originally published as part of a chapbook created for the 2005 The Rolling Darkness Revue.*

—E.D.

Omnibus umbra locis adero: dabis, improbe, poenas.
(My angry ghost, arising from the deep
Shall haunt thee waking, and disturb thy sleep.)

—Virgil

In the end, the car made it more than a mile after leaving the gas station, all the way to the tollgate that marked the outskirts of Rome. Ignoring the horns behind them and the ominous, hacking rattle of the engine, the two Americans dug together through the coins they'd dumped in the dashboard ashtray. Twice, Kellen felt Jamie's sweat-streaked fingers brush his. The horn blasts got more insistent, and Jamie laughed, so Kellen did, too.

When they'd finally assembled the correct change, he threw the coins into the bin, where they clattered to the bottom except for one ten-cent piece that seemed to stick in the mesh. Ruefully, Kellen imagined turning, trying to motion everyone behind him back so he could reverse far enough out of the toll island to open his door and climb out. Then the coin dropped and disappeared into the bottom of the basket.

Green light flashed. The gate rose. Kellen punched the accelerator and felt it plunge straight down. There was not even a rattle, now.

"Uh, Kel?" Jamie said.

As though they'd heard her, or could see his foot on the dead pedal, every car in the queue let loose with an all-out sonic barrage. Then—since this was Italy, where blasting horns at fellow drivers was like showering rice on newlyweds—most of the cars in the queues to either side joined in.

Expressionlessly, Kellen turned in his seat, his skin unsticking from the rental's cracked, roasted vinyl with a pop. The setting sun blazed through the windshield into his eyes. "At least," he said, "it's not like you warned me the car might only take diesel."

"Yes I—" Jamie started, caught the irony, and stopped. She'd been in the midst of retying her maple syrup hair on the back of her neck. Kellen found himself watching her tank top spaghetti strap slide in the slickness on her shoulder as she spoke again. "At least it doesn't say the word DIESEL in big green letters on the gas cap."

He looked up, blinking. "Does it really?"

"Saw it lying on the trunk while that attendant dude was trying whatever he was trying to fix it. What'd he pour in there, anyway?"

Goddamnit, Kellen snarled inside his own head for perhaps the thousandth time in the past week. Jamie and he had been a couple all the way through high school. Three years into their separate college lives, he still considered them one. She said she did, too. And she wasn't lying, exactly. But he'd felt the change all summer long. He'd thought this trip might save them.

A particularly vicious horn blast from the car behind almost dislodged his gaze. Almost. "At least diesel isn't the same word in Italian as it is in English," he said, and Jamie burst out laughing.

"Time to meet more friendly Romans."

Too late, Kellen started issuing his by now familiar warning, cobbled from their parents' pre-trip admonishments about European attitudes toward Americans at the moment, plus the words that had swirled around them all week, blaring from radios, the front pages of newspapers they couldn't read, TV sets in the lobbies of youth hostels they'd stayed in just for the adventure, since their respective parents had supplied plenty of hotel money. Cadavere. Sesto Americano. George Bush. Pavone. Not that Jamie would have listened, anyway. He watched her prop her door open and stick out one tanned, denim-skirted leg.

Instantly, the horns shut off. Doors in every direction popped like champagne corks, and within seconds, half a dozen Italian men of wildly variant ages and decisions about chest hair display fizzed around the Americans' car.

"Stuck," Jamie said through her rolled down window. "Um. Kaput."

"I'm pretty sure that's not Ital—" Kellen started, but before he could finish, his door was ripped open. Startled, he twisted in his seat. The man pouring himself into the car wore no shirt whatsoever, and was already gripping the wheel. The rest of the men fanned into formation, and then the car was half-floating, half-rolling through the tollgate into traffic that made no move to slow, but honked gleefully as it funneled around them. Seconds later, they glided to a stop on the gravel shoulder.

Jamie leaned back in her seat, folding her arms and making a great show of sighing like a queen in a palanquin. Whether her grin was for him or the guy who'd grabbed the steering wheel, Kellen had no idea. The guy hadn't let go, and Kellen remained pinned in place.

What was it about Italian men that made him want to sprout horns and butt something? "I say again," he murmured to Jamie. "Kaput?"

"It's one of those universal words, ol' pal. Like diesel." Then she was lifted out of the car.

Even Jamie seemed taken aback, and made a sort of chirping sound as the throng enveloped her. "*Bella*," Kellen heard one guy coo, and something that sounded like "*Assistere*," and some tongue-clucking that could have been regret over the car or wolfish slavering over Jamie or neither. Kellen didn't like that he could no longer see her, and he didn't like the forearm stretched across his chest.

Abruptly, it lifted, and he wriggled out fast and stood. The man before him looked maybe forty, with black and gray curly hair, a muscular chest, and Euro-sandals with those straps that pulled the big toes too far from their companions. He said nothing to Kellen, and instead watched Jamie slide sunglasses over her eyes, whirling amid her circle of admirers with her skirt lifting above her knee every time she turned. Back home, Jamie was borderline pretty—slim, athletic, a little horse-faced—at least until she laughed. But in Italy, judging from the response of the entire male population during their week in Rome and Tuscany, she was a Goddess. Or else all women were.

Ol' pal. That's what he was, now.

Almost seven o'clock, and still the blazing summer heat poured down. Two more miles, Kellen thought, and he and Jamie could at least have stood in one of Rome's freezing fountains while they waited for the tow truck. Jamie would have left her loafers on the pavement, her feet bare.

"It's okay, thanks guys," he said abruptly, and started around the car. Digging into his shorts pocket for his cell phone, he waved it at the group like a wand that might make them disappear. "*Grazi.*" His accent sounded pathetic, even to him.

Not a single Italian turned. One of them, he noticed, had his hand low on Jamie's back, and another had stepped in close alongside, and Kellen stopped feeling like butting anything and got nervous. And more sad.

"All set, guys. Thanks a lot." His hand was in his pocket again, lifting out his wallet and opening it to withdraw a fistful of five-euro notes. Jamie glanced at him, and her mouth turned down hard as her eyes narrowed. The guy with the sandals made that clucking sound again and stepped up right behind Kellen.

For a second, Kellen went on waving the money, knowing he shouldn't, not sure why he felt like such an asshole. Only after he stopped moving did he realize no one but Jamie was looking at him.

In fact, no one was anywhere near them anymore. All together, the men who'd encircled Jamie and the sandal guy were retreating toward the tollgate. Catching Kellen's glance, sandal guy lifted one long, hairy arm. *Was that a wave?*

Then they were alone. Just he, Jamie, the cars revving past each other as they reentered the laneless *superstrade*, and the other car, parked maybe fifty feet ahead of them. Yellow, encased in grit, distinctly European-box. The windows were so grimy that Kellen couldn't tell whether anyone was in there. But someone had to be, because the single, sharp honk that had apparently scattered their rescuers had come from there.

"What was that bullshit with the money?" Jamie snapped. "They're not waiters. They were help—"

The scream silenced her. Audible even above the traffic, it soared over the retaining wall beyond the shoulder and seemed to unfurl in the air before dissipating. In the first instant, Kellen mistook it for a siren.

Glancing at Jamie, then the retaining wall, then the sun squatting on the horizon, he stepped closer. He felt panicky, for all sorts of reasons. He also didn't want this trip to end, ever. "Got another one of those universal words for you, James. Been in the papers all week. Ready? *Cadaver*."

"*Cadavere*." Jamie said, her head twisted around toward the origin of the scream. "Right."

Together, they collapsed into leaning positions against their rented two-seater. It had been filthy when they got it—cleanliness apparently not the business necessity here that it was back home—and now sported a crust as thick as Tuscan bread.

"Well, you got that thing out." She was gesturing at the cell phone in his hands, and still sounded pissed. "Might as well use it."

Kellen held it up, feeling profoundly stupid. "Forgot to charge."

Instantly, Jamie was smiling again, bending forward to kiss him on the forehead, which was where she always kissed him these days.

"Sorry about the money thing," Kellen said, clinging to her smile. "I didn't mean anything bad, I was just . . ."

"Establishing dominance. Very George Bush."

"Dominance? I was about as dominant as . . . I was being nice. I was showing appreciation. Sincere appreciation. If not for those guys, we'd still be—"

The passenger door of the yellow car swung open, and Kellen stopped talking.

His first thought, as the guy unfolded onto the gravel, was that he shouldn't have been able to fit in there. This was easily the tallest Italian Kellen had seen all week. And the thinnest, and lightest-skinned. The hair on his head shone lustrous and long and black. For a few seconds, he stood swaying with his back to them, like some roadside reed that had sprung up from nowhere. Then he turned.

Just a boy, really. Silvery blue eyes that sparkled even from fifteen feet away, and long-fingered hands that spread over his bare, spindly legs like stick-bugs clinging to a branch. The driver's side door opened, and a second figure tumbled out.

This one was a virtual opposite of his companion, short and stumpy, with curly, dirty hair that bounced on the shoulders of his striped red rugby shirt. He wore red laceless canvas shoes. Black stubble stuck out of his cheeks like porcupine quills and all but obscured his goofy, ear-to-ear smile. He stopped one step behind the reedy kid. All Kellen could think of was *prince* and *troll*.

"*Ciao*," said the troll, his smile somehow broadening as he bounded forward. Unlike everyone else they'd met here, he looked at Kellen at least as much Jamie. "*Ciao*." He ran both hands over the hood of the rental car, then seemed to hold his breath, as though checking for a heartbeat.

"*Parla Inglese?*" Jamie tried.

"*Americano?*"

"Ye—" Kellen started, and Jamie overrode him.

"Canadian."

"*Si. Americano*." Bouncing up and down on his heels, the troll grinned his prickly grin. "George Bush. Bang bang."

"John Kerry," Jamie said, rummaging in her purse and pulling out one of the campaign buttons her mother had demanded she keep there, as though it were mace. She waved it at the troll, who merely raised his bushy eyebrows and stared a question at them.

"What?" Kellen said. "*Non parlo L'Italiano*."

"He didn't say anything, idiot," Jamie said, then gasped and stumbled forward.

Whirling, Kellen found the reedy boy directly behind them, staring down. He really was tall. And his eyes were deep-water blue. *Nothing frightening about him*, Kellen thought, wondering why his heart was juddering like that.

"*Mi dispiace,*" This one's voice rang, sonorous and way too big for its frame, like a bell-peal. From over the retaining wall, another one of those screams bloomed in the air, followed by a second and third in rapid succession.

"Howler monkeys?" Kellen said softly to Jamie. "What the hell is that?"

But Jamie was casting her eyes back and forth between the two Italians. The troll pointed at the hood of their car, then raised his hands again.

"Oh," Jamie said. "The gas. My friend put in . . ."

The troll cocked his head and smiled uncomprehendingly.

Abruptly, Jamie started around to the gas tank and came back with the cap. She pointed it toward the troll. "See? Diesel."

"Diesel. *Si.*"

"No diesel." Forming her fingers into a sort of gun, Jamie mimed putting a pump into the tank. "Gas."

For one more moment, the troll just stood. Then his hands flew to his cheeks. "Ohhh. Gas. No diesel. Ohhh." Still grinning, he drew one of his fingers slowly across his own throat. Then he let loose a stream of Italian.

After a minute or so of that, Kellen held up his cell phone. "You have one?" He was trying to control his embarrassment. And his ridiculous unease.

"Ohhh," the troll said, glancing at his companion.

Reedy boy's smile was regal and slow. He said nothing at all.

"Ohhh." Now, the troll seemed to be dancing as he moved around the front of the car. Instinctively, Kellen stepped a half pace back toward the retaining wall, just to feel a little less like he and Jamie were being maneuvered in between these two. "In America, auto break, call. Someone come." He snapped his fingers. "But *a l'Italia . . .* Ohhh." He smacked his palm to his forehead and made a Jerry Lewis grimace.

The troll's grunting laugh—unlike reedy boy's voice—simply annoyed Kellen. "They'll come. You have?" He waved the cell phone again.

"Why are you talking like that?" Jamie snapped.

"You have one? This one's . . ." He waved the phone some more, looking helplessly at his girlfriend. *Friend,* she'd said. "*Kaput.*"

"Ah!" said prickly guy. "*Si. Si.*" With another glance toward his companion, he raced back to the yellow car and stuck his head and hands inside the window. From the way his body worked, he was still yammering and gesturing as he rummaged around in there. Then he was back, waving a slim, black phone. He flipped open the faceplate, put it to his ears, then raised the other hand in the questioning gesture again.

"I'll do it," Kellen said, reached out, and reedy boy seemed to lean forward. But he made no blocking movement as his companion handed over the phone.

"Thanks. *Grazi,*" Kellen said, while Jamie beamed her brightest naïve, Kerry-loving smile at both Italians. Kellen's father said all Kerry supporters smiled like that. Jamie was quite possibly the only Democrat Kellen's father loved.

He had his fingers on the keypad before he realized the problem. "Shit," he barked.

The troll grinned. "Ohhh."

"What?" Jamie asked, stepping nearer. "Just call someone. Call American Express."

"You know the number?"

"I thought you did."

"It's on speed dial on my phone. My dad programmed it in. I've never even looked at it."

"Get your card."

"They didn't give me that card. They gave me the Visa."

"*Mi scusi*," said the troll, stepping close as yet another of those long, shrieking cries erupted from behind the retaining wall. Reedy boy just looked briefly over his shoulder at the yellow car before returning his attention to Jamie and Kellen. Neither of the Italians seemed even to have heard the screams.

Tapping his red-striped chest, the troll reached out and chattered more Italian. Kellen had no idea what he was saying, but handed him the phone. Nodding, the troll punched in numbers. For a good minute, he stood with the phone at his ear, grinning. Then he started speaking fast into the mouthpiece, turning away and walking off down the shoulder.

"We're pretty lucky these guys are here to help," Jamie said against his ear.

Kellen glanced at her. She had her arms tucked in tight to her chest, her bottom lip curled against her teeth. For the first time, he realized she might be even more on edge than he was. She'd seen the same stories he had, after all. Same photos. The couple left dangling upside down from a flagpole outside the Colisseum, tarred and feathered and wrapped in the Stars and Stripes. The whole Tennessee family discovered laid out on a Coca-Cola blanket inside the ruins of a recently excavated 2000 year-old catacomb near the Forum, all of them naked, gutted from genitalia to xiphoid, stuffed with feathers. The couple on the flagpole had reminded Jamie of a paper she'd written on Ancient Rome, something about a festival where puppets got hung in trees. The puppets took the place of the little boys once sacrificed on whatever holiday that was.

The troll had walked all the way back to his yellow car, now, and he was talking animatedly, waving his free arm around and sometimes holding the cell phone in front of his face and shouting into it. Reedy boy simply stood, still as a sentry, gazing placidly over Kellen and Jamie's head toward the tollgate.

Overhead, the sun sank toward the retaining wall, and the air didn't cool, exactly, but thinned. Despite the unending honks and tire squeals from the A1, Kellen found something almost soothing about the traffic. There was a cheerfulness to it that rendered it completely different from the American variety. The horns reminded him mostly of squawking birds.

On impulse, he slid his arm around Jamie's shoulders. Her skin felt hot but dry, now. Her flip-flopped foot tapped in the dirt. She neither leaned into him nor away. Years from now, he knew, they'd be telling this story. To their respective children, not the children he'd always thought they'd have together. As an excuse to tell it, just once more, to each other.

At least, that's how it would be for him. "Diesel," he muttered. "Who uses diesel anymore?"

"People who care about the air. Diesel's a million times cleaner than regular gas."

"But it stinks." He tried putting a playful arm around her shoulders, but she shook him off.

"You smell anything?"

Kellen realized that he didn't.

"They fixed the smell problem ages ago. You're just brainwashed."

"Brainwashed?"

"Oil company puppet. George Bush puppet. Say W, little puppet."

"W.," said Kellen, tried a smile though he still felt unsettled and dumb, and Jamie smiled weakly back, without taking her eyes off the placid face of the thin boy.

"Okay!" called the troll, waving. He stuck his head into the yellow car, continuing to gesture even though no one could see him, then reemerged. "*Arrivo. Si? Coming.*"

Jamie smiled her thanks. Reedy boy turned his head enough to watch the sun as it vanished. Shadows poured over the retaining wall onto the freeway, and with them came a chorus of shrieks that flooded the air and took a long time evaporating.

Squeezing Jamie once on the elbow in what he hoped was a reassuring manner, Kellen made his way around their dead rental, climbed the dirt incline that rimmed the *superstrade*, and reached the retaining wall, which was taller than it looked. Even standing at its base, Kellen couldn't see over the top. The wall was made of the same chipped, ancient-looking stone that dotted excavation sites all over Italy. What, Kellen wondered, had this originally been built to retain?

Standing on tiptoe, he dropped his elbows on top of the stone, wedged a foot into the grit between rocks, and hoisted himself up. There he hung, elbows grinding into the wall, mouth wide open.

Without letting go, he turned his head after a few seconds. "Jamie," he said quietly, hoping somehow to attract her and not the reedy boy. But his voice didn't carry over the traffic, and Jamie didn't turn around. Against the yellow car, the troll leaned, smoking a thin, brownish cigarette. "*Jamie*," Kellen barked, and she glanced up, and the reedy boy, too, slowly. "Jamie, come here."

She came. Right as she reached the base of the wall, the screeching started once more. Knowing the source, as he now did, should have reassured Kellen. Instead, he closed his eyes and clutched the stone.

"Kel?" Jamie said, her voice so small, suddenly, that Kellen could barely hear it. "Kellen, what's up there?"

He opened his eyes, staring over the wall again. "Peacock Auschwitz."

"Will you stop saying shit like that? You sound like your stupid president, except he probably thinks Auschwitz is a beer."

"He's your president, too."

She was struggling to get her feet wedged into the chinks in the wall. He could have helped, or told her to stay where she was, but did neither.

"Oh, God," she said, as soon as she'd climbed up beside him. Then she went silent, too.

The neighborhood looked more like a gypsy camp than a slum. The tiny, collapsing houses seemed less decayed than pieced together out of discarded tires, chicken wire, and old stones. The shadows streaming over everything now had already pooled down there, so that the olive trees scattered everywhere looked like hunched old people, white haired, slouching through the ruins like mourners in a graveyard.

Attached to every single structure—even the ones where roofs had caved in, walls given way—was a cage, as tall as the houses, lined with some kind of razor wire with the sharp points twisted inward. Inside the cages were birds.

Peacocks. Three, maybe four to a house, including the ones that were already dead. The live ones paced skittishly, great tails dragging in the dust, through the spilled innards and chopped bird feet lining the cage bottoms. There was no mistaking any of it, and even if there were, the reek that rose from down there was a clincher. Shit and death. Unmistakable.

In the cage nearest them, right at the bottom of the wall, one bird glanced up, lifted its tail as though considering throwing it open, then tilted its head back and screamed.

"You know," said the reedy boy, right beneath them, in perfect though faintly accented English, and Kellen and Jamie jerked. Then they just hung, clinging to the wall. "The Ancient Romans sacrificed the *pavone*—the peacock, *si*?—to honor their emperors. They symbolized immortality. And their tails were the thousand eyes of God, watching over our civilization. Of course they also sacrificed humans, to the *Larvae*."

Very slowly, still clutching the top of the wall, Kellen turned his head. The boy was so close that Kellen could feel the exhalation of his breath on the sweat still streaming down his back. Even if Kellen had tried a kick, he wouldn't have been able to get anything on it. Jamie had gone rigid, and when he glanced that way, he saw that her eyes had teared up, though they remained fixed unblinkingly on the birds below.

"Larvae?" he asked, just to be talking. He couldn't think what else to do. "Like worms?"

"Dead men. Demons, really. Demons made of dead, bad men."

"Why?"

"Yes!" The boy nodded enthusiastically, folding his hands in that contemplative, regal way. "You are right. To invoke the *Larvae* and set them upon the enemies of Rome? Or to pacify them, and so drive away ill fortune? Which is the correct course? I would guess even they did not always know. What is your guess?"

That I'm about to die, Kellen thought crazily, closed his eyes, and bit his lip to keep from crying out like the peacocks beneath him. "So Romans cherished their dead bad men?"

"And their sacrifices. And their executioners. Like all human civilizations do."

Carefully, expecting a dagger to his ribs at any moment, Kellen eased his elbows off the stone, let one leg drop, then the other. The birds had gone silent. He stood a second, face to the stone. Then he turned.

The reedy boy was fifteen feet away, head aimed down the road as he walked slowly to his car.

"Jamie," Kellen hissed, and Jamie skidded down the wall to land next to him.

"Ow," she murmured, crooking her elbow to reveal an ugly red scrape.

"Jamie. Are we in trouble?"

She looked at him. He'd never seen the expression on her face before. But he recognized it instantly, and it chilled him almost as much as the reedy boy's murmur. *Contempt*. He'd always been terrified she'd show him that, sooner or later. And also certain that someday she would.

Without a word, she walked down the dirt incline, holding her elbow against her chest. When she reached the car, she stuck out a forefinger and began trailing it through the dirt on the driver's side window.

Okay, Kellen urged himself. *Think*. They had no phone. And who would they call? What was 911 in Italian? Maybe they could just walk fast toward the tollgate. Run out in traffic. People would honk. But they'd also see them. Nothing could happen as long as someone was looking, right?

Then he remembered the way the men who'd helped them to the shoulder had vanished. His mind veered into a skid. *They all know. The whole country. An agreement they've come to. They knew the yellow car, the location. The birds. They knew. They left us here. Put us here. Even the guy at the gas station, just what had he poured in the tank to supposedly save them?*

Peacock screams. A whole chorus of them, as the last light went out of the day. Kellen scrambled fast down the dirt toward the car, toward Jamie, who was crouched on the gravel now, head down and shaking back and forth on her long, tanned neck.

At the same moment, he saw both what Jamie had scrawled in the window grime and the two men by the yellow car starting toward them again. They came side by side, the reedy boy with one long-fingered hand on the stumpy one's shoulders.

AMERICAN MORONS. That's what she'd written.

"I love you," Kellen blurted. She didn't even look up.

The men from the yellow car were twenty feet away, now, ignoring the cars, the bird-screams, everything but their quarry.

Hop the wall, Kellen thought. But the idea of hiding in that neighborhood—of just setting foot in it—seemed even worse than facing down these two. Also, weirdly, like sacrilege. *Like parading with camera bags and iPods and cell phones through places where people had prayed, played with, and killed each* other.

This was what he was thinking, as the two Romans ambled ever nearer, when the truck loomed up, let loose a gloriously throaty, brain-clearing honk, and settled with a sigh right beside them.

"We're saved," he whispered, then dropped to his knees as the first and only girl he'd loved finally looked up. "Jamie, the tow truck's here. We're saved."

In no time at all, the driver was out, surveying the ruined rental, shoving pieces of puffy, cold pizza into their hands. He didn't speak English either, just gestured with emphatic Italian clarity. The cab of his truck was for him and his pizza. Jamie and Kellen could ride in their car. They climbed back in, and as the driver attached a chain and winch to the bumper, began to drag them onto the long, high bed of the truck, Kellen thought about blasting his horn, giving a chin-flick to the yellow car guys.

Except that that was ridiculous. The yellow car guys had called the tow truck. There'd never been any danger at all.

He started to laugh, put his hand on Jamie's. She was shivering, though it was still a long way from cold. The tow truck driver chained them into place, climbed back into his cab. Only then did it occur to Kellen that now they were really trapped.

With a lurch, the truck edged two wheels onto the *superstrade*, answering a volley of horn blares with a bazooka blast of its own. Perched there, eight feet off the ground, chained in the car in the tow truck bed, Kellen had a perfect view of the blue Mercedes coupe as it swerved onto the shoulder directly behind the yellow car. He saw the driver climb out of the blue car, wearing a black poncho that made no sense in the heat.

Stepping away from his own door, this new arrival simply watched as the reedy guy pointed a command and the troll dragged a little boy, bound in rusty wire, kicking and hurling his gagged head from side to side, out of the back seat of the yellow car. All too clearly, Kellen saw the boy's face. So distinctly American he could practically picture it on a milk carton already. Wheat-blond hair, freckles like crayon dots all over his cheeks, Yankees cap still somehow wedged over his ears.

Except it would never wind up on a milk carton, Kellen realized, grabbing at the useless steering wheel. *When he'd called home to tell his father about the murders, his father had snorted and said, "Thus proving there are ungrateful malcontents in Italy just like here." No one else they'd called had even heard the news. This boy would simply evaporate into the new American history, like the dead soldiers lined up in their coffins in that smuggled photograph from the second Gulf War.*

Shuddering himself now, still holding the wheel, Kellen wondered where the boy's face would appear in its Italian newspaper photo. *Drowned in a fountain atop the Spanish Steps? Wedged into one of the slits in the underground walls of Nero's Cryptoporticus? Strewn amid the refuse and scraps of fast-food wrappers and discarded homeless-person shoes along the banks of the Tiber?*

Just as the truck rumbled forward, plowing a space for itself in the traffic, the guy in the poncho closed the door of his Mercedes on his new passenger, and both the troll and the reedy boy looked up and caught Kellen's eyes.

The troll waved. The reedy boy smiled.

Shallaballah

Mark Samuels is the author of two short story collections, The White Hands and Other Weird Tales *and* Black Altars. *His short fiction has been published in the anthologies* A Walk on the Darkside *and* The Mammoth Book of Best New Horror Volume Fifteen *and in* Strange Attractor Journal #2.

"Shallaballah" was originally published in the anthology Don't Turn Out the Light.

—E.D.

A wig covered his bald scalp. His face was a patchwork of skin joined together by ugly black stitches. Mr. Punch told him that, given time, the resulting scars would be scarcely noticeable. Eventually they would almost fade away and leave only thin lines that could not be seen except under an extremely bright light. But as Sogol examined his own features in the mirror, tracing his fingers over the threads that held the flesh together, he found it difficult to believe that what he saw would ever again resemble his old familiar face. His reflection was like a mask, dead and expressionless. Sogol tried to remember that Mr. Punch had told him this was to be expected and that nerve-to-muscle control would take a few days to return, yet he had not really been prepared for the reality of just how ghastly he would appear in the interim. He poked a fingernail into the skin but felt nothing. It was like touching another person.

A gigantic industrial estate with narrow walkways, corridors and alleys. The squat, square buildings are made of concrete. They are run-down and dismal. Many of the windows are broken. On the flat roofs there are crooked TV aerials and grimy satellite dishes. They look like bizarre scarecrows and are framed against an orange-colored sky. Subsidence and age have made the structures lean together. Flights of twisted stairs link one level to another.

Sogol sat on the edge of the camp bed. Its mattress was soiled and hollowed in the center, a reminder of all those who had been here before him. Mr. Punch's "clinic" offered the most meager hospitality, despite the exorbitant cost of his special type of treatment. Those who went under his knife did so in the knowledge that the gentleman was a criminal, possibly even insane. But still his patients came. There was nowhere else for them to go. This horrible little building with its dusty windows and peeling paintwork, hidden away in a run-down ghetto estate, was a recondite Lourdes where one offered up hard cash in exchange for miracles.

He'd heard rumors about the celebrities who had passed through here. Film actresses who, beyond the help of lighting and makeup, even of face-lifts or plastic surgery, had extended their shelf life by more than a decade by utilizing the services of Mr. Punch. One did not approach him. There was no way to contact him. Mr. Punch would call on the telephone offering his services to those he knew were most in need. Celebrities of course. Only ever celebrities who could afford the fees he charged. And then his black ambulance would call in secret at an appointed time.

In Sogol's case it was after the car accident. The TV company had paid a lot of money to hush the thing up. This was, after all, right in the middle of filming the episode that was going to be next year's ratings triumph. Only Mr. Punch could repair the damage that Sogol had suffered in the crash; only Mr. Punch could reconstruct his monstrously burned face in time.

Sogol coked up to the eyeballs, driving a sports car, a bottle of scotch with just a dribble left in it lying beside him on the passenger seat, and a hairpin bend on the hillside road . . . leaving behind some woman . . . who meant nothing to him . . .

Three days ago. Strange to think it had only been less than a week.

The interiors of the dismal buildings are not homes. They contain no dwellings. Inside one would find a series of strange rooms cluttered with all manner of what appears to be junk: pot plants, framed pictures, coat stands, mounds of clothes and painted backdrops.

"You cannot leave," Mr. Punch had told him in a letter passed to Sogol, "until your treatment is complete. You must follow my instructions in each and every detail. If you fail to do so I cannot be held responsible for what might happen to your face."

Sogol had groaned at this statement and crumpled the letter in his hands. He was desperate to leave this anonymous ghetto in a town whose name he could not even recall. God knows in the past he had spent time in enough sleazy hotels in pursuit of fame, playing bit parts where he might be called to the set at any moment in order to wander in front of the cameras and utter a line or two of dialogue. But that was before he had struck it big, before his face was known to everyone he met, before he'd graced the cover of gossip magazines, before interviews with him were sought by all the TV chat-show hosts.

But if he left now people would turn their heads in horror, not in awed recognition, as he passed them by. A man with a cracked face. A freak. A refugee from a side-show who happened to bear a passing resemblance to a famous TV soap opera star.

Sogol, winner of three prestigious awards for best leading male role, one of the most highly paid actors on television, a man whom the public adored, a man who was witty, charming, and handsome. Handsome above all, but now reduced to this intolerable, pitiful state of existence.

There are dusty corridors within the structures of the immense industrial estate. Faded TV schedules are pinned to the walls. The same programs are broadcast at the same time day after day, night after night. The same films, the same episodes of soap operas, the same documentaries, the same panel games and quiz shows. In the photos accompanying the text all the celebrities wear fixed smiles. Their eyes are open too wide as if they regard the camera with fear.

———

Sogol made his way along the passageway outside his room. At the end was the pay phone that he was permitted to use. Mr. Punch had banned mobile phones from his clinic. He confiscated them from patients as soon as they were admitted.

"No distractions," Mr. Punch had explained, "no stress-inducing conversations. Complete rest. If you must make an urgent call, then there is a telephone available. Calls are monitored, however, for your own benefit. Unnecessary exploitation of this service will result in the connection being terminated and the privilege withdrawn."

Up in the corner of the middle of the passageway, in the angle between the far wall and the ceiling, was a surveillance camera. It moved through an arc on its wall-mount base in order to keep Sogol in its line of sight as he passed by. He cradled the receiver between his ear and shoulder, and dialed the number with his right hand as he scanned the little black phone book in his left. Just then he felt the beginnings of a dull pain well up around his forehead and along his jaw-line. A sure sign that the nurse would soon be making her rounds with the drug trolley; strange that he was now marking time by the effects of painkillers wearing off.

"Ketch Entertainments." The sound of a bored, unfamiliar female voice came down the line.

Ketch *what*? Had Sogol heard her right?

"Put me through to Joey," he said through stiffened lips, "tell him it's Sogol."

There was a pause and some tinny Muzak played as his call was transferred. After a few seconds Jackson spoke.

"Hi Joey, it's me."

"Sogol? Where the bloody hell are you?"

What was his problem?

"Where do you think I am, you idiot? Still in the clinic of course."

"What clinic? Why haven't you phoned in? I've gone half-crazy sorting out the seaside shows that have had to be canceled. You've lost us a lot of money. If you think you're still represented by this agency think again."

Had Joey lost his mind? What was this? His idea of a joke?

"I'm having my face reconstructed here and you're acting like an asshole . . ." Sogol hissed through his teeth, but in mid-sentence the line went dead. There was a loud click and then a droning, recorded voice said:

"This call is terminated. Please return to your room at once."

Sogol replaced the receiver and then tried to dial again. However before he'd even completed entering the whole telephone number, he heard the same recorded instruction.

"This call is terminated. Please return to your room at once."

Sogol looked back over his shoulder. The surveillance camera was trained on him. Right now someone was doubtless watching him on one of the pictures from a bank of CCTV screens. Watching and waiting to see whether he would comply. I'm not being treated like some nobody, Sogol thought, I'm not standing for this anymore. I'm Sogol! I'm not in prison!

Just then a set of double doors at the end of the corridor opened, and two huge men clad in three-quarter-length black coats and bowler hats strode purposefully toward him. They looked like undertakers rather than orderlies. Nevertheless, rather than displaying any sign of his being intimidated, Sogol advanced to meet the pair. But within moments, despite his screams of protest, his arms were pinned behind his back and he was frog-marched back along the corridor and thrown into his room. They locked the door behind them once they left. Neither of them had uttered a word to him but had been cold and silent going about their business of restraint and coercion in a mechanical, indifferent fashion. Had the situation required it, Sogol was sure that they would not have balked at actually beating him into submission.

Within the structures with the twisted TV aerials on the roofs one can hear sounds. They echo along the corridors coated with peeling paintwork. There is laughter without any humor in it; shrill, cold laughter. And it is accompanied by a series of groans. The groans seem to come from weakened lungs and throats. When the groans falter there is a horrible tittering, like that of a demented child, and then they begin all over again. This goes on for hours and hours. Finally, the sounds are suddenly replaced by the dim hiss of static. This lasts for a few seconds and then the whole process repeats itself without cessation.

Sogol was perched on the edge of the camp bed waiting for someone to come and attend to him. He'd pushed the summons button over and over again but the nurse had not responded. Was he being punished for his actions? He knew that it was long past the time he was due his medication. The flesh beneath the skin of his face itched unbearably, as if it was infested with spectral bugs, and despite the consequences Sogol could not stop scratching. He felt nothing; the outer layers of his facial skin were as numb as before, but at least it brought some temporary relief further down. Perhaps the bugs stopped crawling when they were sure that he was still alive.

He'd taken off the wig and sat there staring at the shoddy thing as he turned it over repeatedly in his hands. It was made of rough, artificial fibers and the brown fake hair was held together by a mesh that rested next to the scalp when worn. Mr. Punch had advised him that Sogol's own hair would begin to grow back within days but there was no sign of bristle on his skull, simply the same bald mottled patchwork he discovered when he'd awoken after the operation.

Up in the corner of the room was a fixture that he couldn't remember having seen previously. It was a dusty old light fitting with a bulb screwed into the socket. Underneath was a small rectangular panel that was covered in a thick layer of dust. Sogol got up to examine it more closely. He scraped away the debris to reveal the words ON AIR etched into its glass front. The bulb above the lettering was colored a deep red.

Perhaps Mr. Punch had it put there as a tribute to his patients, in recognition of their celebrity status. It was a weird thing to do since in every other detail he had made no similar gestures. How could he possibly consider this seedy flea-pit as suitable for the glitterati? What matter that such an absurd concession had been made when compared to the grubby cells and corridors, the lack of proper heating and basic facilities?

Outside, in the corridor, he could hear the sound of the nurse finally making her rounds with the drugs trolley. It rattled like a jar of nails as she slowly wheeled the thing along the uneven linoleum. Sogol banged ferociously on the door, in an attempt to attract her attention. He began shouting at the top of his voice that he demanded she see to him first and that he was suffering terrible pain.

"I'm next, you old bitch! I'm next! I'm dying in here!"

A grille in the door opened and through the latticework her thin, doll-like head hoved into view. The nurse wore an old-fashioned mobcap. She looked at him with small black eyes, devoid of emotion.

"Stage fright, eh? Stage fright?" The words came from a toothless hole ringed by a gaudy mess of smeared lipstick. Saliva oozed down out of it onto a flabby chin dotted with hairs. "Open wide, ugly. Open wide for Nurse Judy."

She thrust two green-coated pills through the interstices and dropped them. Sogol scrambled to the floor and then swallowed them eagerly. When he looked up, the grille was closed again and he heard her continuing her rounds, whistling a discordant melody.

After fifteen minutes had passed the two grim-faced orderlies entered his room, picked Sogol up from the floor and slung him onto the bed, strapping him down to it. They left the door open, on purpose it seemed, and he stared at the aperture with dry, unblinking eyes. There were moments when the uninterrupted light affecting his retina turned everything into a hazy fog of white blindness.

There is an old television set dating from the 1930s or 1940s. It is housed in a four-foot-tall wooden cabinet with a ten-inch-high flickering blue screen on the front. In a darkened, derelict room a shadowy figure with a patchwork face silently watches the display. The signal that the device is receiving is an image of a long-out-of-date test card. In the center of the image is a circle with vertical lines that thicken from right to left. Outside the circle is a black space that fills the rest of the screen. Written in white lettering on the space are the following words:

Above the circle are a logo and a slogan: SHALLABALLAH, Television IS THE NEW AFTERLIFE. Right: DELAYED IMAGES (GHOSTS) MAY APPEAR ON THE BLACK OR WHITE STRIPS. Left: RECEPTION REPORTS MAY BE SENT TO MR.. PUNCH. COLLEGE OF PROFESSORS. ENG. DIV., LONDON N.19. Underneath: TEST TRANSMISSION.

Accompanying the visual broadcast is a monaural sound; a four-frequency tone that ranges from a very low droning whine to a very high shrill pitch. It is played on a continuous loop. The individual watching and listening to the broadcast is humming to himself, and he eerily mimics the noise coming from the television set's speaker, as if hypnotized.

Sogol heard footsteps and murmuring voices from outside in the corridor. It sounded like someone was conversing with the nurse and he was certain that he heard his name mentioned, though exactly what they were discussing was too indistinguishable to make out. When she came into the room she was carrying an old suitcase, which she set down on the end of his bed. The nurse opened it, and took out items of stage makeup, foundation, powder, and natural skin colorings, as well as a small set of scissors and tweezers. She began to cut and unpick his stitches from his skin. Once she'd finished, she applied some of the makeup to his face, doing her best to mask his blemishes and wounds.

A TV studio with a set designed to look like an operating theater from the 1930s or 1940s. The cameras that the operators are using are as out-of-date as the mock surroundings. Each device requires not only someone to point the lens but also someone else to wheel it around at the base as it closes in on a shot. At the operating table are life-size Punch and Judy puppets in white smocks, masks and gloves. Their movements are stiff and awkward although Punch tries occasionally to caper. Judy passes surgical implements over to him as he tinkers with the exposed brain of a man whose skull has been sawn open. Punch makes incisions in the man's frontal lobe with a scalpel and inserts a series of wires into the holes. The wires are connected to an obsolete television set next to the operating table. The TV is switched on. During the operation a camera draws closer and on the screen next to the table the heavily made-up face of the man being operated on can be seen quite clearly, though the im-

*age is grainy and slightly distorted. His eyes are open. They move from side to side.
Not once does he blink.*

*During the operation Punch and Judy quarrel with each other. Punch throws Judy
to the floor and changes the channel on the TV set, moving a frequency dial until it's
tuned into a station showing a program in which the patient on the table is the star.*

Sogol wandered along the corridors beyond his own room. The effects of the drug
had worn off some hours before although he still suffered from stiffness in his legs
and back, making him walk with a shuffling gait, like that of an elderly man. It
seemed that his treatment was over, for a note left in his room had advised him that
he was to be released after a final interview and examination by Mr. Punch.

He ran his fingers over the flesh of his face. It was almost totally smooth except for
some very thin scar lines and all the lost sensation and movement had now returned.
As the CCTV cameras tracked Sogol's movement through the passageways, he could
not resist turning his gaze upon them so that whoever was observing him could not
help but see him more clearly. Once, he even flashed one of his best trademark
smiles at the indifferent lens. The only thing that continued to trouble him was the
damned wig. But he had to wear it in order to cover the fresh stitches that had been
sewn all the way around his head. Anyway, as soon as he was on the outside it would
be easy enough to find a more sophisticated and comfortable hairpiece.

He passed through a set of double doors. Above the entrance Sogol saw a green
sign that read STUDIO 7. He gazed around him with bemused astonishment at
what he saw in the room. It was dusty and almost bare. At the far end stood a
portable canvas booth, like those used for puppet theater. However, where the stage
opening should be there was instead a television screen. The device inside was
switched on but the picture showed only a card with the words AN ANNOUNCE-
MENT IS BEING MADE IN SOUND on a black background. The sound it emit-
ted was a four-frequency tone, its pitch rising and falling. In the center of the room
a hangman's noose dangled from the ceiling. Directly beneath it was a trapdoor, operated by a lever mechanism fixed onto the bare floorboards.

Then Punch and Judy appeared from behind him. They seized Sogol and although he struggled wildly, the two of them quickly had his hands bound behind his
back with a length of cord. Mr. Punch placed a noose over his neck and tightened
the knot until the rope chafed his throat. Judy dragged his body by its legs into a
standing position above the trapdoor. Neither of them spoke a word, maintaining a
grim, terrifying silence. Mr. Punch beat Sogol about his head viciously with a stick,
until he stopped resisting.

When Sogol was in the right position, the tes-card on the screen faded out although the four-frequency tone continued to be broadcast. The inky blackness
slowly gave way to black and white static. Inside the chaos of the electronic snow features began to coalesce and take shape; a deformed maw that might have been a
mouth and twin holes that might have been empty eye sockets.

Mr. Punch covered Sogol's head with a cloth bag. For some reason it had mouth
and eyeholes cut into the rough material. Then the lever was pulled and Sogol's
flailing body dropped into the opening that appeared beneath him. He fell for fifteen feet before the rope reached its full length and the knot at the base of his skull
snapped his neck.

Up in Studio 7 the face on the television screen in the booth continued to take
shape. Its features became more distinct and more like those of Sogol with each moment that passed.

SARAH MONETTE

Night Train: Heading West

In 2005, Sarah Monette completed her Ph.D. in English Literature, and saw the publication of her debut fantasy novel, first of a quartet of elegant novels of political, magical, and sexual intrigue—the extremely enjoyable Crawford Award finalist Melusine. *This year Monette also published stories in* Tales of the Unanticipated *and* Lady Churchill's Rosebud Wristlet. *"Night Train: Heading West" appeared in the Spring issue of* The Magazine of Speculative Poetry.*

—K.L. & G.G.

In the lounge car, the insomniacs:
a woman playing Solitaire,
the conductor
telling three Minnesota ladies
about his past lives,
a teenage boy, protected
by headphones, staring into the vast
darkness beyond the windows.

The cards
growl through her hands;
she lays them down,
making patterns, looking
for some small meaning.

The Black Death, the conductor
tells the ladies.
It was the third time I had
died in Rome.

The pattern comes to
nothing. She sweeps
the cards together,
shuffles brusquely,
lays them down again.

Egypt, says the
conductor. I
was a priest of Anubis.

I spent my
days among the dead.

A snarl,
a failure.
With impatient hands, she
gathers the cards, lays them down.

The teenage boy rocks
gently to the music only
he can hear. The night
pours past, another river,

like the Mississippi
they have already crossed.
But the night is a river
we are all still crossing.

I was a woman
once, the conductor says.
A Cherokee woman. I died
on the Trail of Tears. I remember
how tired I was, and
how everything tasted of destruction.

She picks up the
cards and deals again.

BRUCE STERLING

Denial

Bruce Sterling's "Denial" was published in the September issue of The Magazine of Fantasy & Science Fiction. Best known as a futurist and science fiction novelist, Sterling has produced a witty fable that touches on natural disasters, marriage, and life after death. Sterling's stories "Bicycle Repairman" and "Taklamaken" won the Hugo. His most recent novels were Distraction, Zeitgeist, and The Zenith Angle, and his nonfiction includes Tomorrow Now: Envisioning the Next Fifty Years and Shaping Things. Last year he became "visionary in residence" at Art Center College of Design in Pasadena, California. He is married to Serbian author and filmmaker Jasmina Tesanovic. Sterling blogs for Wired.com and lives in Austin, Texas.

—K.L. & G.G.

Yusuf climbed the town's ramshackle bridge. There he joined an excited crowd: gypsies, unmarried apprentices, the village idiot, and three ne'er-do-wells with a big jug of plum brandy. The revelers had brought along a blind man with a fiddle.

The river was the soul of the town, but the heavy spring rains had been hard on her. She was rising from her bed in a rage. Tumbling branches clawed through her foam like the mutilated hands of thieves.

The crowd tore splinters from the bridge, tossed them in the roiling water, and made bets. The blind musician scraped his bow on his instrument's single string. He wailed out a noble old lament about crops washed away, drowned herds, hunger, sickness, poverty, and grief.

Yusuf listened with pleasure and studied the rising water with care. Suddenly a half-submerged log struck a piling. The bridge quivered like a sobbing violin. All at once, without a word, the crowd took to their heels.

Yusuf turned and gripped the singer's ragged shoulder. "You'd better come with me."

"I much prefer it here with my jolly audience, thank you, sir!"

"They all ran off. The river's turning ugly, this is dangerous."

"No, no, such kind folk would not neglect me!"

Yusuf pressed a coin into the fiddler's palm.

The fiddler carefully rubbed the coin with his callused fingertips. "A copper penny! What magnificence! I kiss your hand!"

Yusuf was the village cooper. When his barrel trade turned lean, he sometimes patched pots. "See here, fellow, I'm no rich man to keep concubines and fiddlers!"

The fiddler stiffened. "I sing the old songs of your heritage, as the living voice of the dead! The devil's crows will peck the eyeballs of the stingy!"

"Stop trying to curse me and get off this stupid bridge! I'm buying your life with that penny!"

The fiddler spat. At last he tottered toward the far riverbank.

Yusuf abandoned the bridge for the solid cobbles of the marketplace. Here he found more reasonable men: the town's kadi, the wealthy beys, and the seasoned hadjis. These local notables wore handsome woolen cloaks and embroidered jackets. The town's Orthodox priest had somehow been allowed to join their circle.

Yusuf smoothed his vest and cummerbund. Public speech was not his place, but he was at least allowed to listen to his betters. He heard the patriarchs trade the old proverbs. Then they launched light-hearted quips at one another, as jolly as if their town had nothing to lose. They were terrified.

Yusuf hurried home to his wife.

"Wake and dress the boy and girl," he commanded. "I'm off to rouse my uncle. We're leaving the house tonight."

"Oh, no, we can't stay with your uncle," his wife protested.

"Uncle Mehmet lives on high ground."

"Can't this wait till morning? You know how grumpy he gets!"

"Yes, my Uncle Mehmet has a temper," said Yusuf, rolling his eyes. "It's also late, and it's dark. It will rain on us. It's hard work to move our possessions. This may all be for nothing. Then I'll be a fool, and I'm sure you'll let me know that."

Yusuf roused his apprentice from his sleeping nook in the workshop. He ordered the boy to assemble the tools and wrap them with care against damp. Yusuf gathered all the shop's dinars and put them inside his wife's jewelry box, which he wrapped in their best rug. He tucked that bundle into both his arms.

Yusuf carried his bundle uphill, pattered on by rain. He pounded the old man's door, and, as usual, his uncle Mehmet made a loud fuss over nothing. This delayed Yusuf's return. When he finally reached his home again, back down the crooked, muddy lanes, the night sky was split to pieces by lightning. The river was rioting out of her banks.

His wife was keening, wringing her hands, and cursing her unhappy fate. Nevertheless, she had briskly dressed the children and packed a stout cloth sack with the household's precious things. The stupid apprentice had disobeyed Yusuf's orders and run to the river to gawk; naturally, there was no sign of him.

Yusuf could carry two burdens uphill to his uncle's, but to carry his son, his daughter, and his cooper's tools was beyond his strength.

He'd inherited those precious tools from his late master. The means of his livelihood would be bitterly hard to replace.

He scooped the little girl into his arms. "Girl, be still! My son, cling to my back for dear life! Wife, bring your baggage!"

Black water burst over their sill as he opened the door. Their alley had become a long, ugly brook.

They staggered uphill as best they could, squelching through dark, crooked streets. His wife bent almost double with the heavy sack on her shoulders. They sloshed their way to higher ground. She screeched at him as thunder split the air.

"What now?" Yusuf shouted, unable to wipe his dripping eyes.

"My trousseau!" she mourned. "My grandmother's best things!"

"Well, I left my precious tools there!" he shouted. "So what? We have to live!"

She threw her heavy bag down. "I must go back or it will be too late!"

Yusuf's wife came from a good family. Her grandmother had been a landowner's fine lady, with nothing more to do than knit and embroider all day. The grandam had left fancy garments that Yusuf's wife never bothered to wear, but she dearly treasured them anyway. "All right, we'll go back together!" he lied to her. "But first, save our children!"

Yusuf led the way uphill. The skies and waters roared. The children wept and wriggled hard in their terror, making his burden much worse. Exhausted, he set them on their feet and dragged them by the hands to his uncle's door.

Yusuf's wife had vanished. When he hastened back downhill, he found her heavy bag around a streetcorner. She had disobeyed him, and run back downhill in the darkness.

The river had risen and swallowed the streets. Yusuf ventured two steps into the black, racing flood and was tumbled off his feet and smashed into the wall of a bakery. Stunned and drenched, he retreated, found his wife's abandoned bag, and threw that over his aching shoulders.

At his uncle's house, Mehmet was doubling the woes of his motherless children by giving them a good scolding.

As soon as it grew light enough to see again, Yusuf returned to the wreck of his home. Half the straw roof was gone, along with one wall of his shop. Black mud squished ankle-deep across his floor. All the seasoned wood for his barrels had floated away. By some minor quirk of the river's fury, his precious tools were still there, in mud-stained wrappings.

Yusuf went downstream. The riverbanks were thick with driftwood and bits of smashed homes. Corpses floated, tangled in debris. Some were children.

He found his wife past the bridge, around the riverbend. She was lodged in a muddy sandbar, along with many drowned goats and many dead chickens.

Her skirt, her apron, her pretty belt and her needleworked vest had all been torn from her body by the raging waters. Only her headdress, her pride and joy, was still left to her. Her long hair was tangled in that sodden cloth like river weed.

He had never seen her body nude in daylight. He pried her from the defiling mud, as gently as if she were still living and in need of a husband's help. Shivering with tenderness, he tore the shirt from his wet torso and wrapped her in it, then made her a makeshift skirt from his sash. He lifted her wet, sagging body in his arms. Grief and shame gave him strength. He staggered with her halfway to town.

Excited townsfolk were gathering the dead in carts. When they saw him, they ran to gawk.

Once this happened, his wife suddenly sneezed, lifted her head and, quick as a serpent, hopped down from his grip.

"Look, the cooper is alive!" the neighbors exulted. "God is great!"

"Stop staring like fools," his wife told them. "My man lost his shirt in the flood. You there, lend him your cloak."

They wrapped him up, chafed his cheeks, and embraced him.

The damage was grave in Yusuf's neighborhood, and worse yet on the opposite bank of the river, where the Catholics lived. The stricken people searched the filthy streets for their lost possessions and missing kin. There was much mourning, tumult, and despair. The townsfolk caught two looters, pilfering in the wreckage. The kadi had them beheaded. Their severed heads were publicly exposed on the bridge. Yusuf knew the headless thieves by sight; unlike the others, those rascals wouldn't be missed much.

It took two days for the suffering people to gather their wits about them, but common sense prevailed at last, and they pitched in to rebuild. Wounds were bound up and families reunited. Neighborhood women made soup for everyone in big cooking pots. Alms were gathered and distributed by the dignitaries. Shelter was found for the homeless in the mosques, the temple, and the churches. The dead were retrieved from the sullen river and buried properly by their respective faiths.

The Vizier sent troops from Travnik to keep order. The useless troopers thundered through town on horseback, fired their guns, stole and roasted sheep, and caroused all night with the gypsies. Moslems, Orthodox, and Catholics alike waited anxiously for the marauders to ride home and leave them in peace.

Yusuf's wife and the children stayed at his uncle's while Yusuf put another roof on his house. The apprentice had stupidly broken his leg in the flood—so he had to stay snug with his own family, where he ate well and did no work, much as usual.

Once the damaged bridge was safe for carts again, fresh-cut lumber became available. In the gathering work of reconstruction, Yusuf found his own trade picking up. With a makeshift tent up in lieu of his straw roof, Yusuf had to meet frantic demands for new buckets, casks, and water-barrels. Price was no object, and no one was picky about quality.

Sensing opportunity, the Jews lent money to all the craftsmen of standing, whether their homes were damaged or not. Gold coins appeared in circulation, precious Ottoman sultani from the royal mint in distant Istanbul. Yusuf schemed hard to gain and keep a few.

When he went to fetch his family back home, Yusuf found his wife with a changed spirit. She had put old Mehmet's place fully into order: she'd aired the old man's stuffy cottage, beaten his moldy carpet, scrubbed his floors, banished the mice, and chased the spiders into hiding. His uncle's dingy vest and sash were clean and darned. Old Mehmet had never looked so jolly. When Yusuf's lively children left his home, Mehmet even wept a little.

His wife flung her arms around Yusuf's neck. When the family returned to her wrecked, muddy home, she was as proud as a new bride. She made cleaning up the mud into an exciting game for the children. She cast the spoiled food from her drowned larder. She borrowed flour, bought eggs, conjured up salt, found milk from heaven, and made fresh bread.

Neighbors came to her door with soup and cabbage rolls. Enchanted by her charming gratitude, they helped her to clean. As she worked, his wife sang like a lark. Everyone's spirits rose, despite all the trials, or maybe even because of the trials, because they gave people so much to gripe about. Yusuf said little and watched his wife with raw disbelief. With all her cheerful talk and singing, she ate almost nothing. That which she chewed, she did not swallow.

When he climbed reluctantly into their narrow bed, she was bright-eyed and willing. He told her that he was tired. She obediently put her cool, damp head into the hollow of his shoulder and passed the night as quiet as carved ivory: never a twitch, kick, or snore.

Yusuf knew for a fact that his wife had been swept away and murderously tumbled down a stony riverbank for a distance of some twenty arshin. Yet her pale skin showed no bruising anywhere. He finally found hidden wounds on the soles of her feet. She had struggled hard for her footing as the angry waters dragged her to her death.

In the morning she spoke sweet words of encouragement to him. His hard work would bring them sure reward. Adversity was refining his character. The neighbors admired his cheerful fortitude. His son was learning valuable lessons by his manly example. All this wifely praise seemed plausible enough to Yusuf, and no more than he deserved, but he knew with a black flood of occult certainty that this was not the woman given him in marriage. Where were her dry, acidic remarks? Her balky back-talk? Her black, sour jokes? Her customary heartbreaking sighs, which mutely suggested that every chance of happiness was lost forever?

Yusuf fled to the market, bought a flask of fiery rakija and sat down to drink hard in midday.

Somehow, in the cunning pretext of "repairing" their flood-damaged church, the Orthodox had installed a bronze bell in their church tower. Its clangor now brazenly competed with the muezzin's holy cries. It was entirely indecent that this wicked contraption of the Serfish Slaves (the Orthodox were also called "Slavish Serfs," for dialects varied) should be casting an ungodly racket over the stricken town. Yusuf felt as if that great bronze barrel and its banging tongue had been hung inside his own chest.

The infidels were ringing bells, but he was living with a corpse.

Yusuf drank, thought slowly and heavily, then drank some more. He might go to the kadi for help in his crisis, but the pious judge would recommend what he always suggested to any man troubled by scandal—the long pilgrimage to Mecca. For a man of Yusuf's slender means, a trip to Arabia was out of the question. Besides, word would likely spread that he had sought public counsel about his own wife. His own wife, and from such a good family, too. That wasn't the sort of thing that a man of standing would do.

The Orthodox priest was an impressive figure, with a big carved staff and a great black towering hat. Yusuf had a grudging respect for the Orthodox. Look how they'd gotten their way with that bell tower of theirs, against all sense and despite every obstacle. They were rebellious and sly, and they clung to their pernicious way of life despite being taxed, fined, scourged, beheaded, and impaled. Their priest—he might well have some dark, occult knowledge that could help in Yusuf's situation.

But what if, in their low cunning, the peasants laughed at him and took advantage somehow? Unthinkable!

The Catholics were fewer than the Orthodox, a simple people, somewhat more peaceable. But the Catholics had Franciscan monks. Franciscan monks were sorcerers who had come from Austria with picture books. The monks recited spells in Latin from their gold-crowned Pope in Rome. They boasted that their Austrian troops could beat the Sultan's janissaries. Yusuf had seen a lot of Austrians. Austrians were rich, crafty, and insolent. They knew bizarre and incredible things. Bookkeeping, for instance.

Could he trust Franciscan monks to deal with a wife who refused to be dead? Those celibate monks didn't even know what a woman was for! The scheme was absurd.

Yusuf was not a drinking man, so the rakija lifted his imagination to great heights. When the local rabbi passed by chance, Yusuf found himself on his feet, stumbling after the Jew. The rabbi noticed this and confronted him. Yusuf, suddenly thick of tongue, blurted out something of his woes.

The rabbi wanted no part of Yusuf's troubles. However, he was a courteous man, and he had a wise suggestion.

There were people of the Bogomil faith within two days' journey. These Bogomils had once been the Christian masters of the land, generations ago, before the

Ottoman Turks brought order to the valleys and mountains. Both Catholics and Orthodox considered the Bogomils to be sinister heretics. They thought this for good reason, for the Bogomils (who were also known as "Cathars" and "Patarines"), were particularly skilled in the conjuration and banishment of spirits.

So said the rabbi. The local Christians believed that the last Bogomils had been killed or assimilated long ago, but a Jew, naturally, knew better than this. The rabbi alleged that a small clan of the Old Believers still lurked in the trackless hills. Jewish peddlers sometimes met the Bogomils, to do a little business: the Bogomils were bewhiskered clansmen with goiters the size of fists, who ambushed the Sultan's tax men, ripped up roads, ate meat raw on Fridays, and married their own nieces.

Next day, when Yusuf recovered from his hangover, he told his wife that he needed to go on pilgrimage into the hills for a few days. She should have pointed out that their house was still half-wrecked and his business was very pressing. Instead she smiled sweetly, packed him four days of home-cooked provisions, darned his leggings, and borrowed him a stout donkey.

No one could find the eerie Bogomil village without many anxious moments, but Yusuf did find it. This was a dour place where an ancient people of faith were finally perishing from the Earth. The meager village clustered in the battered ruin of a hillside fort. The poorly thatched hovels were patched up from tumbledown bits of rock. Thick nettles infested the rye fields. The goats were scabby, and the donkeys knock-kneed. The plum orchard buzzed with swarms of vicious yellow wasps. There was not a child to be seen.

The locals spoke a Slavish dialect so thick and archaic that it sounded as if they were chewing stale bread. They did have a tiny church of sorts, and in there, slowly dipping holy candles in a stinking yellow mix of lard and beeswax, was their elderly, half-starved pastor, the man they called their "Djed."

The Bogomil Djed wore the patched rags of black ecclesiastical robes. He had a walleye, and a river of beard tumbling past his waist.

With difficulty, Yusuf confessed.

"I like you, Moslem boy," said the Bogomil priest, with a wink or a tic of his bloodshot walleye. "It takes an honest man to tell such a dark story. I can help you."

"Thank you! Thank you! How?"

"By baptizing you in the gnostic faith, as revealed in the Palcyaf Bible. A dreadful thing has happened to you, but I can clarify your suffering, so hearken to me. God, the Good God, did not create this wicked world. This evil place, this sinful world we must endure, was created by God's elder archangel, Satanail the Demiurge. The Demiurge created all the Earth, and also some bits of the lower heavens. Then Satanail tried to create Man in the image of God, but he succeeded only in creating the flesh of Man. That is why it was easy for Satanail to confound and mislead Adam, and all of Adam's heritage, through the fleshly weakness of our clay."

"I never heard that word, *Demiurge*. There's only one God."

"No, my boy, there are two Gods: the bad God, who is always with us, and the good God, who is unknowable. Now I will tell you all about the dual human and divine nature of Jesus Christ. This is the most wonderful of gnostic gospels; it involves the Holy Dove, the Archangel Michael, Satanail the Creator, and the Clay Hierographon."

"But my wife is not a Christian at all! I told you, she comes from a nice family."

"Your wife is dead."

A chill gripped Yusuf. He struggled for something to say.

"My boy, is your woman nosferatu? You can tell me."

"I don't know that word either."

"Does she hate and fear the light of the sun?"

"My wife loves sunlight! She loves flowers, birds, pretty clothes, she likes everything nice."

"Does she suck the blood of your children?"

Yusuf shook his head and wiped at his tears.

The priest shrugged reluctantly. "Well, no matter—you can still behead her and impale her through the heart! Those measures always settle things!"

Yusuf was scandalized. "What would I tell the neighbors?"

The old man sighed. "She's dead and yet she walks the Earth, my boy. You do need to do something."

"How could a woman be dead and not know she's dead?"

"In her woman's heart she suspects it. But she's too stubborn to admit it. She died rashly and foolishly, disobeying her lord and master, and she left her woman's body lying naked in some mud. Imagine the shame to her spirit! This young wife with a house and small children, she left her life's duties undone! Her failure was more than her spirit could admit. So, she does not live, but she stubbornly persists." The priest slowly dipped a bare white string into his pot of wax. "'A man may work from sun to sun, but a woman's work is never done.'"

Yusuf put his head in his hands and wept. The Djed had convinced him. Yusuf was sure that he had found the best source of advice on his troubles, short of a long trip to Mecca. "What's to become of me now? What's to become of my poor children?"

"Do you know what a succubus is?" said the priest.

"No, I never heard that word."

"If your dead wife had become a succubus, you wouldn't need any words. Never mind that. I will prophesy to you of what comes next. Her dead flesh and immortal spirit must part sometimes, for that is their dual nature. So sometimes you will find that her spirit is there, while her flesh is not there. You will hear her voice and turn to speak; but there will be no one. The pillow will have the dent of her head, but no head lying there. The pot might move from the stove to the table, with no woman's hands to move it."

"Oh," said Yusuf. There were no possible words for such calamities.

"There will also be moments when the spirit retreats and her body remains. I mean the rotten body of a woman who drowned in the mud. If you are lucky you might not see that rotten body. You will smell it."

"I'm accursed! How long can such torments go on?"

"Some exorcist must persuade her that she met with death and her time on Earth is over. She has to be confronted with the deceit that her spirit calls 'truth.' She has to admit that her life is a lie."

"Well, that will never happen," said Yusuf. "I never knew her to admit to a mistake since the day her father gave her to me."

"Impale her heart while she sleeps!" demanded the Djed. "I can sell you the proper wood for the sharpened stake—it is the wood of life, *lignum vitae*, I found it growing in the dead shrine of the dead God Mithras, for that is the ruin of a failed resurrection. . . . The wood of life has a great herbal virtue in all matters of spirit and flesh."

Yusuf's heart rebelled. "I can't stab the mother of my children between her breasts with a stick of wood!"

"You are a cooper," said the Djed, "so you do have a hammer."

"I mean that I'll cast myself into the river before I do any such thing!"

The Djed hung his candle from a small iron rod. "To drown one's self is a great calamity."

"Is there nothing better to do?"

"There is another way. The black way of sorcery." The Djed picked at his long beard. "A magic talisman can trap her spirit inside her dead body. Then her spirit cannot slip free from the flesh. She will be trapped in her transition from life to death, a dark and ghostly existence."

"What kind of talisman does that?"

"It's a fetter. The handcuff of a slave. You can tell her it's a bracelet, a woman's bangle. Fix that fetter, carved from the wood of life, firmly around her dead wrist. Within that wooden bracelet, a great curse is written: the curse that bound the children of Adam to till the soil, as the serfs of Satanail, ruler and creator of the Earth. So her soul will not be able to escape her clay, any more than Adam, Cain, and Abel, with their bodies made of clay by Satanail, could escape the clay of the fields and pastures. She will have to abide by that untruth she tells herself, for as long as that cuff clings to her flesh."

"Forever, then? Forever and ever?"

"No, boy, listen. I told you 'as long as that cuff clings to her flesh.' You will have to see to it that she wears it always. This is necromancy."

Yusuf pondered the matter, weeping. Peaceably, the Bogomil dipped his candles.

"But that's all?" Yusuf said at last. "I don't have to stab her with a stick? I don't have to bury her, or behead her? My wife just wears a bracelet on her arm, with some painted words! Then I go home."

"She's dead, my boy. You are trapping a human soul within the outward show of rotten form. She will have no hope of salvation. She will be the hopeless slave of earthly clay and the chattel of her circumstances. For you to do that to another human soul is a mortal sin. You will have to answer for that on the Day of Judgment." The Djed adjusted his sleeves. "But, you are Moslem, so you are damned already. All the more so for your woman, so. . . ." The Djed spread his waxy hands.

The rabbi had warned Yusuf about the need for ready cash.

When Yusuf and his borrowed donkey returned home, footsore and hungry after five days of risky travel, he found his place hung with the neighbors' laundry. It was as festive as a set of flags. All the rugs and garments soiled by the flood needed boiling and bleaching. So his wife had made herself the bustling center of this lively activity.

Yusuf's smashed straw roof was being replaced with sturdy tiles. The village tiler and his wife had both died in the flood. The tiler's boy, a sullen, skinny teen, had lived, but his loss left him blank-eyed and silent.

Yusuf's wife had found this boy, haunted, shivering, and starving. She had fed him, clothed him, and sent him to collect loose tiles. There were many tiles scattered in the wrecked streets, and the boy knew how to lay a roof, so, somehow, without anything being said, the boy had become Yusuf's new apprentice. The new apprentice didn't eat much. He never said much. As an orphan, he was in no position to demand any wages or to talk back. So, although he knew nothing about making barrels, he was the ideal addition to the shop.

Yusuf's home, once rather well known for ruckus, had become a model of sociable charm. Neighbors were in and out of the place all the time, bringing sweets, borrowing flour and salt, swapping recipes, leaving children to be baby-sat. Seeing the empty barrels around, his wife had started brewing beer as a profitable sideline. She also stored red paprikas in wooden kegs of olive oil. People started leaving things at her house to sell. She was planning on building a shed to retail groceries.

There was never a private moment safe from friendly interruption, so Yusuf took his wife across the river, to the Turkish graveyard, for a talk. She wasn't reluctant to go, since she was of good birth and her long-established family occupied a fine, exclusive quarter of the cemetery.

"We never come here enough, husband," she chirped. "With all the rain, there's so much moss and mildew on Great-grandfather's stone! Let's fetch a big bucket and give him a good wash!"

There were fresh graves, due to the flood, and one ugly wooden coffin, still abandoned above ground. Moslems didn't favor wooden boxes for their dead—this was a Christian fetish—but they'd overlooked that minor matter when they'd had to inter the swollen, oozing bodies of the flood victims. Luckily, rumor had outpaced the need for such boxes. So a spare coffin was still on the site, half full of rainwater and humming with spring mosquitoes.

Yusuf took his wife's hand. Despite all her housework—she was busy as an ant— her damp hands were soft and smooth.

"I don't know how to tell you this," he said.

She blinked her limpid eyes and bit her lip. "What is it you have to complain about, husband? Have I failed to please you in some way?"

"There is one matter . . . a difficult matter. . . . Well, you see, there's more to the marriage of a man and woman than just keeping house and making money."

"Yes, yes," she nodded, "being respectable!"

"No, I don't mean that part."

"The children, then?" she said.

"Well, not the boy and girl, but . . . ," he said. "Well, yes, children! Chil-dren, of course! It's God's will that man and woman should bring children into the world! And, well, that's not something you and I can do anymore."

"Why not?"

Yusuf shuddered from head to foot. "Do I have to say that? I don't want to."

"What is it you want from me, Yusuf? Spit it out!"

"Well, the house is as neat as a pin. We're making a profit. The neighbors love you. I can't complain about that. You know I never complain. But if you stubbornly refuse to die, well, I can't go on living. Wife, I need a milosnica."

"You want to take a concubine?"

"Yes. Just a maidservant. Nobody fancy. Maybe a teenager. She could help around the house."

"You want me to shelter your stupid concubine inside my own house?"

"Where else could I put a milosnica? I'm a cooper, I'm not a bey or an aga."

Demonic light lit his wife's eyes. "You think of nothing but money and your shop! You never give me a second glance! You work all day like a gelded ox! Then you go on a pilgrimage in the middle of everything, and now you tell me you want a concubine? Oh, you eunuch, you pig, you big talker! I work, I slave, I suffer, I do everything to please you, and now your favor turns to another!" She raised her voice and screeched across the graveyard. "Do you see this, Grandmother? Do you see what's becoming of me?"

"Don't make me angry," said Yusuf. "I've thought this through and it's reasonable. I'm not a cold fish. I'm living with a dead woman. Can't I have one live woman, just to warm my bones?"

"I'd warm your bones. Why can't I warm your bones?"

"Because you drowned in the river, girl. Your flesh is cold."

She said nothing.

"You don't believe me? Take off those shoes," he said wearily. "Look at those wounds on the bottoms of your feet. Your wounds never heal. They can't heal." Yusuf tried to put some warmth and color into his voice. "You have pretty feet, you have the prettiest feet in town. I always loved your feet, but, well, you never show them to me, since you drowned in that river."

She shook her head. "It was *you* who drowned in the river."

"What?"

"What about that huge wound in your back? Do you think I never noticed that great black ugly wound under your shoulder? That's why you never take your vest off anymore!"

Yusuf no longer dared to remove his clothes while his wife was around, so, although he tried a sudden, frightened glance back over his own shoulder, he saw nothing there but embroidered cloth. "Do I really have a scar on my back? I'm not dead, though."

"Yes, husband, you are dead," his wife said bluntly. "You ran back for your stupid tools, even though I begged you to stay with me and comfort me. I saw you fall. You drowned in the street. I found your body washed down the river."

This mad assertion of hers was completely senseless. "No, that can't be true," he told her. "You abandoned me and the children, against my direct word to you, and you went back for your grandmother's useless trousseau, and you drowned, and I found you sprawling naked in the mud."

" 'Naked in the mud,' " she scoffed. "In your dreams!" She pointed. "You see that coffin? Go lie down in that coffin, stupid. That coffin's for you."

"That's your coffin, my dear. That's certainly not my coffin."

"Go lie down in there, you big hot stallion for concubines. You won't rise up again, I can promise you."

Yusuf gazed at the splintery wooden hulk. That coffin was a sorry piece of woodworking; he could have built a far better coffin himself. Out of nowhere, black disbelief washed over him. Could he possibly be in this much trouble? Was this what his life had come to? Him, a man of circumspection, a devout man, honest, a hard worker, devoted to his children? It simply could not be! It wasn't true! It was impossible.

He should have been in an almighty rage at his wife's stinging taunts, but somehow, his skin remained cool; he couldn't get a flush to his cheeks. He knew only troubled despair. "You really want to put me down in the earth, in such a cheap coffin, so badly built? The way you carry on at me, I'm tempted to lie down in there, I really am."

"Admit it, you don't need any concubine. You just want me out of your way. And after all I did for you, and gave to you! How could you pretend to live without me at your side, you big fool? I deserved much better than you, but I never left you, I was always there for you."

Part of that lament at least was true. Even when their temperaments had clashed, she'd always been somehow willing to jam herself into their narrow bed. She might be angry, yes, sullen, yes, impossible, yes, but she remained with him. "This is a pretty good fight we're having today," he said, "this is kind of like our old times."

"I always knew you'd murder me and bury me someday."

"Would you get over that, please? It's just vulgar." Yusuf reached inside the wrappings of his cummerbund. "If I wanted to kill you, would I be putting this on your hand?"

She brightened at once. "Oh! What's that you brought me? Pretty!"

"I got it on pilgrimage. It's a magic charm."

"Oh how sweet! Do let me have it, you haven't bought me jewelry in ages."

On a sudden impulse, Yusuf jammed his own hand through the wooden cuff. In an instant, memory pierced him. The truth ran through his flesh like a rusty sword. He remembered losing his temper, cursing like a madman, rushing back to his collapsing shop, in his lust and pride for some meaningless clutter of tools. . . . He could taste that deadly rush of water, see a blackness befouling his eyes, the chill of death filling his lungs—

He yanked his arm from the cuff, trembling from head to foot. "That never happened!" he shouted. "I never did any such thing! I won't stand for such insults! If they tell me the truth, I'll kill them."

"What are you babbling on about? Give me my pretty jewelry."

He handed it over.

She slid her hand through with an eager smile, then pried the deadly thing off her wrist as if it were red-hot iron. "You made me do that!" she screeched. "You made me run into the ugly flood! I was your victim! Nothing I did was ever my fault."

Yusuf bent at the waist and picked up the dropped bangle between his thumb and forefinger. "Thank God this dreadful thing comes off our flesh so easily!"

His wife rubbed the skin of her wrist. There was a new black bruise there. "Look, your gift hurt me. It's terrible!"

"Yes, it's very magical."

"Did you pay a lot of money for that?"

"Oh yes. I paid a lot of money. To a wizard."

"You're hopeless."

"Wife of mine, we're both hopeless. Because the truth is, our lives are over. We've failed. Why did we stumble off to our own destruction? We completely lost our heads!"

His wife squared her shoulders. "All right, fine! So you make mistakes! So you're not perfect!"

"Me? Why is it me all the time? What about you?"

"Yes, I know, I could be a lot better, but well, I'm stuck with you. That's why I'm no good. So, I don't forgive you, and I never will! But, anyway, I don't think we ought to talk about this anymore."

"Would you reel that snake's tongue of yours back into your head? Listen to me for once! We're all over, woman! We drowned, we both died together in a big disaster!"

"Yusuf, if we're dead, how can you be scolding me? See, you're talking nonsense! I want us to put this behind us once and for all. We just won't talk about this matter anymore. Not one more word. We have to protect the children. Children can't understand such grown-up things. So we'll never breathe a word to anyone. All right?"

Black temptation seized him. "Look, honey, let's just get in that coffin together. We'll never make a go of a situation like this, it can't be done. That coffin's not so bad. It's got as much room as our bed does."

"I won't go in there," she said. "I won't vanish from the Earth. I just won't, because I can't believe what you believe, and you can't make me." She suddenly snatched the bangle from his hand and threw it into the coffin. "There, get inside there with that nasty thing, if you're so eager."

"Now you've gone and spoiled it," he said sadly. "Why do you always have to do that, just to be spiteful? One of these days I'm really going to have to smack you around."

"When our children are ready to bury us, then they will bury us."

That was the wisest thing she had ever said. Yusuf rubbed the words over his dead tongue. It was almost a proverb. "Let the children bury us." There was a bliss to that, like a verse in a very old song. It meant that there were no decisions to be made. The time was still unripe. Nothing useful could be done. Justice, faith, hope and charity, life and death, they were all smashed and in a muddle, far beyond his repair and his retrieval. So just let it all be secret, let that go unspoken. Let the next generation look after all of that. Or the generation after that. Or after that. Or after that.

That was their heritage.

BARBARA RODEN

Northwest Passage

Barbara Roden was born in Vancouver, British Columbia, in 1963, and moved to England in 1992 where, with her husband Christopher, she founded Ash-Tree Press. In 1997 she returned to Canada, and now lives in the small ranching town of Ashcroft, 200 miles northeast of Vancouver. She is a six-time World Fantasy Award nominee and two-time winner.

Her work—mostly nonfiction—has appeared in journals and magazines in Canada, England, and the United States, and she edits All Hallows, the journal of the Ghost Story Society, in addition to her work with Ash-Tree Press. "Northwest Passage," one of her few works of fiction, is set in an unnamed part of British Columbia which is, in reality, only a few miles from where she now lives, and she has stayed in the cabin which forms the story's central location. The tale sprang from her fascination with the unknown and unknowable wilderness which makes up so much of British Columbia, as well as her interest in people who feel the need to strain against the bonds of civilization, often with devastating results. The story's roots can also be traced back to a comment made by her father many years ago, while looking out at the hillside that features in the story: "I always feel there's something up there watching me."

"Northwest Passage" was first published in Acquainted with the Night, an anthology edited by Ms. Roden.

—E.D.

How then am I so different from the first men through this way?
Like them I left a settled life, I threw it all away
To seek a Northwest Passage at the call of many men
To find there but the road back home again.

—Stan Rogers, "Northwest Passage"

They vary in detail, the stories, but the broad outline is the same.

Someone—hiker, hunter, tourist—goes missing, or is reported overdue, and there is an appeal to the public for information; the police become involved, and search and rescue teams, and there are interviews with friends and relatives, and statements by increasingly grim-faced officials, as the days tick by and hope begins to crack and waver and fade, like color leaching out of a picture left

too long in a window. Then there is the official calling off of the search, and gradually the story fades from sight, leaving family and friends with questions, an endless
round of what ifs and how coulds and where dids pursuing each other like restless
children.

Occasionally there is a coda, weeks or months or years later, when another hiker
or hunter or tourist—more skilled, or perhaps more fortunate—stumbles across evidence and carries the news back, prompting a small piece in the "In Brief" section
of the *Vancouver Sun* that is skimmed over by urban readers safe in a place of
straight lines and clearly delineated routes. They gaze at the expanse of Stanley Park
on their daily commute, and wonder how a person could vanish so easily in a landscape so seemingly benign.

Peggy Malone does not wonder this, nor does she ask herself any questions. She
suspects she already knows the answers, and it is safer to keep the questions which
prompt them locked away. Sometimes, though, they arise unbidden: when outside
her window the breeze rustles the leaves of the maple, the one she asked the Strata
Council to cut down, or the wind chimes three doors down are set ringing. Then the
questions come back, eagerly, like a dog left on its own too long, and she turns on
the television—not the radio, she rarely listens to that now—and turns on the lights
and tries, for a time, to forget.

The road was, as back roads in the Interior go, a good one: Len had always ensured
that it was graded regularly. Peggy, bumping her way up it in the Jeep, added "get
road seen to" to her mental checklist of things to do. She could not let it go another
summer; next spring's meltwater would eat away even further at the dirt and rocks,
and her sixty-three-year old bones could do without the added wear and tear.

She followed the twists and turns of the road, threading her way through stands of
cottonwood and birch and Ponderosa pine. Here and there the bright yellow of an
arrowleaf balsam root flashed into sight beneath the trees, enjoying a brief moment
of glory before withering and dying, leaving the silver-gray leaves as the only evidence of its passing. Overhead the sky was clear blue, but the breeze, when she
pulled the Jeep in front of the cabin, was cool, a reminder that spring, not summer,
held sway.

Peggy opened the rear of the Jeep and began unloading bags of supplies, which
seemed, as always, to have proliferated during the drive. There was nothing to be
done about it, however; the nearest town was an hour away, and she had long since
learned that it was better to err on the side of too much than too little. Even though
she was only buying for one now, the old habits died hard, and she usually managed
to avoid making the journey more than once every two weeks or so.

She loaded the last of the milk into the fridge, which, like the other appliances
and some of the lights, ran off propane; the light switch on the wall near the door
had been installed by Len in a fit of whimsy when the cabin was being built, and
served no useful purpose, as electricity did not extend up the valley from the highway some miles distant. The radio was battery operated, but seldom used: reception
was poor during the day and sporadic at night, with stations alternately competing
with each other and then fading away into a buzz of static. Kerosene lanterns and a
generator could be used in an emergency, and an airtight fireplace kept the cabin
more than warm enough in spring and fall. In winter she stayed with a nephew and
his family on Vancouver Island; Len's brother's son, Paul, a good, steady lad who
had given up urging his aunt to make the move to the Island permanent when he
saw that it did no good. She would move when she was ready, Peggy always replied;

she would know when the time came, and as long as she was able to drive and look after herself she was happy with the way things were.

Supplies unloaded, she set the kettle to boiling. A cup of tea would be just the thing, before she went out and did some gardening. It was not gardening in the sense that any of her acquaintances on the Island would understand it, with their immaculate, English-style flowerbeds and neatly edged, emerald green lawns which would not have looked out of place on a golf course; she called it that out of habit. She had learned, early on, that this land was tolerant of imposition only up to a point, and for some years her gardening had been confined to planting a few annuals—marigolds did well—in pots and hanging baskets.

Of course, she now had the grass to cut, and there were the paths to work on. It was Len who had suggested them, the summer before he had died, while watching her struggle to keep the sagebrush and wild grass at bay. The cabin was built on a natural bench, which overlooked the thickly treed valley, and was in turn overlooked by hills, rising relentlessly above until they lost themselves in the mountains behind. On three sides of the cabin the grassland stretched away to the trees, and Peggy had fought with it, trying, with her lawn and her flowers, to impose some sense of order on the landscape. She had resisted the idea of the paths at first, feeling that it would be giving in; but about what, and to whom, she could not have said. Still, she had started them for Len, who had taken comfort, that last summer, in watching her going about her normal tasks, and then she had continued them, partly because she felt she owed it to Len, and partly to fill the hours.

The paths now wound through a large part of the grassy area around the cabin. They were edged with rocks, and there were forks and intersections, and it was possible to walk them for some time without doubling back on oneself; not unlike, thought Peggy, one of those low mazes in which people were meant to think contemplative thoughts as they followed the path. She was not much given to contemplation herself, but keeping the existing paths free of weeds occupied her hands, and she supposed vaguely that it was good for her mind as well.

Now she stood looking at the paths, wondering whether she should do some weeding or check the mower and make sure it was in working order. It might have seized up over the winter; if so, then a good dose of WD-40 should take care of matters. She knew precisely where the tin was—Peggy knew precisely where everything in the cabin was—and was just turning toward the shed where the mower was stored when she heard the unmistakable sound of a vehicle coming up the road.

It was such an unusual sound that she stopped in her tracks and turned to face the gate, which hung open on its support, the only break in the fence of slender pine logs which encircled the property and served to keep out the cattle which occasionally wandered past. The road did not lead anywhere except to the cabin, and visitors were few and far between, for the simple reason that there was almost no one in the area to pay a visit. Peggy stood, waiting expectantly, and after a few moments a ramshackle Volkswagen van swung round the curve and started up the slight incline that leveled off fifty yards inside the gate, not far from the front of the cabin where her own Jeep was parked.

It pulled to a halt just inside the gate, and Peggy watched it. There were two people in the front seat, and for a minute no one made a move to get out; she got the impression that there was an argument going on. Then the passenger door opened, and a boy emerged, waving a tentative hand at her. She nodded her head, and the boy said something to the driver. Again Peggy got the impression that there was a disagreement of some sort; then the driver's door opened slowly, and another boy emerged.

She would have been a fool not to feel a slight sense of apprehension, and Peggy was not a fool. But she prided herself on being able to assess a situation quickly and accurately, and she did not feel any sense of threat. So she stood and waited as they approached her, taking in their appearance: one tall and fair-haired, the other shorter and dark; both in their early twenties, with longish hair and rumpled clothing and a general impression of needing a good square meal or two, but nothing that made her wish that the .202 she kept inside the cabin was close to hand.

The pair stopped a few feet from her, and the fair-haired boy spoke first.

"Hi. We, uh, we were just passing by, and we thought . . ." He trailed off, as if appreciating that "just passing by" was not something easily done in the area. There was a pause. Then he continued, "We heard your Jeep, and were kinda surprised; we didn't think anyone lived up here. So we thought that . . . well, that we'd come by and see who was here, and . . ."

The trickle of words stopped again, and the boy shrugged, helplessly, as if making an appeal. It was clear the other boy was not about to come to his aid, so Peggy picked up the thread.

"Margaret Malone," she said, moving forward, her hand extended. "Call me Peggy."

The fair-haired boy smiled hesitantly, and stuck out his own hand. "Hiya, Peggy. I'm John Carlisle, but everyone calls me Jack."

"Nice to meet you, Jack." Peggy turned to Jack's companion and looked at him evenly. "And you are . . . ?"

There was a pause, as if the boy was weighing the effect of not answering. Jack nudged him, and he said in a low voice, "Robert. Robert Parker."

Something about the way he said it discouraged any thoughts of Bob or Robbie. The conversation ground to a halt again, and once more Peggy took the initiative.

"So, you two boys students?" she asked pleasantly. Jack shook his head and said, "No, why d'you ask?" at the same moment that Robert said sullenly, "We're not boys."

Peggy took a moment to reply. "To answer you first," she said finally, nodding toward Jack, "we sometimes get students up here, from UBC or SFU, studying insects or infestation patterns, so it seemed likely. And to reply to your comment, Robert," she said, looking him directly in the eye, "when you get to my age you start to look at anyone under a certain age as being a boy; I didn't intend it as an insult. If I want to insult someone I don't leave them in any doubt."

Jack gave a sudden smile, which twitched across his face and was gone in an instant. Robert glared at him.

"If you don't mind my asking, what brings you to this neck of the woods? Seems kind of an out of the way spot for two . . . people . . . of your age, especially this time of year."

Nothing.

Really, thought Peggy, *was my generation as inarticulate as this when we were young? You'd think they'd never spoken to anyone else before.*

Again it was Jack who broke the silence.

"We're just, well, traveling around, you know? Taking some time out, doing something different, that kind of thing." Seeing the look in Peggy's eyes, he added, "We just wanted to go somewhere we wouldn't be bumping into people, somewhere we could do what we wanted. We've been up here for a few weeks now, staying in an old place we found over there." He pointed an arm in an easterly direction. "It was falling to pieces," he added, as if he was apologizing. "No one's lived there for ages, we figured it'd be okay."

Peggy held up a hand. "No problem as far as I'm concerned, if it's the place I think you mean. Used to be a prospector's cabin, but no one's used it for years. You're welcome to it. Last time I hiked over that way was some time ago, and it was a real handyman's special then. You must have done a lot of work to get it fixed up so that you could live in it."

Jack shrugged. "Yeah, but we're used to that. Lots of stuff lying around we could use."

"What do you do about food?"

"We stocked up in town; and there's an old woodstove in the cabin. We don't need a lot; we're used to roughing it."

Peggy eyed them both. "Seems to me you could do with something more than just roughing it in the food line for a couple of days."

"We do okay." It was Robert who spoke, as if challenging Peggy. "We do just fine. We don't want any help."

"I wasn't offering any, just making a comment. Last time I checked it was still a free country."

"Yeah, course it is," Jack said quickly. He glanced at Robert and shook his head; a small gesture, but Peggy noticed it. "Anyway, we heard your Jeep; we were kinda surprised to see someone living up here. We figured it was only a summer place."

"No, I'm up here spring through fall," said Peggy. "Afraid you're stuck with me as your nearest neighbor. Don't worry, I don't play the electric guitar or throw loud parties."

It was a small joke, but Jack smiled again, as if he appreciated Peggy's attempt to lighten the mood. Robert nodded his head in the direction of the van, and Jack's smile vanished.

"Well, we've got to get going," he said obediently. "Nice meeting you, Peggy."

"Nice meeting you two," she said. "If you need anything . . ."

"Thanks, that's really kind of you," said Jack. He seemed about to add something, but Robert cut in.

"Can't think we'll need any help," he said curtly. "C'mon, Jack. Lots to do."

"Yeah, right, lots to do. Thanks again, though, Peggy. See you around."

"Probably. It's a big country, but a small world."

"Hey, that's good." Jack smiled. "Big country, small world."

Robert, who had already climbed into the driver's seat, honked the horn, and Jack turned almost guiltily toward the van. The passenger door had hardly closed before Robert was turning the van around. Jack waved as they passed, and Peggy waved back, but Robert kept his eyes on the road and his hands on the wheel. Within moments they were through the gate, and the curve of the road had swallowed them up.

Over the next few days Peggy replayed this encounter in her head, trying to put her finger on what bothered her. Yes, Robert had been rude—well, brusque, at least—but then a lot of young people were, these days; some old people, too. Their story about wanting to see something different; that wasn't unusual, exactly, but Peggy could think of quite a few places that were different but which didn't involve fixing up a dilapidated shack in the middle of nowhere. Yet Jack had said they'd done that sort of thing before, so it was obviously nothing new for them.

Were they runaways? That might explain why they came to check out who was in the cabin. But if they were running away from someone, they would hardly have driven right up to her front door. Drugs crossed her mind; it was almost impossible to pick up the paper or turn on the news without hearing about another marijuana grow-op being raided by police. Most of them were in the city or up the Fraser Valley, but she had heard about such places in the country, too; and didn't they grow marijuana openly in some rural spots, far away from the prying eyes of the police and neighbors? That might explain why Jack had looked so nervous . . . but, when she recalled the conversation, and the way Jack had looked at his friend, she realized that he was not nervous on his own account, he was nervous for, or about, Robert, who had seemed not in the least bit nervous for, or about, anything. He had merely been extremely uncomfortable, as if being in the proximity of someone other than Jack, even for five minutes, made him want to escape. What had Jack said? They wanted to go somewhere they wouldn't be bumping into people.

Robert must have had a shock when he saw me here, thought Peggy. *Bet I was the last thing he expected—or wanted—to run into.*

She did not see the pair again for almost three weeks. Once she saw their van at the side of the road as she drove out toward the highway and town, but there was no sign of Jack or Robert, and on another occasion she thought she saw the pair of them far up on the hillside above her, but the sun was in her eyes and she couldn't be sure. She thought once or twice about hiking over to their cabin, which was two miles or so away. There had been a decent trail over there at one time, which she and Len had often walked; but the days were getting hotter, and her legs weren't what they once were, and when she reflected on her likely reception she decided she was better off staying put. If they wanted anything, or needed any help, they knew where to find her.

It was late morning, and Peggy had been clearing a new path. A wind had been gusting out of the northwest; when she stopped work and looked up the hill she could see it before she heard or felt it, sweeping through the trees, bearing down on her, carrying the scent of pine and upland meadows before rushing past and down the hill, setting the wind chimes by the front door tinkling, branches bending and swinging before it as if an unseen giant had passed. Sometimes a smaller eddy seemed to linger behind, puffing up dust on the paths, swirling round and about like something trapped and lost and trying to escape. But Peggy did not think of it like this; at least not then. Those thoughts did not come until later.

She straightened up, one hand flat against her lower back, stretching, and it was then that she saw the boy standing at the edge of the property, by the mouth of the trail leading to the prospector's cabin. She had no idea how long he had been standing there, but she realized that he must have been waiting for her to notice him before he came closer, for as soon as he knew he had been spotted he headed in her direction.

"Hello there," she said. "Jack, isn't it? Haven't seen you for a while; I was beginning to wonder if you'd moved on."

"No, we're still here." He gave a little laugh. "Kind of obvious, I guess."

"A bit. Your friend with you?"

"No."

"I'm not surprised. He didn't seem the dropping-in type."

"No." Jack seemed to feel that something more was needed. "He was a bit pissed off when he found someone was living here. He thought we had the place to ourselves, you see, no one around for miles."

"He likes his solitude, then."

"You could say that."

"Still, it's not as if I'm on your doorstep," said Peggy reasonably, "or, to be strictly accurate, that you're on mine. If your friend doesn't want to run into anyone, he's picked as good a spot as any."

"Yeah, that's what I've been telling him, but I think we'll be heading out before the end of the summer."

"Because of me?"

"Well, no; I mean, sort of, but that's not the whole reason. Robert"—he paused, looking for words—"Robert likes to keep on moving. Restless, I guess you could say. He's always been like that; always wants to see what's over the next hill, around the next corner, always figures there's somewhere better out there."

"Better than what?"

Jack shrugged. "I don't know. He gets somewhere, and he seems happy enough for a while, and then, just when I think 'Right, this is it, this is the place he's been looking for,' off he goes again."

"Do you always go with him?"

"Yeah, usually. We've known each other a long time, since elementary school. His family moved from back east and we wound up in the same grade three class."

"Where was that?"

"Down in Vancouver. Point Gray."

Peggy nodded. Point Gray usually, but not always, meant money, respectability, expectations. She could see Robert, from what little she knew of him, being from, but not of, that world. Jack, though, looked like Point Gray, and she wondered how he had found himself caught up in Robert's orbit.

"He's always been my best friend," the boy said, as if reading her thoughts. "We hung out together. I mean, I had other friends, but Robert just had me. It didn't bother him, though. If he wanted to do something and I couldn't, he'd just go off on his own, no problem. It's like he always knew I'd be there when he needed me."

"Has he always liked the outdoor life?"

Jack nodded. "Yeah, he's always been happiest when he's outside." He shook his head. "I remember this one time I got him to go along with a group of us who were going camping for the weekend. We were all eleven, twelve; our parents didn't mind, they figured there were enough of us that we'd be safe." He paused, remembering. "We rode our bikes from Point Gray out to Sea Island; you know, behind the airport." Peggy nodded. "There used to be a big subdivision out there, years ago, but then they were going to build another runway and the houses got . . . what's the word . . . expropriated, and torn down, and then nothing happened, and it all got pretty wild, the gardens and trees and everything.

"Well, we all had the usual shit . . . I mean stuff; dinky pup tents and old sleeping bags and things, and chocolate bars and pop, but not Robert. He had a tarp, and a plastic sheet, and a blanket, matches, a compass, trail mix, bottled water; he even had an ax. You'd've thought he was on a military exercise, or one of those survival weekends, instead of in the suburbs. We goofed around, and ate, and told stories, and then we crawled into our tents, all except Robert. He'd built a fire, and a lean-to out of branches and the tarp, and he said he'd stay where he was, even when it started to rain. Rain in Vancouver: who'd think it?

"Anyway, when morning came round, we were a pretty miserable bunch of kids; the tents had leaked, and our sleeping bags were soaked, and we'd eaten almost everything we'd brought. And there was Robert, dry as a bone, making a fire out of wood he'd put under cover the night before, with food and water to spare. Made us all look like a bunch of idiots."

"Sounds like a good person to have around you in a place like this."

"Yeah, you could say that." He scuffed the toe of one foot against the dirt, watching puffs of dust swirl up into the air.

"So where is he this morning?"

Jack stopped scuffing and looked up at Peggy. "He went off a couple of hours ago; said he needed to get away for a while, be on his own. He gets like that sometimes. I hung around for a bit by myself and then . . ." His look was almost pleading. "It just got so quiet, you know? You don't realize how quiet it is 'til you're by yourself. Robert doesn't mind; sometimes I think he'd rather be by himself all the time, that he wouldn't even notice if I never came back."

Peggy tried to think of something to say. Jack went back to scuffing the dirt, and a breeze picked up the cloud of dust, swirling it in the direction of the paths. Jack followed the cloud with his eyes, and seemed to notice the paths through the grass for the first time.

"Hey, that's pretty cool." He took a couple of steps forward, and she could see his head moving as he followed the curves of the paths with his eyes. "Bet it would look neat from overhead, like in one of those old Hollywood musicals."

Peggy had not recognized the tension in the situation until it was gone; its sudden disappearance left her feeling slightly off-balance, like an actor momentarily surprised by the unexpected ad-lib of someone else on stage. Jack was still gazing out over the paths.

"Must've taken a long time to do this," he said. "What's it for?"

"Nothing, really." Peggy moved forward so that she was standing beside him. "It was my husband's idea; he said he got tired of watching me trying to control the brush, that I should work with it, not against it."

If you can't beat 'em, join 'em, she heard Len's voice say. *And looking at all that—* he had waved his hand toward the expanse of scrub and the hills beyond—*I don't think you're ever going to beat 'em, Peg.*

"If you can't beat them, join them," said Jack, and Peggy started slightly and looked sideways at him. "That's how I feel about Robert sometimes. Can I take a closer look?"

"Go ahead." Peggy looked at her watch. "I'm going to go and make some lunch; nothing fancy, just sandwiches and some fruit, but if you want to stay then you're more than welcome."

"Could I?" he asked eagerly. "I'd really like that. Our cooking's pretty . . . basic."

Peggy, noting Jack's pinched face and pale complexion, could believe it. "I'll go and rustle something up; come in when you're ready."

She stood at the kitchen counter, letting her hands move through the familiar motions of spreading butter and mayonnaise, slicing tomatoes and cucumber, while in her head she went over the conversation with Jack. There were undercurrents she could not fathom, depths she could not chart. She had thought of them as two boys from the city playing at wilderness life, and Jack's words had not dismissed this as a possibility; but there was something else going on, she was sure of it. Were they lovers? Had they had a fight? That could be it, but she did not think so. She could not connect the dark, intense figure she had seen three weeks ago with something as essentially banal as a lovers' tiff.

Through the window she could see Jack moving slowly along one of the paths, his head down as if deep in concentration. He stopped, seemingly aware of her gaze upon him, but instead of turning toward the cabin he looked up at the hillside above, intently, his head cocked a little to one side as if he had heard something. Peggy followed his gaze, but could see nothing on the bare slope, or in the air above; certainly nothing that would inspire such rapt attention.

She stacked the sandwiches on a plate, then sliced some cheese and put it, with some crackers and grapes, on another plate. She wondered what to offer as a drink. Beer would have been the obvious choice, but she had none. Milk or orange juice; or perhaps he'd like a cup of coffee or tea afterward. . . .

Still pondering beverage choices, she put the plates on the table, then went to the door. Jack had not altered his position; he seemed transfixed by something up on the hill. Peggy looked again, sure that he was watching an animal, but there was nothing to be seen.

She called his name, and he turned to her with a startled look on his face, as if he could not quite remember who she was or how he had got there. Then he shook his head slightly and trotted toward her, like a dog who has heard the rattle of the can opener and knows his supper is ready.

"Sorry it's nothing more elegant," said Peggy, pointing to the table, "but help yourself. Don't be shy."

She soon realized that her words were unnecessary. Jack fell on the meal as if he had not eaten in days, and for some minutes the only sound was him asking if he could have another sandwich. Peggy got up twice to refill his milk glass before finally placing the jug on the table so he could help himself, and watched as the cheese and cracker supply dwindled. Finally Jack drained his glass and sighed contentedly.

"Thanks, Peggy, that was great, really. Didn't know how hungry I was until I saw the food. Guess I wouldn't win any awards for politeness."

Peggy laughed. "That's okay. It's been a long time since I saw someone eat something I'd made with that much pleasure. I'm sorry it wasn't anything more substantial."

Jack looked at his watch. "Geez, is that the time? I better be going; Robert'll be back soon, he'll wonder where I am, and I'll bet you've got things to do."

"Don't worry, my time's my own. Nice watch."

Jack smiled proudly, and held up his wrist so Peggy could see it better. Silver glinted at her. "Swiss Army. My parents gave it to me when I graduated. Keeps perfect time." He sat back in his chair and looked around the cabin. "You live here by yourself? You said something about your husband. Is he . . . ?" He stopped, unsure how to continue the sentence to its natural conclusion, so Peggy did it for him.

". . . dead, yes. Four years ago. Cancer. It was pretty sudden; there was very little the doctors could do."

"I'm sorry."

"That's okay. You didn't know him. He went quite quickly, which is what he wanted. Len was never a great one for lingering."

"So you live up here for most of the year on your own? That's pretty gutsy."

Peggy could not recall having been called gutsy before. "You think so?"

"Yeah, sure. I mean, this place is pretty isolated, and you're . . . well, you're not exactly young." His face went pink. "I don't mean that . . . it just must be tough, that's all, on your own. Don't you ever get lonely?"

"No, there's always something to do. I spend the winter with family on the Island; I get more than enough company then to see me through the rest of the year."

Jack nodded. His eyes continued moving around the cabin, and he spotted the light switch. "Hey, I didn't think you had power up here."

"We don't. That's a bit of a joke, for visitors."

"Bet you don't get too many of those."

"You'd be right. My nephew and his family have been up a couple of times, but not for a while. He doesn't like it much up here; says it makes him uncomfortable. This sort of place isn't for everyone."

Jack nodded. "You've got that right." He looked through the screen door toward the hillside and gestured with his head. "You ever feel that something's up there watching you?"

Peggy considered. "No, not really. An animal sometimes, maybe; but we don't get too many animals up there. Odd, really, you'd think it would be a natural place to spot them." A memory came back to her; Paul, her nephew, on one of his rare visits, standing on the porch looking up at the hills. "My nephew said once it reminded him of a horror movie his sons rented; *The Eyes on the Hill* or something."

"*The Hills Have Eyes*," Jack corrected automatically. "Yeah, I've seen it." He was silent for a moment. "Do you believe that?"

"What—that the hills have eyes? No."

"But don't you feel it?" he persisted. "Like there's something there, watching, waiting, something really old and . . . I don't know, part of this place, guarding it, protecting it, looking for something?"

Peggy couldn't keep the astonishment out of her face and voice. "No, I can honestly say I've never felt that at all." She considered him. "Is that what you think?"

"I don't know." He paused. "There's just something weird about this spot. I mean, we've been in some out-of-the-way places, Robert and me, but nowhere like this. I'll be kind of glad when he decides to move on. I hope it'll be soon."

"I thought you wanted him to settle down somewhere."

"Yeah, I do, but not here."

"Why don't you leave? Robert seems able to fend for himself, and he appears to like this sort of life better than you do. Why do you stay with him?"

"I've always stayed with him."

"But you said that he likes to go off on his own, that you don't think he'd notice if you didn't come back."

Jack looked uncomfortable, like a witness caught by a clever lawyer. "Oh, I just said that 'cause I was pissed off. He'd notice."

"Is he your boyfriend? Is that why you stay?"

Jack looked shocked. "God, no! It's nothing like that. It goes back a long way. . . . Remember I told you about that camping trip out to Sea Island? Well, when I went round to Robert's house to get him his mom was there, fussing, you know, the way moms do, and he was getting kind of impatient, and finally he just said 'Bye, Mom' really suddenly and went to get his bike, and his mom turned to me and said 'Look after him.' Which was kind of a weird thing to say, 'cause I was only eleven, and Robert wasn't the kind of kid who you'd think needed looking after—well, we found that out next day. But I knew what she meant. She didn't mean he needed looking after 'cause he'd do something stupid, she meant that he needed someone to . . . bring him back, almost, make sure he didn't go off and just keep on going."

"Is that why you stay with him? So he doesn't just keep on going?"

"I guess." His smile was tinged with sadness. "I'm not doing such a great job, am I?"

"You're a long way from Point Gray, if that's what you mean."

"Yeah, and I can't see us making it back anytime soon. Robert wants to keep heading north, up to the Yukon, and then head east."

"What on earth for?"

Jack shrugged. "He does a lot of reading; he's got a box of books in the van, all about explorers and people who go off into the wilderness with just some matches and a rifle and a sack of flour and live off the land. I think that's what he wants to do; go up north and see what's there, see what he can do, what he can find. He loves reading about the Franklin expedition; you know, the one that disappeared when they were searching for the Northwest Passage, and no one knew for years what happened to them. I think he likes the idea of just vanishing, and no one knows where you are, and then you come out when you're ready, and tell people what you've found."

"The Franklin expedition didn't come out."

"Robert figures he can do better than them."

"Well then, you should break it to him that the Northwest Passage was found a long time ago, and tell him he should maybe stick closer to home."

"He doesn't want to find the Northwest Passage; anyway, he says it doesn't really exist, there is no Northwest Passage, not like everyone thought back in Franklin's time."

"And you'll go with him?"

"I suppose so."

"You do have a choice, you know."

"Yeah, like you said, it's a free country. But I kind of feel like I have to go with him, to . . ."

"Look after him?"

"I guess." He shrugged. "It's like there's something out there, waiting for him, and I have to make sure he comes back okay, otherwise he'd just keep on going, and he'd be like those Franklin guys, he'd never come out."

The conversation was interrupted by the unmistakable sound of a vehicle coming up the road toward the cabin. Jack stood up so quickly his chair fell over.

"Shit, it's Robert."

"Probably," Peggy agreed dryly. "Don't worry, there's nothing criminal about having lunch with someone."

"No, but . . . Robert can be . . . funny, weird, sometimes. Don't tell him what I said about looking after him, he'd be really pissed off."

"Your secret is safe with me."

They went out on to the porch and watched the van drive up. Robert climbed out and glared at Jack.

"Thought you'd be here," he said, ignoring Peggy. "C'mon, let's go."

"Hello to you too," said Peggy. "You're a friendly sort, aren't you? In my day we'd have considered it bad manners to order a person out from under someone else's roof. Guess times have changed. Or are you just naturally rude?" Robert stared at her, but she gave him no chance to speak. "Jack's here as my guest; he's had a good lunch, which I must say he needed, and you look like you could do with something decent inside you, whatever you might think. So you can either stay here and let me fix you some sandwiches, which I'm more than prepared to do if you're prepared to be civil, or you can climb back into your van and drive away, with or without Jack, but I think that's his decision to make, not yours. He found his way here by himself, and I'd guess he can find his way back if he decides to stay a bit longer."

Robert started to say something; something not very pleasant, if the look that flashed across his face was anything to go by. Then he took a deep breath.

"Yeah, you're right. He can stay if he wants. No problem." He turned toward the van.

"Wait a minute," said Jack, moving off the porch. "Don't go. Peggy said you could stay, she'll fix you some sandwiches. Don't be a jerk. You must be as hungry as me."

"We've got food back at our place," said Robert; but he slowed down. Jack turned and threw a pleading look back at Peggy. *What can I do?* was written on his face.

"Robert. *Robert.*" He stopped, but kept his back turned to Peggy. "If you don't want to stay now, that's fine; maybe this isn't a good time, maybe you've got things to do, I don't know. But why don't you both come back over for supper? I've got some steaks in the fridge that need using up, and I can do salad and baked potatoes. Sound good?"

"What do you say, Robert?" said Jack eagerly. "I'll come with you now, then we both come back later and have supper."

Robert looked at Jack, then at Peggy. She put her hands in front of her, palms out, like a traffic policeman. "No ulterior motive, no strings, just a chance to give you both a good meal and talk to someone other than myself. You'd be doing me a big favor, both of you."

"Yeah," said Robert finally, slowly, "yeah, okay, supper would be great."

"Fine! About six, then."

Robert climbed in the driver's seat, and Jack mouthed *Thanks!* and gave a wave; the sun glinted off the face of his watch, making her blink. He got in the other side, and once more she watched as the van rattled out the gate and round the curve.

"I hope I've done the right thing," she said aloud. "Why can't things be simple?"

The afternoon drew on. Peggy did a bit more work on the paths, clearing some errant weeds. She straightened up at last, and glanced down across the valley below. It was her favorite view, particularly in the late afternoon sun, and she stood admiring it for a few moments, watching the play of light and shade across the trees. The wind, which had been playing fitfully about her all day, had at last died down, and everything was still and calm and clear.

Suddenly she turned and looked up behind her. She could have sworn that she heard someone call her name, but there was no one there; at least no one she could see. Still, the feeling persisted that someone was there; she felt eyes on her, watching.

The hills have eyes.

For the first time she realized how exposed she and the cabin were, and how small. Crazy, really, to think that something as essentially puny and inconsequential as a human could try to impose anything of himself on this land. How long had all this been here? How long would it endure after she was gone? *Work with it, not against it,* Len had said. *If you can't beat 'em, join 'em.* But how could you work with something, join with something, that you couldn't understand?

She shook her head. This was the sort of craziness that came from too much living alone. Maybe Paul was right; maybe it was time to start thinking about moving to the Island permanently.

Or maybe you just need a good hot meal, said a voice inside her head. *Those boys will be here soon; better get going.* She took one last look at the hill, then turned toward the cabin. The wind chimes were ringing faintly as she passed, the only sound in the stillness.

Inside, she turned on the radio; for some reason which she did not want to analyze she found the silence oppressive. The signal was not strong, but the announcer's voice, promising "your favorite good-time oldies," was better than nothing. She started the oven warming and wrapped half a dozen potatoes in foil, to the accompaniment of Simon and Garfunkel's "The Sound of Silence," then started on the salad fixings: lettuce, cucumber, radishes, tomatoes, mushrooms. As she scraped the last of the mushrooms off the board and into the bowl, she glanced out the window, and saw a figure standing on one of the paths, looking back at the hillside. *Jack*, she thought to herself, recognizing the fair hair, and looked at her watch. It was ten past five. *They're early. Must be hungry.*

Simon and Garfunkel gave way to Buddy Holly and "Peggy Sue." The oven pinged, indicating it was up to temperature, and she bundled the potatoes into it. When she returned to the window, the figure was gone.

"C'mon in," she called out, "door's open, make yourselves at home." She put the last of the sliced tomatoes on top of the salad, then realized no one had come in. "Hello?" she called out. "Anyone there?" Buddy Holly warbling about pretty Peggy Sue was the only reply.

Peggy went to the door and looked out. There was no one in sight. The van was not there, and it registered that she had not heard it come up the road. *It's such a nice night, maybe they walked.* She looked to her right, to where the trail they would have taken came out of the woods, but no one was there.

A squawk of static from the radio made her jump. For a moment there was only a low buzzing noise; then Buddy Holly came back on, fighting through the static, for she heard "Peggy" repeated. Another burst of noise, then the signal came through more clearly; only now it was the Beatles, who were halfway through "Help!"

"Interference," she muttered to herself. They often got overlapping channels at night; another station was crossing with the first one. She went outside and looked round the corner of the cabin, but there was no one in sight. When she went back in, "Help!" was ending, and she heard the voice of the announcer. "We've got more good-time oldies coming up after the break," he said, and she realized the radio had been broadcasting the same station all along. They must have got their records, or CDs, or whatever they used now mixed up, she decided.

She placed the salad on the table and got the steaks out of the fridge. She was beginning to trim the fat away from around the edges when the radio gave another burst of static, then faded away altogether. She flicked the on/off switch, and tried the tuner, but was unable to raise a signal. *Dead batteries*, she thought. *I only replaced them last week; honestly, they don't make things like . . .*

She broke off mid-thought at the sound of a voice calling her name. *Definitely not Buddy Holly this time*, she thought, and walked to the door, ready to call a greeting. What she saw made her freeze in the doorway.

Robert was running toward her across the grass; running wildly, carelessly, frantically even, as if something was on his tracks, calling out her name with all the breath he could muster. In a moment she shook off her fear and began crossing the yard toward him, meeting him near the back of her Jeep. He collapsed on the ground at her feet, and she knelt down beside him as he gasped for breath.

"Robert! Robert, what's wrong? What's happened?"

"Jack," he gasped; "Jack . . . he's gone . . . got to help me . . . just gone. . . ."

"Gone! What do you mean? Gone where?"

He was still panting, and she saw that his face was white. He struggled to his knees and swung round so that he could look behind him, in the direction of the blank and staring hillside.

"Don't know . . . we were coming over here . . . walking . . . and then he was gone . . . didn't see him. . . ."

"Right." Peggy spoke crisply, calmly. "Just take another deep breath . . . and another. . . . that's it, that's better. Now then"—when his breathing had slowed somewhat—"you and Jack were walking over here—why didn't you come in the van?"

"It wouldn't start; battery's dead or something."

"Okay, so you decided to walk, and Jack went on ahead, and you lost sight of him. Well, as mysteries go it's not a hard one; he's already here."

Robert stared at her. "What do you mean, he's already here?" he almost whispered.

"I saw him, over there." Peggy pointed toward the paths. "I looked out the window and there he was."

"Where is he now?"

Peggy frowned. "Well, I don't know; I went outside, but couldn't see him. I thought you'd both come early and were looking around."

"What time was this?"

"Ten past five; I looked at my watch."

"That's impossible," said Robert flatly, in a voice tinged with despair. "At ten past five he'd only just gone missing, and I was looking for him a mile from here. There's no way he could have got here that fast."

Peggy felt as if something was spiraling out of control, and she made a grab at the first thing she could think of. "How do you know exactly when he went missing?"

"I'd just looked at my watch, to see how we were doing for time; then he was gone."

"Maybe there's something wrong with your watch."

Robert shook his head. "It keeps perfect time." He looked down at his left wrist, and Peggy saw him go pale again.

"What the fuck . . ." he whispered, and Peggy bent her head to look.

The face of the digital watch was blank.

Robert began to shiver. "What's going on?" he said, in a voice that was a long way from that of the sullen youth she had seen earlier. "Where's Jack?"

"I don't know; but he can't have gone far. Did you two have a fight about something? Could that be why he went on ahead?"

"But he didn't go on ahead," said Robert, in a voice that sounded perilously close to tears. "That's just it. We were walking along, and he asked what time it was, and I looked at my watch—it was only for a couple of seconds, you know how long it takes to look at a watch—and then he was just . . . gone."

"Could he have . . . I don't know . . . gone off the trail? Gone behind a tree?"

Robert looked at her blankly. "Why would he do that?"

"I don't know!" Peggy took a deep breath. The boy was distraught enough, without her losing control as well. "Playing a joke? Looking at something? Call of nature?"

He shook his head. "No."

"Think! Are you sure you didn't just miss him?"

"I'm positive. There wasn't time for him to go anywhere, not even if he ran like Donovan Bailey. I'd have seen him."

"Okay." Peggy thought for a moment. "You say you were both a mile from here, at ten past five, which is the same time I looked outside and saw Jack here, at my cabin. I'd say that your watch battery was going then, and it wasn't giving you an accurate time, which is how Jack seemed to be in two places at once."

Robert shook his head again. "No." He looked straight at Peggy. His breath was still ragged; he must have run the mile to her cabin. "Jack's gone." Then, more quietly, "What am I going to do?"

Peggy got him inside the cabin and into an armchair, then went back out on the porch. The clock on the radio had died with the batteries, but her old wind-up wristwatch told her it was almost six. *Time for Jack and Robert to be arriving.* . . .

She called out "Jack!" and the sound of her voice in the stillness startled her. She waited a moment, then called again, but the only reply was the tinkle of the wind chimes. She walked round the cabin, not really knowing why; Jack hadn't seemed the kind to play senseless tricks, and she didn't expect to see him, but still she looked, because it seemed the right—the only—thing to do.

She stood at the front of the cabin, looking down over the valley. All those trees; if someone wandered off into them they could disappear forever. She shivered, then shook her head. Jack hadn't disappeared; there had to be an explanation. He and Robert had had a fight; Jack had stormed off, and Robert was too embarrassed to tell her about it. Jack was probably back at their camp by now . . . but that didn't explain how he had been outside the cabin at ten past five. Unless he had come to the cabin as originally planned, then decided he couldn't face Robert, and gone back to their camp by road . . . no, it was all getting too complex. She took a deep breath and walked round the side of the cabin . . . and stopped short at the sight of a figure over on the paths.

Only it wasn't a figure, she realized a split second later; there was no one, nothing, there. She had imagined it, that was all; perhaps that's what she had done earlier, looked up and remembered the image of Jack standing there from before lunch. He hadn't been there at all; Robert was quite right. In which case . . .

"We need to go looking for Jack."

Robert looked up at her as if he did not understand. Peggy resisted the urge to shake him.

"Did you hear me? I said we need to go look for Jack."

"Shouldn't we . . . shouldn't we call the police?"

"Yes; but first we need to go looking for him." She told him about her mistake with the figure. "He was never here at all. So you must have missed him on the path. And he must be injured, or lost, or he'd be here now. So yes, we'll call the police when we get back. Even if we called them now, though, it would be almost dark before they could get here; they wouldn't be able to start a search until daybreak. We're here now; we have the best chance of finding him."

She turned the oven off—*last thing I need now is to come back and find the place burned down*—then gathered together some supplies: two flashlights, a first aid kit, a couple of bottles of water, a sheath knife. She put them in a knapsack, which she handed to Robert. Then she went into her bedroom and got the .202 out from the back of the cupboard. The sight of it seemed to make Robert realize how serious the situation was.

"What do you need that for?"

"There's all sorts of animals out there, and a lot of them start to get active around this time of day. It's their country, not ours, but that doesn't mean I want to become a meal."

"Do you know how to use it?"

Peggy stared at him levelly. "It wouldn't be much use having it around if I couldn't use it. I'm not an Olympic marksman, but if it's within fifty yards of me I can hit it. Let's go."

They headed out toward the trail, skirting the paths. A little gust of wind was eddying dust along one of them. Peggy was conscious of the hillside above them to their left, and could not shake off the sense that something was watching. What was it Jack had said? *Something there, watching, waiting, something really old . . . part of this place, guarding it, protecting it, looking for something.* No; she had to stop it, stop it now. Thoughts like that were no good. She needed to concentrate.

"Come on, Robert," she called over her shoulder, "let's go. We have a lot of ground to cover, and it'll be dark in another couple of hours. You better go first; it's been a while since I was last through here. Keep yelling Jack's name, and keep your eyes open."

They started along the trail. It was fainter than Peggy remembered, but still distinguishable as such; more than clear enough to act as a guide, even for the most inexperienced eye. They took turns calling, and stared intently about them, looking from side to side, searching for any signs of Jack; but there was nothing, not a trace of his passage, not a hint that he was calling or signaling to them. They stopped every so often to listen, and to give them both a chance to rest; but they only lingered in one place, when Robert indicated that they were at the spot where he had last seen Jack.

"Here," he said, pointing; "I was standing here, and Jack was about fifteen feet in front of me, and then . . . he wasn't."

Peggy looked around, trying to will some sign, some clue into being, but there was nothing that marked the spot out as any different to anywhere else they had passed. Birch and poplar and pines crowded round them, but not so thickly, she thought, that someone could disappear into them and be lost to sight in a matter of seconds. A breeze rustled the branches, and something skittered through the undergrowth; a squirrel, she thought, from the sound. They called, but there was no reply, and searched either side of the trail, but there was no sign of Jack. Without a word they continued on their way.

Robert was still in front, Peggy behind; the trail was not wide enough to allow more than single file passage. *Indian file.* The phrase from her childhood popped unbidden into Peggy's mind, along with the accompanying thought, *I suppose you can't call it that anymore, but Aboriginal file doesn't sound right. Or would it be Native file?* Natives . . . now what did that . . .

"Natives don't like that place." Who had said that? Someone, years before, who she and Len had run into in town, someone who knew the area and was surprised when they told him where they lived. "Natives don't like that place," he had said. "Never have. Don't know why; you can't pin 'em down. Used to be a prospector lived back in there, not far from where you are, I guess, and there was a feeling he was tempting . . . well, fate, I suppose, or the gods, or something. . . . What happened to him? He just up and left one day; disappeared. Some people figured he'd hit it lucky at last and had cleared out with his gold, others said it was cabin fever; whatever happened, it didn't do anything for the place's reputation."

Why had she thought of that now, of all times? She shivered uncontrollably, and was glad that Robert was up ahead and couldn't see her. She hurried to close the distance between them; and although her breath was becoming more ragged, and the ache in her legs more pronounced, she did not stop again until they were at the cabin.

It was much as she remembered it; a low, crudely built structure of weathered pine logs, with a single door and one window in front, and a tin chimney pipe leaning out from the roof at an angle. There was no smoke from the chimney, no movement within or without; only the sound of the wind, and a far-off crow cawing hoarsely, and their own breath. The dying sun reflected off the one window, creating a momentary illusion of life, but neither one spoke. There was no need. Jack was not here.

They checked the cabin, just to be sure, and the van, sitting uselessly in front, and they called until they were hoarse, but they were merely going through the motions, and Peggy knew it. Robert tried the van again, but the battery was irrevocably dead. Still silent, they turned and headed back the way they had come.

They did not call out now, or search for signs; their one thought, albeit an unspoken one, was to get back to Peggy's before dark. The sun had dipped well below the hills now, and the shadows were lengthening fast, and Peggy found herself keeping her eyes on the trail ahead. Once she thought she heard movement in the trees to their right, and stopped, clutching Robert's arm; but it was only the wind. They continued on their silent way, and did not stop again.

They reached the cabin as the last of the light flickered and died in the western sky. Peggy ached in every joint and muscle in her body, but she lit the propane lamps and put water on to boil for coffee while Robert collapsed into a chair and put his head in his hands. Finally, when she could think of nothing else useful to do with her hands, Peggy sat down opposite him.

"Robert." He looked up at her with tired eyes. "Robert, it's time to phone the police. I'll do it, if you'd like."

"Yeah, that'd be good. Thanks."

She would not have thought that this was the same Robert she had seen earlier in the day. He seemed lost, diminished, and she realized with a start that Jack had been wrong, completely wrong, when he had told her that Robert wouldn't have minded if Jack had gone off and never come back. Something inside Robert compelled him, but Jack, she thought, had always been there, a link with the life he had left behind, and a way back to it. As long as Jack had been with him, Robert would have kept moving; now, without him, Peggy had the feeling that there'd be no Northwest Passage. She wished that Jack could know that, somehow.

She moved to the phone, an old-fashioned one with a dial. She picked up the receiver and listened for a moment, then jiggled the cradle two, three, four times, while the look on her face changed from puzzled to worried to frightened. She replaced the receiver.

"No dial tone."

Robert stared at her. "What do you mean, no dial tone?"

"Just what I said. The line must be down somewhere. We can't call out."

"Great. Just fucking great." Anger mixed with fear flashed across his face, and for a moment he looked like the Robert of old. "What do we do now?"

"We have a cup of coffee and something to eat; then we get in my Jeep and drive to town and tell the police what's happened. After that it's in their hands."

"Shouldn't we go now?"

"Frankly, until I get some coffee into me I won't be in a fit state to drive anywhere, and I'd be surprised if you're any different. And the police won't be able to start a search until morning; another half an hour or so isn't going to make much difference now."

Robert looked at her bleakly. "I guess not," he said finally.

She busied herself with the ritual of making coffee. As she measured and poured, something caught her eye at the window, and she looked up automatically.

A face was staring in at her.

She gave a brief, choked cry, and dropped the teaspoon, which clattered on to the counter. It took her a moment to realize that what she saw was her own reflection, framed in the darkness of the window and what lay beyond. That was all it could be. There was no one out there.

But she had seen something at the window, out of the corner of her eye, before she looked up. No, it had been a reflection of something in the room. The cabin was brightly lit, and the windows were acting like mirrors.

From the front of the cabin the wind chimes rang.

Peggy was suddenly conscious of feeling exposed. The little cabin, lights streaming out the windows into the darkness, did not belong here; it was an intruder, and therefore a target. She turned to Robert.

"Close the curtains."

"What?"

She pointed to the picture windows overlooking the valley. "Leave the windows open, but close the curtains."

He did as she asked, while Peggy reached for the blind cord by the kitchen window. The Venetian blinds rattled into place. *That's better,* she thought, and took the coffee in to the living room.

They sat and sipped, both unconsciously seeking refuge in this ordinary, everyday act. There was silence between them, for there was nothing to be said, or nothing they wanted to say. The wind chimes were louder now, the only sound in the vast expanse around them. The only sound. . . .

A thought which had been at the back of Peggy's mind for some time came into focus then, and she looked up, listening intently. She placed her cup on the table in front of her so hard that coffee sloshed over the side. Robert looked up, startled.

"What . . ." he began, but Peggy held up her hand.

"Listen!" she whispered urgently. Robert looked at her, puzzled. "What do you hear? Tell me. . . ."

Robert tried to concentrate. "Nothing," he said finally. "Just that chiming noise, that's all. Why, did you hear something? Do you think it's . . ."

"*Listen.* We can hear the chimes, yes, but there's no wind in the trees; we should be able to hear it in the branches, shouldn't we? And the windows are open, but the curtains aren't moving, they're absolutely still. *So why can we hear the wind chimes, if there isn't a wind?*"

Robert stared at her for a moment, uncomprehending. Then he went pale.

"What are you saying?" he asked; but she saw in his eyes that he already knew the answer, or some of it; enough, anyway.

"I'm saying we have to leave," said Peggy, startled by the firmness in her voice. "Now. Don't bother about the lights. Let's go."

She picked up her purse and keys from the shelf where they lay, and moved to the door. She did not want to go out there, did not want to leave the cabin, and it was only with a tremendous effort of will that she put her hand on the knob and pulled open the wooden door, letting a bright trail of light stream out over the rocky ground. She thought she saw something move at the far end of it, something tall and thin, but she did not, *would not* look, concentrating instead on walking to the driver's door of the Jeep with her eyes on the ground, walking, not running, she would not run. . . .

"Hey!" Robert's voice rang out behind her, and she turned to see him still on the porch, looking, not toward the Jeep, but toward the paths. She followed his gaze, and in the faint light cast by a three-quarter moon could just see a figure standing silent, twenty yards or so from them.

"Jack!" cried Robert, relief flooding his voice. He stepped off the porch and moved toward the figure. "Hey, man, you had us worried! Where've you been? What happened?"

Peggy felt a trickle of ice down her back. "Robert—Robert, come here," she called out, fear making her voice tremble. "Come here now; we have to go."

He stopped and looked back at her. "Can't you see?" he said, puzzled. "It's Jack!" He turned back to the figure. "C'mon, come inside, get something to eat, tell us what happened. You hurt?"

"Robert!" Peggy's voice cracked like a gunshot. "That isn't Jack. Can't you see? *It isn't Jack.*"

"What do you mean? Of course it is! C'mon over here, man, let Peggy take a look at you, you're frightening her. . . ."

All the time Robert had been moving closer to the figure, which remained motionless and silent. Suddenly, when he was only ten feet away from it, he stopped, and she heard him give a strangled cry.

"What the . . . what are you? What's going on?" Then, higher, broken, like a child, "Peggy, what's happening?" He seemed frozen, and Peggy thought for a moment that she would have to go to him, pull him forcibly to the Jeep, and realized that she could not go any closer to that figure. A warning shot, if she had thought to bring the rifle, might have broken the spell, but it was back in the cabin. . . . She wrenched open the driver's door and leaned on the horn with all her might.

The sound made her jump, even though she was expecting it, and the effect on Robert was galvanic. He turned and began moving toward the Jeep in a stumbling, shambling run; as he got closer she could hear him sobbing between breaths, ragged, gasping sobs, and she was glad that she had not been close enough to see the figure clearly.

She had dropped the keys twice from fingers that suddenly felt like dry twigs. Now, on the third try, she slammed the key into the ignition and turned it. Nothing. She turned it again. No response. She tried to turn on the headlights, but there was no answering flare of brightness. The battery was dead, and she realized, deep down in a corner of her mind, that she should have expected this.

Robert turned to her, eyes glittering with panic. "C'mon, get it started, let's go! What are you waiting for?"

"The battery's dead." Her chest was heaving as she tried to bite down the panic welling up inside her. Robert began to moan, a low, keening sound, as Peggy forced her mind back. *Think, think,* she told herself. *There's a way to do this, you know there is, you just have to calm down, remember. . . .*

Len's voice sounded in her ear, so clearly that for a moment she thought he was beside her. "It's not difficult," she heard him say, "as long as it's a standard; automatics are trickier." And she remembered; she had asked him, once, what they'd do if the battery went dead, up here with no other car for miles. "We make sure the battery doesn't go dead," he'd said with a laugh, but when she pressed him—she was serious, it could happen, what would they *do?*—he had replied cheerfully, "Not a problem; just put the clutch in, put it in second, let gravity start to work, let out the clutch, and there you go, easy-peasy. Make sure the ignition's on, and just keep driving for a bit; as long as the engine doesn't stop you'll charge the battery back up."

She had no intention of stopping once she got the engine started.

She took a deep breath. The Jeep was parked on the flat, with the downward slope beginning twenty feet away. She would need help.

"Robert." He was still moaning, looking out the passenger window, and Peggy risked a look too. The figure seemed closer. "Robert! Listen to me!" Nothing. She reached out and shook him, and he turned to her, his eyes wide and scared. She hoped he could hear her.

"You need to get out and push the car," she said, slowly and clearly. He started to say something, and she cut him short. "Just do it, Robert. Do it now."

"I can't get out, I can't, I don't . . ."

"You have to. You can do this, Robert, but you have to hurry. Just to the top of the slope. Twenty feet; then you can get back in."

For a moment she thought that he was going to refuse; then, without a word, he opened his door and half-fell, half-scrambled out. Peggy turned the ignition on, pushed in the clutch, put the Jeep in second, and they began to roll, slowly at first, then faster, Robert pushing with all his strength.

It seemed to take hours to cover the short distance; then Peggy felt the car start to pick up momentum, and Robert jumped in, slamming the passenger door. She said under her breath, "Work, please, work," and let out the clutch.

For one brief, terrible second she thought that it wasn't going to work, that she had done something wrong, missed something out. Then the engine shuddered into life, and she switched on the headlights, and they were through the gate and round the curve, and the cabin had disappeared behind them, along with everything else that was waiting in the darkness.

They did not speak during the drive to town. Peggy concentrated on the road with a fierceness that made her head ache, glad she had something to think about other than what they had left, while Robert sat huddled down in his seat. She did not ask him what he had seen, and he did not volunteer any information. The only thing she said, as they drew near the police station, was "Keep to the facts. That's all they want to hear. Nothing else. Do you understand?" And Robert, pale, shaking, had nodded.

They told their story, for the first of several times, and answered questions, together and separately. Peggy did not know exactly what they asked Robert; she gathered, from some of the questions directed at her, that he was under suspicion, although in the end nothing came of this.

Officialdom swung into action, clearly following the procedures and guidelines laid out for just such a situation. Appeals for help were made; search parties were sent out; a spotter plane was employed. There were more questions, although no more answers. Peggy sometimes wondered where they would fit all the pieces she had not told them: eddies of dust and the ringing of chimes on a windless day, someone (not Buddy Holly) calling her name, the figure they had seen outside the cabin, the battery failures, the phone going dead. She imagined the response if she told the police that they should examine local Native legends and the vanishing of a prospector years earlier, or that she had felt that the hillside was watching her, or that Jack had not disappeared at all, he was still there, watching too, that he had only been looking after Robert.

All the searches came to nothing; no further traces of Jack were found. A casual question to one of the volunteers elicited the information that the phone in the cabin was working perfectly. Peggy herself did not go back; no one expected a sixty-three-year-old woman to participate in the search, and everyone told her they understood why she preferred to stay in a hotel in town. They did not understand, of course, not at all, but Peggy did not try to explain.

Paul came up as soon as he could. He, too, was very understanding, although he was surprised at his aunt's decision to put the property on the market immediately. She was welcome to stay with him and the family for as long as she needed to, that went without saying; but wasn't she being a bit hasty? Yes, it had been a terrible, tragic event, but perhaps she should wait a bit, hold off making a decision . . . she didn't want to do something she would regret. . . .

But Peggy was insistent. If Paul would go with her while she collected some clothing and personal items, she would be grateful; she would arrange with a moving company for everything else to be packed up and put into storage until she had found somewhere to live. She had clearly made up her mind, and although he did not agree with her, Paul did not argue the point any further.

They went up early in the morning, the first day after the search had been called off. Peggy worked quickly, packing up the things she wanted to take with her, while Paul cleared out the food from the fridge and cupboards. When everything had been loaded into his SUV, he went round the cabin, making sure that everything was shut off and locked up, while Peggy waited outside.

Now, in the daylight, with the sun high overhead and birds wheeling against the blue of the sky, everything looked peaceful. A gentle wind ruffled the branches of the trees, and a piece of paper fluttered along—left by one of the searchers, no doubt. It blew across the grass, and landed in the middle of one of the pathways. Out of habit, she walked over to where it lay, picked it up, and put it in her pocket.

She looked up at the hills above her, then back at the cabin, realizing that this was the same spot where she had seen . . . or thought she had seen . . . Jack on the afternoon he had disappeared. She shivered slightly, even though the day was hot, and started toward the SUV, anxious to be gone.

It was as she moved away that she saw it, a glint of something metallic at the edge of the path near her foot. She bent down and picked it up. A Swiss Army watch, silver. Although she knew what she would find, she looked at the face. The hands showed ten past five.

When Paul came out and locked the front door, his aunt was already in the SUV. She did not look back as they drove away.

LAIRD BARRON

Proboscis

Laird Barron was born in Alaska, where he raised and trained huskies for many years. He moved to the Pacific Northwest in the mid-nineties and began to concentrate on writing poetry and fiction. His award-nominated work has appeared in SCI FICTION *and the* Magazine of Fantasy & Science Fiction, *and been reprinted in* The Year's Best Fantasy & Horror, Year's Best Fantasy 6, *and* Horror: The Best of 2005. *Mr. Barron currently resides in Olympia, Washington and is hard at work on many projects, including a novel and his first collection of short fiction.*

"Proboscis" was first published in the Magazine of Fantasy & Science Fiction.

—E.D.

1.

After the debacle in British Columbia, we decided to crash the Bluegrass festival. Not we—Cruz. Everybody else just shrugged and said yeah, whatever you say, dude. Like always. Cruz was the alpha-alpha of our motley pack.

We followed the handmade signs onto a dirt road and ended up in a muddy pasture with maybe a thousand other cars and beat-to-hell tourist buses. It was a regular extravaganza—pavilions, a massive stage, floodlights. A bit farther out, they'd built a bonfire, and Dead-heads were writhing among the cinder-streaked shadows with pagan exuberance. The brisk air swirled heavy scents of marijuana and clove, of electricity and sex.

The amplified ukulele music was giving me a migraine. Too many people smashed together, limbs flailing in paroxysms. Too much white light followed by too much darkness. I'd gone a couple beers over my limit because my face was Novocain-numb and I found myself dancing with some sloe-eyed coed who'd fixed her hair in corn rows. Her shirt said *MILK*.

She was perhaps a bit prettier than the starlet I'd ruined my marriage with way back in the days of yore, but resembled her in a few details. What were the odds? I didn't even attempt to calculate. A drunken man cheek to cheek with a strange woman under the harvest moon was a tricky proposition.

"Lookin' for somebody, or just rubberneckin'?" The girl had to shout over the hi-fi jug band. Her breath was peppermint and whiskey.

"I lost my friends," I shouted back. A sea of bobbing heads beneath a gulf of night sky and none of them belonged to anyone I knew. Six of us had piled out of two cars and now I was alone. Last of the Mohicans.

The girl grinned and patted my cheek. "You ain't got no friends, Ray-bo."

I tried to ask how she came up with that, but she was squirming and pointing over my shoulder.

"My gawd, look at all those stars, will ya?"

Sure enough the stars were on parade; cold, cruel radiation bleeding across improbable distances. I was more interested in the bikers lurking near the stage and the beer garden. Creepy and mean, spoiling for trouble. I guessed Cruz and Hart would be nearby, copping the vibe, as it were.

The girl asked me what I did and I said I was an actor between jobs. Anything she'd seen? No, probably not. Then I asked her and she said something I didn't quite catch. It was either etymologist or entomologist. There was another thing, impossible to hear. She looked so serious I asked her to repeat it.

"Right through your meninges. Sorta like a siphon."

"What?" I said.

"I guess it's a delicacy. They say it don't hurt much, but I say nuts to that."

"A delicacy?"

She made a face. "I'm goin' to the garden. Want a beer?"

"No, thanks." As it was, my legs were ready to fold. The girl smiled, a wistful imp, and kissed me briefly, chastely. She was swallowed into the masses and I didn't see her again.

After a while I staggered to the car and collapsed. I tried to call Sylvia, wanted to reassure her and Carly that I was okay, but my cell wouldn't cooperate. Couldn't raise my watchdog friend Rob in LA. He'd be going bonkers too. I might as well have been marooned on a desert island. Modern technology, my ass. I watched the windows shift through a foggy spectrum of pink and yellow. Lulled by the monotone thrum, I slept.

Dreamed of wasp nests and wasps. And rare orchids, coronas tilted toward the awesome bulk of clouds. The flowers were a battery of organic radio telescopes receiving a sibilant communiqué just below my threshold of comprehension.

A mosquito pricked me and when I crushed it, blood ran down my finger, hung from my nail.

2.

Cruz drove. He said, "I wanna see the Mima Mounds."

Hart said, "Who's Mima?" He rubbed the keloid on his beefy neck.

Bulletproof glass let in light from a blob of moon. I slumped in the tricked-out back seat, where our prisoner would've been if we'd managed to bring him home. I stared at the grille partition, the leg irons and the doors with no handles. A crusty vein traced black tributaries on the floorboard. Someone had scratched R+G and a fanciful depiction of Ronald Reagan's penis. This was an old car. It reeked of cigarette smoke, of stale beer, of a million exhalations.

Nobody asked my opinion. I'd melted into the background smear.

The brutes were smacked out of their gourds on junk they'd picked up on the Canadian side at the festival. Hart had tossed the bag of syringes and miscellaneous garbage off a bridge before we crossed the border. That was where we'd parted ways with the other guys—Leon, Rufus, and Donnie. Donnie was the one who had gotten nicked by a stray bullet in Donkey Creek, earned himself bragging rights if nothing else. Jersey boys, the lot; they were going to take the high road home, maybe catch the rodeo in Montana.

Sunrise forged a pale seam above the distant mountains. We were rolling through certified boondocks, thumping across rickety wooden bridges that could've been thrown down around the Civil War. On either side of busted up two-lane blacktop were overgrown fields and hills dense with maples and poplar. Scotch broom reared on lean stalks, fire-yellow heads lolling hungrily. Scotch broom was Washington's rebuttal to kudzu. It was quietly everywhere, feeding in the cracks of the earth.

Road signs floated nearly extinct; letters faded, or bullet-raddled, dimmed by pollen and sap. Occasionally, dirt tracks cut through high grass to farmhouses. Cars passed us head-on, but not often, and usually local rigs—camouflage-green flatbeds with winches and trailers, two-tone pickups, decrepit jeeps. Nothing with out-of-state plates. I started thinking we'd missed a turn somewhere along the line. Not that I would've broached the subject. By then I'd learned to keep my mouth shut and let nature take its course.

"Do you even know where the hell they are?" Hart said. Hart was sour about the battle royale at the wharf. He figured it would give the bean counters an excuse to waffle about the payout for Piers' capture. I suspected he was correct.

"The Mima Mounds?"

"Yeah."

"Nope." Cruz rolled down the window, squirted beechnut over his shoulder, contributing another racing streak to the paint job. He twisted the radio dial and conjured Johnny Cash confessing that he'd "shot a man in Reno just to watch him die."

"Real man'd swallow," Hart said. "Like Josey Wales."

My cell beeped and I didn't catch Cruz's rejoinder. It was Carly. She'd seen the bust on the news and was worried, had been trying to reach me. The report mentioned shots fired and a wounded person, and I said yeah, one of our guys got clipped in the ankle, but he was okay, I was okay and the whole thing was over. We'd bagged the bad guy and all was right with the world. I promised to be home in a couple of days and told her to say hi to her mom. A wave of static drowned the connection.

I hadn't mentioned that the Canadians contemplated jailing us for various legal infractions and inciting mayhem. Her mother's blood pressure was already sky-high over what Sylvia called my "midlife adventure." Hard to blame her—it was my youthful "adventures" that set the torch to our unhappy marriage.

What Sylvia didn't know, couldn't know, because I lacked the grit to bare my soul at this late stage of our separation, was during the fifteen-martini lunch meeting with Hart, he'd showed me a few pictures to seal the deal. A roster of smiling teenage girls that could've been Carly's schoolmates. Hart explained in graphic detail what the bad man liked to do to these kids. Right there it became less of an adventure and more of a mini-crusade. I'd been an absentee father for fifteen years. Here was my chance to play Lancelot.

Cruz said he was hungry enough to eat the ass end of a rhino and Hart said stop and buy breakfast at the greasy spoon coming up on the left, materializing as if by sorcery, so they pulled in and parked alongside a rusted-out Pontiac on blocks. Hart remembered to open the door for me that time. One glimpse of the diner's filthy windows and the coils of dogshit sprinkled across the unpaved lot convinced me I wasn't exactly keen on going in for the special.

But I did.

The place was stamped 1950s from the long counter with a row of shiny black swivel stools and the too-small window booths, dingy Formica peeling at the edges of the tables, to the bubble-screen TV wedged high up in a corner alcove. The TV was flickering with grainy black and white images of a talk show I didn't recognize and couldn't hear because the volume was turned way down. Mercifully I didn't see my-self during the commercials.

I slouched at the counter and waited for the waitress to notice me. Took a while—she was busy flirting with Hart and Cruz, who'd squeezed themselves into a booth, and of course they wasted no time in regaling her with their latest exploits as hardcase bounty hunters. By now it was purely mechanical; rote bravado. They were pale as sheets and running on fumes of adrenaline and junk. Oh, how I dreaded the next twenty-four to thirty-six hours.

Their story was edited for heroic effect. My private version played a little differ-ently.

We finally caught the desperado and his best girl in the Maple Leaf Country. Af-ter a bit of "slap and tickle," as Hart put it, we handed the miscreants over to the Canadians, more or less intact. Well, the Canadians more or less took possession of the pair.

The bad man was named Russell Piers, a convicted rapist and kidnaper who'd cut a nasty swath across the great Pacific Northwest and British Columbia. The girl was Penny Aldon, a runaway, an orphan, the details varied, but she wasn't impor-tant, didn't even drive; was along for the thrill, according to the reports. They fled to a river town, were loitering wharf-side, munching on a fish basket from one of six jil-lion Vietnamese vendors when the team descended.

Piers proved something of a Boy Scout—always prepared. He yanked a pistol from his waistband and started blazing, but one of him versus six of us only works in the movies and he went down under a swarm of blackjacks, tasers, and fists. I ran the handcam, got the whole jittering mess on film.

The film.

That was on my mind, sneaking around my subconscious like a night prowler. There was a moment during the scrum when a shiver of light distorted the scene, or I had a near-fainting spell, or who knows. The men on the sidewalk snapped and snarled, hyenas bringing down a wounded lion. Foam spattered the lens. I swayed, almost tumbled amid the violence. And Piers looked directly at me. Grinned at me. A big dude, even bigger than the troglodytes clinging to him, he had Cruz in a head-lock, was ready to crush bones, to ravage flesh, to feast. A beast all right, with long, greasy hair, powerful hands scarred by prison tattoos, gold in his teeth. Inhuman, definitely. He wasn't a lion, though. I didn't know what kingdom he belonged to.

Somebody cold-cocked Piers behind the ear and he switched off, slumped like a manikin that'd been bowled over by the holiday stampede.

Flutter, flutter, and all was right with the world, relatively speaking. Except my bones ached and I was experiencing a not-so-mild wave of paranoia that hung on for hours. Never completely dissipated, even here in the sticks at a godforsaken hole in the wall while my associates preened for an audience of one.

Cruz and Hart had starred on Cops and America's Most Wanted; they were celebrity experts. Too loud, the three of them honking and squawking, especially my ex–brother-in-law. Hart resembled a hog that decided to put on a dirty shirt and steel toe boots and go on its hind legs. Him being high as a kite wasn't helping. Sylvia tried to warn me, she'd known what her brother was about since they were kids knocking around on the wrong side of Des Moines.

I didn't listen. *'C'mon, Sylvie, there's a book in this. Hell, a Movie of the Week!'*

Hart was on the inside of a rather seamy yet wholly marketable industry. He had a friend who had a friend who had a general idea where Mad Dog Piers was running. Money in the bank. See you in a few weeks, hold my calls.

"Watcha want, hon?" The waitress, a strapping lady with a tag spelling Victoria, poured translucent coffee into a cup that suggested the dishwasher wasn't quite up to snuff. Like all pro waitresses she pulled off this trick without looking away from my face. "I know you?" And when I politely smiled and reached for the sugar, she kept coming, frowning now as her brain began to labor. "You somebody? An actor or somethin'?"

I shrugged in defeat. "Uh, yeah. I was in a couple TV movies. Small roles. Long time ago."

Her face animated, a craggy talking tree. "Hey! You were on that comedy, one with the blind guy and his seein' eye dog. Only the guy was a con man or somethin', wasn't really blind and his dog was an alien or somethin', a robot, don't recall. Yeah, I remember you. What happened to that show?"

"Canceled." I glanced longingly through the screen door to our ugly Chevy.

"Ray does shampoo ads," Hart said. He said something to Cruz and they cracked up.

"Milk of magnesia!" Cruz said. "And 'If you suffer from erectile dysfunction, now there's an answer!'" He delivered the last in a passable radio announcer's voice, although I'd heard him do better. He was hoarse.

The sun went behind a cloud, but Victoria still wanted my autograph, just in case I made a comeback, or got killed in a sensational fashion and then my signature would be worth something. She even dragged Sven the cook out to shake my hand, and he did it with the dedication of a zombie following its mistress's instructions before shambling back to whip up eggs and hash for my comrades.

The coffee tasted like bleach.

The talk show ended and the next program opened with a still shot of a field covered by mossy hummocks and blackberry thickets. The black and white imagery threw me. For a moment I didn't register the car parked between mounds was familiar. Our boxy Chevy with the driver-side door hanging ajar, mud-encrusted plates, taillights blinking SOS.

A gray hand reached from inside, slammed the door. A hand? Or something like a hand? A B-movie prosthesis? Too blurry, too fast to be certain.

Victoria changed the channel to All My Children.

3.

Hart drove.

Cruz navigated. He tilted a road map, trying to follow the dots and dashes. Victoria had drawled a convoluted set of directions to the Mima Mounds, a one-star tourist attraction about thirty miles over. Cruise on through Poger Rock and head west. Real easy drive if you took the local shortcuts and suchlike.

Not an unreasonable detour; I-5 wasn't far from the site—we could do the tourist bit and still make the Portland night scene. That was Cruz's sales pitch. Kind of funny, really. I wondered at the man's sudden fixation on geological phenomena. He was a NASCAR and *Soldier of Fortune* magazine–type personality. Hart fit the profile too, for that matter. Damned world was turning upside down.

It was getting hot. Cracks in the windshield dazzled and danced.

The boys debated cattle mutilations and the inarguable complicity of the Federal government regarding the Gray Question and how the moon landing was fake and remember that flick from the 1970s, *Capricorn One*, goddamned if O.J wasn't one of the astronauts. Freakin' hilarious.

I unpacked the camera, thumbed the playback button, and relived the Donkey Creek fracas. Penny said to me, "Reduviidea—any of a species of large insects that feed on the blood of prey insects and some mammals. They are considered extremely beneficial by agricultural professionals." Her voice was made of tin and lagged behind her lip movements, like a badly dubbed foreign film. She stood on the periphery of the action, scrawny fingers pleating the wispy fabric of a blue sundress. She was smiling. "The indices of primate emotional thresholds indicate the (*click-click*) process is traumatic. However, point oh-two percent vertebrae harvest corresponds to non(*click-click*) purposes. As an X haplotype you are a primary source of (*click-click*), Lucky you!"

"Jesus!" I muttered and dropped the camera on the seat. *Are you talkin' to me?* I stared at too many trees while Robert De Niro did his mirror schtick as a low frequency monologue in the corner of my mind. Unlike De Niro, I'd never carried a gun. The guys wouldn't even loan me a taser.

"What?" Cruz said in a tone that suggested he'd almost jumped out of his skin. He glared through the partition, olive features drained to ash. Giant drops of sweat sparkled and dripped from his broad cheeks. The light wrapped his skull, halo of an angry saint. Withdrawal's something fierce, I decided.

I shook my head, waited for the magnifying glass of his displeasure to swing back to the road map. When it was safe I hit the playback button. Same scene on the view panel. This time when Penny entered the frame she pointed at me and intoned in a robust, Slavic accent, "Supercalifragilisticexpialidocious is Latin for a death god of a primitive Mediterranean culture. Their civilization was buried in mudslides caused by unusual seismic activity. If you say it loud enough—" I hit the kill button. My stomach roiled with rancid coffee and incipient motion sickness.

Third time's a charm, right? I played it back again. The entire sequence was erased. Nothing but deep-space black with jags of silvery light at the edges. In the middle, skimming by so swiftly I had to freeze things to get a clear image, was Piers with his lips nuzzling Cruz's ear, and Cruz's face was corpse-slack. And for an instant, a microsecond, the face was Hart's too; one of those three-dee poster illusions where the object changes depending on the angle. Then, more nothingness, and an odd feedback noise that faded in and out, like Gregorian monks chanting a litany in reverse.

Okay. ABC time.

I'd reviewed the footage shortly after the initial capture in Canada. There was nothing unusual about it. We spent a few hours at the police station answering a series of polite yet penetrating questions. I assumed our cameras would be confiscated, but the inspector simply examined our equipment in the presence of a couple suits from a legal office. Eventually the inspector handed everything back with a stern admonishment to leave dangerous criminals to the authorities. Amen to that.

Had a cop tampered with the camera, doctored it in some way? I wasn't a filmmaker, didn't know much more than point and shoot and change the batteries when the little red light started blinking. So, yeah, Horatio, it was possible someone had screwed with the recording. Was that likely? The answer was no—not unless they'd also managed to monkey with the television at the diner. More probable one of my associates had spiked the coffee with a miracle agent and I was hallucinating. Seemed out of character for those greedy bastards, even for the sake of a practical joke on their third wheel—dope was expensive and it wasn't like we were expecting a big payday.

The remaining options weren't very appealing.

My cell whined, a dentist's drill in my shirt pocket. It was Rob Fries from his patio office in Gardena. Rob was tall, bulky, pink on top, and garbed according to his impression of what Miami vice cops might've worn in a bygone era, such as the '80s. Rob also had the notion he was my agent despite the fact I'd fired him ten years ago after he handed me one too many scripts for laxative testimonials. I almost broke into tears when I heard his voice on the buzzing line. "Man, am I glad you called!" I said loudly enough to elicit another scowl from Cruz.

"Hola, compadre. What a splash y'all made on page 16. 'American Yahoos Run Amok!' goes the headline, which is a quote of the Calgary rag. Too bad the stupid bastards let our birds fly the coop. Woulda been better press if they fried 'em. Well, they don't have the death penalty, but you get the point. Even so, I see a major motion picture deal in the works. Mucho dinero, Ray, buddy!"

"Fly the coop? What are you talking about?"

"Uh, you haven't heard? Piers and the broad walked. Hell, they probably beat you outta town."

"You better fill me in." Indigestion was eating the lining of my esophagus.

"Real weird story. Some schmuck from Central Casting accidentally turned 'em loose. The paperwork got misfiled or somesuch bullshit. The muckety-mucks are PO'd. Blows your mind, don't it?"

"Right," I said in my actor's tone. I fell back on this when my mind was in neutral but etiquette dictated a polite response. Up front, Cruz and Hart were bickering, hadn't caught my exclamation. No way was I going to illuminate them regarding this development—Christ, they'd almost certainly consider pulling a U-turn and speeding back to Canada. The home office would be calling any second now to relay the news; probably had been trying to get through for hours—Hart hated phones, usually kept his stashed in the glovebox.

There was a burst of chittery static. "—returning your call. Keep getting the answering service. You won't believe it—I was having lunch with this chick used to be one of Johnny Carson's secretaries, yeah? And she said her best friend is shacking with an exec who just frickin' adored you in Clancy & Spot. Frickin' adored you! I told my gal pal to pass the word you were riding along on this bounty hunter gig, see what shakes loose."

"Oh, thanks, Rob. Which exec?"

"Lemmesee—uh, Harry Buford. Remember him? He floated deals for the Alpha Team, some other stuff. Nice as hell. Frickin' adores you, buddy."

"Harry Buford? Looks like the Elephant Man's older, fatter brother, loves pastels, and lives in Mexico half the year because he's fond of underage Chicano girls? Did an exposé piece on the evils of Hollywood, got himself blackballed? That the guy?"

"Well, yeah. But he's still got an ear to the ground. And he frickin'—"

"Adores me. Got it. Tell your girlfriend we'll all do lunch, or whatever."

"Anywhoo, how you faring with the gorillas?"

"Um, great. We're on our way to see the Mima Mounds."

"What? You on a nature study?"

"Cruz's idea."

"The Mima Mounds. Wow. Never heard of them. Burial grounds, huh?"

"Earth heaves, I guess. They've got them all over the world—Norway, South America, Eastern Washington—I don't know where all. I lost the brochure."

"Cool." The silence hung for a long moment. "Your buddies wanna see some, whatchyacallem—?"

"Glacial deposits."

"They wanna look at some rocks instead of hitting a strip club? No bullshit?"

"Um, yeah."

It was easy to imagine Rob frowning at his flip-flops propped on the patio table while he stirred the ice in his rum and coke and tried to do the math. "Have a swell time, then."

"You do me a favor?"

"Yo, bro'. Hit me."

"Go on the Net and look up X haplotype. Do it right now, if you've got a minute."

"X-whatsis?"

I spelled it and said, "Call me back, okay? If I'm out of area, leave a message with the details."

"Be happy to." There was a pause as he scratched pen to pad. "Some kinda new meds, or what?"

"Or what, I think."

"Uh, huh. Well, I'm just happy the Canucks didn't make you an honorary citizen, eh. I'm dying to hear the scoop."

"I'm dying to dish it. I'm losing my signal, gotta sign off."

He said not to worry, bro', and we disconnected. I worried anyway.

4.

Sure enough, Hart's phone rang a bit later and he exploded in a stream of repetitious profanity and dented the dash with his ham hock of a fist. He was still bubbling when we pulled into Poger Rock for gas and fresh directions. Cruz, on the other hand, accepted the news of Russell Piers's "early parole" with a Zen detachment demonstrably contrary to his nature.

"Screw it. Let's drink," was his official comment.

Poger Rock was sunk in a hollow about fifteen miles south of the state capitol in Olympia. It wasn't impressive—a dozen or so antiquated buildings moldering along the banks of a shallow creek posted with NO SHOOTING signs. Everything was peeling, rusting or collapsing toward the center of the earth. Only the elementary school loomed incongruously—a utopian brick and tile structure set back and slightly elevated, fresh paint glowing through the alders and dogwoods. Aliens might have landed and dedicated a monument.

Cruz filled up at a mom and pop gas station with the prehistoric pumps that took an eon to dribble forth their fuel. I bought some jerky and a carton of milk with a past-due expiration date to soothe my churning guts. The lady behind the counter had yellowish hair and wore a button with a fuzzy picture of a toddler in a bib. She smiled nervously as she punched keys and furiously smoked a Pall Mall. Didn't recognize me, thank God.

Cruz pushed through the door, setting off the ding-dong alarm. His gaze jumped all over the place and his chambray shirt was molded to his chest as if he'd been doused with a water hose. He crowded past me, trailing the odor of armpit funk and cheap cologne, grunted at the cashier and shoved his credit card across the counter.

I raised my hand to block the sun when I stepped outside. Hart was leaning on the hood. "We're gonna mosey over to the bar for a couple brewskis." He coughed his smoker's cough, spat in the gravel near a broken jar of marmalade. Bees darted among the wreckage.

"What about the Mima Mounds?"

"They ain't goin' anywhere. 'Sides, it ain't time, yet."

"Time?"

Hart's ferret-pink eyes narrowed and he smiled slightly. He finished his cigarette and lighted another from the smoldering butt. "Cruz says it ain't."

"Well, what does that mean? It 'ain't time'?"

"I dunno, Ray-bo. I dunno fuck-all. Why'nchya ask Cruz?"

"Okay." I took a long pull of tepid milk while I considered the latest developments in what was becoming the most bizarre road trip of my life. "How are you feeling?"

"Groovy."

"You look like hell." I could still talk to him, after a fashion, when he was separated from Cruz. And I lied, "Sylvia's worried."

"What's she worried about?"

I shrugged, let it hang. Impossible to read his face, his swollen eyes. In truth, I wasn't sure I completely recognized him, this wasted hulk swaying against the car, features glazed into gargoyle contortions.

Hart nodded wisely, suddenly illuminated regarding a great and abiding mystery of the universe. His smile returned.

I glanced back, saw Cruz's murky shadow drifting in the station window.

"Man, what are we doing out here? We could be in Portland by three." What I wanted to say was, let's jump in the car and shag ass for California. Leave Cruz in the middle of the parking lot holding his pecker and swearing eternal vengeance for all I cared.

"Anxious to get going on your book, huh?"

"If there's a book. I'm not much of a writer. I don't even know if we'll get a movie out of this mess."

"Ain't much of an actor, either." He laughed and slapped my shoulder with an iron paw to show he was just kidding. "Hey, lemme tell'ya. Did'ya know Cruz studied geology at UCLA? He did. Real knowledgeable about glaciers an' rocks. All that good shit. Thought he was gonna work for the oil companies up in Alaska. Make some fat stacks. Ah, but you know how it goes, doncha, Ray-bo?"

"He graduated UCLA?" I tried not to sound astonished. It had been the University of Washington for me. The home of medicine, which wasn't my specialty, according to the proctors. Political science and drama were the last exits.

"Football scholarship. Hard hittin' safety with a nasty attitude. They fuckin' grow on trees in the ghetto."

That explained some things. I was inexplicably relieved.

Cruz emerged, cutting a plug of tobacco with his pocket knife. "C'mon, H. I'm parched." And precisely as a cowboy would unhitch his horse to ride across the street, he fired the engine and rumbled the one quarter block to Moony's Tavern and parked in a diagonal slot between a hay truck and a station wagon plastered with anti-Democrat, pro-gun bumper stickers.

Hart asked if I planned on joining them and I replied maybe in a while, I wanted to stretch my legs. The idea of entering that sweltering cavern and bellying up to the bar with the lowlife regulars and mine own dear chums made my stomach even more unhappy.

I grabbed my valise from the car and started walking. I walked along the street, past a row of dented mailboxes, rust-red flags erect; an outboard motor repair shop with a dusty police cruiser in front; the Poger Rock Grange, which appeared abandoned because its windows were boarded and where they weren't, kids had broken them with rocks and bottles, and maybe the same kids had drawn 666 and other satanic symbols on the whitewashed planks, or maybe real live Satanists did the deed; Bob's Liquor Mart, which was a corrugated shed with bars on the tiny windows; the Laundromat, full of tired women in oversized T-shirts, and screeching, dirty-faced kids racing among the machinery while an A.M. radio broadcast a Rush Limbaugh rerun; and a trailer loaded with half-rotted firewood for 75 BUCKS! I finally sat on a rickety bench under some trees near the lone stoplight, close enough to hear it clunk through its cycle.

I drew a manila envelope from the valise, spread sloppy typed police reports and disjointed photographs beside me. The breeze stirred and I used a rock for a paper weight.

A whole slew of the pictures featured Russell Piers in various poses, mostly mug shots, although a few had been snapped during more pleasant times. There was even one of him and a younger brother standing in front of the Space Needle. The remaining photos were of Piers's latest girlfriend—Penny Aldon, the girl from Allen Town. Skinny, pimply, mouthful of braces. A flower child with a suitably vacuous smirk.

Something cold and nasty turned over in me as I studied the haphazard data, the disheveled photo collection. I felt the pattern, unwholesome as damp cobwebs against my skin. Felt it, yet couldn't put a name to it, couldn't put my finger on it and my heart began pumping dangerously and I looked away, thought of Carly instead, and how I'd forgotten to call her on her seventh birthday because I was in Spain with some friends at a Lipizzaner exhibition. Except, I hadn't forgotten, I was wired for sound from a snort of primo Colombian blow and the thought of dialing that long string of international numbers was too much for my circuits.

Ancient history, as they say. Those days of fast-living and superstar dreams belonged to another man, and he was welcome to them.

Waiting for cars to drive past so I could count them, I had an epiphany. I realized the shabby buildings were cardboard and the people milling here and there at opportune junctures were macaroni and glue. Dull blue construction paper sky and cotton ball clouds. And I wasn't really who I thought of myself as—I was an ant left over from a picnic raid, awaiting some petulant child god to put his boot down on my pathetic diorama existence.

My cell rang and an iceberg calved in my chest.

"Hey, Ray, you got any Indian in ya?" Rob asked.

I mulled that as a brand new Cadillac convertible paused at the light. A pair of yuppie tourists mildly argued about directions—a man behind the wheel in stylish wraparound shades and a polo shirt, and a woman wearing a floppy, wide-brimmed hat like the Queen Mum favored. They pretended not to notice me. The woman pointed right and they went right, leisurely, up the hill and beyond. "Comanche," I said. Next was a shiny green van loaded with Asian kids. Sign on the door said THE EVERGREEN STATE COLLEGE. It turned right and so did the one that came after. "About one thirty-second. Am I eligible for some reparation money? Did I inherit a casino?"

"Where the hell did the Comanche sneak in?"

"Great grandma. Tough old bird. Didn't like me much. Sent me a straight razor for Christmas. I was nine."

Rob laughed. "Cra-zee. I did a search and came up with a bunch of listings for genetic research. Lemme check this . . ." he shuffled paper close to the receiver, cleared his throat. "Turns out this X haplogroup has to do with mitochondrial DNA, genes passed down on the maternal side—and an X haplogroup is a specific subdivision or cluster. The university wags are tryin' to use female lineage to trace tribal migrations and so forth. Something like three percent of Native Americans, Europeans, and Basque belong to the X group. Least, according to the stuff I thought looked reputable. Says here there's lots of controversy about its significance. Usual academic crap. Whatch you were after?"

"I don't know. Thanks, though."

"You okay, bud? You sound kinda odd."

"Shucks, Rob, I've been trapped in a car with two redneck psychos for weeks. Might be getting to me, I'll admit."

"Whoa, sorry. Sylvia called and started going on—"

"Everything's hunky-dory, All right?"

"Cool, bro." Rob's tone said nothing was truly cool, but he wasn't in any position to press the issue. There'd be a serious Q&A when I returned, no doubt about it.

Cruz's dad was Basque, wasn't he? Hart was definitely of good, solid German stock only a couple generations removed from the mother land.

Stop me if you've heard this one—a Spaniard, a German and a Comanche walk into a bar—

After we said goodbye, I dialed my ex and got her machine, caught myself and hung up as it was purring. It occurred to me then, what the pattern was, and I stared dumbly down at the fractured portraits of Penny and Piers as their faces were dappled by sunlight falling through a maze of leaves.

I laughed, bitter.

How in God's name had they ever fooled us into thinking they were people at all? The only things missing from this farce were strings and zippers, a boom mike.

I stuffed the photos and the reports into the valise, stood in the weeds at the edge of the asphalt. My blood still pulsed erratically. Shadows began to crawl deep and blue between the buildings and the trees and in the wake of low-gliding cumulus clouds. Moony's Tavern waited, back there in the golden dust, and Cruz's Chevy before it, stolid as a coffin on the altar.

Something was happening, wasn't it? This thing that was happening, had been happening, could it follow me home if I cut and ran? Would it follow me to Sylvia and Carly?

No way to be certain, no way to tell if I had simply fallen off my rocker—maybe the heat had cooked my brain, maybe I was having a long-overdue nervous breakdown. Maybe, shit. The sinister shape of the world contracted around me, gleamed like the curves of a great killing jar. I heard the lid screwing tight in the endless ultraviolet collisions, the white drone of insects.

I turned right and walked up the hill.

5.

About two hours later, a guy in a vintage farm truck stopped. The truck had cruised by me twice, once going toward town, then on the way back. And here it was again. I hesitated; nobody braked for hitchhikers unless the hitcher was a babe in tight jeans.

I thought of Piers and Penny, their expressions in the video, drinking us with their smiling mouths, marking us. And if that was true, we'd been weighed, measured and marked, what was the implication? Piers and Penny were two from among a swarm. Was it open season?

The driver studied me with unsettling intensity, his beady eyes obscured by thick, black-rimmed glasses. He beckoned.

My legs were tired already and the back of my neck itched with sunburn. Also, what did it matter anyway? If I were doing anything besides playing out the hand, I would've gone into Olympia and caught a southbound Greyhound. I climbed aboard.

George was a retired civil engineer. Looked the part—crewcut, angular face like a piece of rock, wore a dress shirt with a row of clipped pens and a tie flung over his shoulder, and polyester slacks. He kept NPR on the radio at a mumble. Gripped the wheel with both gnarled hands.

Seemed familiar—a figure dredged from memories of scientists and engineers of my grandfather's generation. He could've *been* my grandfather. I didn't study him too closely.

George asked me where I was headed. I said Los Angeles and he gave me a glance that said L.A. was in the opposite direction. I told him I wanted to visit the Mima Mounds—since I was in the neighborhood.

There was a heavy silence. A vast and unfathomable pressure built in the cab. At last George said, "Why, they're only a couple miles farther on. Do you know anything about them?"

I admitted that I didn't and he said he figured as much. He told me the Mounds were declared a national monument back in the '60s; the subject of scholarly debate and wildly inaccurate hypotheses. He hoped I wouldn't be disappointed—they weren't glamorous compared to real natural wonders such as Niagara Falls, the Grand Canyon, or the California Redwoods. The preserve was on the order of five hundred acres, but that was nothing. The Mounds had stretched for miles and miles in the old days. The land grabs of the 1890s reduced the phenomenon to a pocket, surrounded it with rundown farms, pastures and cows. The ruins of America's agrarian era.

I said that it would be impossible to disappoint me.

George turned at a wooden marker with a faded white arrow. A nicely paved single lane wound through temperate rain forest for a mile and looped into a parking lot occupied by the Evergreen vans and a few other vehicles. There was a fence with a gate and beyond that, the vague border of a clearing. Official bulletins were posted every six feet, prohibiting dogs, alcohol and firearms.

"Sure you want me to leave you here?"

"I'll be fine."

George rustled, his clothes chitin sloughing. "X marks the spot."

I didn't regard him, my hand frozen on the door handle, more than slightly afraid the door wouldn't open. Time slowed, got stuck in molasses. "I know a secret, George."

"What kind of secret?" George said, too close, as if he'd leaned in tight.

The hairs stiffened on the nape of my neck. I swallowed and closed my eyes. "I saw a picture in a biology textbook. There was this bug, looked exactly like a piece of bark, and it was barely touching a beetle with its nose. The one that resembled bark was what entomologists call an assassin bug and it was draining the beetle dry. Know how? It poked the beetle with a razor sharp beak thingy—"

"A rostrum, you mean."

"Exactly. A rostrum, or a proboscis, depending on the species. Then the assassin bug injected digestive fluids, think hydrochloric acid, and sucked the beetle's insides out."

"How lovely," George said.

"No struggle, no fuss, just a couple bugs sitting on a branch. So I'm staring at this book and thinking the only reason the beetle got caught was because it fell for the old piece of bark trick, and then I realized that's how lots of predatory bugs operate. They camouflage themselves and sneak up on hapless critters to do their thing."

"Isn't that the way of the universe?"

"And I wondered if that theory only applied to insects."

"What do you suppose?"

"I suspect that theory applies to everything."

Zilch from George. Not even the rasp of his breath.

"Bye, George. Thanks for the ride." I pushed hard to open the door and jumped down; moved away without risking a backward glance. My knees were unsteady. After I passed through the gate and approached a bend in the path, I finally had the nerve to check the parking lot. George's truck was gone.

I kept going, almost falling forward.

The trees thinned to reveal the humpbacked plain from the TV picture. Nearby was a concrete bunker shaped like a squat mushroom—a park information kiosk and observation post. It was papered with articles and diagrams under plexiglass. Throngs of brightly clad Asian kids buzzed around the kiosk, laughing over the wrinkled flyers, pointing cameras and chattering enthusiastically. A shaggy guy in a hemp sweater, presumably the professor, lectured a couple of wind-burned ladies who obviously ran marathons in their spare time. The ladies were enthralled.

I mounted the stairs to the observation platform and scanned the environs. As George predicted, the view wasn't inspiring. The mounds spread beneath my vantage, none greater than five or six feet in height and largely engulfed in blackberry brambles. Collectively, the hillocks formed a dewdrop hemmed by mixed forest, and toward the narrowing end, a dilapidated trailer court, its structures rendered toys by perspective. The paved footpath coiled unto obscurity.

A radio-controlled airplane whirred in the trailer court airspace. The plane's engine throbbed, a shrill metronome. I squinted against the glare, couldn't discern the operator. My skull ached. I slumped, hugged the valise to my chest, pressed my cheek against damp concrete, and drowsed. Shoes scraped along the platform. Voices occasionally floated by. Nobody challenged me, my derelict posture. I hadn't thought they would. Who'd dare disturb the wildlife in this remote enclave?

My sluggish daydreams were phantoms of the field, negatives of its buckled hide and stealthy plants, and the whispered words *Eastern Washington, South America, Norway*. Scientists might speculate about the geological method of the mounds' creation until doomsday. I knew this place and its sisters were unnatural as monoliths hacked from rude stone by primitive hands and stacked like so many dominos in the uninhabited spaces of the globe. What were they? Breeding grounds, feeding grounds, shrines? Or something utterly alien, something utterly incomprehensible to match the blighted fascination that dragged me ever closer and consumed my will to flee.

Hart's call yanked me from the doldrums. He was drunk. "You shoulda stuck around, Ray-bo. We been huntin' everywhere for you. Cruz ain't in a nice mood." The connection was weak, a transmission from the dark side of Pluto. Batteries were dying.

"Where are you?" I rubbed my gummy eyes and stood.

"We're at the goddamned Mounds. Where are *you?*"

I spied a tiny glint of moving metal. The Chevy rolled across the way where the road and the mobile homes intersected. I smiled—Cruz hadn't been looking for me; he'd been trolling around on the wrong side of the park, frustrated because he'd missed the entrance. As I watched, the car slowed and idled in the middle of the road. "I'm here."

The cell phone began to click like a Geiger counter that'd hit the mother lode. Bits of fiddle music pierced the garble.

The car jolted from a savage tromp on the gas and listed ditchward. It accelerated, jounced, and bounded into the field, described a haphazard arc in my direction. I had a momentary terror that they'd seen me atop the tower, were coming for me, were planning some unhinged brand of retribution. But no, the distance was too great. I was no more than a speck, if I was anything. Soon, the car lurched behind the slope of intervening hillocks and didn't emerge.

"Hart, are you there?"

The clicking intensified and abruptly chopped off, replaced by smooth, bottomless static. Deep sea squeals and warbles began to filter through. Bees humming. A castrati choir on a gramophone. Giggling. Someone, perhaps Cruz, whispering a Latin prayer. I was grateful when the phone made an electronic protest and expired. I hurled it over the side.

The college crowd had disappeared. Gone too, the professor and his admirers. I might've joined the migration if I hadn't spotted the cab of George's truck mostly hidden by a tree. It was the only rig in the parking lot. I couldn't tell if anyone was behind the wheel.

The sun hung low and fat, reddening as it sank. The breeze had cooled. It plucked at my hair, dried my sweat, chilled me a little. I listened for the roar of the Chevy, buried to the axles in loose dirt, high-centered on a stump; or perhaps they'd abandoned the vehicle. Thus I strained to pick my companions from among the blackberry patches and softly undulating clumps of scotch broom which had invaded this place too.

Quiet.

I went down the stairs and let the path take me. I went as a man in a stupor, my muscles lethargic with dread. The lizard subprocessor in my brain urged me to sprint for the highway, to scuttle into a burrow. It possessed a hint of what waited over the hill, had possibly witnessed this melodrama many times before. I whistled a dirge through clenched teeth and the mounds closed ranks behind me.

Ahead, came the dull clank of a slamming door.

The car was stalled at the foot of a steep slope, its hood buried in a tangle of brush. The windows were dark as a muddy aquarium and festooned with fleshy creepers and algid scum.

I took root a few yards from the car, noting that the engine was dead, yet the vehicle rocked on its springs from some vigorous activity. A rhythmic motion that caused metal to complain. The brake lights stuttered.

Hart's doughy face materialized on the passenger side, bumped against the glass with the dispassion of a pale, exotic fish, and withdrew, descending into a marine trench. His forehead left a starry impact. Someone's palm smacked the rear window, hung there, fingers twitching.

I retreated. Ran, more like. I may have shrieked. Somewhere along the line the valise flew open and its contents spilled—a welter of files, the argyle socks Carly gave me for Father's Day, my toiletries. A handful of photographs pinwheeled in a gust. I dropped the bag. Ungainly, panicked, I didn't get far, tripped and collapsed as the sky blackened and a high-pitched keening erupted from several locations simultaneously. In moments all ambient light had been sucked away; I couldn't see the thorny bush gouging my neck as I wriggled for cover, couldn't make out my own hand before my eyes.

The keening ceased. Peculiar echoes bounced in its wake, gave me the absurd sensation of lying on a sound stage with the kliegs shut off. I received the impression of movement around my hunkered self, although I didn't hear footsteps. I shuddered, pressed my face deeper into musty soil. Ants investigated my pants cuffs.

Cruz called my name from the throat of a distant tunnel. I knew it wasn't him and kept silent. He cursed me and giggled the unpleasant giggle I'd heard on the phone. Hart tried to coax me out, but this imitation was even worse. They went down the entire list and despite everything I was tempted to answer when Carly began crying and hiccupping and begging me to help her, daddy please, in a baby girl voice she hadn't owned for several years. I stuffed my fist in my mouth, held on while the chorus drifted here and there and eventually receded into the buzz and chirr of field life.

The sun flickered on and the world was restored piecemeal—one root, one stump, one hill at a time. My head swam; reminded me of waking from anesthesia.

Dusk was blooming when I crept from the bushes and tasted the air, cocked an ear for predators. The Chevy was there, shimmering in the twilight. Motionless now.

I could've crouched in my blind forever, wild-eyed as a hare run to ground in a ruined shirt and piss-stained slacks. But it was getting cold and I was thirsty, so I slunk across the park at an angle that took me to the road near the trailer court. I went, casting glances over my shoulder for pursuit that never came.

6.

I told a retiree sipping ice tea in a lawn chair that my car had broken down and he let me use his phone to call a taxi. If he witnessed Cruz crash the Chevy into the Mounds, he wasn't saying. The police didn't show while I waited and that said enough about the situation.

The taxi driver was a stolid Samoan who proved not the least bit interested in my frightful appearance or talking. He drove way too fast for comfort, if I'd been in a rational frame of mind, and dropped me at the Greyhound depot in downtown Olympia.

I wandered inside past the rag-tag gaggle of modern gypsies which inevitably haunted these terminals, studied the big board while the ticket agent pursed her lips in distaste. Her expression certified me as one of the unwashed mob.

I picked Seattle at random, bought a ticket. The ticket got me the key to the restroom, where I splashed my welted flesh, combed cat tails from my hair, and looked almost human again. Almost. The fluorescent tube crackled and sizzled, threatened to plunge the crummy toilet into darkness, and in the discotheque flashes, my haggard face seemed strange.

The bus arrived an hour late and it was crammed. I shared a seat with a middle-aged woman wearing a shawl and scads of costume jewelry. Her ivory skin was hard and she smelled of chlorine. I didn't imagine she wanted to sit by me, judging from the flare of her nostrils, the crimp of her overglossed mouth.

Soon the bus was chugging into the wasteland of night and the lights clicked off row by row as passengers succumbed to sleep. Except some guy near the front who left his overhead lamp on to read, and me. I was too exhausted to close my eyes.

I surprised myself by crying.

And the woman surprised me again by murmuring, "Hush, hush, dear. Hush, hush." She patted my trembling shoulder. Her hand lingered.

ELIZABETH HAND

Kronia

Elizabeth Hand's evocative and fractured story of alternate personal histories, "Kronia," was published in number 44 of Bard College's Conjunctions, a journal which has, in the last few years, published a great deal of experimental and genre-friendly work. Hand is the author most recently of the novels Mortal Love and Generation Loss (forthcoming). Her latest collection, Saffron And Brimstone: Strange Stories will be published this year by M Press. Hand's stories and novels have won the Tiptree, Mythopoeic, Nebula and World Fantasy Awards. She is a regular contributor to the Washington Post Book World and writes a book review column for Fantasy and Science Fiction. She lives in Maine.

—K.L. & G.G.

We never meet. No, not never; just fleetingly: five times in the last eighteen years. The first time I don't recall; you say it was late spring, a hotel bar. But I see you entering a restaurant five years later, stooping beneath the lintel behind our friend Andrew. You don't remember that.

We grew up a mile apart. The road began in Connecticut and ended in New York. A dirt road when we moved in, we both remember that; it wasn't paved till much later. We rode our bikes back and forth. We passed each other twenty-three times. We never noticed. I fell once, rounding that curve by the golf course, a long scar on my leg now from ankle to knee, a crescent colored like a peony. Grit and sand got beneath my skin, there was blood on the bicycle chain. A boy with glasses stopped his bike and asked was I okay. I said yes, even though I wasn't. You rode off. I walked home, most of the mile, my leg black, sticky with dirt, pollen, deerflies. I never saw the boy on the bike again.

We went to different schools. But in high school we were at the same party. Your end, Connecticut. How did I get there? I have no clue. I knew no one. A sad fat girl's house, a girl with red kneesocks, beanbag chairs. She had one album: The Shaggs. More sad girls, a song called Foot Foot. You stood by a table and ate pretzels and drank so much Hi-C you threw up. I left with my friends. We got stoned in the car and drove off. A tall boy was puking in the azaleas out front.

Wonder what he had? I said.

Another day. The New Canaan Bookstore, your end again. I was looking at a paperback.

That's a good book, said a guy behind me. My age, sixteen or seventeen. Very tall, springy black hair, wire-rimmed glasses. You like his stuff?

I shook my head. No, I said. I haven't read it. I put the book back. He took it off the shelf again. As I walked off I heard him say *Time Out of Joint*.

We went to different colleges in the same city. The Metro hadn't opened yet. I was in Northeast, you were in Northwest. Twice we were on the same bus going into Georgetown. Once we were at a party where a guy threw a drink in my face.

Hey! yelled my boyfriend. He dumped his beer on the guy's head.

You were by a table, watching. I looked over and saw you laugh. I started laughing too, but you immediately looked down then turned then walked away.

Around that time I first had this dream. I lived in the future. My job was to travel through time, hunting down evildoers. The travel nauseated me. Sometimes I threw up. I kept running into the same man, my age, darkhaired, tall. Each time I saw him my heart lurched. We kissed furtively, beneath a table while bullets zipped overhead, beside a waterfall in Hungary. For two weeks we hid in a shack in the Northwest Territory, our radio dying, waiting to hear that the first wave of fallout had subsided. A thousand years, back and forth, the world reshuffled. Our child was born, died, grew old, walked for the first time. Sometimes your hair was gray, sometimes black. Once your glasses shattered when a rock struck them. You still have the scar on your cheek. Once I had an abortion. Once the baby died. Once you did. This was just a dream.

You graduated and went to the Sorbonne for a year to study economics. I have never been to France. I got a job at NASA collating photographs of spacecraft. You came back and started working for the newspaper. Those years, I went to the movies almost every night. Flee the sweltering heat, sit in the Biograph's crippling seats for six hours, Pasolini, Fellini, Truffaut, Herzog, Fassbinder, Weir. *La Jetée*, a lightning bolt: that illuminated moment when a woman's black-and-white face moves in the darkness. A tall man sat in front of me and I moved to another seat so I could see better; he turned and I glimpsed your face. Unrecognized: I never knew you. Later in the theater's long corridor you hurried past me, my head bent over an elfin spoonful of cocaine.

Other theaters. We didn't meet again when we sat through *Berlin Alexanderplatz*, though I did read your review. *Our Hitler* was nine hours long; you stayed awake, I fell asleep halfway through the last reel, curled on the floor, but after twenty minutes my boyfriend shook me so I wouldn't miss the end.

How could I have missed you then? The theater was practically empty.

I moved far away. You stayed. Before I left the city I met your colleague Andrew: we corresponded. I wrote occasionally for your paper. You answered the phone sometimes when I called there.

You say you never did.

But I remember your voice: you sounded younger than you were, ironic, world-weary. A few times you assigned me stories. We spoke on the phone. I knew your name.

At some point we met. I don't remember. Lunch, maybe, with Andrew when I visited the city? A conference?

You married and moved three thousand miles away. E-mail was invented. We began to write. You sent me books.

We met at a conference: we both remember that. You stood in a hallway filled with light, midday sun fogging the windows. You shaded your eyes with your hand, your head slightly downturned, your eyes glancing upward, your glasses black against white skin. Dark eyes, dark hair, tall and thin and slightly roundshouldered. You were smiling; not at me, at someone talking about the mutability of time. Abruptly the sky darkened, the long rows of windows turned to mirrors. I stood in the hallway and you were everywhere, everywhere.

You never married. I sent you books.

I had children. I never wrote you back.

You and your wife traveled everywhere: Paris, Beirut, London, Cairo, Tangier, Cornwall, Fiji. You sent me postcards. I never left this country.

I was vacationing in London with my husband when the towers fell. I e-mailed you. You wrote back:

oh sure, it takes a terrorist attack to hear from you!

That was when we really met.

I was here alone by the lake when I found out. A brilliant cloudless day, the loons calling outside my window. I have no TV or radio; I was online when a friend e-mailed me:

Terrorism. An airplane flew into the Trade Center. Bombs. Disaster.

I tried to call my partner but the phone lines went down. I drove past the farm-stand where I buy tomatoes and basil and stopped to see if anyone knew what had happened. A van was there with DC plates: the woman inside was talking on a cell phone and weeping. Her brother worked in one of the towers: he had rung her to say he was safe. The second tower fell. He had just rung back to say he was still alive.

When the phone lines were restored that night I wrote you. You didn't write back. I never heard from you again.

I was in New York. I had gone to Battery Park. I had never been there before. The sun was shining. You never heard from me again.

I had no children. At the National Zoo, I saw a tall man walking hand in hand with a little girl. She turned to stare at me: gray eyes, glasses, wispy dark hair. She looked like me.

Two years ago you came to see me here on the lake. We drank two bottles of champagne. We stayed up all night talking. You slept on the couch. When I said goodnight, I touched your forehead. I had never touched you before. You flinched.

Once in 1985 we sat beside each other on the Number 80 bus from North Capitol Street. Neither of us remembers that.

I was fifteen years old, riding my bike on that long slow curve by the golf course. The Petro Oil truck went by, too fast, and I lost my balance and went careening into the stone wall. I fell and blacked out. When I opened my eyes a tall boy with glasses knelt beside me, so still he was like a black and white photograph. A sudden flicker: for the first time he moved. He blinked, dark eyes, dark hair. It took a moment for me to understand he was talking to me.

"Are you okay?" He pointed to my leg. "You're bleeding. I live just down there—" He pointed to the Connecticut end of the road.

I tried to move but it hurt so much I threw up, then started to cry.

He hid my ruined bike in the ferns. "Come on."

You put your arm around me and we walked very slowly to your house. A plane flew by overhead. This is how we met.

Nothing sorts out memories from ordinary moments. It is only later that they claim remembrance, when they show their scars.

—Chris Marker, *La Jetée*

KELLY EVERDING

Omens

"Omens" comes from poet Kelly Everding's first chapbook, Strappado for the Devil (EtherDome Press). "Omens" will also be reprinted in a New Rivers Press anthology of Minnesota women poets. Everding's poetry has been published in The Denver Quarterly, Conduit, and The Colorado Review, among others. She lives in Minneapolis and works for the nonprofit literary organization Rain Taxi.

—K.L. & G.G.

A cow lows three times.
Rats leave a house.
A cat spits at midnight,
and a white bird
smashes against a window.
An owl brings tidings.
Furniture creaks without cause.
A church bell strikes
while the parson intones his text.
Children born under a comet.

The lost wax from a candle
is a shroud.
A picture falls from its hook.
Meeting a goat unexpectedly.
A shrew runs across your foot.
January—bad for kings.
A shark following a ship
is a sure sign.

A dead man
knows what is going on
until the last spade-full of earth
touches his grave.
It is dangerous to walk away
and leave a book open.

ELIZABETH BEAR

Follow Me Light

Elizabeth Bear's short stories have been published in The Magazine of Fantasy & Science Fiction, SCI FICTION, The 3rd Alternative, Strange Horizons, and other magazines and webzines and in the anthologies Shadows Over Baker Street and All-Star Zeppelin Adventure Stories. Some of them have recently been collected in The Chains That You Refuse.

The Jenny Casey trilogy, comprising Hammered, Scardown, and World-wired, are near-future science fiction thrillers. Her next two science fiction novels are Carnival and Undertow. She also has a fantasy cycle, "The Promethean Age," beginning in 2006 with Blood & Iron, followed in 2007 by Whiskey & Water.

She cohabitates with approximately three hundred pounds of dog and thirty-nine pounds of cat. Her Web site may be found at http://www.elizabeth bear.com.

"Follow Me Light" was originally published in SCI FICTION.

—E.D.

Pinky Gilman limped. He wore braces on both legs, shining metal and black washable foam spoiling the line of his off-the-rack suits, what line there was to spoil. He heaved himself about on a pair of elbow-cuff crutches. I used to be able to hear him clattering along the tiled, echoing halls of the public defender's offices a dozen doors down.

Pinky's given name was Isaac, but even his clients called him Pinky. He was a fabulously ugly man, lumpy and bald and bristled and pink-scrubbed as a slaughtered hog. He had little fishy walleyes behind spectacles thick enough to serve barbecue on. His skin peeled wherever the sun or the dry desert air touched it.

He was by far the best we had.

The first time I met Pinky was in 1994. He was touring the office as part of his job interview, and Christian Vlatick led him up to me while I was wrestling a five-gallon bottle onto the water cooler. I flinched when he extended his right hand to shake mine with a painful twist intended to keep the crutch from slipping off his arm. The rueful way he cocked his head as I returned his clasp told me he was used to that reaction, but I doubted most people flinched for the reason I did—the shimmer of hot blue lights that flickered through his aura, filling it with brilliance although the aura itself was no color I'd ever seen before—a swampy gray-green, tornado colored.

I must have been staring, because the squat little man glanced down at my shoes, and Chris cleared his throat. "Maria," he said, "This is Isaac Gilman."

"Pinky," Pinky said. His voice . . . oh, la. If he were robbed with regard to his body, that voice was the thing that made up the difference. Oh, my.

"Maria Delprado. Are you the new attorney?"

"I hope so," he said, dry enough delivery that Chris and I both laughed.

His handshake was good: strong, cool, and leathery, at odds with his parboiled countenance. He let go quickly, grasping the handle of his crutch again and shifting his weight to center, blinking behind the glass that distorted his eyes. "Maria," he said. "My favorite name. Do you know what it means?"

"It means Mary," I answered. "It means sorrow."

"No," he said. "It means *sea*." He pointed past me with his chin, indicating the still-sloshing bottle atop the water cooler. "They make the women do the heavy lifting here?"

"I like to think I can take care of myself. Where'd you study, Isaac?"

"Pinky," he said, and, "Yale. Four point oh."

I raised both eyebrows at Chris and pushed my glasses up my nose. The Las Vegas public defender's office doesn't get a lot of interest from Yale Law School grads, *summa cum laude*. "And you haven't hired him yet?"

"I wanted your opinion," Chris said without a hint of apology. He glanced at Pinky and offered up a self-deprecating smile. "Maria can spot guilty people. Every time. It's a gift. One of these days we're going to get her made a judge."

"Really?" Pinky's lipless mouth warped itself into a grin, showing the gaps in his short, patchy beard. "Am I guilty, then?"

The lights that followed him glittered, electric blue fireflies in the twilight he wore like a coat. He shifted his weight on his crutches, obviously uncomfortable at standing.

"And what am I guilty of?"

Not teasing, either, or flirtatious. Calm, and curious, as if he really thought maybe I could tell. I squinted at the lights that danced around him—will-o'-the-wisps, spirit lights. The aura itself was dark, but it wasn't the darkness of past violence or dishonesty. It was organic, intrinsic, and I wondered if it had to do with whatever had crippled him. And the firefly lights—

Well, they were something else again. Just looking at them made my fingertips tingle.

"If there are any sins on your conscience," I said carefully, "I think you've made amends."

He blinked again, and I wondered why I wanted to think *blinked fishily* when fishes do not blink. And then he smiled at me, teeth like yellowed pegs in pale, blood-flushed gums. "How on earth do you manage *that*?"

"I measure the distance between their eyes."

A three-second pause, and then he started to laugh, while Christian, who had heard the joke before, stood aside and rolled his eyes. Pinky shrugged, rise and fall of bulldog shoulders, and I smiled hard, because I knew we were going to be friends.

In November of 1996, I lost my beloved seventeen-year-old cat to renal failure, and Pinky showed up at my door uninvited with a bottle of Maker's Mark and a box of Oreos. We were both half-trashed by the time I spread my cards out on the table between us, a modified Celtic cross. They shimmered when I looked at them; that was the alcohol. The shimmer around Pinky when he stretched his hand out—was not.

"Fear death by water," I said, and touched the Hanged Man's foot, hoping he would know he was supposed to laugh.

His eyes sparkled like scales in the candlelight when he refilled my glass. "It's supposed to be if you *don't* find the Hanged Man. In any case, I don't see a drowned sailor."

"No," I answered. I picked up my glass and bent to look closer. "But there is the three of staves as the significator. Eliot called him the Fisher King." I looked plainly at where his crutches leaned against the arm of his chair. "Not a bad choice, don't you think?"

His face grayed a little, or perhaps that was the alcohol. Foxlights darted around him like startled minnows. "What does he stand for?"

"Virtue tested by the sea." And then I wondered why I'd put it that way. "The sea symbolizes change, conflict, the deep unconscious, the monsters of the Id—"

"I know what the sea means," he said bitterly. His hand darted out and overturned the card, showing the tan back with its key pattern in ivory. He jerked his chin at the spread. "Do you believe in those?"

It had been foolish to pull them out. Foolish to show him, but there was a certain amount of grief and alcohol involved. "It's a game," I said, and swept them all into a pile. "Just a child's game." And then I hesitated, and looked down, and turned the three of staves back over, so it faced the same way as the rest. "It's not the future I see."

In 1997 I took him to bed. I don't know if it was the bottle and a half of shiraz we celebrated one of our rare victories with, or the deep bittersweet richness of his voice finally eroding my limited virtue, but we were good in the dark. His arms and shoulders, it turned out, were beautiful, after all: powerful and lovely, all out of proportion with the rest of him.

I rolled over, after, and dropped the tissue-wrapped rubber on the nightstand, and heard him sigh. "Thank you," he said, and the awe in that perfect voice was sweeter than the sex had been.

"My pleasure," I said, and meant it, and curled up against him again, watching the firefly lights flicker around his blunt, broad hands as he spoke softly and gestured in the dark, trying to encompass some inexpressible emotion.

Neither one of us was sleepy. He asked me what I saw in Las Vegas. I told him I was from Tucson, and I missed the desert when I was gone. He told me he was from Stonington. When the sun came up, I put my hand into his aura, chasing the flickering lights like a child trying to catch snowflakes on her tongue.

I asked him about the terrible scars low on the backs of his thighs that left his hamstrings weirdly lumped and writhed, unconnected to bone under the skin. I'd thought him crippled from birth. I'd been wrong about so many, many things.

"Gaffing hook," he said. "When I was seventeen. My family were fishermen. Always have been."

"How come you never go home to Connecticut, Isaac?"

For once, he didn't correct me. "Connecticut isn't home."

"You don't have any family?"

Silence, but I saw the dull green denial stain his aura. I breathed in through my nose and tried again.

"Don't you ever miss the ocean?"

He laughed, warm huff of breath against my ear, stirring my hair. "The desert will kill me just as fast as the ocean would, if I ever want it. What's to miss?"

"Why'd you come here?"

"Just felt drawn. It seemed like a safe place to be. Unchanging. I needed to get away from the coast, and Nevada sounded . . . very dry. I have a skin condition. It's worse in wet climates. It's worse near the sea."

"But you came back to the ocean after all. Prehistoric seas. Nevada was all underwater once. There were ichthyosaurs—"

"Underwater. Huh." He stretched against my back, cool and soft. "I guess it's in the blood."

That night I dreamed they chained my wrists with jeweled chains before they crippled me and left me alone in the salt marsh to die. The sun rose as they walked away singing, hunched inhuman shadows glimpsed through a splintered mist that glowed pale as the opals in my manacles.

The mist burned off to show gray earth and greeny brown water, agates and discolored aquamarine. The edges of coarse gray cloth adhered in drying blood on the backs of my thighs, rumpled where they had pulled it up to hamstring me. The chains were cold against my cheeks when I raised my head away from the mud enough to pillow my face on the backs of my hands.

The marsh stank of rot and crushed vegetation, a green miasma so overwhelming the sticky copper of blood could not pierce it. The pain wasn't as much as it should have been; I was slipping into shock as softly as if I slipped under the unrippled water. I hadn't lost enough blood to kill me, but I rather thought I'd prefer a quick, cold sleep and never awakening to starving to death or lying in a pool of my own blood until the scent attracted the thing I had been left in propitiation of.

Somewhere, a frog croaked. It looked like a hot day coming.

I supposed I was going to find out.

His skin scaled in the heat. It was a dry heat, blistering, peeling, chapping lips and bloodying noses. He used to hang me with jewels, opals, tourmalines the color of moss and roses. "Family money," he told me. "Family jewels." He wasn't lying.

I would have seen a lie.

The Mojave hated him. He was chapped and chafed, cracked and dry. He never sweated enough, kept the air conditioner twisted as high as it would go. Skin burns in the heat, in the sun. Peels like a snake's. Aquamarine discolors like smoker's teeth. Pearls go brittle. Opals crack and lose their fire.

He used to go down to the Colorado river at night, across the dam to Willow Beach, on the Arizona side, and swim in the river in the dark. I told him it was crazy. I told him it was dangerous. How could he take care of himself in the Colorado when he couldn't walk without braces and crutches?

He kissed me on the nose and told me it helped his pain. I told him if he drowned, I would never forgive him. He said in the history of the entire world twice over, a Gilman had never once drowned. I called him a cocky, insincere bastard. He stopped telling me where he was going when he went out at night.

When he came back and slept beside me, sometimes I lay against the pillow and watched the follow-me lights flicker around him. Sometimes I slept.

Sometimes I dreamed, also.

I awakened after sunset, when the cool stars prickled out in the darkness. The front of my robe had dried, one long yellow-green stain, and now the fabric under my back and ass was saturated, sticking to my skin. The mud seemed to have worked it loose from the gashes on my legs.

I wasn't dead yet, more's the pity, and now it *hurt*.

I wondered if I could resist the swamp water when thirst set in. Dehydration would kill me faster than hunger. On the other hand, the water might make me sick enough that I'd slip into the relief of fever and pass away, oblivious in delirium. If dysentery was a better way to die than gangrene. Or dehydration.

Or being eaten. If the father of frogs came to collect me as was intended, I wouldn't suffer long.

I whistled across my teeth. A fine dramatic gesture, except it split my cracked lips and I tasted blood. My options seemed simple: lie still and die, or thrash and die. It would be sensible to give myself up with dignity.

I pushed myself onto my elbows and began to crawl toward nothing in particular.

Moonlight laid a patina of silver over the cloudy yellow-green puddles I wormed through and glanced off the rising mist in electric gleams of blue. The exertion warmed me, at least, and loosened my muscles. I stopped shivering after the first half hour. My thighs knotted tight as welded steel around the insult to my tendons. It would have been more convenient if they'd just chopped my damned legs off. At least I wouldn't have had to deal with the frozen limbs dragging behind me as I crawled.

If I had any sense—

If I had any sense at all, I wouldn't be crippled and dying in a swamp. If I had any sense *left*, I would curl up and die.

It sounded pretty good, all right.

I was just debating the most comfortable place when curious blue lights started to flicker at the corners of my vision.

I'm not sure why it was that I decided to follow them.

Pinky gave me a pearl on a silver chain, a baroque multicolored thing swirled glossy and irregular as toffee. He said it had been his mother's. It dangled between my breasts, warm as the stroke of a thumb when I wore it.

Pinky said he'd had a vasectomy, still wore a rubber every time we made love. Talked me into going on the Pill.

"Belt and suspenders," I teased. The garlic on my scampi was enough to make my eyes water, but Pinky never seemed to mind what I ate, no matter how potent it was.

It was one a.m. on a Friday, and we'd crawled out of bed for dinner, finally. We ate seafood at Capozzoli's, because although it was dim in the cluttered red room the food was good and it was open all night. Pinky looked at me out of squinting, amber eyes, so sad, and tore the tentacles off a bit of calamari with his teeth. "Would you want to bring a kid into this world?"

"No," I answered, and told that first lie. "I guess not."

I didn't meet Pinky's brother Esau until after I'd married someone else, left my job to try to have a baby, gotten divorced when it turned out we couldn't, had to come back to pay the bills. Pinky was still there, still part of the program. Still plugging away on the off chance that eventually he'd meet an innocent man, still pretending we were and always had been simply the best of friends. We never had the conversation, but I imagined it a thousand times.

I left you.

You wanted a baby.

It didn't work out.

And now you want to come back? I'm not like you, Maria.

Don't you ever miss the ocean?

No. I never do.

But he had too much pride, and I had too much shame. And once I was Judge Delprado, I only saw him in court anymore.

Esau called me, left a message on my cell, his name, who he was, where he'd be. I didn't know how he got the number. I met him out of curiosity as much as concern, at the old church downtown, the one from the thirties built of irreplaceable history. They made it of stone, to last, and broke up petroglyphs and stalactites to make the rough rock walls beautiful for God.

I hated Esau the first time I laid eyes on him. Esau. There was no mistaking him: same bristles and thinning hair, same spectacularly ugly countenance, fishy and prognathic. Same twilight-green aura, too, but Esau's was stained near his hands and mouth, the color of clotted blood, and no lights flickered near.

Esau stood by one of the petroglyphs, leaned close to discolored red stone marked with a stick figure, meaning man, and the wavy parallel lines that signified the river. Old as time, the Colorado, wearing the badlands down, warden and warded of the desert West.

Esau turned and saw me, but I don't think he saw *me*. I think he saw the pearl I wore around my neck.

I gave all the jewels back to Pinky when I left him. Except the pearl. He wouldn't take that back, and to be honest, I was glad. I'm not sure why I wore it to meet Esau, except I hated to take it off.

Esau straightened up, all five foot four of him behind the glower he gave me, and reached out peremptorily to touch the necklace, an odd gesture with the fingers pressed together. Without thinking, I slapped his hand away, and he hissed at me, a rubbery tongue flicking over fleshless lips.

Then he drew back, two steps, and looked me in the eye. His voice had nothing in common with his face: baritone and beautiful, melodious and carrying. I leaned forward, abruptly entranced. "Shipwrack," he murmured. "Shipwrecks. Dead man's jewels. It's all there for the taking if you just know where to look. Our family's always known."

My hand came up to slap him again, halted as if of its own volition. As if it couldn't push through the sound of his voice. "Were you a treasure hunter once?"

"I never stopped," he said, and tucked my hair behind my ear with the brush of his thumb. I shivered. My hand went down, clenched hard at my side. "When Isaac comes back to New England with me, you're coming too. We can give you children, Maria. Litters of them. Broods. Everything you've ever wanted."

"I'm not going anywhere. Not for . . . Isaac. Not for anyone."

"What makes you think you have any choice? You're part of his price. And we know what you want. We've researched you. It's not too late."

I shuddered, hard, sick, cold. "There's always a choice." The words hurt my lips. I swallowed. Fingernails cut my palms. His hand on my cheek was cool. "What's the rest of his price? If I go willing?"

"Healing. Transformation. Strength. Return to the sea. All the things he should have died for refusing."

"He doesn't miss the sea."

Esau smiled, showing teeth like yellow pegs. "You would almost think, wouldn't you?" There was a long pause, nearly respectful. Then he cleared his throat and said, "Come along."

Unable to stop myself, I followed that beautiful voice.

Most of a moon already hung in the deepening sky, despite the indirect sun still lighting the trail down to Willow Beach. The rocks radiated heat through my sneakers like bricks warmed in an oven. "Pinky said he didn't have any family."

Esau snorted. "He gave it the old college try."

"You were the one who crippled him, weren't you? And left him in the marsh to die."

"How did you know that?"

"He didn't tell me. I dreamed it."

"No," he answered, extending one hand to help me down a tricky slope. "That was Jacob. He doesn't travel."

"Another brother."

"The eldest brother." He yanked my arm and gave me a withering glance when I stumbled. He walked faster, crimson flashes of obfuscation coloring the swampwater light that surrounded him. I trotted to keep up, cursing my treacherous feet. At least my tongue was still my own, and I used it.

"Jacob, Esau, and Isaac Gilman? How . . . original."

"They're proud old New England names. Marshes and Gilmans were among the original settlers." Defensive. "Be silent. You don't need a tongue to make babies, and in a few more words I'll be happy to relieve you of it, mammal bitch."

I opened my mouth; my voice stopped at the back of my throat. I stumbled, and he hauled me to my feet, his rough, cold palm scraped the skin of my wrist over the bones.

We came around a corner of the wash that the trail ran through. Esau stopped short, planting his feet hard. I caught my breath at the power of the silent brown river running at the bottom of the gorge, at the sparkles that hung over it, silver and copper and alive, swarming like fireflies.

And standing on the bank before the current was Pinky—Isaac—braced on his canes, startlingly insouciant for a cripple who'd fought his way down a rocky trail. He craned his head back to get a better look at us and frowned. "Esau. I wish I could say it was a pleasure to see you. I'd hoped you'd joined Jacob at the bottom of the ocean by now."

"Soon," Esau said easily, manhandling me down the last of the slope. He held up the hand that wasn't knotted around my wrist. I blinked twice before I realized the veined, translucent yellow webs between his fingers were a part of him. He grabbed my arm again, handling me like a bag of groceries.

Pinky hitched himself forward to meet us, and for a moment I thought he was going to hit Esau across the face with his crutch. I imagined the sound the aluminum would make when it shattered Esau's cheekbone. *Litters of them. Broods.* Easy to give in and let it happen, yes. But litters of *what*?

"You didn't have to bring Maria into it."

"We can give her what she wants, can't we? With your help or without it. How'd you get the money for school?"

Pinky smiled past me, a grin like a wolf. "There was platinum in those chains. Opals. Pearls big as a dead man's eyeball. Plenty. There's still plenty left."

"So there was. How did you survive?"

"I was guided," he said, and the blue lights flickered around him. Blue lights that were kin to the silver lights swarming over the river. I could imagine them buzzing. Angry, invaded. I turned my head to see Esau's expression, but he only had eyes for Pinky.

Esau couldn't see the lights. He looked at Pinky, and Pinky met the stare with a lifted chin. "Come home, Isaac."

"And let Jacob try to kill me again?"

"He only hurt you because you tried to leave us."

"He left me for the father of frogs in the salt marsh, Esau. And you were there with him when he did—"

"We couldn't just let you walk away." Esau let go of my arm with a command to be still, and stepped toward Pinky with his hands spread wide. There was still light down here, where the canyon was wider and the shadow of the walls didn't yet block the sun. It shone on Esau's balding scalp, on the yolky, veined webs between his fingers, on the aluminum of Pinky's crutches.

"I didn't walk," Pinky said. He turned away, hitching himself around, the beige rubber feet of the crutches braced wide on the rocky soil. He swung himself forward, headed for the river, for the swarming lights. "I crawled."

Esau fell into step beside him. "I don't understand how you haven't . . . changed."

"It's the desert." Pinky paused on a little ledge over the water. Tamed by the dam, the river ran smooth here and still. I could feel its power anyway, old magic that made this land live. "The desert doesn't like change. It keeps me in between."

"That hurts you." Almost in sympathy, as Esau reached out and laid a webbed hand on Pinky's shoulder. Pinky flinched but didn't pull away. I opened my mouth to shout at him, feeling as if my tongue were my own again, and stopped. *Litters.*

Whatever they were, they'd be Pinky's children.

"It does." Pinky fidgeted with the crutches, leaning forward over the river, working his forearms free of the cuffs. His shoulders rippled under the white cloth of his shirt. I wanted to run my palms over them.

"Your legs will heal if you accept the change," Esau offered, softly, his voice carried away over the water. "You'll be strong. You'll regenerate. You'll have the ocean, and you won't hurt anymore, and there's your woman—we'll take her too."

"*Esau.*"

I heard the warning in the tone. The anger. Esau did not. He glanced at me. "Speak, woman. Tell Isaac what you want."

I felt my tongue come unstuck in my mouth, although I still couldn't move my hands. I bit my tongue to keep it still.

Esau sighed, and looked away. "Blood is thicker than water, Isaac. Don't you want a family of your own?"

Yes, I thought. Pinky didn't speak, but I saw the set of his shoulders, and the answer they carried was *no.* Esau must have seen it too, because he raised one hand, the webs translucent and spoiled-looking, and sunlight glittered on the barbed ivory claws that curved from his fingertips, unsheathed like a cat's.

With your help or without it.

But litters of *what?*

I shouted so hard it bent me over. "*Pinky, duck!*"

He didn't. Instead, he *threw* his crutches backward, turned with the momentum of the motion, and grabbed Esau around the waist. Esau squeaked—*shrieked*—and threw his hands up, clawing at Pinky's shoulders and face as the silver and blue and coppery lights flickered and swarmed and swirled around them, but he couldn't match Pinky's massive strength. The lights covered them both, and Esau screamed again, and I strained, lunged, leaned at the invisible chains that held me as still as a posed mannequin.

Pinky just held on and leaned back.

They barely splashed when the Colorado closed over them.

Five minutes after they went under, I managed to wiggle my fingers. Up and down the bank, there was no trace of either of them. I couldn't stand to touch Pinky's crutches.

I left them where they'd fallen.

Esau had left the keys in the car, but when I got there I was shaking too hard to drive. I locked the door and got back out, tightened the laces on my sneakers, and toiled up the ridge until I got to the top. I almost turned my ankle twice when rocks rolled under my foot, but it didn't take long. Red rock and dusty canyons stretched west, a long, gullied slope behind me, the river down there somewhere, close enough to smell but out of sight. I settled myself on a rock, elbows on knees, and looked out over the scarred, raw desert at the horizon and the setting sun.

There's a green flash that's supposed to happen just when the sun slips under the edge of the world. I'd never seen it. I wasn't even sure it existed. But if I watched long enough, I figured I might find out.

There was still a hand span between the sun and the ground, up here. I sat and watched, the hot wind lifting my hair, until the tawny disk of the sun was halfway gone and I heard the rhythmic crunch of someone coming up the path.

I didn't turn. There was no point. He leaned over my shoulder, braced his crutches on either side of me, a presence solid and cool as a moss-covered rock. I tilted my head back against Pinky's chest, his wet shirt dripping on my forehead, eyes, and mouth. Electric blue lights flickered around him, and I couldn't quite make out his features, shadowed as they were against a twilight sky. He released one crutch and laid his hand on my shoulder. His breath brushed my ear like the susurrus of the sea. "Esau said blood is thicker than water," I said, when I didn't mean to say anything.

"Fish blood isn't," Pinky answered, and his hand tightened. I looked away from the reaching shadows of the canyons below and saw his fingers against my skin, pale silhouettes on olive, unwebbed. He slid one under the black strap of my tank top. I didn't protest, despite the dark red, flaking threads that knotted the green smoke around his hands.

"Where is he?"

"Esau? He drowned."

"But—" I craned my neck. "You said Gilmans never drown."

He shrugged against my back. "I guess the river just took a dislike to him. Happens that way sometimes."

A lingering silence, while I framed my next question. "How did you find me?"

"I'll always find you, if you want," he said, his patched beard rough against my neck. "What are you watching?"

"I'm watching the sun go down."

"Come in under this red rock," he misquoted, as the shadow of the ridge opposite slipped across the valley toward us.

"The handful of dust thing seems appropriate—"

Soft laugh, and he kissed my cheek, hesitantly, as if he wasn't sure I would permit it. "I would have thought it'd be 'Fear death by water.'"

The sun went down. I missed the flash again. I turned to him in a twilight indistinguishable from the gloom that hung around his shoulders and brushed the flickering lights away from his face with the back of my hand. "Not that," I answered. "I have no fear of that, my love."

JEFFREY FORD

Boatman's Holiday

Jeffrey Ford is the author of six novels: The Physiognomy, Memoranda, The Beyond, The Portrait of Mrs. Charbuque, *and most recently* The Girl in the Glass, *which won the Edgar Award. His short stories have been published in magazines and anthologies, and chosen for several volumes of the* Year's Best Fantasy & Horror. *They are collected in* The Fantasy Writer's Assistant & Other Stories *and in* The Empire of Ice Cream. *Ford is a three time recipient of the World Fantasy Award and won the Nebula Award for best novelette of 2003. His novella,* The Cosmology of the Wider World, *was published as a chapbook in 2006. He lives in South Jersey with his wife and two sons and is a professor of Writing and Literature at Brookdale Community College.*

"Boatman's Holiday" first appeared in the anthology Book of Voices, *which raised money for Sierra Leone's PEN, and was subsequently published in* The Magazine of Fantasy and Science Fiction.

—E.D.

Beneath a blazing orange sun, he maneuvered his boat between the two petrified oaks that grew so high their tops were lost in violet clouds. The vast trunks and complexity of branches were bone white, as if hidden just below the surface of the murky water was a stag's head the size of a mountain. Thousands of crows, like black leaves, perched amidst the pale tangle, staring silently down. Feathers fell, spiraling in their descent with the slow grace of certain dreams, and he wondered how many of these journeys he'd made or if they were all, always, the same journey.

Beyond the oaks, the current grew stronger, and he entered a constantly shifting maze of whirlpools, some spinning clockwise, some counter, as if to negate the passage of time. Another boatman might have given in to panic and lost everything, but he was a master navigator and knew the river better than himself. Any other craft would have quickly succumbed to the seething waters, been ripped apart and its debris swallowed.

His boat was comprised of an inner structure of human bone lashed together with tendon and covered in flesh stitched by his own steady hand, employing a thorn needle and thread spun from sorrow. The lines of its contours lacked symmetry, meandered and went off on tangents. Along each side, worked into the gunwales well above the waterline, was a row of eyeless, tongueless faces—the empty sockets, the gaping lips, portals through which the craft breathed. Below, in the hold, there reverberated a heartbeat that fluttered randomly and died every minute only to be revived the next.

On deck, there were two long rows of benches fashioned from skulls for his passengers, and at the back, his seat at the tiller. In the shallows, he'd stand and use his long pole to guide the boat along. There was no need of a sail as the vessel moved slowly forward of its own volition with a simple command. On the trip out, the benches empty, he'd whisper, "There!" and on the journey back, carrying a full load, "Home!" and no river current could dissuade its progress. Still, it took a sure and fearless hand to hold the craft on course.

Charon's tall, wiry frame was slightly but irreparably bent from centuries hunched beside the tiller. His beard and tangled nest of snow-white hair, his complexion the color of ash, made him appear ancient. When in the throes of maneuvering around Felmian, the blue serpent, or in the heated rush along the shoals of the Island of Nothing, however, he'd toss one side of his scarlet cloak back over his shoulder, and the musculature of his chest, the coiled bulge of his bicep, the thick tendon in his forearm, gave evidence of the power hidden beneath his laconic façade. Woe to the passenger who mistook those outer signs of age for weakness and set some plan in motion, for then the boatman would wield his long shallows stick and shatter every bone in their body.

Each treacherous obstacle, the clutch of shifting boulders, the rapids, the waterfall that dropped into a bottomless star-filled space, was expertly avoided with a skill born of intuition. Eventually a vague but steady tone like the uninterrupted buzz of a mosquito came to him over the water; a sign that he drew close to his destination. He shaded his eyes against the brightness of the flaming sun and spotted the dark, thin edge of shoreline in the distance. As he advanced, that distant, whispered note grew steadily into a high keening, and then fractured to reveal itself a chorus of agony. A few more leagues and he could make out the legion of forms crowding the bank. When close enough to land, he left the tiller, stood, and used the pole to turn the boat so it came to rest sideways on the black sand. Laying down the pole, he stepped to his spot at the prow.

Two winged, toad-faced demons with talons for hands and hands for feet, Gesnil and Trinkthil, saw to the orderliness of the line of passengers that ran from the shore back a hundred yards into the writhing human continent of dead. Every day there were more travelers, and no matter how many trips Charon made, there was no hope of ever emptying the endless beach.

Brandishing a cat-o'-nine-tails with barbed tips fashioned from incisors, the demons lashed the "tourists," as they called them, subduing those unwilling to go.

"Another load of the falsely accused, Charon," said Gesnil, puffing on a lit human finger jutting from the corner of his mouth.

"Watch this woman, third back, in the blue dress," said Trinkthil, "her blithering lamentations will bore you to sleep. You know, she never really meant to add Belladonna to the recipe for her husband's gruel."

Charon shook his head.

"We've gotten word that there will be no voyages for a time," said Gesnil.

"Yes," said Charon, "I've been granted a respite by the Master. A holiday."

"A century's passed already?" said Gesnil. "My, my, it seemed no more than three. Time flies. . . ."

"Traveling?" asked Trinkthil. "Or staying home?"

"There's an island I believe I'll visit," he said.

"Where's it located?" asked Gesnil.

Charon ignored the question and said, "Send them along."

The demons knew to obey, and they directed the first in line to move forward. A bald, overweight man in a cassock, some member of the clergy, stepped up. He was trembling so that his jowls shook. He'd waited on the shore in dire fear and anguish for centuries, milling about, fretting as to the ultimate nature of his fate.

"Payment," said Charon.

The man tilted his head back and opened his mouth. A round shiny object lay beneath his tongue. The boatman reached out and took the gold coin, putting it in the pocket of his cloak. "Next," called Charon as the man moved past him and took a seat on the bench of skulls.

Hell's orange sun screamed in its death throes every evening, a pandemonium sweeping down from above that made even the demons sweat and set the master's three-headed dog to cowering. That horrendous din worked its way into the rocks, the river, the petrified trees, and everything brimmed with misery. Slowly, it diminished as the starless, moonless dark came on, devouring every last shred of light. With that infernal night came a cool breeze whose initial tantalizing relief never failed to deceive the damned, though they be residents for a thousand years, with a false promise of Hope. That growing wind carried in it a catalyst for memory, and set all who it caressed to recalling in vivid detail their lost lives—a torture individually tailored, more effective than fire.

Charon sat in his home, the skull of a fallen god, on the crest of a high flint hill, overlooking the river. Through the left eye socket glazed with transparent lies, he could be seen sitting at a table, a glutton's-fat tallow burning, its flame guttering in the night breeze let in through the gap of a missing tooth. Laid out before him was a curling width of tattooed flesh skinned from the back of an ancient explorer who'd no doubt sold his soul for a sip from the Fountain of Youth. In the boatman's right hand was a compass and in his left a writing quill. His gaze traced along the strange parchment the course of his own river, Acheron, the River of Pain, to where it crossed paths with Pyriphlegethon, the River of Fire. That burning course was eventually quelled in cataracts of steam where it emptied into and became the Lethe, River of Forgetting.

He traced his next day's journey with the quill tip, gliding it an inch above the meandering line of vein blue. There, in the meager width of that last river's depiction, almost directly halfway between its origin and end in the mournful Cocytus, was a freckle. Anyone else would have thought it no more than a bodily blemish inked over by chance in the production of the map, but Charon was certain after centuries of overhearing whispered snatches of conversation from his unlucky passengers that it represented the legendary island of Oondeshai.

He put down his quill and compass and sat back in the chair, closing his eyes. Hanging from the center of the cathedral cranium above, the wind chime made of dangling bat bones clacked as the mischievous breeze that invaded his home lifted one corner of the map. He sighed at the touch of cool wind as its insidious effect reeled his memory into the past.

One night, he couldn't recall how many centuries before, he was lying in bed on the verge of sleep, when there came a pounding at the hinged door carved in the left side of the skull. "Who's there?" he called in the fearsome voice he used to silence passengers. There was no verbal answer, but another barrage of banging ensued. He rolled out of bed, put on his cloak and lit a tallow. Taking the candle with him, he went to the door and flung it open. A startled figure stepped back into the darkness.

Charon thrust the light forward and beheld a cowed, trembling man, his naked flesh covered in oozing sores and wounds.

"Who are you?" asked the boatman.

The man stared up at him, holding out a hand.

"You've escaped from the pit, haven't you?"

The back side of the flint hill atop which his home sat overlooked the enormous pit, its circumference at the top a hundred miles across. Spiraling along its inner wall was a path that led down and down in ever decreasing arcs through the various levels of Hell to end at a pinpoint in the very mind of the Master. Even at night, if Charon were to go behind the skull and peer out over the rim, he could see a faint reddish glow and hear the distant echo of plaintive wails.

The man finally nodded.

"Come in," said Charon, and held the door as the stranger shuffled past him.

Later, after he'd been offered a chair, a spare cloak, and a cup of nettle tea, his broken visitor began to come around.

"You know," said Charon, "there's no escape from Hell."

"This I know," mumbled the man, making a great effort to speak, as if he'd forgotten the skill. "But there is an escape in Hell."

"What are you talking about? The dog will be here within the hour to fetch you back. He's less than gentle."

"I need to make the river," said the man.

"What's your name?" asked Charon.

"Wieroot," said the man with a grimace.

The boatman nodded. "This escape in Hell, where is it, what is it?"

"Oondeshai," said Wieroot, "an island in the River Lethe."

"Where did you hear of it?"

"I created it," he said, holding his head with both hands as if to remember. "Centuries ago, I wrote it into the fabric of the mythology of Hell."

"Mythology?" asked Charon. "I suppose those wounds on your body are merely a myth?"

"The suffering's real here, don't I know it, but the entire construction of Hell is, of course, man's own invention. The Pit, the three-headed dog, the rivers, you, if I may say so, all sprang from the mind of humanity, confabulated to punish itself."

"Hell has been here from the beginning," said Charon.

"Yes," said Wieroot, "in one form or another. But when, in the living world, something is added to the legend, some detail to better convince believers or convert new ones, here it leaps into existence with a ready-made history that instantly spreads back to the start and a guaranteed future that creeps inexorably forward." The escapee fell into a fit of coughing, smoke from the fires of the pit issuing in small clouds from his lungs.

"The heat's made you mad," said Charon. "You've had too much time to think."

"Both may be true," croaked Wieroot, wincing in pain, "but listen for a moment more. You appear to be a man, yet I'll wager you don't remember your youth. Where were you born? How did you become the boatman?"

Charon strained his memory, searching for an image of his past in the world of the living. All he saw was rows and rows of heads, tilting back, proffering the coin beneath the tongue. An image of him setting out across the river, passing between the giant oaks, repeated behind his eyes three dozen times in rapid succession.

"Nothing there, am I correct?"

Charon stared hard at his guest.

"I was a cleric, and in copying a sacred text describing the environs of Hell, I deviated from the disintegrating original and added the existence of Oondeshai. Over the course of years, decades, centuries, other scholars found my creation and added it to their own works and so, now, Oondeshai, though not as well known as yourself or your river, is an actuality in this desperate land."

From down along the riverbank came the approaching sound of Cerberus baying. Wieroot stood, sloughing off the cloak to let it drop into his chair. "I've got to get to the river," he said. "But consider this. You live in the skull of a fallen god. This space was once filled with a substance that directed the universe, no, was the universe. How does a god die?"

"You'll never get across," said Charon.

"I don't want to. I want to be caught in its flow."

"You'll drown."

"Yes, I'll drown, be bitten by the spiny eels, burned in the River of Fire, but I won't die, for I'm already dead. Some time ages hence, my body will wash up on the shore of Oondeshai, and I will have arrived home. The way I crafted the island, the moment you reach its shores and pull yourself from the River of Forgetting, you instantly remember everything."

"It sounds like a child's tale," Charon murmured.

"Thank you," said the stranger.

"What gave you cause to create this island?" asked the boatman.

Wieroot staggered toward the door. As he opened it and stepped out into the pitch black, he called back, "I knew I would eventually commit murder."

Charon followed out into the night and heard the man's feet pacing away down the flint hill toward the river. Seconds later, he heard the wheezing breath of the three-headed dog. Growling, barking, sounded in triplicate. There was silence for a time, and then finally . . . a splash, and in that moment, for the merest instant, an image of a beautiful island flashed behind the boatman's eyes.

He'd nearly been able to forget the incident with Wieroot as the centuries flowed on, their own River of Pain, until one day he heard one of his passengers whisper the word "Oondeshai" to another. Three or four times this happened, and then, only a half century past, a young woman, still radiant though dead, with shiny black hair and a curious red dot of a birthmark just below her left eye, was ushered onto his boat. He requested payment. When she tilted her head back, opened her mouth and lifted her tongue, there was no coin but instead a small, tightly folded package of flesh. Charon nearly lost his temper as he retrieved it from her mouth, but she whispered quickly, "A map to Oondeshai."

These words were like a slap to his face. He froze for the merest instant, but then thought quickly, and, nodding, stepped aside for her to take a seat. "Next," he yelled and the demons were none the wiser. Later that night, he unfolded the crudely cut rectangle of skin, and after a close inspection of the tattoo cursed himself for having been duped. He swept the map onto the floor and the night breeze blew it into a corner. Weeks later, after finding it had been blown back out from under the table into the middle of the floor, he lifted it and searched it again. This time he noticed the freckle in the length of Lethe's blue line and wondered.

He kept his boat in a small lagoon hidden by a thicket of black poplars. It was just after sunrise, and he'd already stowed his provisions in the hold below deck. After lashing them fast with lengths of hangman's rope cast off over the years by certain passengers, he turned around to face the chaotically beating heart of the craft. The large blood organ, having once resided in the chest of the Queen of Sirens, was suspended in the center of the hold by thick branchlike veins and arteries that grew into the sides of the boat. Its vasculature expanded and contracted, and the heart itself beat erratically, undulating and shivering, sweating red droplets.

Charon waited until after it died, lay still, and then was startled back to life by whatever immortal force pervaded its chambers. Once it was moving again, he gave a high-pitched whistle, a note that began at the bottom of the register and quickly rose to the top. At the sound of this signal, the wet red meat of the thing parted in a slit to reveal an eye. The orb swiveled to and fro, and the boatman stepped up close with a burning tallow in one hand and the map, opened, in the other. He back-lit the scrap of skin to let the eye read its tattoo. He'd circled the freckle that represented Oondeshai with his quill, so the destination was clearly marked. All he'd have to do is steer around the dangers, keep the keel in deep water and stay awake. Otherwise, the craft now knew the way to go.

Up on deck, he cast off the ropes, and instead of uttering the word "There," he spoke a command used less than once a century—"Away." The boat moved out of the lagoon and onto the river. Charon felt something close to joy at not having to steer between the giant white oaks. He glanced up to his left at the top of the flint hill and saw the huge skull, staring down at him. The day was hot and orange and all of Hell was busy at the work of suffering, but he, the boatman, was off on a holiday.

On the voyage out, he traveled with the flow of the river, so its current combined with the inherent, enchanted propulsion of the boat made for swift passage. There were the usual whirlpools, outcroppings of sulfur and brimstone to avoid, but these occasional obstacles were a welcome diversion. He'd never taken this route before when on holiday. Usually, he'd just stay home, resting, making minor repairs to the boat, playing knucklebones with some of the bat-winged demons from the pit on a brief break from the grueling work of torture.

Once, as a guest of the master during a holiday, he'd been invited into the bottommost reaches of the pit, transported in a winged chariot that glided down through the center of the great spiral. There, where the Czar of the Underworld kept a private palace made of frozen sighs, in a land of snow so cold one's breath fractured upon touching the air, he was led by an army of living marble statues, shaped like men but devoid of faces, down a tunnel that led to an enormous circle of clear ice. Through this transparent barrier he could look out on the realm of the living. Six days he spent transfixed between astonishment and fear at the sight of the world the way it was. That vacation left a splinter of ice in his heart that took three centuries to melt.

None of his previous getaways ever resulted in a tenth the sense of relief he already felt having gone but a few miles along the nautical route to Oondeshai. He repeated the name of the island again and again under his breath as he worked the tiller or manned the shallows pole, hoping to catch another glimpse of its image as he had the night Wieroot dove into the Acheron. As always, that mental picture refused to coalesce, but he'd learned to suffice with its absence, which had become a kind of solace in itself.

To avoid dangerous eddies and rocks in the middle flow of the river, Charon was occasionally forced to steer the boat in close to shore on the port side. There, he glimpsed the marvels of that remote, forgotten landscape—a distant string of smoldering volcanoes; a thundering herd of bloodless behemoths, sweeping like a white wave across the immensity of a fissured salt flat; a glittering forest of crystal trees alive with long-tailed monkeys made of lead. The distractions were many, but he struggled to put away his curiosity and concentrate for fear of running aground and ripping a hole in the hull.

He hoped to make the River of Fire before nightfall, so as to have light with which to navigate. To travel the Acheron blind would be sheer suicide, and unlike Wieroot, Charon was uncertain as to whether he was already dead or alive or merely a figment of Hell's imagination. There was the possibility of finding a natural harbor and dropping the anchor, but the land through which the river ran had shown him fierce and mysterious creatures stalking him along the banks and that made steering through the dark seem the fairer alternative.

As the day waned, and the sun began to whine with the pain of its gradual death, Charon peered ahead with a hand shading his sight in anticipation of a glimpse at the flames of Pyriphlegethon. During his visit to the palace of frozen sighs, the master had let slip that the liquid fire of those waters burned only sinners. Because the boat was a tool of Hell, made of Hell, he was fairly certain it could withstand the flames, but he wasn't sure if at some point in his distant past he had not sinned. If he were to blunder into suffering, though, he thought that he at least would learn some truth about himself.

In the last moments of light, he lit three candles and positioned them at the prow of the boat. They proved ineffectual against the night, casting their glow only a shallow pole-length ahead of the craft. Their glare wearied Charon's eyes and he grew fatigued. To distract himself from fatigue, he went below and brought back a dried, salted Harpy leg to chew on. In recent centuries the winged creatures had grown scrawny, almost thin enough to slip his snares. The meat was known to improve eyesight and exacerbate the mind. Its effect had nothing to do with clarity, merely a kind of agitation of thought that was, at this juncture, preferable to slumber. Sleep was the special benefit of the working class of Hell, and the boatman usually relished it. Dreams especially were an exotic escape from the routine of work. The sinners never slept, nor did the master.

Precisely at the center of the night Charon felt some urge, some pull of intuition to push the tiller hard to the left. As soon as he'd made the reckless maneuver, he heard from up ahead the loud gulping sound that meant a whirlpool lay in his path. The sound grew quickly to a deafening strength, and only when he was upon the swirling monster, riding its very lip around the right arc, was he able to see its immensity. The boat struggled to free itself from the draw, and instead of being propelled by its magic it seemed to be clawing its way forward, dragging its weight free of the hopeless descent. There was nothing he could do but hold the tiller firm and stare with widened eyes down the long, treacherous tunnel. Not a moment passed after he was finally free of it than the boat entered the turbulent waters where Acheron crossed the River of Fire.

He released his grip on the tiller and let the craft lead him with its knowledge of the map he'd shown it. His fingers gripped tightly into the eye holes of two of the skulls that formed his seat, and he held on so as not to be thrown overboard. Pyriphlegethon now blazed ahead of him, and the sight of its dancing flames, some flaring high into the night, made him scream, not with fear but exhilaration. The boat forged forward, cleaved the burning surface, and then was engulfed in a yellow-orange brightness that gave no heat. The frantic illumination dazed Charon, and he sat as in a trance, dreaming wide awake. He no longer felt the passage of Time, the urgency to reach his destination, the weight of all those things he'd fled on his holiday.

Eventually, after a prolonged bright trance, the blazing waters became turbulent, lost their fire, and a thick mist rose off them. That mist quickly became a fog so thick it seemed to have texture, brushing against his skin like a feather. He thought he might grab handfuls until it slipped through his fingers, leaked into his nostrils, and wrapped its tentacles around his memory.

When the boatman awoke to the daily birth cry of Hell's sun, he found himself lying naked upon his bed, staring up at the clutch of bat bones dangling from the cranial center of his skull home. He was startled at first, grasping awkwardly for a tiller that wasn't there, tightening his fist around the shaft of the absent shallows stick that instead rested at an angle against the doorway. As soon as the shock of discovery that he was home had abated, he sighed deeply and sat up on the edge of the bed. It struck him then that his entire journey, his holiday, had been for naught.

He frantically searched his thoughts for the slightest shred of a memory that he might have reached Oondeshai, but every trace had been forgotten. For the first time in centuries, tears came to his eyes, and the frustration of his predicament made him cry out. Eventually, he stood and found his cloak rolled into a ball on the floor at the foot of his bed. He dressed and without stopping to put on his boots or grab the shallows pole, he left his home.

With determination in his stride, he mounted the small rise that lay back behind the skull and stood at the rim of the enormous pit. Inching to the very edge, he peered down into the spiraled depths at the faint red glow. The screams of tortured sinners, the wailing laments of self-pity, sounded in his ears like distant voices in a dream. Beneath it all he could barely discern, like the buzzing of a fly, the sound of the master laughing uproariously, joyously, and that discordant strain seemed to lace itself subtly into everything.

Charon's anger and frustration slowly melted into a kind of numbness as cold as the hallways of Satan's palace, and he swayed to and fro, out over the edge and back, not so much wanting to jump as waiting to fall. Time passed, he was not aware how much, and then as suddenly as he had dressed and left his home, he turned away from the pit.

Once more inside the skull, he prepared to go to work. There was a great heaviness within him, as if his very organs were now made of lead, and each step was an effort, each exhalation a sigh. He found his eelskin ankle boots beneath the table at which he'd studied the flesh map at night. Upon lifting one, it turned in his hand, and a steady stream of blonde sand poured out onto the floor. The sight of it caught him off guard and for a moment he stopped breathing.

He fell to his knees to inspect the little pile that had formed. Carefully, he lifted the other boot, turned it over and emptied that one into its own neat little pile next to the other. He reached toward these twin wonders, initially wanting to feel the grains run through his fingers, but their stark proof that he had been to Oondeshai and could not recall a moment of it ultimately defeated his will and he never touched them. Instead, he stood, took up the shallows pole, and left the skull for his boat.

As he guided the boat between the two giant oaks, he no longer wondered if all his journeys across the Acheron were always the same journey. With a dull aspect, he performed his duties as the boatman. His muscles, educated in the task over countless centuries, knew exactly how to avoid the blue serpent and skirt the whirlpools without need of a single thought. No doubt it was these same unconscious processes that had brought Charon and his craft back safely from Oondeshai.

Gesnil and Trinkthil inquired with great anticipation about his vacation when he met them on the far shore. For the demons, who knew no respite from the drudgery of herding sinners, even a few words about a holiday away would have been like some rare confection, but he told them nothing. From the look on Charon's face, they knew not to prod him and merely sent the travelers forward to offer coins and take their places on the benches.

During the return trip that morning, a large fellow sitting among the passengers had a last-second attack of nerves in the face of an impending eternity of suffering. He screamed incoherently, and Charon ordered him to silence. When the man stood up and began pacing back and forth, the boatman ordered him to return to his seat. The man persisted moving about, his body jerking with spasms of fear, and it was obvious his antics were spooking the other sinners. Fearing the man would spread mutiny, Charon came forth with the shallows stick and bringing it around like a club, split the poor fellow's head. That was usually all the incentive a recalcitrant passenger needed to return to the bench, but this one was now insane with the horror of his plight.

The boatman waded in and beat him wildly, striking him again and again. With each blow, Charon felt some infinitesimal measure of relief from his own frustration. When he was finished, the agitator lay in a heap on deck, nothing more than a flesh bag full of broken bones, and the other passengers shuffled their feet sideways so as not to touch his corpse.

Only later, after he had docked his boat in the lagoon and the winged demons had flown out of the pit to lead the damned up the flint hill and down along the spiral path to their eternal destinies, did the boatman regret his rage. As he lifted the sac of flesh that had been his charge and dumped it like a bale of chum over the side, he realized that the man's hysteria had been one and the same thing as his own frustration.

The sun sounded its death cry as it sank into a pool of blood that was the horizon and then Hell's twilight came on. Charon dragged himself up the hill and went inside his home. Before pure night closed its fist on the riverbank, he kicked off his boots, gnawed on a haunch of Harpy flesh, and lit the tallow that sat in its holder on the table. Taking his seat there he stared into the flame, thinking of it as the future that constantly drew him forward through years, decades, centuries, eons, as the past disappeared behind him. "I am nothing but a moment," he said aloud and his words echoed around the empty skull.

Some time later, still sitting at his chair at the table, he noticed the candle flame twitch. His eyes shifted for the first time in hours to follow its movement. Then the fire began to dance, the sheets of flesh parchment lifted slightly at their corners, the bat bones clacked quietly overhead. Hell's deceptive wind of memory had begun to blow. He heard it whistling in through the space in his home's grin, felt its coolness sweep around him. This most complex and exquisite torture that brought back to sinners the times of their lives now worked on the boatman. He moved his bare feet beneath the table and realized the piles of sand lay beneath them.

The image began in his mind no more than a dot of blue and then rapidly unfolded in every direction to reveal a sky and crystal water. The sun there in Oondeshai had been yellow and it gave true warmth. This he remembered clearly. He'd sat high on a hill of blond sand, staring out across the endless vista of sparkling water. Next to him on the left was Wieroot, legs crossed, dressed in a black robe and sporting a beard to hide the healing scars that riddled his face. On the right was the young woman with the shining black hair and the red dot of a birthmark beneath her left eye.

"... And you created this all by writing it in the other world?" asked Charon. There was a breeze blowing and the boatman felt a certain lightness inside as if he'd eaten of one of the white clouds floating across the sky.

"I'll tell you a secret," said Wieroot, "although it's a shame you'll never get a chance to put it to use."

"Tell me," said the boatman.

"God made the world with words," he said in a whisper.

Charon remembered that he didn't understand. He furrowed his brow and turned to look at the young woman to see if she was laughing. Instead she was also nodding along with Wieroot. She put her hand on the boatman's shoulder and said, "And man made God with words."

Charon's memory of the beach on Oondeshai suddenly gave violent birth to another memory from his holiday. He was sitting in a small structure with no door, facing out into a night scene of tall trees whose leaves were blowing in a strong wind. Although it was night, it was not the utter darkness he knew from his quadrant of Hell. High in the black sky there shone a bright disk, which cast its beams down onto the island. Their glow had seeped into the small home behind him and fell upon the forms of Wieroot and the woman, Shara was her name, where they slept upon a bed of reeds. Beneath the sound of the wind, the calls of night birds, the whirr of insects, he heard the steady breathing of the sleeping couple.

And one last memory followed. Charon recalled Wieroot drawing near to him as he was about to board his boat for the return journey.

"You told me you committed murder," said the boatman.

"I did," said Wieroot.

"Who?"

"The god whose skull you live in," came the words which grew faint and then disappeared as the night wind of Hell ceased blowing. The memories faded and Charon looked up to see the candle flame again at rest. He reached across the table and drew his writing quill and a sheaf of parchment toward him. Dipping the pen nib into the pot of blood that was his ink, he scratched out two words at the top of the page. My Story, he wrote, and then set about remembering the future. The words came, slowly at first, reluctantly, dragging their imagery behind them, but after a short while their numbers grew to equal the number of sinners awaiting a journey to the distant shore. He ferried them methodically, expertly, from his mind to the page, scratching away long into the dark night of Hell until down at the bottom of the spiral pit, in his palace of frozen sighs, Satan suddenly stopped laughing.

HOWARD WALDROP

The Horse of a Different Color (That You Rode In On)

This year Howard Waldrop produced two original stories for the CapClave convention chapbook: "The Horse of a Different Color (That You Rode in On)" and "The King of Where-I-Go," both inspired by the art of Carol Emshwiller. (Both stories were also published on SCI FICTION.) In "The Horse . . .", Waldrop's secret-history-in-a-showbiz-interview brings together the quest for the Holy Grail, vaudeville, the Marx Brothers, and an oral history of the beginnings of the silver screen. Waldrop is the author of the collections Howard Who?, All About Strange Monsters of the Recent Past, Night of the Cooters, Going Home Again, *and most recently* Heart of Whiteness. *He won the Nebula and World Fantasy Awards for his novelette* "The Ugly Chickens." *Raised in Mississippi, Waldrop lives in Austin, Texas.*

—K.L. & G.G.

A few years before Manny Marks (that's how he insisted his name be spelled) died at the age of 107, he gave a series of long interviews to Barry Winstead, who was researching a book on the death of vaudeville. Marks was 103 at the time, in the spring of 1990. This unedited tape was probably never transcribed.

MARKS:. . . I know it was, because I was playing Conshohocken. Is that thing on? What exactly does it do?

WINSTEAD: Are you kidding me?

MARKS: Those things have been going downhill since the Dictaphone. How well could that thing record? It's the size of a pack of Luckies . . .

WINSTEAD: Trust me, Mr. Marks.

MARKS: Mr. Marx was my father, Samuel "Frenchy" Marx. Call me Manny.

W: Let's start with that, then. Why the name change?

M: I didn't want my brothers riding my coattails. They started calling themselves the Four Marx Brothers, after they quit being the Four Nightingales. Milton—Gummo to you—got it out of his system early, after Julius—Groucho to you. Of course, Leo and Arthur had been playing piano in saloons and whorehouses from the time they were ten and eleven. You'll have to tell me whether you think that's show business or not . . .

W: It's making a living with your talent.

M: Barely.

W: You entered show business when?

M: I was fourteen. Turn of the century. I walked out the front door and right onto the stage.

W: Really?

M: There was a three- or four-year period where I made a living with my talent. Like Gene Kelly says, "Dignity, always dignity." Actually, Comden and Green wrote that—it just came out of Kelly's mouth. I was in a couple of acts like the O'Connor/Kelly one at Dead Man's Fang, Arizona, in that movie.

W: With whom?

M: Whom? You sound like Julius.

W: Would I know any of your partners?

M: In what sense?

W: Would I recognize their names?

M: I wouldn't even recognize their names now. That was almost ninety years ago. Give me a break.

W: What was the act?

M: A little of everything. We danced a little, One partner sang a little while I struck poses and pointed. One guy played the bandoneon—that's one of those Brazilian accordions with the buttons instead of the keys. I may or may not have acted like a monkey; I'm not saying, and I'm pretty sure there aren't any pictures . . .

W: Gradually you achieved success.

M: Gradually I achieved success.

W: Had your brothers entered show business by then?

M: Maybe. I was too busy playing four-a-days at every tank town in Kansas to notice. A letter caught up with me a couple years on from Mom, talking about Julius stranded in Denver and Milton doing god knows what.

W: Did your mom—Minnie Marx—encourage your career as she later did those of your brothers?

M: I didn't hang around long enough to find out. All I know is I wanted out of my home life.

W: Did Al Shean [of Gallagher and Shean] encourage you?

M: Uncle Al encouraged everybody. "Kid, go out and be bad. Come back and see me when you get good, and I'll help you all I can." Practical man.

W: Your compatriot George Burns said, "Now that vaudeville is dead, there's no place for kids to go and be bad anymore."

M: What about the Fox network?

W: You got him there.

WINSTEAD: So by now you were hoofing as a single.

MARKS: No—I moved a little from the waist up, so it wasn't, technically, hoofing. To keep people from watching my feet too much, I told a few jokes. Like Fields in his juggling act or Rogers with his rope tricks. Fields used to do a silent juggling bit. He asked for a raise at the Palace and they said: "You're the highest-paid juggler in the world." He said, "I gotta get a new act."

W: I've heard that story before.

M: Everybody has. I'm just giving you the practicalities of vaudeville. You're the best in the world and you still aren't getting paid enough, you have to do something else, too, to get more money. So I was a dancer and—well, sort of a comic. Not a comic dancer—the jokes are in your feet, then. My act: the top part told jokes—the bottom part moved.

Winstead: What was—who do you think was the best? Who summed up vaudeville?

Marks: That's two questions.

W: Okay.

M: Who summed up vaudeville? The answer's the standard one—Jolson, Cantor, Fields, Foy, Brice, Marilyn Miller. They could hold an audience for ten hours if they'd have wanted to. And you can't point to any one thing they had in common. Not one. There are all kinds of being good at what you do . . .

W: And the best?

M: Two acts. You might have run across them, since you write about this stuff for a living. Dybbuk & Wing: a guy from Canarsie and a guy from Shanghai. Novelty dance act. And the Ham Nag. A horse-suit act.

W: I've seen the name on playbills.

M: Ever notice anything about that?

W: What?

M: Stick with me and I will astound you later.

W: What, exactly, made them so good?

M: Dybbuk & Wing did, among other things, a spooky act. The theater lights would go down, and they'd be standing there in skeleton costumes—you know, black body suits with bones painted on them. Glowed in the dark. Had a scene drop that glowed in the dark, too. Burying ground—trees, tombstones, and so forth. Like in that later Disney cartoon, what was it?

W: The Skeleton Dance?

M: Exactly. Only this was at least twenty years before.

W: So they were like early Melie's—the magician filmmaker?

M: No. They were Dybbuk & Wing.

W: I mean, they used the phantasmagorical in the act. What was it like?

M: It wasn't like anything. It was terrific, is all I can say. You would swear the bones came apart while they were dancing. I was on bills with them on and off for years. They were the only act I know of that never took a bow. The lights didn't come up and they take their skulls off and bow. No matter how much applause. The lights stayed down, the two disappeared, then the lights came back up for the next act. I hated to follow them; so did anyone with a quiet act. They usually put the dog stuff and acrobats on after them, if they had any.

W: Never took a bow?

M: Never.

Winstead: What about the horse act?

Marks: The Ham Nag?

W: What did it/they do?

M: It was just the best goddammed horse-suit act there ever was. Or ever could be. I don't know how to begin to describe it, unless you'd say it was like a cartoon horse come to life. Right there, live, on the boards. When you were watching it you felt like you were in another world. Where there were real cartoon horses.

W: Vaudeville was more varied than people of my generation think.

M: It was more varied than even my generation could think. You had to see it.

MARKS: Dybbuk & Wing set the pattern. Wing—the Chinese guy—never talked. Just like those magicians. Who are they?

WINSTEAD: Penn & Teller?

M: Just like them. I don't mean just in the act, like Harpo. I mean, backstage, offstage, in real life. But I don't think he was a mute, either. I played with them for years and never heard him speak.

Like, one time backstage—we'd moved up to three-a-days somewhere—so we had time to kill. It may have been outside the City of Industry or somewhere. There was only one deck of cards in the whole place, and it was our turn to use them between shows.

"Got any Nine of Cups?" I asked.

Wing shook his head no.

"Go Fish," said Dybbuk.

I mean, Wing could have said something if he'd wanted to. It was just us in the room . . .

MARKS: Okay, the Ham Nag act was, it was always trying to get the one blue apple in a whole pile of green and red ones on a cart. Things kept going wrong. Well, you've seen films from acts back then, like Langdon's exploding car. For some reason, this was hilarious. The Nag made you believe the one goal in its life was to get that apple.

WINSTEAD: You said if I stuck with you, you'd drop a bombshell . . .

MARKS: Oh, you were paying attention, weren't you?

W: Bombs away.

M: I played with Dybbuk & Wing and the Ham Nag on the Gus Sun circuit out of Chicago for at least four years. I think it was at the Arcadia Theater one afternoon when it suddenly clicked.

You remember I told you to look at those posters in your collection? You'll notice that on every one—don't take my word for it—everywhere the Ham Nag played, Dybbuk & Wing were on the bill . . .

W: You mean . . .

M: It took me four years of being on the same bills with them every day before I figured it out. Yeah, they were the Ham Nag, too. It did not come out of their dressing room—they must have changed out in the alleys or the manager's office or somewhere.

That day I went on, did my act, then watched. Dybbuk & Wing were on two spots before me, then suddenly the Ham Nag was on. (The Ham Nag did take four-footed bows and would milk applause. That's why it was called the Ham Nag.) It came offstage. I was going to follow; a chorus girl said something to me; I looked around, and the Ham Nag was gone.

I went to Dybbuk & Wing's dressing room; they were there. Wing was writing a letter and Dybbuk was reading what looked like a two-hundred-year-old book as thick as a cinder block and just as dusty. Like they'd been there all the time.

I finally saw them one night, coming back from the alley after the Ham Nag act. Wing saw me looking at them.

From then on, Dybbuk acted like it was no secret and that I'd known about it all along.

I'm not telling stories out of school here: few people remember either act (though they should), and the acts have been dead half as long as I've been alive. They were supposed to be in that movie I made (*It Goes To Show You*, RKO, 1933, when Manny Marks was forty-seven years old), but they were "hot on the case" by then, as Dybbuk said.

WINSTEAD: What was "the case"?

MARKS: Okay. I'm approaching this as an outsider. Ever read *The Waste Land* by T.S. Eliot? Julius and Eliot had a mutual admiration society—they exchanged photos like International Pen Pals.

W: We had to read it in college.

M: Things will be easier if you go home tonight and read it again. Anyway, there's all this grail imagery in it, and other such trayf. Only you have to work through it, even if you're a Gentile. So where does that leave me? Julius once gave me a book Eliot took a lot of stuff from—somebody named Weston's *From Ritual To Romance*. All this stuff about a wounded king—like Frazer's *The Golden Bough*—look it up.

W: And this has something to do with a horse act?

M: And Dybbuk & Wing's dance act, too. Trust me.

WINSTEAD: So what you're saying here, at the age of 103, is that the Apocalypse may have been averted, and we didn't know it, or something.

MARKS: Or something. No. I'm saying there was some kind of personal Apocalypse ("That which is revealed when the veil is dropped") involving Dybbuk, Wing, the Ham Nag, a couple other vaudeville types, maybe the Vatican, perhaps Mussolini—Stalin and Hitler for all I know. . . .

W: This would have been in . . . ?

M: 1933. When I was making *It Goes To Show You*. Why Dybbuk, Wing, and the Ham Nag couldn't be in the movie.

W: This I'd really like to hear.

M: You will. Hand me that bottle so I can wet my whistle.

MARKS: Now you've got me drunk.

WINSTEAD: I don't think so, Mr. Marks. I've seen you drunk.

M: Where?

W: At Walter Woolf King's wake a few years ago.

M: If you were there, you saw me drunk. I was the oldest drunk there. At my age, I'm the oldest drunk anywhere.

W: You were going to tell me about the Vatican's and Mussolini's interest in a vaudeville horse-suit act?

M: Was I?

W: I think so. I can't be sure.

M: Okay. Is that thing still on?

W: Yes.

M: Here goes.

MARKS: Somewhere around 1927, Coolidge years, the Prohib, vaudeville was already dying. That October would come Jolson in *The Jazz Singer*. It wasn't there yet, but soon the movies would talk, sing, and dance—everything vaudeville could do, only better, because they could spend the money, and every film house could be the Palace, every night.

As I said, you couldn't tell it from *The Jazz Singer*—cantor's son in blackface, jumping around like a fool and disappointing his dad. I saw the play with Jessel back in '25. Trust me, it was just perfect for the movies, and more than perfect for Jolson.

But I had seen the end of, as the paper's named, variety. I knew it as soon as Jolson said "You ain't heard nothin' yet!"

So did Dybbuk. So did Wing.

We had to get new acts.

So this is the context I'm talking about.

What Dybbuk & Wing did between their acts was read and write. Wing probably wrote all the letters for them—he did to me, later—I never saw him actually reading, it was Dybbuk who always had a book open. Where he got them, I don't know—maybe they had a secret card, good at any library anywhere. They only seemed to have one or two books with them at a time. Carrying a bunch around in their luggage would have been prohibitive and tiring, especially on the Sun circuit—if you had it good, you only moved every three days; no split-weeks, and only in the relatively bigger towns.

They must have been reading and writing for years before I ever met them. They were on the trail of something. No telling who they corresponded with, or what attention they attracted.

I believe we were playing the Priory Theater in Zion, Illinois, when Pinky Tertulliano joined the bill. He was an albino comic acrobat—like that guy on Broadway now? [1990—ed.]

WINSTEAD: Bill Irwin?

M: That's him. Anyway, since the Flying Cathar Family was already on the bill, they put him between Edfu Yung and Dybbuk & Wing. Edfu Yung was a Sino-Egyptian bird imitator; quite an act. And he threw his call offstage, like Bergen or Señor Wences. You'd swear the stage flies were full of birds. I don't know that Yung and Wing ever talked over their common heritage, since Wing never talked.

Anyway, Tertulliano—who had a very weird act even for vaudeville—and I'm not kidding—was off before Dybbuk & Wing went on, which is the important thing here.

We found out later he'd come straight over from Italy to the Sun circuit in the Midwest, which was unusual unless Gus Sun was your uncle or something—usually you played whatever you could get on the East Coast—unless you were some real big act brought over by an impresario—Wilson Mizener once said an impresario is someone who speaks all languages with a foreign accent—and if that were the case, what's he doing going on between Edfu Yung and Dybbuk & Wing in Zion?

Anyway, things went swimmingly for a week or two, and the whole bill moved to some other town.

I remember things happened on Friday the Thirteenth—it must have been in May, because a couple of weeks later Lindy made his hop—Dybbuk & Wing came off and stuff had been messed with in their dressing room.

Nothing goes through a theater faster than news that there's a sneak thief around. Suddenly keys are needed for the locks on the doors, and people watch each other's places while they're on. Like with the army, where barracks thieves aren't tolerated; if they're found, there's some rough justice dealt out. Signs go up and things get tense.

They never said what was messed with or taken; they just filed with the theater, Equity, and Gus Sun himself, and spread the word.

Nobody ever proved anything. Tertulliano left the bill about the time Lindbergh took off for France. Nobody else's stuff was ever taken.

Sometime in June, Wing got a letter with lots of odd stamps and dago-dazzler forms all over it; after he read it he gave it to Dybbuk, who told me: "Never act on a bill with Tertulliano; he's trouble."

That's all he said. Fortunately, I nor anyone else ever had to. Far as I know Pinky left vaudeville and went back to Italy. Which is strange, since he had such a good weird act, like the Flying Cathars all rolled into one.

MARKS: . . . so I started noticing stuff about both their acts. Like, in the skeleton dance. I told you there were glow-in-the-dark tombstones and things. One was a big sarcophagus, like in those New Orleans cemeteries. On the side of it was the phrase "Et in Arcadia ego"—"And I too am in Arcadia" is the usual translation, and people think it means death, too, was in pastoral, idyllic settings. I think it was just an ancient "Kilroy was here," myself.

And the horse-suit act, the Ham Nag. "Why is it always trying to get a blue apple?" I asked. Like something out of Magritte. Who ever heard of a blue apple? (Magritte's favorites were of course green.) Dybbuk didn't say anything; he just handed me what turned out to be the thickest, driest book I had ever tried to read in my life. Honest, I tried.

Wing didn't say anything, of course, he just nodded.

MARKS: A week later I brought the book back to them.

"If this is what you guys do for fun," I said, "I think you guys should get out to a movie more often, maybe buy an ice-cream cone."

"You asked," said Dybbuk. "That book explains most of it."

"That book explains my six-day headache," I said. "It's like trying to read Spengler. Better than any Mickey Finn at bedtime. Two paragraphs and I'm sleeping like a baby."

"Sorry," said Dybbuk.

"Besides," I said, "I came from a whole other background. I don't even try to keep trayf for the holidays. I'm not a practicing Jew—much less a Christian. People really believe that stuff? The fight between the Catholics and the Freemasons?"

"Some more than others," said Dybbuk. Wing nodded.

"So why put that stuff in the act if it's so important and so secret?"

And Dybbuk said, "If it's fun, why do it?"

MARKS: I had troubles of my own during all this time, by the way. They tried to slip me down the bill at the next tank town. I needed a new act. The comedy was fine; the dancing and singing never were much, but for vaudeville, it was a wow.

Then I met Marie, who as you know later became Susie Cue.

[Like Burns and Allen, Marks and Susie Cue were a double for the next forty years—in vaudeville, the movie *It Goes To Show You*, in radio and television—anywhere they could work.—ed.]

She was part of a sister act—the only good part. I laid eyes on her and that was it. I was forty-one years old in '27, she was maybe twenty. In two weeks we were a double and her sisters were on the way back to Saskatoon.

So my extracurricular interests changed dramatically. So did the finances, thanks to Susie. We became virtually a house act on the Keith-Albee circuit and did a couple of the last (real) Follies before Ziegfeld croaked, and things got pretty peachy—even with the Crash. Fortunately, as George S. Kaufmann said, all my money was tied up in cash, so I came through it okay.

Meanwhile I heard from Julius that my brothers, except for Milton, were making movies, out in Astoria, of their stage plays. I wished them lots of luck.

But that was just another indication variety was dying. I mean, you have a play run for two years on Broadway and you still gotta make movies to make any more money. The movies, now that they talked—for a while there they talked but didn't move much—see *Singin' in the Rain* for that—were raiding everything—plays, novels, short stories, poems, radio—for that matter, radio was raiding right back—in an effort to get what little money people still had left. Movies did it all the time for a dime; vaudeville did it three times a day for fifty cents. Something had to give.

It was me and Susie Cue, and we went into radio.

Meanwhile, Dybbuk & Wing—I supposed it was Wing—were writing to us.

WINSTEAD: So this was . . . ?

MARKS: We went into radio in late 1931. So did everybody else. We'd tried three formats before we found the right one.

W: My Gal Susie Cue?

M: My Gal Susie Cue. The idea was, it was like having lizards live in your vest and I tried to deal with it.

W: Didn't Dybbuk & Wing appear on it?

M: Exactly twice. Tap dance doesn't come across on radio, especially if there's no patter. Even with a live audience all you hear are the taps—a sound-effect man with castanets can do that—and the oohs and ahhs from the audience.

W: What about the Ham—

M: Even they knew a silent horse-suit act wouldn't work on radio. That would have to wait for *Toast of the Town* on TV, but by then they were gone. I don't even know if there's any film of the horsey act. I once asked them how they did it so well.

Dybbuk gave the classic answer I've seen attributed to other people. He said: "I'm the front of the horse suit, and I act a whole lot. Wing just acts natural."

MARKS: I'm getting ahead of myself. While we were in the Follies and they were still out in the sticks, they wrote me. Letters about other acts, their acts, how bad variety was getting. I did what I could for them, got them a few New York gigs, mostly in olios before movies, that kind of thing. We got together when they were in town. I think they both had crushes on Susie Cue. (Who wouldn't?)

Anyway, when they were on the road they wrote me about their researches, too. It was all too arcane and esoteric for me (those are my two new words of the week from Wordbuilder®), but it seemed to keep them happy. They also made noises about "Pinky types" and "priests with tommy guns" which I took at the time to be hyperbole (my new word from last week), but now I'm not so sure.

The trouble with paranoia (as Pynchon and others—yes, I do read the moderns—said) is the deeper you dig, the more you uncover, whether it's there or not. It's the ultimate feedback system—the more you believe, the more you find to believe. I'm not sure, but I think Dybbuk & Wing may have been in the fell clutch of circumstances of their own making.

That was about the gist of the letters—I haven't looked at them since the late '50s—the century's, not mine—in the late 1950s I was seventy—I was drunk one day and dug them out of an old White Owl box I keep them in. Susie Cue came in and found me crying.

"What's the matter, Manfred?"

"Just reliving the glory days," I said.

"These are the glory days," she said. Maybe for her. She'd just turned fifty.

Anyway, want to jump ahead to where it really gets interesting?

W: Sure.

MARKS: It was early 1933—the week before FDR was inaugurated and the week *King Kong* premiered (that was something people really wanted to see: an ape tearing up Wall Street). We were in LA, making *It Goes To Show You*. Dybbuk & Wing couldn't make it and were having their agent return the advance. I've been in show business for ninety years, and there are only two reasons for an act not to show up and giving money back: 1) You're dead; 2) Your partner's dead. That's it.

I got a confirmation it was them sent the cable.

So no Dybbuk & Wing and no Ham Nag, in their only chance to be filmed. I was more upset about that than about the hole in the movie. We had to get two acts for that—that's why The Great Aerius is in there as a comic acrobat and Gandolfo & Castell are in as the dance act. Then we lucked out and got Señor Wences, with Johnny and Pedro in the box. It was his first American movie. You haven't seen weird til you've seen Señor Wences in 1933 . . .

MARKS: Turn that off a minute.

WINSTEAD: Why?

M: I gotta dig up the letter. I'll read it. It's better than I could tell it.
W: Do you know where it is?
M: Probably it's with the rest. Maybe . . .

MARKS: Did you like the lunch?
WINSTEAD: God, I'm stuffed. Did you find the letter?
M: I think it was written on 1933 flypaper or something. It's pretty brittle. I
    think the silverfish have been at it. Yeah, I got it here.
W: Mr. Marks, I want to know exactly how we got off on this.
M: You asked about vaudeville. This is about vaudeville.
W: A letter dealing with Christian kook cults is about vaudeville?
M: You'd be surprised. Both contain multitudes.
W: Please read it to me.
M: Thursday, March 23, 1933

Dear Knowledge Seeker (they always called me that):
    Sorry about missing the movie deal and (it turns out) we sure could have used
the money. I hope you understand. Who did you get to replace us? I hope they
turned out boffo.
    The easiest way to tell you about it is in order the way it happened. We got to
Yakima on the hottest tip we'd ever gotten the week of FDR's inaugural. The tip
wasn't about Yakima; it was further west, but this is the closest big-train passenger
depot. We'd just done the week in Spokane. Coming in on our heels were the Flying Cathars (you remember them from the Midwest), who are now in a circus
(where they came from and where they are now back). John Munster Cathar gave
us a letter—an answer to someone we'd written to from Denver.
    Let's say it was the most concrete clue we'd ever gotten. Our next booking was in
six weeks in Seattle, after we'd supposedly gotten back from doing your movie in
Hollywood. We called our agent and had him pick up some one-, two-, and three-
nighters between Yakima and Seattle. He cussed us a blue streak for missing the
movie and having to send the money back. But he got on the horn and got us
enough gigs to cover a month of the six weeks anyway.
    The first was the next day in a place called Easton, Washington. We went there
and did a three-a-day, both acts. Then we got on a spur-line train off the B-N and
went to a town called Rosslyn. Which is where we wanted to go in the first place.
    An odd thing we noticed as we got there was that there was a priest waiting at the
depot. Who he met in fact was another priest, both Catholics. The one he met was
young.
    Which is strange, since, believe it or not, most of the priests up here are
Orthodox—left over from when the Pacific Northwest was Russian, and a lot of
Greeks came here around the turn of the century.
    Well, we went down to the theater, Rennie's Chateau. We gave the stagehands
the drops for the skeleton dance, put our trucks and the horse suit in the dressing
room, and asked where we could get breakfast. They told us a block down.
    We walked down there. It was cold. Snow was still two feet high off the side-
walks; guys came by talking about how good the salmon run had been last fall. (The
only water we could see was a small creek that went off back down toward the
Yakima River to the south of us.)
    Dybbuk noticed that the two priests were back down the board sidewalk behind

us, walking the same way we were, talking with animation and blessing people automatically.

We got to the café, and it was full of lumberjacks, which they call loggers up here. There was a bunch of big tables pushed together in the center of the place, and there were twelve or fifteen of them at it, and they were putting away the grub like it was going out of style. There were plates of biscuits a foot high, and if they had been a family, the guys with the shortest arms would have starved to death.

We sat at the counter on the stools by the pies and cakes and such. Dybbuk got coffee, ham, and scrambled eggs. I got chipped beef on toast, coffee, and a couple of donuts.

The waitress yelled to the cook, "Adam and Eve. Wreck 'em. S.O.S. and a couple sinkers. Two battery acids!"

"Yes, Mabel," yelled one of the cooks, lost in clouds of steam and smells.

"More gravy over here, Mabel!" yelled half the table of lumberjacks.

"Eighty-six the gravy," said the cook, "Unless you wanna wash up. I'm outta big bowls."

"Use that old 'un in the high cabinet," yelled Mabel.

The cook went back and rummaged around. The short-order cook moved to his place at the stove; threw water and flour into the giant skillet the bacon and ham had been cooking in. With his free hand he broke six eggs onto the griddle. The main cook came back, moved exactly into the vacated other cook's place, and stirred the gravy with a big ladle.

He put it into a battered old silver server and passed it through the order-hole to Mabel.

Dybbuk paused with his coffee cup halfway to his lips, rolled his eyes, and focused back on the serving bowl.

Wing (me) followed his gaze. The server was what the ancient Greeks would have called a krater: a large, shallow bowl with handles on two sides. There was figurework on the base which extended up the sides of the bowl—it looked like bunches of grapes.

Wing (that's me) nodded to Dybbuk, rolled his eyes, and fixed them on the two priests who had come in and sat down at a window table. They were still talking away and seemed to be paying no attention to anything.

Mabel put the bowl down; six or eight hands filled with biscuits dipped into it and came out with gobs of gravy.

"I s'pose now you'll be wantin' more biscuits?" she asked.

"Mmmmff mmmfmmfs," said the lumberjacks.

"Two doz. hardtack!" she yelled to the cooks.

Back at the dressing room, we thought of a plan. We were going to be at the theater for three days. We got the manager's bill poster to make up a couple of cloth banners advertising the bill. Then we pinned them to both sides of the horse suit. We went out the side door of the theater and up and down the main street, which is called First Street—all the cross-streets are named for states—doing part of the Ham Nag act. We hit the bank, the five-and-dime, the firehouse, the Legion hall; we went past the Masonic Temple across the street from the theater, and of course the café. We went in and bothered Mabel and the cooks. We went back through the kitchen, out the back door, behind the buildings, and back to the theater.

The young priest, who'd been out in front of the theater, gawked at us with the rest of the town (we had quite the little crowd following us down First Street) but stayed in front of the theater, so we figured he wasn't waiting for Dybbuk & Wing.

Later, when we walked back to the hotel on Pennsylvania as ourselves, he followed us as discreetly as a priest can. When we looked outside later, he was still there.

At the theater, Dybbuk went out between our act and the horse act and bought the biggest ceramic bowl the five-and-dime had—it was at least two feet across and weighed a ton. We put it in the cemetery stuff the next performance, leaned it against a tombstone.

The second day the horse suit made more of a nuisance of itself in other parts of town (there were only eight blocks by seven blocks of it, counting Alaska Alley) but ended again annoying the customers and the help at the café.

Once again they were watching the theater—this time the old priest. There was a local-looking kid with him.

When we left for the hotel (as us), it was the kid who wandered that way, and it was either him or some other who stayed outside all night, as far as we knew.

On the third day we took the ceramic bowl with us—me (Wing) carrying it inside his part of the suit. It made for a lumpier horse, I'm sure. After nearly twenty years we move as one, but Dybbuk has to do all the navigating. As they say of huskies, only the lead dog gets a change of scenery.

So we take off down First Street, and even I can tell we're gathering a crowd as we go along. We do some shtick with oil cans at the gas station; I dance around in the back a little, and we move on to the Western Auto hardware store, and then we go down to the café.

This time we came in the back door. "Christ!" says the head cook, "not again!" Dybbuk starts farting with stuff (the laughter was at the Ham Nag flipping pancakes with its front hooves) and rummaging through the cabinets (through the slit in the side of the suit I [Wing] saw everybody in the place up against the counter, looking into the kitchen)—the head cook had taken off and thrown down his apron and walked out into the restaurant in disgust, and then—allez oop!—the ceramic bowl was outside the Ham Nag and the krater was inside, and everybody applauded as we turned and did the double-split bow in the middle of the kitchen floor.

Then we were outside again, at the front door. All I (Wing) heard was Dybbuk say "Trouble!" and grunt before something knocked me off my feet. I jerked back, and some heavy object flattened the suit right between Dybbuk and me. We jumped up and a fist hit me in the jaw and I fell down again. A hand came in the side of the suit and the silver bowl was jerked out of my hands and was gone.

Then something knocked us down again, and we got up and opened the suit to make it a fair fight.

We were surrounded by kids dressed as clowns, including the one I'd seen with the priest. They had what looked like rubber baseball bats and big shoes. There was about half the town around them, clapping and laughing. To them it must have seemed part of the show—the horse suit set on by jokers and clowns. The old priest was standing across from us on the sidewalk, with his hands in his pockets, smiling. He took his hand out and moved it.

I looked way down First Street, and the young priest was just turning out of sight two blocks away with something shiny under his arm.

We got back in the suit and wobbled back toward the theater, the clowns whacking us with rubber bats occasionally. But they hadn't been rubber back in front of the café.

We got back to the dressing room and out of the Ham Nag suit.

"The priest was giving us a Masonic hand signal," Dybbuk said.

Priests don't do that, I (Wing) indicated.

"They do if they're not just priests," Dybbuk said.

We figured, like you did years ago, the kid had doped out we were the Ham Nag too, and the priests laid a plan for us. I'm not sure they knew what we were doing, but someone saw through our misdirection and kept his eye on what was going on.

As Barrymore said, "Never work with kids or dogs."

We almost had it, Knowledge seeker. Now we'll have to start all over again. After all this time, what's a few years more? I mean, the thing has been around for at least one thousand nine hundred and three years . . .

Here's hoping you and Susie Cue are in the pink of health. We'll be here in Seattle at the Summit on Queen Anne Hill from Thursday til the end of next month. Heard your radio show last week; it was a pip.

> Yours in knowledge seeking,
>
> Dybbuk & me (Wing)

WINSTEAD: Can you still talk, after reading all that?

MARKS: I think so, after I get some of this stuff down. (drinks) There, that's better.

W: I don't know what to say. That was a long session. I don't want to wear you out. Will you feel like talking tomorrow?

M: I think so. You wanna hear about the radio show tomorrow?

W: Whatever you want to talk about. Do you think they ever got it?

M: Got the gravy bowl?

W: The thing they were looking for.

M: Your guess is as good as mine.

Manny Marks, the last of the Marx Brothers, died three years later at the age of 107. Barry Winstead's book—*I Killed Vaudeville*—was published by Knopf in 1991. Luke H. Dybbuk died in 1942; John P. Wing is still alive, though he retired from performing in the early years of WWII.

Thanks, Ms. Emshwiller; and Mikes, Walsh and Nelson.

ADAM L.G. NEVILL

Where Angels Come In

Classic source: M. R. James

Adam L. G. Nevill is the author of the acclaimed supernatural thriller, Banquet for the Damned, *published by PS Publishing. His most recent short story and nonfiction appearances can be found in* Gathering the Bones, Poe's Progeny, Bernie Hermann's Manic Sextet, *and* Cinema Macabre. *Both* Banquet for the Damned *and "Where Angels Come In" were written in homage to M. R. James. He lives in London.*

—E.D.

One side of my body is full of toothache. Right in the middle of the bones. While the skin and muscles have a chilly pins-and-needles tingle that won't ever turn back into the warmth of a healthy arm and leg. Which is why Nanna Alice is here; sitting on the chair at the foot of my bed, her crumpled face in shadow. But the milky light that comes through the net curtains finds a sparkle in her quick eyes and gleams on the yellowish grin that hasn't changed since my mother let her into the house, made her a cup of tea and showed her into my room. Nanna Alice smells like the inside of overflow pipes at the back of the council houses.

"Least you still got one 'alf," she says. She has a metal brace on her thin leg. The foot at the end of the caliper is inside a baby's shoe. Even though it's rude, I can't stop staring. Her normal leg is fat. "They took me leg and one arm." Using her normal fingers, she picks the dead hand from a pocket in her cardigan and plops it on to her lap. Small and gray, it reminds me of a doll's hand. I don't look for long.

She leans forward in her chair so I can smell the tea on her breath. "Show me where you was touched, luv."

I unbutton my pajama top and roll on to my good side. Podgy fingertips press around the shriveled skin at the top of my arm, but she doesn't touch the see-through parts where the fingertips and thumb once held me. Her eyes go big and her lips pull back to show gums more black than purple. Against her thigh, the doll hand shakes. She coughs, sits back in her chair. Cradles the tiny hand and rubs it with living fingers. When I cover my shoulder, she watches that part of me without blinking. Seems disappointed to see it covered so soon. Wets her lips. "Tell us what 'appened, luv."

Propping myself up in the pillows, I peer out the window and swallow the big lump in my throat. Dizzy and a bit sickish, I don't want to remember what happened. Not ever.

Across the street inside the spiky metal fence built around the park, I can see the usual circle of mothers. Huddled into their coats and sitting on benches beside pushchairs, or holding the leads of tugging dogs, they watch the children play. Upon the climbing frames and on the wet grass, the kids race about and shriek and laugh and fall and cry. Wrapped up in scarves and padded coats, they swarm among hungry pigeons and seagulls; thousands of small white and gray shapes, pecking around the little stamping feet. Sometimes the birds panic and rise in curving squadrons, trying to get their plump bodies into the air with flap-cracky wings. And the children are blind with their own fear and excitement in brief tornadoes of dusty feathers, red feet, cruel beaks, and startled eyes. But they are safe here—the children and the birds—closely watched by tense mothers and kept inside the stockade of iron railings: the only place outdoors the children are allowed to play since I came back, alone.

A lot of things go missing in our town: cats, dogs, children. And they never come back. Except for me. I came home, or at least half of me did.

Lying in my sickbed, pale in the face and weak in the heart, I drink medicines, read books and watch the children play from my bedroom window. Sometimes I sleep. But only when I have to. Because when I sink away from the safety of home and a watching parent, I go back to the white house on the hill.

For the Nanna Alice, the time she went inside the big white place as a little girl is a special occasion; like she's grateful. Our dad calls her a "silly old fool" and doesn't want her in our house. He doesn't know she's here today. But when a child vanishes, or someone dies, lots of the mothers ask the Nanna to visit them. "She can see things and feel things the rest of us don't," my mom says. Like the two police ladies, and the mothers of the two girls who went missing last winter, and Pickering's parents, my mom just wants to know what happened to me.

At least when I'm awake, I can read, watch television, and listen to my mom and sisters downstairs. But in dreams I have no choice: I go back to the white house on the hill, where old things with skipping feet circle me, then rush in close to show their faces.

"Tell us, luv. Tell us about the 'ouse," Nanna Alice says. Can't think why she's smiling like that. No adult likes to talk about the beautiful, tall house on the hill. Even our dads who come home from the industry, smelling of plastic and beer, look uncomfortable if their kids say they can hear the ladies crying again: above their heads, but deep inside their ears at the same time, calling from the distance, from the hill, from inside us. Our parents can't hear it anymore, but they remember the sound from when they were small. It's like people are trapped and calling out for help. And when no one comes, they get real angry. "Foxes," the parents say, but don't look you in the eye when they say it.

For a long time after what people call "my accident" I was unconscious in the hospital. After I woke up, I was so weak I stayed there for another three months. Gradually, one half of my body got stronger and I was allowed home. That's when the questions began. Not just about my injuries, but about my mate Pickering, who they never found. And now crazy Nanna Alice wants to know every single thing I can remember and all of the dreams too. Only I never know what is real and what came out of the coma with me.

For years, we talked about going up there. All the kids do. Pickering, Ritchie, and me wanted to be the bravest boys in our school. We wanted to break in there and come out with treasure to use as proof that we'd been inside, and not just looked in through the gate like all the others we knew.

Some people say the house and its grounds was once a place where old, rich people lived after they retired from owning the industry, the land, the laws, our houses, our town, us. Others say it was built on an old well and the ground is contaminated. A teacher told us it used to be a hospital and is still full of germs. Our dad said it was an asylum for lunatics that closed down over a hundred years ago and has stayed empty ever since because it's falling to pieces and is too expensive to repair. That's why kids should never go there: you could be crushed by bricks or fall through a floor. Nanna Alice says it's a place "where angels come in." But we all know it's the place where the missing things are. Every street in the miles of our town has lost a pet or knows a family who's lost a child. And every time the police search the big house, they find nothing. No one remembers the big gate being open.

So on a Friday morning when all the kids in our area were walking to school, me, Ritchie, and Pickering sneaked off, the other way. Through the allotments, where me and Pickering were once caught smashing deck chairs and bean poles; through the woods full of broken glass and dogshit; over the canal bridge; across the potato fields with our heads down so the farmer wouldn't see us; and over the railway tracks until we couldn't even see the roofs of the last houses in our town. Talking about the hidden treasure, we stopped by the old ice cream van with four flat tires, to throw rocks and stare at the faded menu on the little counter, our mouths watering as we made selections that would never be served. On the other side of the woods that surround the estate, we could see the chimneys of the big, white mansion above the trees.

Although Pickering had been walking out front the whole time telling us he wasn't scared of security guards or watch dogs, or even ghosts—"cus you can just put your hand froo 'em"—when we reached the bottom of the wooded hill, no one said anything or even looked at each other. Part of me always believed we would turn back at the black gate, because the fun part was telling stories about the house and planning the expedition and imagining terrible things. Going inside was different because lots of the missing kids had talked about the house before they disappeared. And some of the young men who broke in there for a laugh always came away a bit funny in the head, but our dad said that was because of drugs.

Even the trees around the estate were different, like they were too still and silent and the air between them real cold. But we still went up through the trees and found the high brick wall that surrounds the grounds. There was barbed wire and broken glass set into concrete on top of it. We followed the wall until we reached the black iron gate. Seeing the PRIVATE PROPERTY: TRESSPASSERS WILL BE PROSECUTED sign made shivers go up my neck and under my hair. The gate is higher than a house with a curved top made from iron spikes, set between two pillars with big stone balls on top.

"I heard them balls roll off and kill trespassers," Ritchie said. I'd heard the same thing, but when Ritchie said that I just knew he wasn't going in with us.

We wrapped our hands around the cold black bars of the gate and peered through at the long flagstone path that goes up the hill, between avenues of trees and old statues hidden by branches and weeds. All the uncut grass of the lawns was as high as my waist and the old flower beds were wild with color. At the summit was the tall, white house with big windows. Sunlight glinted off the glass. Above all the chimneys, the sky was blue. "Princesses lived there," Pickering whispered.

"Can you see anyone?" Ritchie asked. He was shivering with excitement and had to take a pee. He tried to rush it over some nettles—we were fighting a war against nettles and wasps that summer—but got half of it down his legs.

"It's empty," Pickering whispered. "'Cept for 'idden treasure. Darren's brother got this owl inside a big glass. I seen it. Looks like it's still alive. At night, it moves it's 'ead."

Ritchie and I looked at each other; everyone knows the stories about the animals or birds inside the glass that people find up there. There's one about a lamb with no fur, inside a tank of green water that someone's uncle found when he was a boy. It still blinks its little black eyes. And someone said they found skeletons of children all dressed up in old clothes, holding hands.

All rubbish; because I know what's really inside there. Pickering had seen nothing, but if we challenged him he'd start yelling, "Have so! Have so!" and me and Ritchie weren't happy with anything but whispering near the gate.

"Let's just watch and see what happens. We can go in another day," Ritchie couldn't help himself saying.

"You're chickening out," Pickering said, kicking at Ritchie's legs. "I'll tell everyone Ritchie pissed his pants."

Ritchie's face went white, his bottom lip quivered. Like me, he was imagining crowds of swooping kids shouting, "Piss pot. Piss pot." Once the crowds find a coward, they'll hunt him every day until he's pushed out to the edges of the playground where the failures stand and watch. Every kid in town knows this place takes away brothers, sisters, cats, and dogs, but when we hear the cries from the hill, it's our duty to force one another out here. It's a part of our town and always has been. Pickering is one of the toughest kids in school; he had to go.

"I'm going in first," Pick' said, standing back and sizing up the gate. "Watch where I put my hands and feet." And it didn't take him long to get over. There was a little wobble at the top when he swung a leg between two spikes, but not long after he was standing on the other side, grinning at us. To me, it now looked like there was a little ladder built into the gate—where the metal vines and thorns curved between the long poles, you could see the pattern of steps for small hands and feet. I'd heard that little girls always found a secret wooden door in the brick wall that no one else can find when they look for it. But that might just be another story.

If I didn't go over and the raid was a success, I didn't want to spend the rest of my life being a piss pot and wishing I'd gone with Pick'. We could be heroes together. And I was full of the same crazy feeling that makes me climb oak trees to the very top branches, stare up at the sky and let go with my hands for a few seconds knowing that if I fall I will die.

When I climbed away from whispering Ritchie on the ground, the squeaks and groans of the gate were so loud I was sure I could be heard all the way up the hill and inside the house. When I got to the top and was getting ready to swing a leg over, Pick' said, "Don't cut your balls off." But I couldn't smile, or even breathe. My arms and legs started to shake. It was much higher up there than it looked from the ground. With one leg over, between the spikes, panic came up my throat. If one hand slipped off the worn metal I imagined my whole weight forcing the spike through my thigh, and how I would hang there, dripping. Then I looked up toward the house and I felt there was a face behind every window, watching me.

Many of the stories about the white place on the hill suddenly filled my head: how you only see the red eyes of the thing that drains your blood; how it's kiddy-fiddlers that hide in there and torture captives for days before burying them alive, which is why no one ever finds the missing children; and some say the thing that makes the crying noise might look like a beautiful lady when you first see her, but she soon changes once she's holding you.

"Hurry up. It's easy," Pick' said from way down below. Ever so slowly, I lifted my second leg over, then lowered myself down the other side. He was right; it wasn't a hard climb at all; kids could do it.

I stood in hot sunshine on the other side of the gate, smiling. The light was brighter over there too; glinting off all the white stone and glass up on the hill. And the air seemed weird—real thick and warm. When I looked back through the gate, the world around Ritchie—who stood alone biting his bottom lip—looked gray and dull like it was November or something. Around us, the overgrown grass was so glossy it hurt your eyes to look at it. Reds, yellows, purples, oranges, and lemons of the flowers flowed inside my head and I could taste hot summer in my mouth. Around the trees, statues, and flagstone path, the air was a bit wavy and my skin felt so good and warm I shivered. Closed my eyes. "Beautiful," I said; a word I wouldn't usually use around Pick'. "This is where I want to live," he said, his eyes and face one big smile. Then we both started to laugh. We hugged each other, which we'd never done before. Anything I ever worried about seemed silly now. I felt taller. Could go anywhere, do anything I liked. I know Pick' felt the same.

Protected by the overhanging tree branches and long grasses, we kept to the side of the path and began walking up the hill. But after a while, I started to feel a bit nervous as we got closer to the top. The house looked bigger than I thought it was down by the gate. Even though we could see no one and hear nothing, I also felt like I'd walked into this big, crowded, but silent place where lots of eyes were watching me. Following me.

We stopped walking by the first statue that wasn't totally covered in green moss and dead leaves. Through the low branches of a tree, we could still see the two naked children, standing together on the stone block. One boy and one girl. They were both smiling, but not in a nice way, because we could see too much of their teeth. And their eager faces seemed too old for children. "They's all open on the chest," Pickering said. And he was right; their dry stone skin was peeled back on the breastbone and in their outstretched hands they held small lumps of stone with veins carved into them—their own little hearts. The good feeling I had down by the gate was completely gone now.

Sunlight shone through the trees and striped us with shadows and bright slashes. Eyes big and mouths dry, we walked on and checked some of the other statues we passed. You couldn't help it; it's like they made you stare at them to work out what was sticking through the leaves and branches and ivy. There was one horrible cloth thing that seemed too real to be made from stone. Its face was so nasty, I couldn't look for long. Standing under it gave me the queer feeling that it was swaying from side to side, ready to jump off the stone block and come at us.

Pick' walked ahead of me a little bit, but soon stopped to see another. He shrunk in its shadow, then peered at his shoes. I caught up with him but didn't look too long either. Beside the statue of the ugly man in a cloak and big hat, was a smaller shape covered in a robe and hood, with something coming out of a sleeve that reminded me of snakes.

I didn't want to go any further and knew I'd be seeing these statues in my sleep for a long time. Looking down the hill at the gate, I was surprised to see how far away it was now. "Think I'm going back," I said to Pick'.

Pickering looked at me, but never called me a chicken; he didn't want to start a fight and be on his own in here. "Let's just go into the house quick," he said. "And get something. Otherwise no one will believe us."

But being just a bit closer to the white house with all the staring windows made me sick with nerves. It was four stories high and must have had hundreds of rooms inside. All the windows upstairs were dark so we couldn't see beyond the glass. Downstairs, they were all boarded up against trespassers. "They's all empty, I bet," Pickering said to try and make us feel better. But it didn't do much for me; he didn't seem so smart or hard now; just a stupid kid who hadn't got a clue.

"Nah," I said.

He walked away from me. "Well I am. I'll say you waited outside." His voice was too soft to carry the usual threat. But all the same, I suddenly couldn't stand the though of his grinning, triumphant face while Ritchie and I were considered piss pots, especially after I'd climbed the gate and come this far. My part would mean nothing if he went further than me.

We never looked at any more of the statues. If we had, I don't think we'd have ever got to the wide stone steps that went up to the big metal doors of the house. Didn't seem to take us long to reach the house either. Even taking small, slow, reluctant steps got us there real quick. On legs full of warm water I followed Pickering up to the doors.

"Why is they made of metal?" he asked me. I never had an answer. He pressed both hands against the doors. One of them creaked but never opened. "They's locked," he said.

Secretly relieved, I took a step away from the doors. All the ground floor windows were boarded over too, so it looked like we could go home. But as Pickering shoved at the creaky door again, this time with his shoulder and his body at an angle, I'm sure I saw movement in a window on the second floor. Something whitish. Behind the glass, it was like a shape appeared out of the darkness and then sank back into it, quick but graceful. I thought of a carp surfacing in a cloudy pond before vanishing the same moment you saw its pale back. "Pick'!" I hissed at him.

There was a clunk inside the door Pickering was straining his body against. "It's open," he cried out, and stared into the narrow gap between the two iron doors. But I couldn't help thinking the door had been opened from inside.

"I wouldn't," I said to him. He just smiled and waved at me to come over and help as he pushed to make a bigger space. I stood still and watched the windows upstairs. The widening door made a grinding sound against the floor. Without another word, he walked inside the big white house.

Silence hummed in my ears. Sweat trickled down my face. I wanted to run down to the gate.

After a few seconds, Pickering's excited face appeared in the doorway. "Quick. Come an' look at all the birds." He was breathless with excitement.

I peered through the gap at a big, empty hallway and could see a staircase going up to the next floor. Pickering was standing in the middle of the hall, not moving. He was looking at the ground. At all the dried-up birds on the wooden floorboards. Hundreds of dead birds. I went in.

No carpets, or curtains, or light bulbs, just bare floorboards, white walls, and two closed doors on either side of the hall. On the floor, there were hundreds of pigeons. Most of them still had feathers but looked real thin. Some were just bones. Others

were dust. "They get in and they got nuffin' to eat." Pickering said. "We should collect all the skulls." He crunched across the floor and tried the doors at either side of
the hall, yanking the handles up and down. "Locked," he said. "Both of 'em locked.
Let's go up them stairs. See if there's summat in the rooms."

I flinched at every creak caused by our feet on the stairs. I told him to walk at the
sides like me. He wasn't listening, just going up fast on his plumpish legs. I caught
up with him at the first turn in the stairs and began to feel real strange again. The air
was weird; hot and thin like we were in a tiny space. We were both all sweaty in our
school uniforms from just walking up one flight of stairs. I had to lean against a wall
while he shone his torch up at the next floor. All we could see were the plain walls
of a dusty corridor. Some sunlight was getting in from somewhere upstairs, but not
much. "Come on," he said, without turning his head to look at me.

"I'm going outside," I said. "I can't breathe." But as I moved to go back down the
first flight of stairs, I heard a door creak open and then close, below us. I stopped still
and heard my heart banging against my ear drums from the inside. The sweat turned
to frost on my face and neck and under my hair. Real quick, and sideways, something moved across the shaft of light falling through the open front door. My eyeballs went cold and I felt dizzy. Out the corner of my eye, I could see Pickering's
white face, watching me from above on the next flight of stairs. He turned the torch
off with a loud click.

It moved again, back the way it had come, but paused this time at the edge of the
long rectangle of white light on the hall floor. And started to sniff at the dirty ground.
It was the way she moved down there that made me feel light as a feather and ready
to faint. Least I think it was a *she*. But when people get that old you can't always tell.
There wasn't much hair on the head and the skin was yellow. She looked more like
a puppet made of bones and dressed in a grubby nightie than an old lady. And could
old ladies move so fast? Sideways like a crab, looking backward at the open door, so
I couldn't see the face properly, which I was glad of.

If I moved too quick, I'm sure it would look up and see me. I took two slow side-
steps to get behind the wall of the next staircase where Pickering was hiding. He
looked like he was about to cry. Like me, I knew all he could hear was his own heartbeat.

Then we heard the sound of another door open from somewhere downstairs, out
of sight. We knelt down, trembling against each other, and peered around the corner
of the staircase to make sure the old thing wasn't coming up the stairs, sideways. But
a second figure had now appeared down there. I nearly cried when I saw it skittering
around by the door. It moved quicker than the first one with the help of two black
sticks. Bent right over with a hump for a back, it was covered in a dusty black dress
that swished over the floor. What I could see of the face through the veil was all
pinched and as sickly-white as grubs under wet bark. When she made the whistling
sound, it hurt my ears deep inside and made my bones feel cold.

Pickering's face was wild with fear. I was seeing too much of his eyes. "Is they old
ladies?" he said in a voice that sounded all broken.

I grabbed his arm. "We got to get out. Maybe there's a window, or another door
'round the back." Which meant we had to go up these stairs, run through the building to find another way down to the ground-floor, before breaking our way out.

I took another peek down the stairs to see what they were doing, but wished I
hadn't. There were two more of them. A tall man with legs like sticks was looking up
at us with a face that never changed because it had no lips or eyelids or nose. He
wore a creased suit with a gold watch chain on the waistcoat, and was standing be-

hind a wicker chair. In the chair was a bundle wrapped in tartan blankets. Above the coverings I could see a small head inside a cloth cap. The face was yellow as corn in a tin. The first two were standing by the open door so we couldn't get out.

Running up the stairs into an even hotter darkness on the next floor, my whole body felt baggy and clumsy and my knees chipped together. Pickering went first with the torch and used his elbows so I couldn't overtake. I bumped into his back and kicked his heels. Inside his fast breathing, I could hear him sniffing at tears. "Is they comin'?" he kept saying. I didn't have the breath to answer and kept running through the long corridor, between dozens of closed doors, to get to the end. I looked straight ahead and was sure I would freeze up if one of the doors suddenly opened. And with our feet making such a bumping on the floorboards, I can't say I was surprised when I heard the click of a lock behind us. We both made the mistake of looking back.

At first we thought it was waving at us, but then realized the skinny figure in the dirty nightdress was moving its long arms through the air to attract the attention of the others that had followed us up the stairwell. We could hear the scuffle and swish as they came through the dark behind us. But how could this one see us, I thought, with all those rusty bandages around its head? Then we heard another of those horrible whistles, followed by more doors opening real quick like things were in a hurry to get out of the rooms.

At the end of the corridor, there was another stairwell with more light in it that fell from a high window three floors up. But the glass must have been dirty and greenish, because everything around us on the stairs looked like it was underwater. When he turned to bolt down them stairs, I saw Pick's face was all shiny with tears and the front of his trousers had a dark patch spreading down one leg.

It was real hard to get down them stairs and back to the ground. It was like we had no strength left in our bodies, as if the fear was draining it through the slappy, tripping soles of our feet. But it was more than the terror slowing us down; the air was so thin and dry it was hard to get our breath in and out of our lungs fast enough. My shirt was stuck to my back and I was dripping under the arms. Pick's hair was wet and he was slowing right down, so I overtook him.

At the bottom of the stairs I ran into another long, empty corridor of closed doors and grayish light, that ran through the back of the building. Just looking all the way down it, made me bend over with my hands on my knees to rest. But Pickering just plowed right into me from behind and knocked me over. He ran across my body and stamped on my hand. "They's comin'" he whined in a tearful voice and went stumbling down the passage. I got back to my feet and started down the corridor after him. Which never felt like a good idea to me; if some of them things were waiting in the hall by the front doors, while others were coming up fast behind us, we'd get ourselves trapped. I thought about opening a door and trying to kick out the boards over a window in one of the ground-floor rooms. Plenty of them old things seemed to come out of rooms when we ran past them, like we were waking them up, but they never came out of every room. So we would just have to take a chance. I called out to Pick' to stop. I was wheezing like Billy Skid at school who's got asthma, so maybe Pickering never heard me, because he kept on running toward the end. I looked back at the stairwell we'd just come out of, then looked about at the doors in the passage. As I was wondering which one to pick, a little voice said, "Do you want to hide in here."

I jumped into the air and cried out like I'd trod on a snake. Stared at where the voice came from. I could see a crack between this big brownish door and the doorframe. Part of a little girl's face peeked out. "They won't see you. We can play with my dolls." She smiled and opened the door wider. She had a really white face inside a black bonnet all covered in ribbons. The rims of her dark eyes were bright red like she'd been crying for a long time.

My chest was hurting and my eyes were stinging with sweat. Pickering was too far ahead of me to catch him up. I could hear his feet banging away on loose floorboards, way off in the darkness and I didn't think I could run any further. I nodded at the girl. She stood aside and opened the door wider. The bottom of her black dress swept through the dust. "Quickly," she said with an excited smile, and then looked down the corridor, to see if anything was coming. "Most of them are blind, but they can hear things."

I moved through the doorway. Brushed past her. Smelled something gone bad. Put a picture in my head of the dead cat, squashed flat in the woods, that I found one time on a hot day. But over that smell was something like the bottom of my granny's old wardrobe, with the one broken door and little iron keys in the locks that don't work any more.

Softly, the little girl closed the door behind us, and walked off across the wooden floor with her head held high, like a "little Madam" my dad would say. Light was getting into this room from some red and green windows up near the high ceiling. Two big chains hung down holding lights with no bulbs, and there was a stage at one end with a thick greenish curtain pulled across the front. Little footlights stuck up at the front of the stage. It must have been a ballroom once.

Looking for a way out—behind me, to the side, up ahead, everywhere—I followed the little girl in the black bonnet over to the stage and up the stairs at the side. She disappeared through the curtains without making a sound, and I followed because I could think of nowhere else to go and I wanted a friend in here. The long curtains smelled so bad around my face, I put a hand over my mouth.

She asked my name and where I lived. I told her like I was talking to a teacher who's just caught me doing something wrong, even giving her my house number. "We didn't mean to trespass," I said. "We never stole nothing." She cocked her head to one side and frowned like she was trying to remember something. Then she smiled and said, "All of these are mine. I found them." She drew my attention to the dolls on the floor; little shapes of people I couldn't see properly in the dark. She sat down among them and started to pick them up one at a time to show me, but I was too nervous to pay much attention and I didn't like the look of the cloth animal with its fur worn down to the grubby material. It had stitched-up eyes and no ears; the arms and legs were too long for its body. And I didn't like the way the little, dirty head was stiff and upright like it was watching me.

Behind us, the rest of the stage was in darkness with a faint glow of white wall in the distance. Peering from the stage at the boarded-up windows down the right side of the dance floor, I could see some bright daylight around the edge of two big hardboard sheets nailed over patio doors. There was a breeze coming through. Must have been a place where someone got in before. "I got to go," I said to the girl behind me, who was whispering to her animals and dolls. I was about to step through the curtains and head for the daylight when I heard the rushing of a crowd in the corridor that me and Pickering had just run through—feet shuffling, canes tapping, wheels squeaking and two more of the hooting sounds. It all seemed to go on for ages. A long parade I didn't want to see.

As it went past, the main door clicked open and something glided into the ballroom. I pulled back from the curtains and held my breath. The little girl kept mumbling to the nasty toys. I wanted to cover my ears. Another crazy part of me wanted it all to end; wanted me to step out from behind the curtains and offer myself to the tall figure down there on the dance floor, holding the tatty parasol over its head. It spun around quickly like it was moving on tiny, silent wheels under its long musty skirts. Sniffing at the air. For me. Under the white net attached to the brim of the rotten hat and tucked into the high collars of the dress, I saw a bit of face that looked like skin on a rice pudding. I would have screamed, but there was no air inside me.

I looked down, where the little girl had been sitting. She had gone, but something was moving on the floor. Squirming. I blinked my eyes fast. For a moment, it looked like all her toys were trembling, but when I squinted at the Golly with bits of curly white hair on its head, it was lying perfectly still where she had dropped it. The little girl may have hidden me, but I was glad she had gone.

Way off in the stifling distance of the big house, I then heard a scream; full of all the panic and terror and woe in the whole world. The figure with the little umbrella spun right around on the dance floor and then rushed out of the room toward the sound.

I slipped out from behind the curtains. A busy chattering sound came from the distance. It got louder until it echoed through the corridor and ballroom and almost covered the sounds of the wailing boy. It sounded like his cries were swirling round and round, bouncing off walls and closed doors, like he was running somewhere far off inside the house, in a circle that he couldn't get out of.

I crept down the stairs at the side of the stage and ran across to the long strip of burning sunlight I could see shining through one side of the patio doors. I pulled at the big rectangle of wood until it splintered and I could see broken glass in a doorframe and lots of thick grass outside.

For the first time since I'd seen the first figure scratching about the front entrance, I truly believed I could escape. I could climb through the gap I was making, run around the outside of the house and then go down the hill to the gate, while they were all busy inside with the crying boy. But just as my breathing went all quick and shaky with the glee of escape, I heard a *whump* sound on the floor behind me, like something had just dropped to the floor from the stage. Teeny vibrations tickled the soles of my feet. Then I heard something coming across the floor toward me—a shuffle, like a body dragging itself real quick.

Couldn't bear to look behind me and see another one close up. I snatched at the board and pulled with all my strength at the bit not nailed down, so the whole thing bent and made a gap. Sideways, I squeezed a leg, hip, arm, and shoulder out. Then my head was suddenly bathed in warm sunlight and fresh air.

It must have reached out then and grabbed my left arm under the shoulder. The fingers and thumb were so cold they burned my skin. And even though my face was in daylight, everything went dark in my eyes except for little white flashes, like when you stand up too quick. I wanted to be sick. Tried to pull away, but one side of my body was all slow and heavy and full of pins and needles.

I let go of the hardboard sheet. It slapped shut like a mousetrap. The wood knocked me through the gap and into the grass outside. Behind my head, I heard a sound like celery snapping. Something shrieked into my ear which made me go deafish for a week.

Sitting down in the grass outside, I was sick down my jumper. Mucus and bits of spaghetti hoops that looked all white and smelled real bad. I looked at the door I had fallen out of. Through my bleary eyes I saw an arm that was mostly bone, stuck between the wood and door frame. I made myself roll away and then get to my feet on the grass that was flattened down.

Moving around the outside of the house, back toward the front of the building and the path that would take me down to the gate, I wondered if I'd bashed my left side. The shoulder and hip were achy and cold and stiff. It was hard to move. I wondered if that's what broken bones felt like. All my skin was wet with sweat too, but I was shivery and cold. I just wanted to lie down in the long grass. Twice I stopped to be sick. Only spit came out with burping sounds.

Near the front of the house, I got down on my good side and started to crawl, real slow, through the long grass, down the hill, making sure the path was on my left so I didn't get lost in the meadow. I only took one look back at the house and will wish forever that I never did.

One side of the front door was still open from where we went in. I could see a crowd, bustling in the sunlight that fell on their raggedy clothes. They were making a hooting sound and fighting over something; a small shape that looked dark and wet. It was all limp. Between the thin, snatching hands, it came apart, piece by piece.

In my room, at the end of my bed, Nanna Alice has closed her eyes. But she's not sleeping. She's just sitting quietly and rubbing her doll hand like she's polishing treasure.

ALBERT E. COWDREY

Twilight States

Albert E. Cowdrey was born and grew up in New Orleans toward the end of the Pleistocene Epoch. He earned degrees (in history) from Tulane University and Johns Hopkins and as Teaching Assistant taught at Tulane and the University of New Orleans. While working for the army and living in Anapolis and Washington, DC, he wrote several books on military, medical, and environmental history, most printed by the government, the rest published by university presses and the Free Press.

Upon retirement he returned to New Orleans determined never to fabricate another footnote in this life. He also returned to his lifelong love—fantastic fiction. He had published a story in The Magazine of Fantasy & Science Fiction *in 1968, so tried that magazine again thirty years later and hit it off with Kris Rusch and then with Gordon Van Gelder. His story "Queen for a Day" won the World Fantasy Award in 2002, and his first SF novel,* Crux, *was published in 2004.*

He reports that during Katrina he evacuated early and watched the disaster as most of the world did, on TV. He returned home to find his house miraculously spared by wind, water, and arsonists. He's a loner by nature and dwells there in peace (at least until next hurricane season) with his dog Lagniappe, an amiable mutt whose only flaw is being smarter than his owner.

—E.D.

A dusty shop window, a darkening street outside. Streetlights winking on at three o'clock. A summer storm brewing.

Milton's reflection—dim, bent, somehow older than his fifty-two years—stared at him through backward lettering that said *Sun & Moon Metaphysical Books.*

He sighed and flipped the pages of his desk calendar. June 1979 was drawing to an end. Could he afford to close for the day? A customer might yet be driven in by the threat of rain. . . .

As if summoned, the doorbell jangled and a fat old man carrying a furled umbrella erupted into the shop. He strode to a bookcase, browsed for a moment, then snatched down a faded red volume.

"Why d'you stock a fool like Montague Summers?" he boomed.

"Because he s-sells," Milton answered.

Why the stutter? He hadn't stuttered for years. Decades, maybe. Then he knew why: he'd heard that voice before.

"A superstitious Jesuit who thought vampires were real," the intruder was grumbling. "I'm a scientist myself. . . . Somebody told me you stock old science fiction."

Milton took a deep breath. "Like *Weird Tales, Astounding, Arcana?*"

"That's it. *Arcana.*"

He drew out a ring of keys and unlocked a cabinet. "You're a collector?"

"No. I read for pleasure. And professional interest."

Milton explained that *Arcana* lasted only twenty issues, from mid-1941 until wartime scarcities of paper and ink shut it down. Yet in its brief lifespan it published everybody—big names, promising unknowns.

"Do you have the January '42 issue?"

Milton took another deep breath and offered a flawless copy in its plastic jacket.

"Of course it's pricey. But very rare."

"I'll take it," said the fat man, paying two hundred dollars for a pulp magazine thirty-seven years old. The check he wrote identified him as Erasmus Bloch, M.D., and gave his address and phone number.

The name too rang a bell. An alarm bell, maybe? Yet this was a customer Milton wanted to keep.

"This issue's got a bit of history attached to it," he said, wrapping the package. "My brother Ned was a World War Two hero—Navy Cross—and he got this *Arcana* just about the time of Pearl Harbor. He volunteered so quickly that he never had a chance to read it."

Actually, Milton had bought the copy (and a dozen others) at a newsstand on Royal Street. But people liked pricey purchases to come with a legend.

"Your brother," came that loud, abrupt voice. "Is he still alive?"

Instantly Milton's stutter resurfaced. "No. He was m-murdered. After the war. T-terribly."

Even Bloch seemed to realize he'd put a heavy thumb on an old wound. He touched Milton's bony shoulder with a hand like a flipper.

"This copy will be treasured," he said.

An instant later, the bell jangled, his umbrella deployed with a snap, and the door clicked shut behind him.

Milton folded his arms tight against his concave chest. How could you? he silently berated himself. How could you say so much to a stranger? Worse yet, to somebody who may not be a stranger at all?

By now the French Quarter was adrift in rain. Gutters spouted like whales and ankle-deep water washed the streets clean of tourists. No more customers today.

Milton locked the shop and climbed a circular staircase to his living quarters on the second floor. At the top he paused, wheezing. The hall was deep in shadow and rain streamed down the only window. Four closed doors stood in a row: his parents' bedroom, Ned's, his own, and the bath. Something scratched at Ned's door with a sound like a wire brush.

"It's all right," said Milton. "Don't you be worried. I'm not."

In his room he took off his shoes, stretched out on the bed, and flicked on an old brass lamp. Erasmus, Erasmus. Odd name. Now where—?

In search of an elusive memory, his eyes traveled over the yellow walls, the scarred plaster, the heavy purple furniture, the wall clock missing its pendulum. But no memory came.

Rain drummed on the balcony and rattled the wooden shutters. Gradually Milton's breathing became regular, and sleep fell on him like a coverlet.

He began to dream. Ralph O'Meagan, aged ten, lay in bed listening to his mother curse his father. She was out of the hospital again, and as usual the drying-out treatment hadn't worked for long. She was drinking, and the drunker she got the more she tried to fight with her silent husband, and the more he ignored her the sorrier she felt for herself and the more she drank.

Ralph suffered from nightmares and his parents allowed him to keep a nightlight burning. He lay on his side staring at the wall, at the scars and bumps in the old yellow plaster. "*Why don't you SAY something?*" He concentrated, doing magic, knowing that when his eyes grew tired the wall would seem to move. "*You miserable BASTARD!*"

It was stirring now. Wavering, rippling like a broad flag stirred by a light wind. Then it bellied out like a sail.

Startled, he closed his eyes. Looked again through his lashes. The wall was swollen and straining. When he tried to will it back, it burst in a soundless explosion, flinging sparks in every direction.

The dazzle faded. Ralph was lying on a wet field of grass and reeds. He felt the damp and the cold through his PJs. His breath came quickly and he could hear the beating of his heart.

Bewildered, he sat up, shivering in a raw wind. The sky was blue dusk except for one smear of red in the west and a dim moon rising in the east. Far away, he saw a roller coaster's snaky form outlined in lights. A calliope hooted a popular tune of 1948, "The Anniversary Waltz."

Something scratched and snorted and he turned his head. No more than ten yards away, a giant wild boar was digging at the grass. Its flat bristly nostrils blew puffs of smoke, it braced its thick legs, pulled with orange tusks, and a human arm lifted into view. The fingers moved feebly—

Milton sat up, sweating.

He was safe in his own bed, in his own room where he'd slept all his life. Rain pattered against the shutters. And Ralph O'Meagan was back where and when he belonged, in the January '42 issue of *Arcana*, his name forever attached to an intense and disturbing transdimensional story called "Borderland."

The wire-brush sound came again from Ned's room next door, and Milton muttered, "I told you it's all right."

He got up stiffly, put his shoes on and shuffled downstairs. In a small kitchen behind the bookshop he made green tea on a hot plate and inserted a frozen dinner into a dirty microwave oven.

He sat down at a metal-topped table, sipping the tea, and listened to the fan droning in the microwave. He had no way to avoid thinking about Ned, and about himself.

They'd shared Mama's fair coloring, sharp nose, and prominent chin, but not much else.

The product of an earlier marriage, Ned was a bully and a braggart, a fanatic athlete with an appetite for contact sports. Feared in grade school, worshipped in high school. Milton lived in terror of him, never knowing from day to day whether Ned would use him as a playmate or a punching bag.

Early on, Ned demanded and got a separate room so he wouldn't have to live with The Drip. He warned Milton not to talk to him at school, because he didn't want anybody to know they were related. Ned's door sported a poster of a soldier in a tin helmet and a gas mask. A hand-lettered sign said *POISON! KEEP OUT!*

"I ever catch you in my stuff," Ned warned him, "I'll fix you a knuckle sandwich. You hear that, Drip?"

What was Ned hiding? On December 1, 1941—Milton was an obscure freshman in Jesuit High School, Ned a prominent senior—thinking Ned was out, he fitted a skeleton key into the old-fashioned lock and went exploring.

The yellow walls were exactly like those in his own room, only stuck all over with movie posters of Humphrey Bogart and Edward G. Robinson looking tough. On Ned's desk, athletic trophies towered over a litter of papers and schoolbooks. Magazines—fantasy, sport, muscle, mystery—lay scattered over the rumpled bed.

Not knowing what he wanted to find, Milton began pawing through papers, opening desk drawers. He was still at work when the door crashed against the wall and Ned erupted into the room.

The memory lingered after almost forty years. Milton stopped sipping his tea and ran his fingertips over his ribs, touching the little lumps where cracked bones had healed. He shivered, reliving his terror as Ned's big hands pounded him.

"God damn you, you fucking punk," he bawled, "keep outta here! Keep outta here!"

The boy Milton had hunkered down, trying to shield his face—that was when his ribs took the pounding—and waited for death. But Ned was fighting himself, too. His face and whole body twisted as he tried to regain control.

Milton slipped under his arm and ran away and locked himself in his room, sobbing with rage and shame. Little by little the sparks of acute pain died out and a slow dull throbbing began in his chest, shoulders, arms, face. Blood soaked his undershirt and he tore it off and threw it away.

Later, when Daddy asked him what had happened to him—most of his injuries were hidden by his clothes, but Milton was walking stiffly and sporting a plum-sized black eye and a swollen jaw—he said he'd fallen downstairs at school.

"Clumsy goddamn kid," said Daddy.

By then Pearl Harbor had happened and Daddy was signing papers so that Ned could volunteer for the Navy. "One less mouth to feed," remarked Mr. Warmth.

Ned vanished into the alternate dimension that people called The Service, and Mama locked up his room, saying it must be kept just as he left it or he'd never return alive.

"Crazy bitch," said Daddy, whose comments were usually terse and always predictable.

Night after night for weeks afterward, Milton opened his window, slipped out onto the cold balcony that connected the three bedrooms, lifted the latch on Ned's shutters with a kitchen knife, and silently raised the sash.

One at a time he took Ned's trophies, wrapped them in old newspapers, and put them out with the trash. He threw away Ned's magazines, books, and posters.

He was hoping that Mama was right and Ned would never return. He hoped the Japs would capture him and torture him. He hoped Ned would fall into the ocean and be eaten by sharks. The depth of his loathing surprised even him, and he treasured it as a lover savors his love.

Then he received Ned's first letter. "Hi, Bro!" it started breezily.

Ned told about the weird people he was meeting in the Navy, about the icy wind blowing off the Great Lakes, about learning to operate a burp gun. Milton read the letter dozens, maybe hundreds of times.

More letters came on tissue-paper V-Mail, the APOs migrating westward to San Diego, then to Hawaii. Ned told about the great fleets gathering in Pearl Harbor for the counterpunch against Japan, about the deafening bombardment of Tarawa before the Marines went in. Gifts began arriving for Milton, handfuls of Japanese paper money, a rising-sun flag, a Samurai short sword.

Why had Ned turned from a domestic monster to a brother? Milton never knew. Maybe the war, maybe the presence of death. As the fighting darkened and lengthened, he could see something of the same spirit touching them all.

Mama went to work for the Red Cross and stayed sober until evening. Daddy took the Samurai short sword and hung it over the fireplace in the living room, where everybody could see it. When Ned sent Mama the Navy Cross he'd won, Daddy sat beside her on the sofa, staring at the medal in its little leather box as if a star had fallen from heaven. That was when he stopped calling Ned "my wife's kid" and started calling him "my son."

In the summer of 1945 Ned himself arrived at the naval air station on Lake Pontchartrain. Broad-shouldered and burned mahogany, he burst upon their lives like a bomb blowing down a wall and letting sunlight pour in.

He ordered Mama to stop drinking, and she put her bottles out with the trash. He ordered Daddy to stop insulting her, and he obeyed. At the first sign of backsliding, Ned would fly into one of his patented rages and his parents would hurry back into line. He was still a bully—only now he controlled his chronic abiding fury and used it for good.

Did hatred really lie so close to love? Could God and the devil swap places so easily? Apparently so.

Now Milton loved him and wanted desperately to be like him. An impossible job, of course. But he tried. Out of sheer hero-worship he decided to volunteer for the peacetime Navy and began going to the Y, trying to get in shape for boot camp. The new Ned didn't laugh at his belated efforts to be athletic. Instead, he went running with him at six in the morning, down the Public Belt railroad tracks along the wharves, among the wild daisies, while a great incandescent sun rose and a rank, fresh wind blew off the Father of Waters.

Life seemed to be brightening for all of them. Who could have guessed it would all go so terribly wrong?

Next day Dr. Bloch dropped by the shop to tell Milton how much he's enjoyed reading *Arcana*.

"I love pulp," he confessed. "I like the energy, the violence, the fact that there's always a resolution. The one thing in *The New Yorker* I never read is the fiction."

They chatted cautiously, like strange dogs sniffing each other. Bloch explained he'd retired from practice but still did a little consulting at St. Vincent's, the mental hospital where both of Milton's parents had been patients.

"You're a psychiatrist?" asked Milton, astonished. Bloch was so noisy and intrusive that he wondered how the man got anyone to confide in him.

"The technical term is shrink," Bloch boomed. "I suppose it's all right to say this now. Your brother was a patient of mine long ago. Somebody who knows I'm a fan of old sf told me about your shop, and as soon as I saw your face it all came back. You're very like him, you know."

Milton sat open-mouthed, while—like some cinematic effect—the lines of a younger face emerged from the old man's spots, creases and wattles. How could he have missed it? Dr. Erasmus Bloch was *Dr. Erasmus Bloch*.

"When did you treat Ned?" he asked, his voice unsteady.

"In forty-eight, I think. Gave him a checkup first, naturally. Well set-up young fellow. Athletic. No physical problems at all."

"Was he . . . ah. . . ."

"Psychotic? No. But he was hallucinating, and of course he was scared. We ruled out a brain tumor, drug use, and alcoholism—I don't think he drank at all—"

"No. Because of our mother. I'm the same way. So what was wrong?"

"He was terribly unhappy. He'd grown up isolated, with a drunken mother and a rigid, cold, possibly schizoid father. He had violent impulses that he found hard to control. Frankly, he scared me a bit. These borderline cases can be much more dangerous than the certified screwballs. And he was *strong*, you know?"

"Yes," said Milton, "I remember. . . . You said he was hallucinating?"

"Yes. Quite an interesting case. He believed his frustration and rage had turned him into a god or demon that had created a world. He'd written a story about it, and he loaned me a copy of *Arcana* so I could read it. Matter of fact, I read it again just last night."

Milton nodded. "I've known for years that Ned wrote the story. But I never imagined he thought the—what did he call it? the Alternate Dimension—was real. I mean . . . it's hard to believe he was serious."

"Oh, he was serious, all right. I knew that when I saw the name he'd signed to his story."

"Ralph O'Meagan?"

"It's the closest Ned could come to Alpha Omega. You know, as in *Revelations*: 'I am the Alpha and Omega, the beginning and the end.' Yes, he actually believed he was a god and he'd made a world."

That was a riveting insight. Milton wondered why he'd never seen it himself. His breath came quicker, this was turning out to be the most involving conversation he'd had in decades.

"How do you treat something like that?"

"One technique for dissolving a delusional system is to move into it with the patient. It's such a private thing, it disintegrates when he finds another person inside it. So I told Ned, 'I want to hear more about this world of yours. Perhaps I can go there with you.'

"Something about that scared him. He skipped our next appointment. My nurse tried to call him, but it turned out he'd given her a wrong number. When she looked him up in the phone book, he claimed he'd never heard of me. Sounded as if he really hadn't. Might have been stress-induced amnesia—rather a radical form of denial."

"Yes," murmured Milton. "That does sound radical."

Bloch glanced at his watch, said he was due at the hospital and took his leave. Milton sat for a few minutes hugging his midsection, then got up and locked the door.

This wasn't his regular day to dust Ned's bedroom, but he went upstairs anyway, for the terrible past had taken him in its grip.

His key chain jangled and he sensed something beyond the door as the key turned silently in the well-oiled lock. But the shadowy room held only a faintly sour organic smell.

He opened the window, unbolted the shutters and flung them wide. Light flooded in. The room looked just as it had the week before Christmas 1945, when Ned had thrown his second-to-last tantrum and stormed out of the house.

Milton hadn't actually witnessed it, but he heard about it later. Ned went into a fury because mama, possibly in honor of the season, had disobeyed his orders and started drinking again. After he walked out, of course, she drank more. Milton came home carrying an armful of presents to find her staggering, and Ned forever gone.

God, how he'd hated him that day. Tearing out the underpinnings of his life just when he'd begun to be happy.

On the dresser stood a mirror where Ned had combed his hair, and a tarnished silver frame with a faded picture of him as a young sailor wearing a jaunty white cap. Ned was smiling a fake photographic smile, but his eyes didn't smile. Neither did Milton's as he approached and stared at him.

His face hovered in the mirror, Ned's in the picture. Youth and decay: Dorian Gray in reverse. Suddenly feeling an intolerable upsurge of rage, he growled at the picture, "You were such a lousy stinking bastard."

That was only the beginning. Grinding his teeth, he cursed the picture with every word he'd ever learned from chief petty officers and drunks brawling on Bourbon Street and his own unforgiving heart.

Exhausted by the eruption, trembling, clutching his ribs, Milton staggered back and sat down suddenly on the bed. Little by little he calmed down. After ten minutes he stood up and carefully smoothed the bedspread.

"Time to open the shop again," he said in a quiet voice.

He closed Ned's room and locked it, knowing it would be here when he came again, exactly as it was, never changing, never to be changed. The love and hate of his life, shut up in one timeless capsule.

The afternoon brought few customers, the following morning fewer still.

Milton filled the empty hours as he always did, sitting at his desk with his hollow chest collapsed in upon itself, taking rare and slow and shallow breaths, like a hibernating bear. Musing, dreaming, rearranging the pieces of his life like a chessplayer with no opponent, pushing wood idly on the same old squares.

How much he wanted to put his family into a gothic novel. How often he'd tried to write it, but never could. He smiled ruefully, thinking: Where are you, Ralph O'Meagan, when I need you?

All around him, stacked shelf on shelf, stood haunted books full of demons and starships, the horrors of Dunwich and Poe's Conqueror Worm. But none held the story he longed to tell. He smiled wearily at a dusty print hanging on the wall — Dali's *The Persistence of Memory*, with its limp watches.

He knew now why people talked to noisy Dr. Bloch. It was quite simple: they needed to talk, and he was willing to listen. Shortly after eleven o'clock, Milton dug out his customer file and called Bloch's number. It turned out to belong to a posh retirement home called Serena House.

"This is God's waiting room," the loud voice explained, and Milton moved the phone an inch away from his ear. "God's *first-class* waiting room. Want to join me for lunch?"

Milton found himself stuttering again as he accepted. He locked up, fetched his old Toyota from a garage he rented and drove up St. Charles Avenue to Marengo Street. The block turned out to be one of those old corners of the city where time had stopped around 1890. The houses were old paintless wooden barns, most wearing thick mats of cat's claw vine like dusty habits.

But in their midst sat a new and massive square structure of faux stone with narrow lancet windows. Serena House was a thoroughly up-to-date antechamber to the tomb. After speaking to the concierge—a cool young blonde—Milton waited in a patio that was pure Motel Modern: cobalt pool, palms in large plastic pots, metal lawn furniture, concrete frogs and bunnies and a nymph eternally emptying water from an urn.

"You see what you have to look forward to," boomed Bloch, and they shook hands.

"I can't afford Serena House. Don't you think my shop's a nice place for an old guy to dream away his days?"

"Yes, provided a wall doesn't blow in on you!"

Bloch, that impressively tactless man, laughed loudly at his own wit while leading the way to the dining room. The chairs were ivory enameled with rose upholstery and the walls were festive with French paper. By tacit agreement, they said nothing about Ned until the crème brûlée had been polished off.

Instead they talked sci-fi and fantasy. Milton found Bloch a man of wide reading. He knew the classics by Cyrano and Voltaire, Poe and Carroll and Stoker and Wells. He'd read Huxley's and Forster's ventures into the field. He declared that *Faust* and the *Divine Comedy* were also fantasy masterpieces—epic attempts to make ideas real.

"Because that's what fantasy is, isn't it?" he demanded. "Not just making things up, but taking ideas and giving them hands and feet and claws and teeth!"

After lunch they moved to poolside. Bloch lit a cigar that smelled expensive and resumed grilling Milton. "Your brother—did he die in the room where the story was set?"

He had a gift for asking unexpected questions. Milton cleared his throat, hesitated, then evaded—neatly, he thought—saying where Ned actually did die.

"No. He was found in the marshland out near the lake, about a quarter of a mile from that old amusement park on the shore."

"Any idea what he was doing there?"

"The police thought he'd been killed elsewhere and dumped. I wasn't much help to them—hadn't seen Ned in years. Actually, we'd been on bad terms, and that was sad."

"And your parents . . . what happened to them?"

"Mama drank herself to death. Daddy went senile. Alzheimer's, they'd call it today. He died in St. Vincent's. I got a call one night, and this very firm Negro voice said, 'Your Dad, he ain't got no life signs.' I said, 'You mean he's dead?' 'We ain't 'lowed to use that word,' said the voice. 'He ain't got no life signs is all.'

" 'That's okay,' I said. 'He never did.' "

Bloch smiled a bit grimly, exhaled a puff of blue smoke. "Tell me . . . exactly what killed Ned?"

Milton took a deep breath. He'd left himself open to such probing, and now had no way to evade an answer.

"Hard to say. He was such a mess by the time they found him. It was November, nineteen-forty-eight. The—the damage to his face and body was devastating. There was a nick in one thoracic vertebra that possibly indicated a knife thrust through the chest. But the coroner couldn't be sure—so much of him had been eaten—there were toothmarks on a lot of the bones. . . ."

"Eaten by what?"

Milton squinted at the cobaltpool. Sunstarts on the ripples burned his eyes. He said, "The c-coroner said wild pigs. Razorbacks. The m-marshes were full of them."

Bloch's little pouchy eyes gleamed with interest.

"Amazing. The monster in his story was a wild boar. You're saying he wrote the story in nineteen-forty-one, and seven years later actual wild pigs mutilated his body?"

When Milton didn't answer, Bloch said soberly, "You seem to have lived a Gothic novel, my friend."

"I was thinking the same thing this morning," Milton said, getting up to go. "You know, you're filling your own prescription, Dr. Bloch. You're moving into the fantasy."

"Good Lord," said he, knocking the ash off his cigar as he rose. "I hope not."

By the time he reached the shop, Milton was finding his own behavior incredible. After decades of silence, he couldn't believe the things he'd been saying—to Bloch, of all people.

He was confused as well, angry and fearful yet not sure exactly what he was afraid of. Sitting slumped at his desk, he worked it out.

There was the practical danger, of course. But beyond that lay a metaphysical peril: that he might somehow lose his world. *It's such a private thing*, Bloch had said, *it disintegrates when another person moves into it.*

Rising, Milton unlocked his cabinet and took out a second copy of the January '42 *Arcana*. Six others reposed in the same place, awaiting buyers. He put on white cotton gloves to protect the old brittle pages, and began leafing through them. The words of Ralph O'Meagan were an echo of long ago.

For many long weeks I lived in trembling fear of the night, when I would have to go to my room and see the lamplight on that wall. For now I knew that the world called real is an illusion of lighted surfaces and the resonances of touch, while underneath surges immortal and impalpable Energy, ever ready to create or kill.

There was no possible way of explaining to my father why I should sleep anywhere else, and no way of explaining anything to my mother at all. I tried to sleep without the nightlight, only to find that I feared the demons of the dark even more than those of the light.

Yet I grew tired of waiting and watching for something that never happened, and as time went by I began to persuade myself that what I'd seen that one time was, after all, a mere nightmare, such as I often had.

I was sound asleep, some three or four weeks after my first visit to the Alternate Dimension, when something tickling my face caused me to awaken. At first I had absolutely no sense of fear or dread. Then I felt a prickling on my face and hands like the "pins and needles" sensation when a foot has been asleep—and a memory stirred.

Reluctantly I opened my eyes. I was lying as before in that field of dying grass. One coarse stem was rubbing against my nose, other stems probed my hands and bare feet.

I raised my head and saw the great beast once again. This time I waited until it had finished its horrible meal and had turned away, like an animal well satisfied and ready for sleep.

Trembling, I stood up. I was soaked and shivering and felt as cold and empty as the boar was warm and full. I approached the body it had been mutilating, and it was that of a grown man, with something intolerably familiar about its face—for the face remained: remained, frozen into its last rictus of agony: and I knew that the face one day would be mine.

Milton closed the magazine. Poor Ralph O'Meagan. Poor Alpha Omega. Caught in an eddy of the time process, condemned to return again and again to the same place to undergo the same death and mutilation.

The Alternate Dimension was not the past and not the future. Ralph was encountering Forever.

How extraordinary, Milton thought, that a fourteen-year-old boy should have such ideas and write them so well and then live mute forever afterward. But fourteen, that's the age of discovery, isn't it? Of sexual awakening? Of sudden insights into your fate that you spend the rest of your life trying to understand?

And that rhetoric about immortal and impalpable Energy—was it mere adolescent rubbish? An early symptom of madness? Or a revelation of truth?

That night his sleep was restless. Bloch kept intruding into his dreams, with spotty face thrust forward and eyes staring. Their dialogue resumed, and soon the dream Bloch was breaking into areas the real one hadn't yet imagined.

—*That's what happened, isn't it?* accused the loud metallic voice. *You killed Ned, didn't you?*

—*Christ. Well, yes. I didn't mean to.*

—*No, of course not.*

—*I didn't!*

—*Oh, I think there was a lot of hatred there, plus a lot of rather unbrotherly love. And I don't think you're a forgiving type . . . How'd you do it, anyway?*

—*With a samurai short sword he'd sent me from the Pacific. When he came at me I snatched it off the living room wall and ran it into his chest. Or he did. I mean, he was the one in motion. I was just holding the sword, trying to fend him off. Really.*

—*Why'd he attack you?*

—*He was in one of his rages. It was late at night. Mama was dead and Daddy was in the hospital. I was out of the Navy and living here alone when Ned came bursting into the house, roaring. He'd found out I'd been going to a shrink and using his name instead of my own.*

—*Why'd you do a thing like that?*

—*I was afraid. It was 1948 and people could be committed a lot more easily than they can today. I was afraid I was going crazy and you'd have me put away. It was a dumb trick, but I thought I could find out what was happening to me without running such a risk.*

—*Ah. Now we're getting at it. So you and Ned had your second big fight and—*

—*Just like the first time, he won.*

—*How could he, if you killed him?*

—*He only died. I died but went on living. He became one of the dead but I became one of the undead.*

—*Oh, Lord. Not Montague Summers again.*

—*Yes. Montague Summers again.*

Milton woke up. The clock said 4:20. He got up anyway, and made tea. Except for one light the shop was dark, the books in shadow, all their tales of horror and discovery in suspended animation, like a freeze frame in a movie.

Milton drank green tea, and slowly two images, the dream Bloch and the real one, overlapped in his mind and fused together. What he'd discover in time—the pushy devil.

So, Milton thought. I'll have to get rid of him, too.

He added *too* because over the last three decades there had been other people who seemed to threaten him. He no longer remembered just how many.

Bathed, breakfasted, his long strands of sparse hair neatly combed across his skull, Milton opened his shop as usual at ten. Just before noon Bloch came in, puffing, intruding with his big belly, shaking his veinous wattles.

" 'Welcome to my house!' " Milton quoted, smiling. " 'Enter freely, and of your own will!' "

Bloch chuckled appreciatively. "Thank you, Count."

"That was a fine lunch yesterday," Milton went on warmly, "and the talk was even better than the food."

As usual, they chatted about books. Bloch had been reading an old text from the early days of psychoanalysis, Schwarzwalder's *Somnambulismus und Dämmerzustände*—somnambulism and twilight states. To doctors of the Viennese school, he explained, somnambulism didn't mean literal sleepwalking but rather dissociated consciousness, a transient doubling of the personality.

"Those old boys had something to say," Bloch boomed. "They believed in the reality of the mind. Modern psychiatrists don't. Today it's all drugs, drugs, drugs."

So, thought Milton, Bloch had been analyzing him. He said, "As long as you're here, would you like to see Ned's room? I've kept it exactly as it was when he was alive."

Bloch was enthusiastic. "Indeed I would. I wasn't able to help him, and I seem to remember my failures more than my successes."

"Success always moves on to the next thing," Milton agreed, as Bloch trailed him up the circular stair. "But failure's timeless, isn't it? Failure is forever."

Upstairs the hall was clean and bright, with the sun reflecting through the patio window. There was no sound behind Ned's door.

Bloch stopped to catch his breath, then asked, "I'm invited in here too? Otherwise I wouldn't intrude, you know"—carrying on the Dracula bit in his heavy-handed way.

Smiling, Milton unlocked the door and bowed him in. He opened the window and the shutters, and suddenly the room was full of light. The young sailor's face grinned fixedly from the picture frame, and Bloch approached it, eager as a collector catching sight of a moth he'd missed the last time.

"Ah," he said. "Yes, I remember. He looked a lot like this thirty years ago, when I treated him. Or—"

He paused, confused. Milton had come up behind him and looked over his shoulder. Frowning, Bloch stared at the picture, then at the reflection, then at the picture again. It was the first time he'd seen the brothers together.

"You never really knew Ned, did you?" Milton asked.

"But the man I saw—the one who came for treatment—he was built like an athlete—"

"I spent more than two years in the Navy before they Section-Eighted me. It was the only time in my life I was ever in shape."

That was another bit of news for Bloch to absorb, and for the first time Milton heard him stutter a little.

"And the, ah, r-reason for your d-discharge—"

"Oh, the usual. 'Psychotic.' As far as I could see, the word meant only that they didn't know what they were dealing with. At that time, neither did I."

"The story . . . you wrote it?"

"Have you ever known an athlete who could write, or a bookworm who didn't want to?"

"And the things you told me about Ned—"

"Were true. But of course about me. Hasn't it occurred to you that Ned discharged his rage while I buried mine deep? That if there was a maniac in the family, it was far more likely to be me? What kind of a lousy doctor are you, anyway?"

Despite the harsh words his voice was eerily tranquil, and he smiled when Bloch turned his head to see how far he was from the door.

Then he turned back, staring at Milton's bent and narrow frame, and his thoughts might as well have been written on his face. *This bag of bones—what do I have to fear from him?*

Suddenly his voice boomed out. "Ralph O'Meagan, I'm delighted to make your acquaintance at last!"

He stretched out his fat hand and as he did the yellow wall bellied out and burst, blowing away the room and the whole illusion of the world called real.

Gaping, letting his hand drop nervelessly, Bloch stared now at the smudge of fire in the west, now at the rising moon in the east.

A raw wind blew; delighted shrieks echoed from the roller coaster; the calliope was hooting, and Milton hummed along: *Oh, how we danced on the night we were wed—*

"Welcome to my world," he said, standing back.

Swift trotters were drumming on the earth and splashing in the pools and Bloch whirled as the huge humpbacked beast came at him out of the sunset, smoke jetting from its nostrils, small red eyes glinting like sardonyx.

"What did I do?" Bloch cried, waving his fat hands. "I wanted to help! What did I do?"

The boar struck his fat belly with lethal impact and his lungs exploded like balloons. He lived for a few minutes, writhing, while it delved into his guts. Milton leaned forward, hugging himself, breathlessly watching.

The scene was elemental. Timeless. The beast rooting and grunting, the sunset light unchanging, cries of joy from the roller coaster, and the calliope hooting on: *Could we but relive that sweet moment divine/We'd find that our love is unaltered by time.*

"Now you're really part of the fantasy," he assured Dr. Bloch.

Not that Bloch heard him. Or anything else.

Life returned to normal in *Sun & Moon Metaphysical Books* where, of course, things were never totally normal.

Milton's days went by as before, opening the shop, chatting with the occasional customer, closing it again. Drowsy days spent amid the smell of old books, a smell whose color, if it had a color, would be brownish gray.

Serena House called to inquire about their lodger—Dr. Bloch had left Milton's number when he went out. Milton expressed astonishment over the disappearance, offered any help he could give. Next day a bored policewoman from Missing Persons arrived to take a statement. Milton described how Bloch had visited the shop, chatted, and left.

"He was one of my best customers," he said. "Any idea what might have happened to him?"

"Nothing yet," said the cop, closing her notebook. "It's kind of like Judge Crater."

More than you know, thought Milton. Where Bloch's bones lay it was always 1948, and whole neighborhoods had been built over the spot, a palimpsest of fill and tarmac and buildings raised, razed and raised again. Milton's voice was confident and strong and totally without a stutter as he chatted with the policewoman, and he could see she believed what he told her.

After she left, the afternoon was dull as usual. Around four Milton got up from his desk and took down his copy of Montague Summers's *The Vampire in Europe*. He hefted it, did not open it, put it back on the shelf and addressed its author aloud.

"Reverend Summers, you're a fool. Thinking the undead drink blood. No, we suck such life as we have from rage and memories. It must be a nourishing diet, because we live on. And on. And on. And on. I knew that when I wrote my story."

An hour later, after closing the shop, he entered Ned's room and for a time stood gazing into the mirror. The sun was going down. As the room darkened, he heard the unseen beast rubbing its nap of stiff hair against the wall and smelled the morning-breath odor of unfresh blood that always attended it.

Was it something or somebody? Was it his creature, or himself? Did he dream its world, or did it dream his? Milton brooded, asking himself unanswerable questions while his image faded slowly into the brown shadows, until the glass held nothing, nothing at all.

ANDREW BONIA

Jolly Bonnet

*Andrew Bonia was raised in St. John's, Newfoundland. An actor as well as a
writer, his essays, scripts, short fictions, and poetry have appeared in many
unlikely places, including* TickleAce, The Borgo Post, *and* Comixpedia.com.
*He and his wife Ainsley currently live in Connecticut, where he contributes
columns to* The Newfoundland Independent, *and serves time backstage at
the Long Wharf Theater.*
   "Jolly Bonnet" was published in Jabberwocky.

                                                                    —E.D.

Her new hat
Made of fresh woven straw, and un-scuffed
As she is, (stained red)
Matches the color of night and street;
Two words that, along with 'woman of the'
Comprise her current circumstance.

Straw, cut down when all is ready
Can be formed into many things
From bread (the yardstick of the civilized)
To feed for beasts.
Or sometimes woven within other strands to make a bed,
A placemat, matching coasters
Or a hat.
Or other trifles I've forgotten.

When last seen, she was heading to work
Head strong and confident in her ability to perform
As though she had discovered a new edge, making her special.
Still, she points at her new hat, black and straw-made
And with a grin that comes from sleeping in the dirt
She opens up and shares her final secret;
"See what a jolly bonnet I've got now?"

Night and Street,
Woven within other strands
    Making her special.
    Her new hat
    In the dirt
    (stained red)
    Cut down when all is ready
    As though she had discovered a new edge.
    Night and Street.
    Other trifles I've forgotten.

The Last Ten Years in
the Life of Hero Kai

Geoff Ryman's heroic tale, "The Last Ten Years in the Life of Hero Kai," is an accomplished example of a decidedly eccentric, fairly recent offshoot of genre fiction, "monkpunk." First published in the December issue of The Magazine of Fantasy & Science Fiction, *Ryman's story can plausibly be read as either science fiction or fantasy. In any case, it's utterly unlike anything else we read this past year. One of our favorite writers, Ryman is the author of half a dozen novels, all highly recommended, including* The Child Garden, Was, 253, *and* Air. *His novel* The King's Last Song, *a non-genre, historical novel set in Cambodia, will be published this year in Britain.*

—K.L. & G.G.

Kai was already an old man when he mastered the art of being a hero.
He was a student of war and a student of God. He was a particular follower of the text *The Ten Rules of Heroism.*
The Text is one hundred palm leaves long, but these are the Ten Rules.

1. Heroism consists of action
2. Do not act until necessary
3. You will know that the action is right if everything happens swiftly
4. Do whatever is necessary
5. Heroism is revealed not by victory but by defeat
6. You will have to lie to others, but never lie to yourself
7. Organized retreat is a form of advance
8. Become evil to do good
9. Then do good to earn merit and undo harm
10. Heroism is completed by inaction

The last ten years of Hero Kai's life are considered to be a perfect act of Heroism. One rule is exampled by each of his last ten years.

Heroism consists of action

It is Hero Kai's fiftieth year. He is lean and limber, his gray hair pulled back fiercely. People say his eyes are gray with age. Others say his eyes were always as gray as the eyes of a statue, except for the dark holes of his pupils.

His sword is so finely balanced that it can slice through sandstone walls. Kai himself can run up a vertical surface, or suspend his breathing for hours.

Kai starts each day with his exercises. He stands on tiptoe on the furthest leaf of the highest branch of the tallest mango tree in the region. He holds two swords and engages himself in fast and furious swordplay. He walks on his hands for a whole day.

Yet he takes no action.

He goes to funerals to chant for the dead. Rich men hope to earn merit by paying him to recite the traditional verses called the Chbap or Conduct. This is a Chbap.

> The happy man is one who knows his limitations
> And smiles formally even to a dog
> If a neighbor owes him money
> He applies an even gentle pressure like water falling over rocks . . .

. . . etc., etc. The Chbap are all about being tame and making things easy for superior people.

Kai's kingdom is very badly ruled. The roads have fallen apart; the rivers are choked with weeds; and the King spends his day performing gentle magic for which he has no talent.

The Chbap are the only thing that holds together the Kingdom of Kambu's Sons. The Chbap keep people toiling cheerfully in the rice fields. The verses remind them to give alms to the poor, thus staving off starvation and revolt. They insist that people care for their families, so that everyone can look forward to an honored old age. The Chbap prepare poor people to accept placidly an early and often excruciating death.

Kai believes in the Chbap to the extent that they are useful. He knows them in their thousands and recites one or two of them each evening as he is massaged by the boy he bought. The boy's name is Arun, and he gets up early each morning to sweep the monastery floors—and goes to bed late after scattering dust over those same floors to teach him acceptance.

On the day of his fiftieth birthday, Kai's acolytes present him with a handsome gift.

It is something new and dangerously different. In Kai's language, the words for "different" and "wrong" are nearly identical.

The gift is a tiny round bronze ball and if you fill its tank with water and light a fire under it, it starts to spin.

Alone before going to sleep, Kai thinks about this different miracle long and hard. He decides that there is no magic in it. It is as hard and as fair as drought or pestilence.

The Westerners are building whole engines that work like steamballs.

And the Neighbors are buying them.

The state of Kambu is so weak that the king has to pay to keep the neighboring states from invading. Kambu's king is so powerless that his own army is run by advisers from these states, and so helpless that he enforces their corvées of Kambu labor.

Kambu troops are being used to corral or even kidnap the Chbap-reciting farmers, herding them away to work on a new kind of road in the Commonwealth of the Neighbors.

Hero Kai sits on the beautifully swept floor. His little steamball spins itself to a stop. Candlelight fans its way through the gaps in the floorboards and walls. Everything buzzes and creaks with insects. In the flickering light, Kai thinks.

If only the king were strong. If only the Sons of Kambu stood up as one against the Neighbors. If only there were ten of me. Our army is controlled by our enemies. Our wealth pours out to them and when they want more, they just take it. The king's magic makes girls pretty, fields abundant, and rainfall regular. It holds back disease and the ravages of age.

The Neighbors make the magic of war.

Kai finds he cannot sit still. He stands on one leg and hops so lightly that the floorboards do not shake. He makes many swift passes with his sword, defeating imaginary opponents.

He loses heart and his sword sinks down toward the floor.

The unquiet spirit spends his strength in cutting air. . . .

Kai takes out an incising pen and cuts a letter to the king in a palm leaf. He fills the grooves with ink-powder and burns it so the ink hardens in the grooves but can be brushed away from the surface.

Then he wakes Arun and gives him the letter. Kai tells him to walk to the lake, and take a boat to the distant, tiny, capital.

What can a mouse do when caught by the cat?

Do not act until necessary

A year later Kai stands with the farmers in revolt.

His monk robes are gathered up over his shoulders to free his arms and legs. The cloth is the color of fire. His body is hard and lean, as if cut from marble, with just the slightest creases of age across the belly and splotches around his ankles.

His sword is as long and lean as himself.

The Commonwealth of Neighbors is hot and smells of salt and drains. The sea hammers a coast that used to belong to the Sons of Kambu. The rich plains get all the rain that the mountains block from Kambu. Everything steams and rots.

Kidnapped fathers sweat in ranks, armed with hoes and pickaxes. Some of them simply carry rocks.

They have been starved and beaten until they are beyond caring. Families, fields, home are all hundreds of miles away.

They have nothing to lose.

The Road of Fire grins like an unending smile. The lips are burnished tracks of metal that gleam in mathematically parallel lines. The teeth are the wooden beams that hold the tracks in place. The Road of Fire looks like evil.

The Army of Neighbors looks beautiful.

They are naked except for white folded loincloths. Their bodies are hard but round from food and fighting, and their eyes are gray. Their earlobes are long and stretched, bearing heavy earrings.

Every one of them is a holy man.

The Army of Neighbors is famously small and famously bears no arms. For a moment or two the armies look almost evenly matched.

Then the Neighbors start to chant.

They chant and the sound seems to turn unhappily in place. The air starts to whimper. Kai has time to sniff magic. Magic smells of spit.

The eyes in the head of the man standing next to Kai explode. The man howls and drops the rock he had meant to throw.

There is a ripping sound. Kai turns in time to see the skin being pulled from a young man's body. The air lifts him up and plays with him as he is disrobed of his hide.

A farmer with a lucky mole on his chin is having his intestines pulled rapidly out of his body.

Kai's sword heats up. It becomes as hot as coals. Everywhere about him men scream and drop their hoes or their shovels.

Kai stands his ground. The sword belonged to his master, and his master before that. Kai holds on to it as it scorches his flesh. He focuses his mind on resisting the heat. His skin sears and heals, sears and heals in repeated waves of agony.

The rebels turn and flee.

The dogs of Magic hound them. There is a slathering in the air as magic tastes, selects, destroys.

Magic licks Kai.

All of Kai's skin starts to boil. He can see the fat within bubble. He holds his focus, turns and calmly, somewhat stiffly, walks away. He survives through willpower.

He stumbles down rubble toward cool reeds before having to sit. He steams his way down into damp mud.

In the morning he wakes up after dreams of canoeing on the lake. In a circle all around him plants have burned or shriveled. The dew steams. Kai hears the clink of hammers on rocks and smells a butcher's shop.

He stands. Sons of Kambu work in lines, their heads hanging low. They recite.

> The happy man is one who knows his limitations
> And smiles formally even to a dog

Tears pour down Kai's face, stinging the singed flesh with salt. He stands still, building a wall in his mind against despair.

Oh, familiar kindly Chbap, why do you have no answer to this? Do you have no song to bring victory and not defeat?

And somehow one comes to mind. Why this one? It's called the Problem Chbap, the one nobody understands.

> Magic is the way of men of power
> They do not love kindness and nor does magic.
> Magic perfumes the air and sends men to hell.
> Push the particles of reality far and fast
> And magic will die, succumb to what is likely
> In the land where what you put in tea perfumes
> And magic is what is ground in the pestle.

Kai stands transfixed. Suddenly it makes sense.

A guard struts forward, howling orders. He is a humble Neighbor without magic.

Still contemplating the Problem Chbap, Kai spins on his heel and sends the Neighbor's head still shouting through the air.

Then Kai spins in the opposite direction and starts to march.

What do you put in your tea? Cardamom.

The Cardamom Mountains.

You will know that the action is right if everything happens swiftly

Kai arrives at his old monastery, still smoldering from heat.

The acolytes and the lay preachers and the old masters touch his skin and their fingers hiss. His eyebrows flame and sputter, go out and flame again. The acolytes give him water and it boils in his mouth, but he has to drink it. Tears stream out his eyes and evaporate as steam.

An old master says, "You have become a fulcrum for the universe. I've cast the yarrow and you came up all strong lines, changing to weak ones."

Kai tells them what happened in the lands of the Commonwealth, and of the Problem Chbap.

An acolyte says. "There are many like that. Remember the Dubious Chbap?"

> Even trees mislead,
> The worn path bends the wrong way
> Undo cries the air, undo says the wise men,
> And the trees open up.

Kai realizes. These problem Chbap did not make sense to us because we were not listening. These Chbap bring another kind of wisdom. They provide the balance to others.

These Chbap tell us how to fight.

"And how about this one. The masters love to set this as a test."

> The mind observes and makes happen what it wants to see.
> This is magic.
> The motes of reality coast to what is most likely
> And that is called the real.

Steaming, shuddering, fighting the spell, Kai's mind becomes his sword. For once.

His mind now cuts through a different kind of sandstone wall. This is a wall of beautiful, repetitive images: celestial maidens, virtuous monks, and skilled warriors . . . all that hardened rooster shit.

Kai says, "There is a machine that destroys magic in the Cardamom Mountains. We have to go and find it and use it on the Neighbors."

Immediately, ten young strong warrior monks volunteer. "We pack our bags now."

"No, no, Kai needs to rest," says one old monk, a rival of Kai.

"He should ask the King's permission," says another.

"That old fart!" says one of the warrior monks. "Let him sit at home and make earrings!"

Kai's voice rumbles from the fire within. "We go now. We go slowly, because if I am distracted I will burst into flame."

The young men exclaim: we take nothing! Just clothes, swords, stout shoes. A blanket against the cold in the mountains. We will hunt our food and cut it down from trees.

"More like you'll steal it from the poor peasants," growls Kai's rival.

"You mean like the King does?" The thrill of rebellion has made the acolytes forget respect.

They bustle their packs together.

The boy who Kai bought creeps forward. "Can I come as well?" Arun asks. His name means Morning Sun.

Losing focus, beginning to crackle from heat, Kai can only shake his head.

"Please." Arun begs. "I am so bored here. I learn nothing. I just sweep."

Eyes closed from concentration, Kai nods yes.

So the acolytes, proud sons of significant people, are joined by the slave. "Boy," they say, "Carry this."

Kai growls. "He works for me. Not you."

The acolytes bow and withdraw. They generally do, when faced with power.

They leave that night in the rain. The raindrops sputter and dance on Kai as if on a skillet.

"Swiftly" in a country without roads or waterways can mean many things.

It means you are welcomed in a village, and feted, and asked to wait so that you can chant at the wedding of the headman's daughter. You abide some weeks in preparation.

Arun says, "Teach me how to focus against the heat, Master. That way I can still massage your shoulders."

To Kai's surprise, he does.

One of the young men falls in love with one of the bride's sisters. It takes another week to persuade him to leave.

"Swiftly" means waiting out the rainy season as the plains of Kambu are milled into dough. It means the toes of the young men rot as they squelch through mud.

It means they wait all afternoon under a covered bridge as raindrops pound on the roof.

"Swiftly" means being lured into a welcoming village and then held as bandits, accused of theft and berated for rape.

The trial lasts weeks as all the ills of the village are visited on your head. The wretched people really think they can revenge all the wrongs done to them by killing you.

Kai practices forbearance, calmly pointing out that they were not in the village when the wrongs were done. He looks at the headman playing with Kai's own sword. He waits until the headman tires of admiring it and lays it to one side.

Then Kai stands up and says. "I am so sorry. I am afraid there's nothing we can do now except become another great wrong done to your people."

Kai can sing a note that makes his sword throb in harmony. The sword wobbles, weaves, and bounces itself into his hand.

"Many apologies," he says, and slices a pathway through the villagers, leading his acolytes out the door.

The dry season comes and the rivers shrivel. Kai's men march far out to the muddy borders of the lake, looking for a boat. They are told it will return from the city of Three Rivers within the week.

You swiftly wait sitting in mud, slipping in mud, catching frogs for supper. Each day, the lake is farther way, and you must walk again farther out.

Arun says, "Let me oil and clean your sword, Master, so that it does not rust."

The hissing sword does not burn Arun's fingers. Kai thinks: this Arun has talent.

The noble acolytes look at the fish and frogs they have caught. Must they eat the frogs raw?

"No," says Kai, and cradles the frogs in his hands, passing them back crisp and brown.

Finally the boat comes and sets out through winding channels between reeds. It gets mired behind the abandoned hulk of a bigger boat, and starts to settle sideways in ooze.

Kai walks to the abandoned hull, and blesses it chanting, and where he touches it, the wood catches alight. The wreck burns bright as a torch, down to the waterline. The monks wade in the next day, and clear it.

Their boat proceeds to Three Rivers, the graceful capital.

Their voyage is made even swifter by messengers from Kai's rivals. They rode all night and day to warn the King.

The King's men await them along the marbled waterfront. They greet Kai with distanced politeness and invite him and his men to the Palace. The King himself spares five minutes to greet them. In a silky voice, he insists they must stay and rest.

The acolytes escape the Palace in darkness by running up and over its high walls.

Kai stays behind to rescue Arun who cannot run up vertical surfaces. He loads the boy over his shoulder and walks toward the main gate.

A Neighbor wearing only a loincloth awaits him.

"You dress like that at this time of night?" says Kai. "You must be chilly. Or are you just trolling for trade?"

The Neighbor whispers with disgust and there is a smell of spit.

But once you have been magicked, it is very difficult to magic you again.

Kai says. "Let me warm you."

He embraces the Holy Warrior. He holds the man until his arms have burned to the bone. A burning fist over his face stifles his screams and will scar his mouth permanently closed. Kai and Arun walk flickering with unfocused flame into the night.

Then Arun throws up.

Most swift of all are the Cardamom Mountains.

There was once a great trade route east through Cardamom, to the Tax Haven of the Others. But the Neighbors magnanimously protect the Sons of Kambu from the Others (and most particularly from any haven from taxation). They closed the trade route.

Where once there were broad clear pathways through the forest, Kai and his acolytes have to hack their way through vines, undergrowth, and stinging thorns.

After two months of hacking, mosquitoes, bad water, and ill wind, it becomes evident to even the meanest intelligence that something out of the ordinary is going on.

Steep paths snake their way up a hill, only to end up back at the bottom of the valley.

Kai's followers turn a corner and find that the last man in their caravan is now walking ahead of them all.

Kai cuts his name in the bark of a tree with one long flowing sword-stroke.

They pass that sign again two days later. Kai throws down his sword.

"We stop walking," he says. He sits in meditation thinking about what has happened.

Even trees mislead,
The worn path bends the wrong way
Undo cries the air, undo says the wise men,
And the trees open up.

Kai stands up and shouts "Undo!"

Up and down the valleys, the air echoes "Undo!"

Trees crackle as they unwind, and stand straight. Paths grind as they heave their way back into shape, finally going somewhere.

The air yawns open from relief, being allowed to stretch at last.

Suddenly the path leads to a building, a simple building of red varnished wood. It stands out over the hillside on stilts. Beyond it, on the other side of the valley, rice terraces rise up thousands of feet.

A dog barks. The young nobles advance.

Kai groans. He sinks to the ground and starts to weep. Arun goes to him, takes him by the shoulders and his hands leap back. Arun says, "He's not hot! The spell is broken."

There is a whole village built on stilts over the hillside. There are shaky wooden walkways and windmills. The rice fields go up this side of the valley as well, forming a natural amphitheater. Sounds boom and roll or seem very close to your ear.

The air smells of mud and sweat and smoke.

Kai shudders, then chuckles, and stands up. "There's no magic here."

From out of the houses creep people with terrible broken teeth, spots, and age marks. The younger and more able-bodied of them stand with swords that look like pig iron, cast once and never smelted. Some of the men bear flint scythes that will shatter at the first blow.

"Hello," they say, glumly. "What do you want? We've not got much to take, we can tell you that for free."

Kai smiles with inner peace. "We want to see your machine."

They grin. They need dental magic urgently.

They lead Kai to a stone wall that shores up the cliff face. The whole village is in imminent danger of collapse.

Far below is a circular valley, where perhaps once a whirlpool wore away the rock. In that cavity, as red as tiles, a huge coiled tube stretches at least two hundred arms' lengths across.

"You're welcome to *try* to loot that," the locals say.

"Please," adds one of them, and they all laugh.

"Turning the thing off would be a start," one of them mutters.

The machine is smooth and huge, like a serpent that has swallowed its tail so that both ends merge. There is a series of bolts closing what look like long sideways windows. From this great height, Kai can see that along the top, one window has been left open and unbolted. What look like stars dance over the opening.

"It's never been properly turned on," says one old man.

"Don't give him any ideas," grunts a younger. He uses the tip of his little finger to pump out gross amounts of pus from his ear.

The air and the distance all whisper like defeat.

Kai slumps to the ground. "We can't move it," he says. "We can't take it to fight the Neighbors."

It is a year to the day since he set out on his quest.

Do whatever is necessary

At the gates of the royal palace, Kai hugs another Neighbor. He burns the man right through the middle.

This time Arun maintains his countenance. "Almost surgical," he says.

Kai's noble followers dance through the gates more silently than settling dust.

Two court officials approach in deep discussion, wearing purple cloth with gold embroidered flowers.

With a whisper, swords slip through them. The cuts are so thin that blood seeps slowly. The bodies are arranged on cushions to look as though they are still in conversation.

Kai and his men whisper into the Sycophancy Salon. The Staircase of Effective Entrances sweeps up to the Royal Chambers.

Two strong Sons of Kambu guard the top of the steps.

Kai somersaults up the staircase, gathering speed like an avalanching boulder. He rolls to his feet and elbows their swords out of their hands. He holds his own sword close to their throats. He has lost focus and the sword, even its handle, glows cherry red.

"You are Kambu," says Kai. "We don't want to hurt you. We are here to defeat the Neighbors. To do that we must get the King out of their clutches. Are you with us?"

They say yes. All sons of Kambu, they say, want the King safe from influence, and out of Neighborly attention.

The noble warriors surf up the balustrade of the staircase.

Among them is Arun. "I'll take that," he says and relieves one of the Kambu of his fine imperial sword.

A sword must be either inherited from a master or taken in battle. Arun grins and licks the sword's black laminate.

"Now, master," he says. "I look to you for training."

In the royal apartments, the rooms are stuffed with foreigners—Neighborly advisers who run things, observers who write interesting reports, or guest troops who kill the enemy, i.e., the sons of Kambu.

Kai and his ten are like a bladed whirlwind. They spin through the rooms, harvesting heads.

When they are done, five of the Ten stand guard outside the main doors.

Five plus Arun and his master go into the royal chamber.

The King is hunched over a tiny spinning steamball. "Remarkable this, don't you think?" he says, and only then turns around to look at the swordsmen. "But what use is it, I wonder?"

He is a beautiful man, tall, willowy, and graceful, with long thin fingers that look as though they could pluck heartfelt melodies out of the air. His eyes are full of sympathy for their plight. "Have you come to kill me? You will be reborn as toads."

"We've come," says Kai, "to take you home."

The King flutes some kind of mellifluous reply. It is muffled in Kai's ears. He cannot quite hear what the King says, rather as though his majesty was talking with his mouth full.

Then Kai remembers that he is immune to magic. This includes the magic of charm, of sweetness, of sympathy—the magic of kindly deception.

Whuh, whuh, whuh, the King seems to say. It is not entirely meaningful to say that Kai squints with his ears, but that is more or less what he does. He can just make out the King saying, "You surely don't want to hurt your King. It's a very humble thing to be a King. Your body mirrors the health of the nation. Hurt me and you hurt yourself."

The young men are drawn. "No of course not, Father. Not hurt you. Help you. Get you away from these Neighbors."

"Ah, but these Neighbors are our friends. . . ." Kai lets the words unfocus back into *blah, blah, blah.*

Everyone is entranced. Kai keeps his eyes on them all as he steps carefully backward. There is a cabinet with crystal doors full of items under purple silk. Kai looks, then strikes. His sword cuts through the bolts.

"Oh dear," says the King. "I've been meaning to change those locks."

Kai gathers up the things. The King's voice is entirely unintelligible to him now. It drones like a call to prayers.

His own men turn around and face him, swords drawn.

Kai has a voice as well. "Nobody will hurt you, Father. Isn't that so, boys? We don't want to hurt the King. But he will have to follow these."

The King's eyes go wide and tearful.

Kai hugs to himself the Sacred Sword, the palm-leaf Royal Chronicles, the cymbals, the earrings, and the cup.

"All of this paraphernalia means you are King. Without it you can't give titles and buy the support of nobles. Without it you can't work your magic. Where these go, you have to follow. Or you are not King."

The King falters, looks sad and lonely, an old man, too frail for travel. What Kai has said is true.

Kai strides out of the room with all the symbols of his power and the King trots after him. Kai can make out his tones of sad complaint. Kai's own men stand their ground. Their swords are still drawn.

"Earplugs," sighs Kai. He snatches up four candles, tosses them into the air, and slices them into eight with his sword. He catches them between his toes, and they light themselves from his heat.

Then Kai spins himself into the air, hugging the royal paraphernalia to his chest. Before even his trained acolytes can ward him off, Kai has filled their ears with melted wax.

"Now you can sing as sweetly as you like, King," he smiles.

His acolytes shake their heads, blink in confusion and then shrug.

Kai says, "King, if you call for help, I'll spit down your throat. Your vocal cords will be scalded and you'll never speak again."

Then he and his men jog through rooms soaked in blood and out into the courtyard. All of them run up the walls of the Palace including Arun although he carries a King.

Heroism is revealed not by victory but by defeat

The Neighbors fall for it.

They need the docile Kambu King. He is over-subtle where he should be bold, precise where he should be roughshod but quick.

The horrors of the Palace have shown them that they face a formidable adversary. They abide.

Finally, they hear where the King's new forced capital can be found.

Cardamom.

And so, drawn, they march their magic army into the trap.

Kai stands on the new battlements of what he has renamed the City of Likelihood. Air moves, eagles fly overhead, and far down below at the mouth of the valley, the Army of Neighbors marches.

They number only three thousand. All of them are already through the narrow pass, which looks particularly ragged at the top. The hillside is crowned with heaps of rubble, with logs among them.

Kai smiles.

The Sons of Kambu face the Neighbors in ranks across the valley floor.

This is no ragtag revolt of corvéed labor. These Kambu troops wear armor and carry weapons. The smithies of Likelihood have been busy. The corvéed labor hobbled hundreds of miles to find the new capital, but they have had time to rest and time to train.

Many sons of nobles have come as well, because there is no way for them to get a title but to receive it from the King.

And in flaming orange is a battalion of Kambu warrior monks. They have crossed into Likelihood as well, crying, Undo!

The King stands beside Kai now. Without his magic, the King looks stooped, wizened, and frail. "Are you sure this is a good idea?"

Kai smiles.

Someone must have given the Neighbors the word Undo. That someone hopes to be rescued.

The best argument is action, not words. Kai does not answer him.

Down from the battlements to the valley floor are fine threads of silk, invisible to the Neighbors because they are too real.

Kai utters one piercing shriek, like an eagle's call.

On the distant hillsides, over the pass, teams of oxen drag the great logs. The tree trunks turn sideways, which is all that is needed.

The trees will open.

Oxen hauled those stones up the hillside, but love spurred on their masters.

You could say therefore, thinks Kai, that love moves mountains.

The rocks pour down.

Slowly like a lady's hand putting down her fan, the rubble falls the great distance. The Neighbors have time to turn, elbow each other, and clutch their sides. Their thin laughter wafts across the distance.

How stupid, the Neighbors seem to say. These Kambu wanted to rain down rocks on our heads and waited until we were all through!

The beauty of the Machine, thinks Kai, is that it is *not* a presence. It is an absence. There is nothing for the Neighbors or any of their mages to sense.

Then a cry goes up from the Neighbors.

They have cast their first spell and it hasn't worked.

The stones settle with a crash and a raising of dust, closing the pass. The Neighbors cannot get out.

There is no magic here, only swords. The Neighbors are unarmed.

The ten acolytes of Hero Kai leap from the battlement walls onto the single silken threads, and they slide down. They balance holding out two singing swords in each hand, outstretched like wings. They somersault onto the ground.

Then they whirligig their way across the plain, spinning into the soft and real flesh of the Neighbors.

The monks, the farmers, and the sons without titles advance.

To be sure of victory, the Neighbors sent three thousand of their finest warrior sorcerers.

Within five minutes, all of them are dead.

Again, Kai cries like an eagle and flings his swords over his head. Blood whips from the blades in midair as if the weapons themselves are bleeding.

The Sons of Kambu cheer. They run to Kai, and pat his back. They dip and hold up their hands in prayer toward him. Some of them prostrate themselves on the ground to him, but laughing, he shakes his head, and helps them stand.

"We have all won!" he cries, and all the valley tolls like a giant bell of stone, ringing with many voices.

Kai laughs and turns, and he runs up the silken thread. True he slows somewhat near the summit, but he gains the top of the battlements and the citizens roar all the louder.

He hops down from the wall in front of the King. The King looks like a skeleton.

Kai knows from the man's face. He had thought his only duty was to stay in office. This King liked the Neighbors because they kept him in his palace.

"You are a King for real now," says Kai. "Better start ruling and stop consuming."

The King gives a sad, sick smile. Kai seizes his hand, pulls him to the top of the battlements, and holds the King's hand aloft. All Likelihood cheers its King and all his sacred paraphernalia.

The fiction is maintained.

You will have to lie to others, but never lie to yourself

It has been a year without wonders.

The mountain rice paddies require unending maintenance. Gates have to be opened to let them drain. The gates must be closed promptly or the terraces dry out. Heavy stones must be rolled back into place. Spills of precious topsoil must be scooped back into the fold. The replanting of nursery rice keeps people bent over for a week. The ligaments in the smalls of their backs tear.

The monsoons are late and small. Water has to be pumped up from the valley floor.

Too many people crowd in and there are disputes. The original villagers had no system of land registration. The newcomers steal their terraces only to have them stolen in turn.

So the King assigns fields. What happens when those assigned fields dry out and there are no more fields to register?

The King is pleased. He looks less of a man than ever, like someone recovering from malaria, but he smiles. "Of course, in the old days, I could have called up rain like that." He snaps his fingers.

Kai's reply is placid. "Now you have the opportunity to be responsible in a new way. You will have to join us in thought."

The King chuckles. "Responsible? The King is not supposed to be responsible. The King just is the king. Unless he is prevented from embodying the health of the country."

"You never did. You embodied the disease."

Kai goes for a walk.

He walks through the court that has gathered around the King. It is thriving, full of superior people in blue cloth with gold flowers. They gather murmuring in distinguished groups, and turn and mutter as Kai passes them.

He is relieved to be free of them. He clambers down the wooden ladder that is the entrance to the royal palace. The palace is one of the original, graceful, dilapidated village buildings. He likes it. What better way to say that here everyone shares the wealth and the labor? He himself plants rice.

Kai loves this new Kingdom. Everywhere he sees the work of God, God who hates miracles because they are so unfair.

He smiles at a beautiful Daughter of Kambu. She grins a strange close-lipped smile that looks neither serene nor spontaneous. She is smiling so that she does not show her rotten teeth.

Kai walks through the market. The Neighbors harass caravans bound for Likelihood. The old trade route is kept open only through continuing force of arms. The noble sons who guard the passes come home wrapped in silk for cremation.

The high mountain steppes are good for only one crop of rice each year. They don't support fruit trees. The stall owners sell no longan, rambutan, or jackfruit. The market stinks of rotten old bananas, and aged mushy pineapples. People cover their faces when they walk through it. Everyone looks very lean and fit.

They still greet each other beautifully, and the sun still shines on this glorious day.

It doesn't rain.

The amphitheater of paddies all around them echoes with the sound of labor — axes chopping stone, men grunting as they pump water, an argument because one man threw all his cleared pebbles into another man's field.

Kai himself has tiny new brown spots all over the back of his hand. "I'm getting old," he tells himself. "It is the natural way."

At the far side of the filthy market is one of the hastily constructed new houses, built from cast-off timber and tumbles of stone. Sons of Kambu are not used to building houses out of stone. They are not used to the winter wind that blows through the chinks.

Inside the house, a man is screaming in pain.

Hero Kai does not need to climb the ladder to see in. He can duck his head into the low shelter.

"Can I help?" he asks. He expects surprised pleasure at being visited by a Hero in the making. He imagines polite bowing and hands held up in prayer. A middle-aged woman whose swollen belly is popping the buttons of her shirt looks at him sullenly.

The old man, quivering, sits up. "No you can't!" he says. "Go away, go away and take my pain with you! May it eat your joints!"

Kai is taken aback. "I am so sorry you are ill."

The man shouts again. "I am not an opportunity for you to earn merit!"

Kai feels the blood in his cheeks prickle.

The man drops back. "Curse you, God, for accepting all my offerings and letting me die! Curse you, God, for creating pain. Go away, God, with all your high thoughts and sharp rocks. Blast every living slug, mosquito, spider, snake, civet, all of the thieving, biting things you created! Die, God! Like me! Die!"

Kai feels deafened by the words. He staggers back.

He turns and sees a ring of people around him. They are all grinning smugly. A young man with a particularly nasty smile starts to recite what sounds like a Chbap.

> Oh great wise man with all your strength
> Too big, you crush us like a mill
> Too big, you soak up all our pride
> Too strong, you sit on us like an ox.
> Too clever, you take away all our comfort
> Just because you do not need it.

The circle of people all chuckle. Kai reaches for his sword. He stops himself.

"I will think about what you say," he says. And waits for a respectful response.

"What will you *do*?" asks the smug young man.

Kai acknowledges that with a stiff shake of the head. He feels awkward and foolish as he walks away.

"Die, Big Man! Die!" screams the man in the house.

Kai draws Arun to one side, and takes him for a walk out into the hills where spies can be easily seen.

"It is the way of the world, Arun. You offer people good things, but still they will always complain. To rule, you have to scare them as well as flatter them. We have not used fear. You and the Ten, go out among the town and drink some of these terrible fermentations people brew from the rotten fruit. Pretend to get drunk. Listen to who criticizes."

Kai sighs. "Then we will round them all up and pile stones on top of them."

Organized retreat is a form of advance

Another army pauses at the top of the fallen rubble.

Sunlight glints on metal. They are armored, and some of the armor is Kambu. Banners in the shape of flames flutter in the wind. Gongs and blaring trumpets signal some kind of advance.

The King sits cross-legged on the battlements consulting the Oracle, which of course no longer works here. The yarrow stalks clatter meaninglessly onto the paving. "It seems we have visitors," the King says, croaking and wheedling with an old man's voice.

Kai glares into the distance.

People have formed a long line along the rice terraces over the pass. They appear to be prying free large sections of the cliff face. Huge flat plates of stone break away, land, rock, and settle.

Something like a staircase is being built down from the top of the dam.

This time the Neighbors know magic will not protect them. And they seem to have been joined by Kambu allies.

As he did two years ago, Kai keens like a eagle. It is the call to arms.

There is only silence. A baby wails somewhere.

He keens again and again. Likelihood remains still. Kai hears only wind in response.

The King chuckles and shakes his head.

Kai turns and the King's courtiers block the ladder down. Kai looks at the beautiful superior cloth and imagines it sliced cleanly.

These are not soldiers. Kai puts his hand on the handle of one of his swords, and they flinch and step back. They will not fight him, but they are far from harmless. He walks forward and they step aside to let him through. He beheads them all anyway.

Then he saunters back to the King, hoists him to his feet, and jams a sword to this throat.

"You have the benefit of one escape, because you are my King. But I don't respect you and I have no use for you. Next time, you're dead."

The skinny old man quivers in his grasp bending backward over the edge of the wall.

Kai looks and counts. He sees the Neighbors whose helmets are round with a spike on the top, and he notes the lotus blossom helmets of his own people. He counts them. Superior people outside Likelihood still depend on the King for their titles. They have come to get him, to take him back, to reclaim their superiority.

One thousand he counts. Estimate another thousand there. Three thousand?

There are more Kambu in this army than there are Neighbors.

He darts down the steps and into the Palace.

He can trust his secret police, most of them. He can trust the Ten. He needs nobody else with him.

Underneath the royal palace, on the slope amid its stilts, there hangs a chute for washing waste down over the hills. Kai called it the Tipping of the Balance, and it is the agreed meeting place in case of disaster.

The Ten are all there, with Arun.

Kai explains why they are not fighting. "We did not set out on this great scheme to become killers of the Sons of Kambu."

He is just a little surprised, just a little disappointed, when there is an urgent murmur of assent from even his most loyal.

"Go pack. Gather anyone you see along the way whom we have marked as Likely. Ask them to come with us, but do not wait. Our aim now is to be long gone by the time the new army gets here."

"But the Machine. . . ."

Kai sighs and marvels at his own powers of acceptance. "The Machine is doomed."

All clatter away except for Arun. Arun says, "My only friend is you. The only person I respect is you. I will be with you until the end." The two men hug.

"Brother," declares Kai. This is a promotion.

They go back to the battlements, stepping over a few heads.

The wave of troops advances. They recite the Loyalty Chbap.

> Respect the King, for the job of the King
> Is to eat the country.
> He eats the country so that it can be processed
> Through his sacred alimentary canal.
> It comes out rich fertilizer for us to live on.

Kai chuckles. "And the country is shit."

The loyal Ten come back, bringing, perhaps thirty Likely others with them.

"Enough," says Kai. And with measured pace they begin to climb.

From high in the hills, they look down on misty distance. Elephants have lumbered up and over the heap of stone, hauling a battering ram. Great silk-cotton logs slam repeatedly into the side of the Machine.

Kai can hear the breaking of the clay even from this great distance. A sparkling vapor dazzles its way out of the new mouth. It washes over the elephants and they burn and shrivel. Their great legs twist, collapsing into heaps of ash.

Even on the high mountainside where the Ten stand, the air starts to buzz unpleasantly like a blow to the elbow.

Kai makes one sharp shrill cry. The fat under his skin seethes up and he burns again.

He contorts for a moment, stretching his neck, shoulders and arms. He shivers his way back into normal standing position, mastering himself and the fire.

"Now it's their turn to cheer," he says. He starts to climb again.

Only Arun can lay a comforting hand on his burning flesh.

Become evil to do good

A year later only the Ten are left.

They live in a cave, surviving on what they can hunt. They shiver in furs and spend the long dark hours in meditation. A hard life is what they have come to love, and despite all their virtues, they have become hard men. There are few words and no laughter between them.

Except for Arun. Curiously, he has learned how to laugh. He tells jokes to himself, the Ten, and sometimes even to Kai, when he can find him.

"Master, come back. We need you to warm the walls."

Kai has retreated into the high snows. He perches on icy crags, buffeted by howling winds. The snow sputters on his skin and melts in a perfect circle all around him. The rocks he sits on have the dull metallic look of stones in a steam bath. Trails of vapor hiss from them.

"At least you will be very clean," says Arun again. He crouches near Kai with a pot of stew. Already the stew is icy cold, which is how Kai likes it. It cools his throat as he swallows. Arun feeds him with a spoon he himself has chipped out of stone.

Arun sits in the shelter of Kai's warmth, and places the pot of stew on Kai's lap to heat it up. He tries to make conversation.

"You should come and burn the cave clean for us!" Arun says, but the gale drowns out his words.

"To tell you the truth, the Ten all think I am still a slave. I do all the work!" Still no response. Being with Kai now can be lonelier than being without him. Arun eats his boiling hot stew.

The gray sky edges toward blue. Arun cannot be caught out on icy trails at night. Arun hugs Kai, though it sears his hides and makes them stink.

Kai looks pained and saddened, staring at something quite definite in all that swirling cloud and snow.

Arun stands up, shouts good-bye, gets no answer, and then turns and walks into the blizzard.

Kai sits alone. The wind drives the snow sideways. The world gets bluer, almost turquoise.

Then, swelling out of the storm and the hillside comes a giant stranger made of air and hardship, rock and salt, wind and sleet.

The Buddha was tempted by Mala, the World. Mala offered the Buddha kingship, and the power to do good in the real world.

"Well," says the World. "Here's a fine place for a Hero to end up. Happy in your work?"

"I know who you are," says Kai through broken teeth that glow like embers.

"I know a good dentist," says Mala. "I made him myself."

The World sits down and sighs in a showy, airy way. "Now what do I have here?

Oh, cooling ices. They are made in a city called Baghdad. It's a desert town, quite sophisticated, fiercely hot. They have learned how to transport ice and make sweet delights from it that are colder even that this snow. Magic ices, that would soothe your fiery throat."

Kai chuckles puffing out smoke and ash from his burned windpipe. "Go to hell," he says.

"That's where I am. Hell is wherever you are, my friend," says Mala. "Freezing and burning for the rest of your life? Sounds familiar to me. Myself, I prefer comfort, the here and now, and if a little bit of Magic gets us what we most desire, I, the World-as-it-actually-is, don't see any reason to forego it."

"It is not the will of God."

Mala sighs. "I have no idea what the will of God is. And, my would-be Hero, neither do you. By the way, you have not achieved Heroism."

"I know that."

"Think you'll find it in your navel?"

"Better place to look than up your ass."

"My my, we are sharp this morning, aren't we? A year of agony tends to do that to people. How about looking for Heroism in reality?"

"I do."

"Haven't found it, have you? Look, I'm the entire world and I have many places to be at once. So I'll say this once only and quickly. Your aim was *not* to destroy Magic. Your aim was to free your kingdom from the Neighbors. I'm sorry to have to make this clear to you, but the only way to do that in the World is to destroy the Neighbors. So why not take the most direct and intelligent route? Destroy them through Magic?"

Kai sits unmoved, eyes closed. "All I have to do is give up enlightenment."

The World's laughter melds with the sound of the storm. "You are so far from achieving enlightenment! You've killed too many people! You'll be lucky to reborn as a frog!"

Mala stands up, shaking his head. "You are a complete and total failure. I'll leave the ice cream here. Don't worry, it won't melt. Not up here."

It a particularly stinging blast of wind and snow, Mala leaves . . .

. . . Kai . . .

. . . alone.

He finally eats the ice cream.

He stands, and pauses for thought.

"Good?" asks the World.

Kai trots down the hill.

To Arun, he gives the power of wind, to freeze, or dry or scorch. To the Likely Ten he gives in order:

- pestilence,
- sudden rending of flesh,
- blindness and deafness,
- dazed stupidity and cretinism in all its forms,
- sterility and impotence,
- drought and famine,
- age and the death of children,
- disaster: flood, earthquake, accidents of all kinds
- depression and despair

He himself is already Fire, so he gives himself the power of Kings to make things pretty.

Together with Mala, the Likely Ten descend howling on the Neighbors. Kai stands huge and billowing in flame over the capital city.

Fire torches all their wooden buildings, their finely carved palaces, and the beautiful verse inscribed on palm leaves.

The soldiers of the Neighbors fall where they stand, buboes swelling up and bursting under armpits or in their groins. Others are suddenly split into two. Their fathers go deaf and blind, their faithful wives become so stupid they cannot remember their own names. The young men will find they can't get it up. Their horses and elephants all have rabies, and the vaginas of their women blister with new and fatal contagious diseases. All — all — of their children under twelve die; a million children in one night.

Then the sea rises up to swamp their ports and sink their ships. Earthquakes shake their sacred temples into rubble.

Those few Neighbors who are left alive sit down and weep and surrender to dazed despair.

Kai flies on wings of fire and seizes hold of the King of Kambu. "Remember me?" he chuckles brightly.

He seals the body of the King in amber and uses it for his throne. He makes sure that none of the King's sons, cousins, wives, uncles, or nephews are left alive.

"No nonsense this time," Kai declares from his new and sad-eyed throne. "The Commonwealth of the Neighbors is no more. It is a happy part of the Kingdom of the Sons of Kambu. I am their King."

It is Mala, not Arun, who chuckles and pats his shoulder. No hurricanes blew during the conquest.

"We have swallowed you," Kai admits. "You should have considered the possibility when you tried to swallow us. Now, my dear friends and loyal subjects. It is your turn to build a railway."

All the Neighbors are enslaved.

Then do good to earn merit and undo harm

Women become pretty. The bones in their faces shift subtly and slowly at night. Their teeth straighten. They become pregnant, if they want to be.

Every afternoon, predictably, just before the children go to drive the oxen home, it rains. People finish their wholesome lunches listening to the pleasant sounds of rain on the roof.

The fruits on the market stalls are round, with perfect blushes of ripeness, firm enough but sweet. They scent the air.

Old people suddenly notice that they can stand up straight, and that swinging their legs out of the hammock is easier. They find that standing first thing in the morning no longer hurts. They can dance for joy. They can work in the rice fields as the Chbap advise, and they call to their friends cheerily.

And most strangely of all, whenever they recite the Chbap, good things happen.

Kai chuckles to himself and confides in Arun. "I've given them all magic powers. What was wrong about magic was that it bent the rules unfairly for just a few people. Now, everyone has the power of magic. Everyone has the power to do good. They will realize it, but slowly."

"Whereas," says Arun, his smile a bit thin, "you have a monopoly on doing harm."

"Yes. But I don't have to use it."

"Much," says Arun.

Birds sing, the sun shines, people eat but don't get fat. The Neighbors see that Sons of Kambu have a superior way of life, and envy them. "Well, you know my Grandfather was Kambu," they begin to say, as they stagger under the weight of railway ties. "I always put my superior good fortune down to that."

Kambu words sprinkle their speech. The Neighbors begin to recite the Chbap, and lo! their backaches cease.

"We have a lot to learn from these Sons of Kambu," they agree.

Their few surviving daughters start to wear Kambu fashion. Their eyes follow noble Sons with alluring brightness.

And then the strangest thing of all comes to pass.

To earn merit, Kai orders the rebuilding of temples.

The stones are piled back more or less as they were. Kai is a follower of the Dharma, but he honors the gods that underlie that more clear-headed faith, as he sees it.

All the artisans of the Neighbors are now either dead or senile, so good Kambu craftsmen restore the temples to Vishnu, Siva, and even Brahma. The artists love doing this, for underneath the newer religion, the old gods survived in the hearts of the people. Fine new statues of the gods are made and the monks who were the rivals of Kai are given new jobs. They get to enrobe and feed the statues.

The new enlarged kingdom smells of honey.

The old gods come back.

It starts quietly at first. Whispers are heard in cool stone galleries. The shawls and garlands of flowers that drape the statues flutter, with the wind surely, but as if the stone arm supporting them had moved.

Water poured over the linga and the yoni tastes delicious, poised between sweet and savory. The purified water has the power to restore even Neighbor slaves to health. All anyone has to do to receive a blessing is drink and swear loyalty to the Gods and their earthly representative, King Kai the Merciful.

The temple oracles find that their ingenuity is no longer taxed. They no longer have to invent orotund but ambiguous answers to questions. Instead their heads are thrown back and a godlike voice whispers out of them. Sometimes their listeners look overjoyed by the answer, sometimes they are plunged into despair. But they no longer look baffled.

The Sons of Kambu never quite stopped believing in even older religions. For them, everything has a spirit—a house, a tree, or even a stone.

The food left in spirit houses is found suddenly eaten. The flowers in the beds stir and creep forward, conquering more waste ground. Roofs repair themselves and house fronts seem to adopt cheerful smiling faces.

Finally, at least to superior persons and Brahmins, the gods themselves begin to speak.

"More," the gods ask. They have a great way with simplicity in speech. More sweetmeats, more incense, more garlands, more rice. A little gold or a new temple would be appropriate.

"Well," sniffs Kai, to wealthy dependents. "You heard what the gods told you. Build them a temple."

It is a good way to keep his nobles occupied and leave them no extra cash for private armies.

Suddenly there are hospitals and rest stations for travelers. New roads are built. The King is quick to point out to the gods that roads are necessary if worshippers are to bring offerings.

Roads are also necessary for trade.

A little grudgingly perhaps, the gods do some good. Strong trees, healthy rice, more wildlife to forage, fish in the sea, calm trade routes, and boats that do not leak. Things prosper even more.

"This is a really good deal for you," the gods point out to Kai.

"And for you," he smiles back.

Mala is happiest of all. "I surrender to the superiority of the gods," the World says and keeps himself in the background. The birds sing sweetly.

Heroism is completed by inaction

Late at night, Kai wakes up with Arun's sword at his throat.

A howling gale fills the room and pins Kai to his bed, pushing all his fire down onto the stone mattress.

Arun wants to talk.

He strokes Kai's flaming hair with one hand. "What," he asks Kai, "do you think you're doing? If you swallow the Neighbors, you need to consider the possibility that someone else will turn around and swallow you."

"Arun," says Kai in a tone of voice that embodies the realization that he should have expected this moment to come from him. "Of course I've considered it."

"Of course. But you take no action. You still have a problem taking action, after all these years. But only I know that." Arun lightly plants a kiss on Kai's fiery cheek. He waits for a response. Kai still takes no action.

Arun smiles at him. "Scared old man," he says affectionately. "Who do you think these gods are who are showing up wanting handouts and threatening to turn off the rain if they don't get it? How long do you think they will let you rule?"

"Until I die. They are gods and can afford to be patient."

"No, they can't. Nothing is more fragile than faith."

"Are you warning me of danger, or asking me to retire? Or just threatening to kill me?"

"All three," says Arun. "These gods of yours get bored. They do terrible things. They send plagues just to keep us in line, and make us pray and give more offerings."

"Sounds like the Ten."

"Oh, we are human. They are not. We can still sympathize. They consume. Poor people always get consumed."

"That is the way of the World," sighs Kai.

"Friend of yours, is he?" Arun asks.

"Yes."

Arun goes still. He strokes Kai's head. "You have been serving everything we are taught to shun. So have I."

"Well, there is no guarantee that what we were taught was true. How long can you lie on top of me with a sword at my throat?"

"Until we both die," says Arun, passion in his eyes.

Kai chuckles. "You are so like me when I was young."

Then he says it again in despair. "You are the closest thing I have to a son."

Arun says the obvious. "Then. Make me King."

Kai considers. "There is no such thing as ex-King who is still alive. I have another proposal. I really like this idea by the way. I make you Regent. You rule here. And I? I go on retreat and I try to recover a little bit of merit before I die. Enough to get me out of hell and perhaps be reborn as an insect or a slug."

"You will declare me your legitimate son, fathered in your youth. Your flesh and blood, your rightful heir. You will give me the title of Crown Prince."

"You're making demands and all you have is a sword."

"No, Father. I have your love. And, you don't want to be stuck in hell or reborn as a slug, and I don't want that for you either. I want to see Kai restored to himself."

They look at each other a moment, pat each other's arms, chuckle and sit up.

"What will you do as Regent?" Kai asks.

"I'll make us all Buddhists. But I'll let the worship of the old gods continue. I'll starve them slowly. And I'll make sure that dear old Mala is convinced that I will always give him his due."

"Like father, like son."

"Not always," says Arun.

The next day King Kai declares publicly that Arun is his natural son and heir. He makes him Crown Prince, and announces his retirement from the capital. Arun will rule in his stead. Kai passes him the Sacred Sword. There is wild, ecstatic cheering at this delightful development.

There are some hours of light ceremonials, a bit of singing and dancing and drinking holy water. Then Arun mounts the dais. He looks down at the sad-eyed throne and says, "Get this terrible thing out of here and cremate it with honors."

Kai packs what he took with him on that first quest nine years ago. The Likely Ten, now terrible to behold, safely escort Kai to the gates of the royal precinct, just to be sure that he really has gone. With every step he chuckles.

He walks across the fields, toward the lake and across the kingdom. Everywhere people treat him with respect and kindness. This is due in part to a new Chbap that Arun commissioned and paid to have chanters repeat.

> Imitate the wisdom of the Great King Kai
> Know when to pass responsibility to your son
> Depart in good cheer
> For that quieter kingdom of the world
> Where wisdom is found in small things.

Villagers recognize him, and beg him to stay to chant at weddings. He does so in good cheer. No one accuses him of anything. Women who remember how handsome he once was place garlands of flowers around his neck, and hold up their hands in prayer.

He finally arrives at the place where the paths wind back on themselves, and the trees close over. Undo! he says again.

He finds the City of Likelihood, deserted and forlorn.

He goes to the simple house of unsteady stone in which another old man died in pain. Kai unrolls a mat, and finds a forgotten bowl and spoon. Even after all these years with some of the dikes fallen, sparse rice still whispers in the thousand paddies. They climb toward heaven like stairs.

He gathers rice and stores it, some for seed, for there will be only one crop. The many deserted wooden houses will provide him with firewood. He takes the opportunity to prepare for death and accept the world as it is, and finds that there is surprisingly little to contemplate.

He draws in a breath, and goes down into the valley to carry out his plan.

He goes to the Machine. He is able to step through the breakage into its huge hollow coil. He climbs up the scaffolding and flaps the broken reed panels that once powered its engines. Some clay, some reed, some time—that will be all it needs.

The Machine was built in a dead whirlpool because of the centuries of sediment deposited there. Finding clay is easy. So is finding firewood. Kai hauls huge evergreens down from the hills and lets them dry until they are tinder. He touches them and they catch fire, for Magic now rules everywhere, even in Likelihood. He bakes new sections of tube. He weaves the reed into new blades for windmills.

The machine takes shape, the panels turn in the wind, and Kai sighs with satisfaction. He remembers the original inhabitants.

It's never been properly turned on.

Don't give him ideas!

Too late to avoid that, I'm afraid.

Kai once asked, "What would it do?"

"Buzz the world," said one old man.

Kai slides shut portal after portal. The old machine hums. Kai remembers the one bolted portal at the top that was left open.

Kai the warrior monk stands back and then runs up and over the round smooth sides.

Over the last open portal dances something that looks like stars. Kai, the man of magicked fire, reaches through them, pulls the bolt shut, and locks it. He survives the sparkling blast, where elephants could not. All it does is quench his fire like cooling water.

And all the World is deprived of Magic.

Mala descends howling in rage and grief and betrayal, and Kai smiles at him. Just after his giant wings drop off, Mala melts harmlessly into the ground, personified no longer.

No more miracles.

In all the temples in the lands of Kambu, the voices of the gods whisper once like dust before being blown away. Then their halls are empty. The statues are wrapped, the oracles speak, but with voices that in their hearts they know are their own.

Kai is released for one last time from the fire in his body. He has changed the whole world forever. He made the world in which we now live. Which can hardly be called heroism completing itself through inaction.

Soon after, he gets sick and dies alone in agony in the tiny house of wood and stone.

And what of heroism?

Well the Rules don't understand it, but they sound good, and at least they don't say that you become a hero by being kind and doing your duty.

Heroism consists of the moment that you are cheered by thousands. Heroism resides in the eyes of other people, and what you can get them to believe.

It can also be secret, without praise, and known to no one except you. That kind is a lot less fun.

Heroism, if you want it, resides nowhere, and everywhere, in the air, whether it buzzes with magic or not. In the hard, merciless world of Likelihood, there is no meaning, except in moments. There are also no Rules.

The old gods had been unstitched into ordinary molecules. The pretty magic of Kings no longer worked. Kai's new railway, roads, and cities were an enticement. Steamboats arrived from the West, bearing cannons and ambitious, likely people.

The Souls of Drowning Mountain

Jack Cady was a truck driver, high-tree climber, teacher, and philosopher, as well as the author of eleven novels, five story collections, and the history The American Writer. *He was emeritus writer in residence from Pacific Lutheran University. His novella, "The Night We Buried Road Dog," won the Nebula Award and the Bram Stoker Award. His collection,* The Sons of Noah *won the World Fantasy Award, and his novel,* Inagehi *won the Philip K. Dick Award. He also received a Distinguished Teaching Award from his university. His collection,* Ghosts of Yesterday, *was published in 2002 and his novel/memoir,* The Rules of '48 *was published in 2003. Cady died in 2004.*

"The Souls of Drowning Mountain" was originally published in the anthology Taverns of the Dead.

—E.D.

Mountains in eastern Kentucky have names: Black Mountain, Mingo Mountain, Hangar Mountain, Booger Mountain, and, among a thousand others, Drowning Mountain, which rises above a hollow where sits Minnie's Beer Store. Both mountain and store carry tales, and I'll tell but one. It says too much, maybe, about folks helpless beyond all help, and angry as sullen fires. There will be however, some satisfying murders.

When I first saw Drowning Mountain these many years ago I was "full of piss and vinegar" as old folks used to say. Thought I knew it all. Had knocked off four years of military duty, then worked my way through college. Took a job with a government agency that was partly in the business of welfare, and partly in sanctimonious advice. My assignment was a railroad town in southeast Kentucky.

I'd seen my share of bad stuff in the bars of Gloucester and in Boston's Scollay Square. I'd seen green water over the flying bridge of a cutter. I'd seen fire at sea. I'd dealt with the dead and dying; figured I could handle whatever came.

The day I arrived trains hooted, ladies gossiped in summer heat while fanning themselves on front porches. They stayed away from town. Hatred, downtown, boiled along the streets like ball lightning. It dawned on me that I was the only man in sight who wasn't wearing a pistol.

"We're in the middle of a coal war," my new boss told me. "Keep your head down and stay polite." His name was Bobby Joe and he was from around there. He'd done army time. Rail-skinny, shrewd as a razorback, but smiling. After the army time he'd come back to the hills. Almost everybody from the hills returns sooner or later.

Bobby Joe assigned me a secretary named Sarah Jane, also from around there. She called me Mister James, not Jim, and we did not warm toward each other for weeks and weeks. Sarah Jane was thirtyish, overweight, pale beneath tan freckles, wore frumpish house dresses, and there was nothing about her that would make any preacher claim her a candidate for heaven. She knew her job front and back. I admired her, but didn't understand her anger.

There seemed no end to everybody's anger. My experience with middlewest small towns and large eastern cities meant nothing. I understood ghettos, poverty, welfare, rich bastards, cops, especially rich bastards and cops.

Yet, nothing matched up. There wasn't a kitty-cat's-chance in a dog pound that I could understand Minnie's Beer Store or Drowning Mountain.

"Walk easy," Bobby Joe told me. He spoke slow and southern, but in complete control. "If you bust ass you're courting trouble." He kept me on a short leash for two months. I warmed a chair behind a desk and talked to old men and tired women.

Then Bobby Joe turned me over to a field rep named Tip. We visited small towns, took hardship-claims and gave advice. We visited people who were shut in. When we drove along thin and rutted sideroads we changed from white shirts to chambray shirts, because men in white shirts looked like revenue agents. Men in white shirts got shot.

What thoughts came to pass? These: This is not real. No one lives this way. This place is straight out of medieval times.

Tip was from around there. He looked more like a hill farmer than a government agent. Lank, with longish hair, thin mouth. He could talk tough as barbed wire, and yet the old people we dealt with were crazy about him. "Tell you about Drowning Mountain," he said one day. "Maybe you'll understand why I'm pissed-off ninety percent of the time."

We were outside of Manchester, Kentucky, scouting around the top of a ridge called Pigeon's Roost. Huge broadleaf trees covered the hillside, tangles of bramble, little wisps of smoke on a hot summer day. Smoke, probably from stills.

Tip had a way of explaining the world by telling stories. "Didn't used to be called Drowning Mountain," he told me. "But it sure as sweet-Jesus earned its name."

Even today, all these years later, it breaks my heart to think of it. I'll condense what Tip said.

These mountains are limestone with seams of coal. Sometimes the seam goes straight into the mountain, but not often. It usually angles in and the coal shaft follows one or more seams. Those shafts are propped with timbers, and generally slate lies above the coal. Take out the coal, slate falls, even sometimes, when propped.

Because the limestone is porous there's always ground water. In those days, when miners hit a narrow seam they sometimes had to lie on their backs in the water, underground and between rock, pushing shovels backward over their shoulders to draw out loose coal that had been blasted. In mining camps, even little boys knew how to set a charge of dynamite.

Were these men screwed? You bet they were. Mine owners used up men worse than bad generals killing their own armies. Coal camps were the kinds of hells that made chain gangs look like a vacation. Men actually did owe their souls to the company store. Even if men had enough imagination to leave town they had no money. They were paid in scrip. Plus, they didn't know any better. Lots of those men had gone into the mines at age 12.

So, in a coal camp, way, way back in World War I, they had driven a shaft deep into the heart of the mountain. When the seams played out the shaft was abandoned. Twenty-six years later, no one remembered the shaft was there. The coal company opened a seam on the other side of the mountain. The seam drove in on much the same angle as the old shaft because of a fracture in the rock.

Miners blasted their way in, propped the slate, drove deeper, and deeper; and on a fatal day blasted through to the old, forgotten shaft, which had filled with ground water. Seven men died that day, drowning in darkness in the middle of a mountain.

"Ah, no," I told Tip.

"Helluva note," he said. "Makes you sorta sick, don't it?" Tip was the kind of guy, who if he had been a preacher, would have been a good one. He would not have been hellfire, only tough and kind.

"The reason I tell the story," he said, "is because next week we go to Drowning Mountain."

It was a miserable weekend. The office closed. Nothing to do except keep my head down and wait. The town sat in a dry county. Each election, preachers and bootleggers went to the polls and kept it dry. A wet county was just next door and Tennessee was not all that far off, but there was nothing going on in those directions. I hung out at the drugstore, slurped coffee, listened to gossip.

The main rich bastard in town was named Sims. He ramrodded a coal corporation. Sims was one of those sanitary pieces of crap that wear summer suits and carry perfumed hankies as they walk across the faces of dying men.

Sims's chief armament was a guy named Pook. Pook had the reputation of a real nut-buster. Pook was an actual killer with at least two murders notched to his gun. Gossip said the sheriff was afraid of him.

The two showed up Sunday afternoon, walking Main Street like they owned it. Sims said, "howdy," or even, "howdy, neighbor" to grim-faced men who stepped aside to let him pass. Sims had a bald spot, a sizeable gut, and dainty little feet. He seemed cheery. He had jowls like a pig, and a sneer that could push people backward. On Sunday afternoon he went into the bank. The banker came down and opened up just for him.

Pook stood outside the bank. He looked like Godzilla with a haircut. Or a better description, maybe: he looked like a storm trooper, but with a .45 automatic on his hip, not a Mauser. People didn't talk to him. Pook couldn't out-sneer Sims, but his look told folks that he figured them for dog-dump. When Sims came from the bank the two cruised town in a new Cadillac, snubbing everybody; the Cadillac black and shiny.

On Monday morning Sarah Jane tsked. "You take it slow, now," she told me. "Jim."

It was the first time she ever called me anything but mister.

Bobby Joe talked to Tip, real quiet. Both men looked serious.

"What's the war about?" I asked Tip. We left the office and headed for Drowning Mountain.

"The usual," he told me. "Wages, mechanization, it's pitiful." He kind of hunched over the steering wheel. He kept a low profile in the hills. His car was a beat-up Ford made before WWII. "The men only know one kind of work, and there's no other work. They strike in order to go back into the hole at a bit higher pay, which is like asking to jump smack into hell." He paused. "And there's something worse. Stripping."

I'd heard about it. Strip mining was coming into fashion. It destroyed whole mountains. Strip mining made 6000-foot mountains into smoking piles of rubble. Trees gone. Not a stick of vegetation. Only broken rock. Sulfuric acid rose in the air and washed in the streams. Strip mines were profitable because they needed a few machine operators, but no miners.

"There's something else," Tip told me. "Before we get to Minnie's I gotta prepare you." Even though he was the guy in charge, he looked off-guard and hesitant.

"You might meet some people," he told me, "who you won't know, and maybe I won't either, if they're dead or alive. If you want to stay happy take it for granted. Don't try to study it out. Don't back away."

"Why? Come to think of it, Why and What?"

"Dead or alive, all these folks have is each other. They stick together. There's talk of stripping the mountain."

"Sims?"

"Not all rich men are crap, and not all crap-heads are rich. But, yep. Sims." Tip actually looked relieved . . . probably because I didn't make a deal out of that 'dead or alive' business. I'd come to trust Tip, and if he said don't figure on something, it seemed best not to figure. What he said made no sense. For me, it was wait and see.

"I got more to tell," he said. "There's a history."

He explained that Minnie's Beer Store sat in an abandoned coal camp. Old men were sparsely scattered in cabins along the sides of the hills. Most were widowers, but some had young wives because there were no young men for girls to marry. The young men had gone away, some to the Army, some to other coal camps.

Miners, back then, were more spirits than real by age 40. They moved slow as cold molasses because of black lung, silicosis, violent arthritis. Their hair, if they had any, was white and their faces were black. Coal dust gets under the skin. It doesn't even go away in the grave. When bones become dust, they are still tainted with coal.

"So much anger," Tip murmured. "They're furious about being screwed, but most of them don't know how much they're screwed. They don't know how to fight back. So, they're really furious about not knowing." He slowed the car, making a point. "That dead and alive business. It happened at least once before, and it happened during a coal war."

As we approached, rusting rails ran beside a road of thin macadam once laid by the coal company. The hills were covered with hardwood trees, and here at the end of August a little spot of yellow, leaves changing color, appeared amid stands of green. The narrow road was rutted now. Most of the railroad had been torn away and sold for scrap.

"This is the day when government checks arrive." Tip seemed to be talking to himself. "Things might get pretty lively."

"How can that happen?" It was an honest question. I didn't see how anything could get very lively. We were, approximately, forty miles from nowhere.

"These folks live off the land. They trap small game. Sometimes they have to dig roots." Tip was always in control, but he was angry. "Every month we send each of them a lousy thirty-two bucks. Minnie runs a tab. She cashes their checks. They pay up their owes, mostly for canned goods and liniment. Then they buy a pack of factory-made cigarettes, called tightrolls, and drink. One day a month they get to act like men who don't scratch roots and roll tobacco in newsprint. Around here, that's the main and only use of a beer joint."

Electric lines from earlier days still ran into the hollow, but not to all the cabins. Here and there shelves of rock hovered above what looked like shallow caves. "The people dig out coal for heat," Tip told me. "At least the people who are not too old."

When we turned off the road and up a rutted lane to Minnie's Beer Store, Tip came off the gas. We coasted to a stop. "It looks," he said, "like we got ourselves a goddamn uprising."

The store stood two stories, ramshackle and unpainted. It leaned a little. Upstairs windows had old bed sheets for curtains. Downstairs windows were naked as wind off the mountain. Not much could be seen through the windows because men stood outside the store, blocking the view.

One man packed a silly old over-and-under, a two barrel combination of .22 rifle and .410 shotgun. He pointed it at another man who knelt like in prayer. A half dozen other men stood around, watched, like people stuck in church with the sermon boring. Everybody except the kneeling man wore faded patches on faded clothes. The only man who looked fully alive was the man who knelt. The rest of the men were old and tired. They seemed wispy.

"You are more'n'likely gonna see a shooting," Tip said. "For God's sake keep your mouth shut." He climbed from the Ford. Slammed the door. Knelt like he checked a tire, knelt real easy like he had all the time in the world. He kind of tsked, scratched himself behind the ear, then turned and ambled toward the men like nothing was going on.

"Shitfire, Tom," he said to the man with the gun, "if you shoot the undertaker who's gonna plant him?"

The kneeling man looked about to faint. He dressed in city clothes. His shoes had once been polished. His eyes were wide and scary. Black hair dangled wet over a sweaty forehead. "Tip," he said, "they got it all wrong."

"They probably don't," Tip told him. He turned to me. "This is what comes from too damn much government. The minute we started paying a death benefit, funeral prices went up to match the benefit."

"T'aint that," Tom said. His arm trembled as he held the gun. It looked like the thing would go off just from his shaking. His hair was pure white, his face with black circles around green eyes . . . green but dulled . . . lots of Scots-Irish blood in these hills. Tom seemed feeble, but not at all nervous. "We got graveyard problems," he told Tip.

"Might be fun," Tip said, and sounded droll, "to park him inside. Sweat him a little. You can always shoot him later."

"If you wasn't Tip," Tom said, "I reckon I wouldn't listen." To the kneeling undertaker he said, "Remove your ass. Inside."

I hope to never again see what I saw in Minnie's store. What I heard, I can handle, and tell about. What I smelled was like sweet perfume, the kind that rises from corpses just before they begin to stink. What I saw. . . .

A congregation of weary men, white-haired with faces dark, especially around eyes and noses where coal dust painted faces into masks. Eyes, some brilliant, some flat and dull and deathlike, stared at us from the rings of blackness. Here and there a man wheezed. Others sat quiet, and if they breathed no one could hear. The silent ones seemed to have brighter eyes than the ones who drew breath.

Minnie, rail-skinny, gray-haired and sharp of face, stood behind a bar made of plain boards. Behind her, shelves held chewing tobacco, plus some tobacco leaves, little cans of deviled ham, little cans of sardines. There were a few grocery items plus small bottles of aspirin and some patent medicines. Beer coolers ran beneath the shelves.

When the undertaker came inside he stopped, even though he had a gun in his back. He went wild-eyed, gasped, and literally fell into the nearest chair. He was worth watching, but there was lots else to see so I just listened to him gasp.

"Don't you dare do any shootin' in here," Minnie told Tom. "It makes a mess and it brings the law." Her voice sounded lots nicer than she looked, because she looked like fifty years of hard times. Her oversize man's shirt made her seem small, like a boy. Her worn jeans bagged. Her graying hair was done in a bun. Her voice sounded alert in the surrounding tiredness.

"Now me," Tip drawled, "I drink while on duty." He grinned at Minnie. She looked at me. Tip nodded. Minnie pulled two bottles. The undertaker still gasped, like maybe he would die for want of air.

Tip straddled a chair and looked to Tom. "I ain't come across a good story in a dog's age. Lemme hear it. . . ." He got interrupted.

The undertaker's teeth began to chatter. He kept gasping. Finally, he looked toward one of the sitting men. "Ezekiel, I done buried you."

"And did a piss poor job," Zeke said. Amber eyes flashed like a man alive and angry. Zeke's voice was more like a dry rustle than an actual voice. The rustle did not sound kind. In fact, just the opposite.

Somebody chuckled, but not friendly. Nothing else happened. The undertaker kept gasping. Tom told his story.

"He buried my brother," Tom said. "Buried Ezra. Cheaper coffin than he promised. Coffin got loose. Dropped into the grave, instead of lowered. Cracked open, and Ezra looking at the sky." Tom reached to where he'd leaned the over-and-under. "This bastard threw dirt in Ezra's face, and cussed him."

I couldn't tell whether Tom was dead or alive. He looked mostly alive, and his eyes didn't shine like Zeke's.

"This shootin'-business reminds me," a man said to Minnie. "Give me two cartridges. Might could get a deer."

30-30 cartridges, it turned out, cost thirty-five cents apiece.

"Maybe you wanta wait," Tip said. "Near as I can figure, Ezra might drop in here any minute."

The undertaker was as close to insanity as any man I've ever seen. He hunched in his chair, and when he wasn't gasping for air he sobbed. His face was complete torment. He had badly made false teeth, shiny, but too big and clunky for his face. He whispered to another man, "Why you here, Bill? You're buried."

"The way you laid me out wan't comfortable," Bill said. His voice was a dry whisper. "It ain't right a man's gotta be dead and not comfortable." Bill's eyes were not green, but sharp and glowing blue.

"Preacher," Tip said to another man, "I done heard you'd gone to glory."

"I can't figure it," the preacher whispered. He was a small man. Probably a lay preacher, self-ordained. He wore a frayed, black suit, and his white hair hung to his shoulders. His eyes glowed soft and gray. "Something's goin' on," he whispered. "Maybe the Baptists hogged it all. Might be there's no glory left."

Stillness. From outside a raven chuckled. A cow lowed, a dog barked. It was so quiet I could hear the bubbling of a distant stream that seemed to answer the raven. A way, way off in the distance, maybe two or three mountains to the west, a light plane hummed.

"I reckon," Tom said, like he was talking to himself. "My brother Ezra is out there somewheres and about his own business. Goin' it alone. He had that reputation."

"This all happened once before," Minnie said. "You boys recall that big gom-up durin' the war."

"What gom-up?" Tip sounded just as businesslike and sensible as if he were sitting back at the office. I worked at taking his advice about not studying things. Nobody else seemed troubled. Except, of course, the undertaker.

"When we had those drownings," Minnie said, "it was the same time the company cut wages. Those boys walked out of the hole. People swore they saw 'em. Then the tipple burned. The mine office burned. The company store burned. Rail cars burned. Nary a coal car got loaded for three months. Then those boys disappeared into the forest. People swore they saw 'em." She looked at all of the men, some alive, some dead. "Looks like nobody was lying."

"Which means," Tip said in the direction of Tom and the preacher, "that you gents have been called back to do a hand of work. Instead of going off half-cocked, let's wait it out. I reckon something's about to happen."

What happened was Sims and his pet goon, Pook.

A man lounging in the open doorway looked toward the road. In a voice so tired it quavered he said, "Cadillac car a-coming." He sounded discouraged and beaten. To the preacher he said, "Better get to prayin', for what-dog-good it's gonna do."

Sun sat high but westering. The shadow of Drowning Mountain reached into the hollow and across the road. The Cadillac ran so smooth that nothing could be heard, save the bump of its tires in ruts and potholes. Men stirred, uneasy. "Never to be let alone, never free," someone whispered, ". . . not in this life 'ner any other." The voice filled with sadness.

Pook got from the car first. He came into Minnie's place, looked around, turned back toward the Cadillac. He must have given a signal. Sims got out and stepped toward us. He moved dainty on little feet, and his summer suit was clean as his car. When he spoke his voice was soft. "Very well, Pook. I'll be but a minute." He ignored everyone except Pook. Then he turned to Tip. "Still kneeling, are we," he said to Tip. "Still hugging the poor and unwashed. Were I you, I'd vote Democrat."

"Were I you," Tip told him, "I'd take a bath. Wash off a little-a that snot."

"Watch that mouth." Pook stirred. His hand dropped toward the .45.

"You watch yours," Tip told Pook. "When you threaten me, you threaten my uncle Sammy. Unc will get riled."

"They were about to shoot me." The undertaker's voice quavered like a scared baby. "I gotta get a ride to town."

"You probably got a shootin' comin'." Pook sounded real comfortable.

"He probably does." Sims looked at Pook. "But he's the only one around who handles paupers. The company needs him."

"Get in the car," Pook told the undertaker. "Back seat. Don't drip no sweat."

The undertaker didn't run. He scampered.

"Goddamit, Tip." Tom had his dander up, green eyes coming almost as alive as eyes of the dead.

"Could be I was wrong," Tip murmured, "or maybe not. It's never no trouble to shoot a fella if you give it forethought."

Except for Tip, there wasn't a man in the place who wasn't brow-beat. I exclude myself, since half of what went on breezed right past me. The death smell wasn't quite as strong, or maybe my nose got used to it. There was one woman there, though, and brow-beat she wasn't.

"This is my place," she said to Sims, "and you ain't welcome. Speak your piece and get the hell out." She glanced toward the preacher. "You'll forgive the cuss."

"Yes and no," Sims said pleasantly. "You own the building."

"And the land," Minnie said, "bought fair and square from the company, deed an' all. Twenty bucks a month. Paid in full."

"And the land," Sims agreed. "But the company owns the mineral rights."

Tip pulled me to him. Whispered close in my ear. "Things are gonna get real bad. Keep your mouth shut."

"This is a friendly call." Sims kind-of purred. "Trying to help folks out. You'll be wanting to move. Next month I got machinery coming in."

"Gonna strip," someone whispered.

"My cabin's on that mountain. My woman's buried up there." A man's voice broke.

Pook chuckled. Sims tried to look sad. "Maybe move the grave," he said. "Nothing I can do. It's the company. The company calls the shots."

"Not exactly true," Tip said. "Why are you doing this?"

"Those seams are hardly touched," Sims told Tip. "That mountain has been a curse." He looked toward Minnie. "One month." He turned and walked to his car. Pook followed, but walking kind of sideways so as to cover his back.

Silence. The whir of the Cadillac's starter. The engine purred like an echo of Sim's voice. The car pulled away. Somewhere toward the back of Minnie's place came a dry sob. Men sat stunned, old, tired.

"Give yourselves a minute to breathe," Tip said real quiet. "Those of you with breath. Those without are called back for something."

Silence in the room was as deep as silence outside. No raven, no dog barking, no light plane buzzing. With the shadow of Drowning Mountain reaching across the hollow there should have been a breeze, but not a sound. Not a leaf stirring.

Then, a crack, like doom riding horseback and striking flame from the hooves. I sat straight up. Looked around. Never saw so many happy faces. I tried to place the sound. It was like a three-inch-fifty cannon going off. Sharp. Eardrum buster.

"How in the world," Tip said real pleased and casual, "are me and Jim ever gonna get back to town?"

"Five-stick shot sure'n God's wrath." The preacher looked about to start a sermon.

"That Ezra," Tom said. "By God, Ezra had the nerve to done it. Waste of dynamite. A three-stick would been a-plenty."

Someone laughed out loud. "What do you figger the law will do to Ezra. Kill him?" This, while everybody headed outside to take a look.

The Cadillac, what little was left of it, lay on its back beside a chunk of road that was no longer there. The car was a shiny hunk of black, twisted metal. A body in a summer suit lay sprawled among the weeds, another body big as Godzilla lay without a head, and there were scattered pieces of what had once been an undertaker. Blood stains mixed with burn stains on roadside weeds.

"That Ezra," Minnie said, ". . . now Ezra was always best at setting a shot. He held that reputation."

"Tunneled under the road. Set his charge. Ran his wires to the detonator, and hid on the hill. When the car driv across the charge, he shot those boys straight to hell." The preacher sounded apologetic. "I can't find it in my heart to pray for 'em."

"And now we're gonna catch hell." Tom looked to Tip. "We're gonna get the law."

"Don't give it a first thought," Tip told him. "I got it covered." He turned to the preacher. "Pretty plain why you boys were called back."

A man whispered. The whisper sounded faint, but pleased. He spoke to the preacher. "I reckon brother Sims and his lot feel sorta surprised. They got no experience at being dead." The voice turned mean. "I expect we should show 'em some things. Sort of introduce them around."

"I got a goodly number of things to demonstrate." Another whisper. The whisper sounded most unpleasant.

"I purely agree," the preacher whispered, "an' may The Lord have mercy on my sinful way."

Down by the road an old man limped off the hill. He wore a black burial suit of the cheap kind furnished to the poor. He stood looking at the broken car and broken bodies. Then he scratched his head and looked like a man who figured he had wasted dynamite. Then he looked toward Minnie's.

"That Ezra," Tom said. "I expect you boys better get down there before he has all the fun."

When those who were called back walked to the road, the crowd in front of Minnie's store thinned. We trooped inside. When screaming and torment went on down there, it was not for the living to know or understand.

"Anybody got a peavey?" Tip looked to Minnie. "Me and Jim have got to fix that road a little."

We borrowed the peavey and used it to crack out sleepers from the broken rail bed. For two hours we tossed sleepers into the torn spot of road. With the sun back of the mountain, the old Ford limped across. We made it back to town considerably after dark.

Next day Bobby Joe pulled Tip off to one side. The two men talked, looked toward me. Sarah Jane looked toward me. Lots of questions on faces. Not much said. It seemed clear I was not on trial.

When the sheriff showed up he pulled me and Tip into Bobby Joe's office. He wasn't much of a sheriff.

"Lord only knows who done it," Tip told him. "I can't say who did, but can say who didn't."

"Could-of been someone from town," I mentioned. "But I'm new around here. You might say I didn't see anything except a well-used Cadillac."

When the sheriff left it was clear I'd passed my test. Sarah Jane was lots more friendly. Bobby Joe said that maybe, in a couple months, I could go into the field alone.

"Will those dead stay dead?" I asked Tip once we cleared out of the office.

"Can't imagine that they won't."

"And those alive?"

"They are not off the hook," Tip told me. "You kill a bastard like Sims and ten more just like him come to the funeral."

It fell out that Tip was wrong. The coal company turned the show over to a man wise in the ways of the hills. He wasn't a bit nicer than Sims, but lots smarter. He figured it more economic to strip some other mountain.

I worked out of that office for two more years, then got transferred to Cincinnati. It took all of those two years, a long, long time, for the old men of Drowning Mountain to repair that road. I'm told that they sang church songs as they worked.

This story is in memory of Andy Strunk, coal miner of Gatliff, Kentucky.

ROBERT COOVER

The Last One

*The general framework of the following selection will be immediately famil-
iar, even a leads the reader into deeply strange territory. "The Last One" is
an electric, unexpected and even joyful reworking of* Bluebeard *by Robert
Coover. Coover's first novel won the 1966 William Faulkner Award; more
recently, he was honored by the Dugannon Foundation for his lifetime contribution to the short story. Reading Coover's collection* Pricksongs and Des-
cants, *originally published in 1969, is a bit like sticking your finger into a
light socket; Coover's more recent work, such as the novella "Stepmother,"
published by McSweeney's in a deluxe hardcover edition, and illustrated by
Michael Kupperm still shocks and delights. This year McSweeney's published* A Child Again, *a collection of Coover's retold and remixed fairy tales,
including a story printed on a deck of oversized playing cards which could be
reshuffled and read in any order. The other tales, including this selection,
range from the bawdy to the perversely realistic. Coover continues to write
and to teach at Brown University.*

—K.L. & G.G.

This one asks at breakfast about the first one. My impertinent bride. Impertinent and imprudent (I tell her so and a gentle blush colors her cheeks and
her lashes blink away a dewy mist, though her adoring gaze does not waver).
Of course she will go the way of all the others. Perhaps before the day is over.
Such a pity. But she is young and beautiful, not yet seventeen, and I indulge her.
She was young and beautiful, I say, no older than you, and I indulged her in everything. But she did not respect my wishes.

Are your wishes so terrible then? she asks. There is a hint of a smile on her soft un-
rouged lips. Is she flirting with me?

Not at all, I say with an answering half-smile. You will find me a devoted, atten-
tive, and considerate husband, demanding almost nothing of you and desiring only
to enrich your young life with all the means at my disposal.

Then I shall have to invent your demands that I might please you, she says, putting down her golden fork and fondly covering my hand with hers, for I am like that,
too, and truly love you with all my heart. Her touch seems to find its way directly to
my loins as if her sweet hand held me there and I am deliciously aroused, but I am
also overswept by a sudden sorrow, for, though I have loved and miss them all, I
know I shall miss this one more than any other. Indeed, I am already missing her. I
shall begin by learning prudence and discretion, she adds, and her lips seem to draw

together as though to form a kiss. She lets go my hand and reaches out to touch my blue beard with her fingertips. You are so beautiful! she sighs.

I know that I am not, I reply with a melancholic smile, recalling her ingenuous endearments of the night before, but I love your innocent love and wish that it might last forever.

And so it shall, she says. Why should it not? I am here to serve you in all ways that you might wish until death do us part, exactly as I promised and as is my one desire.

Alas, that's just short of forever, my dear, but I understand your loving intent. So now, to serve me well, please state your other, more intimate desires, that I might have the pleasure of fulfilling them. My entire wealth is at your disposal.

Oh, as your wife, of course, I can and do demand nothing, for that would be an impertinence worse than any other.

You have not a single favor to ask?

No. Well . . . No . . .

Please. Name it. It's yours.

I hope it's not impertinent, too. She lowers her head, peering modestly down into her lap where one hand now enfolds the other. As she does so, she exposes her alluring young nape with its delicate spinal knuckles and skin like silk. It is unutterably precious to me and begs a kiss, not of my ruthless blade (which regretfully I must sharpen before I leave), but of my worshipful lips, and it receives one. But . . . well . . . the nursery . . .

Yes? Inwardly, I am delighted—and flattered—that the thoughts of this playful and sensuous child have been so quickly drawn to aspirations of such maturity, however unlikely it is they can ever be realized. You wish it to be redecorated perhaps? A more cheerful color, a bit more light—?

No, no, it's lovely! It's only . . . well . . . She lifts her head to gaze wistfully up at me, and her soft bosom into which I am peering heaves with a tremulous sigh, and I think: Though I shall leave her today and test her as I always do—and must—we shall perhaps first taste the fruits of love once more . . . It's just that I sometimes feel so lost and inadequate in this grand world of yours, I need a quiet little place all my own to which I might retire to gather my poor childish wits about me and recover my composure. A place where I can be just by myself to reflect upon my love for you and upon ways that I might better please you. The nursery next to our bed chamber is as yet unoccupied— and here she blushes becomingly, and casts her eyes down once again, then timorously looks back up at me—and I feel at home in it, perhaps because I've not been long away from one. Might it just be mine, until . . . until we . . . you know . . . ?

This is not the request that I have anticipated, but it befits her modesty and I recall that when she first arrived she brought with her all her childhood toys—as familiar company for her in this strange place, as she said, begging my pardon for her inability as yet to leave her past behind entirely. I've only brought the little things, she said. Granted, I say now, roguishly arching my brow and taking her hands to draw her up from her chair, provided I might now occupy for a short time that lovely place where I have so come to feel at home.

It is yours to possess without provision, she responds with a shy but welcoming smile.

She is of course vastly disappointed and not a little alarmed when later, clasped still in her arms, I inform her that I must undertake a sudden journey and leave her here to tend the castle while I am gone. We dress and I show her through those parts she has not yet visited, keeping my instructions to a minimum, assuring her that the staff is well trained and accustomed to my frequent absences, providing her with keys to all my strongboxes and personal wealth and all the castle's rooms, including the blue room with the blue door, which I tell her, as I have told them all, she is not on any condition to enter. I add that she is not even to put the key in the lock, for if she does so she might expect the most dreadful of punishments, but though I tell her this with my sword at the whetstone, she seems hardly to be listening, fascinated instead by a pair of songbirds in a gilded cage. When they stroke each other with their bills, she laughs and claps her hands and says: I'm not afraid! I know you will come back to me! Of course I will, I say. You can count on it. And which one of these unlocks the nursery door? she asks.

My invented travels take me, as they always do, to a small inn on a lake nearby, known for the quality of its food and wine, and for its privacy and discretion. I order a platter of succulent plump partridges with wild mushrooms, braised onions, and roasted aubergines and peppers, together with an opulent red wine, perfectly aged, from the north, but I find my appetite has failed me. I have known brief moments of the most intense pleasure and beauty, but my life has not on the whole been a happy one, and on this day I am as unhappy as I have ever been. I am utterly smitten by this pretty child, and I do not want to lose her, although no doubt I shall. I will return and find the bloodstained key and she will lose her head, as have the countless others, and I will lose a wife I dearly love, as I have loved them all. I am reminded in particular on this gray day of a lovely auburn-haired bride, a few years older than the present one, wilier perhaps, and wittier, yet delightfully fresh and childlike in her ways, who tried to stay my hand with story. Her tale, as she knelt there at the chopping block, was of a room with many doors, the rooms beyond them inhabited more by ghostly concepts than by persons and enmazed into a pretty riddle, whose solution, I supposed (we never got that far), was wisdom, or what passes for it in tales like these. Just for a moment I was enthralled and paused, her conjured room or rooms more real to me than my own, and had she not smiled to see me so and so unmasked my passing weakness, she might still wear her comely head. Alas. And it is not obedience I seek, but mere respect. I am a reasonable man, generous to a fault, demanding only this one small thing: that there be no intrusions upon my private quarters. Which, once upon a time, was what the blue room was for me, though now I dread to enter it myself, such a reeking charnel house it has become. So what am I defending? A principle, I suppose, as dead as the heap of headless corpses it has produced and now contains. And yet I can do no other. It is who I am, it is the bleak lot cast for me and for those I love; to do otherwise than as I must would be an act of the most abject cowardice and self-betrayal. I know that (I accept a truffled chocolate from a proffered tray, my appetite somewhat, if only faintly, revived by my recovered resolution). But oh how I long for a wife I might keep with her head on for more than a day or two! I think that I deserve as much.

I return by surprise and am surprised. My bride emerges from the nursery with tears of happiness in her eyes to see me, the blue room has not been entered, the golden key is immaculate, she has not even remembered that I asked her not to go there. She chatters on about her day, the games she's played and how she's missed me, and we enjoy another night together more delightful than the night before, if that is possible. Perhaps at last! I think, and fall asleep with my loved one securely in my arms, her sweet breath (she is alive! alive!) upon my breast.

I am tempted on the morrow to let the matter of the blue room rest. Has she not already proven that she is different from all the others? No, not yet, for she would not be the first to pass the first day's test, only to fall upon the second, and I know that I must do as I have always done. To honor the dead, if for no other reason. So once again I announce my abrupt departure, once again we walk the premises, opening and closing doors, visiting all the treasures of the castle, and once again I show her the key to the blue room and admonish her never to go there. Be not too curious, I say, and she replies, with barely a glance at the forbidden door, Do you know that, when you are being stern, a tiny furrow appears between your brows, exactly like the one that appears there when we are making love? And she pulls my head down with both her hands and kisses it. I love you so! she sighs.

My appetite this second day is much improved, and at the inn I order a handsome fish plucked fresh from the lake, beheaded, gutted, stuffed, and baked, with saffron rice on the side and tender wild asparagus. I am feeling elated. I am convinced I have found a love at last that I may keep. I sip the rich straw-colored wine that I have chosen, served precisely at the temperature of the lake itself, and allow myself to contemplate a future quite unlike my ensanguined past. I often use these mock journeys to seek out and woo a possible future bride, knowing that I must soon lose the one I have, but on this day my thoughts are wholly upon the castle I have left behind and the beautiful and obedient child who awaits me there, more mine than I am mine. Today I have even forgotten, I realize with a pained smile, to hone my monstrous blade. Well, perhaps it will join the mounted antlers, portraits, historic tapestries, and the other useless relics upon the walls. I replay the events of the day before, satisfied that she has satisfied me in all particulars. Excepting perhaps that when she returned the keys the one to the nursery was not among them. But, then, I told her the room was solely hers, did I not, she committed no infraction, broke no command, and I feel certain she will not again today, and so order up a bowl of tiny wild strawberries in a delicate liqueur, brushed with mint, to complete in festive manner my lakeside repast.

I am right. My surprise return does not even wholly surprise her. The blue room has not been invaded, the key's unstained. My bride has spent the day in the nursery, playing with her toys, she explains when she emerges from the room and locks it, and then she throws her arms around me and hugs me with such warm passion, my whole body feels like love's erected organ. Don't go away again! she whispers. Stay here with me always! We spend the rest of the dying day in bed and servants later bring us cheese and wine and fresh fruit, peeled and quartered. She tells me about the serving girl she had to scold for failing to remove the nightcloth from the songbirds' cage (You see, I can be useful to you when you're gone, she exclaims with a teasing smile and plucks a fishbone from my beard) and I provide her a fictitious account of my luncheon visit to a neighboring castellan to discuss proposed changes in the game laws. He is widowed yet again, I say, and is looking for a new young bride, both virtuous and beautiful. I told him to resign himself to cease his search. There was only one such left in the whole world and she is mine.

That night my dreams are free for once of severed heads, fountaining blood, eyes popping with terror from their sockets, and I am returned instead to the happier days of my all-but-forgotten childhood. My dream companion, though also a mere infant, is not unlike my present wife and we play games alone in some wild place that end in shy caresses. I awake in a state of profound joy and gratitude, as though some terrible burden has been lifted, receiving in reality the tender caresses of which I have been dreaming. But then later, after breakfast, when my bride has withdrawn to dress herself for the out of doors (It's a beautiful day! Let's walk the castle grounds! she exclaimed happily, and how could I refuse her, recalling, as I was, a certain sunny wild-flowered meadow where we might at midday lie?), my waking joy fades to despair, for I know that I must test her one more time, a third time, I can do no other, and I fear this day will be the one to break my heart.

Of course she is tearfully disappointed and clings to me, pleading with me not to go, and for a moment my resolution wavers—why must I torture myself this way?—but in the end I do, as I always do, what I must do. I explain: an urgent message, a friend in need, I must leave immediately and am not sure when I might return. We tour the castle and its wealth as before, I warn her about the blue room, I give her the keys. She accepts them without so much as a glance, throws herself into my arms, then tears herself away and runs weeping into the nursery. What have I done? I am weeping, too, unable to stay, unable to leave, wringing my hands, pulling at my beard, pacing the castle corridors. No, I shall not go! And yet I must! I do remember this time to sharpen my sword, not because I wish to use it—oh no, please no!—but because, if I must use it, I wish it to be mercifully swift in its barbarous labors. And perhaps because it gives me something more to do, to delay a departure I am so loathe to make. As the whetstone sings its shrieking song, I think: Of course I must go, this trial is not over and must as always be concluded, but need it be today? Another message might arrive: Stay, my friend. Come tomorrow if you can. Why not? Even should she fail me this third time, we would at least have this last day and night together.

I sheathe my sword and hurry to the nursery to tell her so. It is locked. I lift my hand to knock but am stopped by the sound of voices within, her voice at least. Are you lonely? she is asking. Are you in need of company? Probably she is talking to herself in the mirror. Or to her toys. Yet I am troubled by it, and quietly withdraw. I go outside to peer in through the window, but the drapes are drawn. Now, why would she do that on such a lovely day as this? I ask myself, feeling my suspicions rise, and then as quickly ask· And what am I doing prowling around here outside her window like a common thief, a lowly peeper? I reject my behavior as improper and ungallant—as for the darkened room, she is mourning my departure, after all—and I decide to continue on my way as first announced. It is time to bring this sorry business to an end.

Before I reach the inn, however, I turn back. Was hers the only voice I heard? Almost certainly, and yet . . . I approach the castle from a stand of trees and watch awhile from there. What do I expect to see? I do not know, though disturbing thoughts race through my head and my perspiring hand is on my sword. Of course, nothing happens. Why should it? I begin to feel a fool, all the more so for having passed up that innocent frolic on the meadow, in exchange for such base misery as this, unworthy of my age and of my station. I decide to return immediately: My friend is well, his problem solved, a messenger met me on the way.

My bride greets me as before, throwing herself tearfully into my arms with abject delight as if I've been absent for many days. I try to peek past her shoulder into the nursery, but the door is closed. Locked, no doubt. She strips my shirt away to nuzzle my bare chest as she is wont to do when making love, then tugs me toward our bed chamber, whispering her maidenly endearments. I long for the pleasure that she offers, but am too agitated to perform my part or even to think of doing so. I suggest instead the stroll through the castle grounds we had originally planned and gaily—Oh yes! she cries—she hurries off to the kitchen to arrange a basket lunch. The nursery door is indeed locked, I discover, and I recall now that she has left my side from time to time at night to visit there. A restless sleeper lonely for her lost past? Or . . . ? I put my ear to the door. Nothing. Of course, nothing. What's the matter with me? Standing there, leaning against the locked nursery door with my shirttails dangling like drooping pennants, I suddenly feel desperately old and world-weary, and I know that our walk will not revive my spirits.

It does not. The meadow is there, just as I have remembered it, with its downy bed of soft grasses and silken petals, and naked upon it in the sunlight under the blue breezeless sky, my young bride is a most voluptuous sight, but I am as unaroused as before, and turn quite irritable when she tries to be of help to me. Where has she learned such things? I do not ask her that of course, but complain instead that I feel unwell and fear I may have caught a fever. She could not be more solicitous, insisting that we return to the castle immediately where I shall spend the rest of the day in bed, and she will care for me, and bring me tea and read to me and with her own gentle hands rub all the aches away, but that too, inexplicably, causes my choler to rise and I must bite my beard to refrain from bellowing something at her I would afterward regret.

Only much later, after she has left me, presumably sleeping peacefully following her wifely ministrations, to return to her precious nursery, do I realize I have forgotten to check the blue room key (I do: no stains), that's not the point any longer. Stealthily, I creep once more to that door between us and press my ear against it: She is singing to herself in there, or humming, a kind of marching tune—Step lively now! she says—and now and then a happy little laugh escapes her, a girlish giggle. That she can enjoy such carefree play all by herself, if she is by herself, when I am ill, or presumably ill—I might be dying for all she knows—also stirs my fury and resentment, and to calm myself (I fully intend now to visit the nursery, with or without her invitation, and regardless of any promises to the contrary, but only when in full control of my emotions, now in such turmoil) I take the keys and pace the castle corridors in my nightshirt, counting by candlelight, it would seem to anyone who saw me, my possessions, one madness thus (my possessions are uncountable) concealing another.

At some point in my midnight wanderings, I find myself in front of the infamous blue door, the room beyond it once the very locus of my honor and my integrity, and I wonder at the life that I have made. A man of my wealth and power has certain obligations, of course, but I never meant to be cruel, my intentions always noble and instructive, no matter how my actions may appear. I enter it (the nursery key is missing) but am immediately driven out by the stench within: there are rotting heads and bodies and mutilated limbs everywhere and the floor is covered with clotted blood, the horrid proofs of my severe and lonely existence. I have lived, without remorse, a principled life, and I must be resolutely who I am, else I am no one at all—and yet . . . Well . . . Such a sickening mess here at the center! Even I am excluded from what might be called the very heart of my own being!

This encounter with the ghastly carnage of my past has a sobering and calmative effect, and I return much subdued to our room wherein my bride lies sleeping now, determined that on the morrow I shall seal that fatal chamber up forever and throw away the key, not so much for her sake, or any who might follow, as for my own. My beloved sleeps there peacefully upon her back, herself toylike in her pretty stillness, the faintest traces of a smile upon her lips, as though her dreams were sweet and pleasing her. That I somewhat shape those dreams I know and know that I must treat her always with tolerance and loving kindness, and beware my volcanic temper. I have heard her, alone, secluded, give vent to the loneliness she suffers in my absence and as well to her more playful whims, which in my preceptive solemnity beyond the nursery I have perhaps unwittingly suppressed, and maybe she meant for me to overhear these things that I might learn to remain always by her side and to join her games, however lightsome, with an open and willing heart. To do so is anyway now my firm resolve, and I slip into the bed beside her full of affection and tenderness and easefully enter her and, at peace with myself at last, fall asleep in our locked embrace.

I wake at dawn to an empty bed and think I hear her in the nursery again. I smile sleepily, imagining her there in all her loveliness, surrounded by her little things, and I close my eyes again and think: Let her be. But even as this thought drifts benignly through my mind, I find myself at the door once more, my ear pressed against it, my hand testing the handle. Did I hear a sound within? No, it's someone coming down the corridor! I leap back into bed and pull the covers up just as she enters cheerfully with a breakfast tray. Good morning, my sweet love! I've brought you all your favorite things! I want to make you well again!

I'm much improved, I say, and I rub my eyes and scratch my beard, which I know amuses her. Your kisses have quite revived me, though I think I may require yet another dosage or two.

I am not well trained in the healing arts, she replies with a twinkling smile, setting the breakfast tray aside and crawling in beside me, but you will find me a quick and eager pupil.

I decide to pass the day in bed, close to the nursery door, and I ask my chamberlain to bring me my accounts that I might go over them there, suggesting to my bride that she is free to do as she pleases while I am working. I assume that she will return to the nursery, but she chooses instead to acquaint herself more thoroughly with the running of the castle that she might, as she says, better serve it as its new mistress. Sometimes I hear noises in there, or think I do, and I hurry over to hear what I can hear, but these excursions are often as not interrupted by her sudden arrival from the hallway, and I must make clumsy excuses about a fallen pen or a troublesome insect or a cramp in my leg: Oh let me squeeze the hurt away! she exclaims, and I must feign an appetite, quite vanished suddenly, for her amorous attentions.

Finally there is nothing for it but to arrange her longer absence somehow that I might, leisurely and unobserved, examine her retreat. And so my illness worsens. She must take the carriage and go visit the doctor, some miles hence, and deliver to him the sealed letter which I place into her hands, then bring back to me the potion I request therein. She protests, she cannot bear to leave me alone in my suffering, let a manservant go, she will stay and care for me. Servants are a meddlesome and unreliable lot, I say. A sealed letter is like an open invitation. I trust only you.

She kisses me passionately, almost tearfully. Don't even move till I return! she cries and, hastily tossing a silken shawl over her shoulders for the journey, she dashes away.

I watch the gilded carriage careen at full gallop out of the yard, then try the nursery door. It is locked, as I have supposed, and its key is missing from the ring, also as I have supposed. What surprises me is that my old master key does not work either. I have a drawerful of ancient keys and think to try them, though it means another visit to the stomach-turning horrors of the blue room. They are equally useless, that hellish errand in vain, and I heave the lot across the room, my frustration mounting. Outside, the window is also locked, or stuck. What's worse, there are fresh boot tracks out there, both coming and going, and my mind is suddenly awhirl with the most abominable imaginings. Of course I myself was standing there only yesterday, those tracks are no doubt mine: I try to calm myself. I drop the brick I might in my madness have heaved through the window, without regard for the stories I would have had to invent thereafter, and I return to my bed chamber, now truly ill.

I prepare to retire once more, perhaps this time with a glass of wine, something noble, complex, engaging, that I might free my thoughts from the intolerable virulence that has invaded them, but just as I am about to ring for a servant, I hear whispering inside the nursery. A man! Or men! My worst fears are justified! I try to force the door without success, my fever raging now, but it will not give way. I rush out to get my sword and as I'm hurriedly sharpening its blade, I hear the carriage returning to the yard. There is no time to lose! I am back at the nursery door, hacking wildly at it, when I hear her enter the castle, breathlessly calling out my name: I am here, dear love! I have returned! And, as I break through at last, she appears behind me. Oh my, she says. Whatever are you doing?

Inside the room, her toys are neatly spread about: a miniature roofless castle, richly appointed, set upon parklike grounds made of a green blanket and pebbles from the garden for the drives on which tiny horsedrawn carriages are placed, a mirror for a pond, twisted yarn for trees and shrubs, porcelain figurines standing as statues on wooden blocks, and pillows heaped about to represent the surrounding hills. The rooms inside the toy castle are elegantly carpeted and hung with tapestries and damask, the chairs and sofas are covered with silks and velvet and fringed with gold, the tiny carved dining table set with branched candlesticks and a golden dinner service, and full-length looking-glasses with gilded frames have been mounted in the corridors and private chambers. In one of the these there is a small sign which reads: THE REWARD OF DISOBEDIENCE AND IMPRUDENT CURIOSITY, and the dolls that populate it, all little bearded men, are alive, even the ones whose heads have been taken off and mounted on the walls. Do you like them, my little toys? my bride asks from behind my shoulder. She is smiling tenderly but somewhat wistfully down upon me, and I am touched for a moment by the mystery of her and of all the brides before her. You promised, she says without reproach, though not without a trace of regret, and I feel the withering power of her affectionate disappointment. You were so lovely, she sighs. I so much wished you might at last be the one that I could keep. And she picks me up by my head and sets me inside the castle with the others.

CHINA MIÉVILLE, EMMA BIRCHAM, and MAX SCHÄFER

The Ball Room

China Miéville is the author of several books of fiction and nonfiction, including the novels Perdido Street Station, The Scar, *and* Iron Council. *His novels have won the Arthur C. Clarke award (twice) and the British Fantasy Award (twice). His most recent book is* Looking For Jake, *a collection of short stories, which includes two stories chosen for earlier volumes of* The Year's Best Fantasy and Horror.

Emma Bircham is fabulous, but a bit tired. She lives in London.

Max Schäfer was born in London in 1974 and has been intending to do something ever since.

"The Ball Room" was originally published in Looking for Jake.

—E.D.

I'm not employed by the store. They don't pay my wages. I'm with a security firm, but we've had a contract here for a long time, and I've been here for most of it. This is where I know people. I've been a guard in other places—still am, occasionally, on short notice—and until recently I would have said this was the best place I'd been. It's nice to work somewhere people are happy to go. Until recently, if anyone asked me what I did for a living, I'd just tell them I worked for the store.

It's on the outskirts of town, a huge metal warehouse. Full of a hundred little fake rooms, with a single path running through them, and all the furniture we sell made up and laid out so you can see how it should look. Then the same products, disassembled, packed flat and stacked high in the warehouse for people to buy. They're cheap.

Mostly I know I'm just there for show. I wander around in my uniform, hands behind my back, making people feel safe, making the merchandise feel protected. It's not really the kind of stuff you can shoplift. I almost never have to intervene.

The last time I did was in the ball room.

On weekends this place is just crazy. So full it's hard to walk: all couples and young families. We try to make things easier for people. We have a cheap café and free parking, and most important of all we have a crèche. It's at the top of the stairs when you first come in. And right next to it, opening out from it, is the ball room.

The walls of the ball room are almost all glass, so people in the store can look inside. All the shoppers love watching the children: there are always people outside, staring in with big dumb smiles. I keep an eye on the ones that don't look like parents.

It's not very big, the ball room. Just an annex really. It's been here for years. There's a climbing frame all knotted up around itself, and a net made of rope to catch you, and a Wendy house, and pictures on the walls. And it's full of color. The whole room is two feet deep in shiny plastic balls.

When the children fall, the balls cushion them. The balls come up to their waists, so they wade through the room like people in a flood. The children scoop up the balls and splash them all over each other. They're about the size of tennis balls, hollow and light so they can't hurt. They make little *pudda-thudda* noises bouncing off the walls and the kids' heads, making them laugh.

I don't know why they laugh so hard. I don't know what it is about the balls that makes it so much better than a normal playroom, but they *love* it in there. Only six of them are allowed at a time, and they queue up for ages to get in. They get twenty minutes inside. You can see they'd give anything to stay longer. Sometimes, when it's time to go, they howl, and the friends they've made cry, too, at the sight of them leaving.

I was on my break, reading, when I was called to the ball room.

I could hear shouting and crying from around the corner, and as I turned it I saw a crowd of people outside the big window. A man was clutching his son and yelling at the childcare assistant and the store manager. The little boy was about five, only just old enough to go in. He was clinging to his dad's trouser leg, sobbing.

The assistant, Sandra, was trying not to cry. She's only nineteen herself.

The man was shouting that she couldn't do her bloody job, that there were way too many kids in the place and they were completely out of control. He was very worked up and he was gesticulating exaggeratedly, like in a silent movie. If his son hadn't anchored his leg he would have been pacing around.

The manager was trying to hold her ground without being confrontational. I moved in behind her, in case it got nasty, but she was calming the man down. She's good at her job.

"Sir, as I said, we emptied the room as soon as your son was hurt, and we've had words with the other children—"

"You don't even know which one did it. If you'd been keeping an *eye* on them, which I imagine is your bloody *job*, then you might be a bit less . . . *sodding* ineffectual."

That seemed to bring him to a halt and he quieted down, finally, as did his son, who was looking up at him with a confused kind of respect.

The manager told him how sorry she was, and offered his son an ice cream. Things were easing down, but as I started to leave I saw Sandra crying. The man looked a bit guilty and tried to apologize to her, but she was too upset to respond.

The boy had been playing behind the climbing frame, in the corner by the Wendy house, Sandra told me later. He was burrowing down into the balls till he was totally covered, the way some children like to. Sandra kept an eye on the boy but she could see the balls bouncing as he moved, so she knew he was okay. Until he came lurching up, screaming.

The store is full of children. The little ones, the toddlers, spend their time in the main crèche. The older ones, eight or nine or ten, they normally walk around the store with their parents, choosing their own bedclothes or curtains, or a little desk with drawers or whatever. But if they're in between, they come back for the ball room.

They're so funny, moving over the climbing frame, concentrating hard. Laughing all the time. They make each other cry, of course, but usually they stop in seconds. It always gets me how they do that: bawling, then suddenly getting distracted and running off happily.

Sometimes they play in groups, but it seems like there's always one who's alone. Quite content, pouring balls onto balls, dropping them through the holes of the climbing frame, dipping into them like a duck. Happy but playing alone.

Sandra left. It was nearly two weeks after that argument, but she was still upset. I couldn't believe it. I started talking to her about it, and I could see her fill up again. I was trying to say that the man had been out of line, that it wasn't her fault, but she wouldn't listen.

"It wasn't him," she said. "You don't understand. I can't be *in* there anymore."

I felt sorry for her, but she was overreacting. It was out of all proportion. She told me that since the day that little boy got upset, she couldn't relax in the ball room at all. She kept trying to watch all the children at once, all the time. She became obsessed with double-checking the numbers.

"It always seems like there's too many," she said. "I count them and there's six, and I count them again and there's six, but it always seems there's too many."

Maybe she could have asked to stay on and only done duty in the main crèche, managing name tags, checking the kids in and out, changing the tapes in the video, but she didn't even want to do that. The children loved that ball room. They went on and on about it, she said. They would never have stopped badgering her to be let in.

They're little kids, and sometimes they have accidents. When that happens, someone has to shovel all the balls aside to clean the floor, then dunk the balls themselves in water with a bit of bleach.

This was a bad time for that. Almost every day, some kid or other seemed to pee themselves. We kept having to empty the room to sort out little puddles.

"I had every bloody one of them over playing with me, every second, just so we'd have no problems," one of the nursery workers told me. "Then after they left . . . you could smell it. Right by the bloody Wendy house, where I'd have sworn none of the little buggers had got to."

His name was Matthew. He left a month after Sandra. I was amazed. I mean, you can see how much they love the children, people like them. Even having to wipe up dribble and sick and all that. Seeing them go was proof of what a tough job it was. Matthew looked really sick by the time he quit, really gray.

I asked him what was up, but he couldn't tell me. I'm not sure he even knew.

You have to watch those kids all the time. I couldn't do that job. Couldn't take the stress. The children are so unruly, and so tiny. I'd be terrified all the time, of losing them, of hurting them.

———

There was a bad mood to the place after that. We'd lost two people. The main store turns over staff like a motor, of course, but the crèche normally does a bit better. You have to be qualified, to work in the crèche, or the ball room. The departures felt like a bad sign.

I was conscious of wanting to look after the kids in the store. When I did my walks I felt like they were all around me. I felt like I had to be ready to leap in and save them any moment. Everywhere I looked, I saw children. And they were as happy as ever, running through the fake rooms and jumping on the bunkbeds, sitting at the desks that had been laid out ready. But now the way they ran around made me wince, and all our furniture, which meets or exceeds the most rigorous international standards for safety, looked like it was lying in wait to injure them. I saw head wounds in every coffee-table corner, burns in every lamp.

I went past the ball room more than usual. Inside was always some harassed-looking young woman or man trying to herd the children, and them running through a tide of bright plastic that thudded every way as they dived into the Wendy house and piled up balls on its roof. The children would spin around to make themselves dizzy, laughing.

It wasn't good for them. They loved it when they were in there, but they emerged so tired and crotchety and teary. They did that droning children's cry. They pulled themselves into their parents' jumpers, sobbing, when it was time to go. They didn't want to leave their friends.

Some children were coming back week after week. It seemed to me their parents ran out of things to buy. After a while they'd make some token purchase like tea lights and just sit in the café, drinking tea and staring out of the window at the gray flyovers while their kids got their dose of the room. There didn't look like much that was happy to these visits.

The mood infected us. There wasn't a good feeling in the store. Some people said it was too much trouble, and we should close the ball room. But the management made it clear that wouldn't happen.

You can't avoid night shifts.

There were three of us on that night, and we took different sections. Periodically we'd each of us wander through our patch, and between times we'd sit together in the staffroom or the unlit café and chat and play cards, with all sorts of rubbish flashing on the mute TV.

My route took me outside, into the front car lot, flashing my torch up and down the tarmac, the giant store behind me, with shrubbery around it black and whispery, and beyond the barriers the roads and night cars, moving away from me.

Inside again and through bedrooms, past all the pine frames and the fake walls. It was dim. Half-lights in all the big chambers full of beds never slept in and sinks without plumbing. I could stand still and there was nothing, no movement and no noise.

One time, I made arrangements with the other guards on duty, and I brought my girlfriend to the store. We wandered hand in hand through all the pretend rooms like stage sets, trailing torchlight. We played house like children, acting out little moments—her stepping out of the shower to my proffered towel, dividing the paper at the breakfast bar. Then we found the biggest and most expensive bed, with a special mattress that you can see nearby cut in cross-section.

After a while, she told me to stop. I asked her what the matter was, but she seemed angry and wouldn't say. I led her out through the locked doors with my swipe card and walked her to her car, alone in the lot, and I watched her drive away. There's a long one-way system of ramps and roundabouts to leave the store, which she followed, unnecessarily, so it took a long time before she was gone. We don't see each other anymore.

In the warehouse, I walked between metal shelf units thirty feet high. My footsteps sounded to me like a prison guard's. I imagined the flat-packed furniture assembling itself around me.

I came back through kitchens, following the path toward the café, up the stairs into the unlit hallway. My mates weren't back: there was no light shining off the big window that fronted the silent ball room.

It was absolutely dark. I put my face up close to the glass and stared at the black shape I knew was the climbing frame; the Wendy house, a little square of paler shadow, was adrift in plastic balls. I turned on my torch and shone it into the room. Where the beam touched them, the balls leaped into clown colors, and then the light moved and they went back to being black.

In the main crèche, I sat on the assistant's chair, with a little half-circle of baby chairs in front of me. I sat like that in the dark, and listened to no noise. There was a little bit of lamplight, orangey through the windows, and once every few seconds a car would pass, just audible, way out on the other side of the parking lot.

I picked up the book by the side of the chair and opened it in torchlight. Fairy tales. Sleeping Beauty, and Cinderella.

There was a sound.

A little soft thump.

I heard it again.

Balls in the ball room, falling onto each other.

I was standing instantly, staring through the glass into the darkness of the ball room. *Pudda-thudda*, it came again. It took me seconds to move, but I came close up to the window with my torch raised. I was holding my breath, and my skin felt much too tight.

My torch beam swayed over the climbing frame and out the window on the other side, sending shadows into the corridors. I directed it down into those bouncy balls, and just before the beam hit them, while they were still in darkness, they shivered and slid away from each other in a tiny little trail. As if something was burrowing underneath.

My teeth were clenched. The light was on the balls now, and nothing was moving.

I kept that little room lit for a long time, until the torchlight stopped trembling. I moved it carefully up and down the walls, over every part, until I let out a big dumb hiss of relief because I saw that there were balls on the top of the climbing frame, right on its edge, and I realized that one or two of them must have fallen off, bouncing softly among the others.

I shook my head and my hand swung down, the torchlight going with it, and the ball room went back into darkness. And as it did, in the moment when the shadows rushed back in, I felt a brutal cold, and I stared at the little girl in the Wendy house, and she stared up at me.

The other two guys couldn't calm me down.

They found me in the ball room, yelling for help. I'd opened both doors and I was hurling balls out into the crèche and the corridors, where they rolled and bounced in all directions, down the stairs to the entrance, under the tables in the café.

At first I'd forced myself to be slow. I knew that the most important thing was not to scare the girl any more than she must have been already. I'd croaked out some daft, would-be cheerful greeting, come inside, shining the torch gradually toward the Wendy house, so I wouldn't dazzle her, and I'd kept talking, whatever nonsense I could muster.

When I realized she'd sunk down again beneath the balls, I became all jokey, trying to pretend we were playing hide-and-seek. I was horribly aware of how I might seem to her, with my build and my uniform, and my accent.

But when I got to the Wendy house, there was nothing there.

"She's been left behind!" I kept screaming, and when they understood they dived in with me and scooped up handfuls of the balls and threw them aside, but the two of them stopped long before me. When I turned to throw more of the balls away, I realized they were just watching me.

They wouldn't believe she'd been in there, or that she'd got out. They told me they would have seen her, that she'd have had to come past them. They kept telling me I was being crazy, but they didn't try to stop me, and eventually I cleared the room of all the balls, while they stood and waited for the police I'd made them call.

The ball room was empty. There was a damp patch under the Wendy house, which the assistants must have missed.

For a few days, I was in no state to come in to work. I was fevered. I kept thinking about her.

I'd only seen her for a moment, till the darkness covered her. She was five or six years old. She looked washed out, grubby and bleached of color, and cold, as if I saw her through water. She wore a stained T-shirt, with the picture of a cartoon princess on it.

She'd stared at me with her eyes wide, her face clamped shut. Her gray, fat little fingers had gripped the edge of the Wendy house.

The police had found no one. They'd helped us clear up the balls and put them back in the ball room, and then they'd taken me home.

I can't stop wondering if it would have made any difference to how things turned out, if anyone had believed me. I can't see how it would. When I came back to work, days later, everything had already happened.

After you've been in this job a while, there are two kinds of situations you dread.

The first one is when you arrive to find a mass of people, tense and excited, arguing and yelling and trying to push each other out of the way and calm each other down. You can't see past them, but you know they're reacting ineptly to something bad.

The second one is when there's a crowd of people you can't see past, but they're hardly moving, and nearly silent. That's rarer, and invariably worse.

The woman and her daughter had already been taken away. I saw the whole thing later on security tape.

It had been the little girl's second time in the ball room in a matter of hours. Like the first time, she'd sat alone, perfectly happy, singing and talking to herself. Her minutes were up, her mother had loaded her new garden furniture into the car and come to take her home. She'd knocked on the glass and smiled, and the little girl had waded over happily enough, until she realized that she was being summoned.

On the tape you can see her whole body language change. She starts sulking and moaning, then suddenly turns and runs back to the Wendy house, plonking herself among the balls. Her mother looks fairly patient, standing at the door and calling for her, while the assistant stands with her. You can see them chatting.

The little girl sits by herself, talking into the empty doorway of the Wendy house, with her back to the adults, playing some obstinate, solitary final game. The other kids carry on doing their thing. Some are watching to see what happens.

Eventually, her mother yells at her to come. The girl stands and turns round, facing her across the sea of balls. She has one in each hand, her arms down by her sides, and she brings them up and stares at them, and at her mother. *I won't*, she's saying, I heard later. *I want to stay. We're playing.*

She backs into the Wendy house. Her mother strides over to her and bends in the doorway for a moment. She has to get down on all fours to get inside. Her feet stick out.

There's no sound on the tape. It's when you see all the children jerk, and the assistant run, that you know the woman has started to scream.

The assistant later told me that when she tried to rush forward, it seemed as if she couldn't get through the balls, as if they'd become heavy. The children were all getting in her way. It was bizarrely, stupidly difficult to cross the few feet to the Wendy house, with other adults in her wake.

They couldn't get the mother out of the way, so between them they lifted the house into the air over her, tearing its toy walls apart.

The child was choking.

Of course, of course the balls are designed to be too big for anything like this to happen, but somehow she had shoved one far inside her mouth. It should have been impossible. It was too far, wedged too hard to prise out. The little girl's eyes were huge, and her feet and knees kept turning inward toward each other.

You see her mother lift her up and beat her upon the back, very hard. The children are lined against the wall, watching.

One of the men manages to get the mother aside, and raises the girl for the Heimlich maneuver. You can't see her face too clearly on the tape, but you can tell that it is very dark now, the color of a bruise, and her head is lolling.

Just as he has his arms about her, something happens at the man's feet, and he slips on the balls, still hugging her to him. They sink together.

They got the children into another room. Word went through the store, of course, and all the absent parents came running. When the first arrived she found the man who had intervened screaming at the children while the assistant tried desperately to quiet him. He was demanding they tell him where the other little girl was, who'd come close and chattered to him as he tried to help, who'd been getting in his way.

That's one of the reasons we had to keep going over the tape, to see where this girl had come from, and gone. But there was no sign of her.

Of course, I tried to get transferred, but it wasn't a good time in the industry, or in any industry. It was made pretty clear to me that the best way of holding on to my job was to stay put.

The ball room was closed, initially during the inquest, then for "renovation," and then for longer while discussions went on about its future. The closure became unofficially indefinite, and then officially so.

Those adults who knew what had happened (and it always surprised me, how few did) strode past the room with their toddlers strapped into pushchairs and their eyes grimly on the showroom trail, but their children still missed the room. You could see it when they came up the stairs with their parents. They'd think they were going to the ball room, and they'd start talking about it, and shouting about the climbing frame and the colors, and when they realized it was closed, the big window covered in brown paper, there were always tears.

Like most adults I turned the locked-up room into a blind spot. Even on night shifts when it was still marked on my route I'd turn away. It was sealed up, so why would I check it? Particularly when it still felt so terrible in there, a bad atmosphere as tenacious as stink. There are little card swipe units we have to use to show that we've covered each area, and I'd do the one by the ball room door without looking, staring at the stacks of new catalogues at the top of the stairs. Sometimes I'd imagine I could hear noises behind me, soft little *pudda-thuddas*, but I knew it was impossible so there was no point even checking.

It was strange to think of the ball room closed for good. To think that those were the last kids who'd ever get to play there.

One day I was offered a big bonus to stay on late. The store manager introduced me to Mr. Gainsburg from head office. It turned out she didn't just mean the UK operation, but the corporate parent. Mr. Gainsburg wanted to work late in the store that night, and he needed someone to look after him.

He didn't reappear until well past eleven, just as I was beginning to assume that he'd given in to jet lag and I was in for an easy night. He was tanned and well dressed. He kept using my Christian name while he lectured me about the company. A couple of times I wanted to tell him what my profession had been where I come from, but I could see he wasn't trying to patronize me. In any case I needed the job.

He asked me to take him to the ball room.

"Got to sort out problems as early as you can," he said. "It's the number one thing I've learned, John, and I've been doing this a while. One problem will always create another. If you leave one little thing, think you can just *ride* it out, then before you know it you've got two. And so on.

"You've been here a while, right John? You saw this place before it closed. These crazy little rooms are a fantastic hit with kids. We have them in all our stores now. You'd think it would be an extra, right? A nice-to-have. But I tell you, John, kids love these places, and kids . . . well, kids are really, really important to this company."

The doors were propped open by now and he had me help him carry a portable desk from the show floor into the ball room.

"Kids *make* us, John. Nearly forty percent of our customers have young children, and most of those cite the kid-friendliness of our stores as one of the top two or three reasons they come here. Above quality of product. Above *price*. You drive here, you eat, it's a day out for the family.

"Okay, so that's one thing. Plus, it turns out that people who are shopping for their kids are much more aware of issues like safety and quality. They spend way more per item, on average, than singles and childless couples, because they want to know they've done the best for their kids. And our margins on the bigticket items are way healthier than on entry-level product. Even low-income couples, John, the proportion of their income that goes on furniture and household goods just rockets up at pregnancy."

He was looking around him at the balls, bright in the ceiling lights that hadn't been on for months, at the ruined skeleton of the Wendy house.

"So what's the first thing we look at when a store begins to go wrong? The facilities. The crèche, the childcare. Okay, tick. But the results here have been badly off-kilter recently. All the stores have shown a dip, of course, but this one, I don't know if you've noticed, it's not just revenues are down, but traffic has sunk in a way that's completely out of line. Usually, traffic is actually surprisingly resilient in a downturn. People buy less, but they keep coming. Sometimes, John, we even see numbers go *up*.

"But here? Visits are down overall. Proportionally, traffic from couples with children is down even more. And *repeat* traffic from couples with children has dropped through the floor. That's what's unusual with this store.

"So why aren't they coming back as often? What's different here? What's changed?" He gave a little smile and looked ostentatiously around, then back at me. "Okay? Parents can still leave their kids in the crèche, but the kids aren't asking their parents for repeat visits like they used to. Something's missing. Ergo. Therefore. We need it back."

He laid his briefcase on the desk and gave me a wry smile.

"You know how it is. You tell them and tell them to fix things as they happen, but do they listen? Because it isn't them who have to patch it up, right? So then you end up with not one problem but two. Twice as much trouble to bring under control." He shook his head ruefully. He was looking around the room, into all the corners, narrowing his eyes. He took a couple of deep breaths.

"Okay, John, listen, thanks for all your help. I'm going to need a few minutes here. Why don't you go watch some TV, get yourself a coffee or something? I'll come find you in a while."

I told him I'd be in the staff room. I turned away and heard him open his case. As I left I peered through the glass wall and tried to see what he was laying out on the desk. A candle, a flask, a dark book. A little bell.

Visitor numbers are back up. We're weathering the recession remarkably well. We've dropped some of the deluxe product and introduced a back-to-basic raw pine range. The store has actually taken on more staff recently than it's let go.

The kids are happy again. Their obsession with the ball room refuses to die. There's a little arrow outside it, a bit more than three feet off the ground, which is the maximum height you can be to come in. I've seen children come tearing up the stairs to get in and find out that they've grown in the months since their last visit, that they're too big to come in and play. I've seen them *raging* that they'll never be allowed in again, that they've had their lot, forever. You know they'd give anything at all, right then, to go back. And the other children watching them, those who are just a little bit smaller, would do anything to stop and stay as they are.

Something in the way they play makes me think that Mr. Gainsburg's intervention may not have had the exact effect everyone was hoping for. Seeing how eager they are to rejoin their friends in the ball room, I wonder sometimes if it was intended to.

To the children, the ball room is the best place in the world. You can see that they think about it when they're not there, that they dream about it. It's where they want to stay. If they ever got lost, it's the place they'd want to find their way back to. To play in the Wendy house and on the climbing frame, and to fall all soft and safe on the plastic balls, to scoop them up over each other, without hurting, to play in the ball room forever, like in a fairy tale, alone, or with a friend.

THEODORA GOSS

Nymphs Finding the Head of Orpheus

Theodora Goss has been writing poetry for as long as she can remember. Her poems have been published in magazines such as Mythic Delirium *and* The Lyric, *and reprinted in* The Year's Best Fantasy and Horror. *She recently won a Rhysling Award. Her chapbook of short stories and poems,* The Rose in Twelve Petals & Other Stories, *was published by Small Beer Press, and a short story collection,* In the Forest of Forgetting, *was recently published by Prime Books. She lives in Boston, where she is completing a Ph.D. in English literature, with her husband, daughter, and three cats. Her website address is* http://www.theodoragoss.com.

"Nymphs Finding the Head of Orpheus" was originally published in Jabberwocky.

—*E. D.*

The water has a dim and glassy hue.
A mass of airy bubbles clings to curls
That tumble through the river-bottom's marls,
And cypresses hang heavy with their woe.

Our hair-tips touch the water's urgent tow
As we lift this possessor of blue lips
And single eye that out its substance weeps
From the dark river bound by thorny may.

Now sing, my sisters, piercingly and slow,
And sweetly as the honey of the comb,
For this rank weed, and beat the hollow drum,
And kiss and turn the leperous cheeks away.

DANIEL WALLACE

Vacation

Daniel Wallace is the author of three novels, Ray in Reverse, The Water-melon King, and Big Fish (the latter of which was the basis of the Tim Burton film of the same name), and many short stories. He lives in Chapel Hill, North Carolina, with his lovely wife and brilliant son.

"Vacation" was first published in a chapbook of his stories, Off the Map, published by Two Cranes Press.

—E.D.

You have arrived in Aristea.

The friendly natives of the small island republic welcome you as you step off the plane and into the sweltering midday heat. The sun is high and blinding in its brightness; it's difficult to see anything at first. But you make them out soon enough, there, standing in a line along the edge of the tarmac: the Aristeans. They are small and the color ochre. Their native attire is an odd mix of grass skirts and polo shirts, and hats that once belonged to airline pilots and ocean cruiser tour guides who came here years ago and never left. Many who come here fail to return to their points of origin—such is the magic of Aristea. It says so in the travel guide.

The welcoming ceremony, which begins immediately, is complex, bizarre and macabre. As you walk, suitcase in hand, toward the line of smiling men and women, diminutively precious, they begin to hop up and down to a syncopated beat. They clap their hands and sing a song whose lyrics are at once haunting and cheerful. Then, as if on a cue only they can hear, they disappear into the surrounding brush, all fifteen of them, and return, moments later, holding chickens—live chickens. Some have two. You had been told about this part of the ceremony, but somehow you thought your travel agent had been exaggerating. She wasn't. If anything, she was trying to shield you from the gruesome reality of what is to follow.

They strangle the chickens with their bare hands. One by one the chickens cease their clucking, their wings stop flapping . . . and all is silence. The feathered corpses are held high in the air, triumphantly, for your inspection. The natives proudly display their handiwork. Some of the chickens' heads have been taken right off. Blood drips over the natives' fingers and wrists. You nod, smiling. What else can you do? Then the singing resumes. This ceremony continues for another fifteen minutes, there's more dancing and singing, more hopping around, but after the chickens you don't remember much. Your mind is in a kind of fog. You look around you, suddenly feeling lost, and you wish your wife were here to help, to guide you. You wonder what it was that made you come here, all by yourself, the first vacation you've taken apart from her in years.

Maybe it was this: At home, a thousand miles away, your wife is having an affair with your best friend, Walter. This is not hard to imagine. Walter is actually not a very good friend; to call him your *best* friend implies that there are lots of other friends, and that Walter, among them all, is foremost. It would be more accurate to say that Walter is your only friend. You've lived next door to him for seven years. Prolonged exposure, especially on the weekends, has made him familiar to you in the way you were once familiar with real friends, and thus you have mistaken him for one all this time, when he has actually only wanted to sleep with your wife, a desire he is fulfilling at this very moment.

He is good, too. He is good at sleeping with your wife. Walter is charming in a quiet way, and in bed he knows what to do with his hands, which are big and strong; his fingernails are always clean and cut: perfect crescent moons. He feels good inside your wife, both of them feel good, but it feels especially good to her. She moans, smiling, deeply appreciative of the pleasure Walter affords her. It's not an affair, really, not yet. Now it's just sex. Hot, primitive, wordless sex between your wife and your neighbor.

Suddenly, standing on the tarmac, it all comes to you. This trip was your wife's idea. She said she had heard good things about Aristea. She bought the ticket herself, as a present. After ten years of marriage, she said it was a good time for both of you to rediscover what it was like to be alone, as individuals, and not just half of a couple.

Both of you are discovering what this is like simultaneously, she at home with Walter, and you, on the tarmac, surrounded by fifteen native Aristeans and dozens of freshly killed chickens. You are discovering what it is like to be alone.

After the ceremony, all the natives hug you. Your nice Izod shirt becomes spattered with blood. One native, toothless in a charming way, motions for you to bend over, and when you do he takes a straw hat and fits it, snugly, on your head. With your Bermuda shorts and chalk white legs, you look great. The last man you hug is your driver. His name is Cali—"Like California," he says in a weird accent. His face is dark but his eyes are blue, beautiful but strange, like a doll's eyes. "You from California?" he asks hopefully. "You from Santa Barbara?" But you are not. He shakes your hand anyway. Then, after a deep, meaningful look in the eyes, he takes your bags and throws them into the trunk of his gray taxi, which appears to have been built according to a rumor of what a car might be like. The steering wheel is tied to a broom pole, and the seats are wiry and splintered. The doors don't open but detach, and have to be snapped back into place once you've been seated. After you get in and the car has been reassembled, Cali takes his place in the driver's seat and kicks something, turns the ignition, and the car starts, backfiring and sputtering like a bomb.

"Hair," he says, turning to you as the rumbling car idles in the sun.

"Hair?"

"Hair," he says, "here." But the two words sound almost identical.

He holds up his right arm, which looks like a light brown thin hairless root. He points to his own arm and then to your hairy one. He looks at yours with wonder, and smiles.

"Touch it?" he says. "Okay? To touch?"

"Sure," you say, though you're not sure why it's okay. But it would seem rude somehow to deny him this request. His hand slowly moves to your arm and gently rests there for a moment. You feel his warmth. Then as he lifts his palm, his fingers come together and lightly pull at a tuft of your hair, and just before it is about to hurt he lets go. For a moment he's silent, as though trying to take the experience in, and then he snaps to, smiles at you (he has beautiful teeth; one of them is gold), nods in thanks and turns away and then begins to drive down a winding, unpaved road. This, even though you have yet to tell him where you want to go.

After their first time, Walter and your wife lie together, in your bed, and share an uncomfortable silence. She pulls the pale blue cotton sheets up over her breasts. But the gravity of what they've done settles like a concrete blanket over them both. Everything has changed now. They both know that. Walter is your "friend," but more than that, he's your neighbor. He lives in the bungalow next door. He has made love to your wife, and now he will have to see you every day—wave to you as you are both leaving for work—and know that he has done one of the worst things that one man can do to another. Every time he looks at her, and she looks at him, they will know what they've done. It will be their secret, and as such, it will harm them in ways beyond knowing. It will grow inside them both like a cancer.

Secrets have a way of announcing themselves, though, especially to the person from whom they are being kept. One day you will find out. And what will happen then? Will you fly into a rage? Will you look at your wife and say, "How could you?" Will you kill one of them? Or will you simply get divorced and move away?

Everything has changed. This is the knowledge Walter and your wife share in the silence, after the sex, that first time, as the sunlight angles past the dresser, across the hardwood floor. It's the way Eve felt after taking her first bite of the apple. She felt bad, you know she did.

The second time, however, there are no misgivings, whatsoever. It's all good.

After a few minutes of driving into an increasingly wild and forested countryside, you cough to get his attention, and then say, "Excuse me, Cali? I'm going to the hotel. Hotel Aristea. Is this the way to the hotel?"

Cali looks at you in the rear view mirror and smiles, though you're not sure he can hear you over the sound of the engine.

"No problem," he says and winks.

"The hotel?" you say again.

"I feel," he shouts, and then stops, his face grimaces as he grinds the gears. The car shakes, lurches. "I feel you are like a brother to me," he says.

"Thank you," you say, unsure why you would thank him for saying such a thing. You don't want to be like a brother to Cali. You want to be a passenger in his cab and nothing more. But now you see him lovingly, almost reverently, eyeing you in his rear view mirror, a mirror which is really no more than a shard of glass wired to the ceiling, and you realize that you are much more than just a passenger to Cali. You're like a brother to him, like it or not. You had heard the natives here were friendly, the women, especially. You simply had no idea how friendly they could be.

It would be unfair to your wife to accuse her of encouraging this trip in the hopes that, once you were gone, she could partake in this affair with Walter. At the same time, this is not entirely untrue. She and Walter had never mentioned anything to the other about having an affair, had never spoken in intimate terms in any way. And yet somehow you knew that if you were gone, even for a week, they would fall into bed together. They didn't have to talk about it. The day you left Walter merely knocked on your front door, ostensibly to ask about a dead tree bordering both of your yards, and when their eyes met it was as if a huge conversation took place in less than a second. He walked into your house as though it were his own. She closed the door behind him. And they did it. Do it. Are doing it still. It's great for them both. It's amazing, beyond all hopes, all dreams.

The thing is, you had just lost all that weight. You still had a little tummy, of course, but a man your age, any man your age, is going to have a little tummy. Even Walter has a little tummy. This is what it is, what makes you realize that no matter what she said, no matter how she looked at you, no matter how bad she made you feel about yourself and your body, it was never that. It was always something else. Walter has a nice size tummy, himself. So it was never that.

The Aristean countryside is a florid, volcanic protrusion of flowers and trees, each falling into the next, dark and beautiful and rainforest lush. It is impossible to see into, and, surely, impossible to escape from. Snakes, monkeys, and huge, deadly, virtually unknown insects live in the trees and among the roots within these ancient forests. The travel guide says so.

How could there be a hotel here? Nothing but shanties line the road, and the poor and naked Aristeans wave, apparently happy in their squalor, as you pass. Some chase the cab, and some even catch up with it—they're a speedy little people—and rip off what parts of the cab they can in their hands. To use in the construction of their houses?

"The hotel?" you say again, eternally hopeful. But Cali just drives.

It is hard to believe that your wife is sleeping with Walter—at first. But after thinking about it for a minute, you wonder why you didn't realize how they have always wanted each other, how ready each was for the other, and how your absence has made their union possible, even probable. Face it: your wife is a hot number, seething, wide-eyed, open to the world and its offerings. She married you because you were able to provide her with a safe and secure harbor, a home she could call her own and return to when her adventures *du jour* were over. In other words, you were suitable. Acceptable. Handy. And she, the hot number, seething, wide-eyed. Who knows how many Walter-types she's encountered in the last ten years. But you—you have never found another woman quite like her. You've rarely even glimpsed one except in a magazine. The rest of them, the rest of her kind—it's as if they come from another world, the world of fashion, or airbrushed photographs, of celebrity. You were right to snatch her up. Other men envy you. Yes, they envy you. That's the look you see in their eyes as they watch you with your wife, as they look at you on the street with her, out to eat at a nice restaurant. They shake their heads and smile when they see you. This is envy. You are a very lucky man.

Cali continues to watch you in the rear view mirror. How, you wonder, can he watch you so intently and keep the car on the road? But then, it's not much of a road. In fact it's hard to distinguish what the road is from what it's *not*. It's as if wherever the car happens to go can be considered road, because the car is going over it all, rocks, roots, ravines. Whatever. And you feel every bump.

"Joke?" he says, yelling to you over the grinding noise the engine makes. "You want joke?"

You shrug your shoulders. "Sure," you say. "Tell me a joke."

"Okay," he says, grinning at the thought of it. "Man. This man, he walks into bar. Okay?"

"Okay," you say. Somehow this puts you at ease, that there is humor in a man walking into a bar, even here in Aristea.

"So. Man walks into bar. *Very* sad, this man. Get drunk. Say to bartender, something, 'I feel like *so sad*. I want to see beautiful woman. Where is beautiful woman? Can you show me beautiful woman?' Bartender says, 'I show you beautiful woman.' Takes him to special room. Full of women, full of women, but they are *all* ugly. So ugly. Ugliest women on the earth. So the man says, 'Where are the *beautiful* women?' "

Cali pauses. You wait. You look in the mirror and make eye contact with him, and when you do his smile grows, and he begins to laugh as hard as he can without dislodging an organ, and you realize: that was it. That was the joke.

"I'm sorry," you say. "I don't get it."

"What?" he says.

"The joke," you say. "I don't—where are they?"

"What?" he says. "Where what?"

"The women."

"Who?"

"The women," you say. "The beautiful women."

"Yes?"

"Where are the beautiful women?"

Cali smiles, veers to miss a dog-like creature that has wandered out into the path of the car, and nods, knowingly. "Oh, I seeing. You want I take you to the beautiful women."

"What?"

He meets your eyes in the reflective glass.

"The beautiful women," he says again, a small smile on his lips. "You want I take you to the beautiful women?"

Tired—you are very tired. It was a long flight in a small plane. *No, no, no*, you want to say. *Please, just listen.* But you don't say that. The cab lurches to one side, and something falls off of it (fender? a part of the engine?), and it is against every reflex in your body, but with the overpowering spectral vision of Walter and your wife in bed together a thousand miles away, you nod. It feels right. "Yes," you say. "Yes. Take me to the beautiful women."

Sex: it's not the worst thing, of course. Not for you, not for you as you're thinking about your wife and Walter, your treacherous next door neighbor. The worst is what happens after. Not the first time, or the second, but after the third, and then, more, after the fourth, what happens then.

They *talk*. They talk about themselves to each other.

"My dad was a—I don't know," Walter says. "He messed around a lot. It about killed my mother. It wasn't great for the rest of us either, you know? Just the mood and shit around the house. He traveled a lot. On business. That's when he did it. I hated him."

"You didn't hate him," she says.

"You're right," he says, glancing over at the perceptive and naked woman lying beside him in bed. "I didn't hate him. Not really. I hated the fact that I loved him, and that he was the kind of man who would do that to my mother. Does that make sense?"

"Sure," she says. "I mean, what are you going to do? He's your dad. It's not like—"

"—I can get another," he says.

"Exactly."

"They got divorced when I was sixteen," he says.

"One day," she says, "you'll talk. You have to. Just to get it out of your system. Otherwise—"

"It festers," he says.

"And it kills you."

"It's just—"

"I know," she says.

"Hard," he says.

"I know."

And they don't even touch. They just lie there, together.

This is the worst thing.

Consider this: you are forgetting things you used to know, things you always took for granted knowing, like your telephone number, your mother's maiden name, your favorite place to go for coffee—what was it? You've forgotten. And you've only been here a few hours. You wonder how it will be by the end of the week, what you will have forgotten by then: your wife, her lover, your address, your country of origin. Your own name. You will lie stretched out on the beach in the sun mostly naked, like a slice of bacon in a frying pan, muttering gibberish, laughing for no reason, doing a silly dance.

Your mother never liked your wife. She never said as much because it would be unseemly, but she never warmed up to your wife the way she could have. She never calls her just to chat, never gets her a special present at Christmas. No one's ever mentioned it and you used to resent her for it, but now you don't, you think she has always known something you should have known, but didn't. That one day this would happen. All of this. The affair, Aristea, Cali. The progress of your life. A mother knows these things.

Suddenly the skies begin to darken. In the rear view mirror you watch Cali's eyes narrow, the smile leaves his face stone cold.

"Almost there," Cali says. "Almost there to the beautiful women."

Then it starts to rain. The sky opens and buckets of water fall down all over on the trees and the road and the cab, and all that was once bright and dry and brittle is now wet, dripping, muddy. The cab slides about like a bobsled, and Cali doesn't even appear to be driving anymore; he looks to be hypnotized as the steering wheel rocks back and forth on its own. The wind blows hard, and sheets of rain pour in through the window, which you can't roll up because there isn't one, there is no window, and within seconds your hair is soaked, and you can feel a cool puddle collecting around you in the seat. Everywhere, the world has turned into a gray violent haze of rapidly falling water, as though the ocean were being strained through a filter; and beyond you there is nothing, nothing you can see at all.

And still Cali drives, onward, transfixed as a martyr, with his eyes on his fate.

Back in America, it is a sweet and glossy spring. Perhaps it's the next morning, or the one after that, time is funny the way it changes from place to place—and didn't you fly over the date line to get here? At any rate, it's morning, and Walter is off to work. Your wife is home alone, reading the paper in the sun room, drinking her coffee. She looks up briefly as she hears Walter's car start up, but she doesn't get up to watch him drive away: she just smiles a little smile—for the pleasure she has had or the pleasure that is to come, no one but she could say.

Unbeknownst to you, Walter is a golfing buddy of Nelson, the guy in the cubicle beside yours at work. Your relationship with them both is strangely similar—superficially important—but you never knew that one was acquainted with the other. Walter calls Nelson that morning, from work. "You'll never guess what happened yesterday," he says. "Not in a million fucking years." And Nelson starts guessing, but Walter was right: he would never guess correctly for a very long time. So Walter tells him. He tells him—not everything—but a lot, enough, too much. Husband on trip, wife home alone, et cetera, et cetera. Nelson can't believe it. He can't believe it until he actually tells someone else about it. Over time, as more people tell the story, it becomes more and more believable to everybody.

And so, by the time your vacation is over, everyone will know. As a cuckold, everyone will pity and despise you. Your position at the company will be weakened, your future there, insecure and pointless. So there goes your job along with your wife. There goes everything you ever had. There is no reason, you realize, ever to return.

But just then a light breaks through the darkness—not the sun, but something better: electricity. It's a street lamp. There is a town here, a place, somewhere to be, to rest, shelter from the storm. The hotel must be close. The rain lets up, and you see little buildings. Not the most prepossessing of buildings, but still, with their bamboo awnings and thickly thatched roofs, they are charming, and right out of the travel guide. The cab slows. The streets are deserted in the shower, but as soon as the rain stops—and it does, in the matter of a moment, as if a spigot has been shut off—natives and tourists alike crowd the street, fruit stalls open, a lively excitement bustles all around.

Huge yellow flowers grow from the soil around the sides of buildings, and the women—dressed in almost nothing at all—are beautiful beyond your imagination. They're perfect, from their hair to their breasts to their slender waists and substantial hips. *Wow,* you think. Just *wow* Aristea: you have to admit it now, it's kind of nice. You're kind of glad you came. Beyond the edge of town you can even see the limitless ocean, a shimmering blue, see-through to the sandy bottom, and lovely, just lovely. *Smile, you idiot,* you think to yourself. *Smile.* The strange reception, the alarming driver, and the harrowing cab ride aside, this is a kind of paradise, and you're in it. Pity the poor fuckers at home who have to wake up in the morning to a pine tree and a parking lot. This is the life! Even Cali seems to have settled down: the cab ride is slower now, easy-going, pleasant.

Your eyes meet Cali's in the rear view mirror. You smile, clearly happy, and then he smiles, too.

"My people, we have not so much," he says, in his halting English. "But we try to—we try to how you say—we try to *live,* anyway. Live the good life. No?"

"It's a very beautiful place," you say. "Everything about it now—beautiful."

"Your country," Cali says. "America. America very beautiful too. But America not always good to Aristea. You try to—to *hurt* our country, even though it is *so little.* This big," he says, and holds up a hand with thumb and forefinger just barely apart. "A fly—a fly is bigger than my country."

He looks at you and laughs, though somehow the laugh seems fake, forced. You laugh too.

"It is a small country," you say, nodding. "And America is very big."

For the first time since the ride began, Cali turns to look at you; in the small cab your faces are almost touching.

"So why do you care about hurting us so much?" he says. "Why, my brother?"

This comes as something of a shock.

"*Me?*" you say. "Hurt you?" You don't know what Cali is talking about, but Cali does: his face is set in stone as he stares at you. And then you vaguely remember some articles you read in the paper some time ago, something about the government here: was it overthrown, or did they elect some unsavory character? Was there some military action? You really don't remember. You don't remember because you don't care, you never did and you never will. Why care about Aristea? You're here on vacation, after all.

Cali stops the cab near the side of the road beside what looks like a bar: a martini glass, at any rate, is painted in red on the dirty white brick. There are no windows, however, and only one dark screen door, beyond which there seems to be nothing at all. He turns to you, and studies your face.

"Sit," he says. "Stay here. Wait. I check on women. Back soon."

"Cali," you say, looking at him with all the sincerity you can muster, "I'm your friend."

And Cali smiles. "I know," he says.

He unlatches his door from the sophisticated coat hanger device that holds it on the body of the car, and walks into the building with the martini on the wall. The building appears to swallow him. He's gone for some time. As you wait, you look around and admire the lovely little town that time forgot, the people now swarming the unpaved streets after the rain. Soon this will be you, stepping over puddles, eating bananas, laughing like a hyena.

And this, remarkably, is when you see someone you know. That's Tom Blankenship, for God's sake! You can't remember the last time you saw him, but that's him all right, hasn't changed at all, that's him in a torn and dirty T-shirt, barefooted, wearing a pair of jeans cut off to shorts. He's the guy you always thought of as having it made. Smart, successful, single: if there was fun to be had, Tom Blankenship was having it. Seeing him here confirms that you have come to the right place for a vacation.

"Tom!" you call from the window, and he turns, but only briefly. Then he keeps walking, faster, away from you.

"Tom!" you call again, louder this time. "Tom Blankenship! It's me!"

As he turns a corner, you figure he didn't hear you, or if he did, he couldn't see. You're just some disembodied voice calling his name. So you get out of the cab. He's gone now but you saw where he went and you run after him, calling his name. It's so exciting, in a way you can't describe, this coincidence; you can't wait to share it with him. *You and Tom Blankenship in Aristea!*

Turning the corner, you see him but you're too out of breath to call his name now, and so you just run up and place a hand on his shoulder.

But the man who turns around isn't Tom Blankenship. Not even close. This man isn't even white, he's clearly Aristean, and there's a long scar down one side of his face, and when he smiles you see he's missing most of his teeth, and his tongue writhes around in his mouth like a snake. He looks at your hand on his shoulder as though it were a dead rat, and he grabs it, moving it off of him with a malicious strength, almost breaking your fingers as he does so.

"Sir!"

It is Cali, running toward you as you cringe in pain. The man drops your hand

and, with a cold glare at Cali, walks away. You watch the man go, shaking out your hand to get some feeling back.

"I said, *Sit*," Cali says. "I said, *Stay*. You not stay."

"I thought," you say, but what you thought seems so improbable now that the words can't be spoken, they can't live outside your own mind.

"Thought?" Cali says. He reminds you of your father, the way he says it. "Thought? If you thought, you stay. No thought!" he says. He drags you back to the cab and points to it. "No thought. Look: everything gone!"

"What?"

He is pointing to the trunk. It's open. Inside there is nothing but an old Coke can. This is where your suitcase was. Your passport, your money, all of your clothes, the bathing suit you planned to wear on the beach—gone. All in a minute's time.

"This why I tell you stay," he says, shaking his head sadly, lecturing you. "Some people, they no good. They wait for this, and take everything. Bad men. Bad men here, just like in America. Just like everywhere."

You nod. Cali is right: there are bad men everywhere, here and America, bad men like Walter, Walter who has stolen everything from you, who has destroyed everything you are, or were, your life as you knew it, your wife as you knew her, your place in the world, it's all over now, over and done with. Say goodbye to the old friend that was your life, and say hello to this stranger, this stranger you've become. See him grotesquely reflected in the puddle at your feet. Study him. You will be together for some time.

"But now," Cali says, thumping you on the back and draping an arm over your shoulders, "now is time for women, no?"

You nod, stunned, not knowing the next step here, appreciating Cali's direction. All the familiar guideposts are gone. If he says it is time for the women, it is time for the women. You assent with a nod, and follow your brother, Cali.

And why not? Why not experience something that actually feels good before disappearing into the black numbness of the life that so clearly awaits you back home? Sex with beautiful women is good. It's good in America, and it's good here, in Aristea. You'll do it all week long if you want to. It's not the same as sex with your wife, of course, but you don't really have a wife anymore, do you? She's probably having sex with the neighbor right now. So go for it. Go for the sex with the coffee-colored women.

The room Cali leads you to in the back of the martini bar is windowless and dark. Light from outside soars into it when the door opens, and you can see bodies briefly—women everywhere—and smoke. When the door closes you feel blind for a moment, grasping for something to hold onto, to touch.

Slowly your eyes become adjusted to the darkness. There are little lights everywhere now—the glowing tips of cigarettes. In a corner, a match flares, and a small fire starts, and when it does, you see a woman—part of her face anyway—her long black hair falling across it. "Hello?" you say to her, to everyone, anyone. You feel the presence of lots of people, though no one says anything back to you. Someone laughs. What is *Hello* in Aristean? You can't remember. You can't remember anything. "Hello," you say again. "My name is—" But you stop when you feel a hand around your ankle. It's a small hand but a strong one. And it seems to be pulling you down. "Cali?" you say.

"Sir?" He is right behind you, so close to your ear he only has to whisper. "I am here, sir."

And now the darkness seems to disappear, or to become just another kind of light—a dim, obscure and malevolent kind of light—and the faces and figures of those before you become clearer, even recognizable. These are the people who welcomed you as you got off the plane. These are the people who killed the chickens. Then you see the women, their faces coming close to yours out of the shadows, brightened by the growing fire, and they are as ugly as any you have ever seen or imagined.

"Cali," you say, backing up into his strong, tiny body, your heart about to break wide open it's beating so hard and fast. "What's going on?"

"Man walks into bar," Cali says. "Get it?"

And he laughs, and touches the hair on your arm, pulls it hard until a sharp pain strikes. But you don't cry out, you can't, because someone's hand is covering your mouth. You push it away, and it touches you somewhere else. Out of the darkness other hands find you, touch you, pull your hair.

You don't get it. *Where are the beautiful women?* And yet, somehow, in spite of these people, in spite of Walter and your wife, in spite of everything, you manage a smile. This is not as bad as it looks. You still have your Bermuda shorts, a blood-stained shirt, and a straw hat too small for your own head. Perhaps someone here will be interested in trading for them. *Yes, perhaps a trade*, you think, naïve as always. They do seem interested, though; the natives seem interested in whatever it is you have to share. But trading is not what they have in mind.

NISI SHAWL

Cruel Sistah

"Cruel Sistah" is a striking, contemporary retelling of a traditional ballad. "Cruel Sistah" appeared in the October/November double issue of Asimov's. Shawl's fiction has also appeared in both volumes of the Dark Matter anthology series, So Long Been Dreaming: Postcolonial Science Fiction and Fantasy, Mojo: Conjure Stories, Lenox Avenue, Strange Horizons, and Semiotext(e) SF. 2005 also saw the publication of Nisi Shawl and Cynthia Ward's Writing the Other: A Practical Guide (Aqueduct Press). Shawl writes and reviews for the Seattle Times and is a contributor to The Encyclopedia of Themes in Science Fiction and Fantasy and The Internet Review of Science Fiction. In 2004 and 2005 she edited BEYOND magazine, an online magazine of Afrocentric speculative fiction by teens. Shawl is a founding member of the Carl Brandon Society, an organization which supports the presence of people of color in the fantastic genres, and is currently a board member for the Clarion West Writers Workshop. She has been a guest lecturer at Stanford University and at the Science Fiction Museum and Hall of Fame. She likes to relax by pretending she lives in other people's houses.

—K.L. & G.G.

You and Neville goin out again?"

"I think so. He asked could he call me Thursday after class."

Calliope looked down at her sister's long, straight, silky hair. It fanned out over Calliope's knees and fell almost to the floor, a black river drying up just short of its destined end. "Why don't you let me wash this for you?"

"It takes too long to dry. Just braid it up like you said, okay?"

"Your head all fulla dandruff," Calliope lied. "And ain't you ever heard of a hair dryer? Mary Lockett lent me her portable."

"Mama says those things bad for your hair." Dory shifted uncomfortably on the sofa cushion laid on the hardwood floor where she sat. Dory (short for Dorcas) was the darker-skinned of the two girls, darker by far than their mama or their daddy. "Some kinda throwback," the aunts called her.

Mama doted on Dory's hair, though, acting sometimes as if it was her own. Not too surprising, seeing how good it was. Also, a nervous breakdown eight years back had made Mama completely bald. Alopecia was the doctor's word for it, and there was no cure. So Mama made sure both her daughters took care of their crowning glories. But especially Dory.

"All right, no dryer," Calliope conceded. "We can go out in the back garden and let the sun help dry it. 'Cause in fact, I was gonna rinse it with rainwater. Save us haulin it inside."

Daddy had installed a flexible hose on the kitchen sink. Calliope wet her sister's hair down with warm jets of water, then massaged in sweet-smelling shampoo. White suds covered the gleaming black masses, gathering out of nowhere like clouds.

Dory stretched her neck and sighed. "That feels nice."

"Nice as when Neville kisses you back there?"

"Ow!"

"Or over here?"

"OW! Callie, what you doin?"

"Sorry. My fingers slipped. Need to trim my nails, hunh? Let's go rinse off."

Blood from the cuts on her neck and ear streaked the shampoo clouds with pink stains. Unaware of this, Dory let her sister lead her across the red and white linoleum to the back porch and the creaky wooden steps down to the garden. She sat on the curved cement bench by the cistern, gingerly at first. It was surprisingly warm for spring. The sun shone, standing well clear of the box elders crowding against the retaining wall at the back of the lot. A silver jet flew high overhead, bound for Seatac. The low grumble of its engines lagged behind it, obscuring Calliope's words.

"What?"

"I said, 'Quit sittin' pretty and help me move this lid.' "

The cistern's cover came off with a hollow, grating sound. A slice of water, a crescent like the waning moon, reflected the sun's brightness. Ripples of light ran up the damp stone walls. Most of the water lay in darkness, though. Cold smells seeped up from it: mud, moss. Mystery.

As children, Dory, Calliope, and their cousins had been fascinated by the cistern. Daddy and Mama had forbidden them to play there, of course, which only increased their interest. When their parents opened it to haul up water for the garden, the girls hovered close by, snatching glimpses inside.

"Goddam if that no-good Byron ain't lost the bucket!" Calliope cursed the empty end of the rope she'd retrieved from her side of the cistern. It was still curled where it had been tied to the handle of the beige plastic bucket.

Byron, their fourteen-year-old cousin, liked to soak sticks and strips of wood in water to use in his craft projects. He only lived a block away, so he was always in and out of the basement workshop. "You think he took it home again?" Dory asked.

"No, I remember now I saw it downstairs, fulla some trash a his, tree branches or somethin."

"Yeah? Well, that's all right, we don't wanna—"

"I'll go get it and wipe it out good. Wait for me behind the garage."

"Oh, but he's always so upset when you mess with his stuff!"

"It ain't his anyhow, is it?" Calliope took the porch steps two at a time. She was a heavy girl, but light on her feet. Never grew out of her baby fat. Still, she could hold her own in a fight.

The basement stairs, narrow and uneven, slowed her down a bit. Daddy had run a string from the bare-bulb fixture at their bottom, looping it along the wooden wall of the stairwell. She pulled, and the chain at its other end slithered obediently against porcelain, clicked and snapped back. Brightness flooded the lowering floor joists.

Calliope ignored the beige bucket full of soaking willow wands. Daddy's tool bench, that's where she'd find what she wanted. Nothing too heavy, though. She had to be able to lift it. And not too sharp. She didn't want to have to clean up a whole lot of blood.

Hammer? Pipe wrench? What if Mama got home early and found Calliope carrying one of those out of the house? What would she think?

It came to her with the same sort of slide and snap that had turned the light on. Daddy was about to tear out the railroad ties in the retaining wall. They were rotten; they needed replacing. It was this week's project. The new ones were piled up at the end of the driveway.

Smiling, Calliope selected a medium-sized mallet, its handle as long as her forearm. And added a crowbar for show.

Outside, Dory wondered what was taking her sister so long. A clump of shampoo slipped down her forehead and along one eyebrow. She wiped it off, annoyed. She stood up from the weeds where she'd been waiting, then quickly knelt down again at the sound of footsteps on the paving bricks.

"Bend forward." Calliope's voice cracked. Dory began twisting her head to see why. The mallet came down hard on her right temple. It left a black dent in the suds, a hollow. She made a mewing sound, fell forward. Eyes open, but blind. Another blow, well-centered, this time, drove her face into the soft soil. One more. Then Calliope took control of herself.

"You dead," she murmured, satisfied.

A towel over her sister's head disguised the damage. Hoisting her up into a sitting position and leaning her against the garage, Calliope hunkered back to look at her and think. No one was due home within the next couple of hours. For that long, her secret would be safe. Even then she'd be all right as long as they didn't look out the kitchen windows. The retaining wall was visible from there, but if she had one of the new ties tamped in place, and the dirt filled back in . . .

A moment more she pondered. Fast-moving clouds flickered across the sun, and her skin bumped up. There was no real reason to hang back. Waiting wouldn't change what she'd done.

The first tie came down easily. Giant splinters sprung off as Calliope kicked it to one side. The second one, she had to dig the ends out, and the third was cemented in place its full length by dried clay. Ants boiled out of the hundreds of holes that had been hidden behind it, and the phone rang.

She wasn't going to answer it. But it stopped, and started again, and she knew she'd better.

Sweat had made mud of the dirt on her hands. She cradled the pale blue princess phone against one shoulder, trying to rub the mess clean on her shirt as she listened to Mama asking what was in the refrigerator. The cord barely stretched that far. Were they out of eggs? Butter? Lunch meat? Did Calliope think there was enough cornmeal to make hush puppies? Even with Byron coming over? And what were she and Dory up to that it took them so long to answer the phone?

"Dory ain't come home yet. No, I don't know why; she ain't tole me. I was out in back, tearin down the retaining wall."

Her mother's disapproving silence lasted two full seconds. "Why you always wanna act so mannish, Calliope?"

There wasn't any answer to that. She promised to change her clothes for supper.

Outside again, ants crawled on her dead sister's skin.

Dory didn't feel them. She saw them, though, from far off. Far up? What was going on didn't make regular sense. Why couldn't she hear the shovel digging? Whoever was lying there on the ground in Dory's culottes with a towel over her head, it was someone else. Not her.

She headed for the house. She should be hungry. It must be supper time by now. The kitchen windows were suddenly shining through the dusk. And sure enough, Calliope was inside already, cooking.

In the downstairs bathroom, Daddy washed his hands with his sleeves rolled up. She kissed him. She did; on his cheek, she couldn't have missed it.

The food look good, good enough to eat. Fried chicken, the crisp ridges and golden valleys of its skin glowing under the ceiling light. Why didn't she want it? Her plate was empty.

Nobody talked much. Nobody talked to her at all. There were a lot of leftovers. Cousin Byron helped Calliope clear the table. Daddy made phone calls, with Mama listening in on the extension. She could see them both at the same time, in the kitchen and in their bedroom upstairs. She couldn't hear anything.

Then the moon came out. It was bedtime, a school night. Everyone stayed up though, and the police sat in the living room and moved their mouths till she got tired of watching them. She went in the backyard again, where all this weird stuff had started happening.

The lid was still off the cistern. She looked down inside. The moon's reflection shone up at her, a full circle, uninterrupted by shadow. Not smooth, though. Waves ran through it, long, like swirls actually. Closer, she saw them clearly: hairs. Her hairs, supple and fine.

Suddenly, the world was in daylight again. Instead of the moon's circle, a face covered the water's surface. Her sister's face. Calliope's. Different, and at first Dory couldn't understand why. Then she realized it was her hair, *her* hair, Dory's own. A thin fringe of it hung around her big sister's face as if it belonged there. But it didn't. Several loose strands fell drifting toward Dory. And again, it was night.

And day. And night. Time didn't stay still. Mostly, it seemed to move in one direction. Mama kept crying; Daddy too. Dory decided she must be dead. But what about heaven? What about the funeral?

Byron moved into Dory's old room. It wasn't spooky; it was better than his mom's house. There, he could never tell who was going to show up for drinks. Or breakfast. He never knew who was going to start yelling and throwing things in the middle of the night: his mom, or some man she had invited over, or someone else she hadn't.

Even before he brought his clothes, Byron had kept his instruments and other projects here. Uncle Marv's workshop was wonderful, and he let him use all his tools.

His thing now was gimbris, elegant North African ancestors of the cigar-box banjos he'd built two years ago when he was just beginning, just a kid. He sat on the retaining wall in the last, lingering light of the autumn afternoon, considering the face, neck, and frame of his latest effort, a variant like a violin, meant to be bowed. He'd pieced it together from the thin trunk of an elder tree blown down in an August storm, sister to the leafless ones still upright behind him.

The basic structure looked good, but it was kind of plain. It needed some sort of decoration. An inlay, ivory or mother of pearl or something. The hide backing was important, obviously, but that could wait; it'd be easier to take care of the inlay first.

Of course, real ivory would be too expensive. Herb David, who let him work in his guitar shop, said people used bone as a substitute. And he knew where some was.

Small bits, probably from some dead dog or rabbit. They'd been entangled in the tree roots. He planned to make tuning pegs out of them. There'd be plenty, though.

He stood up, and the world whited out. It had been doing that a lot since he moved here. The school nurse said he had low blood pressure. He just had to stand still a minute and he'd be okay. The singing in his ears, that would stop, too. But it was still going when he got to the stairs.

Stubbornly, he climbed, hanging onto the handrail. Dory's—his—bedroom was at the back of the house, overlooking the garden. His mom kept her dope in an orange juice can hung under the heat vent. He used the same system for his bones. No one knew he had them; so why was he afraid they'd take them away?

He held them in his cupped palms. They were warm, and light. The shimmering whiteness had condensed down to one corner of his vision. Sometimes that meant he was going to get a headache. He hoped not. He wanted to work on this now, while he was alone.

When he left his room, though, he crossed the hall into Calliope's instead of heading downstairs to Uncle Marv's workshop. Without knowing why, he gazed around him. The walls were turquoise, the throw rugs and bedspread pale pink. Nothing in here interested him, except—that poster of Wilt Chamberlain her new boyfriend, Neville, had given her . . .

It was signed, worth maybe one hundred dollars. He stepped closer. He could never get Calliope to let him anywhere near the thing when she was around, but she took terrible care of it. It was taped to the wall all crooked, sort of sagging in the middle.

He touched the slick surface—slick, but not smooth—something soft and lumpy lay between the poster and the wall. What? White light pulsed up around the edges of his vision as he lifted one creased corner.

Something black slithered to the floor. He knelt. With the whiteness, his vision had narrowed, but he could still see it was nothing alive. He picked it up.

A wig! Or at least part of one. Byron tried to laugh. It was funny, wasn't it? Calliope wearing a wig like some old bald lady? Only . . . only it was so weird. The bones. This—hair. The way Dory had disappeared.

He had to think. This was not the place. He smoothed down the poster's tape, taking the wig with him to the basement.

He put the smallest bone in a clamp. It was about as big around as his middle finger. He sawed it into oblong disks.

The wig hair was long and straight. Like Dory's. It was held together by shriveled-up skin, the way he imagined an Indian's scalp would be.

What if Calliope had killed her little sister? It was crazy, but what if she had? Did that mean she'd kill him if he told on her? Or if she thought he knew?

And if he was wrong, he'd be causing trouble for her, and Uncle Marv, and Aunt Cookie, and he might have to go live at home again.

Gradually, his work absorbed him, as it always did. When Calliope came in, he had a pile of bone disks on the bench, ready for polishing. Beside them, in a sultry heap, lay the wig, which he'd forgotten to put back.

Byron looked up at his cousin, unable to say anything. The musty basement was suddenly too small. She was three years older than him, and at least 30 pounds heavier. And she saw it, she had to see it. After a moment, he managed a sickly smirk, but his mouth stayed shut.

"Whatchoodoon?" She didn't smile back. "You been in my room?"

"I—I didn't—"

She picked it up. "Pretty, ain't it?" She stroked the straight hair, smoothing it out. "You want it?"

No clue in Calliope's bland expression as to what she meant. He tried to formulate an answer just to her words, to what she'd actually said. Did he want the wig. "For the bow I'm makin, yeah, sure, thanks."

"Awright then."

He wished she'd go away. "Neville be here tonight?"

She beamed. It was the right question to ask. "I guess. Don't know what he sees in me, but the boy can't keep away."

Byron didn't know what Neville saw in her either. "Neville's smart," he said diplomatically. It was true.

So was he.

There was more hair than he needed, even if he saved a bunch for restringing. He coiled it up and left it in his juice can. There was no way he could prove it was Dory's. If he dug up the backyard where the tree fell, where he found the bones, would the rest of the skeleton be there?

The police. He should call the police, but he'd seen *Dragnet*, and *Perry Mason*. When he accepted the wig, the hair, he'd become an accessory after the fact. Maybe he was one even before that, because of the bones.

It was odd, but really the only time he wasn't worried about all this was when he worked on the gimbri. By Thanksgiving, it was ready to play.

He brought it out to show to Neville after dinner. "That is a seriously fine piece of work," said Neville, cradling the gimbri's round leather back. "Smaller than the other one, isn't it?" His big hands could practically cover a basketball. With one long thumb he caressed the strings. They whispered dryly.

"You play it with this." Byron handed him the bow.

He held it awkwardly: Keyboards, reeds, guitar, drums, flute, even accordion: he'd fooled around with plenty of instruments, but nothing resembling a violin. "You sure you want me to?"

It was halftime on the TV, and dark outside already. Through the living room window, yellow light from a street lamp coated the grainy, gray sidewalk, dissolving at its edges like a pointillist's reverie. A night just like this, he'd first seen how pretty Dory was: the little drops of rain in her hair shining, and it stayed nice as a white girl's.

Not like Calliope's. Hers was as naturally nappy as his, worse between her legs. He sneaked a look at her while Byron was showing him how to position the gimbri upright. She was looking straight back at him, her eyes hot and still. Not as pretty as Dory, no, but she let him do things he would never have dreamed of asking of her little sister.

Mr. Moore stood up from the sofa and called to his wife. "Mama, you wanna come see our resident genius's latest invention in action?"

The gimbri screamed, choked, and sighed. "What on earth?" said Mrs. Moore from the kitchen doorway. She shut her eyes and clamped her lips together as if the awful noise was trying to get in through other ways besides her ears.

Neville hung his head and bit his lower lip. He wasn't sure whether he was trying to keep from laughing or crying.

"It spozed to sound like that, Byron?" asked Calliope.

"No," Neville told her. "My fault." He picked up the bow from his lap, frowning. His older brother had taken him to a Charles Mingus concert once. He searched his memory for an image of the man embracing his big bass, and mimicked it the best he could.

A sweeter sound emerged. Sweeter, and so much sadder. One singing note, which he raised and lowered slowly. High and yearning. Soft and questioning. With its voice.

With its words.

> "I know you mama, miss me since I'm gone;
> I know you mama, miss me since I'm gone;
> One more thing before I journey on."

Neville turned his head to see if anyone else heard what he was hearing. His hand slipped, and the gimbri sobbed. He turned back to it.

> "Lover man, why won't you be true?
> Lover man, why won't you ever be true?
> She murdered me, and she just might murder you."

He wanted to stop now, but his hands kept moving. He recognized that voice, that tricky hesitance, the tone smooth as smoke. He'd never expected to hear it again.

> "I know you daddy, miss me since I'm gone;
> I know you daddy, miss me since I'm gone;
> One more thing before I journey on.
>
> "I know you cousin, miss me since I'm gone;
> I know you cousin, miss me since I'm gone;
> It's cause of you I come to sing this song.
>
> "Cruel, cruel sistah, black and white and red;
> Cruel, cruel sistah, black and white and red;
> You hated me, you had to see me dead.
>
> "Cruel, cruel sistah, red and white and black;
> Cruel, cruel sistah, red and white and black;
> You killed me and you buried me out back.
>
> "Cruel, cruel sistah, red and black and white;
> Cruel, cruel sistah, red and black and white;
> You'll be dead yourself before tomorrow night."

Finally, the song was finished. The bow slithered off the gimbri's strings with a sound like a snake leaving. They all looked at one another warily.

Calliope was the first to speak. "It ain't true," she said. Which meant admitting that something had actually happened.

But they didn't have to believe what the song had said.

Calliope's suicide early the next morning, that they had to believe: her body floating front down in the cistern, her short rough hair soft as a wet burlap bag. That, and the skeleton the police found behind the retaining wall, with its smashed skull.

It was a double funeral. There was no music.

Ding-Dong-Bell

Jay Russell is the author of the novels Celestial Dogs, Burning Bright, *and* Greed & Stuff, *featuring sometime supernatural sleuth Marty Burns. His other books include* Blood, Waltzes and Whispers, *and World Fantasy Award–nominated* Brown Harvest. *His most recent book is the Marty Burns novella* Apocalypse Now, Voyager, *published by Earthling Publications. He teaches creative writing at St Mary's College in London, where he lives with his daughter Rose.*

"Ding-Dong-Bell" was originally published in the anthology Don't Turn Out the Light.

—E.D.

"Mmm-mmm-mmm," the Little Man purred. "Gonna have us a party."

"Party," the Big Man echoed.

"A nekkid lady feast, my very favorite. Umm, yeah!" The Little Man flicked his tongue through chancrous lips and smiled.

"Nekkid," the Big Man said and giggled. He fumbled with the tarnished copper buttons on his faded jeans.

The terrified girl made small-animal noises in the back of her throat. Her gaze darted back and forth between her attackers, then past them. She furiously sought an avenue of retreat, some means of escape.

There was none. They had done this many times before and were very good at it.

She clenched her fists and bared her teeth, determined to go out fighting. The Little Man saw the gesture and laughed meanly, his partner dumbly joining in a moment later, more jocular. A very sharp knife appeared.

"Ding-dong-bell," the Little Man said. "Party time."

The director trailed his hairy knuckles across the ice smooth surface of his mahogany desk. The aroma of fresh paint lingered in the air of the cavernous office. He sucked it in like mother's milk. A self-satisfied anus of a smile crept up his pudgy cheeks.

The Boy Detective makes good, he thought, and the anus blossomed into an elephant's asshole.

The Director drew a fresh Havana cigar from his vest pocket, bit off the end and fired up the stogie. He strolled over to the big picture window to gaze out on what he had already begun to think of as *his* town.

Washington D.C. shimmered in an early spring heat-wave. The Director didn't mind it; where he'd grown up it was hotter than this. He *liked* it warm. The city's gleaming expanse of chiseled marble reflected the harsh sunlight back at him, softened only by the gentle blossoms of the dogwoods and cherry that lined the wide avenues. Through the heat, the phallic totem of the Monument wavered in the distance like some mad pharaoh's barber pole.

Mine, the Director thought, *all mine.*

He flicked the glowing cigar ash out the window, watched it tumble down the five stories of the new headquarters of the Federal Bureau of Investigation —*his* bureau—and alight in the hair of a sweaty gardener. The surprised worker gazed upward, his toothless mouth a gaping "O" of bafflement.

"Stupid monkey," the Director laughed. He sat back down, resting his tiny feet on the massive desk top.

His reverie was broken by a light rapping on the office door. A moment later his secretary walked in, a tall, thin fellow with delicate features and a soft, almost effeminate manner. He wore a baggy gray suit, round, wire-rim glasses, and parted his slick hair down the middle like some western saloon-keeper.

"Afternoon, Sir."

"Yes, Thurmond," the Director said, "I know it's afternoon."

"I've brought up the late mail along with the executive summaries on that Sacco and Vanzetti mess from special agent Mack, Sir."

"Very good. Do we have pictures of the fried eye-ties?"

The secretary nodded as he handed over the papers, then sat down, note pad in hand. The Director casually sorted through them, grinning when he came to the photos of the dead men. He went through it all, dictating the odd response and glancing only briefly at the morass of daily memos and reports as he tossed them into piles of greater or lesser import.

At the very bottom of the stack was a tattered, yellow envelope with no return address. The faded two-cent stamp hung off the weathered paper like a cuticle, the postmark smeared beyond legibility. The thing looked like it had been chewed by a mule and shat back out the other end. He glanced at the hand-written address and his blood froze.

It was amazing that the letter had even found its way to him. It was addressed to a name long since put aside.

"Oh," he whispered, "my."

Thurmond looked up, thin eyebrows arched like quotation marks. "Sir?"

The Director stared at the handwriting and his throat tightened. He blinked— once, twice—but the writing didn't change, wouldn't go away. He exhaled roughly through his mouth as dime-sized drops of sweat oozed out of his big pores. His little hands began to shake.

"Sir?" the secretary asked again.

"Get out!" the Director yelled, his voice breaking. Thurmond slipped quickly and silently out of the room.

Hands trembling, he opened the envelope and spilled the contents out on the desk.

Another photograph. Badly underexposed and slightly out of focus, but all too easy to make out:

A body.

A woman with long dark hair was spread-eagled on a ratty mattress, ankles and wrists bound to the bedposts with barbed wire. Her lips were pulled back in an agonized grimace, but she grinned at the camera through a second, thin smile cut below her chin. Gaping cavities betrayed where fleshy mounds had been scooped out of her torso. The skin on her legs and arms was a latticework of scars, the undoubtedly livid reds and crimsons reproduced in slashes of black and gray on the silvered paper. Her tattered flesh and dark fluids resembled nothing so much as mulligan stew. A stained, upright blade glinted amid the torn folds of skin and exposed, violated viscera.

The Director felt his gorge rise struggled to stave off an eruption of bile. He turned the photograph over and gazed up at his clean, white ceiling as he drew a deep breath. The paint fumes smelled sickly now, coppery and thick in his throat. The heat of the day was suddenly unbearable.

He glanced down again at the tiny square.

Written on the back, in the same, all-too familiar hand, were three little words: DING-DONG-BELL

The Director vomited all over his beautiful polished floor.

The Boy Detective had been tracking clues all over the dusty streets of Salinas, doing his job the way a good lawman should. His brother George and his idiot friend Lenny had been acting strange all week, and though the Boy Detective hadn't figured out what they were doing, knowing George it had to be no good.

Which meant it was probably *real* good.

The Boy Detective could always tell when George was up to something. Reading stories about the Pinkertons and Nick Carter and Old Sleuth had taught him a thing or two about crime and criminal ways. Nasty old George made fun of his dime novels and pulp fictions, but the Boy Detective would get the last laugh. Though his brother had four years, six inches and a whole lot of muscle on him, the Boy Detective had the edge when it came to smarts.

The last time the Boy Detective had sensed something funny going on, just a month before, he'd conducted a careful search through his brother's things. He'd scavenged drawers, turning all the socks inside out, shaking every article of clothing; he'd checked the closets and behind the stored valises; he'd even tailed George home after school, making certain his brother had no secret hidey-holes along the way, or buried treasures in the great sheep meadow behind their house.

When he finally found the evidence, it was purely by accident, in the last place he would ever have thought to look: practically right out in the open, beneath an old school primer that had sat on the same shelf—seemingly untouched—for as long as he could remember.

The Boy Detective thought there was a lesson in that.

He had never seen anything quite like the fuzzy pictures before, but he immediately understood why his brother had hidden them. The photos made *him* feel weird, too—a little queasy, but also a little bit . . . excited. There were nearly a dozen of them, mounted on stiff cardboard, some with crusty yellow stains across them. Naked men and women doing things he had never considered and didn't entirely understand. The Boy Detective had long wondered what women hid beneath their knickers and what you were supposed to do with them when their clothes were off. He had been very confused by the stories his schoolmates loved to tell: impossible sounding things, he'd thought. He knew the matter called for investigation, but hadn't figured out exactly how to go about it. He'd never dreamed that *this* was what was under there.

He had just turned over a postcard of two white women doing something very silly with a big Negro man when George burst into the room. George didn't say a word, just snatched the pictures from his brother's hand. He grabbed the smaller boy by the hair and tossed him onto the bed, pressing a pillow over his face. The Boy Detective could barely breathe, much less make a sound, as George pummeled his stomach and kidneys, occasionally driving a bony knee into his groin. It only lasted a few minutes, but George was very thorough.

"You say a word, pecker," George warned him, "and I'll have Lenny take your eyes for marbles. You'll wander blind *and* stupid through the rest of your days."

The Boy Detective believed it—George had near-total control over his dim-witted pal—and kept his mouth shut. But he never forgot that beating, because detectives have long and perfect memories. He vowed that someday George would pay for his crimes.

And now George was acting funny all over again.

Very funny.

The Boy Detective followed the trail.

High cirrus clouds stretched to the horizon, capturing the deep reds and pinks of the setting sunlight in a thin line of blushing warmth. The Little Man lay on his back on a patch of weed and scrub grass, savoring the end of another hard day of bucking barley. He gazed peacefully at the fading vista and thought about fresh wounds, bleeding holes. He felt the beginnings of a hard-on stir against his coarse jeans.

The Big Man was being unusually quiet. He was almost always mouthing off about something stupid; complaining or laughing or just singing to himself in that unnaturally sweet voice of his. The yammering and whining sometimes drove him crazy, but often as he thought about it, the Little Man couldn't bring himself to get rid of his old partner.

He knew it was a mistake, a bad calculation. Sooner or later the grinning idiot would destroy them both with a careless word or thoughtless action—hell, that was the only kind of which he was capable—but though they weren't related, not brothers or kin of any real kind, there was a bond between them like blood.

The Little Man chuckled at the thought: Hell, it *was* blood between them, it just wasn't *their* blood.

With a sigh he tore his gaze from the dimming sky and looked around for his companion. He spotted him off in the distance, playing some silly game amid a copse of burned-out trees. As he watched, the Big Man hauled himself into the crook of a blackened fir and pulled something out of his pocket.

"What the . . ." the Little Man said and stood up.

The Big Man sang to himself—some nonsense song, all la-las and woo-woos—and stroked what looked like a torn swatch of fabric.

As he got closer, the Little Man took care not to make a sound. His partner had almost superhuman hearing, a talent that came in mighty handy when the law drew near, but had its downsides at moments like these. As the Little Man approached he stepped on a dry twig, invisible in the enveloping night, which snapped sharp and crisp as a child's arm.

The Big Man whirled around, an ugly and menacing snarl on his pasty face. The grimace quickly faded to a look of guilt and cowed submission as he tried to hide what he held in his hand.

The Little Man roughly yanked his partner out of the tree. He landed on his feet, but dropped to a submissive kneel, staring down at the arid soil.

"What you got there?" the Little Man demanded.

The Big Man mumbled unintelligibly.

"Goddamn it, you show me."

"S'nuffim."

"Give it here then. Let me see."

The Big Man started to blubber.

"Now!"

The Big Man trembled, but he handed the item over and burst out with a pathetic defense.

"I'm sorry. I just wanted to stroke it. It feels so soft. I just wanted to touch it."

The Little Man puzzled over it for a minute before recognizing the hairy patch of flesh for what it was. "Jesus Jumping Christ," he whispered. "Do you know what'd happen if anyone saw this?"

The Big Man stared stolidly at the hard ground, his huge frame racked with little boy sobs.

"They'd break every bone in our bodies and then they'd get mean. They'd hang us and shoot us and leave our corpses for the coyotes. How long you been holding this? Who the hell was she?"

"I'm sorry," the Big Man wheezed. He repeated it over and over.

"How long, goddammit?"

"I'm sorry. I'm so bad. I'm sorry, George."

"Mary's holy whelp!" the Little Man yelled.

He yanked his partner's head up by his greasy, tangled hair. The Big Man tried to avoid his friend's icy glare but there was no place else to look. Salty pools welled in his eyes.

"How many goddamn times I gotta tell you, never, never, ever to call me that name no more!"

The Big Man started to cry great syrupy tears. His breath came in gasps as globs of snot bubbled out of his nose.

"I'm sorry, Geor . . . ," he caught himself. Panic jumped across his features like wildfire through a summer meadow.

"I'm so bad. I should go into the hills. You'd do better if I wasn't here. I'll go into the hills. I'm bad."

The Big Man was bawling like a baby. He curled up and thrashed about in the dirt. The Little Man knew there was no use in talking when he got this way. He would have to drill him some more about not using their real names. He knew also that his partner hadn't meant any harm in keeping the souvenir; he really did just like to stroke soft things: dead mice, rabbits, human flesh.

Still, it would have to go.

The Little Man gathered some twigs and branches and set them in a pile. He tossed the hairy skin atop the pyre, struck a match off a gnawed, yellow thumbnail and dropped it onto the kindling.

The dry wood caught instantly and the flesh flared like newsprint. The briefest hint of smoked ham wafted up as it burned and the Little Man sucked in the savory odor.

The Big Man's bawling had subsided to gentle sniffles, which quieted as he watched the fire grow. The Little Man extended his arm and his partner crawled over and laid his head on his buddy's lap. He tossed a few more branches on the blaze and lightly stroked the Big Man's head as the ashes from the crackling flames rose toward Heaven like Lucifer rising from the Pit.

"It's alright, Hoss," he said. "You just gotta try harder to remember. I know you don't mean nothing, but that won't matter if we're swinging from a rope. You just gotta try."

The Big Man nodded his head. He pressed his face against the inside of the Little Man's thigh, feeling a hardness against his cheek.

"Tell me about the rabbits again?" he asked softly.

Curlicues of acrid smoke drifted toward the ceiling. The Director sat at the head of the long conference table, smiling to himself as he eyed the agents one by one. None would meet his gaze.

He rolled the fat cigar around his mouth, savoring the tension in the room. He revelled in taunting these men, many of whom were twice his age, with more years in law enforcement than he had spent in long trousers.

But this was his room, now. His room, his building, his Bureau. To do with as he pleased.

And how pleased he was.

But for the letter.

The Bureau's forensic experts had scrutinized the envelope, but were unable to reach any conclusions as to its origin. He couldn't show them the photograph, of course, not without raising awkward questions.

This was a very delicate matter.

He had planned to simply destroy it at first, but couldn't bring himself to set the paper to flame. He stared at the picture for hours thinking about what he should do, how he might deal with the ancient ghosts that haunted him. *What would the Boy Detective do?*, he wondered.

DING-DONG-BELL

The words shone in bloody headlines in his mind's eye and his pleasure faded. He bit into the cigar, half-chewing off the end then stubbed it out in a sterling silver ashtray. He had played with his little men for long enough.

"Gentlemen," he said, and a dozen heads turned as one in his direction. "You have all read the briefing document and know why we are here. It is time for this bureau to embark on a course of action."

"Excuse me, Mr. Director," Clemmons said from the far end of the table, "but I *have* read the materials, and I must tell you that it is not at *all* clear what this is about or even why the Bureau is getting involved in these arcane matters."

Clemmons was a troublemaker. He'd been around since the Bureau's founding in '08 and was big-league bitter about having been passed over for the top job. But the Director knew that Clemmons had never learned to play the Washington political game and still wouldn't play it. Clemmons did, however, hold the respect and friendship of the other men in the room; a respect that the Director had yet to garner and friendships he envied but would claim to care less about.

"I should think," the Director charged, "that rape, torture and multiple homicide are well within the purview of this agency."

"Forgive me again," Clemmons said, "but this report offers only the most tenuous evidence linking these alleged and bizarre crimes together. They've supposedly occurred over a period of fifteen or more years in half-again as many states. Furthermore, there is no conclusive support for the outlandish notion that these thirty-odd, unrelated crimes are the work of some single individual or, and I quote, 'pair of individuals engaged in *serial* acts.' Serial acts? Who ever heard of such a thing? And where, I ask you *Mr.* Director, where is the evidence for these wild and extravagant claims?"

Several heads nodded in silent agreement. The Director's enemies were legion and he'd have to meet their challenge now. Before he could articulate a response, McCarthy interrupted.

"Point of order, Mr. Director, if I might. Point of order." The Director gestured benevolently toward the jowly young man.

"With all due respect to Chief Clemmons, I believe that there are sources of information to which, for obvious reasons, we cannot all be privy. That has always been the way in the upper echelons of law enforcement and we must trust the Director's discretion and wisdom about such matters."

The Director started to relax as McCarthy worked up a head of steam. The man waved a sheaf of what appeared to be blank pieces of paper.

"I am shocked and appalled by the heinous character of the crimes detailed in this report. The fact that these terrible offenses have been wantonly carried out across state lines and over so very many years necessitates, nay, demands this Bureau's immediate involvement. Frankly, whether these atrocities are the work of one or two men or more, I believe that we have a civic responsibility, nay, I do declare a moral *duty* to investigate this menace. A duty to our wives and to our children and to the good people of this great country."

McCarthy glared around the room before turning an expectant gaze on the Director. The Director had to suppress a smile: wives and children, indeed! The man wasn't married. He didn't even *like* women. The Director had the photographs to prove it.

But the Director recognized ambition when he saw it. It was a face he knew from his own mirror. The others were nodding again, in agreement with McCarthy now. Ignorant lemmings. Clemmons' face had gone bright red.

"Thank you, Joe," the Director said, beaming at the eager man. "I couldn't have said it better myself.

"In fact," he continued, confidently looking up and down the table, "Agent McCarthy is right about the information in this report. Of course, I trust you all implicitly . . ."—he stared coldly at Clemmons—"but I am not free at this time to divulge the source of this document, even to this August assembly. I can only ask that you trust me as much as I trust each and everyone of you."

There were hearty *harrumphs* of agreement around the table. Plans were made, maps were drawn, schemes and traps devised. The Director glanced up several times, and each time found McCarthy looking back at him. The Director nodded, sensing a useful ally in the struggle to focus his new-found power.

This young man might be going places, the Director thought, *and just maybe I'll help him along his way.*

His heart pounded like a bass drum at a Fourth of July parade and his breath came in wheezing rasps as his chest heaved with excitement. Every nerve tingled with prickly sensation. His ankles ached from standing on tiptoe, but he couldn't tear himself away from the window long enough to find a rock or milk box to stand on.

The loud echoing clip-clop of a passing horse and wagon caught his ear and he ducked, afraid that he might be spotted. But he was well-camouflaged by a flowering bougainvillea and the sleepy driver never looked up. Without so much as another glance down the road, the Boy Detective turned back to the remarkable scene unfolding inside the house.

The shade had been drawn nearly all the way down to the peeling window sill, but through a thin gap, as promising as the crack of dawn, he saw George and Lenny and the naked lady.

He wasn't sure who she was, nor did he care. He was too enthralled and amazed by what they were doing. Her back was arched and her head thrown back at a steep angle showing off the alluring whiteness of her neck. The tip of her sharp chin pointed at the slowly turning ceiling fan. She was spread-eagled, her wrists and ankles secured to the bedposts with leather whetting strops. Though a silky gag had been stuffed in her mouth, her frenzied moans penetrated even the leaded panes of the closed window.

George lay on top of her and though the Boy Detective didn't completely understand, he recognized that his brother was aping the actions he'd seen on the picture postcards. He saw the muscles in George's rear flex and tense as the woman raised her midsection as high off the bed as the restraints would allow, meeting George's thrusting movements with equal ferocity.

The Boy Detective glanced over at Lenny sitting on the floor, seemingly unaware of the acrobatic actions on the bed. He was naked, too, but played gleefully with a fine, porcelain doll, holding it by the arms and waltzing it around in circular patterns on the Persian rug as he sang to himself.

George groaned loudly then collapsed on top of the woman. After a minute, George rolled over, untied the woman's ankles and removed the gag from her mouth. In the instant before his brother savagely mashed his lips against hers, the Boy Detective recognized Lenny's Aunt Clara.

He reckoned that Clara must be good fifteen years older than George. He recalled hearing that she and her husband had taken Lenny in after his folks died in a house fire. Clara's husband ran off and left her soon after Lenny moved into the old shed behind their house. The Boy Detective had seen Clara in town once or twice and wondered why ladies whispered and blushed when she walked by.

He heard George bark something at Lenny as he rolled off the bed. George reached back over and slipped two fingers between Aunt Clara's legs, then held the fingers out to his huge friend.

Lenny looked up nervously, clutching the porcelain doll tightly to his chest. He was on the chubby side and his bosoms were near as big as his aunt's. George said something the Boy Detective couldn't hear and Lenny sat the doll delicately back in its place on the shelf before climbing onto the bed. George stuck his fingers under his friend's nose and Lenny sniffed them tentatively, like a dog, before tasting them with his tongue.

George laughed as Lenny's arousal became obvious. The fat boy began to suck on George's salty fingers. Clara looked dumbly on, her face as stiff and blank as the doll's. With some effort, George extricated his digits from Lenny's thick lips and directed his friend's mouth to the source of the salty succor.

George sat in an old rocker in the corner watching Lenny and Clara through half-shut eyes. The Boy Detective tried to follow what was happening, but couldn't see much more than the bobbing of Lenny's fat head. He noticed a mirror hanging above the headboard, slanting slightly downward. In the dirty quicksilver he could just make out the sight of Lenny's pale tongue dancing up and down between Clara's legs. Lenny looked like he was aiming to win the pie-eating contest at the county fair.

Just then, Lenny glanced up into the mirror and caught the younger boy's eyes. With the pleasure of recognition, dim Lenny forgot what he was doing. A dopey smile creaked across his broad features and the Boy Detective saw his lips form the words: "Hi, Johnny."

George was on his feet in a flash and the Boy Detective knew he was in trouble. He turned to run back home, but his legs had gone all pins and needles and he tripped over a tangle of vines. Before he could recover, George, still fastening his jeans, was on top of him.

George dragged his little brother inside the house, cursing a stream of foul invective that shocked the younger boy even through his panic. When the Boy Detective tried to wail in protest, George punched him hard in the throat. The Boy Detective thought his windpipe had been crushed, but after a desperate few seconds, found he could draw a slight breath.

He offered no further resistance.

George dragged his little brother through the house and into the bedroom. Aunt Clara glanced at George with vague interest, but didn't say anything. Lenny said "Hi" again. George threw his brother to the floor and sat back in the rocker, glaring in silence. The Boy Detective clutched at his aching throat and fought off the tears. Finally, George spoke.

"We got us a problem here, Hoss."

Lenny had crawled up his aunt's body, rubbing himself against her soft hair; he snapped-to at the sound of George's voice.

"Whad'ya say George?"

"Ain't no way we can trust this little pissant brother of mine to hold his tongue. Not 'bout this. No way, sir."

The Boy Detective tried to speak, but his brother didn't give him the chance.

"You don't say a word, pecker. I see you even open them lying lips and I'll have your tongue. You know I will."

The Boy Detective whimpered.

"He'fire, Geor'y. Why'nt you say he yer bro'er? Ge'em on up here an' we make it a fam'ly 'fair."

Aunt Clara spoke as if half-asleep. The Boy Detective observed her stilted movements and the filmy glaze in her red eyes.

"Should we, George? Johnny'd like Clara. She's nice and soft. I like to stroke her. Can't Johnny do it, too?"

The Boy Detective lowered his hands from his face and shifted his gaze back and forth between George and Lenny.

"Idiot," George hissed. "We can't trust her neither. Not no slut what'd screw her own dummy nephew. My daddy always says never trust no easy frails."

The Boy Detective couldn't recall their father ever saying anything of the like, but he wasn't about to mention it just then. George continued to rock until a hideous grin took over his face.

The Boy Detective grew very scared.

"Then again, maybe you ain't so dumb after all. Out the mouths of babes comes gems, so's they say." He leered over at his brother. "I think maybe the little pecker *should* share in some of this little party. In fact, I think maybe he's gonna help us solve most *all* our problems."

George strode over and lifted his brother up by his short, black hair.

"You like all them made up stories don't you, pecker? Well, I got one I think you're gonna remember for a real long time."

George carried his little brother over to the bed and threw him onto the mattress. He grabbed a strop and twisted it around the younger boy's wrists, tightening it till it cut into flesh. He yanked his brother's pants and drawers down around his ankles and bent him face-down over the edge of the mattress. Then, eyeing Clara's cast-off sun dress, he picked it up and, laughing like a loon, slipped it over the little boy's shoulders.

"It's a old one, this story, but a damn good one. It's a kiddie story, too, but that seems about right for a pissant pecker like you."

The Boy Detective started to sob.

"It's called: Ding-dong-bell," George said as he unfastened his jeans.

"Ding-dong-bell," Lenny repeated and clapped his hands.

It was a *long* story. And there was no happy ending.

The Little Man watched his friend hack at the torso with a dull axe. The stifling aroma of spilled blood filled the room, though there was little left to spurt from the corpse.

Like a kid eating animal crackers, the Big Man liked to remove the head first, then the arms and legs. The Little Man cradled the head in his naked lap, fingering the whorls of the girl's tiny ear. Her straight black hair was encrusted with blood and brain matter, her features twisted in the oh-so-familiar death's head leer.

Her face was like all the others.

Like Clara's.

The dark hair, the long, thin nose and greenish-gray eyes. He thought back to that first time, as he always did, and the sweet memory of manhood. Manhood achieved not by slipping himself inside her—hell, any idiot could do that, as the big man proved—but by slipping sleek, icy steel into warm flesh. Carving a new woman, a better woman out of the old. A woman who became his not through the brief possession of her sex, but through his eternal signature in her skin and bone and blood.

It was a kind of vow-taking, he thought. Almost like a wedding.

"Jesus Christ, Hoss!" the Little Man shrieked. A razor-sharp bone shard, no bigger than a toenail clipping, exploded out of the corpse from the force of an axe blow, wedging itself in the Little Man's cheek just below the eye.

"You could of done blinded me, you damn fool. How many times I gotta tell you be more careful when you're hacking bone?"

"I'm sorry. I'm real sorry. I didn't mean it." The Big Man started to sob. *Again.*

"All right, all right," the Little Man said. He dabbed at the bloody tears rolling down his cheek and licked his finger. "Don't get yer drawers in a bunch over it."

The Big Man took a deep breath, trying to hold back the sobs. He knew George didn't like it when he cried, but sometimes he couldn't stop himself He forced his thick lips into a smile, but his partner still looked awfully mad so he tried the tactic that never seemed to fail.

"Ding-dong-bell," the Big Man sing-songed.

The Little Man's face relaxed and though he tried to stop it, a grin twisted his lips. He laughed in spite of himself as a fresh drop of blood oozed down his cheek.

He nodded at his friend. "Ding-dong . . ."

. . . *Bell*, The Director mentally recited.

The silly child's rhyme thundered in his head like a fire and brimstone sermon on a hot Sunday morning. Not even the stomach-churning maneuvers of the fragile aircraft could distract him from the images forever linked with those terrible words.

He looked out the small window, saw only the dense, impenetrable gray of the storm front. The dark clouds became a dream screen on which the memories of that terrible, long ago day were projected like a flickering, stag film.

George had forced Clara to drink another laudanum-laced glass of bathtub gin—she had required little coaxing to down the cheap brew—while the Boy Detective cowered beside the bed, bloody and ashamed.

George had secured Aunt Clara's ankles to the sturdy bedposts and stuffed the gag back in her mouth. Clara could barely keep her drugged eyes open and hummed an unknowable tune in her blissful stupor. She didn't respond to the sound of breaking glass or the small boy's fearful gasps.

But her eyes opened wide when George made the first slice in her belly with the tumbler's jagged edge.

The Boy Detective tried to get up and run, but George barked "Hold 'em Hoss," and Lenny sat heavily on his legs, giggling all the while.

"Ding-dong-bell," George hissed.

He slashed her legs

"Pussy's in the well."

Her chest.

"Who put her in?"

Eyes.

"Little Johnny . . ." he said and looked at his brother.

George slashed her throat.

They all watched as she thrashed and moaned and bled—Jesus, how she bled—a smile-cum-grimace on George's lips. When it was over, he thrust a red-spattered hand under his brother's nose and smeared the blood across the boy's cheeks and lips.

"You're in this, too, pecker. You're in deep as us. Blooded."

He pulled the little boy up by the hair and shoved his face within an inch of Aunt Clara's dead eyes.

"You say a word about this, you so much as breathe that you ever been in here and they'll string you up by your scrawny little balls. And if they don't, you *know* that I will."

George threw him back on the floor.

" 'Sides," he said, "you go telling, you'll have to tell it *all*. Including what I done to you. I don't think that's something you want to have getting around. Cause if'n it did, I'd have to say it was all your idea. Say that you got it from one of them clever-clogs books of yours. And they'll believe it, too, won't they? Cause ever'body knows you're so smart and I'm just dumb. Ain't that right, pecker?"

The Boy Detective looked at his brother and saw that there was nothing he could do. He knew he would never say a word; that he could never live with telling all that had happened. What George had done to him.

He nodded and cried.

Lenny watched it all with a gleeful, but hesitant interest. The Boy Detective guessed that George didn't fully understand what had happened, but in an unusually lucid moment, he asked what they were going to do with Aunt Clara now.

"Ding-dong-bell . . ." George said with a smile.

Both boys looked up, not comprehending.

"Pussy's in the well," he concluded and launched into a cackle.

The plane suddenly dropped, jolting the Director out of his nightmare. As the small aircraft bucked, he thought about how the rest of that day had gone. How George made them wait until dark, just sitting in the dim bedroom with Clara's stiffening corpse. How, in the quiet still of night they had unboarded the old well out behind the house and tossed Clara's mutilated body into its black depths.

He remembered the wet thud that echoed up the shaft when Clara struck dried-out bottom.

The plane descended for real now, making its approach to the primitive airport on the fringe of Los Angeles. As it set down with a heart-stopping jolt, the Director thought of the years spent atoning for what had happened that day. For allowing George and Lenny to get away with murder, letting them disappear from Salinas and the iron grip of justice.

His whole life, he knew, had been directed toward the moment at hand. His slavish devotion to duty, his meteoric rise through the Bureau, his surrender of any kind of normal life had been leading him to this moment. This expiation.

Ding-dong-bell, he thought.

The bureau had caught them trying to cross the border into Mexico, trussed them up and shipped them back to a cabin in the hills above the false glitter of Hollywood. It was the same bungalow where Fatty Arbuckle had presented that fatal bottle to Virginia Rapp.

McCarthy met the Director at the airstrip and drove him up to the site.

"You received the message about the big man?" McCarthy asked.

"Yes, damn it. And I told you I wanted them both alive."

"I know, sir, and I am sorry. But he put up an ungodly fight. Incredible strength. We have four men in the hospital. One lost an eye."

"I gave an order."

"Yes sir. I take full responsibility, of course."

Neither said another word along the way.

Two agents stood guard outside the cabin, holstered guns visible. McCarthy dismissed them and opened the door. The Director felt a sudden tide of fear rush through him, a dagger of ice cut into his bowel. He tried to remember who and where he was, and managed to stride in with only the briefest of hesitation.

George looked smaller than he remembered, but then it had been a long, long time and childhood memories are out of scale.

He had been stripped, but for a pair of torn denim trousers, and tied to a heavy wooden chair. His face and body were purple with bruises, the eyes puffy and black and swollen shut. The Director walked a slow circle around him, but George didn't stir. He saw that several of his brother's fingers had been broken; they jutted out from his bound hands at odd angles, like branches tangled in a deadfall.

"Is he alive?" the Director asked, voice cracking.

"Just unconscious."

McCarthy filled a bucket with cold water and dumped it over George's head. George shivered and moaned, but opened his eyes as much as the swelling allowed. After a while his gaze found the Director.

"Pecker!" he spat through a mouthful of broken teeth.

"Long time, George. Long time."

"Still wearing them purty sun dresses?" he said, and coughed or laughed.

The Director felt himself blush, heard McCarthy shuffle behind him. He made himself be strong.

"You shouldn't have sent me that picture, George. Never wake sleeping dogs. Big mistake."

The little man laughed more clearly this time. "Hardly matters, no more," he wheezed. "We was at the end of our trail. Hoss couldn't go no further and I was plum tired of the life. Tired of the living and, aw hell, tired of the dying, too. Figured we had to finish things up right. I see'd your name in the paper, your fancy new job and all, and decided to give you the big score. Kind of circular, like. Least a brother can do."

"There is no big score, George. No one will ever know about you. And I'm already at the top."

"Well, I reckon I put you there, pecker. Me. I made you, didn't I?" George spat a bloody wad of phlegm onto the floor.

"You remember that day at Clara's, pecker? I bet you do. You know what I remember best? Not the way it felt when I shot off in that whore's mouth, nor sliced her titties like a pork loin, nor lapped the blood from her throat.

"What I remember most is you. The look in your eyes while it happened. You was crying and all, but that weren't it. There was fear there—

you always was such a pissant pecker—but I seed something else, too. It were a look of . . ."

The little man didn't know how to finish the thought, but the Director did. It was the last time in his life he would ever be completely honest about anything.

"Understanding," he said.

George nodded. "Understanding. It's the only time I ever felt we truly was brothers."

There was a long still silence. The two men locked eyes and another understanding passed between them.

The Director reached out and McCarthy put the gun in his hand. He pressed the cold, gray barrel against a spot on his brother's forehead, smack dab between his cash-green eyes. He pulled back the hammer.

"Ding-dong-bell, pecker," George said. "Now you're me."

His brains exploded out of the back of his head.

"You'll take care of the disposal?" the Director asked.

"Of course."

The Director trapped McCarthy's gaze. "You're okay with this?"

"Okay with what, sir?"

The Director nodded and walked out.

Many years later, a thousand evil deeds behind him and more blood on his hands than his brother could ever have dreamed of, the Director attended yet another in the endlessly tedious round of Washington social events. A key Congressional ally and possible future presidential candidate was in attendance along with his wife and their cherubic, three-year old son. As the Director happened to walk past them, the little boy playfully sing-songed a very old, very familiar and typically inane nursery rhyme.

The Bureau maintains a file on that boy to this very day.

STACEY RICHTER

A Case Study of Emergency Room Procedure and Risk Management by Hospital Staff Members in the Urban Facility

Stacey Richter is the author of the collection My Date With Satan. *Her work has appeared in many magazines and anthologies, including* The Year's Best Fantasy and Horror, Fourteenth Annual Collection. *She lives in Tucson, Arizona. "A Case Study of Emergency Room Procedure and Risk Management by Hospital Staff Members in the Urban Facility" appeared in the first issue of* Fairy Tale Review.

—K.L. & G.G.

I.

Subject 525, a Caucasian female in her early to mid-twenties, entered an emergency medical facility at around 11 p.m. presenting symptoms of an acute psychotic episode. Paranoia, heightened sensitivity to physical contact, and high volume vocal emanations were noted at triage by the medical staff. The subject complained of the hearing of voices, specifically "a chorus of amphibians" who were entreating the subject to "pretty please guard the product from the evil frog prince." The staff reported that the subject's bizarre behavior was augmented by an unusual sartorial style, commenting that she was "an ethereal young woman wearing a Renaissance-type dress, with huge knots in her long, otherwise flowing hair." She was accompanied by a strange odor, tentatively identified as "cat urine."

During the intake interview, the subject volunteered the information that she had nasally inhaled "crystal," estimating that she had nasally inhaled (snorted) between 50 and 250 mg of "crystal" in the twenty-four hours prior to hospital admission. "Crystal," it was determined, is a slang term for methamphetamine, a central nervous system stimulant similar to prescription amphetamines such as Benzedrine.

Methamphetamine is a "street" drug-of-abuse that has become popular in recent years due to its easy manufacture possibilities (Osborne, 1988). It sometimes referred to by the terms *crystal, speed, zoomazoom*, and *go fast* (Durken, 1972). In a brief moment of lucidity, Subject 525 theorized that her psychotic state might be due to the large quantity of methamphetamine she had "snorted," and the staff agreed to put her in a "nice, quiet, white room" for a period of observation. The head resident thought it advisable to administer antipsychotic medication, but the subject, who by all accounts exhibited an uncanny amount of personal charm, prevailed upon the staff to give her a can of beer instead.

II.

After approximately sixty minutes of observation, a member of the nursing staff noted that the subject had begun to complain that "a be-slimed prince" was causing certain problems for her, namely "using copper fittings" and "not ventilating right." This "prince" was, as the nurse understood it, acting "all mean and horrible" concerning the manufacture of methamphetamine, which the subject had cheerfully volunteered as her occupation during the intake interview. The nurse, who was formerly employed in a Federal prison and had considerable experience treating denizens of the *demimonde*, theorized that "Prince" might by a moniker used by the subject's "old man"; this was particularly likely, the nurse indicated, since the manufacture of methamphetamine is the customary province of "gangs" of motorcycle riders, who often use colorful nicknames as a way of asserting their "outsider" status in society (Ethel Kreztchner, R.N., 2002).

The nurse further asserted that this would explain why the subject had offered, at intake, only the name "Princess," and would indicate no surname. By then the hour had grown rather late, and as the emergency room was quiet, much of the staff gathered around the subject ("Princess") who began to tell a lively tale of capture and imprisonment by a handsome but wicked "prince" who was, in fact, "an evil enchanter." The tradition of shape-shifting sorcerers is a familiar one in old German folk tales (Grimm, ca. 1812), though these tales have been widely regarded as fanciful narratives concocted to intimidate and control unruly juveniles (twelve and under) in diverse cultural contexts, and are rarely considered historical evidence. Nevertheless, the Princess claimed that the Prince had captured her from an orphanage near Eloy, Arizona, where she had spent her days climbing trees in pursuit of nuts. Chasing butterflies, according to the subject, was another activity she enjoyed in her youth. But that all changed when a handsome young man approached the girl and offered her a pony made of candy. The pony was beautiful and delicious, and though the Princess wished to save it forever, she found she devoured it anyway. With every bite the pony grew smaller. And with every bite the handsome "young man" become more fearsome and wicked looking.

The staff gathered close, listening with great interest. The Princess went on to indicate that the Prince/Sorcerer had bewitched her with the candy horse, and had since imprisoned her in a prefabricated "home" near a foul-smelling landfill, where she was kept locked up in a "tin can with carpet taped over the windows." There, the Prince had prevailed upon her to undertake the smelly and dangerous manufacture of methamphetamine by means of his sorcerer's power. All day long, the Princess said, she was forced to "boil down Mexican ephedrine in a triple-neck flask, bubble hydrogen through a stainless steel tank, or titrate ethyl ether out of lock defrosting fluid, dressed only filthy rags," while the Prince rode his shiny "hog" through tall pines in the mountains to the north of town. Or the Prince would "relax and kick back with a can of brew" while the Princess "slaved over a hot chemistry set." The only positive aspect of the experience, the Princess noted, was that she "cooked the best damn product in Arizona," a substance that was uncommonly potent and white, she said, with a "real clean buzz."

The Princess explained, in a sweetly chiming voice, that these endeavors were dangerous, particularly under the conditions imposed by the Prince, who habitually smoked marijuana cigarettes in the vicinity of fumes. She had survived because she was protected by a special angel, one with "gills" who could exist underwater or possibly "inside a solution." She referred to this angel as "Gilbert," (possibly "Gillbert") and noted that Gilbert appeared to her when she imbibed heavily of "the product." The manifestation of angels, seraphim, djinns, and Elvis Presley is common during episodes of psychosis (Hotchkiss, 1969), and much of the staff believed that the Princess was describing an aspect of methamphetamine-induced hallucination. Others on staff found themselves strangely moved by the Princess's story of forced enslavement and the high-risk game of organic chemistry, and wondered if there might be some sort of truth to it.

The head resident, in particular, took an interest in the subject's case, indicating to researchers that he was "bored that night, as usual" and that he found the Princess "interesting." The resident further indicated that his prodigious academic success was based on his above-average intelligence, which was also "a curse" because it led him to feel a feeling of "boredom," and intolerance with all of "the idiots around him," which, he made clear, also applied to the researchers gathering data on this case. Researchers in turn described the resident as rather "vain and haughty," or "arrogant," though most theorized that these traits covered up insecurity about his youth combined with a doomed romanticism undercut by a persistent tendency toward bitterness.

The Princess was exhibiting fewer symptoms of psychosis, and had become quite comfortable in her surroundings, curling up in a nest of pillows "like a cat" (Overhand, 2002). She said that she loved the medical staff and was grateful to them for helping to save her from the evilness of the Prince and the pungent squalidness of methamphetamine manufacture. The head resident shuffled his feet and pointed out that the Princess herself had actually contributed to her own care by wisely seeking medical treatment when she felt overwhelmed by drug-induced psychosis, whereas a lot of "tweaked-out idiots" just went ahead and did something stupid or violent. Then the two stared for a while into each other's eyes.

It was then that lateness of the hour was nervously remarked upon by all, and several staff members complained that they had been on duty for an excessive length of time. The Princess made a "general comment" that her product could "give a person a little pick-me-up" that theoretically might make the staff members feel like "they were operating at one hundred and fifty percent."

The staff was curious about the efficacy of the Princess's homemade methamphetamine, though their enthusiasm abated somewhat after a phlebotomist (a "pretty plump girl who never wore any makeup and never smiled or said hello to nobody beneath her," according to the environmental control officer) recited aloud in a high and quavering voice a list of the possible effects of nasally inhaling methamphetamine, including "nervousness, sweating, teeth-gnashing, irritability, incessant talking, sleeplessness, and the obsessive assembling and disassembling of machinery" (PDR, 2002). Interest swelled once again when the Princess pointed out that the young phlebotomist had mumbled while mentioning one of the chief effects of the substance: euphoria.

After that, the staff cleared from the small room where the Princess was being kept sequestered by herself, though occasionally a lone member would disappear inside, to emerge a few moments later wiping their nose with eyes unusually wild. Such staff members were also observed tidying their work areas, peering into the mirror, smoking cigarettes, and talking to one another with great animation and enthusiasm but little content (Overhand, 2002). The receptionist was observed taking apart a telephone, so that she could "clean it." The overall effect was that the staff was unusually energetic and "happy" (see below).

III.

Shortly before dawn, several nurses returned to the Princess's bedside, where they adjusted the lighting in the small room so a warm glow bathed the subject. They worked with combs to untangle the knots in the subject's hair. The head resident had entered the room as well, and kept his boyish face, so incongruous beneath his balding head, hunched toward his chest while he made notes in the subject's chart.

It was then that the subject began to speak softly about a set of ponies she had made out of old tires. The Princess explained how she had "freed" the ponies from the rubber with a cutting implement, and that a "herd" of such ponies hung from ropes in the trees around her prefabricated housing unit, where they blew back and forth in the breeze, bumping against each other with hollow thuds. They possessed the spirit of "running things," she explained, though they had no "legs to speak of," she could look at them and feel the feeling of "something wild and running away." The subject further explained that nasally inhaling or "skin popping" (subcutaneous injection) of methamphetamine gave her relief from a feeling that "nothing important would ever happen to her," and replaced it with the sensation that she was, like the ponies fashioned from discarded tires, something "wild and running away."

She indicated that these feelings of flight accounted for the only times that she ever truly felt like a princess.

IV.

The notes in the subject's chart at this point become "tiny and very, very neat," according to researchers (Plank et al., 2002). The notes themselves indicate that the subject was "an exceptionally attractive woman," and that the medical staff found her "enchanting." She was "like them but different—more perfect—yet at the same time more glassine and fragile." The chart noted that the subject had become sleepy, perhaps due to the fatigue that often follows the ingestion of methamphetamine (Nintzel, 1982). It was indicated that some members of the staff wished to allow her to sleep, while others had an urgent need to "pester her; to poke her in the leg with a stick over and over," to keep her awake.

Verbal accounts indicate that not all the members of the night staff were equally smitten with the subject. Several members demurred, in particular the phlebotomist, who commented that the subject was "a disgusting drug addict" who was "manipulative." She added that she hated men "who fall for those poor lost creatures," even though such "creatures" were in the process of getting "exactly what they signed up for." The phlebotomist indicated that it was futile to try to help the subject, save medically, because the subject had freely chosen her own seedy destiny, despite her weird story of kidnapping, adding that "not everybody who suffers has a burning need to dramatize it with scarves and eyeliner."

V.

Videotapes from the security cameras in the waiting area provide a clear visual record of the intrusion that occurred at approximately 4:12 a.m. The tapes show a clean, tiled area violently rent by the shiny chrome form of a very large motorcycle (or "hog") piloted by the "Prince," who gained ingress by method of riding through the glass doors, where he continued to gun his motorcycle in circles through a reception area furnished with chairs which became smashed. The Prince was reported to be a large, muscular male of indeterminate race sporting "a pair of sideburns as big as teacups." He was reportedly clad in "enough black leather to denude several cows," though naturally it has not been determined how many cows would have been needed to provide the amount of leather the Prince was wearing. Much of the hospital staff on duty also reported that the intruder had a "tail, slimy and black, sort of like the tail of a tadpole." Careful scrutiny of security videotapes does reveal the presence of a whiplike appendage dangling from the back of the Prince's "hog," though the possibility that this might in fact be a literal "tail" has been discounted by researchers, who have chalked up this and several other aspects of the medical staff's report to group suggestibility (Johansen, 2002). (For example, the hospital staff also reported that the Prince had "eyes that glowed red like coals" and that "lizards and snakes slithered from his boots.")

It was reported that the Prince then parked his "hog" and proceeded past the reception area, stalking the warrenlike halls of the emergency treatment facility in his heavy boots, scuffing the floor, screaming that someone had taken his "woman," and wondering aloud, in a yelling tone, where he could find his "kitten."

At this the Princess and hospital staff fled to a supply closet, where they cowered, leaving the issue of how to properly control the Prince open for resolution. It was agreed that the police, as well as the hospital security guards, should be alerted; it was lamented however that there was no available phone in the supply closet and such action would require someone to dash out into the hallway where the Prince was raging and overturning carts and smashing his hammer-like hands into walls while eating candy reserved for children who were unfortunate enough to wind up in the emergency room. The Princess, whose melodic voice was muffled due to the press of bodies in the supply closet, pointed out that the Prince possessed special evil magic powers and that anyone who challenged him must be good in heart and clever both, and carry with him or her a small silver bell which the Princess kept on a chain around her neck.

As the destructive noises of the Prince's rampage became louder, the head resident indicated that he felt he should be the one to make an effort to save himself, the staff, and the once-psychotic but now quite sweet Princess. The staff was surprised to hear this, as they had never noticed any behavior related to bravery or even simple kindness on the part of the head resident. They continued to be surprised when they heard him say, in a quavering voice, that though it was true he might not be good hearted, he certainly was *clever* enough, so why not give it a go? Everyone in the closet gave him a quiet but heartfelt round of applause. The Princess begged him to be careful and hung the bell around his neck with a trembling hand. She bestowed upon him a soft kiss as he slipped out the door.

The "rescue" of women by handsome, effeminate men is a staple of old folk tales, engineered to reconcile a young woman's inclination's toward feckless independence with the prevailing custom of marriage by casting the potential husband as really nice and sort of harmless and at the very least a whole lot better than the alternative of living with her fucked-up family (cf. *Cinderella*, Grimm, 1812). Despite the tradition of the effeminate male triumphing over the more sexual, "animal" challenger, it seemed uncertain to all present that the head resident could defeat the Prince using the tools at his disposal—a stethoscope, some pens, and a pager. It's difficult to determine, though, what kind of damage the resident may have been capable of inflicting with these devices, since, according to his own account, when confronted with the fierce and gruesome Prince, who "smelled like burning rubber and had white stuff hanging off his beard" he froze, then mutely raised a traitorous arm to point to the supply closet where the Princess and the rest of the staff were hiding.

The Prince wrenched open the door with a huge paw, and out popped the Princess.

According to the staff, the Princess screamed with a high-pitched yelp when the Prince grabbed her, smearing her lovely Renaissance-style dress with grease. The records note that the Prince and the Princess together presented quite an odd picture, one that brought to mind "a nightmare creature clawing a plate of *petit fours*" (Petix, 2002). The Princess is reported to have said, "It's okay," and, "No, but I want to go with him, really," and, "He's my old man!" in a tone of tense brightness, but the staff plainly did not believe her and theorized that she was simply trying to "appease her oppressor" in order to minimize the likelihood of domestic violence. Before the staff was able to contact the authorities, the "Prince" settled himself astride his hog and pulled the Princess up behind him.

The Prince and Princess roared out of the building and vanished into the night in a cloud of exhaust.

Conclusion

After the Prince and Princess had departed, the staff grumbled that the head resident had behaved "most cowardly," and complained that the Princess had been "sacrificed," to be "whisked off to a prefabricated house where everything is always fast and tinged with madness, or else dark and sad and falling asleep." Much of the staff argued that *something* should have been done to help the girl, though some felt it was the curse of the phylum *Princess* to be always at the mercy of one prince-type or another, and that her best chance was to save herself, which seemed unlikely. The resident, for his part, quickly aligned himself with the phlebotomist, agreeing that the Princess was "just an addict" who had come in "exhibiting drug-seeking behavior anyway," and implying, in word and action, that drug addicts were by nature less than human and so deserved whatever nasty fate they got. Then he skulked off down a fluorescent-lit hallway with his hands shoved into his pockets.

Though he wore the silver bell around his neck to the end of his days.

JEFFREY FORD

The Scribble Mind

This year Golden Gryphon will publish Jeffrey Ford's second short fiction collection, The Empire of Ice Cream. *His first collection,* The Fantasy Writer's Assistant, *won the World Fantasy Award. Ford is also the author of a number of novels, most recently the Edgar-winning* The Girl in the Glass *and the short novel* The Cosmology of the Wider World. *He has won the Nebula, as well as two other World Fantasy Awards, the Grand Prix de l'Imaginaire, and the Speculative Fiction Foundation's inaugural Fountain Award. "The Scribble Mind" was published online at Ellen Datlow's* SCI FICTION. SCIFI.COM *recently cut off funding for* SCI FICTION, *but for the time being you can still find several of Ford's best stories there, on the archive. Ford's work is often concerned with the act of artistic creation, whether writing, art, music, or some other creative endeavor. He teaches writing at Brookdale Community College and lives in New Jersey with his family.*

K.L. & G.G.

When I was in graduate school, during the mid-80s, I'd meet Esme pretty much every Sunday morning for breakfast at the Palace A down on Hepson Street. The runny eggs, the fried corn muffins, the coffee, and our meandering conversations carried all of the ritual of a Sunday mass minus the otherwise grim undertones. There was a calm languor to these late-morning meals and something that had to do with the feeling of home.

We'd gone to the same high school, grown up in the same town, and vaguely knew each other back then—friends of friends—but we'd moved in distinctly different social orbits; her's somewhat closer to the sun. Six years had passed since we'd graduated—I hadn't had a single thought about her—and then one day, late in the summer, just before my first semester at the university was about to start, I'd left my flop loft in the seedy First Ward and ventured out for some groceries. I was walking down Klepp Street, and I noticed this good looking girl about my age walking toward me, talking to herself. She was tall and thin with a lot of black curly hair, and dressed in an orange T-shirt and jeans; cheap, plastic beach sandals on her feet. She was smoking a cigarette and mildly gesticulating with her free hand. The fact that she was talking to herself made me think she might be crazy enough to talk to me, so I frantically ran through a few ice breaker lines in my head, searching for one to snag her interest. I immediately got confused, though, because the T-shirt she was wearing bore the name of my high school along with that distinctive rendering of a goofy looking lion. As we drew closer, I saw her face more clearly and knew that I knew her from somewhere. All I could muster when the moment came was, "Hi." She stopped, looked up to take me in, and said, without the least shock of recognition, "Hey, Pat, how are you?" like I'd seen her the day before. Then I realized who she was and said, "Esme, what are you doing here?"

She'd invited me to come along with her to the Palace A to get a cup of coffee. I'd been pretty lonely since arriving in town, what with classes not having started yet and knowing no one. I couldn't have ordered up a better scenario than running into her. We spent an hour at the diner, catching up, filling in the blanks of all the years and miles we'd traveled. She'd been at the university a semester already, but whereas I was there for a master's degree, she'd already gotten one in mathematics at a different school, producing a thesis on fractals and chaos theory, and now was after a second one in art. Coincidentally, art was my major also, and I admitted, with a whisper and a tinge of embarrassment in my voice, that I was a painter. This admission on my part de-animated her for a moment. She cocked her head to the side and stared at me, took a drag of her cigarette, pursed her lips, and then eventually nodded as if she could almost believe it.

Paint, of course, wasn't her thing—all of her work was done on the computer, plotting points and manifesting the rules and accidents of the universe in shape and color. This stuff was new back then and I had no way to conceive of what she was talking about, but the casually brilliant way in which she discussed Mandelbrot sets and strange attractors interested me almost as much as her hair and her smile. When I told her I liked the paintings of Redon and Guston, she laughed out loud, and although I knew she was disparaging my chosen influences, I was enchanted by the sound of it; like a ten year old's giggle.

We'd parted that first day after making plans to meet for breakfast on Sunday. Even then, although I knew we might become good friends, I suspected things would never go further than that. As fascinating as she was, she had a distinct aloofness about her even when staring me straight in the eye and relating the details of her mother's recent death. It was as if a scrupulously calculated percentage of her interest was held constantly in abeyance, busy working the solution to some equation. Besides her affect, I had, at the time, an irrational, Luddite inclination that there was something morally bankrupt about making art with a computer.

The semester began, and I soon discovered that abstract painting was still the order of the day in the university. Most of the professors had come of age in their own work during the late fifties and sixties and were still channeling the depleted spirit of Jackson Pollock; second- and third-rate abstract expressionists tutoring young painters in the importance of ignoring the figure. The canvases were vast, the paint applied liberally, and the bigger the mess the more praise the piece garnered. I was somewhat of an outcast among the students from the start with my crudely rendered cartoon figures frozen in drab scenes that bespoke a kind of world weariness; a mask to hide the fact that I felt too much about everything. I was barely tolerated as a kind of retarded mascot whose work had a throwback charm to it. Esme, for her part, was on similar footing. No one understood, save the people in the computer science division, how she made her glorious paisley whirls, infinite in their complexity or what they represented. The art crowd feared this technological know-how.

I'd done all of my excessive drinking, drug taking, and skirt chasing as an undergraduate, and now threw myself into the work with a commitment that was something new for me. When I think back to that place I had on Clinton Street, I remember the pervasive reek of turpentine, the beat-up mattress someone had put by the curb that became my bed, the dangerous mechanical heater—twisting

Looney-Toons funnel going up through the ceiling—that portioned out warmth by whim, and the bullet hole in the front window I'd covered with duct tape. I worked late into the nights when the crystal meth dealer met his clients under the lamp post across the street in front of the furniture warehouse and after the other tenants of my building had turned off the flames under their relentlessly simmering cabbage pots and fallen from minimum wage exhaustion into their beds. Then I'd make some coffee, put Blossom Dearie low on the old tape machine, and start mixing oils. Each brushstroke carried a charge of excitement. The professors who dismissed my work still had valuable secrets to impart about color and craft and materials, and I brought all of these lessons to bear on my canvases.

The months rolled on and in the midst of my education, I also gleaned a few insights into Esme. Outside of our booth at the Palace A, where the conversation orbited pretty strictly around a nucleus of topics—her diatribes promoting an electronic medium and mine, concerning the inadequacies of abstraction; a few catty comments about our fellow-students' work; the lameness of the professors—she proved to be something of a sphinx. With the exception of her telling me about her mother's bout with cancer that first day, she never mentioned her private life or her family. Anything I learned on that score came through sheer happenstance.

After class one day, I was talking to this guy, Farno, another painter in the graduate program, in the hallway outside a studio and Esme walked by. I interrupted my conversation and said hi to her, and she said, "I'll see you Sunday." When I turned back to the guy, he was shaking his head, and when she was well out of ear-shot, he said, "You know her?"

"Yeah, we went to high school together."

"So you must have fucked her," he said.

I took a step back, surprised at his comment, and said, "What are you talking about? We're just friends."

"I don't think she has any friends," he said.

My sudden anger made me silent.

"Listen, don't get upset," he said. "I'm just trying to warn you. It happened to me just like all the others. She'll come on to you. You go to dinner, or a movie, things wind up back at her place. I mean she's charming as hell, brilliant. You think to yourself, 'Wow, she's great.' You can't help but fall for her. Eventually, it's off to the bedroom. She's aggressive, like she's trying to fuck the life out of you, like she wants to eat your soul. Then, either the next morning, or sometimes even late in the night, you'll wake up and she'll be crying and then yell at you like a kid pitching a tantrum to get the hell out. I've talked to some of the others about her, both guys and girls, even some of the professors. She's whacked."

"Well, we're friends," I said in her defense and walked away.

Later that week, on Sunday, when we went to breakfast, that guy's story was circling in my head like a twister, but I kept my mouth shut about it. Since I'd never gone down that road with Esme, instead of thinking her crazy because of what I'd been told, I just felt, whether I should have or not, kind of bad for her. While all this was going through my head, she was giving me some rap about how chaos theory showed that the universe was both ordered and chaotic at the same time. I could barely concentrate on what she was saying, my mind filled with images of her fucking different people in the art department like some insatiable demon. Finally, she ended her explanation, making a face rife with dissatisfaction for the indecisive nature of creation, and asked me to pass the sugar.

In the next couple of weeks, the indecisive universe dropped two more revelations about her into my lap. I was in the university library one night, looking for a book they supposedly had of Reginald Marsh's Coney Island paintings, when I found myself upstairs where the study carrels were. My department didn't think enough of me to grant me one of these. Department heads doled them out like popes might indulgences to their favorite students. I knew Esme had one, though, granted by the computer science people, and I knew she used it from time to time. I walked along the row of them, peering in the little windows on the doors. Most of them were dark and empty. Eventually I found hers and she was in there, sitting at the desk.

In front of her was a computer with a screen full of numbers. To her right, on the desk was an open book, and, with her right hand, she was intermittently flipping through the pages and working the computer mouse, her attention shifting rapidly back and forth from the page to the screen. At the same time, on her left, on the desk was a notebook and she was writing away to beat the band with a pencil, not even glancing at what she was putting down. While all this was going on, she was also wearing earphones, plugged into a boom box sitting on the floor. When she turned her attention to the book, I caught a glimpse at her eyes. The only way I can describe her look, and this isn't a word I'd normally think to use, is *avaricious*. I was going to knock, but to tell you the truth, in that moment I found her a little frightening.

The second piece of the puzzle that was Esme came to me, from all people, my mother. I'd called home and was chatting with her about how my studies were going and what was up with the rest of the family. True to her mother-self, she asked me if I'd made any friends. I said I had, and then remembering Esme had come from our town, I mentioned her. When I said her name, my mother went uncharacteristically silent.

"What?" I asked.

"Her family . . . sheesh."

"Do you remember them?"

"Oh, yeah, I remember her mother from the PTA meetings and such. A block of ice. You didn't want to get near her for fear of frostbite. And the father, who was much more pleasant, he was some kind of pill addict. At least they had a lot of money."

"She's OK," I said.

"Well, you know best," she said, obviously implying that I didn't.

Esme's *condition*, or whatever you want to call it, haunted me. I don't know why I cared so much. To me she was just a breakfast date once a week, or was she? She was fun to talk to and I enjoyed meeting her at the Palace A for our rendezvous, but when I started to find myself thinking about her instead of thinking about painting, I made a determined effort to ignore those thoughts and dive back into my work.

On a Sunday afternoon in my second semester, somewhere right at the cusp between winter and spring, we were sitting in the diner celebrating with the steak and egg special a positive review of my recent work by my committee. I held forth for Esme on the encouraging comments of each of the professors. When I was done she smiled and said, "Pat, that's terrific, but think how much weight you put behind what they say now. I remember a few months ago when by your own estimation they were fools," and that took a little of the wind out of my sails. Still, I could undeniably feel the paintings were coming together and the creativity just seemed to flow down my arm and through the brush onto the canvas. I knew I was on to something good, and nothing Esme said could completely dampen my spirits. Instead, I laughed at her comment.

She got up to go to the bathroom, and I sat paging through the catalog of a spring show that was to hang in the university gallery and would include some graduate student pieces and some by well-established professionals. I'd been asked to put a piece in that show, and I was ecstatic. When she returned, I was looking at a page with a reproduction of a painting by the artist, Thomas Dorphin, the best known of the artists who would be at the opening.

"What's that you're looking at?" she asked as she slid into the booth.

"A piece by that guy, Dorphin. Do you know his stuff?"

She shook her head.

"It's kind of like that Cy Twombly crap, only it looks three-dimensional, sort of like a mix between him and Lichtenstein." Twombly had done a series of pieces that were scribbles, like a toddler loose with a crayon, on canvas and the art world was still agog over them. The painting by Dorphin was also a scribble, only the line was rendered with a brush and the illusion of three dimensionality, as if instead of obviously being a line from a crayon, it appeared a piece of thick twine. The technique was pretty impressive, but it left me cold.

"Let me see," she said.

I turned the catalog around to her and she drew it closer.

She looked at it for about two seconds, and I noticed a nearly undetectable tremor of surprise. Then her complexion went slightly pale.

"What's wrong?" I said.

Still clutching the catalog, she slid out of the booth and stood up. She reached into the pocket of her jeans and pulled out a wad of bills, too much for what we'd both had, and threw it on the table.

"I want you to come with me to my place," she said, looking a little frantic.

Immediately, I thought that my time had come to be fucked like she was eating my soul. I got nervous and stammered about having to get back to work, but she interrupted me and said, "Please, Pat, you have to come. It won't take long. I have to show you something."

I was leery, but she seemed so desperate, I couldn't let her down. I nodded, got up, and followed. Her apartment was only two blocks from the diner in a renovated warehouse on Hallart Street. I'd never been there before, but I knew where it was. She walked in front of me, keeping a quick pace and every now and then looked over her shoulder to see that I was still behind her. When she glanced back at me, I smiled, but she made no expression in return. With the rate we were walking, it took only minutes to get to the front door. She retrieved her keys and let us in. There was an old freight elevator you had to take to get to her rooms on the fifth floor. As we ascended, I said to her, "What's all this about?"

"You won't believe it," she said and then lifted the catalog and flipped it open to the page with the Dorphin on it for another look.

She unlocked the door to her place and we entered. If order and chaos existed simultaneously in the universe, her apartment was one of the places where order hid out. It was a nice space, with a huge window view of the river in the distance. There was a big Persian carpet on the floor with a floral mandala design. The walls were painted a soothing sea green, and hung with framed pieces of her fractal art. However it was done, the lighting made the room seem a cozy cave. I was in there for no more than a minute, and I felt the tension just sort of slough off me like some useless outer skin. On the desk, next to a computer was a row of sharpened pencils lined up in descending order of length from right to left. The sight of them gave me a sudden flashback to the crusted dishes piled in the sink back at my place.

"Beautiful," I said to her as she hung her jacket up in a closet near the entrance.

"It's OK," she said absentmindedly. "Stay here for a minute, I have to look for something in the bedroom."

In her absence, I went to the nearest bookcase and scanned the titles. My gaze came to rest not on one of the many volumes of art books, but upon a photograph on the top shelf. It was in a simple, silver frame—the image of a severe looking middle-aged woman with a short, tight permanent and her arms folded across her chest. She was sitting at a table in front of a birthday cake, its candles trailing smoke as if just having been extinguished. The woman's jaw and cheekbones were no more than cruel, angular cuts, as if her face had been hacked from granite with a blunt pick, and her eyes stared directly through mine and out the back of my head. I surmised she was the Snow Queen of the PTA my mother had told me about.

When Esme emerged from the other room, she called me over to a card table with two chairs set on opposite sides near the back of the apartment in front of the window. The sun was bright that day, and I remember squinting out at the view of the light glinting in diamonds off the river just before taking the seat across from her. In addition to the catalog, her cigarettes, an ashtray and lighter, she laid on the table-top what appeared to be a plastic Mylar bag, the kind that comic book collectors keep their treasures in. From where I sat, it looked as if it held only a sheet of white paper, $8\frac{1}{2}$ by 11.

She lit a cigarette, and while clamping it in the corner of her mouth as she returned her lighter to the table, began speaking. "Remember where the 7-11 was downtown back in Preston?" she asked.

I nodded. "Yeah, it was the only place in town that would sell us beer."

"I think I might remember seeing you in there," she said. "Well, if you made a right at that corner and headed down toward the municipal garage, do you recall on the left side of the road that little day-care center?"

I couldn't really picture it, but I nodded anyway.

"I worked in that center the summer after senior year. It was one of those places where parents drop their kids off when they go to work. Mostly toddlers, some a little older. I liked the kids but there were too many of them and not enough of us."

"Never work with animals or children," I said.

"Not if you mind wiping noses and asses all day," she said. "It was a good introduction to chaos theory, though." She paused, took a drag of her cigarette and shook her head as if remembering the scene. "Anyway, one day near the end of the summer, about an hour before the parents came to pick the kids up, I was sitting on a tiny kid's chair, completely exhausted. I was so motionless for so long, I think the kids kind of forgot that I was there. They had the dress-up trunk out, and hats and masks and old tattered costume stuff was flying all over the place.

"There was this one strange little kid who was there every day. He was really young, but he had an amazing sense of presence, like he was a little old man. The other kids all loved being around him, and sometimes they just stared for the longest time into his eyes, which were like a crystal, turquoise color. His name was Jonathan. So this other kid, a little bit older walks up to Jonathan, and I'm sitting there quietly, watching this go down. The other kid seems sad or tired. Keeping his voice a little low, he says, 'Tell me what it was like inside your mommy, I'm starting to forget'."

"What?" I said.

"Yeah," said Esme, and nodded, smiling.

"That's wild."

"Right after the kid said this to Jonathan, another little girl, who'd dressed up in a fairy princess outfit—she had a little tiara on her head and was carrying a wand, walked between them, turned to the kid who asked the question, waved the wand and said in a soft chant, 'Go away. Go away. Go away.'"

"Did he?"

"Yeah. I swear I thought he was going to start crying. Then for a little while, I guess my mind was preoccupied, trying to think back and see if I remembered my earliest memory. If I could recall being in the womb. Nothing. I got a big, frustrating blank. When I looked up I noticed Jonathan and the kid had met up again off in the corner of the room. The kid was leaning down and Jonathan, hand cupped around his mouth and the kid's ear, was whispering something to him. The kid was smiling."

"What do you think he was telling him?"

"I don't know," she said, "but just then my boss came in and saw that the other kids were getting wild. She had me calm them down and hand out paper for them to draw on until it was time to leave. She always liked them quiet for when the parents came to get them. Time was finally up and the parents showed and when the last of the little crumb snatchers was gone, I started cleaning up. Most of them had left their drawings behind on the table tops. I went around and collected them. I always got a charge out of seeing their artwork—there's just always a sense of rightness about the pictures from kids who haven't gone to school yet—fresh and powerful and so beautifully simple.

"When I got to the place where the kid who wanted to remember his mother's womb sat, I found that he'd left this big scribble on his paper. I can't really describe it, but it was like a big circular scribble, overlapping lines, like a cloud of chaos, in black crayon. I remarked to myself that that wasn't such a good sign after what I'd witnessed. But check this out," she said and drew the Mylar bag next to her closer and opened the zip top. "When I got to Jonathan's picture, it lay face down on the desk. I turned it over, and . . ." Here she reached into the bag and pulled out two sheets of drawing paper. As she laid them down in front of me I saw there was black crayon on both. "The same exact scribble. Absolutely, exactly the same."

"Nah," I said, and looked down at the two pages.

"You show me where they differ," she said.

My glance darted back and forth from one to the other, checking each loop and intersection. Individually, they appeared to have been dashed off in a manner of seconds. There was no sense that the creators were even paying attention to the page when they did them. Eventually, I laughed and shook my head. "I give up," I said. "Are you pulling my leg? Did you do these on the computer?"

"No," she said, "but even if I had, now check this out." Here she opened the catalog to the page with the reproduction of the Dorphin painting. "It's rendered as if three-dimensional, but look closely. It's the same damn scribble made to look like a jumble of twine."

I looked and she was right. Reaching across the table, I took one of her cigarettes and lit it. I sat and smoked for a minute, trying to get my mind around her story and the pictures before me. For some reason, right then, I couldn't look into her eyes. "So what are you trying to tell me?" I finally said.

"I'm not *trying* to tell you anything," she said. "But I've seen it in other places. Once when I was in New York City, I was on the subway. It was crowded and I took a seat next to a guy who had a drawing pad with him. I looked over and he was sketching some of the other passengers, but down in the corner of the page was that same scribble. I pointed to it and said to him, 'That's an interesting design.' He looked at me and asked, 'Do you remember?' I didn't answer, but I was taken aback by his question. He must have seen the surprise in my eyes. Without another word, he closed the book, put it in his knapsack, stood up and brushed past me. He moved through the crowd and went to stand by the door. At the next stop, he got off."

"Get out," I said. "That really happened?"

"You'll see it," she said. "If you don't know what to look for, you'd never notice it. It just looks like a scribble, like somebody just absent-mindedly messing around with a crayon or pen. But you'll see it now."

"Where am I going to see it?" I asked.

"Hey, don't believe me, just call me when you do and tell me I was right."

"Wait a second . . . , and so you think it has to do with . . . what?" I asked, not wanting to say what I was thinking.

"It's some kind of sign or symbol made by people who remember all the way back to the womb," she said.

"Is that even possible?" I asked, stubbing out my cigarette in the ashtray.

She shrugged, "I don't know. What do *you* make of it?"

I didn't answer. We sat there for quite a while, both looking at the two drawings and Dorphin's painting.

"You kept these drawing all these years?" I said, breaking the silence.

"Of course, in case I wanted to tell someone. Otherwise they wouldn't believe me."

"I still don't believe you," I said.

"You will," said Esme.

During the walk back to my apartment and all afternoon, I thought about the drawings and their implications. What Esme'd really been hinting at, but didn't come out and say, was that there was afoot in the world a conspiracy of in-utero-remembering scribblers. Was there some secret knowledge they were protecting, did they have powers far beyond those of mortal men, were they up to no good? The concept was so bizarre, so out of left field, my paranoia got the better of me and I had to wonder whether Esme had concocted the whole thing, having first seen the Dorphin painting and knowing I'd eventually show her the catalog or we'd come across it at the university. If that was true, then it represented an outlandish effort to dupe me, and for what? A momentary recollection of her in the library carrel gave me a shiver.

That night, I found I couldn't paint. The great ease of conception and movement of the brush I'd felt in recent weeks was blocked by the chaotic scribble of my thoughts. I lay on the mattress, staring at the ceiling, trying to think back to my own beginning. The earliest experience I could recall was being in a big rubber snow suit out in our backyard, sitting atop a snow drift, staring at a red, setting sun and my mother calling from the back door for me to come in. When my thoughts hit the wall of that memory, they spun off in all directions, considering what exactly it might be that the scribblers were remembering. A state of mind? A previous life? Heaven? Or just the underwater darkness and muffled sounds of the world within the belly?

By Wednesday, I'd seen that damn scribble three times. The first was in the men's room of the Marble Grill, a bar down the street from my apartment where I ate dinner every once in a while. The place was a dive, and the bathroom walls were brimming with all kinds of graffiti. I'd gone in there to take a piss, and while I was going, I looked up, and, there, just above the plumbing of the urinal, staring me right in the face, was a miniature version of that tumbleweed of mystery. Recognizing it gave me a jolt, and I almost peed on my sneaker. I realized that in the dozen or so other times I'd stood there, looking directly at it, it might as well have been invisible.

I saw it again, later that very night, on the inside back cover of a used paperback copy of this science fiction novel, *Mindswap*, I'd bought a few weeks earlier at a street sale. The book was pretty dog-eared, and I don't know what made me pick it up that night out of all the others I had laying around. On the inside front cover, written in pencil, in a neat script, was the name, *Derek Drymon*, whom I surmised was the original owner. Whoever this guy was, where ever he was, I wondered if he was *remembering* as I lay there on my mattress wishing I could simply forget.

The last instance, which happened two days later, the one that drove me back to Esme's apartment, was a rendition of the scribble on a dollar I whipped out at the university cafeteria to pay for a cup of coffee. The girl behind the cash register reached toward me, closed her fingers on the bill, and at that moment I saw the design. She tugged, but I couldn't let go. My gaze remained locked on it until she said, "You paying for this, or what?" Then I released my hold, and it was gone.

Later that afternoon, I found myself on Hallart street, standing on the steps of Esme's building, waiting for her to buzz me in. In the elevator, I prepared myself to eat crow. When the elevator opened, she was standing there waiting for me in the doorway to her apartment. She had a smile on her face and the first thing she said was, "Go ahead."

"What do you mean?" I asked.

"An apology, perhaps? Esme, how could I have doubted you?" she said.

"Fuckin' scribble," I muttered.

She laughed and stepped back to let me in. As I passed, she patted me on the back and said, "Maddening, isn't it?"

"Well," I said, "you're right, but where does that get us? It's got me so I can't paint."

"Now that we both know, and I know I'm not crazy," she said, "we're going to have to figure out what it's about."

"Why?" I asked.

"Because the fact that you don't know will always be with you. Don't you want to know what you're missing?"

"Not really," I said, "I just want to get past it."

She took a step closer to me and put her palms on my shoulders. "Pat, I need you to help me with this. I can't do it by myself. Someone has to corroborate everything."

I shook my head, but she pulled me over to her desk. "Before you say anything, check this out." She sat down in the chair, facing the computer. With a click of the mouse, the machine came to life.

"OK, now," she said, spinning on the seat so she could look up at me. She took my left hand in both of hers, more than likely so that I couldn't escape. "After you were here last Sunday, and I had the pictures out, I studied them closely for the first time in a long while. I can't believe I didn't think of this before, but in concentrating on the intersections of the lines, I wondered what these points would reveal if plotted on a graph. So I scanned the drawing into the computer, and erased the lines, leaving only the points of intersection."

She clicked the mouse once, and an image of the scribble appeared on the screen. After letting that sit for a few seconds, she then clicked again, and revealed only the points, like a cloud of gnats.

"I set them on a graph," she said. Another click and the entire swarm was trapped in a web. "Then for a long time, I looked for sequences, some kind of underlying order to them. It wasn't long before I saw this." She gave another click, and there appeared a line, emanating from a point close to the center of the cluster and looping outward in a regular spiral, like the cross section of a nautilus shell.

"Interesting," I said, "but it only utilizes some of the dots. You could easily make just as many irregular designs if you linked other dots."

"Yes," she said. "But do you know what that shape represents?" she asked.

"It's the Golden Section," I said. "We studied it earlier in the year when we were covering Leonardo. You can find it in all of his paintings, from St. Jerome and the Lion to the *Mona Lisa*. A lot of painters swore by it—Jacopo, Seurat, . . ."

Tracing the spiral on the screen with her index finger, she said, "You're good. It's a Fibonacci series. Consciously used in art and architecture but also found occurring spontaneously everywhere in Nature. To the ancients the existence of this phenomenon was proof of a deity's design inherent in the universe. It's Holy. It's Magic."

"Back up, though," I said. "It doesn't utilize all of the dots, and there's so many dots there that connected in the right way you could come up with a shit load of different designs as well."

"True," she said, "but look . . ." She clicked the mouse again. "At any one time, depending on what you choose as your starting points, you can plot five Golden Sections within the scribble, the five using all of the dots except one. Order in chaos, and the one representing the potential of the chaotic amidst order."

The picture on the screen proved her point with lines, I could easily follow curling out from central points. She clicked the screen again.

"Change the originating points and you can make five different Golden spirals," she said.

Just as I was able to take in the next pattern, she clicked the mouse again, waited a second, and then clicked it again. She clicked through twelve different possible designs of spiral groups before stopping. Turning on the seat, she looked up at me.

"That's all I had time for," she said.

"You're industrious as hell," I told her and took a step backward.

She stood up and came toward me. "I have a plan," she said.

By the time I left Esme's place, it was dark. She'd unfurled her plan for me. "Who do we know for sure Remembers?" she'd asked, and I'd told her, "No one." But as she'd revealed, that wasn't true. "Dorphin," she said, and then told me how she was going to take one of the scribble drawings she had to the opening at the university gallery and try to convince him she'd done it and was one of *them* in an attempt to get him to talk. I'd told her I wanted nothing to do with it and, after long arguments both reasonable and passionate, when I'd still refused, she'd kicked me out. As I walked along the night streets back to my apartment, though, it wasn't her scheme I thought about. What I couldn't help remembering was that brief period before she turned on the computer when she'd held my hand.

That Sunday, when I got to the Palace A, she wasn't there, and I knew immediately she wouldn't be coming. I took a seat anyway and waited for an hour, picking at a corn muffin and forcing down a cup of coffee. Her absence was palpable, and I realized in that time how much I needed to see her. She was my strange attractor. I finally left and went by her apartment. Standing on the steps, I rang the buzzer at least six times, all the while picturing her at her computer, tracing spirals through clouds of dots. No answer. When I got back to my place, I tried to call her, but she didn't pick up.

There were many instances in the following week where I considered writing her a note and leaving it in her mailbox, telling her I was sorry and that I would gladly join her in her plan to flush out Dorphin, but each time I stopped myself at the last second, not wanting to be merely a means to an end, another Fibonacci series used to plumb the design of the ineffable. Ultimately, what exactly I wanted, I wasn't sure, but I knew definitely I wanted to see her. I hung around campus all week, waiting for her outside of classes I knew she had, but she never showed herself.

Saturday night came, the night of the opening, and I should have been excited with the prospect of so many people seeing my painting hanging in the university gallery alongside those of well known artists, but I was preoccupied with whether or not she would be there. Still, I had the presence of mind to clean myself up, shave, and throw on my only jacket and tie. The place was packed, wine was flowing, and quite a few people had approached me to tell me how much they admired the piece I had hanging. Dorphin was there, and the neo-cubist, Uttmeyer, and Miranda Blench. Groups of art students and faculty clustered around these stars. Just when I'd had a few glasses of wine and was letting myself forget Esme and enjoy the event a little, she walked in. She wore a simple, low-cut black dress and a jeweled choker. I'd never seen her in anything beside jeans and a T-shirt. Her hair glistened under the track lighting. She walked toward me, and when she drew near, I said, "Where were you on Sunday?" Without so much as a blink, she moved past me, heading for Dorphin, and I could feel something tear inside me.

Moving out of the crowd, I took up a position next to the wine and cheese table, where I could keep a surreptitious eye on her. She bided her time, slowly circling like a wily predator on the outskirts of Dorphin's crowd of admirers, waiting for just the right moment. I noticed that she carried a large manila envelope big enough to hold one of the drawings. The artist, himself, a youthful looking middle-aged guy with sandy hair, seemed shy but affable, taking time to answer questions and smiling through the inquisition. Now that Esme was on his trail, I was disappointed that he didn't come off a self-centered schmuck. Behind him hung his painting, and from where I stood, a view that put his slightly bowed head directly at the center of the scribble, its aura appeared a halo of confusion.

A half hour passed in which other students stopped to say hello and congratulate me on my painting making the show, and each time I tried to dispatch them as quickly as possible and get back to spying on Esme. It was right after one of these little visits that I turned back to my focal point, and saw that in the brief few minutes I was chatting, she'd made her move. The first thing I noticed was a change in Dorphin's look. His face was bright now, and he no longer slouched. He was interested in her—who could blame him? They were already deep into some conversation. She was smiling, he was smiling, she nodded, he nodded, and then I saw her lift that manila envelope and open it. Pulling out a sheet of white paper, no doubt one of the drawings, she offered it to him. He turned it around, took a quick look at the picture and then over each shoulder to see if anyone else was near. He spoke some short phrase to her, and she hesitated for only an instant before nodding.

One of my professors walked over to me then and I had to turn away. What started as a friendly conversation soon turned into a gas bag disquisition on his part, and he was one of those talkers who takes a breath at odd times so you can't follow the rhythm and intuit the free moment when you can get a word in and escape. I managed to remain in the realm of polite respect and still steal a couple of glances into the crowd. On my first, I noticed that Esme and Dorphin had moved off into a corner and were talking in what seemed to me to be conspiratorial whispers. The next I looked, he had his hand on her shoulder. And when my professor had spent his brilliance on me and gone in search of another victim, I looked to that corner again and they were gone.

I stepped into the crowd and spun around, trying to find them again. Two rotations and it appeared they were no longer in the gallery. I walked the perimeter once to make sure I hadn't missed them in my survey while a growing sense of desperation blossomed in my gut. I went out in the hallway and checked up and down, but they weren't there either. At that moment, I couldn't have put in words what I was feeling. I was certain I'd lost Esme, not that I had ever really had her. The realization made me stagger over to a bench and sit down. What came to mind were all of those Sunday mornings at the Palace A, and as each memory appeared it as suddenly evaporated and was gone as if it had never happened.

"Where is she?" I heard a voice ask through my reverie. I looked up to see a tall, thin guy with blonde hair, standing over me.

"Who?" I asked, only then realizing it was Farno.

"Did Esme leave with Dorphin?" he asked.

"Why?" I asked.

"Yes or no?" he said, seeming agitated.

"I think she did, what of it?"

He leaned down and whispered to me, "She's in danger. Dorphin's an imposter."

"What do you mean?" I said.

Instead of answering, he pulled a pen out of his pocket, moved over to the wall where there was a flyer hanging, and, in a second, had made a mark on the paper. I stood and walked up behind him. When he noticed me there, he lifted the pen and pointed to what he'd drawn. It was a miniature facsimile of the scribble. I'd seen the design enough times to know his was authentic.

"Look, I'm sure she told you about the scribble," he said. "Dorphin is passing himself off as someone who Remembers as a way of drawing us out. He's working for someone else. I can't explain now. You've got to trust me. I'm telling you, she's in serious trouble."

I stood there stunned. "OK," was all I could say.

"I have a car," said Farno. "He's from out of town but close enough where I doubt he'd have booked a room. Where would she take him?"

"Her place," I said.

He was already running down the hallway toward the exit that led to the parking lot. "Come on," he yelled over his shoulder.

Running to Farno's car in the parking lot, I don't remember what, if anything, I was thinking at the time. The entire affair had become just too bizarre. Once we were in the old four-door Chevy, and he was pulling out of the parking lot, he turned to me and said, "She still lives on Hallart, right? That renovated warehouse building?"

I nodded.

"They're only a few minutes ahead of us," he said. He was driving within the speed limit, but I could see his anxiety in the way he hunched up over the dashboard and nervously tapped the steering wheel at the first red light we stopped at.

"What exactly is going on?" I finally asked. "Dorphin is dangerous?"

"I shouldn't be telling you any of this, but I might need your help," he said, "so try to keep it to yourself, OK?"

"I can do that," I said.

"I can Remember," he said. "You know what that means."

I nodded.

"That time I told you about that Esme had me to her place, she revealed the drawings to me and her theory. So I was aware she'd stumbled onto the scribble, something she wasn't supposed to know about. She's not the first, but for the most part it's gone unrecognized for centuries. When I saw you two hanging out together, I tried to make you think she was crazy so that if she told you about it, you'd dismiss it as just some delusion."

"You mean all that stuff you told me about her fucking all of those people wasn't real?" I asked.

"No," he said. "That part's true, but I thought if I told you, you'd be more circumspect about her theory."

"Jeez," I said. "What about Dorphin? Where does he come in?"

"Like I said, some people have gotten hip to the scribble over time. You can't keep something like this a complete secret for eternity. In the past, even if people were suspicious, they just wrote it off to mere coincidence or some innocuous aberration of reality. But somewhere in the late 1960s, somebody put things together and decided that the ability to Remember and all that went with it was something that was either dangerous to the rest of the populace or could be mined for economic benefit. We don't really know what their motivations are, but there is a group, as secretive as we are, who want to get to the bottom of the phenomenon."

"Dorphin's been a painter for years," I said.

"He's been co-opted by this group. A lot of people with the scribble mind turn out to be artists—painters, musicians, writers—not all of them. So they either paid Dorphin a huge sum of money or blackmailed him or something to work for them. They gave him the design, no doubt, which it's obvious they now know, and he produced this painting and took it on the road to try to flush us out. Believe me, no one who Remembers would go that public with the *Vundesh*. I knew it was a ploy when I saw the catalog and that painting, and I knew Esme would see it."

"The Vundesh?"

"That's the name of the scribble design."

"This is completely insane," I said. "What will they do to Esme?"

"Well, if Dorphin believes she really Remembers, she could disappear for good," he said. "It all depends if he has this device with him or not."

"What device?" I asked, but I felt the car stopping. I looked and saw that Farno was pulling up to the curb in front of Esme's building. There was another car parked a few yards up in front of the Chevy.

We jumped out and ran up the steps. The moment we were at the door, I reached up and hit the buzzer for her apartment. We waited and there was no answer. I hit it three more times with no response from above.

"Look out," said Farno, and he gently moved me to the side and scanned the names next to the buzzers. "I think Jenkins from our Life class lives here too." He must have found his name there, because he pressed one of the buzzers and held it down.

Before long, a window opened two stories up and Jenkins stuck his head out. "Who's there?" he said looking down.

Farno took a step back and looked up. "Hey man, it's me," he said and waved.

"Yo," said Jenkins.

"Shay's here with me. We're going up to Esme's place but I think she's got her headphones on or something. Buzz us in, ok?"

I heard the window close, and a few seconds later the door buzzed. I grabbed the handle and Farno and I ran in. I was heading for the stairs, which I thought would be quicker, but he said, "it's probably locked down here. We've got to take the eleva-tor." The ascent was excruciatingly slow.

"Let's avoid fisticuffs and heroics," said Farno. "I want to get through this without anyone getting hurt, especially me."

When the elevator came to rest at Esme's floor, I pulled back the heavy door, and just as I got a view of her apartment and that it was wide open, I saw someone bolt out of it and head down the short hallway. It could have been Dorphin, but all I saw was a blur. Stepping into the hall, I turned and saw the door to the stairway swing shut and lock. I bounded across the hall and into Esme's place. She was stretched out on the floor in the middle of her apartment, not moving. I dropped down next to her and took her arm to feel for a pulse, but as I groped along her wrist, I realized she was breathing.

"She's alive," I said over my shoulder.

"Let's get her up on the couch," said Farno.

I took her arms and he her legs and we hoisted her up where she'd be more com-fortable. He went to get her some water, and I sat holding her hand and calling her name.

She eventually came around, shaking her head as if to clear it. When she opened her eyes, she saw me and said in a groggy voice, "Hey, Pat." A moment passed, and then she suddenly sat straight up, and looked around nervously.

"Where is he?" she asked.

"Dorphin? He's gone," I said.

"He put this thing on my head, and then . . . everything went black."

Farno walked in with the water then. She looked up at him. "What are you doing here?" she asked. "What are the two of you doing here?"

She held her head in both hands as we filled her in. "Are you getting this?" I asked.

She nodded.

Farno explained that the device he had her wear was something that helps them, whoever they are, to determine if you actually Remember. According to him it was something new and it indicated some anomaly in the natural electro-magnetic field emanating from the brain which was at the heart of the phenomenon.

"Did he have like a television remote control?" asked Farno.

Esme nodded. "My god, it zapped me like an electric shock."

"He probably knows you don't have it, if he used that. That's a good thing," said Farno. "If he thought you had it, you might not be here still."

Esme took her hands away from her head and looked up. "Here's what I want to know," she said. "What is *it*?"

I turned to Farno and said, "Yeah, let's have it. We know too much already."

He got up and went over and shut the door to the apartment. On the way back, he pulled up the chair from the computer desk and straddled it, leaning over the back. "OK," he said. "It's not like it's gonna change anything for you to know. Just, please, try to keep it a secret from here on out. Can you promise me that?"

Esme and I both agreed.

"There are some people, why these people and not others, it seems completely random, but there are some people who are born with the ability to remember, after they are born, what it was like in the womb."

"Dorphin told me it was Heaven—blue skies and dead relatives and omnis-cience, and that his device would allow me to see it," said Esme.

"Dorphin's an imposter. He's not even close to what the memory is. And in fact, it's something that I truly can't describe to you. There just aren't words. It makes you different, though. It makes you experience the world differently than people without it. There's no special powers that come with it, no grand insights, but just a calm sense of well-being. All I can tell you is that you feel in your heart that you belong to the universe, that you know you have a purpose. That's it."

"What about the scribble?" I asked.

"I can make it automatically. I could make it ever since I could hold a crayon; perfect every time. It's a physical manifestation of the phenomenon. I don't understand it, only that it's a sign to others who have it that you also Remember. There's something to knowing you're not the only one, and so we communicate this to each other. There's nothing more to it than that. There's no dark conspiracy. We're not out to take over the world or any of that silly shit."

"If it's so simple," said Esme, "then why keep it a secret?"

"First off," said Farno, "there's an understanding that comes with the Remembering, sort of built in with it, and that is that it's better to keep it a secret from those who don't experience it. Look at Dorphin and the people he works for—the government; some pharmaceutical company, maybe, wanting to bottle and exploit that sense of purpose I mentioned; perhaps a vigilante group desperate to eradicate our difference from humanity. If you told people, they'd think we were talking about a memory of heaven, or the afterlife, or some realm in the course of reincarnation—start projecting onto it what they wanted it to be and become jealous they'd missed out. They couldn't be farther off the mark. Think of how the religious would abuse it. It has nothing to do with God in the pedestrian sense. The anti-abortionists would have a field day with it, never understanding the least bit of what it was. The truth is, if you have it, you have it, you know, and if you don't, you'll never know."

I had a thousand more questions, but Farno said he had to leave. "She should probably stay somewhere else for a couple of days just in case they come again," he said to me. "If by then no one has broken into the apartment here, it's probably a good sign that they know she's not authentic. No sense in calling the cops; they're not gonna believe you." He got up and headed for the door, and I thanked him for helping us. Without looking back, he simply waved his hand in the air. I thought Esme should also have said something to him, but she never opened her mouth. When he was gone, I looked at her and saw she was crying.

She remained silent while I helped her put a few things together and got her into her coat. It was as if she was drugged or drunk or sleep walking. I told her I was taking her to my place, and I thought she would refuse to go, but she didn't. On the walk to my apartment, I kept my arm around her. She leaned against me, and I could feel her shivering. "Are you all right?" I'd asked her every couple of blocks, and instead of answering me, she'd put her hand on my side for a moment. The only sign that she was conscious at all was when we got to my apartment and climbed the impossibly long set of steps. I opened the door and flipped on the light switch, and when she saw it, she said, "Beautiful." I laughed, but she didn't.

She left my side and walked over to where the mattress lay on the floor. Unhitching the back of her dress, she let it drop right there, and wearing only a pair of underpants got into bed and curled into a fetal position beneath the two blankets. She closed her eyes, and I turned the lights off so she could sleep. Instead of trying to find a place to sleep, I sat in the dark in front of my easel and had a beer, thinking through what had happened that night. I wondered why she seemed so beaten. This experience had changed her in some way, flipped a switch inside of her and turned off the manic energy. I pondered how and why, but it never came clear to me. Finally, I just laid down on the floor at the foot of the mattress and wadded a jacket up for a pillow. The floor was hard as hell, but I was exhausted.

My eyes hadn't been closed five minutes when I heard her voice, whispering. "Pat, come over here with me," she said. I didn't argue, but got to my knees and crawled over to the empty side of the mattress. Once I was under the covers, she turned to me and said, "Just hold me." So I did, and that's how we slept all night.

I was late getting up the next morning and had to rush to get ready for school. She was still asleep when I left. All day I wondered how long Esme would stay with me or if she'd be gone when I got home. I saw Farno in class and he completely ignored me. To show him I was true to my word of secrecy, I also said nothing to him. When class was over, though, and we passed in the hallway, he subtly nodded and smiled to me. I took the first bus home I could catch and stopped at the Chinese place up the street from my apartment, buying enough for two. On the walk from there to my place, it struck me that I hadn't done a painting in a long time. I made a mental note to force myself back to work.

Esme was there when I came in. She'd done the dishes and straightened the place up a bit—a very welcome sight indeed. Her demeanor was lighter, at least more cognizant. It wasn't that I still could not recognize that change I'd noticed the other night, but she was talkative and smiled at the fact that I'd bought us dinner. Instead of my usual, eating right out of the white cartons, we cleared the table and she found a couple of plates I couldn't remember owning. She asked me what happened at school, and I thanked her for doing the dishes and cleaning. After that, though, things went quiet.

Unable to take the silence, I asked her, "So did you go out today?"

"No," she said, "but I'll show you what I did." She got up and walked over by the window to stand next to an old drawing board I had set up there. I followed her, and when I got there, she pointed down at the board.

On one side, taped to the slanted surface, was one of the old drawings of the scribble she had collected at the daycare. Lying next to it was a stack of drawing paper, the top sheet of which also had a scribble on it, but not *the* scribble.

"What are you doing?" I asked, smiling.

"I'm trying to draw the scribble freehand."

"Why?" I asked.

"I thought that if I could get it just right, I'd be able to Remember. Some times things work in both directions," she said. Her smile became tenuous.

"Do you think that's a good idea?" I asked.

"It could work," she told me.

She seemed too fragile for me to try to talk reason to her, as if she'd implode if I called into question her process. Instead, I said, "Well, there's a lot of paper there," pointing to the 500-sheet box of copier paper I'd ripped off from the school that lay on the floor.

She nodded and sat down. Picking up a pencil, she leaned over and grabbed a new sheet of paper from the box. "I'll use both sides," she said.

"Thanks," I said and went back to the table to finish my dinner.

She worked away relentlessly at reproducing the scribble. I sat, pretending to paint, and witnessed her mania, trying to decide what to do. Eventually, late into the night, she stood up, took off her clothes and got down on the mattress under the blankets.

The next morning when I awoke, she was already at the drawing board. I took a shower and got dressed for school, and when I told her I had to get going, she barely looked up. The sheets of paper holding the rejected scribbles had originally been neatly stacked, but now that stack was spilling onto the floor, and the chair she occupied was surrounded by them.

"How's it going?" I asked, trying to get a response from her before leaving.

"Good," she said, holding up her latest attempt. "Look, I'm getting really close." She laid the picture down next to the one taped to the board. "Don't you think?"

"Yeah," I said. "You're making progress." To be honest, it looked to me like she was further from the mark than when she'd started. I said goodbye to her, but she was already beginning on the next one and didn't acknowledge my leaving.

That evening, when I returned home, I found a blizzard of copier paper covering the floor around the drawing table; the box was empty. The original drawing, from the day-care center, and the small suitcase she'd packed the night she came to stay were gone and so was she. For the first time since I began living there, the apartment felt empty. I left and ran over to her place. After not being able to rouse her, I buzzed for Jenkins. A minute later, he was sticking his head out the window above.

"What do you want, Shay?" he asked upon seeing me.

"Have you seen Esme?"

"Yeah," he said. "About three hours ago. She had a pile of suitcases, right there on the curb. A cab came and got her."

"Buzz me in, man," I said to him.

He did and I went up to her apartment. The door was unlocked. She'd left her computer and all of her books. I wondered if that meant she'd be back. Then I noticed, lying on the floor in the corner, the picture of her mother. It'd been taken out of its frame, which lay nearby in a pile of broken glass. I picked up the photo and brought it closer. Then I noticed that the face of the severe looking woman had been covered with a scribble.

I went religiously to the Palace A every Sunday morning for a late breakfast, but she never joined me again. Later on, I learned from one of the professors that she'd dropped out. Making a phone call home, I told my mother to keep a lookout for her in town in case Esme'd decided to return to her father's house. Finishing that semester was one of the hardest things I've ever done. At the eleventh hour, when it looked like I wouldn't be able to come up with any new paintings for my final review, I had a breakthrough one night and dashed off a portrait of a little girl, sitting alone by an open window. Outside the sun is shining and the sky is blue. She's drawing at a table, and although the pencil in her hand is drawing a scribble on the paper before her, her eyes are closed. I called it "The Scribble Mind." It was only one piece, but it was good enough to get me through the semester.

After graduate school I kept painting, year in and year out, with a show here and there but never to any great acclaim. When I was younger, that bothered me, and then I forgot about it, and the work itself became its own reward. Still, in all of those hundreds of canvases I'd covered not one ever gave me a hint as to what my true purpose was. Living without knowing was not so bad, especially after I'd married and had two daughters. I had all the purpose I needed in my family, and the art was just something I did and will always do.

I did see Esme one more time, years later. It wasn't that I'd forgotten her, that would have been impossible, but more that I packed that time away and painted through it. I was in a small gallery down in Soho in New York City where I'd had a few pieces in a show. I'd gone in that afternoon because the show was over and I had to take my work down. The owner of the place was back in her office, and the gallery was empty. I was just about to remove a painting from the wall when the door opened and in walked a woman with a young girl following. As I turned to see who it was, the woman said, "Hey, Pat." I noticed the black hair and her eyes and something stirred in my memory, although the expensive coat and boots weren't right. "Esme, what are you doing here?" I said.

She laughed. "I live uptown, and I saw this show advertised and your name along with it and thought I'd come down and see what your paintings looked like. I never suspected you'd be here."

"It's great to see you," I said.

She introduced me to her daughter, who stood by the front window, looking out at the people walking by. Her name was Gina, and she seemed a kind of quiet and sad kid. I said hi to her and she turned and waved. She must have been about six.

I showed Esme my work and she praised it unconditionally; told me how glad she was to see I was still painting after all these years. We talked about a lot of things — the Palace A, and our hometown, the university, the fact that she no longer bothered with her computer art — but neither of us mentioned the scribbles or the night involving Dorphin or what happened afterward. It was strange dancing around those memories, but I was more than happy to.

Finally she said she had to go, and she leaned close to me and gave me a quick kiss on the cheek. "Thanks for coming," I said. Before she called to her daughter and they left the gallery, though, she made a kind of dramatic pause, and brought her hand up to trace a quick scribble in the air. Then she winked at me and said in a whisper, "Pat, . . . I Remember." I put on a face of envy and excitement, though I felt neither inside. I knew she was lying, because the whole time she was there, the kid never came within eight feet of her. There are some mysteries in this world you can learn to live with and some you just can't.

TOM BRENNAN

Scarecrow

Tom Brennan lives on the coast in Liverpool with his wife, Sylvia, and many cats.

He enjoys a wide variety of fiction, and his short stories have appeared in Writers of the Future XVIII, Story House, Indy, The Harrow, *and* Baen's Universe. *His first mystery novel,* The Debt, *is out now through Gale/Five Star.*

"Scarecrow" was originally published in the U.K. magazine Crimewave 8.

—E.D.

When Marc walked back from the hens' coop at sunrise, he found footprints in the damp red soil below the girls' bedroom window. He set the wicker tray of warm eggs on the sill. The deep footprints led through the farmyard, up to the house, then past the chestnut trees toward the road. As he followed the tracks, a line of watching crows erupted from the fence rail, cawing.

Marc counted the imprinted cleats of work boots and trainers. Almost the same tracks as before.

He carried the eggs into breakfast but didn't tell Yvonne or the girls about the footprints. They might worry. But later that day, when Boncourt came to help set the fox snares, Marc mentioned the tracks. Boncourt reminded Marc about the meeting at Morisault's farm. This time, Marc agreed to go.

On the fourth Sunday in October, after morning Mass, Marc followed the other men up to Morisault's farm. It was the largest in the village, and close to the foothills and the border. In the kitchen, Morisault stood with his wide back to the roaring blue-tiled stove, stooping a little, his head brushing the oak beams.

The men sat on worn pine benches around the table. Rain dripped from jackets onto flagstones. It mixed with the dark red soil tramped in on their boots. Morisault's wife poured wine for everybody before she left them, closing the door behind her. Rain attacked the windows, hammering the glass. The men drank from glasses and clay mugs. They waited.

Morisault spoke first. "My grandfather built this farm. He planted up these fields. At first, he lost half his seeds to the birds. Then, one day at sunset, he nailed a fat, dead crow to a post in the big field."

Someone coughed. A hand reached out for the cracked yellow jug of wine.

"The other birds would circle but they wouldn't land. They'd move on to some other field, some other village, and ruin the crops there."

For a few minutes, no sound other than the rain. Then Boncourt said, "I caught two of the bastards in my hayloft, smoking. I could've lost the barn. Maybe the house, too."

As if a sluice gate had opened, everyone wanted to speak:

"Three of them followed my eldest, Marie, home from school. If she hadn't called the dogs out of the yard, God knows what would have happened."

"They helped themselves to my lad's bike, and a crate of wine!"

"We lost half our crop of apples."

"Louise won't go to the village alone any more."

Everyone had a story. Marc told them about the footprints and the stolen food and hens. Eventually, someone mentioned Thierrot. "That didn't have to happen." Late one night, three weeks before, Thierrot had gone out to check his animals. His sons had found him the next morning beside the stables, stabbed in the chest. Marc's village lay beneath a pass, a notch in the mountains; they had always had immigrants of every nationality coming over. But it had never been this bad before.

Marc said, "I don't think that was the immigrants. It was the runners, the ones that guide them over."

Morisault shook his blunt gray head. Thierrot had been his cousin. "It wouldn't have happened if the immigrants didn't come here. We have to stop them."

Nobody could argue with that. Every man in the room had been to Thierrot's funeral. They had seen his family, his two sons not yet twenty years old. When Marc had looked into the face of Thierrot's wife, he could see his own wife standing there, red-eyed and dazed, dressed in black.

"You think it will work?" Boncourt asked.

"It will work," Morisault said.

Still, Marc hesitated. But he thought of Yvonne and the girls sitting alone in the farmhouse. The nearest policeman thirty kilometers away. Their nearest neighbor, Lucas, more than seventy years old. Marc had put locks on the windows, another bolt on the back door. But who wanted to live in a cage?

The men looked up at Morisault. One after another, every man in the room nodded. But how would they choose one of the immigrants? It had to be a man, that much they knew. Not too young, but not old enough to have his own family, his own children. They didn't want that.

Morisault split the men into two groups. Marc took the first night. When Yvonne asked him where he was going, he told her he'd be at Morisault's. All the men would say the same. The wives knew.

That first night, nothing. They played cards in Boncourt's Peugeot, parked up by the old loggers' road. Boncourt brought his dogs along, wiry Lurchers that slept at the men's feet. With the farmers Givre and Chasset, the men took turns to patrol the woods but heard nothing. It felt good to be out in the cold air, with the smell of rich, damp earth. Above them, a field of diamond stars.

The second night, just before Morisault and his shift took over, they caught two men coming down from the pass. The immigrants stood in the beams of Boncourt's and Givre's flashlights, staring at the shotguns and the straining dogs. But the men looked too old, late thirties or early forties. One of them wore a wedding ring. Marc and the others let them go and watched them run away without looking back.

At home, Yvonne stopped asking Marc where he was going. Like everyone else in the village, she waited. When she found Marc awake early in the morning, she didn't comment. Marc had always been a restless sleeper.

October became November.

They found the man on the seventh night, close to twelve o'clock. Marc heard Boncourt's whistle and ran over, his shotgun ready.

The man stood in a clearing, shielding his eyes against the flashlight. Wearing frayed wet jeans and a black leather jacket, he clutched a woman's yellow woven shopping bag in his left hand. He had no ring on the third finger.

Boncourt told him to drop his hand. Then Marc saw the man's face: eyes screwed almost shut, hair black as oil falling across his forehead. Skin like mahogany. He looked about twenty years old. From his lips, quick bursts of breath that turned to mist. Morisault and the others arrived. The men stood in a circle around the immigrant, glancing at each other. Above them, restless birds or squirrels rustled in the trees. Far away, a car revved its engine, then faded. Boncourt locked his dogs in his Peugeot. When he returned and stood next to Marc, he stank of brandy.

Most of the men had brought flashlights or lanterns. They turned them off until only one beam lit the immigrant in the clearing. He stood there, clutching his shopping bag. Maybe he didn't understand. Maybe he understood too well.

For a moment, he looked at Marc. Marc looked away, then remembered his two girls getting off the school bus and walking back to the farmhouse. They had to walk almost two kilometers from the bus stop, in the winter darkness. There were no houses close to the lane. Nobody to help them.

Marc raised his eyes and stared back at the man.

Morisault stepped forward. In his right hand, the knife he used on the pigs. The curved blade flickered in the torch beam.

Still clutching his bag, the immigrant tried to run through the circle of men. Someone knocked him down. He dropped the bag and fell on all fours.

In one movement, Morisault grabbed the man's hair in his left hand and tugged the head back. Morisault's right hand drew the blade across the man's throat. Blood hissed across the clearing.

The immigrant tried to stand. Trying to push the blood back with his hands, he stumbled to his feet. He made a sound halfway between sobbing and swallowing. He stared at the men, swaying. Then he fell onto his back. After a few minutes, he didn't move. The men stood around the clearing. The wind threshed the trees. Someone fetched a green plastic sheet from a car. Another produced blue nylon rope. The men bound the body and carried him to Morisault's Renault. Morisault spread old newspapers inside the car before they slid the body in.

The men washed their hands in the stream below the clearing, then drove down to the village. Marc rode with Boncourt. The dogs stayed quiet in the back, their heads down, ears flat and eyes staring. With one hand on the wheel, Boncourt drank from the brandy bottle, then offered it to Marc. Marc took a long gulp, then another.

In the darkness, he saw the taillights of the other cars leading the way, like animals' red eyes staring back. Below the men, the village lay silent. A few streetlights glowed yellow. The men had already agreed where they should leave the body.

As they drove into the main square, nobody watched them. No windows opened. No curtains parted. The fountain had stopped.

Morisault parked in front of the town hall's heavy wooden doors. To the right of the main entrance, the third glass door along wore signs and stickers in five languages. The immigrants congregated there for help, for money and information.

The men dragged the body from Morisault's car and rolled it from the sheet. With more of the blue rope, they tied the man's hands to the advice center's door.

Nobody spoke. Slumped against the door, with his legs draped across the stone pavement and his face and neck in shadow, the dead man looked drunk. Or asleep. But none of the other immigrants could avoid seeing him.

One of the men had picked up the yellow shopping bag; he set it beside the body. It fell over and two green apples rolled out. Inside, Marc saw a sweater and a rag doll, almost the same type of doll his girls had played with years before.

One by one, the men drove away. Boncourt dropped Marc near the farmhouse. Yvonne sat in a pool of light at the kitchen table. She looked up from her book, then down at Marc's boots and trousers. She nodded once and poured him a glass of brandy. As Marc drank that, he heard her running the bath. Sophie, their youngest, asked Yvonne if she could come down to see Marc. Yvonne told her to go back to bed.

The next day, the Spanish news teams arrived first, at ten o'clock. The French and English teams arrived after lunch. But all of them left before nightfall. When Marc came in from the fields, he caught the evening news. Blue and white screens blocked off the site of the body. Behind the woman with the microphone, some of the village boys waved into the camera. One boy turned a cartwheel and landed on his backside in the mud.

Yvonne switched off the TV and called the girls in to dinner. The family didn't talk over their food. As Marc watched the girls eating, he wanted to reach out and pull them to his chest, smooth their hair and hold them. He couldn't imagine life without them. And how would they cope without him?

The next morning, the news announced that the immigrant had been married. He'd had a son and a daughter, both a year old.

"We weren't to know," Morisault said. After the news, most of the men had made for Morisault's farm.

"That's true," Boncourt said. "He looked young, didn't he? And he didn't have a wedding ring on, right? Right?"

Nobody disagreed. They drank Morisault's wine and talked about crop prices and the winter ahead. On their way out, Morisault said, "It's done now. It'll be shown on Spanish TV; everyone will see it and understand. We can rest easy."

And the village lay quiet for a while, undisturbed. People talked about Christmas, about parties and celebrations. They didn't see any immigrants.

Then, the second week in December, when he couldn't sleep, Marc found new footprints by the kitchen door and the bedroom window. Someone had stolen all of the eggs from the coop. Boncourt said he saw three men at the edge of his yard, just watching him. Givre found his dog killed, stabbed through the neck.

Morisault called another meeting. Boncourt drove around just before sunset to collect Marc. Marc hesitated; he told Boncourt he didn't want to let the men down, but he wouldn't be going. Boncourt nodded and said he understood.

From the kitchen window, Marc watched Boncourt drive away. He could see flocks of birds darting and circling over the lower field, black specks against the orange sky. As soon as the sound of Boncourt's engine faded away, the crows came down to land.

CHAZ BRENCHLEY

Going the Jerusalem Mile

Chaz Brenchley has been making a living as a writer since he was eighteen. He is the author of nine thrillers, most recently Shelter, *and two major fantasy series:* The Books of Outremer, *based on the world of the Crusades, and* Selling Water by the River, *set in an alternate Ottoman Istanbul. A winner of the British Fantasy Award, he has also published three books for children and more than five hundred short stories in various genres. His time as Crimewriter-in-Residence at the St Peter's Riverside Sculpture Project in Sunderland resulted in the collection* Blood Waters. *He is a prizewinning expoet, and has been writer in residence at the University of Northumbria, as well as tutoring their MA in Creative Writing. His novel* Dead of Light *is currently in development with an independent film company;* Shelter *has been optioned by Granada TV. He lives in Newcastle upon Tyne with a lopsided cat and a famous teddy bear.*

"Going the Jerusalem Mile" was originally published in the UK magazine The Third Alternative.

—E.D.

Ten days in every year—Easter week, the solstices, All Souls'—the canons of the cathedral have a great many chairs removed and a vast square of canvas taken up from beneath them, to reveal a maze laid out in lines of bronze and time on the stone flags of the floor there, a channel worn by centuries of barefoot and chilly faith.

I think they're mad, entirely insane, and I have told them so. That cursed measure should be dug up and melted down, it should be ripped out and filled in, plowed under and cemented over. That tainted bronze that marks the path should be cast into ingots and then into the sea, into the deepest trench of the deepest sea, where no man might ever see or touch it. Let it do harm to demon-fish in the darkness, I don't care. The maze should be deleted, expunged, destroyed; beyond that, I dare not go.

No blame to the good canons, I guess, that it is not. Small lives are small concern to them, who overlook a thousand years of history in stone and height and symbol. Easter congregations flock to walk the maze, jostling each other from its concentricity; its fame draws in tourists and townsfolk with forbidden cameras and outré shoes, both tolerated for that short season for the sake of money in the offertory boxes. In winter, pilgrims walk from the north, from distant Scottish churches, timing their long marches to reach us on the shortest day. Our maze is the end, the point and purpose of all that walking; by candlelight and prayer they shuffle, round and round and back and forth like dancers to a spoken beat resounding down the generations. The summer solstice looks southerly, to churches from the chalky lands, the lands of flint and furrow. Their pilgrims burn candles too when they come to us, and carry crosses as a sign of fealty.

They hardly need to do that. It gives them pleasure, I suppose, to give themselves a little pain. Their coming is token enough that this is a crusade, Crusading-Lite, in search of a diet deliverance. They'll find no pain else, beyond what they bring on their own behalf.

It's called the Jerusalem Mile, our precious maze, this way they walk, white-worn stone with brass edgings polished to a razor's edge. It's carried a special dispensation for the better part of a thousand years: the old or the infirm who walk this way are reckoned to have walked enough. No need to go further. They count equivalent to palmers, as though they too had been to the Holy Land and prayed in the holy places and scattered greenery in the dust and been forgiven for their pains. Form is function; the intent is taken for the deed and carries the same remittance. So a thirteenth-century pope said, at least, declaring a local indulgence which the church has maintained through the Dissolution and all points since. The current dispensation doesn't actually speak about indulgence, far less purgatory, but they will still insist that a special blessing attaches, especially to the elderly and sick. How God might feel about it all is not recorded.

So they have their special pilgrimages at the turnings of the year, they have their mass migrations over Easter; all that gives them license to have postcards by the font and local TV every now and then, mentions in dispatches and a presence on the Web.

What happens for All Souls' is very different, and they keep it quiet when they can.

On the second day in November—or the third, when the second is a Sunday; like Easter, All Souls' is a movable feast—the massive doors of the cathedral are locked against the world. Visitors and worshipers both are redirected to other churches in the diocese. Those who must be let in, those with authority or special dispensation find no service before the great altar nor any chairs in that greater space beneath the tower, where transept crosses nave. Only a wide circle of candles burning, and a patrol of sidesmen to lead the faithful to the Mary Chapel in the apse.

They preach a shortcut to heaven, a lesser gate to which they hold the key; and they do guard it, you see, on All Souls' Day when the desperate turn their avid eyes on any key that turns. They just don't guard it well, not well enough.

She was my wife, she was my love, and she was stained with acid failure, the vitriol of lack. That was almost the first thing I loved about her, how she wore her defeats like tattoos on her skin and on her tongue. How she was as a child I can't say, we met first at university; but the way her family used to watch her, mongoose-wary before a cobra's spite, I think that says a lot. That a watchful, wary mongoose is always a good bet against a cobra, that possibly says more. Whatever she took on, always, she did expect to lose.

I overreached myself to win my place at Durham; she did the opposite, bidding for Oxbridge and failing, falling short. That was the inherent lesson of her life, that she could never learn her lesson. She must always aim high, and always be disappointed. She would have stayed to read for a master's and a doctorate, to have been a don, but that her academic ambitions couldn't survive her second-class degree.

She would have been a management trainee and afterward a manager, she could have been head-hunted around the world from corporation to multinational corporation, but that she never quite made it through the selection process. I guess the interview boards could read that hint of second-best in her CV, could measure how she burned passionately but somehow not quite bright enough.

I think she would have married another man than me, except that none of them would offer. I know she dated plenty. Even after I left Durham, even after she followed me down, still it took her a long time to settle for what she'd got. I don't know yet, will never know how far she felt she had to fall, before she could fall for me.

We did marry, though, and I at least was happy. I like a bitter marmalade, a green apple, a touch of sour to underlie the sweet. I liked it that her dreams outran her frantic grasp, whichever way she snatched; I liked it that she could not keep from snatching.

She was my wife; she wanted to be the perfect wife, homemaker, and helpmeet. She learned to cook, grimly. She learned to sew, to keep house, to serve coffee and biscuits to my friends, to smile of a sort while she did it. She learned to knit, before ever she had anyone to knit for.

That was the next, near the last and near the most perfectly dreadful of her failures. Perfect wife must needs be perfect mother; for the longest time, the worst time she could not quicken. That was the word she used herself, *quicken*, as though to underscore its opposite, herself. The opposite of quick is not slow, but dead. She began to speak of herself as shriveled, barren, bereft. She never suggested that I should take a sperm count; like everything, this had to be her inadequacy. All her bitterness was turned against herself, like a scorpion that stings its own body in its frenzy.

Doctors tried to help her, but they could not; their failures were expensive. In the end, despairing, she fell back on childhood certainties and went to church.

Threw herself on the church, rather, on the fickle mercies of God. Even this she had to do in full measure, to perfection, to extremes: as though only monomania or fanatical devotion could store up enough treasure in Heaven to buy her the child she burned for. Sunday worship at our parish church would never do, it must needs be the cathedral and services daily, twice daily when she could. And flower rosters, polishing the brass and speaking to the bishop, prayer meetings and bible classes and retreats. The Dean was an old high Anglo, who seemed to hear the shiver of a bell when the Host was lifted; she went to him for private confession, and learned to cross herself and bob toward the altar.

I'd go with her Sundays and holy days, no more. I had no greater trust in God than I did in doctors or thermometers or hope, blind hope. Some women are not made fertile; children are no more a right than life or liberty or luck. At last, I thought, she must accept that, and turn her fevered eyes elsewhere. Meanwhile, I loved her for her hunger, for this latest face of pain.

April, come she will, and Easter with her. Of course my love, my wife, my dear despairing wanted to walk the Jerusalem Mile. Many a woman has made pilgrimage for the sake of a child, to confound an arid womb; some have come back pregnant. We could not afford the Holy Land, but this petty substitute was easy.

On Palm Sunday, all the congregation can be palmers. The chairs and canvas are all cleared away before the doors are flung open to let the people in for Matins; in lucky years the sun beats in through stained windows to throw the colors of the saints across the floor there, and those who sit behind can watch the quest of light across shimmering brass and stone. Then during the recessional the bishop leads his ministers, his choirs, and his flock in that same quest, down the aisle and through the maze in a long, long line all searching for their very own and golden city, all marching to Jerusalem. Some carry palms or other greenery in token.

It is not, of course, truly a maze. It could not be; we're dealing in symbols here, and there are no false turnings, no dead ends for those who take the high and narrow way to God. No, the path defines the great circle quadrant by quadrant, as though it were a compass rose, not so much a spiral as a succession of switchbacks. The way into it comes from the north, from the cold, hard not to shiver at the thought of it, ice at your back; turn clockwise and follow the rim around until suddenly you're sent back, don't step over the line and you retrace your course just a short pace closer to the center, bumping shoulders with those who come behind. And come back almost to where you started and so turn again, and again and yet again; each time a shorter walk and a more sudden turn, and you come at last to where a single step could have you standing on the central cross, X marks the spot, except that you may not cross that thin brass filament and so it leads you through to another quadrant and the start of a slow unwinding that takes you back toward the rim again.

Four quadrants, in and out and the same again, like the steps of a country dance; and indeed this is country religion, old-time religion, and in the end there is a simple procession, for the path strikes clean and clear from the western edge to the heart of the circle and you can walk it with your eyes uplifted, fixed on the high altar and the rose window beyond, the east and the everlasting dawn beyond that, the rise of a hope imperishable.

My wife cherished a hope she could not believe in, but still she did hope, she needed to, she had to yearn and stretch. Faith does not accumulate, but blessings are heaped up upon the faithful. Persistence might pay off, she thought, she hoped. She never gave it credence.

I went with her, of course, to the cathedral. I was her witness, her counterpoint; I might not share her vision nor her need, but everything else I shared. We sat, we stood, we knelt in proper order, we sang hymns and heard the sermon and said Amen. She crossed herself and took communion, and so did I, though it was only she who shivered under the momentous weight of it all. It was her own dark stare that made me shiver, how her eyes followed every movement of the ministers while all the time I knew that her attention, all her focus lay on the great open space behind us, the revealed mystery on the ageworn flags of the floor.

After the final blessing, Bach rolled over us more sonorous than the bishop's voice, and more imperative. The organist was alone, left out, the only one who could not walk to mercy; perhaps he thought his fingers on the manuals, his feet on the pedals would be fit substitute if he only worked them hard, a double substitution, a pilgrim playing in lieu of a pilgrim maze in lieu of a proper pilgrimage. I had heard him often, but I never heard him find such power. It set my skin to shiver again, just to listen to it.

My wife was shivering, fidgeting at my side for another reason altogether. She could always do patience until it came to the point, the purpose, the last sprint to the line. Then she would rush, and stumble, and so fall. She could blame exam nerves, poor interview technique, any number of superficial causes; the truth of it went deeper, to her soul. When she saw what she wanted, she must snatch, she must hurl herself at it; and what she wanted was always out of reach. Deliberately so, I thought sometimes. She set herself impossible targets in order to fail because that was what she did, that defined her. Or else she was simply afraid to succeed, afraid of what might follow. She was not desperate for children, I thought, until it was clear that they would not come easy to her; they were not crucial to her happiness until it was clear to her that they would not come at all.

I knew this, I think she knew it too. And yet she was desperate, and they were crucial. That was the heart of her unhappiness, that she truly did suffer, even where it was suffering of her own construction. And so she fidgeted and fretted at my side while the bishop paraded down the aisle in stately measure, and all his clergy and the robed choirs behind. Then came the sidesmen, slowly down the lines of pews and the massed ranks of chairs, gesturing out the faithful row by row.

Our turn and she was up and eager, into the shuffling single file, jostling the man ahead in her impatience. He was broad, impassive, ideal; unable to elbow him aside, she fell quickly into step, into that near-mindless state that the English call a queue.

More like a slow conga line, perhaps, with no kicking. We did move in time with the music; like queuing, counterpoint is hypnotic, in a way that harmony can never be. And I did settle my hands on her hips, in a purely protective gesture, *don't jog the guy ahead, be steady, be calm*, though she shrugged me off, twitched away in short order. This was a holy place, not made for mauling. Besides, I'd never been given license to offer that kind of protection. I could follow behind her if I chose, but she always went alone to face her demons, her failures, the precise measure of her falling short.

Shuffle-step weaving back and forth within the narrow brass lines that defined the maze, within the footworn channel, easy for the blind to find their way. So many of us that we might as well have been blind, we couldn't see our feet for the crush of others' bodies, just trust the one ahead and follow close as the turns got tighter, toward the center of the circle.

Clergy and choir and congregation, filled out with the vapid and the curious: too many people already in that slow dance to the music of time. And then they let the children in, the Sunday-school children who usually picked up their parents after service; of course they could not be excluded, today of all days.

Most tagged on obediently at the rear, still some distance short of the Jerusalem Mile. Others did not. They spotted their parents somewhere in the slow-grinding mill of the maze, or else they pretended to, for the simple fun of squirming through the crowds. We had been tight but organized, a steady state, slow water in the channel set; now suddenly we were buffeted unpredictably from any side, squeezed and shoved out of line and it was hard even to keep our feet, let alone be sure where they were treading.

Once warned already, I didn't reach out to wrap shielding arms around my wife. That was my failure, although later she would call it hers. So I was too slow to help, I was helpless when a boy cannoned heedlessly into her legs. She was knocked out of step, out of line, sent stumbling across the brass fillet that divided one quadrant from the next.

Kind hands caught her, gripped her, held her upright. I stepped across and put my arm around her, too late; looked back to the line that we had come from, but already our place was gone, the gap closed up and our neighbors moving on. Meanwhile these generous folk were making room for us in this new channel; I nudged my wife to take it. There was no going back.

She had lost the easy rhythm of the dance. All her movements were stiff and spasmodic now; her head kept twisting as she cast wild glances over her shoulder, trying to see where we should have been, how much we'd cut across.

"It won't matter," I whispered, a useless litany. "How can it matter? God will understand, God saw . . ."

She didn't, she couldn't believe me; but God perhaps was listening to my distraction, or else to her distress. We came eventually to the circle's center and the cross set into the stonework there, where it points due east toward the altar. Those ahead of us moved on, following the straight path out of the maze. We stepped forward, she set her foot deliberately at the focal point of the cross, the center where the two arms meet—and she gasped, and clutched abruptly at her belly.

"What is it, what's wrong?"

"Nothing," she whispered, straightening slowly and feeling, probing with nervous fingers below her waistline. "Nothing's wrong, no . . ."

"But you were hurt, something hurt you."

"Not hurt. I felt, I don't know, a shifting? As though some little part of me had moved, fallen into place after a long time twisted . . ."

And she stared at me with a wild, frantic hope that seemed to plunder all the logic of the world and leave it, me, entirely bereft.

"Just wait," I said, all that I could say. "Wait and see, that's all. It might be nothing," a torn muscle from the shove, wishful thinking, constipation, anything. "Come on, I'll take you home."

"Not yet, not now." Her eyes moved toward the Mary Chapel in the apse. "I said a particular rogation to Our Lady, I need to go and thank her . . ."

"No. You need to lie down, you need to rest," *you look insane, and sound it*, although I would not tell her that, how could I? "We don't know yet if there's anything to thank her for. Even if there's been a miracle," she'd like the thought of that, I thought, "we still have work to do, you haven't quickened yet. Unless you're following Mary all the way, like a virgin?"

"Hush, not here, you can't talk like that here," but she was giggling breathily, like the girl she must once have been, digging her way out through accreted years of disappointments. That was miracle enough for me; I gazed on in wonder. It was like a transformation in reverse, the chrysalis tearing open to release someone much younger, much less formed . . .

And uncertain, and easy to direct. She came home with me, because I told her to; she went to bed in the middle of the day there, because I said that it was best. I let her doze behind the curtains for an hour or so, then took her a bowl of soup and a cup of Earl Gray with lemon, sharp and scented and suggestive. I sat on the bed and took my shoes off while she spooned the soup, my shirt and tie while she drank the tea. She looked at me doubtfully; I grinned at her.

"How are you feeling?"

"Fine. Rested. Thank you . . ."

"No pain, no discomfort?"

"No, nothing."

"Good, then. Only one way I can think of, to learn whether it really was that miracle you've been praying for. Yes?"

"Oh, yes. Please . . ."

So we did, and it was, or it seemed so. For a while. Almost immediately, she announced that she was pregnant. Except that a month later, it seemed that she wasn't after all. She insisted that she'd lost a baby, and our doctor said that very possibly she had; many women lost their first, he said, especially where they'd had such trouble conceiving. Keep trying, he said, stay hopeful.

So we did that too, at my insistence against her revitalized depression, her overweening misery: "We don't know for sure that you did miscarry, but if you did, it's only proof that you can carry to begin with. You can quicken. And if you can carry, you can keep it. So we try again, and next time we'll be more careful . . ."

Months of that, and at last I proved a prophet, against my own expectation. She was pregnant, this time the home tests and the doctor's both confirmed it; and she was determined, this time there would be no more disasters.

A hard time she had of it none the less, though she stayed at home and often stayed in bed, like a woman of her grandmother's generation playing out the rules of a classic confinement. She was sick every morning and not well at any time, pale and anemic and distressed. She ate despite her lack of appetite; she demanded special diets from midwives and nutritionists, anything that would benefit her baby regardless of what it did to her. She tried to drag herself and me to antenatal classes, but was too unwell too often; in the end they told her not to come again, and it had taken little persuasion from me to have them do it.

She sat out the last trimester of her pregnancy entirely at home. I only wished that she could have enjoyed it more, a rare treat, an indulgence. She was anxious, always, for the baby; otherwise she was simply sickly, enjoying nothing, only enduring, her gaze fixed ferociously on the closing goal, full term, the point and purpose of all this suffering.

It came as it must, with the rotation of the calendar. She was in no fit state to attempt a normal birth; I had booked her in for a Cesarean months before, and she'd barely had the strength to argue. Her lips twitched, though, as she accepted it, and I knew she'd write it down as yet one more of her failures, that she couldn't bring a child into this world without medical intervention. Not a great failure, though, surely not significant against the achievement of the child itself, the grail discovered . . .

And so the taxi ride to hospital in the fortieth week, the overnight bag at last needed overnight, surgery in the morning. Scrubbed and gloved and gowned, I was there to watch; I saw her opened up and her baby, ours, scooped out slimy, weakly kicking, wet and froglike with a frog's thin croak of a voice to match.

It was a boy, hers, ours, our son; we delighted in him, of course, what could we else?

But he was not well, not vigorous, more gray than pink and undersized, ill-fed by her placenta. They kept him days apart from us, in an incubator, breathing bottled air and feeding from a tube. My wife had no milk to offer him, in any case. She needed special care as much as he did; when she saw him, it was from a chair where I was wheeling her.

She recovered slowly, and so did he; they both gained strength, and won an exeat at last. I brought them home together, he cradled in her arms, and then fed him from a bottle while she slept off the effort of the journey. He was thin and jaundiced still, his skin flaking and a disturbing dullness to his eyes, an air of being exhausted already by the world and finding no good in it.

Weeks, months later he had not improved. He was still scrawny, yellow, uninvolved, showing little interest in food or the world or us, barely moving in his cradle, barely crying. He seemed to endure, and nothing more than that: as though there was no more than that, and nothing to be hoped for.

My wife grew stronger in her body, but that was little help. No strength could ever be enough to shoulder the weight she dragged behind her, the intolerable burden of her guilt.

She blamed herself, of course, she had to. One more failure, more terrible than any: our son's weakness must necessarily be his mother's fault. She might have blamed her diet, but did not. She might have blamed her exercise or lack of it, her lying in bed, her constant sickness; she did not. She blamed the Jerusalem Mile, where she'd met her blessing.

Her broken blessing, as she explained it now, because she had made a broken pilgrimage. "I should have gone back," and never mind the crush, the impossibility of it, "I should have walked the proper route, the full route. You can't cheat God and not be punished for it."

"You believe that God would punish our child," I said, "because you got jostled in a maze?"

"Because I let myself be knocked from the proper path," she said, "oh, yes. Besides, it's not his punishment. Look at him; he doesn't suffer. It's we who pay the price, in watching him. That's how it is."

Almost, the doctors seemed to agree with her. They could find no other cause for his disconnection. He was in no pain, he carried no infections; I asked to see his notes, and what they said was *failure to thrive*. It sounded not too dreadful, until a specialist told me that a child could die from failure to thrive; it could be a cause of death on the certificate.

I did not tell that to my wife, but she knew it anyway. She didn't need the diagnosis. And if she knew what ailed him, she knew the cure too. She must walk the maze again: no worse than that. With our child in her arms, and properly this time, prayerfully and undisturbed.

We were too late for Easter, even if she'd been prepared to risk the crowds again, which she was not. She petitioned the Dean and Chapter, that she might be allowed a private, solitary passage; they refused her. They turned down many such requests, they said, each year. Reluctantly, they had to. If they allowed one, they must allow them all; it was not their task to act as arbiters, to say who deserved the privilege and who did not. The work, they said, would be unfeasible, so much time and labor it took to clear the cathedral floor. . . .

Privately, to me alone they said they thought we should look otherwhere for causes and for cures. This was not Lourdes, they said, there were no miracles at the heart of the Jerusalem Mile; it was a gesture of faith, not a task undertaken for reward. If God chose to bless the pilgrims, that was his affair. There were no guarantees, from the cathedral or from heaven.

I knew all of that already, but my wife did not and would not learn it.

She asked to join the summer pilgrimage, when the southern churches sent their devotees to walk up for the solstice. Again, she was refused. She was not strong enough, they said, to join the march; or if she was, her baby most certainly was not. And this was an opportunity for others, not for local people. The bishop and congregation would pray for our baby, gladly, next Sunday and every Sunday; let her be content with that.

She was not, of course, though obedience demanded that she should be. She subsided, largely onto her knees; it was God and the Virgin she pleaded with now, not the unresponsive diocese. She threw herself even more vigorously into cathedral life, as though she struggled to make herself indispensable. If she hoped that way to change their minds, I thought she was wasting her effort in a losing battle; but my judgment was based on those private conversations, which I could not admit to her.

I stayed quiet, stayed at home, cared for the baby in so far as he needed or allowed it, which was not far at all. He remained unresponsive, uninvested in the world.

Came the autumn, late autumn, first blast of winter weather; first touch of chill to my soul, as at last I understood my wife.

"You can't. You can't do that."

"I must."

Oh, we said more, we said it otherwise and often, but that was the gist, the thrust of everything we said. What I thought impossible, she thought imperative. I argued all the dangers, but in the end there was no argument. It takes two to argue, and she would not; she was simply resolute, determined, immovable.

Vulnerable too, open to betrayal. She understood that and expected it, I think. It would be another manifestation of failure, that she had hidden her purposes too scantily, betrayed herself to a man who must betray her.

So of course I did not, I kept quiet and only watched as she manipulated herself onto one more rota, the long night's vigil for All Souls'. Simple fire precautions demanded that a watch be kept on all those candles, but that was only common sense, not a religious obligation; it was the sidesmen who drew up the list of volunteers, and neither Dean nor Chapter thought to oversee it.

My wife put her name forward, and my own. They were so used to her volunteering, there was no question to it, no surprise. When she said we'd take the dogwatch, alas, she said it to a retired Navy man, who laughed at her. He knew what she meant, though, even before she stammeringly explained it, and he put us down quite happily for the graveyard shift.

I could not be happy, but only force could prevent her, force or treachery, and I was capable of neither.

So I helped her wrap our sleeping son against the weather and myself carried him out to the car, as I had carried him in, his first day home. I settled him into her lap and saw them both securely belted before I drove the short distance to the high stark vision that was the cathedral, so lit against the darkness that there was no way to tell that simpler lights burned within.

It was a little before four in the morning. Only the wicket door was open, a private way into solemnity, *like a side door into heaven,* I thought and did not say. This was not a night for symbols, not All Souls' in the cathedral with the candles aflame and my wife setting her feet, our child's welfare on a perilous path. I wanted nothing to mean anything beyond the thing that it was. *This is a door and nothing more, it leads into the cathedral, nowhere else; and there, that circle of little lights, those are candles and nothing more. They are not guards, nor wards. The shadows that surround them are not, are most certainly not moving except as the flames move, flickering in the draft of our arrival . . .*

They were altar candles, as fat around as the span of my two hands together, knee-high against me as they stood on the stones. The couple we were relieving, students from the theological college, said that none had needed attention during the four hours of their watch; they had prayed and read psalms to each other, kept a casual eye on the candles, felt themselves cheerfully redundant and wished us more of the same. Then they went away to their no doubt separate beds—all this great space to play in, and they read psalms to each other!—and left us to our own more dangerous occupations.

The wicket had barely slammed behind them before my wife was moving toward the candles, our son so muffled up in blankets against her chest, so habitually still and silent that the students hadn't even realized we had a baby with us.

"Wait," I said, and went to throw the bolts that fixed the little door within the greater, to keep us private and undisturbed. That done, I turned round to find that she had been overtaken again by that terrible hurry that would not brook any proper preparation, had not waited at all.

She had moved two candles, the two most crucial, those two that stood tall guard at the entrance to the maze. She had set those two aside, set her feet between brass and brass, set off again to walk the Jerusalem Mile.

Set off alone, without me, unprotected: this night of all nights, this most deadly, with our child in her arms.

All Souls' is the day of prayer for those in purgatory, those souls doomed but not damned for the sins of their lives. They must suffer a given time, perhaps a long time; but the prayers of the church are effective, they can win remission for the faithful departed, and on this one day all the churches pray together. The priests wear black vestments, and say the office for the dead; in some places, monasteries, houses of the holy, they start at midnight and pray for twenty-four unbroken hours. Laying up treasure in heaven, perhaps, hoping to reduce their own future sentence by serving time for others now.

When it's four in the morning in England, it's midday or later in the far east, there are powerhouses of prayer out there that have been running a good twelve hours already. There are souls in purgatory that have felt an easing, a lifting, a glimmer of hope unlooked-for; and now they look, now they're hungry for it, now they will swarm to any chink of light.

That's why the cathedral is closed, why the Jerusalem Mile is guarded by prayer and candle in this vulnerable time. There are uncountable souls in purgatory, they are immeasurably suffering, we cannot know how many or how much; but this we do know, that they crave release as water craves to flow. Whoever can offer a shortcut to God's grace, whoever holds the key to a way out does well to guard it well, All Souls' Day when it comes.

It had come, and my wife had opened the way in her own desperation. Against all policy and all advice, against my urgent pleading she had let loose a world of spirits for the sake of our sickly child; and she had done it without me, ahead of me, alone.

Not let them loose on our world, she wouldn't and couldn't be that irresponsible. Set them free to run heavenward, rather, along the selfsame path as herself; she knew the risk to herself, and had discounted it.

The risk to the baby had to be discounted in its turn. Children die, from failure to thrive . . .

By the time I reached the circle, she was advanced far into the first quadrant, but it was heavy going. She walked as though braced against a wind that blew on her back, as though she waded thigh-deep in a force of water. I have said, it was no good night for symbols; I mean this almost literally. Almost. Her long hair licked and whipped about her face; even as I approached the entrance to the maze, I could feel the tug, the chilly flow around and past my legs as if all the cold thoughts in the world had massed together and plunged toward the warm.

How many sly souls could race that path to glean an undeserved forgiveness, seizing this rare chance before some wiser vigilant came to close the way against them? I cannot answer that. Uncountable numbers, at any rate. I felt them like wind and water, like the bite of a vicious storm; I could barely stand amidst their hurry.

I could watch my wife ahead of me, see the precious care she took to walk within the lines of brass, see how her loose clothes only emphasized her weakness as they were pressed against her skin, clinging to her body, showing her spare flesh and bone as if they were sodden wet. I could wonder how ever she managed to keep upright, where it was so hard for me who was so much stronger; I couldn't see the baby at all, but I could wonder also about him, how he would survive this. Whether he would survive it.

Before long I felt a button go, I heard my first seam rip. Before either one of us had reached the second quadrant, we walked in rags. My wife was hunched over what she carried, to offer to his blankets the poor shelter of her back, as though she had not given him enough, too much already.

Well, we could go naked and cold in a cathedral. There must have been holy fools run skyclad here before. Worse, far worse were the cramps that jerked and twisted my muscles with every step, the pains that danced electric along my nerves, that lashed me from toes to teeth. I know I sobbed, I may have screamed; I must have cursed God and the devil and all souls trapped between. I felt like Caliban, tormented by cruel Prospero and his untame spirits: a creature of mud and mockery, whose suffering could count for nothing in this mad dash to redemption so why not make him suffer?

Or perhaps it was not so deliberate, perhaps it simply happened, perhaps a human body must bleed and break caught up in so much spirit, too solid to hold together. Perhaps our every cell yearns for disintegration. I cannot tell. I only know that I left bloody footprints smeared in the stone channel where I trod, smeared over gleaming brass where I stumbled. I know that I ached, I hurt, I suffered every step of the way, as though like Christ I shouldered all the sins of the world on my way to a sham Jerusalem, and paid the price of every one.

And my wife was ahead of me, who had suffered too much already; and she held my baby in her arms, whose life had seemed to be a dreary weight of suffering, and I did not think my wife's body was any protection to him. No more was I, I could not even reach them.

Back and forth, up and down, the path contained within its wider circle: I trod on knives, there was broken glass in every joint and ground glass in every breath, I was buckled and bowed before ever I came to its end, almost crawling by the time I toppled at last into the center.

Here was blessed stillness, the unblinking eye of the storm, relief from pain; here the spirits fled, were lifted up, were gone to their cheap-bought deliverance, forgiven us and all sins else.

Here I fell full length on ice-cold stone, and for a while only breathed, because I could.

Slowly, slowly I pushed myself up onto trembling hands and knees, crawling for real now; and crawled the little distance to where my wife lay crumpled, collapsed, ripped and raw like the rags still clutched about her, the bundle still held to her belly.

She was breathing too, but barely: the faintest flutter of air at her lips, weak as a dying wick's flicker before it drowns in wax.

Somehow she found enough air, just enough to shape a word, our child's name, no more.

I had to force her hands apart, where her clawed fingers had sunk deep into the tattered tangle of what had been good woolen blankets. *Rigor mortis conturbat me;* it seemed premature, if barely so.

I took the bundle, and unwrapped it.

Looked once, just the once, to see what my wife's desperate miracle had made of her child, ours; and heard the soft rattle of her dying beside me and was glad of it, rejoiced at it almost, that she might never have to face what she had done. A baby's bones are weak, are soft; they can be snapped like candles, or they can be shaped like warm wax, squeezed and moulded.

I cradled what remained, what had been boy as it snuffled at me, as it stirred; and I gazed down at where my wife was slumped and gone, and thought her greedy beyond redemption, though we lay at the heart of the Jerusalem Mile and fresh from a bitter pilgrimage. Some sins, I thought, can never be forgiven. I could hope only that God agreed with me.

WILLA SCHNEBERG

Grief

We read Willa Schneberg's poem "Grief" in the excellent anthology Chance of a Ghost: An Anthology of Contemporary Ghost Poems *edited by Gloria Vando and Philip Miller. Schneberg is the author of* Box Poems *and* In the Margins of the World *(winner of the Oregon Book Award for Poetry). Her poems have appeared in* Salmagundi, Michigan Quarterly Review, *and* American Poetry Review. *For her new collection,* Storytelling in Cambodia, *Schneberg drew on her experience as a UN volunteer in Cambodia in the early 1990s. She is a ceramic sculptor and a photographer whose work has been widely exhibited. She works as a private practice clinical social worker.*
—K.L. & G.G.

The sorcerers are bored and frustrated
standing in their glittery robes and pointy hats
in the corner of my parents' small kitchen
where the cupboards never close properly,
the pilot light always goes out and
my father remains spindly and mute
as before he died.

They kill time rolling small glass balls
in their palms and conjuring
the electric can opener
to delid all the tuna cans,
but finally the incantations and
wand waving work.

My father is morphing
into his debonair self, tall of carriage
as if a picture were about to be taken
in three-quarter profile, a pipe in his mouth.

He vanishes.
Ashes burn in an ashtray,
The room thick with sweet smoke.

He reappears plumper, but still translucent
holding a bowl with a puddle
of vanilla ice-cream and canned peach juice.

He floats down and sits.
The index cards are still
where he left them
waiting for names of uncracked books
and Dewey decimals.

The sorcerers do my bidding
and free him to be
who he never was in life.
Today he knows origami.
Under his hands
library index cards moonlight
as snails, whales and kangaroos.

(2)

The sorcerers are delighted with themselves.
Now, in search of my mother
they squish together for a ride
in the motorized stair chair
my father used at the end.

They find her fast asleep in the den
bent over a crossword puzzle.
When she awakens
all the empty squares are filled-in with:

I LOVE YOU

I
L
YOU
V
I WILL ALWAYS LOVE YOU

PENTTI HOLAPPA

Boman

Pentti Holappa has long been known in his own country, Finland, for his wide-ranging body of work. Born in 1927, in his fifty years of writing he has published fiction, essays, plays, and most recently, several collections of poetry. His 1998 novel, Ystävän muotokuva (Portrait of a Friend) *was awarded the Finlandia Literary Prize. In "Boman," Holappa uses fantastical underpinnings to examine the ethics of modern, middle-class life. "Boman" was originally published in the collection* Muodonmuutoksia (Metamorphoses, 1959), *and was translated into English by David Hackston for the 2005 anthology,* The Dedalus Book of Finnish Fantasy, *edited by Tiptree-winning writer Johanna Sinisalo.*

—K.L. & G.G.

Translated from the Finnish by David Hackston

I might begin my story by saying: I once owned a dog called Boman. But I might also begin by saying: I was once owned by a dog called Boman. These two sentences reveal two different truths about the same matter and this a good way to begin the story of Boman, as what happened to her has often caused me to doubt many things I once held to be true. Allow me to point out that I was by no means the only person who thought they owned Boman. As far as I am aware, many people believed they had that particular privilege. This often happens to creatures that are well-liked.

Boman was a female mongrel. She had a shining black coat, a tail with a joyful curl and two ears that stood up vigilantly. She was small. Initially I had thought taking her in was merely a animal-friendly gesture: I had thought I was saving an abandoned puppy from certain death. I had no idea of the significance this was to have. Enjoying a somewhat macabre sense of humor, a group of friends and I christened her after a poem telling the story of a civilized animal. Needless to say, this name proved far more than simply an omen.

People have always assured me that dogs need to be trained, and perhaps I did not have the strength of character to take this claim with a grain of salt. Thus by chiding, complimenting, rewarding, and disciplining her, I began to teach Boman civilized manners, I began to shape her in my own image. I had no comprehension whatsoever of the bewildered look in her brown eyes, I merely persisted with her training, even though the initial results were nothing special. Boman had to ask to be let out when she needed, Boman was not allowed to bark, Boman was not allowed to chew my slippers, Boman was not allowed to run about the neighbor's garden, and so the list went on. A dog living in a civilized society has to learn a surprising number of different things. And because dogs cannot ask "why," they cannot be given any explanations. They simply have to accept these demands as they are, as if they were humans—a race whose entire culture is based on mindless submission.

My bookshelves contained a variety of books with detailed accounts of how best to instill a dog with human values. Of an evening I would often leaf through these books while Boman lay at my feet. Every now and then she would give an unfriendly growl and look me right in the eyes. It seemed that she was behaving as if she had understood what I was doing. I decided to tell my friends about this to show them what an intelligent dog I had. However, I had not had the chance to do so before Boman gave me a most unpleasant surprise.

On the day in question I had shut her in my study as I had gone into town to run some errands. When I arrived back home the room was covered in mutilated shreds of paper, and there was Boman lying on the floor with part of a book cover in her mouth. Of course the first thing I did was give her a thorough telling off. Boman accepted this punishment as if it were perfectly natural: she did not try to defend herself or even hide under the bed. She clearly understood the matter and I gullibly believed this would suffice. Every one of the dog training books states that once a dog knows what is permissible and what is not, it will start to behave properly. I finished telling her off and began to tidy the room. Only then did I notice that the only books missing from the shelf were those dealing with dog training. All the other books were still stacked neatly exactly where they had been left. An odd coincidence, I thought, and decided to tell my friends all about it.

At that time Boman was about six months old. It was summer, though I decided not to travel anywhere, staying instead at home working and not going outdoors very often. To put it plainly, I was gloomy. There is however no point in talking about this any further; after all, human sorrows differ very little from one another. I tried using books to, as it were, vaccinate myself spiritually: I would seek out gloomy books, something which was hardly difficult. Almost all good books are gloomy. I read stories about people who committed murders and suicides; people who suffered from famine and illnesses; people who rotted away in prison and died with not a soul to remember them; people who refuse to accept the so-called joys of life, who flagellate themselves, who indulge in other sacred rites and who gradually wither away in their studies. Surrounded by such novels and other entertaining reading I revitalized my spirit with philosophy, which convinced me all the more that all people are essentially evil, that life is meaningless, and that our every action merely brings about more suffering. Still, sometimes it occurred to me that my own fate was after all reasonably bearable, and to tell you the truth I took some amount of delight in the plight of those fellow beings worse off than myself. Nonetheless this offered me only mild comfort and did not bring me any true enjoyment. After work each day I would often spend the evenings gripped in a melancholy stupor. When Boman became restless and started scratching pointedly at the door, I would begrudgingly leave the house, and walking through the woods or along the shore I would try to shut out the sound of the birds singing or the roar of the waves, and I would blind my eyes so as not to see the grass, the trees or the sky dotted with stars.

I cannot say how long this would have continued if Boman had not awoken me. She declared open war on my books, the very foundations of my existence. After the books dealing with dog training, she chose to tear up my books on popular psychology, then philosophy, steeped in the sweet smell of death, then the gloomiest of my novels. Naturally I was incensed at the dog's barbaric behavior. I was no longer content with merely reprimanding her, but became furious and enraged at Boman, who always remained perfectly calm during my outbursts. I did not know how to shake her self-assured animality and had therefore to resort to the sorts of measures common only to bad educators.

I began hiding the books I thought to be in the greatest danger. At first Boman was unperturbed. Instead of those hidden away, she destroyed books within her reach. I realized that I had categorized my books wrongly. The books Boman had destroyed were of greater value to me that those I had hidden. Finally I was left with no option but to lock all my books away. It was an extremely time-consuming, frustrating job, and I was made all the crosser by the sight of Boman lounging on the floor with an openly mischievous glint in her eyes as I toiled. I took to reading in much the same way that secret drinkers practice their vice. I would attempt to creep up to the locked bookshelf without Boman's noticing, I would hide the title of the book I had chosen and would not put it down while lighting a cigarette, going to the kitchen or answering the telephone. This was an awful lot of bother, but it meant I was enjoying reading more than ever. Many's the time I would spend the wee hours of the morning with a book in my hand in the grip of a wicked, clandestine excitement.

Once, as dawn was approaching, I startled upon noticing Boman's muzzle peering inquisitively over my shoulder at the book in my hand. I gave a start and snapped: "You're just pretending. You can't read."

Everyone talks to their dogs; there is nothing out of the ordinary about it. Be that as it may, it is perhaps less common for the dog then to reply. In fact, it may very well be that such a thing has never happened—never before. In any case, Boman replied in a beautiful, cultivated voice, with perfect diction:

"Of course I can read. I learned the alphabet when I was three months old."

"Then you did it without my knowledge," I snapped angrily. "It's inappropriate for a dog to learn things it isn't taught. You might have kept your skills to yourself, but of course with your vanity you had to tell me. Don't you remember that modesty is a dog's greatest virtue? Dogs should lie down at their masters' feet and dutifully obey his commands."

What a fine sermon, I thought, and was surprised to hear quite how beautifully a little moral indignation made my voice resound. Boman listened politely, but did not seem the least bit disturbed, not to mention showing any signs of slinking under the bed in shame. After my speech she replied politely, yet with an ironic smirk:

"I'm surprised that all those books haven't instilled you with a greater love of the truth. To keep your self-esteem intact—something which, I must say, seems to be built on very shaky foundations—I am prepared to remain silent, though you will have to forgive me if I yawn from time to time. Your company can be very dull. I do have one request, however. When we go for walks, please do not throw sticks expecting me to retrieve them for you. I find it a most tedious and unimaginative game."

I had already raised my hand and was about to teach my rude dog a lesson she would not forget, but the calm look in Boman's eyes made me relent. Instead I shrugged my shoulders, picked up my book once again and tried to read. I had in fact proved the existence of a very rare phenomenon—talking, literate dogs were not to be found in every household. Not for a moment did I think I was delusional, or that I had been swept away by hallucinations. Besides, there was no reason I would conjure up "voices" to speak to me in such a haughty, offensive manner—the way Boman had spoken to me. A moment passed, and once I felt slightly calmer I turned to look at the dog.

"Let's agree that you may only use these linguistic skills of yours when we're alone. I do however expect a certain amount of respect, and a polite tone of voice. I am your master, after all."

"And so do I. After all, I am your dog."

Another argument was about to erupt, but I managed to control myself.

"In fact, your powers of speech could be very useful indeed," I said in a more friendly tone. "You know very well that my finances are not in the best possible shape, and this might just be the answer. People will pay a great deal of money to see anything new and out of the ordinary. I would say that a talking dog, who can also read, is fairly out of the ordinary. You could recite beautiful poems in front of an audience—that way we would also be doing the arts a noble favor. You could read texts handed in by the audience: we have to prove that you really can read, you see, and that you haven't just learned it all off by rote. Perhaps we could even hire you a singing coach. This has true potential: we need to appeal to a young audience, and nowadays all they seem interested in is popular music. Italian songs are very much in fashion. You might want to liven up your performance with a little dance routine: you would become the first dog in the world to dance the mambo."

'"Yes, a splendid idea," said Boman. "You should hire an enormous circus tent. It would be full to capacity every night."

"Absolutely," I cried excitedly. "Soon we won't have a care in the world."

Boman carried on talking calmly despite my enthusiasm.

"I can see it all in my mind's eye. The tent is packed full, the crowd is waiting eagerly. Then suddenly you appear in the spotlight, with me on the lead, and urge me up on to the stage. Thunderous applause. You bow to the audience. But what happens next?"

"You'll begin your performance, of course."

"Yes," said Boman. "If I feel like it. I can't say for certain whether I'll always be in the right mood."

"You mean you'd refuse?" I shouted angrily. "You're the most ungrateful creature I think I've ever met. I saved you from a certain death, I've shared my dinner with you, sometimes I even allow you to sleep at the end of my bed. And this is how you repay me for the trouble!"

"I didn't say anything final, I merely wanted to highlight a likely scenario. A true friend will never give too rosy a picture of the future, but will always remind others of its shortcomings. And a dog is a man's best friend; I'm your best friend. In any case, you might think of becoming a ventriloquist just in case. Masters of ventriloquism are very rare indeed."

At this I was very hurt.

"Me, a ventriloquist? I hope you don't think I'd turn myself into a clown just for money. I do have some self-respect, you know."

"You would only have to be my stand-in," Boman gently pointed out.

For a while I said nothing to her. I needed all the self-control I could muster, because it was not easy dealing with a dog which, in addition to all its other attributes, can think. This plainly obvious fact was the most difficult for me to accept, as my dog training books, all written by skilled animal psychologists, had imprinted upon me the tenet that dogs necessarily lack such symbolic cognition. They did not, however, appear to be right.

As I sat there Boman's slender muzzle brushed against my knee and her brown eyes looked up at me as gently as only a dog can. Those eyes had made me forgive the destruction of many of my most beloved books, and her self-deprecating gaze did not go unnoticed this time either. I lay my hand on her neck and scratched her gently under the collar. We were friends again and, as if by mutual agreement, decided to forget our previous conversation.

"You should take better care of yourself," said Boman in a friendly tone. "To tell the truth, I've often been worried about the state of your body and soul. You're a young man, yet here you are wasting the best years of your life surrounded by books, many of which—if you'll forgive me—are of questionable quality."

"Perhaps you're right. I don't see other people very often and I'm on edge rather a lot."

"I'm not surprised. People no less than dogs ought not to neglect their needs during the mating season."

"The mating season. Who told you about things like that? As far as I can see you're still a minor."

"Mother Nature is an excellent teacher," she said with a smile in her eyes.

We talked for a long time and had a very pleasant conversation. An untamed animal instinct sometimes shone through Boman's opinions and this upset me a bit, but still I tried my best to tolerate it. I had noticed that Boman did not find my humanity entirely pleasant either. We avoided the subject of philosophy, as we held utterly opposing views. Boman only had to remind me of the inspired words of one of the great thinkers of our age, referring to "the stars up above and humankind down below," and I realized that, ultimately, human wisdom was not intended for wise dogs.

I'm sure I need not point out that Boman was anything but a well-behaved dog. Being too well-behaved would have become tedious after a while and Boman could certainly not be accused of that. Now that we were on a level pegging, so to speak, she began to take ever greater liberties. She would pass the time by chewing at my slippers or lounging in my favorite armchair leafing through my books. She flicked the pages over with her long tongue, often complaining that the paper and ink tasted foul. This made Boman almost as uncomfortable as the bad style of certain writers.

The duality of Boman's life gave rise to many amusing games. When in other people's company she very much enjoyed pretending to be a normal dog. While walking outside I would let her off the lead and she would walk by my side, behaving impeccably. I lived in a small residential area on the outskirts of Helsinki and only a few steps away from my garden there was a path leading to a quiet pond in the woods and beyond that to an uninhabited part of the coastline. This was our everyday route and we very rarely met other people along the way. On one occasion the lady from next door walked past us; Boman did not like her. The reason for this was perfectly understandable: the woman had once kicked Boman when she was a puppy because, despite her friendly smile, she did not like dogs. I greeted her politely, but Boman started to growl. She drew back her muzzle in a snarl revealing her great set of teeth—an imposing sight indeed. Boman then began to approach the woman and leaned back on her hind legs as if preparing herself for an attack. The lady gave out a shrill, frightened cry and leaped off the path and into the woods with Boman barking frantically at her heels. What a sight it was! A sophisticated woman, dressed in a tight skirt, stumbling comically among the thicket. I laughed so much it echoed through the forest. After a while Boman appeared once again, winked mischievously and said:

"I didn't lay a paw on her, I just got a bit carried away."

After this incident the woman next door never said hello again and her husband would scowl at me every time we met.

There were many other people whom Boman very much enjoyed winding up. On sunny days she would lie out in the garden and frighten debt collectors, the most malicious old gossip-mongers in the town and several of our neighbors who were known to be teetotallers. Boman did not hold any personal grudges against these people, rather she acted out of a sense of duty, knowing my natural antipathy. Over time she acquired quite an array of fervent enemies, and it would hardly have surprised me if someone had tried to offer her a treat laced in deadly poison. Boman would not have been tricked by such a thing. She never accepted treats from the hands of nasty strangers. Despite this Boman never turned general opinion against herself, because she could be as adorable as only profoundly mischievous creatures know how. Children were Boman's sworn friends, so she had nothing to fear: children are the true rulers of suburbs like these.

It was during this time that Boman first met Pertti, a schoolboy who lived on the other side of the woods. I never met the boy myself, and all I know about him is what Boman has told me. Pertti's story was so appalling that it sounded almost like an old-fashioned fairytale, the kind that people nowadays find slightly trivial.

Pertti's mother had died and so his father had married a nasty woman, who became Pertti's wicked stepmother, and who had soon filled their little apartment with children, Pertti's wretched half-brothers and sisters. Even Pertti's father no longer cared for his eldest son. That in itself was a sad enough story.

Boman had first met Pertti down by the shore. It was a beautiful Sunday afternoon and Pertti's eyes had lit up as he stood looking out at the yachts, which seemed to be flying through the blue sky, as in the bright sunshine he could not tell where the sea and the sky met.

"They're flying," he said to himself.

Boman sat down next to him and the boy continued:

"Why don't humans have wings? Why can't they fly too?"

"Why don't people just grow themselves wings?"

Only then did Pertti notice Boman; he turned and looked at her reproachfully.

"But they can't."

"Have you tried?"

"I've sometimes wished for them."

What followed was such a truly beautiful conversation about wings that only the most gifted poets would be able to repeat it. I listened in silence. When Boman told me about this encounter, I saw a romantic gleam in her eyes for the very first time, as she would not normally allow tears to cloud her intelligent eyes. Even now she seemed annoyed at how moved she was, and who else could she turn to to talk about such a thing if not to me?

"Why do the bourgeois insist on having pets?" she asked. "Animals have an imagination of their own; they have fantastic, wild dreams; and all the bourgeois offer them are sweet pastries and a warm home. In return they expect their pets to whimper as their master leaves the house and to jump with joy when he returns, because people like that do nothing for free."

There was something very endearing about Boman's outburst, and I did not have the heart to remind her that she too was especially fond of sweet pastries and more often than not demanded that I procure them.

I had to admit, however, that Boman's position as my dog was far from easy. I believe the majority of my friends to be moderately intelligent, but they too have their limits. Those of my friends who considered it a great merit to have been born a human put me in a very awkward situation. With them, it was human-this and human-that from start to finish: "We humans . . . human rights . . . humanity . . . humane . . . superhuman." Only rarely did the word *animal* interrupt this stream of humanity, and at this the speaker's voice would become tainted with disgust. Once in a while I would become indignant on Boman's behalf, but this was in fact unnecessary. In her intellectual independence my dog did not require the help of others. Boman proved this convincingly to me and a guest of mine, who thought himself a genius as he proclaimed that dogs do not understand the meaning of words, rather they respond to the speaker's tone of voice.

"And is that then less praiseworthy?" I asked. "Many humans only understand the meanings of words, but they don't listen to the tone of voice. Tone is also a part of speech."

My guest listened neither to my words nor to my tone of voice, so excited was he over his revelation.

"Let's see," he said. "I'll demonstrate that I'm right."

He bowed down to Boman and very softly said:

"Go to hell. Go to hell."

Boman had dozed off during our conversation. She looked my guest up and down, but after noticing my warning glance, she decided not to resort to violence. She got up, stretched, trotted over to my guest and lifted her hind leg at his shin as if it were a lamp-post. This of course was merely a harmless gesture, as Boman was a bitch, but my guest failed to understand the joke, despite being an intelligent and well-read man. He put on his jacket and left, and I have not seen him since.

"Training humans is very hard work," Boman complained. "They never seem to learn anything from their experiences."

She gave me a friendly look and added: "Still, with some perseverence one can achieve astounding results. Sometimes I almost forget that, for instance, you are a human. And I haven't completely ruled out the possibility that one day you might even begin to think."

It was not often that Boman in any way complimented me and I felt flattered. I was grateful for any attention Boman showed me, because her life had begun to fill up with other matters. More and more often she would spend entire days and nights out on her own. I was worried about her, but I also knew she would not put up with any infringement of her freedom. There were many times she would come home and tell me astonishing things. She had talked to many different people, and I wondered how it was possible that the newspapers were not running stories about a mysterious talking dog. Clearly a talking dog was not considered an appropriate topic of discussion in our society: it was one of those things that everyone was aware of, but that no one dared talk about. This, of course, was very convenient for both me and Boman.

A suicidal young man was one of the many people Boman had met on her lonely treks. There was a time when it seemed that hanging oneself was something of a national pursuit. Local legend and numerous folk songs are testimony to this. Whenever I have traveled through the beautiful Finnish countryside, the locals have always pointed out some protected tree growing by the side of the road, saying: "That's where John So-And-So hanged himself in the year such-and-such by the full moon in autumn." Any story beginning like that is then told in full, the speaker reveling in every detail, and often ends with the fact that the lost soul in question has never found lasting peace, but to this day haunts the cowshed behind his old house. On the whole they are young men or men in the prime of their lives. I have seen young people abroad, all of them brimming with vitality, and I felt envious on behalf of the young people back home, whose duty it seems is to at least attempt to commit suicide. Over the years hanging has made way for sleeping pills, gas and other modern methods, but Boman's story revealed that the old tradition is still going strong.

Boman had just taken Pertti home, but decided to run about the woods out of sheer canine joy. All of a sudden she noticed a young man sitting in a tree placing a noose around his neck. Boman did not have time to intervene before the young man jumped from tree, but the jump did not go quite as expected. The rope was far too long, so the young man did not hang from the branch; instead he fell to the mossy ground with a thud. There he sat dejectedly and burst into tears. Boman carefully approached him and said:

"What bad luck you've had."

"Yes, and this is my third attempt," replied the young man, sobbing.

"Dear oh dear," said Boman. "Isn't that too much? Maybe you should measure the rope before jumping."

"What do you mean?"

"Check that you can stand freely under the rope while it's dangling from the branch."

Only then did the young man realize that he was talking to a dog. He hurriedly removed the noose from around his neck and backed off from Boman. He had stopped crying and with a shrewd and suspicious look in his eyes he said:

"Why, you're a talking dog, and you're very keen to help me kill myself. I know who you are."

"Yes, I am a talking dog."

The young man was not listening; he continued speaking, his teeth clenched together the way bad actors often do: "You came here to wait for my demise, but it seems you've shown yourself too soon."

"Too late, I would say. You said this was your third attempt, and I sincerely believe that both people and dogs succeed in everything they do on the first attempt. Though it has to be said, dogs very rarely hang themselves."

"I'll make the sign of the cross and you will disappear."

"I could disappear without it, but I could also stay. You might still need my help—in measuring the rope, perhaps."

"No, don't go," said the young man. "I've never met the Devil himself before. I'd like to talk to you."

"Thank you," Boman replied. "I've always liked nicknames, but I don't have very many. Devil sounds good."

"That's it, I see you're trying to be funny. Well, humor is the Devil's work, I've always known that. But you still wish me dead."

"No I don't, quite the contrary. Bodies hanging from trees are not a pretty sight."

"In that case you're the first creature not to wish me ill."

The young man looked almost moved, but Boman interrupted him.

"I don't wish you good or bad. I don't know you. Only a moment ago I didn't know you even existed. I can only tell you what I wish you after we've got to know one another. So let's get to know one another. You could start by telling me why you tried to kill yourself."

The young man readily began to explain; all he needed was a listening ear. He had committed a grave sin, a crime. He had stolen. The previous evening he had gone to visit his elderly uncle, an old sea captain who had sailed the seven seas. His uncle was as miserly as the Devil himself (at this, the young man glanced sheepishly at Boman), but still the young man knew that one day he would inherit his uncle's wealth. This was not an insignificant amount, it would be enough for him to live happily for the rest of his days. That night they had sat up talking, as on many occasions before. Suddenly, over his uncle's shoulder on top of the bookshelf, the young man had noticed a golden Buddha staring down at him. The statue, about a span high, had probably been there for years, but the young man had never noticed it before. Now he felt that the Buddha's mysterious smile was meant for him alone, and the metal statue began to glow, its dazzling light filling the room. The young man was convinced that there was a secret power hidden within the statue, and that it would bring both wisdom and happiness to its owner. After all, did not his own uncle think of old age and his approaching death with surprising calm? This explained everything. And because the Buddha was clearly made of gold, it was surely priceless. So once he had pondered on these thoughts for a moment, it was not surprising that he began to covet the small golden statue for himself. Acquiring that statue became vitally important to him. So when his uncle was not looking he slipped the Buddha into his pocket, bid the old man farewell and hurried off into the night with his new treasure. As soon as he got home, he took the statue out of his pocket and spent that whole summer's night sitting on the edge of his bed staring at the Buddha. Its smile had captivated him, and the night seemed to pass in a daze. It was only in the morning that the young man realized what a serious crime he had committed, and at his job in an office he spent the whole day on edge. He was convinced that there would be no way of making up for his deeds; there was only one solution. Death.

As he recounted his story the young man had taken the fateful statue out of his pocket and was now staring at it fixedly. He had clearly forgotten all about Boman, and gave a start as she said:

"Can I have a closer look?"

The young man held the statue out toward Boman; she inspected the Buddha carefully and asked to see underneath it.

"You're right," she said finally. "In its own way it is a very beautiful statue. I can see it has enchanted you. It's impossible to explain that smile; I don't think there's anything there, but I can imagine how it might contain a secret I can never reach."

"It does contain a secret," he replied instantly. "That smile doesn't just hold the key to life, but to existence itself."

"I believe you," Boman agreed. "If there is a secret, its key may just as well be hidden in that smile as anywhere else. The key to your secret is, however, hidden right here."

The young man clutched the statue tightly against his chest and shouted half sorrowfully, half rejoicing:

"Think how unhappy my uncle must be. He has lost the meaning of his life, the key to his existence. I don't believe he will ever recover from this blow; he'll die soon."

"Oh I don't think so. I rather suspect that this statue only holds special significance for you. Your uncle probably hasn't even noticed it's missing."

"That's impossible. Even if he hasn't understood the statue's significance, he'll still be frantic, out of greed. He'll be thinking of the money he could have made by selling the statue, and now he'll think it's lining my pocket."

"Yes, I noticed," Boman replied. "But as far as I can see you have overestimated the value of this statue. This metal isn't gold, it's brass. Bite it and see; it's an old method for identifying gold. In addition, the words 'Made in England' are printed on the statue's base. You know what this means. To anyone else your treasure is just junk, but this doesn't matter to you. What's most important is that for you it is the key to existence."

At first the young man did not understand Boman's words, then he began to shake as if he were consumed with a terrible fever. His hands trembling, he turned the statue over, squeezed it and finally let it fall to his feet.

"I've been cheated, cheated," he shouted, hopping up and down with rage. "I've been terribly deceived."

"I don't understand what you mean. Surely you're not angry at yourself."

"You damned cur, get out of my sight," shouted the young man. "You're the Devil himself and this is all your doing."

In his rage the young man tried to kick Boman, though naturally he missed as Boman was able to move very nimbly indeed.

"And here I thought I was doing you a favor," said Boman feigning innocence. "I'm sure your uncle would gladly give you that statue, or at least he would sell it to you for next to nothing. Just think—once you owned the Buddha of Secrets you would be both wise and happy. You would be able to think more calmly about death, as it draws closer every moment, though you're still so young."

Boman uttered those final words to herself, as the young man had bounded off deep into the woods and would not have been able to hear Boman for the gnashing of his teeth. The brass Buddha lay on the ground. Boman would gladly have taken it home with her, but carrying a metal object in her mouth would have been most unpleasant. There was also nothing she could do about the noose still hanging from the branch above.

"I do hope it doesn't prove a fateful discovery for some other desperate chap," said Boman solemnly as she rounded off her story.

Boman spent the vast majority of her time with Pertti. He had nothing to do during the long summer months and people at home were glad the longer he stayed out of their sight. I am not sure quite what the two of them got up to, but I am certain that a little boy and a dog see far more on their walks in the woods than adults. Pertti and Boman were both so close to the ground that nothing could escape their notice among the trees, the bushes and the moss. And they both had a very similar imagination. I knew that Boman dreamed of running through great forests, across open fields and along high cliffs. At times like this her paws would tremble restlessly and her nostrils would sniff around for strong new scents arising from the depths of her dream.

When autumn came Pertti had to go to school. After this Boman spent days on end in my company and looked frightfully bored, even though I very often neglected my work to spend time with her. I did what I could, but because starting a conversation was suddenly so difficult I decided to read her stories and poetry. Though I went out of my way to entertain her she was not the least bit grateful, but instead made derisive comments about my choice of texts, which eventually made me feel a certain distaste toward writers and poets whom I had previously held in high regard.

"I'm bored to tears by your stories," she grumbled. "The suspense stories are ridiculous, because who on earth would feel suspense at a mere story? All the tragedies have the same lofty ending—something offered to the reader like a sugar cube to sweeten the pill. The only function of the bawdy stories is to titillate those with one set of morals for the living room and another for the bedroom. And as for the poetry! These old-fashioned poems with their clumsy rhymes creak like a rusty set of cogs and modern poets are just as pretentious as poets throughout the ages. They whine on and on about the same old things: the setting sun and the morning dew, lost innocence, even though no living creature is ever innocent, and wise old men, even though wise old men are merely tired human beings."

I gradually realized that it was not within my power to make Boman happy. I left her to her own devices and did not notice that she would slip out of the open window when the children were let out of school. Sometimes Boman would show her affection by telling me how sorry she was for Pertti. Strangers did not think Pertti was handsome, they found him rather sickly and they did not understand that the glint in his eyes was a sign of his wild imagination. It was not only at home that Pertti was made to suffer: the boys at school teased him and his teachers thought he was stupid and badly raised.

"They're proud of their own excellent upbringing," Boman scoffed, "and by this they mean that they have all learned to speak, behave and think in exactly the same way."

One day Boman informed me that she and Pertti had decided to run away together. In telling me she was in fact breaking her promise. It was a secret. Boman's eyes smiled at me and she looked happy for the first time in a long while. I understood that it was a secret for Pertti's sake, thus I was flattered I had been told and took as much comfort from this as I could.

At first however I did not think of myself; I was worried for the young pair of conspirators. I tried to explain that their plan was insane and highly dangerous. Boman was responsible for a boy too young to understand the consequences of his actions.

"Does anyone understand the consequences of their actions?" asked Boman nonchalantly. "Did you understand what you were doing when you took me in?"

Eventually this conversation ended like every conversation in which Boman and I had differing opinions: Boman finally had her way.

"This is my gift to him," she deigned to point out. "Pertti needs an adventure he can remember for the rest of his life. It doesn't matter if things turn out badly, but when he becomes an adult he will remember the time he grabbed hold of freedom, something which would never have been offered him otherwise. It'll give him strength."

I tried to question Boman's noble arguments. I said that it was she who needed the adventure—she had always rebelled against the security of the bourgeois lifestyle. But these were empty words. I was already packing Pertti a knapsack I had bought in town especially. I made sure to pack warm clothes and enough food for a little boy and a dog. As night drew in I took the knapsack outside and placed it on the step, left the door ajar and bid Boman farewell.

"Think of me, won't you," I said and did not dare look at her.

I shut myself in my study. When I appeared a few hours later Boman was gone and the knapsack was no longer on the step.

Needless to say, the days that followed were very upsetting for me. I tried to read, I made more of an effort to spend time with my friends, but nothing seemed to amuse me. After they had bombarded me with their wit for a number of hours they began to look askance at me, thinking I was hopelessly demented. I was sad. A few days later I read a small announcement in the newspaper about the disappearance of a little boy called Pertti. This told me very little and it was only much later that I heard about their adventures in more detail.

First off they had gone into town. Although it was only some ten kilometers from our suburb into the center of town, to Pertti Helsinki was an unknown city. Its streets, restaurants, and cinemas excited his imagination. Boman had accompanied me into town on a few occasions, but had never particularly enjoyed it. She had complained of people stepping on her toes, and in general she looked down upon people who flocked together in this manner.

The journey into town had been an adventure in itself. Walking along the street they had to be careful not to talk within other people's earshot, and at first they had found this secrecy a fun new game. As they arrived in town they stopped outside display windows and cinemas looking in awe at advertisements and foreign pictures. Their glances and gestures convinced one another that everything was incredible, fun and exciting. Boman acquired a taste for straining at the leash and running up to lampposts, which she then sniffed with exaggerated enthusiasm. No one walking by could have imagined what a fun game this was.

Once they arrived in the center of town the adventurers were a little confused. They had reached their destination and there was nowhere to continue their journey. Before they had set out Pertti had tried to explain to Boman that adventures would come along of their own accord; they would meet weird and wonderful people and they would be carried away by the very flow of events. But now most people hurriedly darted past them, and those leaning on lampposts or loitering around the streets looked so hostile that the pair dared not approach them. Pertti and Boman tried to play at the railway station. They would walk along with the crowds of people arriving, then with those leaving on a train and try to look hurried and important, but before long they became tired of this and sat down on a bench in the waiting room. Now they had the time to see that these travelers were all gray and weary. Being on the move did not feel fun or exciting any more; they would much rather have been asleep in their own beds thinking of nothing. The little boy and the dog tried to escape their melancholy in the cold park, where they sat eating from their knapsack.

The park was empty and they could have talked freely without fear of anyone overhearing them, but they had nothing to say to one another. Such a thing had never happened to them before. Boman silently examined Pertti's thin face, blue with the cold, and for the first time in her life she felt guilty of a terrible deed. Boman had steeled her wits against the human sense of guilt, something she had often referred to as cheap, useless emotional rubbish. Now she felt responsible for not dashing Pertti's expectations from the outset, for not drawing the gray curtain of reality over his future.

In silence the adventurers returned to the streets, loitered aimlessly by a hot dog stand and witnessed a number of street fights. They then began to look for a place to spend the night and before long they found an open stairwell. They climbed up to the top of the stairs and lay down to sleep huddling next to one another. The darkness was impenetrable and in its protection Pertti plucked up the courage to speak to Boman.

"I shouldn't have dragged you along with me. You have a good master and a safe home."

"A safe home can seem like a prison to someone who wants to help his friend discover a new world."

Boman's voice was gentle but defiant. It made Pertti speechless and Boman felt a few warm tears drop on her muzzle. After he had calmed down, Pertti said:

"There is no new world. We saw that this evening."

"If it doesn't exist, we'll have to create it," said Boman without a shadow of hesitation in her voice.

In only a few sentences they had said all that needed to be said. There they fell asleep and awoke in the morning under a glaring light to find someone trying to wake them up, bellowing angrily. It was the caretaker.

"Up you get, boy, and be gone with you. Quick smart! And take that dog with you, unless you want me to call the police."

The fright woke Pertti and Boman in a flash. Pertti grabbed the knapsack and the adventurers flew down the stairs. The chortling of the caretaker boomed around them and followed them out into the street as they instinctively ran away from the town center and out toward the sea and the park land along the shore. Once in the park they stopped and took a bewildered look around. They were welcome here. The trees were decorated in a wonderful display of colors to celebrate their arrival: red, yellow, and orange leaves lay scattered along the path forming a soft carpet beneath their feet. A fresh sea breeze caught Pertti's hair and caressed Boman's shining coat.

All of a sudden both the little boy and the dog were once again filled with the joy which had died out the day before; they could enjoy the luxury of their freedom. They frolicked about the park laughing, at times holding ceremonious silences. They irritated the seagulls by mimicking their cawing and tried to tame the already tame squirrels as, startled by Boman, they darted up into great tall trees. Then they would laugh at the arrogant little sparrows. In the harbor, gray, asthmatic boats wheezed their own importance, dainty yachts, stripped naked, swayed back and forth around the pavilions and lonely island fortifications sulked out at sea.

"What an angry man," said Pertti referring to the caretaker.

"Let's forget about him," said Boman. "Let this be our revenge. We'll forget all about the angry caretaker and the old world."

"Yes, let's," Pertti agreed.

On they frolicked through parks and docks and over bridges. They gradually left the town behind them and found that walking around here was far easier. The sea played with them, momentarily disappearing behind hills and capes, then suddenly swelling back beside them, accompanying them on their journey, the waves beating in time with their steps, leading them over bridges across the bay. Further out to sea they could make out small, friendly looking islands, also decked out in resplendent autumn colors.

"That's where I'd like to go, to those islands," said Pertti.

"I've been waiting all this time for you to start wishing to go there."

They winked at one another and left the road to follow the shore. They soon discovered a cove containing lots of little boats, but only in one of them were the oars unlocked. They decided to take that one.

"I really ought to warn you," said Boman. "This is a crime and you'll be held responsible for it. I'm a dog, I can't be accused of anything."

"I'm sure an owner who has left his oars unlocked can't be mean. He'll understand that someone else might need his boat."

Thus began their journey through the archipelago. They decided not to go ashore on the first island, as they did not want to barge their way in; instead they waited for an invitation, a sign. Before long one of the islands revealed a friendly cove, and the wind gently blew their boat toward it. They hauled the boat safely on to the shore, sheltered under a group of spruce trees, and set off along the paths on the island. The firm, dry land supported their steps, the forest was almost silent. The most skilled summer songbirds had already flown south, and in the silence the solitary chirping of the remaining gray singers resounded with desolate calm.

There were many summer houses on the island, but not one of them contained any inhabitants. The owners were in town, but their houses were glad to welcome the small travelers. In each of the houses there was an opening just big enough for a dog, a simple latch, steps and a door opening silently. So the houses welcomed them with open arms, laid out soft carpets in front of them, offered them armchairs and sofas, bathrooms and balconies. Pertti and Boman welcomed the houses' hospitality and in return they created a history for every one of them. They conjured up noble masters living in the houses, each with a sprightly dog of his own; they imagined strong bonds between the different households, bringing them together and keeping them apart. They charted every inch of the island, its knolls, its spruce groves and bays, and gave each of these places an ambiguous name. And all this time their senses were aroused by the smell of salt and they were caressed by the icy hand of the wind coming in across the sea.

In this way the little boy and the dog created their new world, but all the time they knew that danger was not far away. Every now and then they would take a cautious look out across the open sea between the island and the mainland and as evening drew in they saw a motor boat heading toward the island. They quickly hid themselves near the boat concealed in among the spruces, and before long they could hear the sound of strange footsteps thumping the ground. Soon afterward they heard angry shouts and cursing, people rushing past them. Cold and hungry, Pertti and Boman huddled against one another and waited for night to fall. Protected by the darkness they pushed the boat out to sea and headed off toward new islands.

All in all Pertti and Boman lived this precarious life for a few weeks: at times they were welcome guests, for whom houses opened their doors and offered the wonderful treats in their pantries and cellars, at others they were fugitives, spending days on end hidden in the forest or among the rushes. They learned that there were two realities on the islands; one was of their own creation and the other was a strange and brutal reality, something in which they wanted no part. They spoke only of their own reality, of banquets and high dramas played out in the great rooms of these houses and on the shores, decked out in festive splendor.

Over time they became too tired to try and forget about the cold, the hunger and the fear attacking them from the old world, and one night Pertti no longer had the energy to row the boat to the safety of another island, but lay down instead at the bottom of the boat and fell asleep next to Boman. The sea rocked them first gently, then with ever greater waves, and they dreamed of sailing along far off shores on a ship with enormous sails. When they awoke the following morning all they could see was blue, the cold blue of the sea and the sky. The waves had died down to a soft swell, lazily rocking back and forth out toward the horizon. High above them were sparse clouds, which the wind had combed into thin trails across the sky. Both boy and dog were exhausted. It had been a long time since their last meal and their hunger had gradually turned to weariness.

"There is another shore on this sea, isn't there?" Pertti whispered softly into Boman's ear. "Do you think we'll ever reach it?"

"The shore will find us soon enough. We simply have to wait," Boman replied just as softly.

They fell asleep once again. A patrol boat spotted a small boat, which looked empty, drifting out to sea. It was only once they came closer that the patrol men noticed a little boy and a black mongrel sleeping next to each other at the bottom of the boat.

Boman had been on her travels for about three weeks. One day there came a knock at my door; outside was a policeman in uniform holding Boman on a leash. He told me that they had seen from her collar that Boman belonged to me. Some little rascal had stolen the dog and taken her with him. I thanked the policeman, he saluted me and went on his way. Only then did I dare take a closer look at Boman. The end of her muzzle was dry and she looked generally ill and feverish. I stroked her gently, but did not want to show her quite how happy I was to see her again. I placed her on my bed and she fell asleep in an instant; she slept there for a long time, semiconscious, her legs twitching. I guessed she was dreaming about continuing her flight at Pertti's side. Boman recovered from her fever a few days later with the help of the penicillin prescribed by the vet. After eating the first square meal since her return, she told me she was going out. I did not try to stop her.

This time she was not away for long. She returned with a small letter in her mouth, left for her at an agreed hiding place by Pertti. I was allowed to read the letter, which read simply in heavy, childish lettering: "They're sending me to a borstal. Pertti." The letter also contained the name of the borstal and a clumsy, hand-drawn map showing where it was situated.

Once I had read the letter, Boman and I looked at each other in silence.

"It's a long journey," she said.

"It's too long," I said, as I could see what she was thinking.

We did not speak about Pertti for a long time after this. Boman tried as best she could to adapt once again to her role as my dog, but as I listened to her witty banter I would often turn and look out of the window, and I would feel like crying. It was as if we were playing out a tragedy, in which the function of the lines is merely to hide the characters' pain. Boman had lost the happy, mischievous gleam in her eyes, she no longer smirked like a naughty young rogue. Sometimes she would ask me to read her poems about the sea, the wind and friendship. As she listened she would often remain silent for entire evenings at a time.

"I think your taste is falling to ruin,' I said, trying to sound jovial. 'You never used to like literature with such pathos."

Boman did not reply.

On our walks she would plod compliantly by my side, she no longer ran around under the trees sniffing at the moss and the tussocks. On one occasion we stopped by the shore and watched the seagulls' noisy capers.

"Seagulls can fly very fast," said Boman.

"And they are beautiful," I added.

I had hoped that Boman was gradually beginning to see beyond herself, so I was not overjoyed when she said:

"I wonder whether it's difficult to grow oneself wings."

"It's impossible."

Boman sneered and glanced over at me.

That same evening I was reminded of the fact that Boman was almost a fully grown dog. As we had left the house I had caught a glimpse of some dogs running loose near our garden. I did not pay any particular attention to this, because Boman had said something and my attention had been drawn elsewhere. As we arrived back at the house I realized that she had done this on purpose. It was dark and in the garden I could see several pairs of eyes shining motionlessly. I sensed that they were staring at us and quickened my step. Boman reluctantly followed me, but followed nonetheless.

Once we had got inside I asked almost angrily:

"What were they?"

"Dogs. Males."

"I didn't know you were that way inclined."

Boman did not respond, and despite her normal ready wit she seemed at a loss for words. I remained silent for a moment, then asked reticently:

"Would you like to go out?"

"I don't think so," she said.

She struggled against herself, asked me to read poetry to her again and tried hard to listen, but suddenly gave a start at a sound from outside and began pacing restlessly around the house until she finally went up to the front door in the hallway and started sniffing it. Every now and then she would let out a coarse, mournful sound, then a reply would be heard from outside. She glanced over at me, then crept into a corner of the study.

This indecision lasted two days and two nights and throughout that time the dogs kept a vigil outside the door. At night the scraping of their paws could be heard on the front steps and during the day they would retreat into the woods, remaining in view the whole time.

On the third evening after we got back from our walk Boman said:

"You and your books have taught me that one always has to choose between two or more options."

"That's true," I replied. "Life is about making choices."

'Maybe your life and your truth. I want to choose both options, so I'd like to go outside.'

"By all means," I said. "Please, no one is stopping you."

"Then would you open the door," Boman growled angrily.

"Sorry, I didn't realize it was shut. Please remember to be careful, it would be terrible if those wild beasts were to bite you."

"I will take care of myself, and I know those wild beasts. I am a wild beast too. You don't know anything about these things."

I opened the door and Boman disappeared.

In the morning she returned looking awful, covered from head to toe in dirt and with blood stains matted in her coat. She had prepared herself for a dressing down, so she was behaving as arrogantly as when she had left, but in her eyes I could see her silent distress.

"You see?" she said. "Nothing out of the ordinary went on."

"Really?" I retorted and went into the kitchen.

I made her a substantial meal and she tucked in heartily, then walked over to the darkest corner of my study and went to sleep. I thought she was just resting after the events of the previous night, it was only later that evening, when she refused to leave the house for our daily walk, that I began to worry. The same happened the following day as well. Boman did not want to stay outside for more than a few minutes at a time, and when I offered her food, she would turn her head and slink off to the furthest corner of the room. There she spent day upon day, not sleeping, but staring blindly in front of her. She responded to my speech the way dogs normally do: she stared at me with questioning eyes, and it was impossible to tell whether she had understood anything at all.

In my mind I was beginning to formulate tragic theories of how moral decline can destroy the spiritual fabric of a well-developed being. Boman had given in to the beast inside her, and because of this had returned to her base animal level and had lost her ability to speak and most probably her ability to think. I returned to my books, which had lain untouched for some time, and they supported this view in every respect. For safety's sake I never spoke out loud about these thoughts, because you never could tell with Boman. Perhaps she would still understand what I was saying. After a while I became worried about the state of her health. Regardless of whether she was once again a normal dog, tied to her animal needs, things were not at all the way they should have been. As a dog, surely she should recover from her moral crisis and wait calmly for its natural consequences. In no way was she behaving like a healthy dog and I began to worry whether she might have received a serious internal injury during her adventure that night. I decided it was best to call the doctor and as I picked up the telephone I told Boman my decision, the way I had always informed her of such matters in the past. To my surprise she raised her head sharply and said simply:

"No."

So she could still speak after all. I did not know quite what to think. Had I yet again tried to find too simple an explanation for things with all my books and life experience? Nonetheless I left the dog in peace and waited.

A week later Boman became tormented, she began whimpering quietly to herself and there was a pained look in her eyes. At first I pretended not to notice anything, but after a while I could restrain myself no longer. I approached her and she made no attempt to run away. She allowed me to rest my hand on her neck and stroke it. It was then that I noticed for the first time that two large lumps were growing on her back, right on top of her shoulder blades. As my hand lightly touched them she winced and turned to give me a stern look.

At that moment I understood. I remembered the seagulls along the shore and I remembered the first time Pertti and Boman met. "Why don't people just grow themselves wings?" Boman had asked. She had said she wanted to choose both options and had then opted for her nocturnal fall from grace. I looked at her fondly and tears welled in my eyes.

"My friend, you are the first true hero I have ever met," I said.

At last I understood how to relate to Boman. I talked to her a lot, even though she just lay silently in the corner and did not respond. I tried to encourage her: I told her that her will was stronger than that of any other living creature and every day I remarked on how the lumps had grown. The day her wings would hatch was drawing close.

Boman appeared to perk up when I kept her company and it seemed that the worst of the pain was over. She had stopped whimpering, and although she still refused to talk she would give me signs and make it clear when she wanted to go outside. On our walks she would lead me toward the shore. We would often stand on the rocks by the shore as evening approached, the surrounding landscape was deserted and pale gray light trickled from the sky. The seagulls had not disappeared, they continued to swoop noisily above the shore, their delicate wings like sails sketching masterful patterns in the wind. Boman sat on the rocks watching the birds for hours at a time. Sometimes she looked as if she might have wanted to join them, but then she remembered and looked at her back, and her eyes would fill with helplessness.

It only took a few weeks for her wings to mature. First of all, her coat around the lumps disappeared to reveal soft, silken skin, through which two small black wings protruded. On the day the wings hatched came the first snowfall. Boman had again been very restless the previous night, she had whined to herself and paced up and down through the house. In the morning she came to show me her wings; she was both humble and proud, like a mother showing off her newborn child or an artist who is convinced of the unique qualities of a new work. The wings themselves were still very small and delicate and were a shade of bluish black, like the feathers of splendid woodland birds.

"I knew you could do it," I said.

Boman turned her head and examined her wings, then lay down on the floor and slept solidly for two days. I bought her a jacket made of red fabric, as I did not want the neighbors to see me walking about with a winged dog.

When she awoke Boman seemed to be herself once again. She chatted happily and intelligently and we would go out for many a long walk. She had nothing against wearing the jacket, because she could not yet fly, even though her wings were growing visibly bigger. Still she was impatient.

"They're growing so slowly," she complained. "I'm in a hurry."

I too was restless. I was worried that Boman's adventure that night would not be without its consequences. I suggested she practice flying—this would help strengthen her wings.

One moonlit night we went into the woods and Boman climbed up a small hill, while I remained down below waiting. Once at the top Boman stretched out her wings, shook them and finally dared to let them carry her weight. On her first attempt she only managed to fly a few meters before falling to the ground and rolling down the hill with her wings still outstretched. She yelped excitedly and stood up, nothing serious had happened. I very much enjoyed watching these practice flights, though I was not having as much fun as Boman. I think I was slightly envious of her, and sometimes I secretly touched my own shoulder blades, but the slightest lump did not appear to be growing.

The day soon came when Boman could fly impeccably. Although it was highly risky we even started going out during the daytime. Boman would jump from the rocks and with only a few flaps of her wings she would rise up among the seagulls. She had hoped to make playmates of the seagulls, but they were startled, cawed loudly in distress and swooped out of Boman's path. Then they flew away to a distant shore frantically flapping their wings. The seagulls' panic was perfectly understandable as Boman's wing span was almost two meters and in the air she was a frightening and awesome sight.

As she returned to me Boman was dissatisfied.

"It baffles me that creatures as stupid as birds should be blessed with such noble limbs."

"Perhaps flying alone does not make us blessed," I replied dryly.

"There is of course a difference between flying and flying. For some it is merely a way of moving, for others it represents freedom."

I was happy for Boman's triumph, I felt that I had had some part in the birth of her wings, but at the same time I was uncomfortable. I knew she had not grown wings for the sheer sake of it. Several times I found her examining a map, and would try to back off as quietly as possible. On one of these occasions she noticed me and followed me into the study; she lay her head on my knee and said:

"Don't be sorry."

"I'm not," I lied. "We're still friends."

"Of course we are. I don't want to make excuses, but it's not easy being a dog with wings, a talking dog and a normal dog all at once. Many things have become inevitable. My adventure that night, you remember, was inevitable and soon I will inevitably have to fly away."

I nodded and we sat there for a long time, neither speaking nor moving. I gradually moved my hand on to her neck and rested it there. Boman gave a start and said:

"In fact, I will have to go now."

"Wait a moment, I'll open the door."

This was the only farewell we bade each other. On that day the clouds were very low in the sky, dragging across the treetops, and Boman flew hidden safely among them for the majority of the journey. Only a few times did she fly low enough to take her bearings from certain landmarks: lakes, railway tracks, towns. Someone idly wandering the streets noticed her black wings outstretched against the clouds and shouted: "Look, a black swan!" But no one heard him and so the wanderer was branded a liar as he told his friends and neighbors that evening that he had seen a black swan flying north at this time of year. Such a thing is impossible.

Only once did Boman land to rest. She chose a bare hilltop amidst the great wilderness, where all the eye could see was dirty brown pine swamps and bluish forests. Everything was still, never before had Boman heard a stillness like this.

It was late evening by the time she reached her destination. She circled above the borstal several times before landing in a nearby forest, where she spent her first night. The forest floor was covered in spruce branches and the remnants of the felling season, and from these Boman made herself a shelter and hiding place. In the morning she made an early start, crept up toward the edge of the forest and followed any movement from the borstal. The building looked just like any country house, it was not cut off from the outside world by a wall or a high fence. The boys, still drowsy with sleep, assembled in the forecourt, they were given tools and split into groups, after which they went off in different directions toward the field, each group under the close supervision of one of the masters. The boys moved slowly and from a distance it looked as if they were wearing shoes far too big for them. Sometimes while the masters were not looking the boys would push and shove one another, not so much to let off steam, but simply because they resented those with whom destiny had thrown them together.

Boman spent a few days watching these events from a distance before she caught sight of Pertti, who appeared with one of the groups near the edge of the forest. The fields were narrow and the ditches in between covered in thick willow bushes. Boman had already concluded that she would have to use those ditches to her advantage. Now she put her plan into action; she easily managed to come close to the group, but had to wait for a while until Pertti was far enough away from the others that she could speak to him. Before long a suitable opportunity presented itself.

Pertti managed to conceal his excitement from the other boys and the masters, for he had long since learned the art of pretending. He was only able to whisper a few words, but Boman spoke to him for a long time. I do not know what they talked about, but I do know that there was no chance for the two of them to meet in private. Pertti may have wanted to try and escape, but that would have been a desperate thing to do and Boman did not wish to cause her friend any fresh difficulties. Even so, the mere knowledge that Boman was nearby gave Pertti strength. He stood up straight, the former bluish gleam returned to his eyes and he laughed happily at the taunting of the other boys and masters. "He's been taken by the Devil," said the nastiest of them. The others simply wondered what had come over him.

On her first excursion, Boman spent about a week with Pertti, sleeping hidden away in her shelter under the spruce branches. She also had to fend for herself. Boman had never acquired a taste for raw meat and she had never before killed a living being. Now, however, she had no choice in the matter and began with stupid, ugly animals; her diet thus consisted for the most part of crows. She could catch them easily in flight and force herself to eat, though the taste of blood disgusted her.

After a week had gone by Boman returned to me, not to stay but to rest at my house. She gave me only a scant outline of what she had been doing. Sometimes we would chat generally or talk vividly about our shared memories, but at other times Boman seemed strangely wild. On days like this she would sleep through the daylight, while at night her eyes would begin to glow. She would not let me brush her and if I came too close she would growl angrily. The next day she would once again be like any other dog: playful, mischievous but always considerate. She would also not want to talk about the previous day whatsoever. Sometimes she would ask me to read aloud to her, poetry about wings, clouds and friendship, and at times like this she seemed to cry to herself—without shedding a tear.

Boman made many subsequent visits to Pertti, though these visits were not as long as the first. I was worried about her and kept a close watch on her, and before long I realized she was expecting puppies. Soon she would be unable to fly at all.

Talking about hunches is normal between humans, but what humans had mere hunches about, Boman knew as fact. Of course, she had nothing to hide from herself; her role as both a dog with a collar and a winged animal were in constant interaction. Boman knew this and made sure I also knew this as she softly began to speak.

"I don't seem to have complimented you very often," she said.

"But why would you have offended me?"

We both sneered quietly, sadly, both of us understanding. Then Boman continued:

"If you had no imagination, I wouldn't exist. I would have been born, of course, but imagine what would have happened if I'd had a master who couldn't believe his eyes or his ears! He would have predefined the limits of my being. In that respect I would never have existed."

"My friend," I said. "You're making this conversation very difficult for me. Perhaps it's my turn to tell you what a great service you have done me, a dog who can cross the boundary between the possible and the impossible as if it weren't there."

"Oh I believe you, I'm hardly modest. To tell you the truth, I have also fulfilled my nature as a dog, in everything I've done. It's because of you that I learned to speak, and you also played an important part in my wings—they belong equally to you, although they are on my back.'

"In my mind I've often flown with them. This is not a gift many dogs have given their masters."

"Most dogs would be only too happy to do so, but such a gift needs a recipient, or else it won't exist. In any case, I hope that, even as you walk alone, you will always hear the patter of my paws beside you."

These words, which sounded so like a farewell, dispelled the smile which had rippled across our eyes throughout this solemn exchange. I wanted to ask, to implore her for an explanation, but could not bring myself to do so. Boman left that same day without my noticing, leaving me alone to spend my time longing for her. I did not read very much during this time; I found the self-importance of books, searching for something eternal, somewhat objectionable. I settled instead for newspapers and numbed my brain by reading their every last word. Soon after she had left I noticed a small announcement in the paper warning people of a wolf or a wild Alsatian moving in the vicinity of Borstal K. The local authorities were to arrange a hunt, in which the military would also take part. The paper fell from my hands.

The following day the newspaper reported the wolf as fact. There had been many reported sightings of the animal and people were afraid it would break into a barn and ravage their cattle. A wolf hunt was underway. Dozens of men, each of them armed, combed their way through the forest from dawn till dusk. The wolf was behaving strangely: it did not flee the area, as many unarmed people had seen it, and it refused to be caught in meticulously laid traps. Newspaper articles gradually became more and more fanatical, the wolf was suddenly front page news, men in both the forest and in the editorial office were in a frenzy. An animal, which so skilfully evaded its pursuers, had to be dangerous. One person even used the word "criminal" to refer to this stubborn animal, which refused to give itself up and be killed.

I waited and thought of Boman. I knew she could have fled if she had wanted to. She could have spread out her black wings and risen out of reach, but I also knew that she would not flee. I remembered the glow in her eyes of late, I understood why she had kept quiet about certain matters. She was free, she had grown herself a set of wings, she could fly and be with her friend in a fantasy land, a free land. Yet at the same time she was tied. She was tied to me and she was tied to her pregnancy. Boman lived in a world in which all three of these levels cannot be realized at once: while one represented freedom, the others were shackles. Two represented crime, only one making amends. Boman firmly believed in the strength of her own will. She had grown herself a set of wings, she wanted to force the men on the wolf hunt to accept the fact that the animal they were hunting would not be trapped, that it was smarter, more cunning, and freer than the people stalking it. I could imagine Boman, emerging triumphant from this furor, landing one day in the market place, gathering her black wings and walking off calmly along the high street.

This is what I imagined as I waited. I thought that by her very existence she might force people to accept certain truths: there is a dog with wings, there is a dog which soars above our heads toward freedom, descending once again into our midst, or joining other dogs in their untamed games.

I did not sleep well at night, but despite this my hearing was far from acute. One morning I opened the door and found Boman lying on the step. She was already cold, there was a wound in her right side. Her black wings lay disheveled, helpless, beside her.

RALPH ROBERT MOORE

The Machine of a Religious Man

Ralph Robert Moore was born in New England and moved to California in his twenties, where he met his wife Mary. After traveling around North America for a number of years, they settled in Texas, where they currently live.

Moore's fiction has been published in America, England, Ireland, and Australia in many magazines, including Albedo One, Chizine, Lullaby Hearse, Midnight Street, Porcupine, Redsine, Roadworks, Space and Time, *and* The Los Angeles Times Calendar Magazine, *as well as in the anthologies* Dark Delicacies *and* Darkness Rising.

His novel Father Figure *was published in 2003. A wide selection of his writings can be found at: http://www.ralphrobertmoore.com.*

"The Machine of a Religious Man" was originally published in Spring 2005 issue of the British magazine Midnight Street.

—E.D.

You find yourself racing through the desert on the coldest, darkest night. Birds splash against the speed of your windshield. Beaks, talons, blood. The world has shrunk to your bouncing headlights.

Your hands are on the steering wheel, but it's not your car. You don't know who owns the car.

The tall man sitting next to you, Bonay, red, wind-raw face, jutting forehead, drooping black mustache, jabs your knee again. Points past the yellow dust of the windshield to an Indian walking alongside the road, under the purple moon.

"Ask him! Ask this one, man!"

You pull over the car. As with the others, this one keeps walking. You creep the hood of the purple car forward, honking the horn.

Bonay leans out the window, lips parting to show his snaggled teeth. "Hey, partner! Partner! Will you help us a minute?"

The Indian shuffles over, hands in pockets, young, round-faced, long, straight black hair.

"My friends are looking for the Indian reservation. Do you know where the Indian reservation is at?"

The Indian shakes his head, hands still in his pockets. "No, man. I don't know."

"You're Indian, right?"

The young man grins, teeth missing. "Yeah, but I don't know."

You speed off. Bonay takes another swig from the bottle of whiskey wedged between his dungaree legs.

In the back seat, Gordon keeps weeping. Big hands over his face. Broad, old man's shoulders rocking as the car cuts a spray of dust down the cold roads outside town.

Up ahead, in the silent hush of night, a group of kids are trudging along the road. Throwing dirt at each other.

Bonay jabs your knee. "Ask these kids, man."

You pull the car off the side of the road, onto the spurning shoulder.

The kids look over, a half dozen of them. All on one side or the other of pubescence, all black-haired.

"Hey, you kids! How do we get to the Indian reservation?"

They look at each other, deciding who will answer. If anyone.

Bonay slips his hand around the inside latch of his passenger side door. "Hey you gangbangers, I'm talking to you. Show respect for your elders. Who knows how to get to the Indian reservation?"

No one answers.

Bonay pulls the bottle of whiskey out from his crotch. Leans his elbow on the sill of his passenger side window, holding the bottle up for the kids, waving it by its neck.

"I give a long drink of whiskey to know that. Hurry up and help us."

One of the boys, the smallest, heads over. "Why do you want to know?"

"Don't fuck with me, Junior. You know where that reservation is?"

The boy kicks up an explosion of yellow dirt. "How much whiskey you got in that bottle?"

"Shit, man, this bottle's three-quarters full. You drink all you want, but I hold the bottle. Now where's that fucking reservation?"

"Fuck you, man."

Bonay jerks up the handle, gets out, tall, loose-limbed. The kids start to run, but Bonay, lanky, is faster than any of them. He shoves the boy against the purple side of the car. "Where's it at, little pig man?"

The boy, frightened, looks for his friends, who stay out in the gray-green brush away from the road. Squinches his eyes, readying himself to be hit.

"You tell to me where it is, and you can drink all the whiskey you want, but I hold the bottle."

The boy opens his mouth.

"Wait a minute, wait a minute, little man. Whisper it into Bonay's ear."

The boy puts his small right hand against Bonay's ear, whispering.

"You did good, son. Maybe. Maybe, you did good." Bonay pulls his pistol out of his waistband, aims it at the oldest, a black-haired girl. "Come here."

The girl shakes her head.

"Come here to me or I fucking shoot you. You want to die, out here in the desert at night? The wolves will eat you. They'll go back up in the hills with little bits of your body and some of the buttons of your dress between their teeth."

The girl comes over, walking sideways.

"That's a good sweetheart for Bonay. Tell to me where the Indian reservation is, but don't look at your brother."

"He's not my brother."

"I don't give a fuck who he is. Tell to Bonay."

She twists her small hands in the dark air as she gives directions. "Go to Route 43 which is down there, it's about ten minutes, then turn right and go up into the mountains, until you get to the sign for Salado County, then turn left and keep driving."

"That's exactly what this little boy says. That's what he whispered to me." Bonay looks in the car's back seat, at Gordon. Gordon nods through his tears.

"Okay, my little accomplice. I'm going to hold the bottom end of this bottle, and you can drink all you can until you pull your mouth off the bottle. A deal's a deal."

You rocket the old purple car along Route 43 up into the black jaggedness of the mountains. The car's sides dip left, right, through the ruts.

The headlights sweep across the small sign for Salado County. You slam on the brakes, car fish-tailing in the dust, turn left.

"Those gangbangers were telling to us the truth," Bonay says, nodding his head, righteous. Out of the darkness rises the large, flat parking lot for the Money Wishing Casino and Entertainment Complex.

You park the car as close to the entrance as you can, in a fire lane.

Gordon, still weeping in the back seat, weakly waves a hand. He can't go in, you and Bonay must do this.

The two of you walk across the darkness of the dirt lot to the wide entrance. Giant orange and blue neon dice tumble perpetually above the double doors.

Inside, all the employees are in black tuxedoes, short black hair. Some of them look handsome. Bonay goes up to one of the large-nosed ones.

"Tell to me where I find Chief Black Foot."

The male employee smiles, black-eyed, looking at Bonay, looking at you. Elderly men and women in casual clothes, ranchers, wander around the slot machine aisles, bells ringing. "Do you know the Chief?"

"You bet I do. So where do I find this guy?"

"The Chief's not here."

"Where he be, then?"

"So how do you know him?"

Bonay gives out a hearty laugh, looks around under his jutting forehead.

Helps the doubled-over employee outside, away from the big pulsing dice, to the left, to dirt and darkness.

Bonay pulls out of his waistband a knife the size of his forearm. He leans his height against the tuxedoed employee. Breathes into his face, waits until he has the employee's dilated eyes. "Do you know how easy it is for me to be jabbing this knife up and up inside your asshole? I could be turning your asshole into a red asterisk, man, and the asterisk would refer down to a footnote that says this guy ain't never going to shit normal again, you know? This Chief Black Foot, he ain't gonna keep you in his employ if you're disfigured that way."

"The chief's not here."

"Okay, so where is the fucker?"

"He's home, man. He's in his home tonight."

"So where is his home at, fucker?"

"He lives down in the valley. He's on El Cuendo Drive. I don't know the number, but it's the last house there, a real hacienda. He's got cacti by the arch of his driveway. You can't miss it."

"Give me your driver's license."

"I don't have it on me, man."

"I'm gonna stick my big knife up your asshole, and then you won't be so fancy."

The tuxedoed employee hands over his driver's license.

"So let's look at this. It says here you're Peter Proud Hand and you live at 2394 Sebring Way in Gallup. I know where that is, Mister Rooster. I can drive there with just one hand on the steering wheel. Maybe, if this information you give to me is not correct, I take a Sunday drive over there and I tie you and your family up. I make you watch me fuck everybody in your family before I kill them in the bathtub, huh? I'm real messy, Pete. Do you want to change what you tell me?"

"That's the truth. I told you the truth. That's where the chief lives."

"We'll see about that. Meantime, I'm gonna keep this driver's license, and every time you wonder where your license is, and then you remember, you pray to your God you did tell me the truth, because the thing about me is, I can get very vindictive, even without alcohol or other drugs. You understand me, friend?"

"I do."

"I could be the breath of horror and chaos in your life, or I could be nothing more than a desert wind to you. But I never give second chances."

You speed the car out of the dirt parking lot. Head over the mountains again, rattling through the night down into the valley, swinging through the intersections, cruising dark and silent until you come to the street sign that reads, El Cuendo Drive.

The purple car glides down the paved road, past all the mailboxes.

The property at the end of the street has an arch made of adobe, tall, green cacti on either side.

Bonay pats the air next to him, telling you to stop.

He scurries out with wire cutters in his hand. A moment later you see him scrambling up the telephone pole above the entrance, snipping.

You pull the car up to the front door. It's almost midnight.

Gordon is still crying in the back seat. Bonay puts his large face inside the car. "This is it, Gordon."

You accompany Bonay to the tall front door. Carved wood. Bonay lifts the big brass knocker, bangs it several times.

Nothing.

Lifts it again, bang, bang, bang, bang.

A light goes on behind the stained glass transom above the entrance.

One of the two doors opens. A sleepy-eyed Mexican woman, white robe pulled around her.

"What you want?"

"I want Chief Black Foot."

"He not here."

"Bring him to me, Señorita."

"He not here. Good-bye."

She starts to close the door. Bonay leans against it, forcing it open.

He walks into the house, looking around, jutting forehead, lanky black mustache.

"I bet he's upstairs, in bed, counting his money."

"He not here!"

Bonay gets halfway up the curving stairs when Chief Black Foot appears at the top, in a nightgown, long black and gray hair disheveled. Leveling a shotgun at Bonay.

"Don't take another step!"

Bonay holds up his hands. "I always planned on stopping on this here step. Your first name is John, right?"

"Ramona, call the police."

"Ramona cannot call the police, John, because I cut all the telephone lines. Check and checkmate."

The chief goes down a couple of steps, still aiming the shotgun at the broad chest between Bonay's big, upraised hands. "What do you want?"

Bonay, keeping his hands up, walks backward down the staircase. "I need your cattle, John. I need to use your cattle for a night, to have them stampede."

The chief follows Bonay down the stairs, still squinting his eye behind the sight of the shotgun. "Why do you need my cattle?"

"Let's go to your bar and discuss this, John. It's a good story."

"I don't want to discuss nothing. I want you out of my house."

Bonay, still holding his hands up, dips his shoulders, looking through the different archways off the main hall. "It's a good story, John. You know what I think? I think your bar is in there." He starts walking through one of the archways, into the living room.

"Stop! Stop or I'll shoot you!"

"John, I don't think you're going to shoot a man who is doing nothing more than walking toward your bar. I'll meet you there."

Bonay continues into the living room, turning on lights. Floor lamps with tasseled shades, gooseneck lights snaking out from the walls, a circular halogen lamp that pops white light on his hand and wrist.

Sure enough, opposite the floor to ceiling fireplace, made of round native stones, pink and gray, there's a large, mahogany bar backed into a corner of the room, glass shelves behind holding bottles.

The chief follows Bonay into the living room. Still leveling his shotgun.

Bonay sits at one of the barstools. "I'd like a beer, John. Let's you and me sit like a couple of fellas drinking a beer together, and I'll tell you this whole sad story."

He gestures for you to settle into one of the many easy chairs facing the bar.

The chief lowers the shotgun. Red, wrinkled face surrounded by his uncombed black and gray hair appraising Bonay. "Do you think you can just walk into my home?"

"I have a reason to do it, John. I'm not here to rob you. I don't want to kill you."

"I'm the one with the shotgun."

"Sit on the other side of the bar, John. Let's you and me open a couple of Tecates, get some lemon slices going."

The chief walks behind the bar. Puts the shotgun sideways underneath. He pulls open the white door of the refrigerator, takes out two cans of Tecate, and a white plate of lemon slices. "I have a pistol back here too. You're a big one, but my bullets hit big ones, too. I killed three men in my life. I never went to prison. You could be number four."

Bonay uses the curved bottom of his beer can to crush a cockroach on the mahogany bar, popping off its head. The tiny black head keeps wriggling, as if still running. "They don't like the light, John. You need exterminators out here."

"What do you want?"

Bonay squeezes a lemon slice over the triangular opening in his can of Tecate. "In my car out front, I have my boss, Gordon, in the back seat. My boss is crying. He has been crying one full day, twenty-four hours."

"Why is he crying?"

"He's an old man now, but a rough and tumble man all his life. A deeply religious man. A rancher. He works the land for sixty years. Sometimes God is in the sky over his ranch, looking down, but most of the time, his ranch does not do well."

"Like everybody."

"So what keeps him going, Chief Black Foot? Why does he plow those furrows each winter? He has a wife, and he has a daughter, and he has a little granddaughter. His wife's name is Sarah, his daughter's name who they had late in life is Sarah also, and guess what, Chief? His granddaughter's got the same name. The three Sarahs. Big Sarah and Sarah and Little Sarah. Big Sarah, she sews all their clothes for them, mends his socks, makes little Sarah's Halloween costumes, stays with him through all the bad times, right? A man can last forever if he has the right woman, right?"

The Chief takes a swig of his beer, sunken black eyes watching Bonay. "You should have told me that forty years ago."

"Man to man, what's the worse of that arrangement, Chief? When Gordon was so young, and he first courted Big Sarah, he tried to impress her with how wonderful their future together would be. They'd be rich, living off his ranch. Get the new truck each year, and go to Europe eventually. Big Sarah went to college. She read Andre Gide and James Joyce and John Updike. 'We pattern our Heaven on bright butterflies, but it must be that even in earth Heaven lies. The worm we uproot in turning a spade returns, careful brute, to the peace he has made.' She recited that to me one day, Chief, on the front porch while she was serving us lunch. It impressed me about her. Not that she wrote it, which she hadn't, but that she had read it. Gordon never knew anybody that read poetry. That was like knowing someone who could make an elephant appear behind a handkerchief. She could have gone to a city, but she stayed here in New Mexico with him. And what she could have been, an editor at some magazine, a college professor, or maybe just a secretary who weeps over poetry at lunch, she gave all that up, to be with him.

"And over the years, it got harder and harder. She was a beautiful woman, maybe even a little vain when she was younger, brushing her hair every night, you know how that is, Chief, you look like you had a couple hair brushers yourself in your glorious youth, but she adjusted to the bad times. She had to have some teeth pulled, because Gordon couldn't afford to pay for crowns. She agreed to it, never complained. Still smiled just as wide, with those gaps showing. She was loyal. She saw what was, but she also saw what could have been, and she never blamed Gordon about that difference.

"Sometimes when Gordon and me were out working in the fields, getting those furrows deeper, that's hard work, right, Chief? Or mending his chicken wire fences up in the hills, and he'd get tired, and discouraged, and maybe have an existential moment like we all do, I'd see him bow his head a moment, sweat dripping off that thinning hair of his, then raise his head and keep on keeping on, and I knew that in that moment his head was bowed, he'd be thinking about Big Sarah back down there in the farmhouse, and that thought of her squared his shoulders.

"So here we got the perfect marriage, better than you or me wound up with, right, Chief? And one day the three of us are sitting on the front porch after dinner, Gordon and me aren't really talking, we're just looking out over the ranch, thinking about what we got to do tomorrow, and Big Sarah, she's in her rocking chair beside Gordon, she's white-haired by now, got her long white hair in a braid, and she's fallen asleep. I can tell she's asleep in her rocker because when she drifts off, her mouth opens. So it's time to go in, and Gordon, he leans over to gently wake his Big Sarah, right? And she's dead, Chief. Just like that. One moment, everything's the way it should be, and the next moment, that happy little world is gone forever. Gordon, he keeps trying to wake her up, very gently, but her head's going sideways this way and that, profile like a lioness, so I see that and know she's dead, but I have to tell him very carefully, and even then, he don't believe me at first, he keeps trying to wake her up, for them to go inside.

"He wanted to bury her on the ranch, where they lived their life, where he could go out there alone without seeing other people, and talk to her, but the town says you can't do that, Gordon. Your deceased wife got to be buried in the cemetery like everyone else."

"Someday somebody's gonna put a bullet smack in the foreheads of everyone in town who wears a suit, and it may not be an Indian who does that."

"You and me see eye to eye on that one, Chief. It may not even be a bullet. It may be a knife about the size of the one I showed you.

"So here's our Gordon, he's seventy-nine years old, he's a strong man, he helped build the Alaskan-Canadian Highway during World War II, he was at Contact Creek when the boys on both ends joined up, he's tough, his hands and back got scars all over, and here he is watching this long box get lowered down into the ground, and he knows his wife of fifty-five years is inside that box, and he knows once they get the box the way they like it down in that hole, these strangers are gonna throw dirt on top of it, shovel after shovel, until she's buried six feet under, and he's trying not to cry, just standing there with his big hands at his side, wondering what she's thinking inside that box as the dirt lands on the lid.

"Gordon doesn't drink, because he learned in his youth he was one of those men who can't control whiskey once they let that heat inside them, so he needs something else to keep him going. That something else is Sarah, his and Big Sarah's daughter. Now we're gonna talk about her a little bit.

"Sarah was home-schooled for the first eight grades by Big Sarah, but then when it got to high school time, Gordon and Big Sarah felt like Sarah should go to a regular school with the other rancher kids, so she'd fit better into the world. She's real smart in school, better than the other students they got there, with her mother's good looks, but Gordon, he couldn't afford new clothes for her, so Big Sarah made clothes. Bought some fabric through the mail, but some of the clothes she made from curtains and bed sheets. That was the problem. She was great with the needle, but you know yourself, Chief, it's not enough to have the needle. You got to have something to put the needle in.

"So Sarah, she's in that high school every day, maybe a little shy because she was home-schooled. All the girls there, they got jeans on and blouses in what passes for the latest style out here in the desert, but Sarah, she's got to wear the stuff her mom made, which is all old-fashioned dresses down to the knees. They look good, Chief, but maybe it's not what girls are wearing in high school now, right? So one day, there's Sarah sitting by herself at a table in the cafeteria, eating the lunch her mom made her, apple slices dipped in lemon juice, and a cold beef pot pie, and these girls sit down around her. One of the girls, whose daddy owns the gas station in town, so she's always got new clothes, she keeps trying to reach behind Sarah's head, laughing and rolling her eyes, and our poor Sarah, she's thinking maybe she's got a bug in her hair and this girl's trying to be helpful, right? Until the girl manages to peel down the back of Sarah's dress, and she sees there's no label there, like giving the manufacturer's name, or how you wash the dress. So these girls, they all start to call Sarah 'Kitchen Curtain Sarah'. They just whisper it at first, looking at her behind their hands, but soon enough, it's in the halls and on the bus. I don't think a person grows up until they lose that streak of cruelty from childhood.

"So Sarah, now she keeps to herself all the time, right? Doesn't go to the school dances no more, stalls around in the gym until all the other girls have left the showers, the whole cock-a-doodle. One day, she meets this new guy who just started at the school. He's a grade behind her, he's from a poor family just like her. They talk, pretty soon he's helping out at the ranch. He's not a handsome one like me, Chief, but he takes good care of her, looks out for her, gets into a couple of fist fights to defend her precious honor, loses almost all of them, but even so, we both know most big dogs, they don't want to fist fight, because even the winner gets hit, so after a while all the sports heroes leave him and her alone.

"You're an old man, Chief, but you still remember what happens when a young boy and girl fall in love, and they got a whole ranch full of hay lofts and sweet-smelling grass fields, the kind with yellow dandelions, right? So Sarah tells her mother she's pregnant. They have a little wedding right at the ranch, some pretty good pot roast afterward, and a dutch oven full of steamed potatoes. Three years later, he leaves her over some girl with a ring in her nostril who giggles a lot, a waitress at the luncheonette next to his work.

"Sarah's strong, her parents taught her that, so she cries, cries, cries to herself for a month or so, but keeps working, keeps raising that baby girl right, talking about maybe moving to a city some day, where there won't be as much prejudice held against her among the young eligible men for having a baby.

"And then one day, about a year after Big Sarah's death, Sarah gets a little red dot, about halfway down her back, and that dot just grows and grows. Gordon, he prays that it will go away. It doesn't. He tries soap on it, and some expensive ointment he sends away for, I say expensive but it was only a couple of dollars, expensive to him, when a couple of dollars could buy a big bag of fertilizer. None of that works. By the time he and Sarah finally go to the clinic, and they go there thinking this is just a minor annoyance, Chief, just one more thing to get through before going back to hoping life will turn around, the cancer has got its tentacles into so many organs inside her there is nothing they can do. Gordon let the corn and the strawberries go to seed that year, so he could buy painkillers for her. I worked for free, that Summer, but even then I didn't have nothing to do but sit on the front porch.

"So what do you think, Chief? Do you think Gordon's daughter miraculously recovered, or do you think she died?"

The Chief nurses his can of beer, both big hands around it. "Strangers only come to my house in the middle of the night because of death."

"That's right, Chief. She died in the bed in which she was born, right there on the ranch. Couldn't even talk with dignity to say her last words, because she was so full of dope."

"That's a sad story, but there's a lot of sad stories in the desert."

"What do you think keeps this man going after his wife's death and his daughter's death, Chief?"

"I don't know."

"You forgot about little Sarah, Chief. You're not paying attention."

"How old is this little Sarah?"

"Twelve years old. Eleven when her mom died. Death affects people in a lot of different ways, Chief, but nobody is more affected by death than a young daughter when her mother dies. You agree with me, Chief?"

"Does this Gordon need money for his daughter?"

"Gordon doesn't need money for nothing now, Chief. Let me tell you about little Sarah. She's at school when her mom died, so the bus lets her off out in front of the ranch at the end of the day and Gordon, his daughter's only dead an hour, he has to walk down that long, dirt driveway to meet his little granddaughter to tell her her mother's dead. Only he doesn't need to say a word, she sees the tears on his face, she looks puzzled, then she lets out a cry, she lets out this terrible cry, it's too big a cry for a little girl, a cry that big shouldn't come out of her until she's forty or fifty, and she curls down in the dirt, sobbing and shaking. Gordon has to stoop over and gather up her books for her, bring her back to the house, her clinging to him, crying that suffocating way a child cries.

"Gordon gets the local funeral director to do the job for free, in exchange for Gordon putting a new roof on the man's house, and laying down a paved driveway for the man. Gordon builds his daughter's casket himself, because he don't have no money. And they bury her.

"But Gordon, he stands as straight as he can, for their little granddaughter. They talk to each other every evening, by the fireplace, about remember this, and remember when we did that, and they cry and hug each other, trying to keep her memory alive, trying to use the memories of the good times to get them through this, right? They are like two animals out in the desert night, huddling against each other to stay warm."

"They're lucky to have each other. There's good luck in bad luck."

Bonay wipes his eyes. "Tell that to Gordon when you meet him, Chief. Because last night his granddaughter died."

The Chief crushes his empty beer can, says nothing.

"Gordon and me, we were out gathering wood last evening, because it's been so cold this Winter. We get back in time to meet little Sarah when she gets dropped off by the school bus, so she doesn't have to walk into that big, quiet ranch house alone, only the bus just drives past Gordon's driveway. It doesn't stop.

"Gordon and I look at each other. That's the scary thing about death, Chief. It always tells you when it's come back, but it always does it in a way you never expected. Not like howling winds, or a mirror that drops, right? But some weird way of its own, like that school bus not slowing down as it went past us.

"Gordon calls the school and they say little Sarah decided to walk home. On a cold night like last night? And she's only twelve?

"But last night was her mother's birthday.

"We found her about two o'clock in the morning. Down by the pond behind Gordon's property. Why was she there?" Bonay shrugs. "Last year, when her mother was still alive, she and little Sarah and Gordon went to that same pond this same time of year, and there were snapdragons in bloom along its shore. That's unusual. What I think, maybe she went back there, on her mother's birthday, to see if the snapdragons had returned, to pick some to bring home for the kitchen table. And maybe she got confused, in the cold and the darkness, and stepped across the pond thinking she was still on solid ground."

Bonay crushes his own beer can. "Where she fell in, it didn't make that big a hole in the ice. But maybe the shock of the cold she fell into confused her some more, or maybe it was so cold in the slush of the pond it numbed her too quickly, before she could try to climb out. When your hands get red and numb, especially if you're a little girl, you don't have the strength no more to pull yourself out, before your body gets too cold, and the heat goes out."

"What does this friend of yours, Gordon, want?"

"Gordon wants to get his granddaughter out of that pond. He wants to hold her against him, and talk to her. He wants to think of himself taking her home. Laying her in her bed, where it's warm, not cold and dark and underwater and frightening and lonely.

"The mind knows how to torture itself. It knows where to look inside for the rack and the whips, and Gordon, his mind is no different. After the shock, and the grief, I see him sitting at the kitchen table, with the three empty chairs, and I know he's going to that place inside for his torture. After Sarah died, Gordon was walking with little Sarah one day last Summer, out behind the barn, explaining to her about butterflies, and darn if little Sarah didn't step on the tines of a rake, and stepping on it like that, it tilted the handle of the rake up fast as a snake, to where that wooden handle smacked little Sarah right in the middle of her face. Now she had a happy look on her face just before, her granddaddy telling her about butterflies, but the disoriented look she gets on her face right after she gets smacked by that rake, that's all Gordon sees now, it's what he replays over and over in his mind, he can't get it out of his mind, because he figures that smacked look must have been the look she had just as she collapsed through the ice surface of the pond. The happy look of searching around for snapdragons, maybe feeling her mom near, then that smacked look as she dropped into that cold blackness."

"It's a sad story, man. But what can I do? Do you want me to help dig her out?"

Bonay shakes his head. "Nobody's digging her out. The ice has set. We tried, with pickaxes. That pond's made of stone now, and it won't thaw until next year. Gordon isn't going to leave his granddaughter in that frozen pond until then, her face just below the surface, her two arms sticking up in the air. We were chasing the birds away from those exposed arms. We were chasing big, black crows away."

"So what do you want me to do, man?"

Bonay straightens up on his stool. "You're going to put on an overcoat and come with us to your ranch in the valley, Chief. You're going to get your men to release your cattle. The four of us are going to drive those cows over the hill to that pond, and onto that pond, so their weight breaks the ice, and Gordon's little granddaughter floats free."

The chief says nothing, staring back with his old face at Bonay. He tosses his crumpled beer can in a white waste basket behind the bar. "Tell this Gordon I am sorry about his granddaughter. Tell him I could get some men together to try to dig her out, but you say that won't work. So I can't do anything to help you. But I will pray for her soul tonight."

Bonay pulls out his knife, long as his forearm.

The Chief lifts a revolver from under the bar. Points it at Bonay's chest. "You finished your beer, friend. I want to go back to bed now."

Bonay shakes his head. "I would do anything for Gordon. You're coming with me, Chief. Guess to yourself how fast my hands are."

Bonay leads the chief out to the purple car, its engine still running.

He steers the chief by the old man's shoulders down into the driver's seat, behind the wheel.

Getting in himself, on the passenger side, Bonay twists around to Gordon, the black and red bloom of a bullet hole in Bonay's left shoulder. "We're on schedule, Gordon. Start driving, Chief."

The chief keeps his hands in his lap. "No."

Bonay pulls out his long knife, pushes the top two inches through the Chief's overcoat, through his nightshirt, pushes it between two ribs, pushes it into the cavity of the chief's chest. The chief sits up, sucking air in, rapidly.

"Start driving, Chief."

The chief, bleeding a dark red out of his right side, puts his left hand on the wheel, right hand on the shift to go into reverse. "Maybe a couple of days from now we're going to reverse this situation. I take you for a ride in my pickup, with a couple of my boys in back, off the road and out into the desert where there's only scorpions and the sun."

Bonay leans his tall body against the chief, knife blade riding between those ribs. "Maybe I'm on a road you don't got the shoes to walk down, chief. There is a terrible machine that has been started up, and I don't approve of this machine, but we got to let its pistons and pendulums take us to where Gordon wants to be."

The Chief doesn't have an answer.

Bonay starts singing as the purple car hurtles toward the chief's ranch in the valley.

> Brother, Sister,
> It's mystical, magical
> It's monstrosity-filled
> It's a moon in the night over a corn field
> It's a minute of madness
> It's a monkey in a mansion
> It's melons outside a monastery
> It's a mouse munching cheese in a maze
> It's a nun who eats pickles for a nickel

The chief turns toward you, old hands grasping the wheel. "What's your part in this rumble-dumble?"

You say nothing.

The chief tries to tenderly adjust himself in his seat around the knife blade stuck in his ribs. He looks at you again. "I can smell my own deodorant. I hate that smell."

Around four in the morning, the purple car slows down at the entrance to the Chief's cattle ranch.

A red and white striped barricade floats across the entry.

An Indian comes out of the boxed light of the guard booth. Blinking his eyes. Bonay slides another wide inch of knife between the chief's ribs. The chief sits up even straighter, farting, letting out into the seat of his pants a pool of hot diarrhea.

The guard walks over, holding an unlit flashlight.

He lowers his broad face to the opened driver's side window. Wide nose, black hair. Switches his dark eyes around, looking into the interior. Takes in the chief at the wheel. Bonay snuggled next to the chief. You sitting by the passenger side door. Gordon weeping in the back seat.

"You're here late, Chief Black Foot."

The chief lolls his head toward the rolled-down window. "I'm selling these will o' the wisps some cattle. Raise the barrier for me, and you can go home. Sneak into bed with your wife and wake her up."

The guard grins at the chief. Crunches over to the barricade. Manually raises the long, flimsy striped post.

"You sure you don't need me, Chief Black Foot?"

The chief closes his eyes, shakes his head. "You go home. They give you a heater in there?"

The guard looks back at the lit booth. "No, sir."

"I'm gonna get you a heater. It's too cold to stand in there all night."

The four of you drive down the long dirt road, through the tunnel of night. In the dark distance, but you can't tell exactly where, rises up a cow's solitary bellow.

As you get near, the drawn-out moo sounds erupt more frequently, from dozens of stretched throats.

The ripe smell of the cattle starts filling the car.

"It's right up here."

The headlights wash across horizontal fence rails, a chicken wire gate. Around the headlights' periphery, dark shapes shamble.

The chief stops the car. Pulls up the handbrake. "I got some prize steers in there. You don't need them."

Bonay steps out of the car, tall and wiry, shrinking his nose at the smell. "How many cows you got that aren't steers?"

The chief stands up out of the driver's seat in his dark overcoat and white night-gown, holding the wound in his right side. "Hundred and thirty, maybe a hundred and forty."

"That's enough." Bonay switches his head around, squinting his eyes. "How many trucks you got here, Chief?"

"Just that one on the side."

"That the one you gonna give me my Sunday drive in?"

"That's it."

"That's a nice pickup for a Sunday drive. All gleamy. Probably got a nice heater inside, I hope. But tonight, you and me are gonna ride in that truck alone, Chief. Same arrangement as before, you driving, only this time I don't stick my big knife in you, unless you want me to."

Bonay gestures for you to get back in the purple car, behind the steering wheel.

"What I want for you to do is this. I am going to go into the corral and start slapping the rumps of these cows, get them shuffling out of the pen. Once they're all out, then you start herding them with your car up over that hill there, just like I'm gonna do with the pick-up. We get them over the hill, then we bully them down into the valley, to the pond. We get to the pond, the first few are gonna go out over that ice no problem, but then the rest of the herd, they see the front lines sinking in the ice, they're gonna rear up. That's when you got to start ramming those timid cows with the bumper of your car. Bang them hard enough to force them to move forward, out over the ice, but don't bang them so hard you cripple their back legs, or kill them. I don't want to be dragging dead cows to the pond. They're heavy."

Through your windshield, you see Bonay open the chicken wire fence, all the way wide. He wades into the shifting herd, bumping past heads and rumps, looking down to avoid the piles of cow dung. Works toward the rear of the enclosure. Once there, a tiny figure, you watch as his right hand smacks down on the cows' rumps, a disproportionately loud sound in the night, then left hand, right hand, then punching them, pushing them.

The first few cows exit through the opened gate, mooing, dipping their heads down, foraging for grass. They get bumped from behind by the next wave of cows. Some of the first cows turn sideways, others trot heavily a few yards away from the increasing crowd. One stands off by itself, shit dribbling down from underneath its tail.

The cows exit slowly at first. But after about half of them are outside the pen, the remaining ones quickly rush out, spilling around the gate. One ambles over to your car, long pink tongue tasting the side mirror.

Bonay, shutting the chicken wire gate behind him on the now-empty corral, takes off his shirt, wipes his chest with it, his arms, wandering cows banging against him, puts his shirt back on. He grabs the chief's arm, helps him to the pickup.

You back the car up. Twist the steering wheel to get behind the herd. This is the first time you've been alone in the car with Gordon. You look up into the rearview mirror. He's not watching any of this. His hands are in his lap, head bowed, still crying.

You hear a honk.

The pickup jerks forward, aiming at the rumps of the nearest cows, bumping them. They start shambling forward, mooing.

You get behind the other side of the herd, bang a bit roughly against their tails. Brake. Back up. Bump them again.

A few stragglers trot away sideways.

Reverse, swing the car ahead of them. Reverse, twist the steering wheel toward their sides. Brake. Give it some gas, collide against the cows' ribs. Brake. Heads down, they waddle back into the herd.

The cattle drive up the hill is slow, tedious. You hear Bonay on the other side of the herd, swearing at the cows as his gears grind back and forth between reverse and forward.

It takes an hour to get most of the herd up over the crest of the hill, and started down the other side. About a dozen escape, wandering back down the slope, and one is on its side, next to a tree, dying, because you hit it too hard, but Bonay doesn't go back for those stragglers, so you don't, either.

Pausing in your car on the top of the hill, you look down into the valley. There it is, about a mile from here, the small stand of bare trees, the large, dark oval of the pond in its center.

Even though it's after five in the morning by now, the sky is overcast, so the rising sun is dim, diffused in the low gray clouds.

Herding the cattle down the hill is much easier, because of gravity. You find you don't have to collide against the cows anymore to keep them tightly together. It's enough to ride up alongside one that looks like it might bolt, and keep honking your horn.

But at the bottom of the hill, the front of the herd tries to spill sideways across the valley. You in your car, Bonay in his pickup, are back to grinding gears, shaping the front of the cattle drive again, funneling it toward those bare trees.

Your forearms are getting tired from steering the tires through the wet grass and mud. But you can't stop.

The front of the herd merges into the trees, rubbing their ribbed sides against the tree trunks. The bare tops of the trees shake.

The herd crackles over the black branches that have broken off, fallen to the ground during the winter freezes. One cow among the black tree trunks rears up, eyes wild, bellowing. Its hoof must be caught. The undulating backs of the other cows knock it over, out of sight, trundling over its screams.

"I'll get out, here."

You look up into the rear view mirror. It's Gordon talking. The first time you hear him speak. His voice surprisingly mild, well-educated.

You brake the old purple car.

Gordon leans forward, face wet. Jerks up the handle to the left rear door.

His legs are unsteady at first. How long had he been sitting in that back seat?

The herd clops out noisily across the pond.

A few cows slip, scream as others clop over them.

At first, it looks like the ice will hold. Then pops, cracking sounds. Three cows drop down under the surface. Zig-zags crackle across. A huge, jagged section of ice tilts up whitely toward the bare treetops. Cattle slide down its plane, landing on their heavy sides in the black water.

Gordon is stumbling along the shore of the pond, arms out, blowing kisses at the pond's far side.

You see the two small red arms jutting up from their elbows out of the ice.

More cows plow forward into the cold water, walking and slipping on the backs of the drowning ones beneath them. Twenty cow heads whipping around above water, forelegs paddling uselessly, nostrils shooting vapor. Mouths bellowing, gurgling.

Gordon steps across the ice at the far end, still crying, his tall, board-shouldered, old man's body staggering past the crashes and bellows toward his granddaughter's forearms.

Where's Bonay? Why doesn't he warn Gordon to wait until it's safe, until the chaos has subsided?

Even more cattle piles into the black pond. Stampeding through the floes, over the bodies of those dead on the pond's bottom. Climbing over the dead, clacking their front hooves on the remaining section of ice, hauling up onto it, shaking their bodies like huge, shaved dogs.

The remaining ice splits thunderously apart.

Gordon pitches forward, hands instinctively out to break his fall.

Slips under. Slips down into the world of his granddaughter, cold, black, lonesome.

You watch his body glide facedown around the drowning cattle. Wonder if he's dead, or if his arms will start swinging, to swim toward his granddaughter's forearms. You watch his body glide under the water long enough to know his arms aren't going to move. His feet aren't going to kick.

The ice around the granddaughter's forearms breaks up. The forearms fall over, sliding separately away, across the erupting white ice. Beneath them, the little body, freed, blurs down into the darkness.

The chief is sitting on the ground, back propped against the pick-up's front tire, holding his side, watching. Coughing.

Bonay stands next to you. He raises his voice to be heard over the cries of the cows, the snapping of the ice. He's crying. "Gordon asked for me to put this terrible machine into motion for him, and we both knew without speaking of it why this machine was built, and where it would take him, but I would do anything for him. He couldn't do it himself, not unless it was an accident. Be in peace, Gordon. I did your favor."

Amid the rage within the pond, cows struggling to keep their nostrils afloat, ice snapping apart, the body of Gordon, facedown, arms spread, like a statue, floats silently toward the blackness at the bottom.

CHUCK PALAHNIUK

Hot Potting

*Chuck Palahniuk is of French and Russian descent but his last name is from
the Ukraine. He won recognition with his first novel* Fight Club, *which was
later made into a film. He has since gained greater popularity with the subsequent books* Survivor, Invisible Monsters, Choke, Lullaby, *and* Diary.

*He has also written a travel book about his hometown Portland, Oregon
entitled* Fugitives & Refugees, *and a collection called* Stranger Than Fiction: True Stories. *He lives in Washington State.*

*"Hot Potting" is, if possible, even more gruesome than his story "Guts"
from last year's volume of* The Year's Best Fantasy and Horror, *so readers
beware. It was originally published in his book,* Haunted: A Novel in Stories.

—E.D.

C ome February nights," Miss Leroy used to say, "and every drunk driver was a
blessing."

Every couple looking for a second honeymoon to patch up their marriage. People falling asleep at the steering wheel. Anybody who pulled off
the highway for a drink, they were somebody Miss Leroy could maybe talk into renting a room. It was half her business, talking. To keep people buying another next
drink, and another, until they had to stay.

Sometimes, sure, you're trapped. Other times, Miss Leroy would say, you just sit
down for what turns out to be the rest of your life.

Rooms there at the Lodge, most people, they expect better. The iron bed frames
teeter, the rails and footboards worn where they notch together. The nuts and bolts,
loose. Upstairs, every mattress is lumpy as foothills, and the pillows are flat. The
sheets are clean, but the well water up here, it's hard. You wash anything in this water, and the fabric feels sandpaper-rough with minerals and smells of sulfur.

The final insult is, you have to share a bathroom down the hall. Most folks don't
travel with a bathrobe, and this means getting dressed just to take a leak. In the morning, you wake up to a stinking sulfur bath in a white-cold cast-iron claw-foot tub.

It's a pleasure for her to herd these February strangers toward the cliff. First, she
shuts off the music. A full hour before she even starts talking, she turns down the
volume, a notch every ten minutes, until Glen Campbell is gone. After traffic turns
to nothing going by on the road outside, she turns down the heat. One by one, she
pulls the string that snaps off each neon beer sign in the window. If there's been a
fire in the fireplace, Miss Leroy will let it burn out.

All this time, she's herding, asking what plans these people have. February on the White River, there's less than nothing to do. Snowshoe, maybe. Cross-country ski, if you bring your own. Miss Leroy lets some guest bring up the idea. Everybody gets around to this same suggestion.

And if they don't, then she brings up the notion of hot potting.

Her stations of the cross. She walks her audience through the road map of her story. First she shows herself, how she looked most of her life ago, twenty years old and out of college for the summer, car camping up the White River, begging for a summer job, what back then was the dream job, tending bar here at the Lodge.

It's hard to imagine Miss Leroy skinny. Her skinny with white teeth, before her gums started to pull back. Before the way they look now, the brown root of each tooth exposed, the way carrots will crowd each other out of the ground if you plant the seed too close together. It's hard to imagine her voting Democrat. Even liking other people. Miss Leroy without the dark shadow of hair across her top lip. It's hard to imagine college boys waiting an hour in line to fuck her.

It makes her seem honest, saying something funny and sad like that, about her-self.

It makes people listen.

If you hugged her now, Miss Leroy says, all you'd feel is the pointy wire of her bra.

Hot potting, she says, is, you get a gang of kids together and hike up the fault side of the White River. You pack in your own beer and whiskey and find a hot-springs pool. Most pools stand between 150 and 200 degrees, year-round. Up at this eleva-tion, water boils at 198 degrees Fahrenheit. Even in winter, at the bottom of a deep icy pit, the side of snowdrifts sloping into them, these pools are hot enough to boil you alive.

No, the danger wasn't bears, not here. You wouldn't see wolves or coyote or bob-cat. Downriver, yes, just one click away on your odometer, just one radio song down the highway, the motels had to chain their garbage cans shut. Down there, the snow was busy with paw prints. The night was noisy with packs howling at the moon. But here, the snow was smooth. Even the full moon was quiet.

Upriver from the Lodge, all you had to worry about was being scalded to death. City kids, dropped out of college, some stay around a couple years. Some way, they pass down the okay about which pools are safe and where to find them. Where not to walk, there's only a thin crust of calcium or limestone sinter that looks like bedrock but will drop you through to deep-fry in a hidden thermal vent.

The scare stories, they pass along also. A hundred years back, a Mrs. Lester Ban-nock, here visiting from Crystal Falls, Pennsylvania, she stopped to wipe the steam from her smoked glasses. The breeze shifted, blowing hot steam in her eyes. One wrong step, and she was off the path. Another wrong step, and she lost her balance, landing backward, sitting in water scalding hot. Trying to stand, she pitched forward, landing facedown in the water. Screaming, she was hauled out by strangers.

The sheriff who raced her into town, he requisitioned every drop of olive oil from the kitchen at the Lodge. Coated in oil and wrapped in clean sheets, she died in a hospital, still screaming, three days later.

Recent as three summers ago, a kid from Pinson City, Wyoming, he parked his pickup truck and out jumped his German shepherd. The dog splashed dead center, jumping into a pool, and yelped itself to death mid–dog paddle. The tourists chew-ing their knuckles, they told the kid, don't, but he dove in.

He surfaced just once, his eyes boiled white and staring. Rolling around blind. No one could touch him long enough to grab hold, and then he was gone.

The rest of that year, they dipped him out with nets, the way you'd clean leaves and dead bugs out of a swimming pool. The way you'd skim the fat off a pot of stew.

At the Lodge bar, Miss Leroy would pause to let people see this a moment in their heads. The bits of him left all summer skittering around in the hot water, a batch of fritters spitting to a light brown.

Miss Leroy would smoke her cigarette.

Then, like this is something she's just remembered, she'd say, "Olson Read." And she'd laugh. Like this is something she doesn't think about part of every minute, every hour she's awake, Miss Leroy will say, "You should've met Olson Read."

Big, fat, virtuous, sin-free Olson Read.

Olson was a cook at the Lodge, fat and pale white, his lips too big, blown up with blood and squirming red as sushi against the sticky-rice-white skin of his face. He watched those hot pools. The way he'd kneel beside them all day, watching it, the bubbling brown froth, hot as acid.

One wrong step. One quick slide down the wrong side of a snowdrift, and just hot water would do to you what Olson did to food.

Poached salmon. Stewed chicken and dumplings. Hard-boiled eggs.

In the Lodge kitchen, Olson used to sing hymns so loud you could hear them in the dining room. Olson, huge in his flapping white apron, the ties knotted and cutting into his thick, deep waist, he sat in the bar, reading his Bible in the almost-dark. The beer-and-smoke smell of the dark-red carpet. If he joined your table in the staff break room, Olson bowed his head to his chest and said a rambling blessing over his baloney sandwich.

His favorite verb was "fellowship."

A night when Olson walked into the pantry and found Miss Leroy kissing a bellhop, just some liberal-arts dropout from NYU, Olson Read told them kissing was the devil's first step to fornication. With his rubbery red lips, Olson told everyone he was saving himself for marriage, but the truth was, he couldn't give himself away.

To Olson, the White River was his Garden of Eden, the proof his God did beautiful work.

Olson watched the hot springs, the geysers and steaming mud pots, the way every Christian loves the idea of hell. The way every Eden had to have its snake. He watched the scalding water steam and spit, the same way he'd peek through the order window and watch the waitresses in the dining room.

On his day off, he'd carry his Bible through the woods, through the clouds and fog of sulfur. He'd be singing "Amazing Grace" or "Nearer My God to Thee," but only the fifth or sixth verses, the parts so strange and unknown you might think he made them up. Walking on the sinter, the thin crust of calcium that forms the way ice sets up on water, Olson would step off the boardwalk and kneel at the deep edge of a spitting, stinking pool. Kneeling there, he'd pray out loud for Miss Leroy and the bellhop. He'd pray to his Lord, our God Almighty, Maker of Heaven and Earth. He'd pray for the immortal soul of each busboy by name. He'd inventory the sins of each hotel maid out loud. Olson's voice rising with the steam, he prayed for Nola, who pinned up the hem of her skirt too high and committed the act of oral sex with any hotel guest willing to cut loose a twenty-dollar bill. The tourist families standing back, safe on the boardwalk behind him, Olson begged mercy for the dining-room waiters, Evan and Leo, who assaulted each other with lewd acts of sodomy every night in the men's dorm. Olson wept and shouted about Dewey and Buddy, who breathed glue from a brown paper bag while they washed the dishes.

There at the gates of his hell, Olson yelled opinions into the trees and sky. Making his report to God, Olson walked out after the dinner shift and shouted your sins at the stars so bright they bled together in the night. He begged for God's mercy on your behalf.

No, nobody very much liked Olson Read. Nobody any age likes a tattletale.

They'd all heard the stories about the woman wrapped in olive oil. The kid cooked to soup with his dog. And Olson especially would listen, his eyes bright as candy. This was proof of everything he held dear. The truth of this. Proof you can't hide what you've done from God. You can't fix it. We'd be awake and alive in Hell, but hurting so bad we'd wish we could die. We'd spend all eternity suffering, someplace no one in the world would trade us to be.

Here, it would be, Miss Leroy would stop talking. She'd light a new cigarette. She'd draw you another beer.

Some stories, she'd say, the more you tell them, the faster you use them up. Those kind, the drama burns off, and every version, they sound more silly and flat. The other kind of story, it uses you up. The more you tell it, the stronger it gets. Those kind of stories only remind you how stupid you were. Are. Will always be.

Telling some stories, Miss Leroy says, is committing suicide.

It's here that she'd work hard to make the story boring, saying how water heated to 158 degrees Fahrenheit causes a third-degree burn in one second.

The typical thermal feature along the White River Fault is a vent that opens to a pool crusted around the edge with a layer of that crystallized mineral. The average temperature of thermal features along the White River being 205 degrees Fahrenheit.

One second in water this hot, and pulling your socks off will pull off your feet. The cooked skin of your hands will stick to anything you touch and stay behind, perfect as a pair of leather gloves.

Your body tries to save itself by shifting fluid to the burn, to dissipate the heat. You sweat, dehydrating faster than the worst case of diarrhea. Losing so much fluid your blood pressure drops. You go into shock. Your vital organs shut down in rapid succession.

Burns can be first-degree, second-, third-, or fourth-degree. They can be superficial, partial-thickness, or full-thickness burns. In superficial or first-degree burns, the skin turns red without blistering. Think of a sunburn and the subsequent desquamation of necrotic tissue—the dead, peeling skin. In full-thickness, third-degree burns, you get the dry, white leather look of a knuckle that bumps the top heating element when you take a cake out of the oven. In fourth-degree burns, you're cooked worse than skin deep.

To determine the extent of a burn, the medical examiner will use the "Rule of Nines." The head is 9 percent of the body's total skin. Each arm is 9 percent. Each leg is 18 percent. The torso front and back are each 18 percent. One percent for the neck, and you get the whole 100 percent.

Swallowing even a mouthful of water this hot causes massive edema of the larynx and asphyxial death. Your throat swells shut, and you choke to death.

It's poetry to hear Miss Leroy spin this out. Skeletonization. Skin slippage. Hypokalemia. Long words that take everybody in the bar to safe abstracts, far, far away. It's a nice little break in her story, before facing the worst.

You can spend your whole life building a wall of facts between you and anything real.

A February just like this, most of her life ago, Miss Leroy and Olson, the cook, were the only people in the Lodge that night. The day before dropped three feet of new snow, and the plows hadn't come through yet.

The same as every night, Olson Read takes his Bible in one fat hand and goes tramping off into the snow. Back then, they had coyotes to worry about. Cougar and bobcat. Singing "Amazing Grace" for a mile, never repeating a verse, Olson tramps off, white against the white snow.

The two lanes of Highway 17, lost under snow. The neon sign saying *The Lodge* in green neon, free-standing on a steel pole anchored in concrete with a low brick planter around the base of it. The outside world, like every night, is moonlight black and blue, the forest just dark pine-tree shapes stretched up.

Young and thin, Miss Leroy never gave Olson Read a second thought. Never realized how long he was gone until she heard the wolves start to howl. She was looking at her teeth, holding a polished butter knife so she could see how straight and white her teeth looked. She was used to hearing Olson shout each night. His voice shouting her name followed by a sin, real or imagined, it came from the woods. She smoked cigarettes, Olson shouted. She slow-danced. Olson screamed at God on her behalf.

Telling the story now, she'll make you tweeze the rest out of her. The idea of her trapped here. Her soul in limbo. Nobody comes to the Lodge planning to stay the rest of their life. Hell, Miss Leroy says, there's things you see happen worse than getting killed.

There's things that happen, worse than a car accident, that leave you stranded. Worse than breaking an axle. When you're young. And you're left tending bar in some little noplace for the rest of your life.

More than half her life ago, Miss Leroy hears the wolves howl. The coyotes yip. She hears Olson screaming, not her name or any sin, but just screaming. She goes to the dining-room side door. She steps outside, leaning out over the snow, and turns her head sideways to listen.

She smells Olson before she can see him. It's the smell of breakfast, of bacon frying in the cold air. The smell of bacon or Spam, sliced thick and hissing crisp in its own hot fat.

At this point in her story, the electric wall heater always comes on. That moment, the moment the room's got as cold as it can get, Miss Leroy knows that moment, can feel it make the hair stand up on her top lip. She knows when to stop a second. To leave a little way of quiet, and then—voom—the rush and wail of warm air out of the heater. The fan makes a low moan, far away at first, then up-close loud. Miss Leroy makes sure the barroom's dark by now. The heater comes on, the low moan of it, and people look up. All they can see in the window is their own reflection. Their own face not recognized. Looking inside at them is a pale mask full of dark holes. The mouth is a hanging-open dark hole. Their own eyes, two close-together staring black holes through to the night behind them.

The cars parked just outside, they look a hundred cold miles away. Even the parking lot looks too far to walk in this kind of dark.

The face of Olson Read, when she found him, his neck and head, this last 10 percent of him was still perfect. Beautiful even, compared to the peeling, boiled-food rest of his body.

Still screaming. As if the stars give a shit. This something left of Olson, dragging itself down this side of the White River, it stumbled, knees wobbly, staggering and coming apart.

There were parts of Olson already gone. His legs, below his knees, cooked and drug off over the broken ice. Bit and pulled off, the skin first and then the bones, the blood so cooked inside there's nothing going off behind him but a trail of his own grease. His heat melting deep in the snow.

The kid from Pinson City, Wyoming, the kid who jumped in to save his dog. Folks say that when the crowd pulled him out his arms popped apart, joint by joint, but he was still alive. His scalp peeled back off his white skull, but he was still awake.

The surface of the seething water, it spit hot and sparkling rainbow colors from the kid's rendered fat, the grease of him floating on the surface.

The kid's dog boiled down to a perfect dog-shaped fur coat, its bones already cooked clean and settling into the deep geothermal center of the world, the kid's last words were, "I fucked up. I can't fix this. Can I?"

That's how Miss Leroy found Olson Read that night. But worse.

The snow behind him, the fresh powder all around him, it was cut with drool.

All around his screams, fanned out around behind him, Miss Leroy could see a swarm of yellow eyes. The snow stamped down to ice in the prints of coyote feet. The four-toe prints of wolf paws. Floating around him were the long skull faces of wild dogs. Panting behind their own white breath, their black lips curled up along the ridge of each snout. Their little-root teeth meshed together, tight, tugging back on the rags of Olson's white pants, the shredded pants legs still steaming from what's boiled alive inside.

The next heartbeat, the yellow eyes are gone and what's left of Olson is what's left. Snow kicked up by back feet, it still sparkles in the air.

The two of them, in the warm cloud of bacon smell, Olson pulsed with heat, a big baked potato sinking deeper into the snow beside her. His skin was crusted now, puckered and rough as fried chicken, but loose and slippery on top of the muscle underneath, the muscle twisting, cooked, around the core of warm bone.

His hands clamped tight around her, around Miss Leroy's fingers, when she tried to pull away, his skin tore. His cooked hands stuck, the way your lips freeze to the flagpole on the playground in cold weather. When she tried to pull away, his fingers split to the bone, baked and bloodless inside, and he screamed and gripped Miss Leroy tight.

He was too heavy to move. Sunk there in the snow.

She was anchored there, the side door to the dining room only twenty footprints away in the snow. The door was still open, and the tables inside set for the next meal. Miss Leroy could see the dining room's big stone mountain of a fireplace, the logs burning inside. She could watch, but it was too far away to feel. She swam with her feet, kicking, trying to drag Olson, but the snow was too deep.

Instead of moving, she stayed, hoping he would die. Praying to God to kill Olson Read before she froze. The wolves watching with their yellow eyes from the dark edge of the forest. The pine-tree shapes going up into the night sky. The stars above them, bleeding together.

That night, Read Olson told her a story. His own private ghost story.

When we die, these are the stories still on our lips. The stories we'll only tell strangers, someplace private in the padded cell of midnight. These important stories, we rehearse them for years in our head but never tell. These stories are ghosts, bringing people back from the dead. Just for a moment. For a visit. Every story is a ghost. This story is Olson's.

Melting snow in her mouth, Miss Leroy spit the water into Olson's fat red lips, his face the only part of him that she could touch without getting stuck. Kneeling there beside him. The devil's first step to fornication. That kiss, the moment Olson had saved himself for.

For most of her life, she never told anyone what he yelled. Holding this inside was such a burden. Now she tells everyone, and it's no better.

That boiled, sad thing up the White River, it screamed, "Why did you do this?" It screamed, "What did I do?"

"Timber wolves," Miss Leroy says, and she laughs. We don't have that trouble. Not here, she says. Not anymore.

How Olson died, it's called myoglobulinaria. In extensive burns, the burned muscles release the protein myoglobulin. This flood of protein into the bloodstream overwhelms each kidney. The kidneys shut down, and the body fills with fluid and blood toxins. Renal failure. Myoglobulinaria. When Miss Leroy says these words, she could be a magician doing a trick. They could be a spell. An incantation.

This way to die takes all night.

The next morning, the snow plow came through. The driver found them: Olson Read dead and Miss Leroy asleep. From melting snow in her mouth all night, her gums were patched with white Frostbite. Read's dead hands were still locked around hers, protecting her fingers, warm as a pair of gloves. For weeks, the frozen skin around the base of each tooth, it peeled away, soft and gray from the brown root, until her teeth looked the way they do. Until her lips were gone.

Desquamating necrotic tissue. Another magic spell.

There's nothing out in the woods, Miss Leroy would tell people. Nothing evil. It's just something so sad and alone. It's Olson Read not knowing, still, what he did wrong. Not knowing where he's at. So terrible and alone, even the wolves, the coyotes are gone from up that end of the White River.

That's how a scary story works. It echoes some ancient fear. It recreates some forgotten terror. Something we'd like to think we've grown beyond. But it can still scare us to tears. It's something you'd hoped was healed.

Every night's scattered with them. These wandering people who can't be saved but won't die. You can hear them at night, screaming out there, up this side of the White River Fault.

Some February nights, there's still the smell of hot grease. Crisp bacon. Olson Read not feeling his legs but still getting tugged back. Him screaming. His fingers hooked claws into the snow, getting tugged back into the dark by all those clenched little teeth.

JOE HILL

My Father's Mask

Joe Hill's short stories have been published in the magazines Postscripts, Subterranean, The Third Alternative, *and* Crimewave, *and in the anthology* The Many Faces Of Van Helsing. *Those stories and several new ones comprise his brilliant debut collection,* 20th Century Ghosts, *winner of the William L. Crawford Award for best first fantasy book. His stories have been reprinted in* The Mammoth Book of Best New Horror. *His first novel,* Heart-Shaped Box, *will be published in 2007. He is a past recipient of the Ray Bradbury Fellowship and the A.E. Coppard Fiction Prize. He lives in New England with his wife and children.*

About the story, Hill says:

"I wrote a lot of this story while my wife was pregnant with our third boy, during the last trimester, when neither of us could sleep, and we spent our nights wandering the darkened house, the both of us edgy and anxious, and our relationship with reality growing increasingly tenuous. So what follows is mostly the result of a feverishly overtired imagination. Not everything, though. The cottage on Big Cat Lake was real, although not long ago it was demolished, plowed into the earth, so thoroughly wiped away it might never have been."

"My Father's Mask" was originally published in 20th Century Ghosts.

—E.D.

O n the drive to Big Cat Lake, we played a game. It was my mother's idea. It was dusk by the time we reached the state highway, and when there was no light left in the sky, except for a splash of cold, pale brilliance in the west, she told me they were looking for me.

"They're playing card people," she said. "Queens and kings. They're so flat they can slip themselves under doors. They'll be coming from the other direction, from the lake. Searching for us. Trying to head us off. Get out of sight whenever someone comes the other way. We can't protect you from them—not on the road. Quick, get down. Here comes one of them now."

I stretched out across the backseat and watched the headlights of an approaching car race across the ceiling. Whether I was playing along, or just stretching out to get comfortable, I wasn't sure. I was in a funk. I had been hoping for a sleepover at my friend Luke Redhill's, ping-pong and late night TV with Luke (and Luke's leggy older sister Jane, and her lush-haired friend Melinda), but had come home from school to find suitcases in the driveway and my father loading the car. That was the first I heard we were spending the night at my grandfather's cabin on Big Cat Lake. I couldn't be angry at my parents for not letting me in on their plans in advance, because they probably hadn't made plans in advance. It was very likely they had decided to go up to Big Cat Lake over lunch. My parents didn't have plans. They had impulses and a thirteen-year-old son and they saw no reason to ever let the latter upset the former.

"Why can't you protect me?" I asked.

My mother said, "Because there are some things a mother's love and a father's courage can't keep you safe from. Besides, who could fight them? You know about playing card people. How they all go around with little golden hatchets and little silver swords. Have you ever noticed how well armed most good hands of poker are?"

"No accident the first card game everyone learns is War," my father said, driving with one wrist slung across the wheel. "They're all variations on the same plot. Metaphorical kings fighting over the world's limited supplies of wenches and money."

My mother regarded me seriously over the back of her seat, her eyes luminous in the dark.

"We're in trouble, Jack," she said. "We're in terrible trouble."

"Okay," I said.

"It's been building for a while. We kept it from you at first, because we didn't want to scare you. But you have to know. It's right for you to know. We're—well, you see—we don't have any money anymore. It's the playing card people. They've been working against us, poisoning investments, tying assets up in red tape. They've been spreading the most awful rumors about your father at work. I don't want to upset you with the crude details. They make menacing phone calls. They call me up in the middle of the day and talk about the awful things they're going to do to me. To you. To all of us."

"They put something in the clam sauce the other night, and gave me wicked runs," my father said. "I thought I was going to die. And our dry cleaning came back with funny white stains on it. That was them too."

My mother laughed. I've heard that dogs have six kind of barks, each with a specific meaning: *intruder, let's play, I need to pee.* My mother had a certain number of laughs, each with an unmistakable meaning and identity, all of them wonderful. This laugh, convulsive and unpolished, was the way she responded to dirty jokes; also to accusations, to being caught making mischief.

I laughed with her, sitting up, my stomach unknotting. She had been so wide-eyed and solemn, for a moment I had started to forget she was making it all up.

My mother leaned toward my father and ran her finger over his lips, miming the closing of a zipper.

"You let me tell it," she said. "I forbid you to talk anymore."

"If we're in so much financial trouble, I could go and live with Luke for a while," I said. *And Jane,* I thought. "I wouldn't want to be a burden on the family."

She looked back at me again. "The money I'm not worried about. There's an appraiser coming by tomorrow. There are some wonderful old things in that house, things your grandfather left us. We're going to see about selling them."

My grandfather, Upton, had died the year before, in a way no one liked to discuss, a death that had no place in his life, a horror movie conclusion tacked on to a blowsy, Capraesque comedy. He was in New York, where he kept a condo on the fifth floor of a brownstone on the Upper East Side, one of many places he owned. He called the elevator and stepped through the doors when they opened—but there was no elevator there, and he fell four stories. The fall did not kill him. He lived for another day, at the bottom of the elevator shaft. The elevator was old and slow and complained loudly whenever it had to move, not unlike most of the building's residents. No one heard him screaming.

"Why don't we sell the Big Cat Lake house?" I asked. "Then we'd be rolling in the loot."

"Oh, we couldn't do that. It isn't ours. It's held in trust for all of us, me, you, Aunt Blake, the Greenly twins. And even if it did belong to us, we couldn't sell it. It's always been in our family."

For the first time since getting into the car, I thought I understood why we were *really* going to Big Cat Lake. I saw at last that my weekend plans had been sacrificed on the altar of interior decoration. My mother loved to decorate. She loved picking out curtains, stained glass lamp-shades, unique iron knobs for the cabinets. Someone had put her in charge of redecorating the cabin on Big Cat Lake—or, more likely, she had put herself in charge—and she meant to begin by getting rid of all the clutter.

I felt like a chump for letting her distract me from my bad mood with one of her games.

"I wanted to spend the night with Luke," I said.

My mother directed a sly, knowing look at me from beneath half-lowered eyelids, and I felt a sudden scalp-prickle of unease. It was a look that made me wonder what she knew and if she had guessed the true reasons for my friendship with Luke Redhill, a rude but good-natured nose-picker I considered intellectually beneath me.

"You wouldn't be safe there. The playing card people would've got you," she said, her tone both gleeful and rather too-coy.

I looked at the ceiling of the car. "Okay."

We rode for a while in silence.

"Why are they after me?" I asked, even though by then I was sick of it, wanted done with the game.

"It's all because we're so incredibly superlucky. No one ought to be as lucky as us. They hate the idea that anyone is getting a free ride. But it would all even out if they got ahold of you. I don't care how lucky you've been, if you lose a kid, the good times are over."

We were lucky, of course, maybe even superlucky, and it wasn't just that we were well off, like everyone in our extended family of trust-fund ne'er-do-wells. My father had more time for me than other fathers had for their boys. He went to work after I left for school, and was usually home by the time I got back, and if I didn't have anything else going on, we'd drive to the golf course to whack a few. My mother was beautiful, still young, just thirty-five, with a natural instinct for mischief that had made her a hit with my friends. I suspected several of the kids I hung out with, Luke Redhill included, had cast her in a variety of masturbatory fantasies, and that indeed, their attraction to her explained most of their fondness for me.

"And why is Big Cat Lake so safe?" I said.

"Who said it's safe?"

"Then why are we going there?"

She turned away from me. "So we can have a nice cozy fire in the fireplace, and sleep late, and eat egg pancake, and spend the morning in our pajamas. Even if we are in fear for our lives, that's no reason to be miserable all weekend."

She put her hand on the back of my father's neck and played with his hair. Then she stiffened, and her fingernails sank into the skin just below his hairline.

"Jack," she said to me. She was looking past my father, through the driver's side window, at something out in the dark. "Get down, Jack, get down."

We were on route 16, a long straight highway, with a narrow grass median between the two lanes. A car was parked on a turnaround between the lanes, and as we went by it, its headlights snapped on. I turned my head and stared into them for a moment before sinking down out of sight. The car—a sleek silver Jaguar—turned onto the road and accelerated after us.

"I told you not to let them see you," my mother said. "Go faster, Henry. Get away from them."

Our car picked up speed, rushing through the darkness. I squeezed my fingers into the seat, sitting up on my knees to peek out the rear window. The other car stayed exactly the same distance behind us no matter how fast we went, clutching the curves of the road with a quiet, menacing assurance. Sometimes my breath would catch in my throat for a few moments before I remembered to breathe. Road signs whipped past, gone too quickly to be read.

The Jag followed for three miles, before it swung into the parking lot of a roadside diner. When I turned around in my seat my mother was lighting a cigarette with the pulsing orange ring of the dashboard lighter. My father hummed softly to himself, easing up on the gas. He swung his head a little from side to side, keeping time to a melody I didn't recognize.

I ran through the dark, with the wind knifing at me and my head down, not looking where I was going. My mother was right behind me, the both of us rushing for the porch. No light lit the front of the cottage by the water. My father had switched car and headlights off, and the house was in the woods, at the end of a rutted dirt road where there were no streetlamps. Just beyond the house I caught a glimpse of the lake, a hole in the world, filled with a heaving darkness.

My mother let us in and went around switching on lights. The cabin was built around a single great room with a lodge-house ceiling, bare rafters showing, log walls with red bark peeling off them. To the left of the door was a dresser, the mirror on the back hidden behind a pair of black veils. Wandering, my hands pulled into the sleeves of my jacket for warmth, I approached the dresser. Through the semi-transparent curtains I saw a dim, roughly formed figure, my own obscured reflection, coming to meet me in the mirror. I felt a tickle of unease at the sight of the reflected me, a featureless shadow skulking behind black silk, someone I didn't know. I pushed the curtain back, but saw only myself, cheeks stung into redness by the wind.

I was about to step away when I noticed the masks. The mirror was supported by two delicate posts, and a few masks hung from the top of each, the sort, like the Lone Ranger's, that only cover the eyes and a little of the nose. One had whiskers and glittery spackle on it and would make the wearer look like a jeweled mouse. Another was of rich black velvet, and would have been appropriate dress for a courtesan on her way to an Edwardian masquerade.

The whole cottage had been artfully decorated in masks. They dangled from doorknobs and the backs of chairs. A great crimson mask glared furiously down from the mantle above the hearth, a surreal demon made out of lacquered papier-maché, with a hooked beak and feathers around the eyes—just the thing to wear if you had been cast as the Red Death in an Edgar Allan Poe revival.

The most unsettling of them hung from a lock on one of the windows. It was made of some distorted but clear plastic, and looked like a man's face molded out of an impossibly thin piece of ice. It was hard to see, dangling in front of the glass, and I twitched nervously when I spotted it from the corner of my eye. For an instant I thought there was a man, spectral and barely there, hovering on the porch, gaping in at me.

The front door crashed open and my father came in dragging luggage. At the same time, my mother spoke from behind me.

"When we were young, just kids, your father and I used to sneak off to this place to get away from everyone. *Wait*. Wait, I know. Let's play a game. You have until we leave to guess which room you were conceived in."

She liked to try and disgust me now and then with intimate, unasked-for revelations about herself and my father. I frowned and gave what I hoped was a scolding look, and she laughed again, and we were both satisfied, having played ourselves perfectly.

"Why are there curtains over all the mirrors?"

"I don't know," she said. "Maybe whoever stayed here last hung them up as a way to remember your grandfather. In Jewish tradition, after someone dies, the mourners cover the mirrors, as a warning against vanity."

"But we aren't Jewish," I said.

"It's a nice tradition though. All of us could stand to spend less time thinking about ourselves."

"What's with all the masks?"

"Every vacation home ought to have a few masks lying around. What if you want a vacation from your own face? I get awfully sick of being the same person day in, day out. What do you think of that one, do you like it?"

I was absent-mindedly fingering the glassy, blank-featured mask hanging from the window. When she brought my attention to what I was doing, I pulled my hand back. A chill crawled along the thickening flesh of my forearms.

"You should put it on," she said, her voice breathy and eager. "You should see how you look in it."

"It's awful," I said.

"Are you going to be okay sleeping in your own room? You could sleep in bed with us. That's what you did the last time you were here. Although you were much younger then."

"That's all right. I wouldn't want to get in the way, in case you feel like conceiving someone else."

"Be careful what you wish for," she said. "History repeats."

The only furniture in my small room was a camp cot dressed in sheets that smelled of mothballs and a wardrobe against one wall, with paisley drapes pulled across the mirror on the back. A half-face mask hung from the curtain rod. It was made of green silk leaves, sewn together and ornamented with emerald sequins, and I liked it until I turned the light off. In the gloom, the leaves looked like the horny scales of some lizard-faced thing, with dark gaping sockets where the eyes belonged. I switched the light back on and got up long enough to turn it face-to the wall.

Trees grew against the house and sometimes a limb batted the side of the cottage, making a knocking sound that always brought me awake with the idea someone was at the bedroom door. I woke, dozed, and woke again. The wind built to a thin shriek and from somewhere outside came a steady, metallic ping-ping-ping, as if a wheel were turning in the gale. I went to the window to look, not expecting to see anything. The moon was up, though, and as the trees blew, moonlight raced across the ground, through the darkness, like schools of those little silver fish that live in deep water and glow in the dark.

A bicycle leaned against a tree, an antique with a giant front wheel, and a rear wheel almost comically too small. The front wheel turned continuously, ping-ping-ping. A boy came across the grass toward it, a chubby boy with fair hair, in a white nightgown, and at the sight of him I felt an instinctive rush of dread. He took the handlebars of the bike, then cocked his head as if at a sound, and I mewed, shrank back from the glass. He turned and stared at me with silver eyes and silver teeth, dimples in his fat cupid cheeks, and I sprang awake in my mothball-smelling bed, making unhappy sounds of fear in my throat.

When morning came, and I finally struggled up out of sleep for the last time, I found myself in the master bedroom, under heaped quilts, with the sun slanting across my face. The impression of my mother's head still dented the pillow beside me. I didn't remember rushing there in the dark and was glad. At thirteen, I was still a little kid, but I had my pride.

I lay like a salamander on a rock—sun-dazed and awake without being conscious—until I heard someone pull a zipper on the other side of the room. I peered around and saw my father, opening the suitcase on top of the bureau. Some subtle rustling of the quilts caught his attention, and he turned his head to look at me.

He was naked. The morning sunshine bronzed his short, compact body. He wore the clear plastic mask that had been hanging in the window of the great room, the night before. It squashed the features beneath, flattening them out of their recognizable shapes. He stared at me blankly, as if he hadn't known I was lying there in the bed, or perhaps as if he didn't know me at all. The thick length of his penis rested on a cushion of gingery hair. I had seen him naked often enough before, but with the mask on he was someone different, and his nakedness was disconcerting. He looked at me and did not speak—and that was disconcerting too.

I opened my mouth to say hello and good morning, but there was a wheeze in my chest. The thought crossed my mind that he was, really and not metaphorically, a person I didn't know. I couldn't hold his stare, looked away, then slipped from under the quilts and went into the great room, willing myself not to run.

A pot clanked in the kitchen. Water hissed from a faucet. I followed the sounds to my mother, who was at the sink, filling a tea kettle. She heard the pad of my feet, and glanced back over her shoulder. The sight of her stopped me in my tracks. She had on a black kitten mask, edged in rhinestones, and with glistening whiskers. She was not naked, but wore a MILLER LITE T-shirt that came to her hips. Her legs, though, were bare, and when she leaned over the sink to shut off the water I saw a flash of strappy black panties. I was reassured by the fact that she had grinned to see me, and not just stared at me as if we had never met.

"Egg pancake in the oven," she said.

"Why are you and dad wearing masks?"

"It's Halloween isn't it?"

"No," I said. "Try next Thursday."

"Any law against starting early?" she asked. Then she paused by the stove, an oven mitt on one hand, and shot another look at me. "Actually. *Actually.*"

"Here it comes. The truck is backing up. The back end is rising. The bullshit is about to come sliding out."

"In this place it's always Halloween. It's called Masquerade House. That's our secret name for it. It's one of the rules of the cottage, while you're staying here you have to wear a mask. It's always been that way."

"I can wait until Halloween."

She pulled a pan out of the oven and cut me a piece of egg pancake, poured me a cup of tea. Then she sat down across from me to watch me eat.

"You have to wear a mask. The playing card people saw you last night. They'll be coming now. You have to put a mask on so they won't recognize you."

"Why wouldn't they recognize me? I recognize you."

"You think you do," she said, her long-lashed eyes vivid and humorous. "Playing card people wouldn't know you behind a mask. It's their Achilles heel. They take everything at face value. They're very one-dimensional thinkers."

"Ha ha," I said. "When's the appraiser coming?"

"Sometime. Later. I don't really know. I'm not sure there even is an appraiser. I might've made that up."

"I've only been awake twenty minutes and I'm already bored. Couldn't you guys have found a babysitter for me and come up here for your weird mask-wearing, baby-making weekend by yourselves?" As soon as I said it, I felt myself starting to blush, but I was pleased that I had it in me to needle her about their masks and her black underwear and the burlesque game they had going that they thought I was too young to understand.

She said, "I'd rather have you along. Now you won't be getting into trouble with that girl."

The heat in my cheeks deepened, the way coals will when someone sighs over them. "What girl?"

"I'm not sure which girl. It's either Jane Redhill or her friend. Probably her friend. The person you always go over to Luke's house hoping to see."

Luke was the one who liked her friend, Melinda; I liked Jane. Still, my mother had guessed close enough to unsettle me. Her smile broadened at my stricken silence.

"She is a pert little cutie, isn't she? Jane's friend? I guess they both are. The friend, though, seems more your type. What's her name? Melinda? The way she goes around in her baggy farmer overalls. I bet she spends her afternoons reading in a treehouse she built with her father. I bet she baits her own worms and plays football with the boys."

"Luke is hot for her."

"So it's Jane."

"Who said it has to be either of them?"

"There must be some reason you hang around with Luke. Besides Luke." Then she said, "Jane came by selling magazine subscriptions to benefit her church a few days ago. She seems like a very wholesome young thing. Very community minded. I wish I thought she had a sense of humor. When you're a little older, you should coldcock Luke Redhill and drop him in the old quarry. That Melinda will fall right into your arms. The two of you can mourn for him together. Grief can be very romantic." She took my empty plate and got up. "Find a mask. Play along."

She put my plate in the sink and went out. I finished a glass of juice and meandered into the great room after her. I glanced at the master bedroom, just as she was pushing the door shut behind her. The man who I took for my father still wore his disfiguring mask of ice, and had pulled on a pair of jeans. For a moment our eyes met, his gaze dispassionate and unfamiliar. He put a possessive hand on my mother's hip. The door closed and they were gone.

In the other bedroom, I sat on the edge of my bed and stuck my feet into my sneakers. The wind whined under the eaves. I felt glum and out of sorts, wanted to be home, had no idea what to do with myself. As I stood, I happened to glance at the green mask made of sewn silk leaves, turned once again to face the room. I pulled it down, rubbed it between thumb and forefinger, trying out the slippery smoothness of it. Almost as an afterthought, I put it on.

My mother was in the living room, fresh from the shower.

"It's you," she said. "Very Dionysian. Very Pan. We should get a towel. You could walk around in a little toga."

"That would be fun. Until hypothermia set in."

"It is drafty in here, isn't it? We need a fire. One of us has to go into the forest and collect an armful of dead wood."

"Boy, I wonder who that's going to be."

"Wait. We'll make it into a game. It'll be exciting."

"I'm sure. Nothing livens up a morning like tramping around in the cold foraging for sticks."

"Listen. Don't wander from the forest path. Out there in the woods, nothing is real except for the path. Children who drift away from it never find their way back. Also—this is the most important thing—don't let anyone see you, unless they come masked. Anyone in a mask is hiding out from the playing card people, just like us."

"If the woods are so dangerous for children, maybe I ought to stay here and you or Dad can go play pick up sticks. Is he ever coming out of the bedroom?"

But she was shaking her head. "Grown-ups can't go into the forest at all. Not even the trail is safe for someone my age. I can't even see the trail. Once you get as old as me it disappears from sight. I only know about it because your father and I used to take walks on it, when we came up here as teenagers. Only the young can find their way through all the wonders and illusions in the deep dark woods."

Outside was drab and cold beneath the pigeon-colored sky. I went around the back of the house, to see if there was a woodpile. On my way past the master bedroom, my father thumped on the glass. I went to the window to see what he wanted, and was surprised by my own reflection, superimposed over his face. I was still wearing the mask of silk leaves, had for a moment forgotten about it.

He pulled the top half of the window down and leaned out, his own face squashed by its shell of clear plastic, his wintry blue eyes a little blank. "Where are you going?"

"I'm going to check out the woods, I guess. Mom wants me to collect sticks for a fire."

He hung his arms over the top of the window and stared across the yard. He watched some rust colored leaves trip end-over-end across the grass. "I wish I was going."

"Then come."

He glanced up at me, and smiled, for the first time all day. "No. Not right now. Tell you what. You go on, and maybe I'll meet you out there in a while."

"Okay."

"It's funny. As soon as you leave this place, you forget how—pure it is. What the air smells like." He stared at the grass and the lake for another moment, then turned his head, caught my eye. "You forget other things too. Jack, listen, I don't want you to forget about—"

The door opened behind him, on the far side of the room. My father fell silent. My mother stood in the doorway. She was in her jeans and sweater, playing with the wide buckle of her belt.

"Boys," she said. "What are we talking about?"

My father didn't glance back at her, but went on staring at me, and beneath his new face of melted crystal, I thought I saw a look of chagrin, as if he'd been caught doing something faintly embarrassing; cheating at solitaire maybe. I remembered, then, her drawing her fingers across his lips, closing an imaginary zipper, the night before. My head went queer and light. I had the sudden idea I was seeing another part of some unwholesome game playing out between them, the less of which I knew, the happier I'd be.

"Nothing," I said. "I was just telling Dad I was going for a walk. And now I'm going. For my walk." Backing away from the window as I spoke.

My mother coughed. My father slowly pushed the top half of the window shut, his gaze still level with mine. He turned the lock—then pressed his palm to the glass, in a gesture of goodbye. When he lowered his hand, a steamy imprint of it remained, a ghost hand that shrank in on itself and vanished. My father drew down the shade.

I forgot about gathering sticks almost as soon as I set out. I had by then decided that my parents only wanted me out of the house so they could have the place to themselves, a thought that made me peevish. At the head of the trail I pulled off my mask of silk leaves and hung it on a branch.

I walked with my head down and my hands shoved into the pockets of my coat. For a while the path ran parallel to the lake, visible beyond the hemlocks in slivers of frigid-looking blue. I was too busy thinking that if they wanted to be perverted and un-parent-like, they should've figured a way to come up to Big Cat Lake without me, to notice the path turning and leading away from the water.

I didn't look up until I heard the sound coming toward me along the trail: a steely whirring, the creak of a metal frame under stress. Directly ahead the path divided to go around a boulder, the size and rough shape of a half-buried coffin stood on end. Beyond the boulder, the path came back together and wound away into the pines.

I was alarmed, I don't know why. It was something about the way the wind rose just then, so the trees flailed at the sky. It was the frantic way the leaves scurried about my ankles, as if in a sudden hurry to get off the trail. Without thinking, I sat down behind the boulder, back to the stone, hugging my knees to my chest.

A moment later the boy on the antique bike—the boy I thought I had dreamed—rode past on my left, without so much as a glance my way. He was dressed in the nightgown he had been wearing the night before. A harness of white straps held a pair of modest white-feathered wings to his back. Maybe he had had them on the first time I saw him and I hadn't noticed them in the dark. As he rattled past, I had a brief look at his dimpled cheeks and blond bangs, features set in an expression of serene confidence. His gaze was cool, distant. Seeking. I watched him expertly guide his Charlie-Chaplin-cycle between stones and roots, around a curve, and out of sight.

If I hadn't seen him in the night, I might have thought he was a boy on his way to a costume party, although it was too cold to be out gallivanting in a nightgown. I wanted to be back at the cabin, out of the wind, safe with my parents. I was in dread of the trees, waving and shushing around me.

But when I moved, it was to continue in the direction I had been heading, glancing often over my shoulder to make sure the bicyclist wasn't coming up behind me. I didn't have the nerve to walk back along the trail, knowing that the boy on the antique bike was somewhere out there, between myself and the cabin.

I hurried along, hoping to find a road, or one of the other summer houses along the lake, eager to be anywhere but in the woods. Anywhere turned out to be less than ten minutes walk from the coffin-shaped rock. It was clearly marked—a weathered plank, with the words "**ANY-WHERE**" painted on it, was nailed to the trunk of a pine—a bare patch in the woods where people had once camped. A few charred sticks sat in the bottom of a blackened firepit. Someone, children maybe, had built a lean-to between a pair of boulders. The boulders were about the same height, tilting in toward one another, and a sheet of plywood had been set across the top of them. A log had been pulled across the opening that faced the clearing, providing both a place for people to sit by a fire, and a barrier that had to be climbed over to enter the shelter.

I stood at the ruin of the ancient campfire, trying to get my bearings. Two trails on the far side of the camp led away. There was little difference between them, both narrow ruts gouged out in the brush, and no clue as to where either of them might lead.

"Where are you trying to go?" said a girl on my left, her voice pitched to a good-humored hush.

I leaped, took a half-step away, looked around. She was leaning out of the shelter, hands on the log. I hadn't seen her in the shadows of the lean-to. She was black-haired, a little older than myself—sixteen maybe—and I had a sense she was pretty. It was hard to be sure. She wore a black sequined mask, with a fan of ostrich feathers standing up from one side. Just behind her, further back in the dark, was a boy, the upper half of his face hidden behind a smooth plastic mask the color of milk.

"I'm looking for my way back," I said.

"Back where?" asked the girl.

The boy kneeling behind her took a measured look at her outthrust bottom in her faded jeans. She was, consciously or not, wiggling her hips a little from side-to-side.

"My family has a summer place near here. I was wondering if one of those two trails would take me there."

"You could go back the way you came," she said, but mischievously, as if she already knew I was afraid to double back.

"I'd rather not," I said.

"What brought you all the way out here?" asked the boy.

"My mother sent me to collect wood for the fire."

He snorted. "Sounds like the beginning of a fairy tale." The girl cast a disapproving look back at him, which he ignored. "One of the bad ones. Your parents can't feed you anymore, so they send you off to get lost in the woods. Eventually someone gets eaten by a witch for dinner. Baked into a pie. Be careful it's not you."

"Do you want to play cards with us?" the girl asked, and held up a deck.

"I just want to get home. I don't want my parents worried."

"Sit and play with us," she said. "We'll play a hand for answers. The winner gets to ask each of the losers a question, and no matter what, they have to tell the truth. So if you beat me, you could ask me how to get home without seeing the boy on the old bicycle, and I'd have to tell you."

Which meant she had seen him and somehow guessed the rest. She looked pleased with herself, enjoyed letting me know I was easy to figure out. I considered for a moment, then nodded.

"What are you playing?" I asked.

"It's a kind of poker. It's called Cold Hands, because it's the only card game you can play when it's this cold."

The boy shook his head. "This is one of these games where she makes up the rules as she goes along." His voice, which had an adolescent crack in it, was nevertheless familiar to me.

I crossed to the log and she retreated on her knees, sliding back into the dark space under the plywood roof to make room for me. She was talking all the time, shuffling her worn deck of cards.

"It isn't hard. I deal five cards to each player, face-up. When I'm done, whoever has the best poker hand wins. That probably sounds too simple, but then there are a lot of funny little house rules. If you smile during the game, the player sitting to your left can swap one of his cards for one of yours. If you can build a house with the first three cards you get dealt, and if the other players can't blow it down in one breath, you get to look through the deck and pick out whatever you want for your fourth card. If you draw a black forfeit, the other players throw stones at you until you're dead. If you have any questions, keep them to yourself. Only the winner gets to ask questions. Anyone who asks a question while the game is in play loses instantly. Okay? Let's start."

My first card was a Lazy Jack. I knew because it said so across the bottom, and because it showed a picture of a golden-haired jack lounging on silk pillows, while a harem girl filed his toenails. It wasn't until the girl handed me my second card—the three of rings—that I mentally registered the thing she had said about the black forfeit.

"Excuse me," I started. "But what's a—"

She raised her eyebrows, looked at me seriously.

"Nevermind," I said.

The boy made a little sound in his throat. The girl cried out, "He smiled! Now you can trade one of your cards for one of his!"

"I did not!"

"You did," she said. "I saw it. Take his queen and give him your jack."

I gave him the Lazy Jack and took the Queen of Sheets away from him. It showed a nude girl asleep on a carved four-poster, amid the tangle of her bedclothes. She had straight brown hair, and strong, handsome features, and bore a resemblance to Jane's friend, Melinda. After that I was dealt the King of Pennyfarthings, a red-bearded fellow, carrying a sack of coins that was splitting and beginning to spill. I was pretty sure the girl in the black mask had dealt him to me from the bottom of the deck. She saw I saw and shot me a cool, challenging look.

When we each had three cards, we took a break and tried to build houses the others couldn't blow down, but none of them would stand. Afterward I was dealt the Queen of Chains and a card with the rules of Cribbage printed on it. I almost asked if it was in the deck by accident, then thought better of it. No one drew a black forfeit. I don't even know what one is.

"Jack wins!" shouted the girl, which unnerved me a little, since I had never introduced myself. "Jack is the winner!" She flung herself against me and hugged me fiercely. When she straightened up, she was pushing my winning cards into the pocket of my jacket. "Here, you should keep your winning hand. To remember the fun we had. It doesn't matter. This old deck is missing a bunch of cards anyway. I just knew you'd win!"

"Sure she did," said the boy. "First she makes up a game with rules only she can understand, then she cheats so it comes out how she likes."

She laughed, unpolished, convulsive laughter, and I felt cold on the nape of my neck. But really, I think I already knew by then, even before she laughed, who I was playing cards with.

"The secret to avoiding unhappy losses is to only play games you make up your-self," she said. "Now. Go ahead, Jack. Ask anything you like. It's your right."

"How do I get home without going back the way I came?"

"That's easy. Take the path closest to the 'any-where' sign, which will take you anywhere you want to go. That's why it says anywhere. Just be sure the cabin is really where you want to go, or you might not get there."

"Right. Thank you. It was a good game. I didn't understand it, but I had fun play-ing." And I scrambled out over the log.

I hadn't gone far, before she called out to me. When I looked back, she and the boy were side-by-side, leaning over the log and staring out at me.

"Don't forget," she said. "You get to ask him a question too."

"Do I know you?" I said, making a gesture to include both of them.

"No," he said. "You don't really know either of us."

There was a Jag parked in the driveway behind my parents' car. The interior was pol-ished cherry, and the seats looked as if they had never been sat on. It might have just rolled off the dealership floor. By then it was late in the day, the light slanting in from the west, cutting through the tops of the trees. It didn't seem like it could be so late.

I thumped up the stairs, but before I could reach the door to go in, it opened, and my mother stepped out, still wearing the black sex-kitten mask.

"Your mask," she said. "What'd you do with it?"

"Ditched it," I said. I didn't tell her I hung it on a tree branch because I was em-barrassed to be seen in it. I wished I had it now, although I couldn't have said why.

She threw an anxious look back at the door, then crouched in front of me.

"I knew. I was watching for you. Put this on." She offered me my father's mask of clear plastic.

I stared at it a moment, remembering the way I recoiled from it when I first saw it, and how it had squashed my father's features into something cold and menacing. But when I slipped it on my face, it fit well enough. It carried a faint fragrance of my father, coffee and the sea-spray odor of his aftershave. I found it reassuring to have him so close to me.

My mother said, "We're getting out of here in a few minutes. Going home. Just as soon as the appraiser is done looking around. Come on. Come in. It's almost over."

I followed her inside, then stopped just through the door. My father sat on the couch, shirtless and barefoot. His body looked as if it had been marked up by a sur-geon for an operation. Dotted lines and arrows showed the location of liver, spleen and bowels. His eyes were pointed toward the floor, his face blank.

"Dad?" I asked.

His gaze rose, flitted from my mother to me and back. His expression remained bland and unrevealing.

"Sh," my mother said. "Daddy's busy."

I heard heels cracking across the bare planks to my right, and glanced across the room, as the appraiser came out of the master bedroom. I had assumed the appraiser would be a man, but it was a middle-aged woman in a tweed jacket, with some white showing in her wavy yellow hair. She had austere, imperial features, the high cheekbones and expressive, arching eyebrows of English nobility.

"See anything you like?" my mother asked.

"You have some wonderful pieces," the appraiser said. Her gaze drifted to my fa-ther's bare shoulders.

"Well," my mother said. "Don't mind me." She gave the back of my arm a soft pinch, and slipped around me, whispered out of the side of her mouth, "Hold the fort, kiddo. I'll be right back."

My mother showed the appraiser a small, strictly polite smile, before easing into the master bedroom and out of sight, leaving the three of us alone.

"Do you miss your grandfather, Jack?" the appraiser asked.

The question was so unexpected and direct it startled me a little; or maybe it was her tone, which was not sympathetic, but sounded to my ears too-curious, eager for a little grief. Also, I didn't like that she knew my name.

"I guess. We weren't so close," I said. "I think he had a pretty good life, though."

"Of course he did," she said.

"I'd be happy if things worked out half as well for me."

"Of course they will," she said, and put a hand on the back of my father's neck and began rubbing it fondly.

It was such a casually, obscenely intimate gesture, I felt a sick intestinal pang at the sight. I let my gaze drift away—had to look away—and happened to glance at the mirror on the back of the dresser. The curtains were parted slightly, and in the reflection I saw a playing card woman standing behind my father, the queen of spades, her eyes of ink haughty and distant, her black robes painted onto her body. I wrenched my gaze from the looking-glass in alarm, and glanced back at the couch. My father was smiling in a dreamy kind of way, leaning back into the hands now massaging his shoulders. The appraiser regarded me from beneath half-lowered eyelids.

"That isn't your face," she said to me. "No one has a face like that. A face made out of ice. What are you hiding?"

My father stiffened, and his smile faded. He sat up and forward, slipping his shoulders out of her grip.

"You've seen everything," my father said to the woman behind him. "Do you know what you want?"

"I'd start with everything in this room," she said, putting her hand gently on his shoulder again. She toyed with a curl of his hair for a moment. "I can have everything, can't I?"

My mother came out of the bedroom, lugging a pair of suitcases, one in each hand. She glanced at the appraiser with her hand on my father's neck, and huffed a bemused little laugh—a laugh that went *huh* and which seemed to mean more or less just that—and picked up the suitcases again, marched with them toward the door.

"It's all up for grabs," my father said. "We're ready to deal."

"Who isn't?" said the appraiser.

My mother set one of the suitcases in front of me, and nodded that I should take it. I followed her onto the porch, and then looked back. The appraiser was leaning over the back of the couch, and my father's head was tipped back, and her mouth was on his. My mother reached past me and closed the door.

We walked through the gathering twilight to the car. The boy in the white gown sat on the lawn, his bicycle on the grass beside him. He was skinning a dead rabbit with a piece of horn, its stomach open and steaming. He glanced at us as we went by and grinned, showing teeth pink with blood. My mother put a motherly arm around my shoulders.

After she was in the car, she took off her mask and threw it on the backseat. I left mine on. When I inhaled deeply I could smell my father.

"What are we doing?" I asked. "Isn't he coming?"

"No," she said, and started the car. "He's staying here."

"How will he get home?"

She turned a sideways look upon me, and smiled sympathetically. Outside, the sky was a blue-almost-black, and the clouds were a scalding shade of crimson, but in the car it was already night. I turned in my seat, sat up on my knees, to watch the cottage disappear through the trees.

"Let's play a game," my mother said. "Let's pretend you never really knew your father. He went away before you were born. We can make up fun little stories about him. He has a Semper Fi tattoo from his days in the marines, and another one, a blue anchor, that's from—" her voice faltered, as she came up suddenly short on inspiration.

"From when he worked on a deep-sea oil rig."

She laughed. "Right. And we'll pretend the road is magic. The Amnesia Highway. By the time we're home, we'll both believe the story is true, that he really did leave before you were born. Everything else will seem like a dream, those dreams as real as memories. The made-up story will probably be better than the real thing anyway. I mean, he loved your bones, and he wanted everything for you, but can you remember one interesting thing he ever did?"

I had to admit I couldn't.

"Can you even remember what he did for a living?"

I had to admit I didn't. Insurance?

"Isn't this a good game?" she asked. "Speaking of games. Do you still have your deal?"

"My deal?" I asked, then remembered, and touched the pocket of my jacket.

"You want to hold onto it. That's some winning hand. King of Pennyfarthings. Queen of Sheets. You got it all, boy. I'm telling you, when we get home, you give that Melinda a call." She laughed again, and then affectionately patted her tummy. "Good days ahead, kid. For both of us."

I shrugged.

"You can take the mask off, you know," my mother said. "Unless you like wearing it. Do you like wearing it?"

I reached up for the sun visor, turned it down, and opened the mirror. The lights around the mirror switched on. I studied my new face of ice, and the face beneath, a malformed, human blank.

"Sure," I said. "It's me."

ISABEL ALLENDE

The Guggenheim Lovers

Translated by Margaret Sayers Peden, Isabel Allende's story of a rather unusual consummation of a rather unusual marriage within the walls of the Guggenheim Museum, was first published in the summer issue of the Virginia Quarterly Review. *Born in Chile, Allende now lives in the United States. A journalist in Chile and Venezuala for many years, Allende is the author of many novels including* House of Spirits, Eva Luna, Daughter of Fortune, My Invented Country, *a young adult fantasy series, and* Zorro, *in which the writer imagines "the origins of the legend." In 1996 she created the Isabel Allende Foundation, in honor of her late daughter, Paula Frias. The Foundation supports organizations that help women and children in need by providing education, healthcare, protection and the means to empowerment.*
—K.L. & G.G.

A night watchman found the lovers fast asleep in a knot of arms and hair, wrapped in a froth of ruined bridal gown in one of the galleries of the Guggenheim Museum in Bilbao. That was at five A.M., as first the watchman and then the police confirmed. Detective Aitor Larramendi added in his report that there was unmistakable evidence of a bacchanal scattered throughout the building. Although he had never participated in one—a fact he secretly lamented—his experience in every manner of human vice allowed him to detect the signs without a smidgen of doubt. The way the daring couple had got into the museum, and stayed there, was never clarified. They insisted they had spent the night inside the building, but the indignant guards swear to this day that they couldn't have, that it was impossible, considering that they make regular rounds. Besides, they explained, the television monitors detect every movement down to the most secret thought, and infrared alarms clang at the least provocation. The museum is fitted with magic eyes, and if they so much as blink they set off a commotion that would wake the dead, alerting policemen, firemen, and the director, a man wearied by the weight of his responsibility and cursed with a nervous constitution. Not even a cockroach can slip by unseen in the Guggenheim, the security experts avow, much less a pair of crazy kids as wild as that couple.

"I didn't see anyone the whole night," the girl said eleven hours later, after she regained consciousness in the rehab clinic.

The paramedics had carried her out on a stretcher, covered up like a cadaver, but anyone could make out the curves of her body beneath the sheet. The train of her dress and her dark, siren's hair dragged the floor. In the meantime, two uniformed policemen led the young man, naked and handcuffed, to a police car. Witnesses were moved and envious.

"Watchmen? No way, man. Those guys had to be playing cards or watching television. Half the world was in front of the TV last night because of that scandal about the Pope. Right? She and I were chasing each other through all the rooms like rabbits, me as naked as when my mother brought me into the world, and she still in her bridal gown because I couldn't undo those teeny little buttons," the young man corroborated later, after he was arrested and held in the police tank.

Detective Larramendi collected the faded flowers of the bridal bouquet—that too scattered around different floors. Rose petals, which had been white in their virginal state, dotted the marble floors like beds of pale clams, perfuming the air of the Guggenheim with the impossible odor of a courtesan's tomb. The dress, all forty yards of diaphanous tulle, which when new must have been a cloud imprisoned by seams, was reduced to tatters stained by the incontrovertible traces of love. The skirt and three layer petticoat had served as a pillow, and the queenly train had swept sixty-six percent of the marble floors, as the detective determined following a minute examination. Larramendi, not for nothing called "the Bilbao mastiff," is a man who inspires respect, with his five-foot stature, his lizard skeleton, and an enormous walrus mustache pasted on his face like a barber's joke. This same official found shreds of organza, curly hairs, and traces of bodily fluids. With his bloodhound instinct, he sniffed out the memory of the suspects' caresses, shivers, and sighs floating in the still air of the museum, from the front entrance to the last, right rear gallery, but he couldn't find a single empty bottle, forgotten cork, joint, or heroin syringe despite his legendary capacity for picking up a trail of guilt even where there was none. Larramendi could not prove, therefore, that the couple had violated any museum rule in that regard. The girl in the bridal dress must have been intoxicated before entering the building, he deduced with masterly skills of detection. As for the man with her, when Larramendi examined him he found only minimal traces of marijuana in his urine. Since the rule of the museum does not specifically refer to fornication in any of its variants, the only offense punishable by law was that the couple had remained inside the building after closing hour, a minor charge. He had to acknowledge that except for slightly littering the floors they had done no damage; just the opposite, according to the testimony of the employees, the next day everything shone as if bathed in sunshine, although it was raining pitilessly outside. It had rained all week.

"That's why we went in, because of the rain," the girl said. "Humidity always makes my hair kinky."

"Why were you dressed like a bride?" Aitor Larramendi queried.

"Because I didn't have time to change."

"Where were you married?"

"Who?"

"You and Pedro Berastegui," the policemen muttered, making a tremendous effort to stay calm.

"And who is he?"

"Who do you think, woman! Your husband? Your fiancé? Well, anyway, the fellow you were with in the museum."

"His name is Pedro? Nice name. It's a very manly name, don't you think, Inspector?"

"Let's go back to the beginning. How and when did you two meet?"

"I don't remember. I don't hold my drinks very well, I have two and I get totally silly."

"That is obvious. You were completely intoxicated."

"With love. . . ."

"Love, you say, but you have no idea who it was you were fucking in the museum.

"Not a clue."

"How did you get in?"

"Through the door, of course."

"You mean don't you, that you went into the building at a time when it was still open to the public?"

"No, I believe it was already closed . . ."

In his statement, Pedro Berastegui, the fortunate young man whom the press had labeled as "the magus of love," also assured the detective that the museum seemed to be closed, but that they'd had no problem at all going in: they pushed the doors and they softly swung open. Inside, it was dark and cozy, and the heating system must have been on because they were never cold for a minute, he said.

"That's because of the art works, we have to maintain a constant temperature and humidity," a prostrate museum director explained to Larramendi, and he added that the accused could not have got into the building as they said, because at five-fifteen precisely the doors are locked down by an electronic system.

"We walked in, with no problem," Pedro repeated for the hundredth time, faithful to his first version.

"And then what happened?" Larramendi inquired.

"Do you want me to tell you the details, Inspector? We made love all night, that's what we did."

"Where and when did you meet Elena Etxebarria?"

"So that's her name! Elena. Hélène. Helen. Like Helen of Troy. . . ."

Aitor Larramendi concluded that the transgressors hadn't known each other prior to committing their crime, and he had to admit, grumblingly, that there was no premeditation or mischief in their acts.

That memorable Saturday Elena Etxebarria had plans to marry her lifelong sweetheart, a good man who worked in her father's modest bakery and who had the distinction of having been the goalie for the Colegio San Ignacio de Loyola soccer team. Nonetheless, as the Inspector found out in his astute interrogations of the Jesuit priest who was going to marry them, as well as various witnesses present, the wedding of Elena Etxebarria and the soccer player never came off. He was told how the bride stumbled into the church leaning heavily on the strong arm of her older brother, an hour late and sobbing like a widow. She was crying so hard they could barely hear the chords of the wedding march. Another indication that the bride was not in her right mind was that before she got to the altar she kicked off her shoes and sent them flying, and the final evidence of her unhappiness came when suddenly she turned and shot from the church, leaving the soccer player, the priest, and the rest of those attending with their mouths agape. Nothing more was heard from her until the next day when her photograph appeared in El Correo Español under the headline "The Mysterious Guggenheim Lovers."

"I repeat," the detective insisted, "Where did you meet?"

"At the counter in Iñigo's bar. She caught my eye the minute I walked in," Pedro Berastegui said in his statement.

"Why is that?" asked detective Aitor Larramendi.

"Why is what?"

"Why did she catch your eye?"

"Well, it's not every day you see some knockout in a bar, dressed in a wedding gown, crying and tossing back drinks like a Cossack."

"What did you do then?"

"I spoke to her."

"Go on."

"She threw me a look and I fell for her. Just like that, I swear to you. Her make-up was streaming down her face. She looked like a clown, but those Cleopatra green eyes nailed me. I'm telling you, Inspector, nothing like that had ever happened to me. I felt this ferocious jolt, like sticking your finger in a wall socket."

"And she?"

"She leaned her head against my chest and went on crying like a baby. I didn't know what to do. After a while I took her into the bathroom and washed her face. I asked her why she was crying so hard and she told me that her fiancé was a hopeless idiot. Then I offered to marry her, right there."

"You both were drunk, of course."

"She was a little tipsy, but I don't drink. I'm a teetotaler, you might say. I'd smoked a joint, but alcohol? Not a drop. I went back to the bar alone to collect a bet from Iñigo we'd made on the Holy Father."

"What did she say?"

"She said swell, that she'd marry me in order not to waste the dress. Then she kissed me right on the mouth."

"And you?"

"I kissed her back. Wouldn't you have done the same? We couldn't let each other go, we kissed and kissed and kissed. It was love at first sight, just like in the movies."

"Then?"

"Then that jerk Iñigo interrupted and threw us out. He told us to go to a motel, that we were shameless. All to keep from paying off the bet."

"Go on."

"We left. We just started walking, we were looking for somewhere to rest a while—and a bite to eat wouldn't have hurt—but we didn't find anything. It started to rain, real gentle, but we didn't have an umbrella. I put my jacket around her, but there was no way to keep from ruining the dress. I wanted to take her to my apartment, but I remembered that my mother would be there watching television with my uncles. The scandal about the Pope, you know?"

"Yes, man, I know about the scandal."

"Then I saw the museum, right in front of us, like a magician's trick. A miracle!" And Pedro Berastegui fell quiet, lost in memories of his splendid night.

"Go on, for Christ's sake," the detective ordered.

"Well, it occurred to me that we could get out of the rain there, and we ran across that large terrace in front of the museum doors. You know it, don't you?"

"No one stopped you? Where were the guards?"

"There weren't any. I tell you, no one, Inspector."

"And?"

"I told you, we barely touched the door and it swung open, inviting us to come in. She kissed me again and told me she wanted to be carried over the threshold, like a real bride. I tried to pick her up, but I got tangled in her train, and we fell in the door, dying laughing. We tried to stand up but kept slipping, so finally we crawled in on all fours, kissing and laughing and feeling each other all over. Now I know what they mean by crazy in love, Inspector. I'd never . . ."

"Are you going to tell me that you didn't try to find out her name or why she was wearing that dress?" the detective interrupted, who had endured twenty-three years of a boring marriage and deep down didn't want to hear about pleasures he might never experience.

"It never occurred to me, and that's the truth, Inspector. Besides, I'm not much for words, I get right down to brass tacks, if you get my meaning."

Larramendi is pretty much a brass tacks man himself, and later, as he was questioning Elena Etxebarria, he decided to be subtle and not alarm her.

"Are you a whore?" he asked.

The girl, sitting stiffly in a chair in the rehab clinic, wrapped in a patient's robe and with her hair pulled back in a long ponytail, was humiliated, and burst out crying. Between hiccups she declared she had been educated by the nuns, had guarded her virginity until that night in the museum, and that she did not intend to let some ape with a big mustache and bigger paunch get away with insulting her. What was he thinking? He'd see what her three brothers had to say when they found out.

"All right, girl, calm down. It's a routine question, I don't mean anything by it. But it seems a little strange to me that Berastegui and you did what you did right off the bat, without ever being introduced, without knowing each other's name, nothing. . . ."

"It was as if we'd known each other forever, Inspector, as if we'd been together in another life. Do you believe in reincarnation?"

"No, I'm a Christian."

"I am too, but one thing doesn't exclude the other, if you think about it. The minute we crossed the threshold of the museum it was as if we'd been married in the eyes of God and the civil registry," said Elena, and proceeded to tell him that with her groom, the first one, the soccer player, she didn't feel anything.

"Can you imagine, Inspector? Now that's fate. If I hadn't run out of the church and if I hadn't gone into that bar, I would never have known true love," she added.

"That isn't love, woman, that's lust, pure high octane madness. How do you explain the fact that you two spent the whole night galloping through the museum but were never caught on the video cameras?"

"Maybe we were invisible. . . ."

"Better watch that smart mouth!"

"Don't you know the Guggenheim is bewitched, Inspector?"

"What a bunch of nonsense! The Guggenheim is the most modern museum in the world!" Detective Aitor Larramendi interrupted, although he knew all too well what the girl with the green eyes was referring to. Rumors had begun to circulate almost as soon as construction began on the building: the talk was that it was humanly impossible to make something that beautiful without making a pact with the forces of the Other Side.

"That building is bristling with alarms. I can't understand how none of them went off."

"Are you sure we were in the museum?"

"Are you pulling my leg?"

"I'm asking in all seriousness, Inspector. If it was closed, as you say, and if the alarms didn't go off, maybe we were never there. The truth is that the place where we made love didn't look like a museum. I remember it as a crystal palace, a castle from another planet, like the ones you see in the movies."

"And how was that?" asked Larramendi, routinely, because he was tired of the whole matter.

"Through the windows we could see diamonds falling, and we heard the music of a waterfall . . ."

"Rain, child, it was rain."

"And a faint perfume of ripe plums."

"That would be the roses of your bouquet."

"No. Plums. Haven't you smelled plums in the summertime, Inspector? It's a heavy fragrance, it leaves your mouth hungry for something."

"All right, it smelled like plums."

"You say we went into the Guggenheim, but I tell you we were in a magic place; there were no walls, only space, bright and open."

"The walls are cement, Elena."

"Believe me, these walls were imaginary, pulsing and smooth. Not only could you hear the water, I'm sure that something was vibrating in the air, like a murmur, like that river of words that just come out when you're making love. You know what I mean."

"No.

"Too bad. Well, then we began to float."

"What do you mean by float?"

"Haven't you ever been in love, Inspector?"

"I'm the one asking the questions here, understood?"

"We were floating, hand in hand, carried by the breeze billowing the layers of my dress."

"There's no breeze inside the building. It must have been the hot air circulating."

"Must have been, Inspector. Pedro—isn't that what you said his name is?—took off his trousers and shirt and undershorts, and his clothing was floating, too, like birthday balloons."

"Lewd and indecent behavior in a public place," the inspector spit out.

"There wasn't any public. Pedro tried to get my dress off, but he couldn't unbutton it. Those little buttons are impossible, you know?"

"Are you telling me you were flitting around like flies?"

"Just like flies. Once we'd been through all the galleries and had stepped inside the paintings and had drunk the colors and had played in the labyrinth and danced with the sculptures, then we came back down."

"Where exactly?" Aitor Larramendi asked.

"How do I know!"

The Bilbao Mastiff sighed: the girl had about as much brains as a chicken. He went back to the cell where Pedro Berastegui, still in handcuffs, was drinking coffee and discussing the scandal about the Pope with two on-duty detectives. Larramendi did not favor fraternizing with the prisoners; you lost authority and it was, after all, against the rules. After taking the paper cup from the young man's hands, he led him by one wing to the green interrogation room. "So then, you never asked the girl her name," he attacked, picking up his questioning from the point he had left it hours before.

"There wasn't time for much conversation, we were sort of busy, you know?"

"Making love like rabbits," the inspector interrupted.

"More like angels, I'd say."

"Out of your head, I'd say, and buck naked."

"I was, I admit, but she had her dress on and was covered by her long hair. Did you see what pretty hair she has? Pure silk, like a doll's hair."

"You can spare me the metaphors, Berastegui. How did you disconnect the alarms and survey cameras?"

"I didn't touch anything. Strange things happen in that museum. My uncle, the lame one, my mother's brother, had to go repair the elevator on the night of Good Friday, and he says that with his own eyes he saw a statue move."

"Which one?"

"One of those in a tangle like intestines."

"What is your uncle's name?"

"Keep my family out of this, Inspector," Pedro Berastegui replied emphatically.

He corroborated Elena Etxebarría's statement point by point. Despite Aitor Larramendi's legendary wiliness in catching out suspects in fatal contradictions, he had to admit that he didn't have enough proof to send that pair to jail for several months—which they richly deserved. However, his failure did not leave him in a bad mood, just the opposite; he had to make an effort to control the little hop in his step and the twitch of a smile struggling to betray his true state of mind. For the first time, his rusted policeman's heart was celebrating an unpunished crime. What the devil, he reasoned, the only vice was love. Many people, like Pedro Berastegui's lame uncle, believed that every night in the museum the statues danced the conga, figures leaped from the paintings to wander through the galleries, and the entire museum was filled with playful spirits. Among the savvy detective's conjectures was the possibility that the lovers had entered the Guggenheim at the precise instant the building was entering the dream dimension and so had unintentionally fallen into that time that isn't measured on clocks. It would be difficult to explain this theory to his superiors, the detective concluded, grinding out his cigarette butt beneath his shoe, but with a little luck maybe he wouldn't have to. It was election time; there had been problems with terrorists and the National Health Service strike, conditions that didn't leave much room for magic lovers. The Guggenheim was just a museum, who was going to care about art? If the kids had broken the security of the Banco de Bilbao, now that would be a different matter.

A few days later, Aitor Larramendi closed the file on the case and stuck it in the bottom of the cabinet where he kept indefinitely shelved cases, and where the slow mill of bureaucracy would eventually grind it to powder. The press, still occupied with the scandal in the Vatican, quickly forgot the mysterious Guggenheim lovers. The person most affected was the museum director, who couldn't stop worrying even though he replaced the watchmen, installed a new security system, and contracted a celebrated Dutch psychic to exorcise the museum. As for the protagonists of that scandal of love, let us just say that when Elena Etxebarria picked up her bridal gown from the cleaner's, Pedro Berstegui was waiting on the corner with a bouquet of fresh roses in his hand.

THEODORA GOSS

A Statement in the Case

Theodora Goss's much-anticipated first collection, In the Forest of Forgetting, *will be published this year by Prime Books. She is currently working on
a novel, while also coediting, with Delia Sherman, a short fiction anthology
for the Interstitial Arts Foundation. In 2005 Goss's stories appeared in
Strange Horizons, Flytrap, and Polyphony 5. "A Statement in the Case,"
which first appeared in the August issue of* Realms of Fantasy, *is Goss's fifth
appearance in this series. Her stories are enchanting, deft, and sly. She
teaches at Boston University and lives in Boston, Mass., with her scientist
husband, Kendrick, and their daughter Ophelia Philippa. Her Web site is
www.theodoragoss.com.*

—*K.L. & G.G.*

S ure, I know István Horvath. We met about a year before Eva died. That's my
wife, Eva. You knew that? Yeah, I figured you were pretty thorough.
   It was the year of the blizzard, when snow covered the cars parked on the
streets and even the Post Office shut down. I didn't have to go to work for a
week. So one night, I think it was Thursday, Eva says, "Mike, I only have one of the
blue pills left." This was when we still thought the chemo was doing something.
When we discovered it wasn't, she turned her head toward me on the pillow—she
was so beautiful, like the day we got married—and said, "Mike, I think the Lord
wants me home." After that, she refused to take the pills. But I couldn't throw them
out. Every morning I opened the medicine cabinet, and there they were, the blue
ones, the orange ones that made her throw up, the green ones that made her hair fall
out, the purple ones that caused constipation. When she died, I flushed them down
the toilet. But you don't want to hear about Eva. I was talking about the day I met
István Horvath.
   Well, there she was saying there were no more blue pills, and how was I going to
get to Walgreens? The snow was up to my armpits, and the subway wasn't running.
Then Eva said, "What about that store around the corner?" Now, we always went to
Walgreens. You know the guy in Alabama who sold aspirin as that stuff you take for
cholesterol? So we were always careful. We never went to the store around the corner. For one thing, the sign said Apothecary, which looked kind of foreign, and we
wanted our pills one hundred percent American. For another, the front of the store
was kind of dirty. You know, like nobody washed the windows.
   But we had to have the blue pills. So I put on my boots and walked through the
snow to the Apothecary. And I tell you, it was just around the corner, but by the time

I got there I felt like I was going to have a heart attack. It was some work, walking through all that snow.

I figured the store would be closed, and I'd have to knock on the other door, the one for the apartment above the store, which had a sign on it that said Pharmacist. But the sign in the window—which was written in magic marker, can you believe it—said Open. So I walked in.

When the bell on the door rang, István stood up from behind the counter. Not that I knew his name, then. He was wearing a white coat, so I figured he was the pharmacist. "Hello," he said, in a foreign kind of voice, like I'd expected. I figured he was probably Russian. We had a lot of Russians in the neighborhood, in those days. Nothing wrong with that. My grandfather came through Staten Island. We're all immigrants, right? Even the Indians came from someplace else. Now Gorski, what's that, Polish? Ernie at the Post Office, he's Polish. Do you mind if I get some water, Sergeant Gorski? I'm not used to talking so much, since Eva died. Nowadays, you get these lawyers and doctors moving in. They like the "neighborhood atmosphere." Then the old people can't afford it anymore, so they go to Florida, to the retirement communities. And suddenly there's nobody to talk to. But Eva and I had some savings, and with my pension—well, I'm not ready to leave the neighborhood yet.

So István stands up from behind the counter and says, "Hello. Today, I did not expect customers. I was setting traps for the mice. Not to hurt them, you understand. I take them outside, to the cemetery."

Later, I told him they would come back. Mice are smart, they know their way home. But he said, "Then I will trap them again. It is pleasant in the cemetery, with the grass and trees. I will leave them bread, and perhaps they will learn to like it there." Can you imagine? A regular mouse vacation. But that was István all over. He wouldn't swat the flies on the walls. He'd catch them and put them outside, and half an hour later they'd get in again through the holes in the screen. So you're not going to convince me that he murdered his wife.

Now, I have to admit I didn't like the look of the place, when I first came in. There was dust on the shelves, and the boxes of Ace bandages looked like they'd been there a while. Toward the back there were bottles of what looked like dried leaves and flowers, with labels—in magic marker, what did you expect—saying things like Tansy, Agrimony, Rue. But the bottle of blue pills he gave me looked just like it came from Walgreens. When he handed it to me he said, "Tell her to take it always with a piece of bread, so the nausea is not so bad." And you know, he was right.

I won't say I stopped going to Walgreens after that, but I got to buying little things at the Apothecary. Tweezers, antacids, Vicks VapoRub. One day I noticed a chess board on the counter. "Colonel Borodin, she left it," he told me. He could never get his genders right. To him, everyone was a she. "She has a problem with the liver, all that vodka. But she cannot pay the bill, so she gives me this. It is beautiful, no?"

It was beautiful, with ebony and ivory pieces. My grandfather taught me to play chess. He said, in Italy all the men would play in the park, while the women were cooking Sunday dinner. That was the way to live, he said. I sure wouldn't mind living that way.

So István and I started to play together. Usually we played in the Apothecary, on the counter, but a couple of times I invited him over to meet Eva. That was when I found out he was Hungarian. Eva's grandmother was Hungarian, and she knew a few words: yes, no, hello, goodbye, thank you. I think he liked to hear them. Once, he brought a plastic bag full of yellow and white flowers. "Chamomile," he said. "It helps the stomach." Later, he showed me where he dried things, in the basement. He had racks down there, with plants hanging from them. I know that's not what you found. Don't they teach you patience, at the police academy? Chamomile tea was the only thing Eva drank, the month before she died. Toward the end, when she couldn't talk, he told her stories. About girls who lived in rivers, and hens that laid eggs covered with diamonds and rubies. They were so fancy, they were sent to the Russian Tsar. He said he had learned them from his mother. Eva loved those stories. She would smile, and then for a while she'd be able to sleep. She didn't sleep much, in those days.

Before she died, we didn't have a lot of friends. She hadn't gone out for a long time, except to the hospital, and I didn't want to invite the guys from the Post Office to the funeral. Ernie, for example, he can't stand hallways, especially if they're narrow. Stan doesn't like bushes. And none of us like going to funerals. Your father was in Vietnam? Yeah, you know what I'm talking about.

Our parents, they died a while back, and her brother was out in Tucson. So it was just me and István at the cemetery. He brought a bunch of Easter lilies, exactly the kind of flowers Eva would have liked.

I didn't see him for a while after that. I felt like keeping to myself. I went to work, came home, opened a bottle of beer, and watched TV. I didn't even answer the telephone. It was always someone trying to sell me something, like a time share in Florida, or asking what I thought about the mayor. And István left me alone. That's the kind of guy he was, sensitive. Like Eva.

But one day, he knocked on the door. "Mike," he said, after I'd let him in and asked if he wanted a beer, "I have to go to Budapest. My mother, she is dying. The doctors are not so good there. And now I think they will not put me in prison."

See, the Berlin Wall had come down. I watched them take it down on TV. I figured, this was what we had fought for. To defeat the Commies, right? That's what Ernie said: the day that wall came down, we won the Vietnam war. I don't know. It didn't feel won to me.

"The first time I tried to escape," he told me—I was drinking beer, he was drinking chamomile tea—"they found me. I was stupid, I tried to escape on the train. I was only fifteen. The guards, they laughed and beat the soles of my feet. They sent me back to my mother and told her I would not run away any more. The second time, I was a pharmacist, finished with university. A German friend came to Budapest on vacation. His car, the back seat, it was hollow. I stayed there until we crossed the border into West Germany."

He sat with his hands wrapped around the mug. "I wonder if I was wrong to leave my country. A pharmacist, she is useful everywhere." He looked down into his tea. "I do not know what my mother looks like, now. When I left, her hair was brown. Perhaps it is white."

"You can't change the past," I said. And you can't. It's the one thing you can't do.

He asked if I would take care of the store, just check on it once in a while to make sure no one broke in and the mice didn't eat everything. Then he gave me the key.

I didn't see him again for a couple of months. Then one day I heard a knock on the door. It was him, even thinner than usual, like he hadn't been eating. And standing next to him was this girl.

Of course it was her. Don't worry, I'm getting to that. She had on this coat that looked like it came from the Salvation Army, and a cap on her head that was the color of—well, anyway, it was brown. She was ugly, then. Pale, like she hadn't been out in the sun in years. And she had dark circles under her eyes. I mean, she looked like she'd been raised in a box.

István said, "My friend Mike!" and kissed me on both cheeks. Now, I don't hold with men kissing, you understand. But he'd been away for a while, and they do things different in those foreign countries.

"This is Ildiko," he said, "my wife." She'd been taking care of his mother, he explained. After his mother died, she had nowhere to go. She had no family, and there were no jobs in Budapest. If the country became Communist again, the borders would close, and she'd have no way out. Now isn't that István all over. He marries this girl because he feels sorry for her. He might as well have invited the flies into his apartment.

The first thing I noticed, when I went to the Apothecary for some Pepto Bismol and maybe a game of chess, was the sign. It wasn't in magic marker any more. It was one of those regular signs that other stores had, the Pizza Express and Lou's Shoe Repair and the Vacuum Emporium. The window had been cleaned. In it were a row of combs and brushes, and some of those plastic things women put in their hair. Clips and things. Not the sorts of things Eva would ever have worn. Though toward the end, she almost always wore a turban.

Ildiko was standing behind the counter, with her hair back in one of those plastic clips. "István not here," she said, and rang me up. She was looking a little better, like she'd gotten some sleep. But I don't like skinny women, or ones that don't say hello or thank you. She stared at me like I had no right to be in that store. I tell you, I knew even then that something was wrong. You don't believe me? Well, you're the one trying to figure out who burned down the Apothecary.

About a week later, István invited me over to play chess. He told me he'd been at a pharmacist's convention. It had been Ildiko's idea, like the combs and brushes. Everything was Ildiko's idea, then.

This time there was a rack of magazines by the register: *Woman's Day, Soap Opera Digest, The National Inquirer*. Those bottles of leaves and flowers that he'd dried himself—they'd been replaced on the shelves with soap and shampoo. There were jars of face cream. It was cleaner, sure, and more like Walgreens. But I didn't like it.

Ildiko was behind the counter again, but I almost didn't recognize her. For one thing, she'd dyed her hair. It was blond, like Marilyn Monroe, though you could still see the roots. And she was wearing bright red lipstick. Her fingernails were bright red too. She was something to look at, all right. But I sure wouldn't have wanted to be her husband.

István, he thought she was wonderful. "She loves America," he told me, setting up the chess pieces. We were upstairs, in the apartment. She didn't want him playing chess on the counter. It would make the customers think there wasn't enough business. "She wants this to be a real American store. She thinks we should name it Drug Mart. You see, she is so clever about the window. We need a display, she says. Something to bring in the women. And her Russian is better than mine. The old men, the majors and colonels, they like her." I bet they did. "I wish she and Eva could have met. I'm certain they would have liked each other." I wasn't so certain. Eva was—well, she was a lady, if you know what I mean. And Ildiko Horvath—well, I don't want to say what she was.

At that moment we heard her laughing, and a "Da, da" coming from downstairs.

You think I'm being unfair? One night, this was about two weeks later, I was walking down the street, smoking a cigarette. Eva would never let me smoke in the apartment, and I still go outside. I don't know why. I guess I imagine her saying, "Mike, you're going to get that smoke all over my curtains."

Anyway, when I passed the Apothecary, I heard her voice from the upstairs window. "Do you think I enjoy taking care of that stupid woman? Do you think I enjoy cleaning up when she cannot go to the toilet? And then I find out she doesn't leave me a forint, not a forint!" She was shouting so loud I thought she would wake up Lou. He still lives above the Shoe Repair, though he retired last year. István answered her in Hungarian, or that's what I figured it was. "Why you think I marry you?" I had to give her one thing, her English was getting better. "I deserve—yes, *deserve*, every forint of that money!"

So don't get on your high horse to me about Ildiko Horvath. The *Herald* can go on about the tragic story: young wife found in a basement, burned to death. But I know what kind of woman she really was.

We started playing chess every week, me and István, and every week there was something new at the store. Boxes of Whitman's Samplers. Marlboro Lights. Those pantyhose in eggs. Ildiko sat at the counter with her blond hair and red nails, in dresses I'd be ashamed to see on Eva.

All right, all right, I'll stick to the facts. That day, I went over to play chess. She wasn't at the counter. István was there instead, with a liquor bottle open beside him. I'd never seen him drink anything stronger than chamomile tea. "Come join me, friend Mike," he said, and poured some into a glass. It was called—now, what was it? Pálinka. Peach brandy, though it didn't taste much like peaches. It burned my throat going down.

Yeah, I guess it could account for the smell. So the firemen noticed that, did they?

"We've been friends for a long time, no?" he said, and I nodded. I guess he was as close to a friend as I had. "I can tell you, things are not well." His speech was slurred, and it was hard figuring out what he was saying, with that accent. He was drunk of course, and I figured I was in for the whole story. That's what guys do when they're drunk, they tell you the whole story. And then they cry in their beer. Waste of good beer, if you ask me. But he got up from the counter and said, "Come, I will show you. She said she will shop for dresses at Filene's, and then she will watch a movie. She said I should not expect her until evening."

He was swaying from side to side, like one of those toys that kids punch, and they don't fall down. But he managed to unlock the door to the basement. I followed him down the stairs.

When he switched on the light, I saw that the racks of drying plants were gone. Instead—how can I describe it? Eva liked movies where people wore costumes. You know, *Dr. Zhivago*. In those movies, rich people always have tables with things on them, like statues. That basement was full of tables and chairs, and on them were statues, of women dancing, and all kinds of dogs. There were pieces of lace, just lying on the tables. Silver teapots and trays, piles of teaspoons. Glass bowls and vases, dark red and that yellow color, what do they call it? Amber. The legs of the tables were carved so they had feet, and the backs of the chairs were inlaid. You know, where they use a different wood to make designs, like birds or flowers. Stan does it as a hobby, but I've never seen him do anything like that. On one table there was a box filled with jewelry, rings and necklaces and what looked like a crown. The kind Miss America wears. On another there was a collection of eggs, and I knew what those were. Eva took me to the museum once, to see those eggs. Fabergé, they call them.

The most expensive eggs in the world. The whole room looked like it belonged in Las Vegas.

"What the hell?" I said. I couldn't think of anything else to say.

"My country is poor now," said István. "Many people sell what belonged to their parents or grandparents. And Ildiko knows people who will carry these things across the border. I don't know how, she does not tell me. Mike, how can she know such people?"

"What the hell is she going to do with all this?" I couldn't stop staring. I picked up the crown. It was heavier than I'd expected.

"She sells to Americans. First she sold only a few pieces, then with the money she bought more, and now she sells the treasures of my country." He held out his hands, as though he didn't know what to say. "She tells me, this is America, land of opportunity. I have been here so long, I should be rich by now. But this is not the worst. No—"

Above us, I heard the store bell ring.

"I must go see the customer," he said, "or Ildiko will be angry." He swayed up the stairs, leaving me in the basement.

I looked around me. All that stuff in the light of one bare bulb, shining off the carved wood, the polished silver. It was like being in Aladdin's cave.

Then I heard something. Don't ask me to describe it to you. It came from the back of the basement, behind the tables. Where the light didn't exactly reach. I heard it again.

You think it was Ildiko Horvath? You mean, you think he knocked her on the head, hid her in the basement, then took me down to see what she'd been doing? What kind of fool would do a thing like that? No offense, Gorski, but I don't know how you made sergeant. Sure, he might have been too drunk to care. But that's not what happened. I told you she'd gone to the movies. I saw her come home myself, around six o'clock.

No, what I saw were cages. Cages stacked on top of each other, in the darkness. Now, I'm going to tell you what was in those cages. But I want you to remember, I'd been drinking that pálinka. I was probably drunk. Would a sober man have seen a goat with the head of a boy, maybe fifteen, sixteen? Or a girl, but only about three feet tall, and covered with scales? She had gills on the sides of her neck, just like a fish. There wasn't enough room in the cage for her to stand, so she sat there, rocking back and forth like a monkey at the zoo. There was a cage full of snakes, except they had wings, a bunch of them on some of the bigger ones. There wasn't room to fly, but they beat the air with their wings, and hissed at me. There was a hen with only one leg, not on one side as though the other had been chopped off, but right in the middle. When I looked in that cage, I realized where all those Fabergé eggs had come from. Then the goat boy bleated—that was the sound I'd heard—and something in a cage I'd thought was empty, except for what looked like a rubber poncho on the floor, opened its eyes. Its hell of a lot of eyes, all different colors, blue and gray and green. I turned and ran out of that basement, up the stairs and past the counter where István was ringing up a customer. He looked up, startled, as I ran past him and out the door. I didn't stop until I was across the street and smoking a cigarette. I stood there, across the street from the store, until it got dark, smoking most of a pack, not wanting to go home to the empty apartment, not wanting to return to the Apothecary. I think István realized why I had run out of there, because after that customer left he went upstairs to the apartment and sat at the kitchen table with his head in his hands. Yeah, he went down again once, but then he went back to the kitchen. A couple more customers came by, but he didn't answer the bell.

That's how I saw when Ildiko came home, right around six o'clock as I said. She went upstairs and said something to him. When he didn't answer she threw her coat down on the chair, and her purse on top of it. Then she turned on the stove and started cooking dinner.

Now what you want to know is, how did the store burn down, with her body in the basement? I'll tell you what I'm going to swear to in court. I'm going to swear that I saw Ildiko Horvath go down to the store and open the basement door, then go down to the basement. You can see the door through the store window. And I'll swear that I saw István fall asleep on the kitchen table, spilling the bottle of pálinka. Remember, the stove was on. It was a small kitchen—easy enough for some of the pálinka to spill on thc flames. That would explain why the firemen smelled peaches. You don't think I could see that far? Check my army record. I was a sniper in Vietnam. My vision's still better than twenty twenty.

Oh, but I wasn't drunk by then. I'd been standing out there about an hour. I'd had plenty of fresh air. All right, so Ildiko had a bruise on her head. Maybe she got that trying to escape the fire. It spread so fast, I barely got István out. Someone should talk to the mayor about these old buildings.

I thought you would find the cages. Of course they were empty. You don't think I actually saw those things? István probably kept the cages for catching raccoons.

But I'm going to tell you something, Sergeant. Off the record. You don't have one of those wires, do you? I've watched cop shows on TV. That's why I wanted to meet here, instead of at the station. István Horváth, he wouldn't hurt a fly. Those things— I don't know what they were, but I think he cared about them. Remember the stories he told Eva. I think that's what he really meant, when he talked about the treasures of his country. I mentioned how he let the mice out in the cemetery? Once, when I was sitting there by Eva's grave, I saw her. The scaled girl. She was sitting on the grass by the pond, and sort of humming. And once I saw the biggest bat I've ever seen. Two feet across, it must have been, like a black kite. I don't even want to talk about its eyes. But it was getting dark, so I could have been mistaken.

What if, off the record now, István did start that fire? First, he would have set those things free. Some things shouldn't be in cages. You can understand that, right? You're Polish, your people are from the old country. And Ildiko Horvath? Like I said, István wouldn't hurt a fly. But she wasn't a fly, more like a spider in her web, or a cat waiting for the mouse to come out of its hole. What if, when she went down to the basement, István followed her, with the bottle of pálinka in his hand? What if he showed her the empty cages, then poured what was left in the pálinka bottle over those pieces of lace, and told her he would burn the things in the basement before he'd let her sell them? And then he lit a match. I figure she would fly at him with those red nails of hers. If he hit her with the bottle, well, that's self-defense. It wouldn't be his fault that the fire spread so quickly. But hey, I'm just telling a story. There are no windows in the basement. If something happened down there, I wouldn't have seen it, even if I wanted to. Anyway, I tell you, whatever she got she deserved. And I think Eva would agree.

But that's between you and me. István's not talking. I told him, this is America. We have rights in this country. So I'm your only witness. As far as I'm concerned, the fire was an accident. And I'm not going to say different, not if I have to swear on the Bible, so help me God.

DAVE HUTCHINSON

The Pavement Artist

Dave Hutchinson was born in Sheffield in 1960. He majored in American Studies at the University of Nottingham, and since 1984 he's worked as a journalist in London. He and his wife, Bogna, live in North London with their three cats.

He's the author of five collections of short stories: Thumbprints, Fools Gold, Torn Air, The Paradise Equation, *and* As The Crow Flies; *one novel,* The Villages; *coeditor (with John Grant) of* Strange Pleasures 2, *and editor of* Strange Pleasures 3 *and* Strange Pleasures 6.

"The Pavement Artist" was originally published in As the Crow Flies.

E.D.

Coypu and I only met once, in the accepted sense of the word, at his first—and as it turned out, his only—exhibition.

Fricke's had organized a private viewing for members of the trade, minor politicians, Arts Council hangers-on, and certain soap opera stars. I didn't want to go, partly because the presence of such semi-celebrities would attract magazine prismers and I hate having my photograph taken, but mainly because Fricke and I had had a falling-out some weeks previously over the sale of an early Angus Bouton monotype and the thought of being in the man's presence turned my stomach sour.

Eve, my wife, prevailed, though. "He sent you an invitation," she pointed out. "Perhaps he wants to kiss and make up."

"I doubt that," I said. "He just wants to parade his new wünderkind and pretend he knows the actors from *Hope Estate*."

"It can't hurt just to turn up and see what all the fuss is about, though, can it?"

Indeed. For months now Fricke's crafty publicity machine had been releasing—like a secret agent releasing a poison gas—rumors of a new, original talent in town. There are always rumors like that. For my own purposes, I had been responsible for some of them in the past. However, there was always a chance that one day the rumors might turn out to be true. And it would be nice to be present at Fricke's if they weren't.

It may have been that I wasn't the only art dealer in London who was keen to watch Fricke fall on his face, because his little gallery was bustling with people who had even better reason to dislike him than I did, wandering round gossiping about each other over wine and canapés.

Eve and I arrived unfashionably late, to find Fricke himself in an alcove talking to a prismer from the *Illustrated London News*. The journalist was holding her camera easily on one shoulder and asking quiet questions, which Fricke answered with much hand waving. I heard him mouth a number of superlatives as we went by.

In the gallery's main room a space had been roped off in the middle of the floor, at the center of which stood a large bulky object entirely covered with a paint-stained gray sheet, like something left behind by a careless firm of decorators. Guests slowly circulated around the roped-off area, telling bad jokes, spreading rumors, lying about each other.

A waiter in punk drag provided us with two glasses of white wine and indicated that as far as food was concerned it was "help yourself."

"Supermarket plonk," I commented, sipping the wine.

Eve dug me in the ribs with her elbow. "If he does want to kiss and make up, I want you to accept."

"Whatever for?"

"Because this stupid feud of yours is driving me mad. I'm sick of listening to you thinking up fresh insults about the poor man."

"That 'poor man' cost me a commission which would have paid to redecorate the house," I reminded her. "If I want to insult him, I'll insult him."

"Oh look, Carolyn's here," she said, drifting away across the room waving her hand above her head at someone in the crowd. I watched her for a moment, then looked around for the food.

It was then that I heard a huge voice behind me say, "Thomas, my man!"

I smiled. "Hello, Bill."

Bill From Chicago ("Hi, I'm Bill from Chicago.") was involved in a complicated juggling act involving half a bottle of wine, two glasses, and a plate piled with tiny pastries. I hadn't seen him in some months, and it seemed to me that he had lost weight. He also appeared to be wearing a clown's suit.

"What on earth are you wearing?" I said.

He grinned. "Thought I'd inject a little color into the proceedings."

"I bet that pleased Fricke."

"He was pleased speechless. Here, try one of these." He somehow managed to offer me the vol-au-vents without dropping everything else he was carrying. "The salmon ones are pretty good."

"I can see you're fond of them." The pockets of his clown suit were bulging with food; the sharp points of dozens of cocktail sausage sticks had pierced the cloth, and protruded from his hip like an imaginative antipersonnel device.

"Man's gotta eat, Thomas. How've you been?"

"Busy. You?"

He unloaded his plate and one of the glasses onto a passing waiter, refilled the other glass and stood holding the bottle by the neck. "Jesus Christ, Thomas, look at these kids," he said, nodding at the waiter, dressed in torn green fishnet stockings, a pair of suspenders and a black lace tutu, hair shaved into a tight mohawk. "Who the hell dresses like that any more? You reckon they're faggots?"

"I don't think you're in any position to be critical of how other people dress," I said.

"Eve here?" he asked, craning his bull-neck to look out over the crowd. "I don't see her."

"She spotted Carolyn, I think."

"Carolyn?"

"The one with the two hyphens. Carolyn-Something Something-Something. I forget."

Bill shook his head. "Christ, what a country. I been *real* busy, Thomas. Lots of new stuff. Fresh stuff. Come over and see it sometime."

I nodded, but I knew a trip to his little studio in Islington would be fruitless. For all his disparagement of Britain, he had been here almost fifteen years, had arrived young and full of energy, a powerful talent in portraiture. But it was almost five years since he had produced anything of note, and that, even his friends agreed, had been a pale shadow of his former work. Most dealers and gallery owners regarded him as a burnout. His hair was thinning and going gray, and there was a bloom to his cheeks which from a distance might be mistaken for the flush of rude health, but closer to revealed itself as a fine patchwork of broken capillaries.

"What's the word on Fricke's new toyboy?"

"Nobody seems to know anything much," I said, letting him refill my glass. "He's young and he's hot, you know the kind of thing."

"Cagey bastard, that Fricke."

I nodded agreement, watching the cagey bastard working his way through the crowd toward us. He was wearing a sober gray business suit, the effect somewhat spoiled by a huge floppy bow tie which appeared to have been dipped in vomit.

"I see you have brought your jester, Thomas," he said to me, sparing Bill a poisonous glance. Bill guffawed and bowed deeply, spilling wine on the floor.

"We thought you might need the entertainment, Waldtar," I said coolly.

"I must talk with you about that Bouton business," he said, dropping his voice conspiratorially and trying to lead me by the arm away from Bill.

"I don't think we have anything to talk about," I said, standing my ground.

He looked hurt. "But this was business, Thomas! There is no reason why we cannot be friends."

I gently removed his hand from my arm. "There is *every* reason, Waldtar." I didn't know why he looked so hurt; I was the one who had been cheated.

His expression changed, his eyes hardened. "You will regret this, Thomas. I have something here that everyone will want."

"Waldtar," I told him, "there is nothing here that *I* want."

He tipped his head back and snorted and strode away into the crowd.

"It was worth coming here just to see that," said Bill. "Eve, *baby*!" He gave her a huge hug as she came back to us.

"Hello, Bill," she said, looking small and crushed in his huge arms but returning the hug. "Well?"

"Well what?" I asked innocently.

"Did you and Waldtar kiss and make up?"

"Oh yes," I said. "Oh yes, we kissed and made up."

She looked back through the crowd, searching for Fricke. "He didn't look very happy."

"Under a lot of strain," Bill said. "Big night for him."

Eve gave me a long cool stare. "Mm," she said. I smiled at her.

"Ladies and gentlemen! Ladies and gentlemen!" Fricke's voice went up in the room.

"It's showtime, folks," Bill rumbled as we all turned to face Fricke.

He was standing by the roped-off area. Beside him was a slight figure dressed all in black and topped off with a great floppy mat of black hair.

"Ladies and gentlemen," said Fricke, acting up for the cameras, "you have been invited here tonight to witness the emergence of a new talent in the world of art, a fresh voice embracing both technology and artistry. Ladies and gentlemen, please allow me to present Coypu."

The figure beside him, sallow-faced under his unruly shock of black hair, just stared at the assembly with tiny blue eyes. He didn't speak, but his attitude, his body language, suggested some huge, baffling hostility.

There was a subdued ripple of applause, which Fricke raised his hands to quieten. When all attention was back on him, he stepped over to the rope barrier and approached the draped shape.

"Ladies and gentlemen," he said, "The Decline of Western Civilization!"

With a grand gesture, he took a corner of the paint-spattered sheet and tugged it away from what it covered, and for a moment the only sound in the gallery was of Bill howling with laughter.

Under the sheet was a washing machine. An old-fashioned Zanussi model, to be sure, but still just a washing machine. I looked across at Coypu and was disturbed to find his little eyes locked with mine.

Then there was a faint whirring sound, and when I looked back at the washing machine it had started to move.

A small flap had popped up on the side of the machine, and from this emerged a skeletal articulated arm nearly a meter long, tipped with a little screwdriver. The arm waved sinuously at us as other panels flipped up and more arms emerged. Bill, beside me, stopped laughing. He blew a raspberry, but it sounded half-hearted and uncertain.

There were over a dozen arms growing out of the machine by now, ending in wrenches and screwdrivers and Allen keys and spanners and little grasping metal claws, waving slowly in the air accompanied by the barest whirring of servomechanisms. For a moment, it seemed as if the Zanussi had transformed itself into some bizarre white insect.

Then, with monstrous grace and in almost total silence, it proceeded to take itself apart.

Powered screwdrivers withdrew screws, side panels were removed and lowered gently to the floor, tiny wrenches and spanners undid nuts and bolts, small components were plucked out and placed beside the machine in some outrageous act of self-surgery. And no one said a word.

In the end, all that remained of the Zanussi was the chassis, with the washing drum nestled inside among the servos and motors and processors Coypu had installed to make the thing work.

The arms stilled, drooped as if in salute, and there was a burst of applause from the audience, in which Bill and I did not participate.

But *The Decline of Western Civilization* had one last surprise.

The hollow drum suddenly flooded with blue-white light, and when the light had faded away there was a human head in the drum. A little girl's head, with blonde curls and a tiny snub nose. The applause grew ragged and died away, and I heard gasps from the other side of the room, where the soap opera actors had congregated.

Then the little girl's eyes opened, and they were unnaturally blue, like neon sapphires.

"It's a fucking cracker," Bill murmured.

"It can't be," I said.

The head regarded us from the innards of the gutted washing machine. Then, in an old man's ruined whiskey voice, it said, "Help me, Daddy. Help me, Daddy. Help me, Daddy," over and over again, the voice growing fainter and fainter until at last we could no longer hear it, only see the girl's lips moving. Then even this stopped; she closed her eyes, the disembodied head bowed forward, and she faded away.

There was a long moment of silence, then someone—I will always be certain it was Fricke himself—began to clap. Others took up the applause until it was appallingly loud. I stood where I was, arms folded, while Eve clapped and cheered beside me. Bill was not clapping either; he was staring at the gutted Zanussi with a look on his face I couldn't identify. All of a sudden he was no longer a crafty satirical gatecrasher. All of a sudden he looked exactly the way he was dressed: a clown.

The applause went on for an embarrassingly long time, and with a sinking sensation I watched Fricke leading Coypu through the admiring throng toward me.

They reached us as the applause degenerated into excited conversation. Fricke gave Bill a superior sneer, bowed low to Eve, and said to Coypu, "My boy, this is the man I told you about. Mr. Thomas MacDougal."

Coypu barely inclined his head toward me. "I know you," he said in a clipped New Zealand accent. His eyes were like glass, little azure marbles, their gaze so discomforting and direct that I had to look away.

"Oh?"

"Yeah. Got a good gallery. Got a good reputation." He turned his gaze on Eve. "Got a nice wife." Eve smiled and started to examine her wineglass.

"One always likes to feel appreciated," I said lightly.

"Oh sure," he said, his voice a sneering approximation of my own. "*Doesn't* one just."

I just stared. Eve, always less prepared to be judgmental than me, said, "Have you been in London long, Mr. Coypu?"

He tipped his head to one side and regarded my wife as if she was a biological specimen. Then he leaned forward and, putting his mouth close to her ear, whispered something I didn't catch.

Eve gasped and took a step back, putting one hand to her mouth. With the other hand, she slapped Coypu across the face.

I started forward, but Bill, somehow accommodating all his plates and bottles and glasses in one hand, grabbed my upper arm and held me back.

Coypu hadn't moved. A red imprint of my wife's hand was appearing on his white cheek, and he was smiling. His upper lip curled back, and I saw that his teeth were a dirty orange color. "Come down here to watch Fricke's little pet," he sneered. "What were you expecting? Someone nice?"

"You're lucky I don't thump you, you little shit," I said, shaking free of Bill's hand.

He gave me a long calculating look, as if evaluating me as an opponent. "You're a pimp, Tom," he said. "Just living off people like me."

I truly believe that if his behavior hadn't surprised me so much I would have knocked him entirely across the room. Instead, I said, "If it wasn't for pimps like Waldtar and me, you'd be doing chalk drawings on the pavements, you little bastard."

And he grinned. I swear he grinned a huge happy grin. "But they'd be fucking brilliant chalk drawings, all the same."

Fricke, who had watched all this with a satisfied look on his face, put a hand on Coypu's arm and steered him away from us. As they turned away, I saw Fricke grin. I wanted to go after them and punch him, but Eve took hold of my wrist. "Let's go, Thomas," she said. "I don't want to stay here with that horrible little man."

Bill sighed. "Well he sure as hell won't be able to exhibit anywhere after *that*."

Bill was wrong. In the beginning, Coypu's constructions only had a minority appeal, mainly among those easily fooled by what others told them was fashionable. The constructions appeared time and again that summer at Fricke's gallery. They sold for interesting sums, but they did not sell often.

Then, slowly, word began to leak out into the larger world; more and more people were fooled by what they believed was genius. I watched the process, wishing there was something I could do to stop it.

There were magazine documentaries. A few at first, then an increasing flood. Coypu began to make the transition from Artist to Celebrity. His work sold more and more often, for increasing sums.

As his Celebrity gained intensity, so did the stories about him. There were rumors of outrageous drug use, of dreadful behavior in restaurants, a case of common assault that was thrown out of court because the alleged victim declined to give evidence, soap starlets eager to get a tan under the bright light of his fame. He became a hero to the young. One magazine program described him as 'the last true critic of Consumerism.'

There seemed no escaping him. To my mild surprise, I even found him in science magazines, in articles about crackers.

Bill had been wrong; the girl's head in *The Decline of Western Civilization* was not a cracker. It was just a hologram, but of such sophistication that most people assumed it was a real personality structure. The assumption was so widespread that I even read of people who claimed they knew the little girl whose personality structure had been used.

There was a point, twenty years ago, just after the Japanese first devised a procedure for recording human personalities, when people had asked what possible purpose it could have. It was only when details of the technique emerged—the neuroelectrical and chemical stimulation of the brain involved causing irreversible brain damage in eighty-six percent of subjects and death in the remaining fourteen percent—that excitement about cracking died down. It was obviously far too dangerous to be of use to anyone but the terminally ill.

Then a number of American and European states instituted personality structuring in place of the death penalty. It had the advantage of salving liberal consciences: the body dies, but the personality survives. It began to be known as personality distillation. Cracking. Death Row became known as The Distillery. I understand that there is a possibility that crackers may be used to pilot spacecraft, but this seems unlikely.

I believe there is a rumor among civil rights organizations that cracking is being used by the police and security services to interrogate suspects, but it seems highly unlikely to me; only a terminally stupid police force would use an interrogation technique that killed fourteen percent of its subjects and left the rest irretrievably brain-damaged.

Coypu's opening night somehow caused a shift in the public perception of cracking. I began to see cracker-imitation holograms used more and more often in sculpture. Some of these works were offered to me. I always refused them, but the legend that Coypu seemed determined to build rolled inexorably onward.

I was working in my office at the gallery one afternoon in late July when I heard a commotion in the main room, shouts and crashes, and, implausibly, singing.

Going out into the gallery, I found one of my assistants struggling to restrain a filthy, leather-clad young woman with a spider's web tattooed across her face. The young woman wore electric-blue tights and biker boots, and a combat jacket so ingrained with dirt that its original color was impossible to discern. Her hair had been hacked haphazardly into the semblance of a Mohawk crest, and in one grimy hand she held a large tool of some kind, a species of wrench.

My assistant was trying to back her into a corner, but the girl kept attempting to lunge past him toward the gallery's exhibits. She had already managed some damage; a small Allan Benedict statuette lay in pieces on the floor, and my one remaining Saul de Bono watercolor was ruined, smashed to bits.

I dashed over and grabbed the girl, revolted by the smell of excrement and solvents rising from her. She tossed her head as she tried to shake herself free, and I saw that her eyes were completely crazy. She was singing a song in a language I did not recognize, and I was fairly sure that she was not even wholly aware of where she was.

My assistant ran off to call the police, and as he did so I looked out through the window of the gallery and saw a familiar black-clad figure standing in a shop doorway across the road. He was smiling; I could see his orange teeth, even from the other side of the street.

He was gone by the time the police arrived, of course. The girl, high on something or other, was taken away and charged with malicious damage. She couldn't remember why she had attacked the gallery, or who had given her the drugs. She was fined several hundred euros, and since she could not pay she was sent to prison for a year.

I knew who had given her the drugs, but I had no proof, and I began to see him hanging around on the opposite side of the street. Sometimes he was just walking past, but it was not unusual for him to stand staring at the gallery for hours at a time, smiling.

"Why us?" Eve said one evening. "Why pick on us?"

"Fricke told him to," I said. "Because I wouldn't forgive him for that Bouton business."

Eve shuddered. "They deserve each other." She had never told me what Coypu had whispered to her, the night of his exhibition. She grew quiet if I asked her, and eventually I had given up asking.

"Besides, it isn't just us," I said. "He's been wandering around some of the other galleries as well, making himself unpleasant. Fricke must think he has a lot of scores to settle."

"Can't the police do anything?"

"Not without evidence. And I don't want to give Fricke the satisfaction of being able to act the outraged innocent." I smiled. "And you wanted to make friends with him."

She gave me a long cool look. "This might not be happening if you had."

Perhaps she was right. I never told her about the notes which had begun to appear on the gallery's doormat, all of them in the clear flowing anonymous copperplate of a Canon Voicewriter, all of them saying the same thing: *the american is fucking your wife, tom*. I had torn them all up and burned the pieces.

Coypu made a recording with some dreadful reggae revival band that topped the national charts; the promotional video showed all his constructions taking the places of the band, the little girl's head in the Zanussi singing the lyrics. Eve wouldn't watch it. At the band's live performances, Coypu was seen to slash his body with broken bottles, fling himself repeatedly into his adoring audience, and, occasionally, to physically assault himself with his microphone stand.

And yet through all his excesses he seemed to return fresh and undamaged, his creative faculties unharmed and even enhanced. It was as if he was trying to prove to the world that he was indestructible, that he thrived on the chaos that attended him.

He was wrong.

One morning in early October, Fricke arrived at his gallery and found Coypu lying on his back across the top of *The Decline of Western Civilization*.

Fricke was used to Coypu's irregular comings and goings, his sudden drunken arrivals, he said later, and he found nothing very unusual about his artist's presence in his gallery, apparently insensible.

It was only when he tried to rouse Coypu, and saw the cyanotic color of his skin, the lumpy mass of vomit in his gaping mouth, the foam of blood and mucus which had poured from his nostrils, that Fricke panicked.

He told the police that he had not been thinking clearly, that his only concern was to protect his gallery and his good name from scandal. And that was why, when he was stopped in Soho for dangerous driving, Coypu's body was in the boot of his car.

The trial was the high spot of the autumn. The autopsy revealed a cocktail of various illegal substances in Coypu's bloodstream, and the verdict of the inquest was that these had probably caused the artist's death.

Fricke's defense was that he knew nothing of Coypu's habit. He believed the young man had drunk very heavily, but he said that was part and parcel of the bohemian lifestyle Coypu was leading, and he had no reason to suspect it went any further than that.

There were character witnesses to testify that Fricke was a fine upstanding member of the community. I was gratified to note that the defense did not approach me to act as a character witness.

The prosecution, however, brought forward two witnesses who testified to having sold Fricke drugs on several occasions, and one who said he had seen both Fricke and Coypu snorting cocaine. Fricke said his own drug habit—for which he was now receiving treatment—was a matter of common knowledge. This was news to me, as it was to a number of other owners I spoke to.

Finally, Fricke did some kind of deal with the prosecution, turning king's evidence against the network of drug dealers he had used, and entered a witness support program under which he presumably vanished with a new name and face. He was lucky; had he been tried in France or Spain or Germany, he would have been sentenced to death and cracked, and might have wound up as part of somebody's sculpture, which would have been poetic justice.

His gallery was bought by a firm of theatrical suppliers. They held a sale of the contents, and I was able—by greasing a few palms—to obtain *The Decline of Western Civilization*, which Fricke had never sold. Eve didn't like it, so I kept it in my office at the gallery, as a trophy.

Despite the age of Information Technology in which we live, we still suffer the vagaries of the postal service, and it was some days after the end of Fricke's trial that a plain yellow envelope was delivered to the gallery containing a standard-size holofiche, such as dealers send to each other to show examples of artworks.

I slipped the fiche into my projector and pressed the READ button. On the projector stage there appeared what seemed to be a small electronic device, a holo-prism camera of some kind. A peculiar kind of thing to send anyone.

I pressed the reader's SCAN button, and there appeared a rapid sequence of still images, each one slightly different from the last, so the effect was of a jerky animated film. As I watched, a line of gooseflesh traveled up my forearms.

Tiny arms appeared on the sides of the camera. They proceeded to take it to pieces, then put it back together again in a different configuration so that it resembled a fat spider. Then it got up and took a few steps before sitting down again and reassembling itself as a camera.

I ran the sequence again, swearing under my breath. It was Coypu's final gesture, I was sure of it. He was offering me one of his pieces, cynically, mockingly. I tore the fiche from the reader and burned it in my ashtray. It was printed on cheap stock and burned with a bright yellow flame that tailed off into greasy acrid smoke.

During Fricke's trial I had started to hear more and more from Bill. There were letters, postcards, e-mails, messages on my phone service. Doing wonderful work, Thomas. Come up and see me sometime. Islington the Heart of the Universe. Much new work: come see. Where are you, you moody old shit?

I was in no hurry; Bill had never been a special friend, and his work had declined alarmingly. Besides, these were busy times for the gallery; I had discovered several new artists of potential greatness, and my time was taken up in shepherding them out into the public gaze. Bill could wait.

It was Eve who finally got me to go and see him. She found one of his postcards on my desk at the gallery.

"Oh, Thomas," she said. "For shame. You could at least see what he wants."

"It's a waste of time," I said. "Really, Eve. There's no point."

"How can you say that? You used to be friends."

"Acquaintances," I corrected absently, attending to the month's budget sheet.

"You're behaving shamefully," she said. "Go and see him."

"There won't be anything there worth seeing," I said.

"So go and see Bill, you bastard." She shook her head in wonderment. "Sometimes I think you believe people are only here to make art for you to sell."

I looked up. "Aren't they?" She glared at me. "Joke."

She was still glaring. "It better have been."

Bill's studio was in a converted garage on a street off the Caledonian Road, an area where gentrification had made some tentative steps a decade or so ago and then given it up as a bad job. Now rubbish blew along the pavements and groups of youths huddled in shop doorways and watched as I drove past.

He didn't answer the front door bell. I walked along the side of the old garage, trying to peer through the grimy wire-reinforced windows. I thought I saw movement inside and I carried on round to the back.

The big double doors at the back of the garage were open onto the little courtyard. Bill was sitting in the doorway in a faded deck chair, wearing wire-framed sunglasses which hid his eyes entirely.

"Thomas," he said when I emerged from around the side of the garage.

"Hello, Bill."

"Bit off the beaten track today, aren't you?"

I squatted down beside the deckchair. "I got an invitation I couldn't refuse."

He seemed lost in thought for a moment. "Oh, yeah," he said finally. His voice sounded very tired.

"You said something about some new work."

He nodded. "Yeah. They're in back. Going to buy something?"

"I won't know until I've seen them."

"How's Eve?"

"She's all right."

He shook his head. "You don't treat that girl right, Thomas," he said distantly.

For a second, I thought irrationally of the anonymous notes shoved through the gallery's letterbox, and I was about to mention them to him when there was a whirring noise and the little camera-spider I had seen in the fiche stepped uncertainly through the doors and into the weak sunshine. It swung its body from side to side, panning its three sensor-eyes around the yard, then turned and toddled back into the garage. I heard something fall over inside, followed by a nearly human squeak. Bill and I looked at each other.

"Bill," I said.

I saw his face screw up as if in intense concentration. Then he sat back in the deckchair. "I let him work here," he said.

"What? Why?"

I watched him sitting there. With the sunglasses on, he looked like a blind man, finding the sun's position in the sky by the miniscule heat on his face. Finally he said, "I went to him after Waldtar's show, offered him a place to work. Offered him the money my family sends me. He couldn't resist it, rubbing my face in it."

I shook my head. "I don't understand."

He didn't answer for a long time. When he did, he said, "He was magic, Thomas. I knew that the first time I set eyes on him. Magic. I was starting to work again, just being around him. Good work, too."

"He was an outrage, Bill," I said, genuinely mystified. "He was scum. The world's better off without him."

"Ah, Thomas." He smiled up into the sky. "You just think that because he was Waldtar's boy. If you'd found him he would only have been a step or so down from Jesus."

"No," I said, shuddering. "Not a chance."

"I've seen you work, Thomas," he said. "You're not that different from Waldtar, not really. Coypu was different. Not like most of the kids today. At least he tried to be different."

"Coypu was vile, Bill," I said. "I wouldn't have touched him with a barge pole."

"He was magic, though," he said dreamily. "Magic."

And Bill had thought he could recapture the power of his younger days by warming himself beside Coypu's talent. It was so pathetic it wasn't even sad.

I rubbed my eyes, stood up, and went into the garage. When my eyes had adjusted to the dimness I saw that the spider had somehow got itself caught up in a dangling tangle of wire threaded with antique resistors. In its efforts to untangle itself, the spider had somehow managed to pull a heavy piece of computer hardware off a workbench onto itself. The module had caught one of its legs, and it was sitting on the concrete floor mewing gently, unable to pull free. I lifted the module and picked up the little machine and looked around the studio.

Canvases and boards were stacked haphazardly around the walls, propped up on benches and bits of furniture, laid flat on the floor, standing on worktops. There were sculptures in a dozen different media, there were oils, watercolors, gouaches, acrylics, landscapes, portraits, abstracts. It was as if he had literally tried *everything* in a desperate attempt to reinvent himself. And it was all awful. The paintings were frantic slashes of color; the sculptures were hopeless blobs. I sighed and went back outside, the spider under my arm.

"How many have you sold?" I asked.

"Not one," he replied without looking at me. "Oh, people come up here, but they get here and they just pussy out of buying anything. They just come . . . oh, I don't know. Maybe they just come to look." He sighed. "What a stupid business for a good Illinois boy to get himself into."

I put the spider down. One of its legs appeared to be broken, uncoordinated. It sat on the concrete and ran two of its legs over the damaged one. It seemed almost comically sad; its tiny stupid sound chip made forlorn little meeping sounds.

"It's his," Bill said, looking down at the little machine. "Last thing he ever made."

"You sent me that fiche, didn't you?" I said.

He waved a hand. "I was trying to sell the fucking thing. Thought you might go for it, maybe buy it through an agent if it offended you so much." He looked at the spider, its legs waving weakly. "It's broken?"

"It had an accident."

"I'll never sell it now. Probably have to junk it." For a moment, the spider seemed to pause in the forlorn examination of its broken leg, tilt its body from one side to the other, then resume its hopeless investigation. Bill sighed. "Sometimes I swear it understands every word I say."

"How much money do you have?"

"I don't want your charity, Thomas," he said.

"How much?"

He craned his neck back, looking at the sky. "I won't make this month's rent."

I took out my organizer, typed out a transfer of five thousand euros. I still had his account details on file from the last time I had bought something from him; I entered them, added the requisite code words, and made the transfer.

"Take a holiday, Bill," I said, handing him the hardcopy. "Go home to Chicago for a while."

He looked at the printed slip and his throat seemed to close up. He made a little croaking sound.

"It's all right. I lost more than that when Fricke sold that Bouton from under me, remember?"

He smiled and nodded; tears were emerging from beneath the mirrored lenses of the sunglasses and making grimy trails on his cheeks. "Wonder what happened to old Waldtar."

"I don't care so long as he stays away from me." I picked up the spider and tucked it under my arm. "Send me a postcard, eh?"

"Sure," he said, not looking at me, the slip crumpled in one huge dirty fist.

The little camera-spider toddled about the gallery for two months or so, mewing and tugging at visitors' ankles until they bent down and patted it. Sometimes it would sit down and attempt to reconfigure itself into a camera again, but each time the damaged leg defeated it. It would sit there for hours with apparently infinite patience, the job half done, neither one thing nor another, with the leg jutting out at an angle. Then all of a sudden it would seem to shrug, turn itself back into a spider, and limp off looking for an ankle to tug at. Eve thought it was creepy, but I could quite happily watch it all day.

Finally, its batteries ran down. It proved very difficult to find replacements, so the spider sat on my desk, legs in the air, all through Christmas and over New Year.

I was in the gallery one morning in February, contemplating the dead spider and trying to think where I might find its peculiar type of battery, when my post arrived. Among the usual circulars and sales fiches there was a simple postcard, the kind tourists can buy almost anywhere in London, a view of the Houses of Parliament from Waterloo Bridge. I turned it over and found that the space for the message had been left blank. The address, however, was handwritten in a familiar emphatic style.

I saw the drawings first, a line of them along the pavement on Victoria Embankment. Each stone had a representation in colored chalk of some painting. Leonardos, Michaelangelos, Hockneys, in a line which stretched out into the distance from Waterloo Bridge toward Blackfriars. There was a Mona Lisa, a detail from the Sistine ceiling, the face of a girl from a Tissot portrait I vaguely recognized. There must have been hundreds of them. At this end, they were faded and blotched by the drizzle, but they grew stronger and fresher as I walked toward Blackfriars and the figure working there.

He was on his knees on the pavement, dressed in a shirt, jeans, cardigan and a crumpled shapeless beige jacket. His hair was wet and tousled from the rain. About him lay scattered nubs of chalk. He was drawing another Mona Lisa on the paving stone beneath him; there was a fresh Hals portrait on the one to his right, and on the one to the left I could make out the faded outline of a man's face. Beyond, running toward Blackfriars Bridge, I could see other faded representations. I wondered how many times he had gone up and down the Embankment.

"So how was the holiday?" I asked.

He looked up. His eyes were sunken, his cheeks hollow, his shoulders rounded from bending over the chalk drawings. "Hello, Thomas," he said.

I squatted down beside him. "The batteries ran down on the construction I bought from you. I can't find replacements."

He looked blankly at me. "There's some at the studio," he said. "Big box. Last you forever."

"Maybe you could let me have some. I'd pay for them."

He shook his head. "Take them."

"Thanks for the postcard, by the way."

"Least I could do." He stood slowly, reluctantly, like a tired puppet, and I stood with him, seeing the tattered knees of his jeans, the raw friction sores on the skin underneath. He looked down at his drawings. "Shall we prise a couple up for the gallery, Thomas? Would the council let us do that?"

I waved my hand along the line of chalk pictures. "What on earth are you doing this for?"

He dug around in a pocket of his jacket and found a lighter and a packet of cigarettes. He lit one, shielding the lighter flame from the wind with his hand. "Well, Thomas, I guess I needed the money. The family cut me off. Called me a black sheep, can you imagine that?"

"What about the money I gave you?"

He laughed, a bitter shadow of his old guffaw that came out shrouded in cigarette smoke. "That lasted me about a week." He turned away from me and walked to the wall of the Embankment. "I got debts coming out of my ears. Your money didn't hardly dent them."

I went over to stand beside him, arms resting on top of the wall, staring out across the river at the buildings along the South Bank. "You should have said something. Got in touch. I'd have helped."

He looked at me. "The way you came running as soon as I told you I'd been working again?" He shook his head. "Sorry, Thomas, I couldn't wait that long."

A young couple came walking along the pavement, he in jeans and a combat jacket, she in a short flowered skirt, orange jacket, and floppy red boots. As they passed us, the girl laughed and tossed a couple of euros at my feet. The boy laughed too, and they walked on.

"It's surprising how much you can make on a good day," Bill said, regarding the little coins on the pavement. He stooped and picked them up. "Of course, it's surprising how little you can make as well."

"Bill, I'm sorry," I said, quite appalled at how far he had fallen.

He gave me a strange little lopsided smile. "Why sorry, Thomas? You're not your brother's keeper, after all." He put a big hand on my shoulder. "Even if I had gotten in touch, you'd have been busy, am I right?" When I looked away, he chuckled. "Old Bill, he isn't such a *close* friend, is he," he went on, lifting his hand away from my shoulder and brushing his hair back from his forehead. "Old Bill, he isn't *talented* any more, is he. Am I right?"

"I haven't done anything to deserve this, Bill."

"Oh?" He stepped back in mock amazement, toes scuffing across the Mona Lisa's smile. "And I have? What have I done to deserve this, Thomas? Tell me that." He looked tiredly along the line of pictures. "Fuck, even Coypu would have deserved better than *this*," he said quietly.

"Coypu would have enjoyed it," I said, thinking about what he had said to me the night of his exhibition.

Bill smiled thoughtfully. "Yeah. Maybe he would, at that." He looked at me. "I killed him, you know."

I stared. "Beg pardon?"

He leaned back against the wall and crossed his arms. "I killed the little shit." He looked about him. "And a whole lot of good it did me."

"You what?"

He was watching me solemnly. "Were the words too difficult for you or something?" he inquired.

Unwittingly, I had crossed the distance between us until we were almost toe-to-toe. "What do you mean you killed him?" I said under my breath.

"I mean I killed him," he said, leaning down toward me. "Have you suddenly become very very stupid, Thomas?"

"It was drugs," I said. "An overdose."

"Well, sure, it *looked* that way."

I suddenly realized I had one hand against his huge barrel chest; I could feel his heartbeating under my palm. "What?" I said, baffled.

He gave me a long-suffering look. "I got hold of a cracking deck and I killed him with it," he said slowly and distinctly, as if I was hard of hearing or slow in the head. I think the look on my face must have convinced him I was the latter, because he straightened up and folded his arms again. "Don't look at me like that, Thomas. I just went ahead and did what everybody else was dreaming of doing."

I stepped away, studying his face for some sign that he was lying or crazy, and knowing he was neither. "Where did you get a cracking deck?"

He laughed. "Oh come on, Thomas. Where do you think I was before I came here? I've got contacts you never dreamed of. The deck came through Korea. Cost me everything I had. Best buy I ever made." He took a few steps away from me along the pavement, dropped his cigarette end and ground it into the Hals face with his toe. "He was working real late one night; he'd been coked to the eyeballs for days, and he just fell asleep on the cot in the studio." He smiled at me. "He looked real innocent lying there asleep."

I said, "Bill . . ."

He watched the crowds of office girls and baggy-suited youths passing their lunchtime with a walk along the Embankment. "I nearly changed my mind, right there. He looked like a normal person when he was asleep. He just looked like a kid." He walked back toward me and sighed. "But he was dreaming of making more of those fucking clever things, so I put the machine on him and I pressed the button. Sucked him right out of his head and structured his personality onto a half-dozen terabyte ROM chips. It was real poetic. I hope it made him happy."

All I could do was stare.

Bill sniffed and wiped his nose on the sleeve of his jacket. "I was going to dump him in the river when it was finished, let him drown. Suicide. But it turned out he was one of the unlucky fourteen percent the machine kills outright. He had a key to Fricke's gallery, so I trucked the body down there and left it."

"Fricke was on trial," I whispered.

"Oh, Thomas, please. Don't tell me you're sorry for *Fricke*."

"No, but . . ."

He spread his hands. "No argument then."

I shook my head to try and clear it. "I don't understand . . . Why are you telling me all this?"

Bill grinned. "The Master Criminal always confesses his Evil Plan in the final reel, doesn't he?"

I wanted to take him by the lapels and shake him, but I knew I wouldn't be able to budge him. "This isn't a film, Bill. And you're no master criminal."

"Oh, but I am." And for a moment the old, familiar twinkle returned to his eyes. "I committed the perfect murder. A regular work of art, in fact. He never told anyone he was working at my place; the police never even phoned me. They cremated his body, I paid cash for the machine and bought it under a false name through a middleman, and when I'd finished I broke it up and incinerated the bits. There's no evidence." He leaned forward slightly again. "And anyway, you don't believe me."

But I did. It was outrageous and horrible, but I believed every word. And I believed I knew why he had done it.

"He was sending me letters saying you and Eve were having an affair," I blurted.

Bill nodded solemnly. "I guess we'll never know how he found out about that," he said, and I was struck completely dumb. He regarded me steadily and shook his head. "Was over a long time ago, Thomas. Years. You never treated that girl right; don't hold it against her. And it's not why I killed him, if that's what you're thinking. Though it helped, I have to admit."

"The chips," I managed to say.

He cocked his head to one side. "The what?"

"You said you structured Coypu's personality onto six terabyte ROM chips. What happened to them?"

He put his head back and guffawed, the familiar Bill guffaw. "Good Christ,

Thomas," he laughed. "I tell you I'm a murderer who was sleeping with your wife, and all you can think about is ROM chips?"

"Where are they? What did you do with them?"

He screwed up his face and shook his head. "Nah. Maybe if you think about it hard enough, you'll figure it out for yourself."

I was appalled at his composure. I wanted to punch him, kick him, throw him screaming into the Thames. Instead I said, "Tell me where they are."

"Pimp to the very end, eh, Thomas?" he said with a grin. "Imagine what those chips are worth now, eh?" The grin mellowed into a smile. "You could figure it out, you know. You're smart enough. Maybe." He checked his watch and then set about gathering his chalks together and putting them into his jacket pockets. "If you'll excuse me, I have to be somewhere else." He straightened up and put a hand on my shoulder. "Stay sharp, eh, Thomas?"

I could think of nothing more to say to him. Not then, not ever again. I just watched him go, angry at myself for not knowing what was the right thing to do, and for not being strong enough to do it. And all the time I was thinking, *You always meant to do it, didn't you; you already had the cracking deck, didn't you; you always meant to do it. . . .*

He walked away, but he had only gone a couple of meters when the stopped and looked back. "They're pretty good, though. Aren't they?"

I looked along the line of drawings. "Yes," I said. "Yes, they are."

It wanders around the floor, dragging its injured leg, day after day after day, mewing for human companionship, nipping ankles which ignore it. Sometimes it sits down and tries to remake itself, but the injury prevents it and it just gets up again and goes looking for someone to love it, poor half-machine, going round and round and round. . . .

KIM NEWMAN

The Gypsies in the Wood

"The Gypsies in the Wood" was one of our favorite stories of the year. Despite its length, we couldn't imagine not introducing Newman's admittedly dark-fantasy novelette of Victorian detectives, children's literature, and fairy abductions to a new audience. "The Gypsies in the Wood" was first published in The Fair Folk, *edited by Marvin Kaye, an all-original novella anthology from the Science Fiction Book Club. Every story in it was worthy of consideration for this anthology, and we especially enjoyed the selections by Patricia A. McKillip and Megan Lindholm. Kim Newman lives in London, England. His work includes the classic vampire novel,* Anno Dracula, The Original Dr. Shade and Other Stories, *and, with coeditor Stephen Jones, 2005's* Horror: 101 Best Books.

—K.L. & G.G.

Act I: The Children of Eye

1: "we take an interest"

"M r. Charles Beauregard?" asked Dr Rud, squinting through *pince-nez*.
Charles allowed he was who his *carte de visite* said he was.
"Of . . . the Diogenes Club?"
"Indeed."

He stood at the front door. The Criftins, the doctor's house, was large but lopsided, several buildings close together, cobbled into one by additions in different stone. At once household, clinic, and dispensary, it was an important place in the parish of Eye, if not a noteworthy landmark in the county of Herefordshire. On the map Charles had studied on the down train, Eye was a double-yolked egg: two communities, Ashton Eye and Moreton Eye, separated by a rise of trees called Hill Wood and an open space of common ground called Fair Field.

It was mid-evening, full dark and freezing. His breath frosted. Snow had settled thick in recent weeks. Under a quarter-moon, the countryside was dingy white, with black scabs where the fall was melted or cleared away.

Charles leaned forward a little, slipping his face into light-spill to give the doctor a good, reassuring look at him.

Rud, unused to answering his own front door, was grumpily pitching in during the crisis. After another token glance at Charles's card, the doctor threw up his hands and stood aside.

A Royal Welsch Fusilier lounged in the hallway, giving cheek to a tweeny. The maid, who carried a heavy basin, tolerated none of his malarkey. She barged past the guard, opening the parlor door with a practiced hip shove, and slipped inside with an equally practiced flounce, agitating the bustlelike bow of her apron ties.

Charles stepped over the threshold.

The guard clattered upright, rifle to shoulder. Stomach in, shoulders out, eyes front, chin up. The tweeny, returning from the parlor, smirked at his tin soldier pose. The lad blushed violet. Realizing Charles wore no uniform, he relaxed into an attitude of merely casual vigilance.

"I assume you are another wave of this *invasion?*" stated the doctor.

"Someone called out the army," said Charles. "Through channels, the army called out us. Which means you get me, I'm afraid."

Rud was stout and bald, hair pomaded into a laurel-curl fringe. Five cultivated strands plastered across his pate, a sixth hanging awry—like a bellpull attached to his brain. Tonight, the doctor received visitors without ceremony, collarless, in shirtsleeves and waistcoat. He ought to be accustomed to intrusions at all hours. A country practice never closed. Charles gathered the last few days had been more than ordinarily trying.

"I did not expect a curfew, sir. We're good, honest Englishmen in Eye. And Welshmen too. Not some rebellious settlement in the Hindu Kush. Not an enemy position, to be taken, occupied, and looted!"

The guard's blush was still vivid. The tweeny put her hands on her broad hips and laughed.

"Your 'natives' seem to put up a sterling defense."

"Major Chilcot has set up inspection points, prohibited entry to Hill Wood, closed the Small Man . . ."

"I imagine it's for your protection. Though I'll see what I can do. If anything is liable to lead to mutiny, it's shutting the pub."

"You are correct in that assumption, sir. Correct."

Charles assessed Rud as quick to bristle. He was used to being listened to. Hereabouts, he was a force with which to be reckoned. Troubles, medical and otherwise, were brought to him. If Eye was a fiefdom, the Criftins was its castle and Dr Rud—not the vicar, justice of the peace, or other local worthy—its Lord. The doctor didn't care to be outranked by outsiders. It was painful for him to admit that some troubles fell beyond his experience.

It would be too easy to take against the man. Charles would never entirely trust a doctor.

The bite mark in his forearm twinged.

Pamela came to mind. His wife. His *late* wife.

She would have cautioned him against unthinking prejudice. He conceded that Rud could hardly be expected to cope. His usual run was births and deaths, boils and fevers, writing prescriptions and filling in certificates.

None of that would help now.

This sort of affair rang bells in distant places. Disturbed the web of the great spider. Prompted the deployment of someone like Mr. Charles Beauregard.

A long-case clock ticked off each second. The steady passage of time was a given, like drips of subterranean water forming a stalactite. Time was perhaps subjectively slower here than in the bustle of London—but as inevitable, unvarying, inexorable.

This business made the clock a liar. Rud did not care to think that. If time could play tricks, what *could* one trust?

The doctor escorted Charles along the hallway. Gas lights burned in glass roses, whistling slightly. Bowls of dried petals provided sweet scent to cover medical odors.

At the parlor door, the soldier renewed his effort to simulate attention. Rud showed the man Charles's card. The fusilier saluted.

"Not strictly necessary," said Charles.

"Better safe than sorry, sah!"

Rud tapped the card, turning so that he barred the door, looking up at Charles with frayed determination.

"By the bye, how precisely does membership of this institution, this *club*—with which I am unfamiliar—give you the right to interview my patient?"

"We take an interest. In matters like these."

Rud, who had probably thought his capacity for astonishment exhausted, at once caught the implication.

"Surely this case is singular? Unique?"

Charles said nothing to contradict him.

"This has happened before? How often?"

"I'm afraid I really can't say."

Rud was fully aghast. "Seldom? Once in a blue moon? Every second Thursday?"

"I really can't say."

The doctor threw up his hands. "Fine," he said, "quiz the poor lad. I've no explanation for him. Maybe you'll be able to shed light. It'll be a relief to pass on the case to someone in authority."

"Strictly, the Diogenes Club has status rather than authority."

This was too much for Rud to take aboard. Even the mandarins of the Ruling Cabal could not satisfactorily define the standing of the Diogenes Club. Outwardly, the premises in Pall Mall housed elderly, crotchety misanthropes dedicated only to being left in peace. There were, however, other layers: sections of the club busied behind locked steel doors, *taking an interest*. Gentlemanly agreements struck in Whitehall invested the Diogenes Club as an unostentatious instrument of Her Majesty's government. More often than the public knew, matters arose beyond the purview of the police, the diplomatic service, or the armed forces. Matters few institutions could afford to acknowledge even as possibilities. *Some* body had to take responsibility, even if only a job lot of semi-official amateurs.

"Come in, come in," said Rud, opening the parlor door. "Mrs. Zeals has been feeding the patient broth."

The Criftins was low-ceilinged, with heavy beams. Charles doffed his hat to pass under the lintel.

From this moment, the business was *his* responsibility.

2: "my mother said I never should"

The parlor had fallen into gloom. Dr Rud turned the gas key, bringing up light as if the play were about to begin. *Act I, Scene 1: The parlor of the Criftins. Huddled in an armchair by the fire is . . .*

"Davey Harvill?"

The patient squirmed at the sound of Charles's voice, pulling up and hugging his knees, hiding his lower face. Charles put his hat on an occasional table and took off his heavy ulster, folding it over a high-backed chair.

The patient's eyes skittered, huge-pupiled.

"This gentleman is . . ."

Charles waved his fingers, shutting off the doctor's preamble. He did not want to present an alarming, mysterious figure.

The patient's trousers stretched tight around thin shanks, ripped in many places, cuffs high on the calf like knee-britches. He was shirtless and shoeless, a muffler wrapped around bird-thin shoulders. His calloused feet rested in a basin of dirtied water. His toenails were like thorns. Many old sores and scars made scarlet lakes and rivers on the map of his very white skin. His thatch of hair was starched with clay into the semblance of an oversized magistrate's wig; his beard matted into peltlike chest hair, threaded through with twigs; his mustaches hung in twisted braids, strung with beadlike pebbles.

Glimpsing himself in a glass, Rud smoothed his own stray hair strand across his scalp.

Charles pulled a footstool close to the basin.

The patient looked like Robinson Crusoe after years on the island. Except Crusoe would have been tanned. This fellow's pallor suggested a prisoner freed from an *oubliette*. Wherever he had been marooned was away from the sun, under the earth.

An animal smell was about him.

Charles sat on the stool and took the patient's thin hands, lifting them from his knees. His fingernails were long and jagged.

"My name is Charles. May I talk with you?"

The eyes fixed on him, sharp and bright. A tiny flesh-bulb, like a drop of fresh blood, clung to the corner of the right eyelid.

"Talk, mister?"

The voice was thin and high. He spoke as if English was unfamiliar, and his native tongue lacked important consonants.

"Yes, just talk."

"Frightened, mister. Been so long."

The face was seamed. Charles would have estimated the patient's age at around his own, thirty-five.

Last week, Davey Harvill had celebrated his ninth birthday.

The patient had a child's eyes, frightened but innocent. He closed them, shutting out the world, and shrank into the chair. His nails pressed into the meat of Charles's hands.

Charles let go and stood.

The patient—Davey, he had to be called—wound a corner of the muffler in his fingers, screwing it up close to his mouth. Tears followed runnels in his cheeks.

Mrs Zeals tried to comfort him, with coos and more broth.

"Rest," said Charles. "You're safe now. Talking can wait."

Red crescents were pressed into the heels of Charles's hands, already fading. Davey was not weak.

The patient's eyes flicked open, glittering in firelight. There was a cunning in them, now. Childlike, but dangerous.

Davey gripped Charles"s arm, making him wince.

"My mother said, I never should . . . play with *the gypsies in the wood* . . . it I did, she would say, '*naughty girl to disobey*'!"

Davey let him go.

The rhyme came in a lower voice, more assured, almost mocking. Not a grown-up voice, though. A feathery chill brushed Charles's spine. It was not a boy's rhyme, but something a girl would sing. Davey smiled a secret smile, then swallowed it. He was as he had been, frightened rather than frightening.

Charles patted his shoulder.

"Has he an appetite?" he asked the housekeeper.

"Yes, sir."

"Keep feeding him."

Mrs. Zeals nodded. She was part-nurse, probably midwife too. The sort of woman never missed until she was needed, but who then meant life or death. If a Mrs Zeals had been in the Hill Country, Charles might still be a husband and father. She radiated good sense, though this case tested the limitations of good sense as a strategy for coping.

"We shall talk again later, Davey. When you're rested."

Davey nodded, as much to himself as Charles.

"Dr. Rud, do you have a study? I should like to review the facts."

The doctor had hung back by the door, well out of reach.

"You're in charge, Mrs. Zeals," he said, stepping backward out of the room, eyes on the patient. "Mr. Beauregard and I have matters of import to discuss. Have Jane bring up tea, a light supper and a bottle of port."

"Yes, doctor."

Rud shot a look at the soldier. He disapproved of the invasion, but at present felt safer with an armed guard in his home.

"It's this way," he told Charles, indicating with his hands, still watching the patient. "Up the back stairs."

Charles bowed to Mrs. Zeals, smiled again at Davey, and followed the doctor.

"Extraordinary thing, wouldn't you say?" Rud gabbled.

"Certainly," Charles agreed.

"Of course, he can't be who he says he is. There's some *trick* to this."

3: "pebble in a pond"

Rud's consulting room was on two levels, a step running across the floor raising a section like a small stage. One wall was lined with document boxes. Locked cabinets held vials of salves, balms, cures and patent potions. A collection of bird and small mammal skeletons, mounted under glass domes, were posed upon items— rocks, branches, green cloth representing grass—suggestive of natural habitat.

On the raised area was a desk of many drawers and recesses. Above this, a studio photograph of Dr. and Mrs. Oliver Rud was flanked by framed documents, the doctor's diploma, and his wife's death certificate. Glancing at this last item, careful not to be seen to do so, Charles noted cause of death was down as *diphth*, and the signature was of another physician. He wondered if it was prominently displayed to caution the doctor against medical hubris, or to forewarn patients that miracles were not always possible.

Where was Pamela's death certificate? India?

Rud sat by the desk, indicating for Charles an adjustable chair in the lower portion of the room, obviously intended for patients. Charles sat down, suppressing a thought that straps could suddenly be fixed over his wrists, binding him at a mad surgeon's mercy. Such things, unfortunately, were within his experience. The doctor rolled up the desk cover and opened a folder containing scrawled notes.

"Hieroglyphs," he said, showing the sheaf. "But I understand them."

A maid came in with the fare Rud had ordered. Charles took tea, while the doctor poured himself a full measure of port. A plate of precisely cut sandwiches went untouched.

"If you'll start at the beginning."

"I've been through this with Major Chilcot, and . . ."

Charles raised a finger.

"I know it's tiresome to rehash over and over, but this is a tale you'll retell for some years, no matter how it comes out. It'll be valuable to have its raw, original form before the facts become, as it were, *encrusted* with anecdotal frills."

Rud, vaguely offended, was realist enough to see the point.

"The yarns in circulation at the Small Man are already wild, Mr. Beauregard. By the end of the month, it'll be full-blown myth. And heaven knows what the newspapers will make of it."

"We can take care of that."

"Can you, indeed? What useful connections to have . . . at any rate, the facts? Where to begin?"

"Tell me about Davey Harvill."

Rud adjusted his *pince-nez* and delved into the folder.

"An ordinary little boy. The usual childhood ailments and scrapes, none fatal. Father was well set-up for a man of his stripe. Cabinetmaker. Skilled craftsman. Made most of the furniture in this room."

"*Was* well set-up? Past tense."

"Yes, cut his arm open with a chisel and bled out before anything could be done. Two years ago. Undoubtedly an accident. Risk of the trade, I understand. By the time I was summoned, it was too late. Davey and his sisters, Sairey and Maeve, were raised by their mother, Mrs. Harvill. Admirable woman. Her children will have every chance in life. Would have had, rather. Now, it's anyone's guess. Sairey, the eldest child, is married to the local baker, Philip Riddle. She's expecting her first this spring. Maeve . . . well, Maeve's an unknown quantity. She is—was—two years older than her brother. A quiet, queer little girl. The sort who'd rather play by herself. Davey, or whoever this vagrant might be, says Maeve is still 'in the wood'."

Charles sipped strong tea.

"Tell me about Davey's birthday."

"Last Wednesday. I saw him early in the morning. I was leaving Mrs. Loll. She's our local hypochondriac. Always dying, secretly fit as a horse. As I stepped out of her cottage, Davey came by, wrapped up warm, whipping a hoop. A new toy, a birthday present. Maeve trailed along behind him. "If I don't watch him, doctor, he'll get run over by a cart," she said. They were walking to school, in Moreton."

"Along Dark Lane?"

Rud was surprised. "You know the area?"

"I looked at the map."

"Ah, *maps*," said Rud, touching his nose. "Dark Lane is the road to Moreton *on the map*. But there's a cart track through Hill Wood, runs up to Fair Field. From there, you can hop over a stile and be in Moreton. Not everything is on the map."

"That's an astute observation."

"Davey was rolling his hoop. There was fresh-fallen snow, but the ruts in Fair Field Track were already cut. I saw him go into the wood, his sister following, and that was it. I had other calls to make. Not something you think about, is it? Every time someone steps out of your sight, it could be the last you see of them?"

"Were you the last person to see the children?"

"No. Riddle, Sairey's husband, was coming down the track the other way, with the morning's fresh-bake. He told them he had a present to give Davey later, when it was wrapped—but gave both children buns, warm from the ovens. Then, off they went. Riddle hasn't sold a bun since. In case they're cursed, if you can credit it. As we now know, Davey and Maeve didn't turn up for school."

"Why weren't they missed?"

"They were. Mrs. Grenton, the teacher, assumed the Harvills were playing truant. Giving themselves a birthday treat. Sledging on Fair Field or building a snowman. She told the class that when the miscreants presented themselves, a strapping would be their reward. Feels dreadful about it, poor woman. Blames herself. The Harvills had perfect attendance records. Weren't the truant sort. Mrs Grenton wants me to prescribe something to make her headaches go away. Like a pebble in a pond, isn't it? The ripples. So many people wet from one splash."

Rud gulped port and refilled the measure. His hand didn't shake, but he gripped the glass stem as if steadying his fingers.

He whistled, tunelessly. Davey's rhyme.

"*Are* there gypsies in the wood?" asked Charles.

"What? Gypsies? Oh, the rhyme. No. We only see Romanies here at Harvest Festival, when there's a fair on Fair Field. The rhyme is something Maeve sings . . . used to sing. One of those girls' things, a skipping song. In point of fact, I remember her mother asking her not to chant it during the fair, so as not to offend actual gypsies. I doubt the girl took any notice. The gypsies, neither, come to that. No idea where the song comes from. I doubt if Violet Harvill ever had to warn her children against playing with strangers. This isn't that sort of country."

"I've an idea the gypsies in the rhyme aren't exactly gypsies. The word's there in place of something else. Everywhere has its stories. A ghost, a dragon, a witch's ring. . . ."

Rud thought a moment.

"The local bogey tale is *dwarves*. Kidnapping children to work in mines over the border. Blackfaced dwarves, with teeth filed to sharp points. 'Say your prayers, boyo, or the Tiny Taffs will away with you, into the deep dark earth to dig for dirty black coal.' I've heard that all my life. As you say, everywhere has its stories. Over Leintwardine way, there's a Headless Highwayman."

"All Eye lives in fear of Welsh dwarves?"

"No, even children don't—didn't—pay any attention. It came up again, of course. When Davey and Maeve went missing. There was a stupid scrap at the Small Man. It's why the Major closed the pub. English against Welsh. That's the fault line that runs through the marches. Good-humored mostly, but sharp-edged. We're border country, Mr. Beauregard. No one is wholly one thing or the other. Everyone has a grandparent in the other camp. But it's fierce. Come Sunday, you might hear 'love thy neighbor' from the pulpit, but we've three churches within spitting distance, each packed with folk certain the other congregations are marching in step to Hell. The Harvills call themselves English, which is why the children go to school in Moreton. The Ashton school is 'Welsh,' somehow. The schoolmaster is Welsh, definitely."

Charles nodded.

"Of course, all Eye agrees on something now. Welsh soldiers with English officers have shut down the pub. I'm afraid the uniting factor is an assessment of the character and ancestry of Major Chilcot."

Charles considered this intelligence. He had played the Great Game among the squabbling tribes of India and Afghanistan, representing the Queen in a struggle with her Russian cousin to which neither monarch was entirely privy, exploiting and being exploited by local factions who had their own Byzantine causes and conflicts.

It was strange to find a Khyber Pass in Herefordshire, a potential flashpoint for an uprising. In border countries the world over, random mischief could escalate near-forgotten enmities into riot and worse.

"When were the children missed in Ashton?"

"About five o'clock. When they didn't come in for their supper. Because it was the lad's birthday, Riddle had baked a special cake. Davey's friends came to call. Alfie Zeals, my housekeeper's son, was there. Even if brother and sister *had* played truant, they'd have been sure to be home. Presents were involved. The company waited hours. Candles burned down on the cake. Mrs. Harvill, understandably, got into a state. Riddle recounted his story of meeting the children on Fair Field Track. Alfie also goes to Moreton School and admitted Davey and Macve hadn't been there all day. Mrs Harvill rounded on the boy, who'd kept mum to keep his friend out of trouble. There were harsh words, tears. By then, it was dark. A party of men with lanterns formed. They came to me, in case a doctor was needed. You can imagine what everyone thought."

Charles could.

"Hill Wood isn't trackless wilderness. It's a patch between fields. You can get through it in five minutes at a stroll. Even if you get off Fair Field Track and have to wade through snow. The children couldn't be *lost* there, but mishaps might have befallen. A twisted ankle or a snapped leg, and the other too afraid to leave his or her sibling. The search party went back and forth. As the night wore on, we ventured further, to Fair Field and beyond. We should have waited till morning, when we could see tracks in the snow. By sun-up, the wood was so dotted with bootprints that any made by the children weren't noticeable. You have to understand, we thought we'd find them at any moment. A night outside in March can be fatal for a child. Or anyone. We run to bone-freezing cold here. Frost forms on your face. Snow gets hard, like a layer of ice. Violet Harvill had to be seen to. Hysteria in a woman of her age can be serious. Some of our party had come directly from the Small Man and were not in the best state. Hamer Dando fell down and tore a tendon, which should put a crimp in his poaching for months. Came the dawn, we were no better off."

"You summoned the police?"

"We got Throttle out of bed. He's been Constable in Eye since Crimea. He lent his whistle to the search. The next day, he was too puffed to continue, so I sent for Sergeant High, from Leominster. He bicycled over, but said children run off all the time, dreaming of the South Seas, and traipse back days later, crying for mama and home cooking. I don't doubt he's right, usually. But High's reassurances sat ill with these circumstances. No boy runs away to sea when he has a birthday party to go to. Then, Davey's new whip was found in the wood, stuck into a snow bank."

"A development?"

"An unhappily suggestive one. The mother began insisting something be done, and I was inclined to support her. But what more *could* be done? We went over the ground again, stone cold sober and in broad daylight. My hands are still frozen from dismantling snowdrifts. Every hollow, every dead tree, every path. We looked. Riddle urged we call out the army. Stories went round that the children had been abducted by foreign agents. More foreign than just Welsh. I had to prescribe laudanum for Violet."

"This was all five days ago?"

Rud checked his notes. "Yes. The weekend, as you can appreciate, was a terrible time. Riddle got his way. Major Chilcot's fusiliers came over from Powys. At first, they just searched again, everywhere we'd looked before. Violet was besieged by neighbors offering to help but with no idea what to do. I doubt a single soul within five miles has had a night's uninterrupted sleep since this began."

Rud's eyes were red-rimmed.

"Then, yesterday morning," said the doctor, "Davey—or whoever he might be—came to his mother's door, and asked for his blessed cake."

Rud slapped his folder on his desk. An end to his story.

"Your patient claims to be Davey Harvill?"

"Gets upset when anyone says he can't be."

"There is evidence."

"Oh yes. Evidence. He's wearing Davey's trousers. If the army hadn't been here, he'd have been hanged for that. No ceremony, just hanged. We're a long way from the assizes."

Charles finished his tea and set down the cup and saucer.

"There's more than that," he said. "Or I wouldn't be here. Out with it, man. Don't be afraid of being laughed at."

"It's hard to credit . . ."

"I make a speciality of credulousness. Open-minded, we call it."

Gingerly, Rud opened the file again.

"The man downstairs. I would put his age at between thirty-five and forty. Davey is nine years old. *Ergo*, they are not the same person. But, in addition to his own scars, the patient has *Davey's*. A long, jagged mark on his calf. Done hauling over a stile, catching on a rusty nail. I treated the injury last year. The fellow has a perfect match. Davey has a growth under the right eye, like a teardrop. That's there, too."

"These couldn't be new-made."

"The scar, just maybe—though it'd have to be prepared months in advance. The teardrop is a birthmark. Impossible to contrive. It's not a family trait, so this isn't some long-lost Harvill popping up at the worst possible moment."

Upon this development, Chilcot, like all bewildered field commanders, communicated with his superiors, who cast around for some body with special responsibility for changelings.

Which would be the Diogenes Club.

"Where does he claim to have been?"

"Just 'in the wood.'"

"With the gypsies?"

"He sings that rhyme when the mood takes him, usually to end a conversation he's discomfited by. As you said, I don't think gypsies really come into it."

"You've examined him. How's his general health?"

Rud picked up a note written in shiny new ink. "What you'd expect from a tramp. Old wounds, untended but healed. Various infestations—nits, lice, the like. And malnutrition."

"No frostbite?"

Rud shook his head.

"So he's not been sleeping out of doors this past week? In the cold, cold snow?"

Rud was puzzled again. "Maybe he found a barn."

"Maybe."

"There's another . . . ah, anomaly," ventured the doctor. "I've not told anyone, because it makes no sense. The fellow has good teeth. But he has two missing at the front, and new enamel growing through the gums. Normal for a nine-year-old, losing milk teeth and budding adult choppers. But there is no third dentition. That's beyond freakish."

Rud slipped the paper back into the folder.

"That's Davey Harvill's file, isn't it?"

"Yes, of course . . . oh, I see. The patient should have a fresh folder. He is not Davey Harvill."

Rud pulled open desk drawers, searching for a folder.

"Follow your first instincts, Dr. Rud. You added notes on this patient to Davey's folder. It seemed so natural that you didn't even consider any other course. Logic dictated you proceed on an assumption you know to be impossible. So, we have reached the limits of logic."

4: "Silas Gobbo"

In the snug of the Small Man, after breakfast, Charles read the riot act to the army. Though the reason for closing the pub was plain, it did not help Major Chilcot's case that he had billeted himself on the premises and was prone to "requisitioning" from the cellar.

"Purely medicinal," Chilcot claimed. "After a spell wandering around with icicles for fingers, a tot is a damn necessity."

Charles saw his point, but suspected it had been sharpened after a hasty gulp.

"That's reasonable, Major. But it would be politic to pay your way."

"We're here to *help* these ungrateful bounders . . ."

The landlord glared from behind the bar.

"Just so," said Charles.

The major muttered but backed down.

The landlord, visibly perked, came over.

"Will the gentleman be requiring more tea?"

"No, thank you," said Charles. "Prepare a bill for myself and the Major. Keep a running tally. You have my word you will not be out of pocket. Tonight, you may reopen."

The landlord beamed.

"Between sunset and ten o' clock," insisted Chilcot.

A line appeared in the landlord's forehead.

"That's fair," said Charles.

The landlord accepted the ruling. For the moment.

The major was another local bigwig, late in an undistinguished career. This would be the making or breaking of a younger, more ambitious officer.

While he stayed cozy in the Small Man, his men bivouacked on Fair Field under retreat-from-Moscow conditions. They were diamond-quality. Sergeant Beale, an old India hand, had rattled off a precise report of all measures taken. It wasn't through blundering on the part of the fusiliers that Maeve Harvill still hadn't turned up.

Charles left the pub and walked through Ashton Eye. Snow lay thick on roofs and in front gardens. Roads and paths were cleared, chunky drifts stained with orange mud piled at the sides. By day, the occupation was more evident. Soldiers, stamping against the cold, manned a trestle at the bottom of Fair Field Track. Chilcot, probably at Beale's prompt, had established a perimeter around Hill Wood.

At the Criftins, Charles was admitted—by a manservant, this time. He joined a small company in the hallway. A fresh fusilier stood guard at the parlor. Dr. Rud introduced Charles, vaguely as "from London," to a young couple, the woman noticeably with child, and a lady of middle years, obviously in distress.

"Philip and Sairey Riddle, and Mrs. Harvill . . . Violet."

He said his good mornings and shook hands.

"We've asked you to here to put the man purporting to be Davey to the test," Charles explained. "Some things are shared only among family members. Not great confidences, but trivial matters. Intelligence no one outside a home could be expected to have. Remarks made by someone to someone else when they were alone together. An impostor won't know that, no matter how carefully he prepared the fraud."

Mrs. Harvill sniffled into a kerchief. Her daughter held her shoulders.

"He is still in the parlor?" Charles asked Rud.

"Spent the night there. I've got him into a dressing gown. He's had breakfast. I had my man shave him, and make a start on his hair."

The doctor put his hand to the door.

"It is best if we hold back," said Charles. "Allow the family to meet without outsiders present."

Rud frowned.

"We'll be here, a moment away, if needs arise."

The doctor acquiesced and held the door open.

"Mam," piped a voice from inside. Charles saw Davey, in his chair, forearms and shins protruding from a dressing gown a size too small for him. Without the beard, he looked younger.

Mrs. Harvill froze and pulled back, shifting out of Davey's eyeline.

"Mam?" almost a whine, close to tears.

Mrs. Harvill was white, hand tightly gripping her daughter's, eyes screwed shut. Her terror reminded Charles of Davey's, last night, when he felt threatened. Sairey hugged her mother, but detached herself.

"You stay here, Ma'am. Me and Phil'll talk with the lad. The gentlemen will look after you."

Sairey passed her mother on to Rud.

Mrs. Harvill embraced the practitioner, discomfiting him, pressing her face to his shoulder. She sobbed, silently.

Sairey, slow and graceful in her enlarged state, took her husband's arm and stepped into the parlor. Davey started out of his seat, a broad smile showing his impossible teeth-buds.

"Sairey, Phil . . ."

Charles closed the door.

Rud sat Mrs. Harvill on a chair and went upstairs to fetch a something to calm her. The woman composed herself. She looked at Charles, paying him attention for the first time.

"Who are you?" she asked, bluntly.

"Charles Beauregard."

"Oliver said that. I mean what are you?"

"I'm here to help."

"Where are my children? Are they safe?"

"That's what we are trying to determine, Mrs. Harvill."

The answer didn't satisfy. She looked away, ignoring him. In her pettishness, she was like Davey. Charles even thought he heard her crooning, "My mother said . . . ," under her breath. She had found a fetish object, a length of rope with a handle. She bound her hand until the fingers were bloodless, then unwound the rope and watched pink seep back.

Rud returned and gave Mrs. Harvill a glass of water into which he measured three drops from a blue bottle. She swallowed it with a grimace and he rewarded her with a sugar-lump. If her son *had* been transformed into an adult, this business had turned her—in some sense—into a child.

A muffle of conversation could be heard through the door. The temptation to eavesdrop was a fishhook in the mind. Charles saw the doctor felt the tug even more keenly. Only the soldier was impassive, bored with this duty but grateful to be inside in the warm.

"What *can* be keeping them?" said Mrs Harvill.

She fiddled again with her fetish, separating the rope into strands as if undoing a child"s braid. The rope was Davey's new whip, which had been found in Hill Wood.

Charles could only imagine how Violet Harvill felt.

Pamela had died, along with their newborn son, after a botched delivery. He had blamed an incompetent doctor, then malign providence, and finally himself. By accepting the commission in the Hills, he had removed his family from modern medicine. A hot, hollow grief had scooped him out. He had come to accept that he would never be the man he was before, but knew Pamela would have been fiercely disappointed if he used the loss as an excuse to surrender. She had burst into his life to challenge everything he believed. Their marriage had been a wonderful, continuous explosion. In the last hours, clinging to him—biting deep into his forearm to stanch her own screams—and knowing she would die, Pamela had talked a cascade, soothing and hectoring, loving and reprimanding, advising and ordering. In London fog, he had lost the memory for a while. An engagement to Pamela's cousin, Penelope Churchward, had been his first effort at reforming a private world, and its embarrassing termination the spur to think again on what his wife had tried to tell him. As he found himself deeper in the affairs of the Diogenes Club, Pamela's voice came back. Every day, he would remember something of hers, something she had said or done. Sometimes, a twinge in his arm would be enough, a reminder that he had to live up to her.

Looking at Mrs. Harvill, he recalled the other loss, eclipsed by Pamela's long, bloody dying. His son, Richard Charles, twelve years dead, had lived less than an hour and opened his eyes only in death, face washed clean by the *ayah*. If he had been a girl, she would have been Pandora Sophie. Charles and Pamela had got used to calling the child "Dickie or Dora." As Pamela wished, he had served mother and child in the Indian manner, cremating them together. Most of the ashes were scattered in India, which she had loved in a way he admired but never shared. Some he had brought back to England, to placate Pamela's family. An urn rested in the vault in Kingstead Cemetery, a proper place of interment for a proper woman who would have been disowned had she spent more time at home expressing her opinions.

But what of the boy?

Losing a child is the worst thing in the world. Charles knew that, but didn't *feel* it. His son, though born, was still a part of Pamela, one loss coiled up within the other. If he ached for Dickie or Dora, it was only in the sense he sometimes felt for the other children Pamela and he would have had, the names they might have taken. The Churchwards ran to Ps and there had yet to be a Persephone, Paulus, Patricia, or Prosper.

Now he thought of the boy.

It was in him, he knew, wrapped up tight. The cold dead spot. The rage and panic. The ruthlessness.

Violet Harvill would do *anything*.

She seemed to snap out of her spell, and tied Davey's whip around her wrist, loose like a bracelet. She stood, determined.

Rud was at the parlor door.

"If you feel you're up to this, Violet . . ."

She said nothing but he opened the door. Sairey was laughing at something Davey had just said. The lad was smiling, an entirely different person.

"Mam," he said, seeing Mrs. Harvill.

Charles *knew* disaster was upon them. He was out of his chair and across the hall, reaching for Mrs. Harvill. She was too swift for him, sensing his grasp and ducking under it. A creak at the back of her throat grew into a keening, birdlike cry. She flew into the parlor, fingers like talons.

Her nails raked across Davey's face, carving red runnels. She got a grip on his throat.

"What've you done with them?" she demanded.

A torrent of barrack abuse poured from her mouth, words Charles would once have sworn a woman could not even know—though, at the last, Pamela had used them too. Violet Harvill's face was a mask of hate.

"What've you *done?*"

Sairey tried to shift from her chair, forgetting for a moment her unaccustomed shape. With a yelp, she sat back down, holding her belly.

Riddle and Rud seized Mrs. Harvill and pulled her away. Charles stepped in and prised the woman's fingers from Davey's throat, one by one. She continued to screech and swear.

"Get her out of the room," Charles told the doctor. "Please."

There was a struggle, but it was done.

Davey was back in his huddle, knees up against his face, eyes liquid, sing-songing.

"Naughty girl to disobey . . . *dis-o-bey!* Naughty girl . . ."

Sairey, careful now, hugged him, pressing his head to her full breast. He rocked back and forth.

Charles's collar had come undone and his cravat was loose.

He was responsible for this catastrophe.

"He'm Davey, mister," said Sairey, softly. She didn't notice she was weeping. "No doubt 'bout it. We talked 'bout what you said. Family things. When I were little, Dad do made up stories for I, stories 'bout Silas Gobbo, a little wood-carver who lives in a hollow tree in our garden and makes furniture for birds. Dad'd make tiny tables and chairs from offcuts, put 'em in the tree and take I out to the garden to show off Silas's new work. Dad told the tales over, to Davey and Maeve. Loved making little toys, did Dad. No one but Davey could've known 'bout Silas Gobbo. Not 'bout the tiny tables and chairs. Even if someone else heard the stories, they couldn't *love* Silas. Davey and Maeve do. With Dad gone, loving Silas is like loving him, remembering. Maeve used to say she wanted to marry Silas when she grew up, and be a princess."

"So you're convinced?"

"Everythin' else, from last week and from years ago, the boy still has in 'en. Mam'll never accept it. I don't know how I can credit it, but it's him."

She held her brother close. Even shaved, he seemed to be twice her age.

Charles fixed his collar.

"What does he say about Maeve?"

"She'm with Silas Gobbo. He'm moved from our tree into Hill Wood. Davey says Maeve be a princess now."

5: "filthy afternoon"

It was a dreary, depressing day. Clouds boiled over Hill Wood, threatening another snowfall. The first flakes were in circulation, bestowing tiny stinging kisses.

Charles walked down Dark Lane, toward Fair Field Track. A thin fire burned in a brazier, flames whipped by harsh, contradictory winds. The fusiliers on guard were wrapped in layers of coat and cloak. The youth who had tried to make time with Rud's tweeny was still red-cheeked, but now through the beginnings of frostbite.

Sergeant Beale, elaborately mustached and with eyebrows to match, did not feel the cold. If ordered to ship out, Beale would be equally up for an expedition through Arctic tundra or a trail across Sahara sands. Men like Major Chilcot only thought they ran the Empire; men like Beale actually did.

"Filthy afternoon, sir," commented the Sergeant.

"Looks like snow."

"Looks and feels like snow, sir. Is snow."

"Yes."

"Not good, snow. Not for the little girl."

"No."

Charles understood. If this Christmas card sprinkle turned into blizzard, any search would be off. Hope would be lost. The vanishing of Maeve Harvill would be accepted. Chilcot would pack up his soldiers and return to barracks. Charles would be recalled, to make an inconclusive report. The Small Man could open all hours of the night.

An April thaw might disclose a small, frozen corpse. Or, under the circumstances, not.

Charles looked over the trestle and into the trees.

The men of Eye and the fusiliers had both been through Hill Wood. Now, Charles—knowing he had to make sure—would have to make a third search. Of course, he wasn't just looking for the girl.

"I'll just step into the wood and have a look about, Sergeant."

"Very good, sir. We'll hold the fort."

The guard lifted the trestle so Charles could pass.

He tried to act as if he was just out for a stroll on a bracing day, but could not pull it off. Pamela nagged: it was not just a puzzle; wounded people surrounded the mystery; they deserved more than abstract thought.

Footprints were everywhere, a heavy trample marking out Fair Field Track, scattering off in dispersal patterns to all sides. Barely a square foot of virgin white remained. The black branches of some trees were iced with snow, but most were shaken clean.

Charles could recognize fifteen different types of snake native to the Indian subcontinent, distinguishing deadly from harmless. He knew the safest covert routes into and out of the Old Jago, the worst rookery in London. He understood distinctions between specter, apparition, phantasm, and revenant—knowledge the more remarkable for being gained first-hand rather than through dusty pedantry. But, aside from oak and elm, he could identify none of the common trees of the English countryside. Explorations of extraordinary fields had left him little time for ordinary ones.

He was missing something.

His city boots, heavily soled for cobbles, were thin and flexible. Cold seeped in at the lace holes and seams. He couldn't feel his toes.

It was a small wood. No sooner was he out of sight of Beale than the trees thinned and he saw the khaki tents pitched on Fair Field. Davey and Maeve had been *detained* here, somehow. Everyone was convinced. Could the children have slipped out unnoticed, into Fair Field and over the stile or through a gate, disappearing into regions yet to be searched? If so, somebody should have seen them. No one had come forward.

Could they have been stolen away by passing gypsies?

In Eye, gypsies or any other strangers would be noticed. So, suspicion must range closer to home. Accusations had begun to run around. Every community had its odd ones, easy to accuse of unthinkable crimes. P.C. Throttle still said it was the Dandos, a large and unruly local clan. Accusing the Dandos had solved every other mystery in Ashton and Moreton in the last thirty years, and Throttle saw no reason to change tactics now. The fact of Davey's return had called off the witch hunt. Even those who didn't believe Davey was who he claimed assumed he was at the bottom of the bad business.

If Davey was Davey, what had happened?

Charles went over the ground again, off the track this time, zigzagging across the small patch. He found objects trampled into muddy snow, which turned out to be broken pipes, a single man-sized glove, candle stubs. As much rubbish was tossed here as in a London gutter. The snowfall was thickening.

Glancing up, he saw something.

Previous searches had concentrated on the ground. If Maeve had flown away, perhaps Charles *should* direct his attention upward.

Snowflakes perished on his upturned face.

He stood before a twisted oak. A tree he could identify, even when not in leaf. An object ringed from a branch, just out of his reach. He reached up and brushed it with his fingers.

A wooden band, about a eighteen inches in diameter, was loose about the branch, as if tossed onto a hook in a fairground shy. He found footholds in the trunk and climbed a yard above the ground.

He got close enough to the band to see initials burned into its inner side. *D.H.* Davey's birthday hoop.

Charles held the branch with gloved hands and let go his knee grip on the trunk. He swung out and the branch lowered, pulled by his weight. His feet lightly touched ground, the branch bent like a bow. With one hand, he nudged the hoop, trying to work it free. The branch forked and the hoop stuck.

That was a puzzle.

The obvious trick would be to break the hoop and fix it again, around the branch. But there was no break, no fix. In which case, the toy must have been hung on the tree when it was younger, and become trapped by natural growth.

The oak was older than Davey Harvill, by many human lifetimes. It was full-grown when Napoleon was a boy. The hoop had not been hung last week, but must have been here since the Wars of the Roses.

He let go of the branch. It sprang back into place, jouncing the hoop. Snow dislodged from higher up.

The tree creaked, waving branches like a live thing.

Charles was chilled with more than cold.

About twenty feet from the ground, packed snow parted and fell away, revealing a black face. A pattern of knotholes, rather, shaped into a face.

We see faces in everything. It is the order we attempt to put on the world—on clouds, stains on the wallpaper, eroded cliffs. Eyes, a nose, mouth. Expressions malign or benevolent.

This face seemed, to Charles, puckish.

"Good afternoon to you, Mr. Silas Gobbo," he said, touching his hat brim.

"Who, pray, is Silas Gobbo?"

Charles turned, heart caught by the sudden, small voice.

A little girl stood among the drifts, braids escaping from a blue cap, coat neatly done up to her muffler.

His first thought was that this was Maeve!

It struck him that he wouldn't recognize her if he saw her. He had seen no picture. There were other little girls in Eye.

"Are you looking for Maeve Harvill?" he asked. "Is she your friend?"

The little girl smiled, solemnly.

"I am Maeve," she said. "I'm a princess."

He picked her up and held her as if she were his own. Inside, he melted at this miracle. He was light-headed with an instant, fast-burning elation.

"This is not how princesses should be treated, sir."

He was holding her too tight. He relaxed into a fond hug and looked down at the fresh footprints where she had been standing. Two only, as if she was set down from above, on this spot. He looked up and saw a bramble-tangle of black branches against dirty sky.

He cast around for the face he had imagined, but couldn't find it again.

Maeve's dad would have said Silas Gobbo had rescued Maeve, returned her to her family.

It was the happy ending Charles wanted. He ran through his joy, and felt the chill again, the cold chill and the bone chill. He shifted the little girl, a delicate-boned miniature woman, and looked into her perfect, polite face.

"Princess, have you brothers and sisters?"

"David and Sarah."

"Parents? Mam and Dad."

"Father is dead. My mother is Mrs. Violet Harvill. You would do me a great service if you were to take me home. I am a tired princess."

The little bundle was warm in his arms. She kissed his cheek and snuggled close against his shoulder.

"I might sleep as you carry me."

"That's all right," he told her.

He trudged along Fair Field Track. When the guards saw him, they raised a shout.

"'E's gone and done it!"

Charles tried a modest smile. The shout was taken up, spread around. Soon, they became hurrahs.

6: "something about the little girl"

Dr. Rud's parlor was filled with merry people, as if five Christmases had come along together and fetched up in a happy, laughing pile.

Mrs. Harvill clung to her princess, who had momentarily stopped ordering everyone as if they were servants. Philip and Sairey, stunned and overjoyed, pinched each other often, expecting to wake up. Sairey had to sit but couldn't keep in one place. She kept springing up to talk with another well-wisher, then remembering the strain on her ankles. Philip had made another cake, with Maeve's name spelled out in currants.

Rud and Major Chilcot drank port together, laughing, swapping border war stories.

People Charles had not met were present, free with hearty thanks for the hero from London.

"We combed Hill Wood and did all we could," said the Reverend Mr. Weddle, Vicar of Eye. "Too familiar, you see, with the terry-toree. Could not see the wood for the trees, though acts of prayer wore the trews from our knees. Took an outsider's eye in Ashton Eye, to endeavor to save the Princess Maeve. Hmm, mind if I set that down?"

Weddle had mentioned he was also a poet.

P.C. Throttle, of the long white beard and antique uniform, kept a close eye on the limping, scowling Hamer Dando—lest thieving fingers stray too close to the silverware. Hamer's face was stamped on half a dozen other locals of various ages and sexes, but Throttle was marking them all.

Charles's hand was shaken, again, by a huge-knuckled, blue-chinned man he understood to be the Ashton schoolmaster, Owain Gryfudd.

"Maeve's coming to the Welsh school now," he said, in dour triumph. "No more traipsing over the stile to that Episcopalian booby in Moreton. We shall see a great improvement."

Charles gathered Gryfudd captained an all-conquering rugby team, the Head-Hunters. They blacked their faces with coal before going onto the pitch. The teacher still had war paint around his collar and under his hairline, from frequent massacres of the English.

Cake was pressed upon Charles. Gryfudd clapped his back and roared off, bearing down on a frail old lady—Mrs. Grenton, of Moreton Eye school—as if charging for a match-winning try.

Whenever Mrs. Harvill saw Charles, she wept and—if Maeve wasn't in her arms—flung an embrace about him. She was giddy with joy and relief, and had been so for a full day.

Her princess was home.

As Sairey had said, she would never accept Davey as Davey. But Maeve's return ended the matter.

That, among other things, kept Charles from entering into the spirit of this celebration.

In this room, he sensed an overwhelming desire to put Davey and the mystery out of mind. Davey was upstairs, shut away from the celebration.

All's well that ends well.

But Charles knew nothing had ended. And nothing was well.

He could do no more. In all probability, his report to the Ruling Cabal would be tied with pale green ribbon and filed away forever.

He left the parlor. In the hallway, soldiers and maids sipped punch. Smiles all round.

But for Sergeant Beale.

"I suppose you'll be back to London now, sir?"

"I see no other course."

"There's something about the little girl, isn't there?"

"I fear so."

"Where *were* those kids? What happened to the boy?"

"Those, Sergeant, are the questions."

Beale nodded. He took no punch.

Charles left the Sergeant and walked to the door. A tug came at his arm. Sairey held his sleeve. The woman was bent almost double. It was nearly her time. That was all this party needed: a sudden delivery and a bouncing, happy baby.

"Phil and I'll take in Davey."

"I'm glad to hear that, Sairey. I know it won't be easy."

She snorted. "Neither one'll take him in class, not Gryfudd nor Grenton. So that's an end to his schooling. And he's a clever lad, Davey. Give him a pencil and he can draw anything to the life. Mam . . . she's daffy over Maeve, hasn't any left for Davey. Won't have him in the house."

Charles patted her hand, understanding.

"And what *is* it about Maeve? She calls I 'Sarah.' I've been 'Sairey' so long I forgot what my name written down in the family Bible were."

"She doesn't know Silas Gobbo."

Sairey closed her eyes and nodded.

"She frightens I," she said, so quietly no one could overhear.

Charles squeezed her fingers. He could give no reassurance.

Riddle came into the hallway, looking for his wife. He escorted her back into the warmth and light. A cheer went up. Someone began singing . . .

> "A frog he would a wooing go . . .
> *Heigh-ho, says Rowley!*
> And whether his mother would let him or no . . ."

Other voices joined. One deep bass must be Gryffud.

> "With a roly poly gammon and spinach . . .
> *Heigh-ho, says Anthony Rowley!*"

Charles put on his hat and coat and left.

Act II: Uncle Satt's Treasury for Boys and Girls

1: "Lady of the Leprechauns"

"If that's the Gift," commented a workman, "I'd likes ter know as 'oo gave it, and when they're comin' ter fetch it back."

Kate jotted the words into a notebook, in her own shorthand. The sentiment, polished through repetition, might not be original to the speaker. She liked to record what London thought and said, even when the city thought too lightly and said too often.

"Dunno what it thinks it looks like," continued the fellow.

In shirtsleeves, cap on the back of his head, he perspired heavily.

Freezing winters and boiling summers were the order of the '90s. This June threatened the scorch of the decade. She regretted the transformation of the parasol from an object of utility into a frilly aid to flirtation. As a consequence of this social phenomenon, she didn't own such an apparatus and was just now feeling the lack — and not because she wished the attention of some dozy gentleman who paid heed only to females who flapped at him like desperate moths. Like many blessed (or cursed) with red hair, too much sun made her peel hideously. Her freckles became angry blood-dots if she took a promenade *sans* veiled hat. Such apparel invariably tangled with her large, thick spectacles.

At the South end of Regent's Park, the Gift shone, throwing off dazzles from myriad facets. Completed too late for one Jubilee, it was embarrassingly early for the next. To get shot of a White Elephant, the bankrupt company responsible made a gift of it (hence the name) to the Corporation of London. Intended as a combination of popular theater, exhibition hall and exotic covered garden, the sprawling labyrinth had decoration enough for any three municipal eyesores. The thing looked like a crystal circus tent whipped up by a color-blind Sunday painter and an Italian pastry chef.

It was inevitable that someone would eventually conceive of a use for the Gift. That visionary (buffoon?) was Mr Satterthwaite Bulge, "Uncle Satt" to a generation of nieces and nephews, *soi-disant* Founder of Færie and Magister of Marvels (his spelling). This afternoon, she had an invitation to visit Bulge's prosperous little kingdom.

"Katharine Reed, daredevil reporter," called a voice, deep and American.

A man in a violently green checked suit cut through gawping passersby and wrung her hand. He wore an emerald bowler with shining tin buckle, an oversize crepe four-leafed clover *boutonniere*, a belt of linked discs painted like gold coins and a russet beard fringe attached to prominent ears by wire hooks.

"Billy Quinn, *publicist*," he introduced himself, momentarily lowering his false whiskers.

She filed away the word. Was it a coinage of Quinn's? What might a publicist do? Publicize, she supposed. Make known personalities and events and products, scattering information upon the public like lumps of lava spewn from Vesuvius. She had a notion that if such a profession were to become established, her own would be greatly complicated.

"And, of course, Oi'm a leprechaun. Ye'll be familiar with *the leettle people*."

Quinn's Boston tones contorted into an approximation of Ould Oireland. Inside high-button shoes, her toes curled.

"There's not a darter of Erin that hasn't in her heart a soft spot for Seamus O'Short."

She was Dublin-born and Protestant-raised. Her father, a lecturer in Classics at Trinity College, drummed into her at an early age that *pots o' gold* and *wee fair folk* were baggages that need only trouble heathen Papists dwelling in the savage regions of dampest bog country. Whenever anyone English rabbited on about such things (usually affecting speech along the lines of Quinn's atavistic brogue), she was wont to change the subject to Home Rule.

"You're going to love this, Kate," he said, casually assuming the right to address her by a familiar name. She was grateful that he had reverted to his natural voice, though. "Here's your fairy sack."

He handed over a posset, with a drawstring. A stick protruded from its mouth, wound round with tinsel.

"That's your fairy wand. Inside, there's magic powder (sherbet) and a silver tiara (not silver). Tuppence to the generality, but *gratis* to an honored rep of the Fourth Estate."

Rep? Representative. Now, people were *talking* in shorthand. At least, people who were Americans and *publicists* were.

Quinn led her toward the doors of the Gift.

A lady in spangled leotards and butterfly wings attracted a male coterie, bestowing handbills while bending *just so* to display her *décolletage* to its best advantage, which was considerable. The voluptuous fairy had two colleagues, also singular figures. Someone in a baggy suit of brown fur and cuirass, sporting an enormous plaster bear's head surmounted by an armored helm. A dwarf with his face painted like a sad clown.

"Come one, come all," said Quinn. "Meet Miss Fay Twinkledust, Sir Boris de Bruin, and Jack Stump."

The trio posed *en tableau* as if for a photograph. Miss Fay and Jack Stump fixed happy grimaces on their powdered faces. Sir Boris perked up an ear through tugging on a wire. In this heat, Kate feared for the comfort and well-being of the performer trapped inside the costume.

Children flocked around, awed and wondered.

Jack Stump was perturbed by affections bestowed on him by boys and girls taller and heftier than he. Kate realized she'd seen the dwarf, dressed as a miniature mandarin, shot out of a cannon at the Tivoli Music Hall. This engagement seemed more perilous.

In the offices of the *Pall Mall Gazette*, she had done her homework and pored through a year's worth of *Uncle Satt's Treasury for Boys and Grils*. She was already acquainted with Miss Fay Twinkledust, Sir Boris de Bruin, Jack Stump, Seamus O'Short, and many others. Gloomy Goat and his cousins Grumpy (her favorite) and Grimy; Billy Boggart of Noggart's Nook; Bobbin Swiftshaft, Prince of Pixies; Wicked Witch-Queen Coelacanth. The inhabitants of Uncle Satt's Færie Aerie were beloved (or deliciously despised) by seemingly every child in the land, to the despair of parents who would rather their precious darlings practiced the pianoforte or read Euripides in the original in exactly the way they hadn't when they were children.

Kate was out of school, and near-disowned for following her disreputable Uncle Diarmid into "the scribbling trade," well before the debuts of Miss Fay *et al.* but her younger brother and sisters were precisely of an age to fall into the clutches of Mr. Satterthwaite Bulge. Father, whose position on the *wee fair folk* was no longer tenable, lamented he was near financial ruin on Uncle Satt's account, for a mere subscription to the monthly *Treasury* did not suffice to assuage clamor for matters færie-related. There was also *Uncle Satt's Færie Aerie Annual*, purchased in triplicate to prevent unseemly battles between Humphrey, Juliet, and Susannah over whose bookshelf should have the honor of supporting the wonder volume. Furthermore, it was insisted that nursery wallpaper bear the likenesses of the færie favorites as illustrated by the artist who signed his (or her?) works "B. Loved," reckoned by connoisseurs to be the true genius of the realm which could properly be termed Uncle Satt's Færie Empire. In addition, there were china dolls and tin figures to be bought, board games to be played, pantomime theatrical events to be attended, sheet music to be performed, Noggart's Nook sugar confections to be consumed. Every penny doled out by fond parent or grandparent to well-behaved child was earmarked for the voluminous pockets of Uncle Satt.

As a consequence, Bulge could afford the Gift. On his previous record, he could probably turn the White Elephant into the wellspring of further fortunes. Pots of gold, indeed.

The Gift was not yet open to the general public, and excited queues were already forming in anticipation. No matter how emetic the Uncle Satt *oeuvre* was to the average adult, children were as lost to his Færie as the children of Hamelin were to the Pied Piper.

A little girl, no more than four, hugged Sir Boris's leg, rubbing her cheek against his fur, smiling with pure bliss.

"We don't pay these people," Quinn assured her. "We don't have to. To be honest, we would if we did but we don't. This is all gin-u-wine."

Some grown-ups were won over to the enemy or found it politic to claim so, lest they be accused of stifling the childish heart reputed to beat still in the breasts of even the hardest cynics. Many of her acquaintance, well into mature years and possessed of sterling intellects (some *not even parents*), proclaimed devotion to Uncle Satt, expressing admiration if not for the literary effulgences then for the talents of the mysterious, visionary "B. Loved." Even Bernard Shaw, whose stinging notice of *A Visit to the Færie Aerie* led to a splashing with glue by pixie partisans, praised for the illustrations, hailing "B. Loved" a titan shackled by daisy chains. The pictures, it had to be said, were haunting, unusual and impressive, simple in technique, yet imbued with a suggestiveness close to disturbing. Their dreamy vagueness would have passed for *avant-garde* in some salons but was paradoxically embraced (beloved, indeed) by child and adult alike. Aubrey Beardsley was still sulking because B. Loved declined to contribute to a færie-themed number of *The Yellow Book*, though it was bruited about that the refusal was mandated by Uncle Satt, who had the mystery painter signed to an exclusive contract. It was sometimes hinted that Bulge *was* B. Loved. Other theories had the illustrator as an asylum inmate who had sewn his own eyes shut but continued to cover paper with the images swarming inside his broken mind, a spirit medium who gave herself up to an inhabitant of another plane as she sat at the board, or a factory in Aldgate staffed by unlettered Russian immigrants overseen by a knout-wielding monk.

"Come inside," said Quinn. "Though you must first pass these Three Merry Guardians."

The publicist opened a little gate and ushered Kate into an enclosure that led to the main doors. The entrance was painted to look like the covers of a pair of magical books. Above was a red-cheeked, smiling, sparkle-eyed caricature of Uncle Satt, fat finger extended to part the pages.

Envious glares came from the many children not yet admitted to the attraction. Cutting comments were passed by parents whose offers of bribes had not impressed the Three Merry Guardians. Kate had an idea that, if his comrades were looking the other way, Jack Stump would not have been averse to slipping a half-crown into his boot and lifting a tent corner.

"This is a Lady of the Leprechauns," said Quinn, to appease the crowds, "on a diplomatic visit to Uncle Satt. The Gift will open to one and all this very weekend. The Færie Aerie isn't yet ready to receive visitors."

A collective moan of disappointment rose.

Quinn shrugged at her.

Kate stepped toward the main doors. Long, hairy arms encircled her, preventing further movement. Sir Boris de Bruin shook with silent laughter.

This was very irritating!

"I had almost forgotten," said Quinn. "Before you enter, what must you do?"

She was baffled. The bear was close to taking liberties.

"What must she do, boys and girls?" Quinn asked the crowd.

"Færie name! Færie name!"

"That's right, boys and girls. The Lady of the Leprechauns must take her færie name!"

"Katharine Reed," she suggested. "Um, Kate, Katie?"

"*Nooooo*," said Quinn, milking it. "A new name. A true name. A name fit for the councils of Bobbin Swiftshaft and Billy Boggart."

"Grumpia Goatess," she ventured, quietly. She knew her face was red. The bear's bristles were scraping.

"I have the very name! Brenda Banshee!"

Kate, surprised, was horrified.

"Brenda Banshee, Brenda Banshee," chanted the children. Many of them booed.

Brenda Banshee was the sloppy maidservant in the house of Seamus O'Short, always left howling at the end of the tale. It struck Kate that the leprechaun was less than an ideal employer, given to perpetrating "hi-larious pranks" on his staff then laughing uproariously at their humiliations. In the real world, absentee landlords in Ireland were *boycotted* for less objectionable behavior than Seamus got away with every month.

"What does Brenda Banshee do?" asked Quinn.

"She howls! She howls!"

"If you think I'm going to howl," she told Sir Boris quietly, "you're very much mistaken."

"Howl, Brenda," said Quinn, grinning. "Howl for the boys and girls."

She set her lips tight.

If Brenda Banshee was always trying to filch coins from her employer's belt o' gold, it was probably because she was an indentured servant and received no wages for her drudgery.

"I think you'd howl most prettily," whispered Sir Boris de Bruin.

It dawned on her that she knew the voice.

She looked into the bear's mouth and saw familiar eyes.

"*Charles?*"

"If I can wear this, you can howl."

She was astounded, and very conscious of the embrace in which she was trapped. Her face, she knew, was burning.

"Please howl," demanded Quinn, enjoying himself.

Kate screwed her eyes shut and howled. It sounded reedy and feeble. Sir Boris gave her an encouraging, impertinent squeeze.

She howled enough to raise a round of applause.

"Very nice, Brenda," said Quinn. "Howl-arious. Shall we go inside?"

The book covers opened.

2: "details, young miss"

What *did* Charles Beauregard think he was about?

She scarcely believed an agent of the Diogenes Club would take it into his head to supplement his income by dressing up as a storybook bear in the service of Mr. Satterthwaite Bulge. She recalled John Watson's story in the *Strand* of the respectable suburban husband who earned a healthy living in disguise as a deformed beggar. Kate wondered at the ethics of publicizing such a singular case; it now served as an excuse for the smugly well-off to scorn genuine unfortunates on the grounds that "they doubtless earn more than a barrister." Money would not come into this. Charles was of the stripe who does nothing for purely financial reward. Of course, he could afford his scruples. He did not toil in an underpaid calling still only marginally willing to accept those of her sex. The profession Neville St. Clair had found less lucrative than beggary was her own, journalism.

Sir Boris hung back as Quinn escorted her along a low-ceilinged tunnel hung with green-threaded muslin. Underfoot was horsehair matting, dyed dark green to approximate forest grass.

"We proceed along the Airy Path, to Noggart's Nook . . ."

Quinn led her to a huge tree trunk that blocked the way. The plaster creation was intricate, with grinning goblin faces worked into the bark. Their eyes glowed, courtesy of dabs of luminous paint. An elaborate mechanical robin chirruped in the branches. Quinn rapped three times on the oak. Hidden doors opened inward.

". . . and into the Realm of Bobbin Swiftshaft, Prince of the Pixies . . ."

Kate stepped into the tree, and down three shallow steps. Cloth trailed over her face.

"Mind how you go."

She had walked into a curtain. Extricating herself, she found she was in a vaulted space: at once cathedral, Big Top, and planetarium. The dome sparkled with constellations, arranged to form the familiar shapes of B. Loved creatures. Miss Fay, Bobbin Swiftshaft, Jack Stump, Sir Boris, Seamus, and the rest cavorted across the painted, glittering ceiling. Tinsel streamers hung, catching the light. All around was a half-sized landscape, suitable for little folk, created through tamed nature and theatrical artifice. Kate, who spent most of her life peering up at people, was here taller than the tallest tree—many were genuine dwarves cultivated in the Japanese manner, not stage fakery—and a giant beside the dwellings. The woods were fully outfitted with huts and palaces, caves and castles, stone circles and hunting lodges. Paths wound prettily through miniature woodland. Water flowed from a fountain shaped like the mouth of a big bullfrog, whose name and station escaped her. The respectable torrent poured prettily over a waterfall, agitated a pond beneath, and passed out of the realm as a stream which disappeared into a cavern. An iron grille barred the outflow, lest small persons tumble in and be swept away.

All around were strange gleams, in the air and inside objects.

"The light," she said, "it's unearthly."

Looking close, she found semi-concealed glass globes and tubes, each containing a fizzing glowworm. Some were tinted subtle ruby-red or turquoise. They shone like the eyes of ghosts.

"We're mighty proud of the lighting," said Quinn. "We use only Edison's incandescents, which burn through the wizardry of the age, *electricity*. Beneath our feet are vast dynamos, which churn to keep the Aerie illuminated. The Gift quite literally puts the Savoy in the shade."

Mr. d'Oyly-Carte's Savoy Theater had been fully electrified for over a decade. Some metropolitan private homes were lit by Edison lamps, though the gas companies were fighting a vicious rearguard campaign against electrification, fearing the fate of the candle makers. Despite scare stories, the uninformed no longer feared lightning strikes from new-fangled gadgetry. They also no longer gasped in wonder at the mere use of an electrical current to spin a wheel or light a room. There was a risk that electric power would be relegated to quack medicinal devices like the galvanic weight-loss corset. In America, electrocution was used as a means of execution; in Britain, the process was most familiar from advertisements for the miracle food Bovril—allegedly produced by strapping a cow into an electric chair and throwing the switch. From H.G. Wells, the *Pall Mall Gazette*'s scientific correspondent, Kate gathered the coming century would be an Era of Electricity. At present, the spark seemed consigned to trivial distraction; that was certainly the case here.

A bulb atop a lantern pole hissed, flared and popped. A tinkling rain of glass shards fell.

"Some trivial teething troubles," said Quinn.

A lanky fellow in an overall rushed to attend to the lantern. He extracted the burned-out remains, ouching as his fingers came into contact with the hot ruin. He deftly screwed in a replacement, which began at once to glow, its light rising to full brightness. Another minion was already sweeping the fragments into a pan for easy disposal.

"Unusual-looking elves," she commented.

"It takes a crew of twenty-five trained men to keep the show going," said Quinn. "When the Gift is open, they *will* be elves. Each will have his own character and place."

Uncle Satt was insistent that in Færie, as in mundane society, there was a strict order of things. If a woodsman wed a fairy princess, it was a dead cert He was a prince in disguise rather than a real peasant. The reader was expected to guess as much from a well-born character's attention to personal cleanliness. Children knew the exact forms of protocol in Uncle Satt's imaginary kingdom, baffling adults with nursery arguments about whether a knight transformed into a bear by Witch-Queen Coelacanth outranked a tiger-headed maharajah from Far Off Indee.

Charles had shambled in and was sitting on a wooden bench, head inclined so he could talk quietly with one of the worker elves. Quinn had not noticed that Sir Boris had abandoned the other Merry Guardians.

When Mr. Henry Cockayne-Cust, her editor, sent Kate to the Gift, she had considered it a rent-paying exercise, a story destined for the depths of the inside pages. Much of her work was fish wrap before it had a chance to be read. It was a step up from "Ladies' Notes"—to which editors often tried to confine her, despite an evident lack of interest in the intricacies of fashionable feminine apparel or the supervision of servants—but not quite on a level with theater criticism, to which she turned her pen in a pinch, which is to say when the *Gazette*'s official reviewer fell asleep during a first night.

An item ("puff piece") about the Færie Aerie seemed doomed to fall into the increasingly large purview of Quinn's profession. She lamented the colonization of journalism by organized boosterism and the advertising trade. In some publications, people were deemed worthy of interest because of a happenstance rather than genuine achievement. The day might come when passing distraction was valued higher than matters of moment. She held it a sacred duty to resist.

If Mr. Charles Beauregard, if *the Diogenes Club*, took an interest in the Gift, an interest was worth taking. Some aspect of the endeavor not yet apparent would likely prove, in her uncle's parlance, "newsworthy."

Quinn's jibe about "daredevil" lady reporters had niggled. Now, she wondered whether there might not be a Devil here to dare.

"This, dear Brenda, is Uncle Satt."

While she was thinking, Mr. Satterthwaite Bulge had come up out of the ground.

Illustrations made Bulge a cherubic fat man, a clean-shaven Father Christmas or sober Bacchus, always drawn with gleam a-twinkle in his bright eye and smile a-twitch on his full, girlish lips. In person, Bulge was indeed stout but with no discernible expression. His face was the color of thin milk, and so were his longish hair and thinish lips. His eyes were the faded blue of china left on a shelf that gets too much sun. He wore sober clothes of old-fashioned cut, like a provincial alderman who stretches one good suit to last a lifetime in office. Bulge seemed like an artist's blank: a hole where a portrait would be drawn. More charitably, she thought of actors who walked through rehearsals, hitting marks and reciting lines without error, but withheld their *performance* until opening night, saving passion for paying customers.

Bulge had climbed a ladder and emerged through a trap-door, followed by another elf, a clerkish type with clips on his sleeves and a green eyeshade.

"This is Katharine Reed, of the *Pall Mall Gazette*," said Quinn.

"What's the circulation?" asked Bulge.

"Quite large, I'll wager," she said. "We're under orders not to reveal too much."

That, she knew, was feeble. In fact, she had no idea.

"I know to the precise number what the *Treasury* sells by the month. I know to the farthing what profit is to be had from the *Annual*. Details, young miss, that is the stuff of my enterprise, of *all* enterprises. Another word for *detail* is *penny*. Pennies are hard to come by. It is a lesson the *dear children* learn early."

She did not think she would ever be able to call this man "Uncle." The instant Bulge used the phrase "the *dear children*" and slid his lips into something he fondly imagined to be a smile, Kate knew his deepest, darkest secret. Mr. Satterthwaite Bulge, Uncle Satt of *Uncle Satt's Treasury for Boys and Girls*, greatly disliked children. It was an astonishing intuition. When Bulge used the word "dear," his meaning was not "beloved" but "expensive." Some parents, not least her own, might secretly agree.

"Do you consider the prime purpose of your enterprise to be educational?" she asked.

Bulge was impatient with the attempt at interview.

"That's covered in the, ah, what do you call the thing, Quinn . . . the *press release*. Yes, it's all covered in that. Questions, any you might ask, have already been answered. I see no purpose in repeating myself."

"She has the press release, Mr. Bulge," said Quinn.

"Good. You're doing your job. Young miss, I suggest you do yours. Why, all you have to do to manufacture an article is pen a general introduction, copy out Quinn's *release* and sign your name. Then you have your *interview with Uncle Satt* at a minimum of effort. A fine day's work, I imagine. A pretty penny earned."

The flaw, of course, was that she was not the only member of the press to receive the "release." If an article essentially identical to her own appeared in a rival paper, she would hear from Mr. Harry Cust. The editor could as devastatingly direct disapproval in person at one tiny reporter as, through editorial campaign, at an entire segment of society or tier of government. For that reason, the excellent and detailed brochure furnished by Quinn lay among spindled documents destined for use as tapers. The "press release" would serve to transfer flame from the grate to that plague of cigarettes which rendered the air in any newspaper office more noxious than the streets during the worst of a pea-soup fog.

"If I could ask a few supplementary questions, addressing matters touched upon but not explored in the release . . ."

"I can't be doing with this now," said Bulge. "Many things have to be seen to if the Gift is to open to the *dear children* on schedule."

"Might I talk with others involved? For instance, B. Loved remains a man of mystery. If the curtain were lifted and a few facts revealed about the artist, you could guarantee a great deal of, ah, *publicity*."

Bulge snorted. "I *have* a great deal of publicity, young miss."

"But . . ."

"There's no mystery about Loved. He's just a man with a paint box."

"So, B. Loved *is* a man then, *one* man, not . . ."

"Talk with Quinn," Bulge insisted. "It's his job. Don't bother anyone else. None can afford breaks for idle chatter. It's all we can do to keep everyone about their work, without distractions."

Quinn, realizing his employer was not making the best impression, stepped in.

"I'll be delighted to show Kate around."

"You do that, Quinn."

"She has her fairy sack."

Kate held it up.

"Tuppence lost," said Bulge. "Quinn's extravagances will be the ruin of me, young miss. I am surrounded by spendthrifts who care nought for *details.*"

"Remember, sir," said Quinn, mildly, "the matter we discussed . . ."

Bulge snorted. "Indeed, I do. More jargon. *Public image*, indeed. Arrant mumbo jumbo and impertinence."

If Uncle Satt wrote a word published under his name, Kate would be astounded. On the strength of this acquaintance, she could hardly believe he even *read* his own periodicals.

Which begged the question of what exactly he did in his empire.

See to details? Add up pennies?

If B. Loved was a man with a paint box, was he perhaps on the premises? If not painting murals himself, then supervising their creation. She had an intuition that the trail of the artist might we worth following.

A nearby tower toppled, at first slowly with a ripping like stiff paper being torn, and then rapidly, with an almighty crash, trailing wires that sparked and snapped, whipcracking toward the stream.

Bulge looked at Kate darkly, as if he suspected sabotage.

"You see, I am busy. These things *will* keep happening . . ."

Wires leaped like angry snakes. Elves kept well away from them.

"Accidents?" she asked.

"Obstacles," responded Bulge.

Bulge strode off and stared down the cables, which died and lay still. The electric lamps dimmed, leaving only cinder ghosts in the dark. Groans went up all around.

"Not again," grumbled an elf.

Someone struck a match.

Where the tower had fallen, a stretch of painted woodland was torn away, exposing bare lath. Matches flared all around and old-fashioned lanterns lit. It was less magical, but more practical.

"What is it this time, Sackham?"

"Been chewed through, Uncle," diagnosed the clerk, examining the damage. "Like before."

Bulge began issuing orders.

Kate took the opportunity to slip away. She hoped Bulge's attention to details would not extend to keeping track of her.

These things will *keep happening.*

That was interesting. That was what they called a lead.

3: "goblins"

"Is this a common event?" she asked an idling elf.

"Not 'arf," came the reply. "If it ain't breakin' down, it's fallin' down. If it ain't burnin' up, it's messin' up."

This particular elf was staying well out of the way. Several of his comrades, under the impatient supervision of Uncle Satt, were lifting the fallen tower out of the stream. Others, mouths full of nails and hammers in their hands, effected emergency repairs.

"They says it's the *goblins*."

Kate wanted to laugh, but her chuckle died.

"No, ma'am," said the elf, "it's serious. Some 'ave seen 'em, they say, then upped and left, walkin' away from good wages. That's not a natural thing, ma'am, not with times as they are and honest labor 'ard to come by."

"But . . . goblins?"

"Nasty little blighters, they say. Fingernails like teeth, an' teeth like needles. Always chewin' and clawin', weakenin' things so they collapse. Usually when there's someone underneath for to be collapsed upon. The craytors get into the machinery, gum up the works. Them big dynamos grind to a 'alt with a din like the world crackin' open."

She thought about this report.

"You mean this is sabotage? Has Satterthwaite Bulge deadly rivals in the færie business? Interests set against the opening of the Gift?"

"What business is it of yours?"

The elf realized for the first time he had no idea who she was. Her relative invisibility was often an aid in her profession; many forgot she was there even as they talked to her. Now, her spell of insignificance was wearing off.

"Miss Reed is a colleague, Blenkins," came a voice.

They had been joined by a bear. His presence reassured the elf Blenkins.

"If you say so, Sir Boris," he allowed. "My 'pologies, ma'am. A bloke 'as to be careful round 'ere."

"A bloke always has to be careful around Miss Reed."

She hoped that, in the gloom, Charles could not discern the fearful burning of her cheeks. When he first strolled into her life, Kate was thirteen and determined to despise the villain set upon fetching away her idol, Pamela Churchward. Father was lecturing at London University for a year, and Kate found herself absorbed into the large, complicated circle of the Churchwards. The beautiful, wise Pamela was the first woman ever to encourage Kate's ambitions. Her engagement seemed a treacherous defection, for all the bride-to-be insisted marriage would not end her independent life. Penelope, Pamela's ten-year-old cousin, said bluntly that Kate's complexion meant she would end up a governess or, at best, palmed off as wife to an untenured, adenoidal lecturer. Just then, as Kate was trying in vain not to cry, Pamela introduced her princely fiancé to her protégé.

Of course, Kate had fallen *horribly* in love with Charles. She doubted she had uttered a coherent sentence in his presence until he was a young widower. By then, courtesy of interesting, if brief, liaisons with Mr. Frank Harris, another editor, and several others, none of whom she regretted, she was what earlier decades might have branded *a fallen woman*.

Now, with Pamela gone and pernicious Penelope in retreat, she knew the thirteen-year-old nestled inside her thirty-two-year-old person remained smitten with the Man from the Diogenes Club. As a grown-up, she was more sensible than to indulge such silliness. It irritated her when he pretended to think she was still a tiny girl with rope braids down to her waist and cheeks of pillar-box red. It was, she knew, *only* pretense. Like his late wife (whom she still missed *so*), Charles Beauregard was among the select company who took Katharine Reed seriously.

"Sir Boris, you do me an injustice."

The bear head waved from side to side.

For once, she was not the most ridiculous personage in the room.

"Still, I'm sure you intended to be a very gallant bear."

She reached up and tickled the fur around his helm. It was painted plaster and she left white scratches. She stroked his arm, which was more convincing.

Blenkins slipped away, leaving them alone.

"There's a catch at the back," Charles said, muffled. "Like a diver's helmet. If you would do me the courtesy . . ."

"You can't get out of this on your own?"

"As it happens, no."

She found the catch and flipped it. Charles placed his paws over his ears and rotated his head ninety degrees so the muzzle pointed sideways, then lifted the thing free. A definite musk escaped from the decapitated costume. Charles's face was blacked like Mr. G.F. Elliott, the music hall act billed as "the Chocolate-Colored Coon." She found Elliott only marginally less unappealing than those comic turns who presented gormless, black-toothed caricatures of her own race. Charles's makeup was to prevent white skin showing through Sir Boris's mouth.

He whipped off a paw and scratched his chin.

"I've been desperate to do that for hours," he admitted.

He used his paw-glove to wipe his face. She took pity, produced a man-size handkerchief from her cuff and set about properly cleaning off the burned cork. He sat on a wooden toadstool and leaned forward so she could pay close attention to the task.

"Thank you, mama," he teased.

She swatted him with the blacked kerchief.

"I could leave you looking like a Welsh miner."

He shut up and let her finish. The face of Charles Beauregard emerged. Weary, to be sure, but recognizable.

"You've shaved your cavalry whiskers," she observed.

His hand went to his neatly trimmed mustache.

"A touch of the creeping grays, I suspect," she added, wickedly.

"Good grief, Katie," said Charles, "you're worse than Mycroft's brother!"

"I'm right, though, am I not?"

"There was a certain *tinge* of dignified white," he admitted, shyly, "which I estimated could be eliminated by judicious barbering."

"Considering your calling, I'm surprised every hair on your person hasn't been bleached. It's said to be a common side effect of stark terror."

"So I am reliably informed."

He undid strings at the back of his neck and shrugged the bear suit loose, then stepped out of the top half of the costume. The cuirass, leather painted like steel, unlaced down the back to allow escape from straitjacket-like confines. Underneath, he wore a grimy shirt, with no collar. High-waisted but clownishly baggy furry britches stuck into heroic boots that completed the ensemble.

"The things you do for Queen and Country, Charles."

He looked momentarily sheepish.

"*Charles?*"

"I'm at present acting on my own initiative."

This was puzzling and most unlike Charles. But she knew what had brought him here. She had seized at once on the "newsworthy" aspect of the Gift.

"It's the *goblins*, isn't it?"

He flashed a humorless smile.

"Still sharp as ever, Kate? Yes, it's Blenkins's blinkin' goblins."

The hammering and tower raising continued. The electric lights fizzled on again, then out. Then on, to burn steady. Charles instinctively stepped back, into a shadowed alcove, drawing Kate with him.

Bulge flapped a list of "to do" tasks at the elves. Mr Sackham was presently at the receiving end of the brunt of Uncle Satt's opprobrium.

"What do you know that I don't?" she asked Charles.

"That's a big question."

She hit him on the arm. Quite hard.

"You deserved that."

"Indeed I did. My apologies, Katie. Life inside a bear costume is, I'm afraid, a strain on any temperament. When the Gift opens to the public, I should not care to let a child of my acquaintance within easy reach of anyone who is forced, as the "show-business" slang has it, "to wear a head." An hour of such imprisonment transforms the most patient soul into Grendel, eager for a small, helpless person upon whom to slake his wrath."

"You have my promise that I shall write a blistering exposé of this cruel practice. The cause of the afflicted "head wearers" shall become as known as, in an earlier age, was that of the children employed as human chimney brushes or, as now, those drabs sold as "maiden tributes of modern Babylon." A committee shall be formed and strong letters written to Members of Parliament. Fairies will chain themselves to the railings. None shall be allowed to rest in the Halls of Justice until the magic bears are free!"

"Now *you're* teasing *me*."

"I have earned that right."

"That you have, Katie."

"Now this amusing diversion is at an end, I refer you back to my initial question. What do you know that I don't?"

Charles sighed. She had sidestepped him again. She wondered if he ever regretted that she was no longer tongue-tied in his presence.

"Not much," he admitted, "and I can't talk about it here. If you would meet me outside in half an hour. I am acting on my own initiative and honestly welcome your views."

"This goblin hunt?"

"That's part of it."

"Part only?"

"Part only."

"I shall wait half an hour, no longer."

"It will take that to become presentable. I can't shamble as a demi-bear among afternoon promenaders."

"Indeed. Panic would ensue. Men with nets would be summoned. As an obvious chimera, you would be captured and confined to the conveniently nearby London Zoo. Destined to be stuffed and presented to the Natural History Museum."

"I'm so glad you understand."

He kissed her forehead, which reddened her again. She was grateful her blushes wouldn't show up under the electric lamps.

4: "a pale green ribbon"

A full forty-five minutes later, Kate was still waiting in the park. On this pleasant afternoon, many freed from places of employment were not yet disposed to return to their homes. A gathering of shopgirls chirruped, competing for the attention of a smooth-faced youth who sported a cricket cap and a racy striped jacket. Evidently quite a wit, his flow of comments on the peculiarities of passersby kept his pretty flock in fits.

"With her colorin' and mouth," drawled the champion lad, "it's a wonder she ain't forever bein' mistook for a pillar box."

Much hilarity among the *filles des estaminets*.

"Oh Max, you are so *wicked* . . . you shouldn't ought to say such things . . ."

Kate supposed she *was* redder than usual. The condition came upon her when amused, embarrassed or—as in this case—annoyed.

"I 'magine she's waitin' to be emptied."

"The postman's running late today," ventured the boldest of the girls.

"Bad show, what. To leave such a pert post box unattended."

Charles emerged from the Gift at last, more typically clothed. Most would take him for a clubman fresh from a day's idleness and up for an evening's foolery.

As he approached, the girls' attention was removed entirely from Max. Their eyes followed Charles's saunter. He did such a fine job of pretending not to notice that only Kate was not fooled.

"He must have a letter that *desperately* needs postin'," said the amusing youth.

"If you will excuse me," said Charles, raising a finger.

He walked over to the group, who fluttered and gathered around Merry Max. Charles took a firm grip on the youth's ear and dragged him to Kate. The cap fell off, revealing that his cultivated forelock was a lonely survivor on an otherwise hairless scalp.

"This fellow has something to say to you, Kate."

"Sorry," came the strangled bleat, "no 'ffence meant."

Now someone was redder than she. Max's pate was practically vermilion.

"None taken."

Charles let Max go and he fell over. When he sat up again, his congregation was flown, seeking another hero. He snatched up his cap and slunk off.

"I suppose you expect me to be grateful for your protection, Sir Boris?"

Charles shrugged. "After a day in the bear head, I had to thump *someone*. Max happened to be convenient. He was making 'short' jokes about Jack Stump earlier."

"I believe you."

He looked at her, and she was thirteen again. Then she was an annoyed grown-up woman.

"No, really. I do."

Charles glanced back at the Gift.

"So, Mr. Beauregard, what's the story? Why take an interest in Uncle Satt?"

"Bulge is incidental. The mermaid on the front of the ship. Oh, he's the one who's made the fortune. But he's not the treasure of the *Treasury*. That's the other fellow, the mysterious cove . . ."

"B. Loved?"

Charles tapped her forehead. "Spot on. The artist."

"What does the B stand for?"

"David."

"Beloved. From the Hebrew."

"Indeed. Davey Harvill, as was. B. Loved, as is."

The name meant nothing to her.

"Young Davey is a singular fellow. We met eight years ago, in Herefordshire. He had an unusual experience. The sort of unusual that comes under my purview."

It was fairly openly acknowledged that the Diogenes Club was a clearing house for the British Secret Service. Less known was its occult remit. While the Society for Psychical Research could reliably gather data on cold spots or fraudulent mediums, they were hardly equipped to cope with supernatural occurrences that constituted a threat to the natural order of things. If a spook clanked chains or formed faces in the muslin, a run-of-the-mill ghost finder was more than qualified to provide reassurance; if it could hurt you, then the Ruling Cabal sent Charles Beauregard.

"Davey was lost in the woods and found much older than he should be. I don't mean aged by terrible experience, your "side effects of stark terror." He disappeared a child of nine and returned a full-grown man, as if twenty years had passed over a weekend."

"You established there was no imposture?"

"To my satisfaction."

Kate thought, tapping her teeth with a knuckle. "But not to everyone's?"

Charles spread his hands. "The lad's mother could never accept him."

She had a pang of sympathy for this boy she had never met.

"What happened after he was returned?"

"Interesting choice of words. 'Was returned'? Suggests an agency over which he had no control. Might he not have *escaped*? Davey was taken in by his older sister, Sarah Riddle. Maeve Harvill, Davey's other sister, also went into the woods. She came out like her normal self and was embraced by the mother. Sadly, Mrs. Harvill died some time afterward. I have questions about that, but we can get to them later. Sarah, herself the mother of a young son, became sole parent to both her siblings. By then, Davey was drawing."

"The færie pictures?"

"They poured from his pencils," said Charles. "He does it all with pencils, you know. Not charcoal. The pictures became more intense, more captivating. You've seen them?"

"Who hasn't?"

"Quite. That's down to Evelyn Weddle, the vicar of Eye. He took an interest, and brought Davey's pictures to the attention of a Glamorgan printer."

"Satterthwaite Bulge?"

"Indeed. Bulge, quite against his nature, was captivated. The pictures have strange effects, as the whole world now knows. Bulge put together the first number of his *Treasury*. It made his name."

"Who writes the copy?"

"At first, Weddle. He's the sort of the poet, alas, who rhymes 'pixie' with 'tipsy' and 'færie' with 'hurry.' Don't you hate that diphthong, by the way. It's one step away from an umlaut. What's wrong with f-a-i-r-y, I'd like to know? The vicar was so flattered to see his verses immortalized by typesetting that he cared not that his name wasn't appended. He fell by the wayside early on. Now, Bulge has many scribbling elves—though he oversees them all, and contrives to imprint his own concerns upon the work. All that business about washing your hands, respecting princes and punishing servants. Leslie Sackham, whom you saw dancing attendance, is currently principle quill-pushing elf. They are interchangeable and rarely last more than a few months, but there's only one B. Loved."

"Is this golden egg-laying goose chained to an easel?"

Charles shook his head. "His artistry is of a *compulsive* nature. The *Treasury* can't keep up with the flow. Even under a hugely unfair personal contract the Harvills knew no better than to accept, Davey has become very well off."

She thought of the illustrations, wondering if she would see them differently now she had some idea about their creator. They had always seemed portals into another, private world.

"What does Davey say about the time he was away?"

"He *says* little. He claims an almost complete loss of memory."

"But he draws. You think not from imagination, but from life?"

"I don't suppose he is representing a literal truth, no. But I am certain his pictures spring from the place he and his sister were taken—and I do believe they were *taken*—whether it be a literal Realm of Færie or not."

"You know the stories . . ."

Charles caught her meaning. ". . . of the little people, and babies snatched from their cribs? Changelings left in their stead? Very Irish."

"Not in the Reed household. At least, not until the rise of Uncle Satt. But, yes, those stories."

"They aren't confined to the emerald isle. Ten years ago in Sussex, a little girl named Rose Farrar was allegedly spirited away by 'angels.' That's an authenticated case. We took an interest. Rose is still listed among the missing."

"It's not just leprechauns. Someone is always accused of child abduction. Mysterious folk, outsiders, alien. Dark-complected, most like. Wicked to the bone. There are the stories of the Pied Piper and the Snow Queen. Robbers, imps and devils, Red Indians, the gypsies . . ."

"Funny you should mention gypsies."

"Tinkers, in Ireland. Have they ever *really* stolen babies? Why on earth would they want to? Babies are bothersome, I'm given to understand. Nonsense is usually spouted about strengthening the blood stock of a small population, but surely you'd do better taking grown-up women for that. No, it seems to me that the interest of the stories is in the people who tell them. There is a *purpose*, a lesson. Don't go wandering off, children, for you might fall down a well. Don't talk to strangers, for they might eat you."

Afternoon had slid into evening. One set of idlers had departed, and a fresh crowd come upon the scene. This was a park, not wild woods. Nature was trimmed and tamed, hemmed in by city streets and patrolled by wardens. Treetops were black with soot.

A shout went up nearby, a governess calling her charge.

"Master Timothy! Timmy!"

Kate felt a clutch of dread. Here, in the press of people, was more danger than in all the trackless woods of England. Scattered among the bland, normal faces were blood-red, murderous hearts. She had attended enough coroner's courts to know imps and angels were superfluous in the metropolis. Caligula could pass, unnoticed, in a celluloid collar.

Master Timothy was found and smothered with tearful kisses. He didn't look grateful. Catching sight of Kate, he stuck out a fat little tongue at her.

"Beast," she commented.

Charles looked for a moment as if he was going to serve the ungracious little perisher as he had Merry Max. She laid a hand in the crook of his arm. She did not care to be complicit with another assault. Charles laid his hand on hers and tapped, understanding, amused.

"The Diogenes Club has a category for everything," he said, "no matter how outré. Maps of Atlantis—we have dozens of them, properly catalogued and folded. Hauntings, tabulated and subcategorized, with pins marked into ordnance survey charts and patterns studied by our learned consultants. Witch Cults, ranked by the degree of unpleasantness involved in their ritual behavior and the trouble caused in various quarters of the Empire. There's also a category for mysteries without solution. Matters we have looked into but been unable to form a conclusion upon. Like the diplomat Benjamin Bathurst, who 'walked around the horses' and vanished without trace. Or little Rose Farrar."

"The *Mary Celeste?*"

"Actually, we did fathom that. It remains under the rose for the moment. We've no pressing desire to go to war with the United States of America."

She let that pass.

"Unsolved matters constitute large category," he continue. "Most of my reports are inconclusive. A strategy has formed for such cases. We tie a pale green ribbon around the file and shelve it in a windowless room behind a door that looks like a cupboard. The Ruling Cabal, which is to say you-know-who, disapproves of fussing with green ribbon files. As he says, 'when you are unable to eliminate the impossible, don't waste too much time worrying about it.' The ribbons are knotted tight and difficult to unpick—though, from time to time, further information comes to light. Of course, it's easier to work in the green ribbon room if you think of *people* as *cases.*"

"And you can't?"

"No more than you can. No, I don't mean that, Katie. You, more than anyone, are immune to that tendency. I am not. I concede that sometimes it helps to consider mysteries purely as puzzles. Pamela would nag me about it. She always thought of *people* first, last and always."

Pamela's name did not come up often between them. It did not need to.

"So, in her memory and for fear of disappointing you, I tied the pale green ribbon loosely around Davey Harvill. I had thought the whole thing buried in Eye, a local wonder soon forgotten. However, here we are in the heart of London, before Davey's færie recreated. There are the goblins to consider. Blenkins's goblins. How did they creep into the picture?"

Kate snapped her fingers. "That's how B. Loved draws goblins, hidden as if they've crept in. You have to look twice, sometimes very closely, to see them, disguised against tree-bark or peeping out of long grass. In the *Annual*, there's a plate entitled 'How many goblins are being naughty in this picture?' It shows a country market in an uproar."

"There are twenty-seven goblins in the picture. All being naughty."

"I found twenty-nine."

"Yes, well, that's a game. This is not. Workmen have been injured. Nipped as if by tiny teeth. Rats, they say. The thing is, when it's rats, parties involved usually say it isn't. *That's* when they talk about mischievous imps. No one who wants to draw in crowds of children likes to mention the tiniest rat problem. But here everyone says it's rats. Except Blenkins, and he's been told to shut up."

". . . if it can hurt you . . ."

"I beg your pardon."

"Just something I was thinking of earlier."

There was another commotion. Kate assumed Timmy had fled his governess again, but that was not the case.

"Speak of the Devil . . ."

Blenkins was running through the crowds, clearly in distress.

He saw Charles and dashed over, out of breath.

"Mr B," he said, "it's terrible what they done . . ."

Police whistles shrilled nearby.

"I can't credit it. 'appened so quick, sir."

Cries went up. "Fire!" and "Murder!"

"You better take us in," said Charles.

"Not the lady—beggin' your pardon, ma'am—it's too 'orrible."

"She'll be fine," said Charles, winning her all over again—though the casual assumption of the strength of her constitution in face of the truly 'orrible gave her some pause. "Come on, quick about it!"

Blenkins led them back toward the Gift.

5: "the scene of the occurrence"

There was a rumble, deep in the ground, like the awakening of an angry ogre. The doors of the Gift were thrown open, and people—some in costume—poured through. Bulge, collar burst and a bruise on his forehead, was carried out by a broken-winged fairy and a soot-grimed engineer.

Charles held Kate's arm, holding her back.

Bulge caught sight of her and glared as if she were personally to blame.

Blenkins took off his cap and covered his face with it.

Something big broke, deep inside the Gift. Cries and screams were all around.

Quinn, beard awry and hat gone, staggered into the evening light, dazed.

The elves stumbled into an encircling crowd of curious spectators. Kate realized she was in danger of belonging to this category of nuisance.

A belch of smoke escaped and rose in a black ring.

The doors clattered shut.

Breaths were held. There was a moment of quiet. No more smoke, no flames or explosions. Then, everyone began talking at once.

The police were on the scene, a troop of uniformed constables throwing up a picket around the Gift. Kate recognized Inspector Mist of Scotland Yard, a sallow man with a pendulous mustache.

Mist caught sight of Charles and Kate. He shifted his bowler to the back of his head.

"Again we meet in unusual circumstances, Inspector," said Charles.

"Unusual circumstances are an expected thing with you, Mr. Beauregard," said the policeman. "I suppose you two'll have the authority of a certain body to act as, shall we say, observers in this investigation."

Charles did not confirm or deny this, a passive sort of mendacity. She had a pang of worry. Her friend stood to lose a hard-to-define position. She had dark ideas of what form expulsion from the Diogenes Club might take.

"We're not sure any crime has been committed," she said, distracting the thoughtful Mist. "It might be some kind of accident."

"There is usually a crime somewhere, Miss Reed."

Mist might look the glum plodder, but was one of the sharpest needles in the box.

"Hullo, Quinn," said the inspector, spotting the publicist. "Not hawking patent medicines again, are we?"

Quinn looked sheepish and shook his head.

"I'm relieved to hear it. I trust you've found respectable employment."

The former leprechaun was pale and shaking. His green jacket was spotted with red.

Mist ordered his men to disperse only the irrelevant crowds. He told the elves not to melt into the throng just yet. Questions would have to be answered. More policemen arrived, then a clanking, hissing fire engine. Mist had the Brigade stand by.

"Let's take a look inside this pixie pavilion, shall we?"

Quinn shook his head, insistently.

Mist pulled one of the book covers open, and stepped inside. No one from Bulge's troupe was eager to join him. Blenkins hid behind Miss Fay, whose wand was snapped and leotards laddered. Kate followed the inspector, with Charles in her wake. In the murk of the tunnel, Mist was exasperated. He pushed the main door back open.

"Who's in charge?" he called out.

Some elves moved away from Uncle Satt, who was fiddling with his collar, trying to refasten it despite the loss of a stud.

"Mr. Bulge, if you would be so kind . . ."

The inspector beckoned. Bulge advanced, regaining some of his composure.

"Thank you, sir."

Bulge entered his realm, joining the little party.

"If you would lead us to the scene of the occurrence . . ."

Bulge, even in the shadows, blanched visibly.

"Very well," he said, lifting a flap of black velvet. A stairwell wound into the ground. Smell hung in the air, ozone and machine oil and something else foul. Arhythmic din boomed from below. Kate felt a touch of the quease.

Mist went first, signaling for Bulge to follow. Kate and Charles waited for them to disappear before setting foot on the wrought-iron steps.

"Into the underworld," said Charles.

"I didn't realize Noggart's Nook harbored circles of damned souls."

"Children who don't wash their hands before *and* after meals, maids who sweep dust under the carpets . . ."

Beneath the Gift were large, stone-walled rooms, hot and damp. Electric lamps flickered in heavily grilled alcoves.

"Good God," exclaimed Inspector Mist.

The dynamos were still in motion, though slowed and erratic. Huge cast-iron engines, set in concrete foundations, spat sparks and water droplets as great belts kept the drums in motion. Wheels and pistons whirled and pounded, ball valves spun and somewhere below a hungry furnace roared. The central dynamo was grinding irregularly, works impeded by a limp suit of clothes filled with loose meat.

Kate gasped and covered her mouth and nose with her hand, determined not to be overcome.

Flopping from the suit collar was a deflated ball with a bloody smear for a face.

"Sackham," cried Bulge.

She could not recognize this rag as the clerkish elf she had seen earlier, scurrying after his master.

"What's been done to you?!" howled Bulge, with a shocking, undeniable grief.

The human tangle was twisted into the wheels of the machine, boneless legs caught in cogs. A ball-valve whined to a halt and shook off its spindle. With a mighty straining and gouts of fire, the central dynamo died. Its fellows flipped over inhibitors and shut down in more orderly fashion. The lamps faded.

In the dark there was only the *stench*.

Kate felt Charles's arm around her.

Act III: Færie

1: "events have eventuated"

After a day as Sir Boris and a night at a police station, Charles needed to sleep. The situation was escalating, but he was no use in his present state. He had told Inspector Mist as much as he could and done his best to spare Kate further distress.

He was greeted at the door of his house in Cheyne Walk.

"Visitors, sir," said his man, Bairstow. "I have them in the reception room. Funereal gentlemen."

He considered himself in the hall mirror. Unshaven, the gray Kate—clever girl!—had deftly intuited was evident about his gills.

These visitors would not care about his appearance.

"Send in tea, Bairstow. Strong and green."

"Very good, sir."

Charles stepped into his reception room, as if he were the intruder and the others at home.

The two men were dressed like undertakers, in long black coats and gloves, crepe-brimmed hats, and smoked glasses.

"Beauregard," said the senior, Mr. Hay.

"Gentlemen," he acknowledged.

Mr. Hay took his case in the best armchair, looking over the latest number of the *Pall Mall Gazette*, open to an article by Kate. Not a coincidence.

Mr. Effe, younger and leaner, stood by a bookcase, reading spines.

Charles, not caring to be treated like a schoolboy summoned before the beak for a thrashing, slipped into a chair of his own and stretched out, fingers interlaced on his waistcoat as if settling down for a nap.

(Which would be a good idea.)

Two sets of hidden eyes fixed on him.

"Must you wear those things?" Charles asked.

Mr. Hay lowered his spectacles, disclosing very light-colored, surprisingly humorous eyes. Mr. Effe did not follow suit. Charles amused himself by imagining a severe case of the cross-eyed squints.

At this hour in the morning, a maid would have opened the curtains. The visitors had drawn them again, which should make protective goggles superfluous. He wondered what his visitors could actually see. It was no wonder Mr. Effe had to get so close to the shelves to identify books.

"The salacious items are under lock and key in the hidden room," said Charles. "Have you read *My Nine Nights in a Harem?* I've a rare *Vermis Mysteriis*, illustrated with brass rubbings that'd curl your hair."

"That's a giggle," snarled Mr. Effe. "Of course, you *do* have hidden rooms."

"Three. And secret passages. Don't you?"

He couldn't imagine Mr. Hay or Mr. Effe—or any of their fellows, Mr. Bee, Mr. Sea, and Mr. Dee, all the way to Mr. Eggs, Miss Why, and Mr. Zed—*having* homes, even haunted lairs. He assumed they slept in rows of coffins under the Houses of Parliament.

Mr. Effe wiped a line down a mediocre edition of *The Collected Poems of Jeffrey Aspern* and pretended to find dust on his gloved finger.

Charles knew Mrs. Hammond, his housekeeper, better than that.

"You've been acting on your own initiative," said Mr. Hay. "That's out of character for an active member of the Diogenes Club. Not that there are enough of you to make general assumptions. Sedentary bunch, as a rule."

"Did you think we wouldn't notice?" sniped Mr. Effe.

Mr. Hay raised a hand, silencing his junior.

"We're not here for recriminations."

Millie, the second prettiest maid, brought in the tray. He approved; Lucy, the household stunner, was in reserve for special occasions. After thanking the by no means unappealing Millie, he let her escape. Mr. Effe's attempt at a charming smile had thrown a fright into the girl. Charles poured a measure of Mrs. Hammond's potent brew into a giant's teacup, but did not offer hospitality.

"Events have eventuated," said Mr. Hay. "Your Ruling Cabal was shortsighted to green-ribbon the Harvill children. You, however, were perceptive in continuing to take an interest. Even if *unsanctioned*."

"Bad business under Regent's Park," commented Mr. Effe.

Charles expected these fellows to be up on things.

"Your assumption is that this is the same case?" asked Mr. Hay.

He swallowed tea. The Undertaking knew full well this was the same case.

"Mr. Effe, if you would do the honors," said Mr. Hay, snapping his fingers.

Mr. Effe unbuttoned his coat down the front, and reached inside.

Charles tensed, ready to defend his corner.

Mr. Effe produced a pinch of material, which he unravelled and let dangle. A pale green ribbon.

"Removed from the Harvill file," said Mr. Hay. "With the full cooperation and consultation of the Ruling Cabal."

"You're official again, pally," snapped Mr. Effe.

Charles relaxed. He would have to make explanation to the Cabal in time, but was protected now by approval from on high (rather, down below). There was a literal dark side to this. For all its stuffinesses and eccentricities, he understood the Diogenes Club: it was a comfort and shelter in a world of shadows. The Undertaking was constituted on different lines. Rivalry between the Club and the men in smoked glasses held a potential for outright conflict. It had been said of Mycroft Holmes, chairman of the Ruling Cabal, that sometimes he *was* the British Government; the troubling thing about the Undertaking was that sometimes it *wasn't*.

"We'll see your report," said Mr. Hay.

He remembered how tired he was. He closed his eyes.

When he opened them again, he was alone.

Something tickled on his face. He puffed it away, and saw it was the ribbon.

2: "thrones, powers and principalities"

Kate's story dominated the front page of the *Pall Mall Gazette*. An affront to a national treasure (for so Uncle Satt was reckoned), a gruesomely mysterious death, and rumors of supernatural agency meant Harry Cust had no choice but to give her piece prominence. However, it was rewritten so ruthlessly, by Cust himself at the typesetting bench, that she felt reduced to the status of interviewee, providing raw material shaped into journalism by other hands.

She was cheered, slightly, by a telegram of approval from Uncle Diarmid, who *ought* to be reckoned a national treasure. It arrived soon after the mid-morning special was hawked in the streets, addressed not to the *Gazette* offices but the Cheshire Cheese, the Fleet Street watering hole where Kate, and four-fifths of the journalists in London, took most meals. Uncle Diarmid always said half the trick of newspaper reporting was getting underfoot, contriving to be present at the most "newsworthy" incidents, gumming up the works to get the story.

The image conjured unpleasant memories. She had ordered chops, but wasn't sure she could face eating—though hunger pangs had struck several times through the long night and morning.

Reporters from other papers stopped by her table, offering congratulations but also soliciting unrefined nuggets of information. Anything about Satterthwaite Bulge was news. Back files were being combed to provide follow-up pieces to fill out this afternoon and evening editions. The assumption was that the notoriously close-mouthed Inspector Mist would not oblige with further revelations about the death of Mr. Leslie Sackham in time to catch the presses.

Kate had little to add.

The story about the goblins was out, and sketches already circulated ("artists' impressions," which is to say unsubstantiated, fantastical lies) depicting malicious, oval-headed imps tormenting Mr. Sackham before tossing him to the dynamo. Most of Uncle Satt's elves had come forth with tales of goblin sightings or encounters in the dark. Blenkins was charging upward of ten shillings a time for an anecdote. The rumor was the Scotland Yard were looking for dwarves. Jack Stump was in hiding. Kate wondered about other little people—like Master Timothy, the obnoxious child. How far could such a prankster go? Surely, nursery ill manners did not betoken a heart black enough for murder. It made more sense to look for goblins. The sensation press had already turned up distinguished crackpots willing to expound at length about the vile habits of *genus goblinus*. Soon, there would be organized hunting parties, and rat-tail bounties offered on green, pointed ears.

Kate's chops were set before her. She had ordered them well-cooked, so that no red showed. Even so, she ate the baked potato first.

There was the problem of Mr. Sackham's obituary, which was assigned to her. The most interesting thing about the man's life was its end, already described at quite enough length. His injuries were such that it was impossible to tell whether he had been thrown (or fallen) alive into the dynamo. Indeed, the corpse was mutilated to such an extent that if the incident were encountered in a penny dreadful, the astute reader would assume Mr. Sackham not to be dead at all but that the body was a nameless tramp dressed in his clothes and sacrificed in order to facilitate a surprise in a later chapter. The second most interesting thing about Sackham was that he had penned many of the words recently published under the byline of Uncle Satt, but Cust forbade her to mention this. Exposing hypocrites was all very well, but no newspaper could afford to suggest that Satterthwaite Bulge was less than the genial "Founder of Færie and Magister of Marvels" for fear of an angry mob of children invading their offices to wreak vengeful havoc. She was reduced to padding out a paragraph on Sackham's duties at the Gift and the fact that he very nearly could legitimately call Uncle Satt his uncle; Leslie Sackham had been the son of his employer's cousin.

She finished her copy and her chops at about the same time, then gave a handy lad tuppence to rush the obit. to the *Gazette* in the Strand. As Ned made his way out of the Cheese, he was entrusted with a dozen other scribblings—some on the reverse of bills, most on leaves torn from notebooks—to drop off at the various newspapers on his route.

Now, she might snatch a snooze.

"Kate."

She looked up, not sure how long (or if) she had dozed in her chair.

"Charles."

He sat down.

"Scotland Yard is saying it was an accident," he said.

Kate sensed journalistic ears pricking up all around.

"That doesn't sound like Mist," she observed.

"I didn't say, 'Mist,' I said, 'Scotland Yard.'"

She understood. Decisions had been made in shadowed corridors.

"The Gift is declared 'unsafe' for the moment," he continued. "No grand opening this weekend, I'm afraid. There'll be investigations, by the public health and safety people and anyone else who can get his oar in. It turns out that the Corporation of London still owns the site. Uncle Satt is lessee of the ground, though he has deed and title to all structures built on and under it. There'll be undignified arguments over whose fault it all is. In the mean time, the place is under police guard. As you can imagine, Regent's Park is besieged by aspirant goblin hunters. Some have butterfly nets and elephant guns."

She looked around. The cartoonist responsible was lurking somewhere.

"I was given this," he said, producing a length of green ribbon.

"The Ruling Cabal want you to continue to take an interest?"

"They've no choice. Another body has made its desires known. There are thrones, powers, and principalities in this. For some reason beyond me, this matter is important. My remit is loose. While the police and the safety fellows are concerned with Sackham's death, I am to pull the loose ends. I have leeway as to whom I choose to involve, and I should like to choose you."

"*Again?* You'll have to put me up for membership one day."

She was teasing, but he took it seriously. "In a world of impossibilities, that should be discussed. I shall see what I can do."

Previously, when Charles involved her (or, more properly, allowed her to become involved) in the business of the Diogenes Club, she had gathered stories that would make her name if set in type but which wouldn't even pass the breed of editor willing to publish 'artist's impressions,' let alone Henry Cockayne-Cust. Still, she had an eternal itch to draw back the curtain. Association with Charles was interesting on other levels, if often enervating or perilous.

"If the Gift is being adequately investigated, where should we direct our attentions?"

Charles smiled.

"How would you like an audience with B. Loved?"

3: "the Affair of the Dendrified Digit"

"So this is the house that Færie built?" said Kate.

"Bought," he corrected.

"Very nice. Pennies add up like details, indeed."

They were on a doorstep in elegant Broadley Terrace, quite near Regent's Park and a long way from Herefordshire.

"What's that smell?" asked Kate, nose wrinkling like a kitten's.

"Fresh bread," he told her.

The door was opened by a child with flour on his cheeks and a magnifying glass in his hand. The boy examined Charles's shoes and trouser cuffs, then angled his gaze upward. Through the lens, half his face was enlarged and distorted.

"I be a 'tective," he announced.

"What about the flour?" asked Charles.

Kate had slipped a handkerchief out of her tightly buttoned cuff, possessed of a universal feminine instinct to clean the faces of boys who were perfectly happy as they were.

The boy touched his forehead, then examined the white on his fingertips.

"I be a baker too, like my Da. I be baker by day, 'tective by night."

"Very practical," said Kate. "In my experience, detectives often neglect proper meals."

"Are you a 'tective too, mister?"

Charles looked at Kate, for a prompt.

"Sometimes," he admitted. "But don't tell anyone. Affairs of state, you know."

The boy's face distorted in awe.

"A *secret agent* . . . Come in and have some of my boasters. I made them special, all by myself. Though Da helped with the oven."

Charles let Kate step into the hallway and followed, removing his hat.

A woman bustled into the hall.

"Dickie," she said, incipiently scolding, "who've you let in now?"

The woman, neat and plump, came to them. Sairey Riddle, well shy of thirty, had gray streaks. In eight years, she had filled out to resemble her late mother.

She remembered him.

"It's you," she said, face shaded. "You found *her*."

"Maeve."

"Her."

He understood the distinction.

"This is my friend, Miss Katharine Reed. Kate, this is Sairey Riddle."

"Sarah," she said, careful with the syllables now.

Dickie was clinging to his mother's skirts. Now, he looked up again at Charles.

"You be *that* 'tective. Who found Auntie when she were lost? In the olden days?"

"He means before he were . . . was born. It's all olden days to him. Might as well a' been knights in armor and fire-breathing dragons."

"Yes, Dickie. I found your Aunt Maeve. One of my most difficult cases."

Dickie looked through his magnifying glass again.

"A proper *'tective*," he breathed.

"I do believe you've found a hero worshiper," whispered Kate, not entirely satiri-
cally.

Charles was intently aware of a sudden responsibility.

"Don't mind our Dickie," said Sarah. "He's not daft and he means well."

For the first time in months, Charles felt the ache in his forearm, in the long-
healed bite. It was the name, of course. By now, his son would have been almost an
adult; he would have been Dickie as a child, Dick as a youth, and be on the point of
demanding the full, respectful Richard.

"Are you all right?" inquired Kate, sharp as usual.

"Old wound," he said, not satisfying her.

"Have you come about the business in the park?" prompted Sarah. "We heard
about poor Mr. Sackham."

"I'm afraid so. We were wondering if we might see Davey?"

Sarah bit her lower lip. He noticed a worn spot, often chewed. She glanced up at
the ceiling. The shadow that had fallen over this family in Hill Wood had never been
dispelled.

"It's not been one of his good days."

"I can imagine."

"We never did find out, you know, what *happened* to him. To them both."

"I know."

Sarah led them into a reception room. She left Dickie with them while she went
to look in on her brother.

"Do you want to see my *clues*?" asked the boy, tugging Charles's trouser pocket.

Kate found this hilarious but stifled her giggles.

Dickie produced a cigar box and showed its contents.

"This button 'nabled me to solve the Case of the Vanishing Currant Bun. It were
the fat lad from down the road. He snitched it from the tray when Da weren't looking. This playin' card, a Jack of Hearts with one corner bent off, is the key to the
Scandal of the Cheatin' Governess. And this twig that looks 'zactly like a 'uman finger is a mystery whose solution no man yet knows, though I've not 'bandoned my in-
quiries."

Dickie examined the twig, which did resemble a finger.

"What do you call the case?" he asked the boy.

"It hasn't a name yet."

"What about the Affair of the Dendrified Digit?" suggested Kate.

Dickie's eyes widened and he ran the words around his mouth.

"What be a 'dendrified digit'?"

"A finger turned to wood."

"Very 'propriate. Are you a 'tective too, lady?"

"I'm a reporter."

"A *daredevil* reporter," Charles corrected.

Kate poked her tongue out at him while Dickie wasn't looking.

"Then you must be a 'tective's *assistant*."

Kate was struck aghast. It was Charles's turn to be amused.

Dickie reached into his box and produced a rusty nail.

"This be . . ."

He halted mid-sentence, swallowed, and stepped back, positioning himself so
that Kate stood between the door and him.

The handle was turning.

Into the room came a little girl in blue, as perfectly dressed as a china doll on display. She had an enormous cloud of stiff blonde hair and a long, solemn, pretty face.

Beside her, Dickie looked distinctly shabby.

The girl looked at Charles and announced, "We have met before."

"It's Auntie," whispered Dickie. Charles saw the wariness the lad had around the girl; not fear, exactly, but an understanding, developed over years, that she could hurt him if she chose.

"Maeve," Charles said. "I am Mr. Beauregard."

"The man in the wood," she said. "The hero of the day. *That* day."

Kate's mouth was open. At a glance from Charles, she realized her lapse and shut it quickly. Dickie wasn't quite hiding behind Kate's skirt, but was in a position to make that retreat if needed.

Maeve wandered around the room, picking up ornaments, looking at them and putting them down in exactly the same place. She didn't look directly at Charles or Kate, but always had a reflective surface in sight to observe their faces.

Instinctively, Charles wanted to know where she was at any moment.

If Dickie were seven or eight, Maeve should be nineteen or twenty. She was exactly as she had been when he first saw her, in Hill Wood.

"I thought you'd be taller," said Kate.

The girl arched a thick eyebrow, as if she hadn't noticed Kate before.

"Might you be *Mrs.* Beauregard?"

"Katharine Reed, *Pall Mall Gazette*," she said.

"Is it *common* for ladies to represent newspapers?"

"Not at all."

"Oh, really? I rather thought it was. Most *common*."

She turned, as if dismissing a servant.

Maeve Harvill did not act like a carpenter's daughter or a baker's niece. She was a princess. Not an especially nice one.

"You'll have come to see poor David."

'Poor' David owned this house and was the support of his whole family. Charles wondered if Davey even knew that.

"About the unpleasantness in the park."

"You know about that?"

"It was in the *newspapers*," she said, tossing a glance at Kate. "Do you know Mr. Satterthwaite Bulge? He's *ghastly*."

That was the first child thing she had said.

"Does Uncle Satt call here often?" asked Kate.

"He's not *my* uncle. He stays away unless he absolutely can't help it. Will he go to jail? I'm sure what happened to Leslie is all his fault."

"You knew the late Mr. Sackham?" he asked.

Maeve considered Kate and then Charles, thinking. She pressed an eyetooth to her lower lip, carefully not breaking the skin, mimicking Sarah—whom it was hard to think of as the princess's sister.

"Is this to be an *interrogation*?"

"They be 'tectives, Auntie," said Dickie.

"How exciting," she commented, as if on the point of falling asleep. "Are we to be arrested?"

She held out her arms, voluminous sleeves sliding away from bird-thin wrists.

"Do you have handcuffs in my size?"

She spied something on a small table. It was Dickie's twig-clue. She picked it up, held it alongside her own forefinger, and snapped it in half.

"Dirty thing. I can't imagine how it got in here."

Dickie didn't cry, but one of his eyes gleamed with a tear-to-be.

Maeve made a fist around the twig fragments as if to crush them further, then opened her hand to show an empty palm. With a flourish she produced the twig—whole—in her other hand.

Kate clapped, slowly. Maeve smiled to herself and took a little bow.

"I be a 'tective," said Dickie, tears gone and delight stamped on his face. "Auntie Maeve be a *conjurer.*"

"She should go on the halls," said Kate, unimpressed. "Mystic, Magical Maeve, the Modern Medusa."

The girl flicked the twig into a grate where no fire would burn till autumn. Neither of her hands was dirty, the neatest trick of all.

"She makes things vanish, then brings 'em back," said Dickie.

"That seems to happen quite often in this family," commented Charles.

"More things vanish than come back," said Maeve. "Has he told you about the Bun Bandit from two doors down?"

"A successful conclusion to a baffling case?"

Maeve smiled. "Sidney Silcock might not think so. He was thrashed and put on bread and water. Dickie has to keep out of the way when Sidney pays a call. A retaliatory walloping has been mentioned. There's a fellow who knows how to bide his time. I shouldn't be surprised if he waits *years*, until everyone else has forgotten what it was about. But the walloping will be *heroic.* Sidney is one to do things on an heroic scale."

"He sounds a desperate villain."

"He's desperate all right," said Maeve, smiling her secret smile again.

"Greedy Sid's sweet on 'er," said Dickie.

She glared calmly at her nephew.

Sarah came into the room, took in the scene, and nipped her lip again.

"Sarah, dear, I have been renewing a friendship. This, I am sure you realize, is Charles Beauregard, the intrepid fellow who rescued me from the *gypsies in the wood.*"

"Yes, Maeve, I realize."

Sarah was not unconditionally grateful for this rescue. Sometimes she wished Charles had left well enough alone, had not lifted the princess from the snow, not carried her out of the wood.

"Davey says he'd like to see you," Sarah told Charles, quietly—like a servant in her mistress's presence. "And the lady."

"You are privileged," said Maeve. "My brother rarely likes to see me."

She was playing with a glass globe that contained a miniature woodland scene. When shook, it made a blizzard.

"Happy memories," she commented.

"Davey's upstairs, in his studio," said Sarah. "Drawing. He's better than he was earlier."

Sarah held the door open. Kate stepped into the hall, and Charles followed. Sarah looked back, at her son and her sister.

"Dickie, come help in the kitchen," she said.

Dickie stayed where he was.

"I can see he stays out of trouble while we have visitors," said Maeve. "I've been practicing new tricks."

Sarah was unsure. Dickie was resigned.

"I be all right, Ma."

Sarah nodded and closed the door on the children. A tear of blood ran down the groove of her chin, unnoticed.

"Maeve hasn't changed," said Charles as Sarah led them upstairs.

"Not since you saw her," she responded. "But she *did* change. When she were away. As much as Davey, not that anyone do listen to I. Not that Mam listened, God rest her."

From the landing, Charles looked downstairs. All was quiet.

"Come through here," said Sarah. "To the studio."

4: "industry is a virtue"

Kate was expecting Ben Gunn—wild hair, matted beard, mad eyes. Instead, she found a presentable man, working in a room full of light. Beard he had, but neatly trimmed and free of beetles. One eye was slightly lazy, but he did not seem demented. Davey Harvill, B. Loved, sat on a stool, over paper pinned flat to a bench. His hand moved fast with a sharp pencil, filling in intricate details of a picture already sketched. To one side was a neat pile of papers, squared away like letters for posting. By his feet was a half-full wastepaper basket.

This was the neatest artist's studio she had ever seen: bare floorboards spotless, walls papered but unadorned. Uncurtained floor-to-ceiling windows admitted direct sunlight. The expected clutter was absent: no books, reference materials, divans for models, props. Davey, in shirtsleeves, had not so much as a smudge of graphite upon him. He might have been a draper's clerk doing the end-of-day accounts. It was as if the pictures were willed into being without effort, without mess. They came out of his head, whole and entire, and were transmitted to paper.

Mrs. Riddle let Kate and Charles into the room, coughed discreetly, and withdrew.

Davey looked up, nodded to Charles and smiled at Kate. His hand moved at hummingbird speed, whether his eye was upon the paper or not. Some mediums practiced automatic writing; this could be automatic drawing.

"Charles, hello," said Davey.

As far as Kate knew, the artist had not seen Charles in eight years.

"How have you been?" asked Charles.

"Very well, sir, all things considered."

He finished his drawing and, without looking, freed it from its pinnings and shifted it to the pile, neatening the corners. He unrolled paper from a scroll, deftly pinned it in place and used a penknife to cut neatly across the top. A white, empty expanse lay before him.

"Busy, of course," he said. "Industry is a virtue."

He took a pencil and, without pause, began to sketch.

Kate moved closer, to get a look at the work in progress. Most painters would have thrown her in the street for such impertinence, but Davey did not appear to mind.

Davey's pencil point flew, in jagged, sudden strokes. A woodland appeared, populated by creatures whose eyes showed in shadows. Two small figures, hand in hand, walked in a clearing. A little boy and a girl. Watched from the trees and the burrows.

"This is my friend Kate Reed," said Charles.

Davey smiled again, open and engaging, content in his work.

"Hello, Kate."

"Please forgive this intrusion," she ventured.

"It's no trouble. Makes a nice change."

His pencil left the children, and darted to the corners of the picture, shading areas with solid strokes that left black shadows, relieved by tiny, glittering eyes and teeth. Kate was alarmed, afraid for the safety of the boy and the girl.

"I still haven't remembered anything," said Davey. "I'm sorry, Charles. I have tried."

"That's all right, Davey."

He was back on the central figures. The children, alone in the woods, clinging together for reassurance, for safety.

"What subject is this?" she asked.

"I don't know," said Davey, looking down, seeing the picture for the first time, "the usual."

Now his eyes were on the paper, Davey stopped drawing.

"*Babes in the Wood?*" suggested Charles. "Hansel and Gretel?"

Something was wrong about the children. They did not fit either of the stories Charles had mentioned.

"Davey and Maeve," said the artist, sadly. "I know everything I draw comes from *that time*. It's as if it never ended, not really."

Charles laid a hand on the man's—the boy's—shoulder.

Davey began to work again on the children, more deliberately now.

Kate saw what was wrong. The girl was not afraid.

As Davey was doing the girl's eyes, the pencil lead broke, scratching across her face.

"Pity," he said.

Rather than reach for an india rubber and make a minor change, he tore the paper from the block and began to make a ball of it.

"Excuse me," said Kate, taking the picture from its creator.

"It's no use," he said.

Kate spread the crumpled paper.

She saw something in it.

Charles riffled through the pile of completed illustrations. They were a sequence. The children entering the woods, taking a winding path, walking past færie dwellings without noticing, enticed ever deeper into the dark

Kate looked back at the rejected picture.

The girl was exactly the child-woman Kate had met downstairs, Maeve. Her brother had caught the sulky, adult turn of her mouth and made her huge brush of hair seem alive. A princess, but a frightening one.

In the picture, the children were not lost. The girl was *leading* the boy into the woods.

"This is your sister," said Kate, tapping the girl's scratched face.

"Maeve," he said, not quite agreeing.

"And this is you? Davey?"

Davey hesitated. "That's not right," he said. "Let me fix it . . ."

He reached for his pencil, but Charles stayed his hand.

They all looked closely at the boy in the picture. He was just beginning to worry, starting to consider unthinkable things—that the girl who held his hand was, in a real sense, a stranger to him, a stranger to *everyone*, that this adventure in the woods was taking a sinister turn.

It *might* be Davey, as he was when he went into the woods eight years ago, as a nine-year-old.

But it looked more like Dickie, as he was now.

5: "Richard Riddle, Special Detective"

"If *I* were a real detective," said Auntie Maeve, "I shouldn't be content to waste my talents tracking down bun thieves. For my quarry, I should choose more desperate criminals. Fiends who threaten the country more than they do their own trouser buttons."

Dickie trailed down the street after his aunt.

"I should concentrate exclusively on cases which constitute a challenge, on mysteries *worth* solving. Murders, and such."

Maeve led him past the Silcock house, which gave him a pang of worry. Greedy Sid was, like the Count of Monte Cristo, capable of nurturing over long years an impulse to revenge. Behind the tall railings, bottom still smarting, the miscreant would be brooding, plotting. Dickie imagined Sidney Silcock, swollen to enormous size, become his lifelong nemesis, the Napoleon of Gluttony.

"The mystery of Leslie Sackham, for instance."

The name caught Dickie's mind.

He remembered Mr. Sackham as a bendy minion, hair floppy and cuffs ink-stained, trailing after Mr. Bulge in attitudes of contortion. A tall man, he tried always to look up to his employer, no matter what kinks that put into his neck and spine. Sometimes, Mr. Sackham told stories to children, but got them muddled and lost his audience before he reached the predictable endings. Dickie remembered one about Miss Fay Twinkledust, who put all her sparkles into a sensible investment portfolio rather than tossing them into the Silver Stream to be gobbled by the Silly Fish. Mr. Sackham had been a boring grown-up. Now he was dead, the limits of his bendiness reached inside the works of a dynamo, Dickie felt guilty for not having liked him much.

It would be fitting if he were to solve the mystery.

Everyone would be grateful. Especially if it meant the Gift could open after all. Mr. Bulge's business would be saved from the Silly Fish. Dickie understood the fortunes of the Harvill household depended in some mysterious way on the enterprises of "Uncle Satt"—though only babies and girls read that dreary *Treasury* for anything but Uncle Davey's pictures.

Maeve took his hand.

"Where are we goin'?"

"To the park, of course."

"Why?"

"To look for *clues.*"

At this magic word, Dickie was seized by the *rightness* of the pursuit. Whatever else Maeve might be, she was clever. She would make a valuable detective's assistant, with her sharp eyes and odd way of looking at things. Sometimes, she frightened people. That could be useful too.

Though it was too warm out for caps, scarves and coats, Maeve had insisted they dress properly for this sleuthing expedition. They might have to go *underground,* she said.

Dickie wore his special coat, a "reversible" which could be either a loud check or a subdued herringbone. If spotted by a suspected criminal one was "tailing," the trick was to turn the coat inside-out and so seem to be another boy entirely. He even had a matching cap. In addition, secret pockets were stuffed with the instruments of his calling. About his person, he had the magnifying glass, measuring calipers, his catapult (which he was under strict orders from Ma not to use within shot of windows), a map of the locality with secret routes penciled in, a multipurpose penknife (with five blades, plus corkscrew, screwdriver, and bradawl) and a bottle of invisible ink. He had made up cards for himself using a potato press, in visible and invisible ink: "Richard Riddle, Special Detective." Da approved, saying he was "a regular Hawkshaw." Hawkshaw was a famous detective from the olden days.

Maeve, with a blue bonnet that matched her dress, was a touch conspicuous for "undercover" work. She walked with such confidence, however, that no one thought they were out on their own. Seeing the children—not that Aunt Maeve was *exactly* a child—in the street, people assumed there was a governess nearby, watching over them.

Dickie didn't believe in governesses. They came and went so often. Ma lamented that most found it difficult to work under a baker's wife, which proved the stupidity of the breed. He might bristle at parental decrees, especially with regards to the overrated virtues of cleanliness and tidiness, but Ma knew best—better than a governess, at any rate. Some were unaccountably prone to fits of terror. He suspected Maeve worked tricks to make governesses vanish on a regular basis, though she never brought them back again. He even wondered whether his aunt hadn't had an unseen hand in one of his greatest triumphs, the Mystery of the Cheating Governess. Despite overwhelming evidence, Miss MacAndrew had maintained to the moment of her dismissal that she had done no such thing.

In the park, children were everywhere, playing hopscotch, climbing anything that could be climbed, defending the North-West Frontier against disapproving wardens, fighting wild Red Indians with Buffalo Bill. Governesses in black bombazine flocked on the benches. Dickie imagined a cloud of general disapproval gathering above them. He pondered the possibility that they were in a secret society, pledged to make miserable the lives of all children, sworn to inflict *etiquette* and *washes* on the innocent. They dressed alike, and had the same expression— as if they'd just been made to swallow a whole lemon but ordered not to let it show.

He shouldn't be at all surprised if governesses were behind the Mystery of the Mangled Minion.

Mr. Sackham had died in the park. There were always governesses in the park. They could easily cover up for each other. In their black, they could blend in with the shadows.

He liked the theory. Hawkshaw would have found it sound.

A pretty child with gloves in the shape of rabbit heads approached, smiling slyly. She had ribbons in her hair and to her clothes. She was overdecorated, as if awarded a fresh ribbon every time she said her prayers.

"Little boy, my name is Becky d'Arbanvilliers," said the girl, who was younger than him by a year or more. "When I gwow up and Papa cwoaks, I shall be *Lady* d'Arbanvilliers. If you do something for me, I'll let you kiss my wabbits."

Maeve took the future Lady d'Arbanvilliers aside, lifted a curtain of ribbons, and whispered into her ear. Maeve was insistent but calm. The girl's face crumpled, eyes expanding. Maeve finished whispering and stood back. Becky d'Arbanvilliers looked up at her, trembling. Maeve nodded and the girl ran away, exploding into screams and floods of tears.

"Hey presto, Hawkshaw," she told Dickie. "Magic."

Becky d'Arbanvilliers fled to the coven of governesses, too hysterical to explain, but pointing in the direction where Maeve had been.

An odd thing was that two men dressed like governesses, not in long skirts but all in black with dark spectacles and curly hat-brims, were nearby. Dickie pegged them as sinister individuals. *They* paid attention to the noisy little girl.

"How cwuel," said Maeve, imitating perfectly. "To be named 'Rebecca' and yet pwevented by nature fwom pwonouncing it pwoperly."

Dickie laughed. No one else noticed his aunt could be funny as well as frightening. It was a secret between them.

Maeve led him toward the Gift.

A barrier of trestles was set up all around the building, hung with notices warning the public not to trespass. A policeman stood by the front doors, firmly seeing away curiosity seekers. Dickie and Maeve had visited while Uncle Davey was helping Mr. Bulge turn the Gift into the Færie Aerie, and knew other ways in and out. Special Detectives always had more information the poor plods of the Yard.

Maeve led Dickie round to the rear of the Gift. A door there supposedly only opened from the inside, so the used-up visitors could leave to make room for fresh ones. Unless you knew it was there, you wouldn't see it. The wall was painted with a big color copy of one of Uncle Davey's drawings, and the door hid in a waterfall, like goblins in a puzzle.

They slipped under an unguarded trestle.

Commotion rose in the park, among governesses. Becky d'Arbanvilliers had been able to explain. Though the governess instinct was to distrust anything a child told them, *something* had upset the girl. A hunt would have to be organized.

The men dressed like governesses took an interest.

Dickie was worried for his aunt.

Maeve smiled at him.

"I shall spirit us to safety, with more magic," she announced. "Might I borrow your catapult?"

He was reluctant to hand over such a formidable weapon.

"I shall return it directly."

Dickie undid his secret pocket and produced the catapult.

Maeve examined it, twanged the rubber appreciatively and pronounced it a fine addition to a detective's arsenal.

She made a fold in the rubber and slipped it into the crack in the falling waters that showed those who knew what to look for where the door was. She worked with her fingers for a few moments.

"This is where a conjurer chats to the audience, to take their minds off the trick being done in front of their eyes."

Dickie watched closely—he always did, but Maeve still managed tricks he could not work out.

"I say, what are you children doing?"

It was a *governess*, a skeleton in black.

"Have you seen a horrid, *horrid* little girl . . . ? Dipped in the very essence of wickedness?"

Maeve did one of her best tricks. She put on a smile that fooled everyone but Dickie. She seemed like all the sunny girls in the world, brainless and cheerful.

"I should not like to meet a wicked little girl," she said, sounding a little like Becky d'Arbanvilliers. "No, thank you very much."

"Very wise," said the governess, fooled entirely. "Well, if you see such a creature, stay well away from her."

The woman stalked off.

Maeve shrugged and dropped the smile.

"I swear, Hawkshaw, these *people*. They're so *stupid*. They deserve . . . ah!"

There was a click inside the wall. Maeve pulled the catapult free and the door came open.

She handed him back the catapult and tugged him inside, into the dark.

The door shut behind them.

"This is an adventure, isn't it?"

He agreed.

6: "intelligence reports"

Sarah Riddle, over the first shock, slumped on a hall settee, numb and cried out.

Charles understood.

The worst thing was that this was a *familiar* anxiety.

Maeve and Dickie were missing.

"It's *her*," said Sarah. "I always knew . . ."

The house had been searched. Kate turned up Bitty, a maid who recalled noticing Dickie and his aunt, dressed as if to go out. That she had not actually seen them leave the house saved her position. Charles knew that even if Bitty had been there, she would not have been able to intervene. Maeve treated her family like servants; he could imagine how she treated servants.

"It's like before," said Philip Riddle, standing by his wife. "Only then it were Hill Wood. Now, it's a whole *city*."

Charles reproached himself for not considering Dickie. He had given a lot of thought to Davey and Princess Cuckoo, but rarely recalled this household harbored one proper child. When Charles was in Eye, Dickie had not been born, was not part of the story.

Now, Charles saw where Dickie fit.

Davey had escaped *something*. Dickie would do as replacement.

"Charles," said Kate, from the top of the stairs. "Would you come up?"

He left Sarah and Philip, and joined Kate. She led him into the studio.

Davey was still drawing.

Kate showed him finished pictures in which the children ventured deeper into the woods. A smug bunny in a beribboned pinafore appeared in a clearing. The girl, more Maeve than ever, loomed over the small, terrified rabbit. In one picture, her head was inflated twice the size of her body, hair puffed like a lion's mane. She showed angry, evil eyes and a toothy, dripping shark's maw. The rabbit fled, understandably. In the next picture, Maeve was herself again, though it would be hard to forget her scary head. She was snatching the boy, Dickie, away from a clutch of old-womanish crows who sported veiled hats and reticules. Then the children came to a waterfall. Maeve used long-nailed fingers to unlock a door in the cascade—a door made of *flowing* water, not ice—to open a way into wooded underworld.

"What does this mean, Davey?"

He drew faster than ever. Tears spotted his paper, blotching the pencilwork. His face shut tight, he rocked back and forth, crooning.

"*My mother said . . . I never should . . . play with the gypsies . . . in the wood.*"

Another picture was finished and put aside.

The children were in a forested tunnel, passing a fallen tower. Goblins swarmed in the undergrowth, ears and tongues twitching, flat nostrils a-quiver.

"I know that ruin," said Kate. "It's in the Gift. We were there when it collapsed."

"And *I* know the waterfall door."

Kate began searching the studio.

"What are you looking for?" he asked her.

"A sketchpad. Something he can carry. We have to take him to the park. All this is happening *now*. The pictures are like *intelligence reports*."

Kate opened a cupboard in the workbench and found a package of notebooks. She took several and shoved one opened under Davey's pencil, whispering to him, urging him to shift to a portable medium. After a beat of hesitation, he began again, drawing still faster, pencil scoring paper. Kate gathered the completed pictures into a sturdy artists' folder.

"Stay with him a moment," he told her, leaving the study.

Dickie's parents were at the foot of the stairs, looking up.

"Is this household on the telephone?" Charles asked.

"Mr. Bulge insisted," said Philip Riddle. "The apparatus is in the downstairs parlor."

"Ring up Scotland Yard and ask for Inspector Henry Mist. Tell him to meet us at the Gift."

Riddle, a solid man, didn't waste time asking for explanations. He went directly to the parlor.

Kate had Davey out of his studio and helped him downstairs. He still murmured and scribbled.

"Bad things in the woods," Kate reported. "Very bad."

Charles trusted her.

"Have you called a cab?" she asked.

"Quicker to walk."

Sarah reached out as Kate and Charles helped Davey past, pleading wordlessly. Her lip was bleeding.

"There's hope," he told her.

She accepted that as the best offer available.

On the street, he and Kate must have seemed the abductors of a lunatic. When Davey finished a picture, Kate turned the page for him.

From a window peered the fat face of a sad little boy. He alone took notice of the peculiar trio. People on the street evaded them without comment. Charles did his best to look like someone who would brook no interference.

Every pause to allow a cart or carriage primacy was a heart-blow.

The streets were uncommonly busy. People were mobile trees in these wilds, constantly shutting off and making new paths. London was more perilous than Hill Wood. Though it was a sunny afternoon and he walked on broad pavement, Charles recalled snow underfoot.

"What's in the pictures now?" he asked.

"Hard to make out. Children, goblins, woods. The boy seems all right still."

Maeve and Dickie must have taken this route, perhaps half an hour earlier. This storm had blown up in minutes.

If it weren't for Kate's leap of deduction, the absences might have gone unnoticed until teatime. Another reason to propose her for membership.

In the park, there was the expected chaos. Children, idlers, governesses, dogs. A one-man band played something from *The Mikado*.

"The crows," said Kate.

Charles saw what she meant. Some governesses gathered around a little girl, heads bobbing like birds, veiled hats like those in Davey's illustration.

"And that's the frightened bunny," he pointed out.

He remembered Maeve's temporary scary head. Davey's drawings weren't the literal truth, he hoped. They hinted at what really happened.

"Ladies," he began, "might I inquire whether you've seen two children, a girl of perhaps eleven and a slightly younger boy? You would take them for brother and sister."

The women reacted like Transylvanian peasants asked the most convenient route to Castle Dracula, with hisses and flutterings and clucks very like curses.

"That horrid, *horrid* girl . . ." spat one.

Even in the circumstances, he had to swallow a smirk.

"That would be the miss. You have her exactly."

The governesses continued, yielding more editorial comment but no hard news.

"Why is that man dwawing?" asked the ribboned girl.

"He's an artist," Charles told her.

"My name is Becky d'Arbanvilliers," she said proudly. "When I gwow up and Papa cwoaks, I shall be *Lady* d'Arbanvilliers."

Few prospective heirs would be as honest, he supposed. At least, out loud. In cases of suspicious death, the police were wont to remember such offhand remarks.

"Did you meet a bad girl, Becky?"

She nodded her head, solemnly.

"And where is she now?"

Becky frowned, as angry as she was puzzled.

"I *told* Miss Wodgers, but she didn't believe me. The bad girl and the nasty boy went to the waterfall in that house."

She pointed to the Gift.

"There was a girl," said the governess, whose name he presumed was Miss Rodgers. "But not the one who so upset Becky. This was a nice, polite child."

Becky looked at Charles, frustrated by her governess's gullibility.

"It was her," she insisted, stamping a tiny foot.

Davey finished one notebook and started on the next. Kate took the filled book and leafed through, then found a picture.

"*This* girl?" she asked. "And this boy."

"That's them," said Becky. "What a pwetty picture. Will the man dwaw me? I'm pwettier than the bad girl."

"Miss Rodgers," he prompted.

The governess looked stricken.

"Yes," she admitted. "But she *smiled* so . . ."

Recriminations flew around the group of governesses.

"*Will the man dwaw me?*"

Kate leafed through the folder and found a picture of the children meeting the ribboned rabbit, the one in which Maeve was not showing her scary head. She handed it over. Becky was transported with delight, terrors forgotten.

Miss Rodgers saw the picture, puzzled and disturbed.

"How did he do this? It was drawn before he set eyes on Rebecca . . ."

They left the governesses wondering.

From the corner of his eye, Charles glimpsed a couple in black who weren't governesses. Mr. Hay and Mr. Effe. Since this morning, he had been aware of their floating presence. The Undertaking was playing its own game and had turned up here before he did. He would worry about that later, if he got the chance. Right now, he should be inside the Gift.

By the time they found the door concealed in the waterfall design, Inspector Mist was on the scene.

"Mr. Beauregard, what is all this about?"

7: "stage snow"

Kate knew Charles would make a token attempt to dissuade her from continuing. The argument, a variation on a theme with which she was bored, was conducted in shorthand.

Yes, it might be dangerous.

Yes, she was a woman.

No, that wouldn't make a difference.

Settled.

Mist of the Yard was distracted by Davey's compulsive sketching.

"Is this fellow some sort of psychic medium?"

"He has a connection with this business," Charles told Mist. "This is Davey Harvill."

"The boy from Eye."

The Inspector evidently knew about the Children of Eye. She was not surprised. Whisper had it that Mist was high up in the Bureau of Queer Complaints, an unpublicized Scotland Yard department constituted to deal with the "spook" cases.

Mist posted constables to keep back this afternoon's crowds. Rumors circulated. The Gift was about to be opened to the public. Or razed to the ground. No one was sure. Helmeted bobbies assumed their usual attitudes, bored resignation to indicate nothing out of the ordinary taking place behind the barriers and truncheon-tapping warning that no monkey business would be tolerated. Popular phrases were recited: "move along, now" and "there's nothing to see 'ere."

Two men in black clothes augmented by very black spectacles sauntered over. At the flash of a card, they were admitted to the inner circle.

They chimed with another whisper, about funereal officials seen pottering about new-made meteor craters or the sites of unnatural vanishments. Another high-stakes player at this table, in competition or alliance with the Diogenes Club and the BQC. The poor plodders of the Society for Psychical Research must feel left out, stuck with only the least mysterious of eternal mysteries, trivial table rappings and ghosts who did nothing but loom in sheets and say "boo!" to handy geese.

Charles made rapid introductions, "Mr. Hay and Mr. Effe, of the Undertaking. Mist you know. Katharine Reed . . ."

Mr. Effe bared poor teeth at her. Even without sight of his eyes, she could gauge his expression.

"Do we need the press, Beauregard?" he asked.

"I need *her.*"

Argument was squashed. She was proud of him, again. More than proud.

"The missing boy is in there," said Mist. "And his . . . sister?"

"*Aunt,*" corrected Charles. "Maeve. Don't be taken in by her. She's not what she seems. The boy is Richard. Dickie. He's the one in danger. We must get him out of the Gift."

"The girl too," prompted Mr. Hay.

Charles shook his head. "She's long lost," he said. "It's the boy we want, we *need . . .*"

"That wasn't a suggestion," said the Undertaker.

Charles and Mist exchanged a look.

"Get that door kicked in," Mist told two hefty bobbies.

They shouldered the waterfall, shaking the whole of the Gift.

"It's probably unlocked and opens outward," she suggested.

The policemen stood back. The dented door swung slowly out, proving her point. Inside, it was darker than it should be. This was a bright afternoon. The ceiling of the Gift was mostly glass. It should be gloomy at worst.

White powder lay on the floor, footprints trodden in.

"Is that snow?" asked Mist.

"Stage snow," said Charles. "Remember, nothing in there is real. Which doesn't mean it's not dangerous."

"We'll need light. Willoughby, hand over your bull lantern."

One of the bobbies unlatched a device from his belt. Mist lit the lamp. Charles took it and shone a feeble beam into the dark. Stage snow fell from a sky ceiling. It was a clever trick—reflective sparkles set into wooden walls. But she did not imagine the cold wind that blew from the Gift, chilling through her light blouse. She was not dressed to pay a call on the Snow Queen.

Charles ventured into the dark.

Kate helped Davey follow. He had stopped chanting out loud but his neck muscles worked as he subaudially repeated his rhyme.

In his pictures, goblins gathered.

Mist came last, with another lamp.

Mr. Hay and Mr. Effe remained outside, in the summer sunshine.

This was not a part of Færie she had seen yesterday, but Charles evidently knew his way. The walls were theatrical flats painted with convincing woodlands. Though the corridor was barely wide enough for two people side by side, scenery seemed to extend for miles. In the minimal light, the illusion was perfect. She reached out. Where she was sure snow fell through empty air, her fingers dimpled oiled canvas.

They could not be more than fifty feet inside the Gift, which she knew to cover a circle barely a hundred yards across, but it seemed miles from Regent's Park. Glancing back, she saw the Undertakers, scarecrows against an oblong of daylight. Looking forward, there was night and forest. Stars sparkled on the roof.

The passage curved, and she couldn't see the entrance any more.

Of course, the Gift was a fairground maze.

Charles, tracking clear footprints, came to a triplicate fork in the path. Three sets of prints wound into each tunnel.

"Bugger," said Mist, adding, "pardon me, miss."

She asked for light and sorted back through Davey's pictures. She was sure she had seen this. She missed it once and had to start again. Then she hit on sketches representing this juncture. On paper, Maeve led Dickie down the left-hand path. In the next picture, goblins tottered out of the trees on stilts tipped with child-sized shoes which (horribly) had disembodied feet stuffed into them. The imps made false trails down the other paths, smirking with mean delight, cackles crawling off the paper.

Kate was beginning to *hate* Davey's goblins.

Charles bent low to enter the left-hand tunnel, which went under two oaks whose upper branches tangled, as if the trees were frozen in a slapping argument. Disapproving faces twisted in the bark.

Even Kate couldn't stand up in this tunnel.

They made slow, clumsy progress. It was hard to light the way ahead. All Charles and Mist could do was cast moon circles on the nearest surface, infernally reflecting their own faces.

The tunnel angled downward.

She wondered if this led to the dynamo room. The interior of the Gift was on several levels. Yesterday, it had been hot here. Now snowflakes whisped on her face like ice-pricks.

"That's not likely," said Mist, looking at snowmelt in his palm.

Davey stumbled over an exposed root. Kate reached out to catch him. They fell against a barbed bramble and staggered off the path, tumbling into a chilly drift. Painted walls had given way to three-dimensional scenery, the break unnoticed. The snow must be artificially generated—ice chips sifted from a hidden device up above—but felt unpleasantly real.

Mist and Charles played their lamps around.

Kate assumed they were in the large, central area she had visited, but in this minimal light it seemed differently shaped. Everything was larger. She was now in proportion with trees that had been miniature.

A vicious wind blew from somewhere, spattering her spectacles with snow dots. The waterfall was frozen in serried waves, trapping bug-eyed, dunce-capped Silly Fish in a glacier grip.

Charles took off his ulster and gave it to her. She gratefully accepted.

"I never thought I'd miss my Sir Boris costume," he said.

Mist directed his lamp straight up. Its throw didn't reach any ceiling. He pointed it down, and found grass, earth and snow—no floorboards, no paving, no matting. In the wind, trees shifted and creaked.

"Bloody good trick," said the policeman.

Davey hunched in a huddle, making tinier and tinier pictures.

There was movement in the dark. Charles turned, pointing his light at rustles. Wherever the lantern shone, all was stark and still. Outside the beam, things were evilly active. The originals of Davey's goblins, whatever they might be, were in the trees. The illustrations, satirical cartoons, were tinged with grotesque humor. She feared there would be nothing funny about the live models.

"*Dickie*," shouted Charles.

His echo came back, many times. Charles's breath plumed. His shout dissipated in the open night. She could have sworn mocking, imitative voices replaced the echo.

"There's a castle," said Kate, looking at Davey's latest drawings. "No, a *palace*. Maeve is leading Dickie up steps, to meet . . . I don't know, a prince?"

Davey was still working. His arm was in the way of a completed picture. Gently, she shifted his wrist.

In a palatial hall, Dickie was presented to a mirror, looking at himself. Only, his reflection was different. The boy in the glass had thinner eyes, pointier ears, a nastier mouth.

Davey went on to another book.

Kate showed Charles and Mist the new sequence.

"We have to find this place, quickly," said Charles. "The boy is in immediate danger."

8: "the game is up"

Maeve had turned her ankle. Dickie's aunt did not usually act so like a girl. After helping as best he could, he left her wrapped up by the path. She kept their candle. When the mystery was solved, he could find his way back to her light. Bravely, Maeve urged him on, to follow the clues.

In the middle of the Gift, she said, was a palace.

Inside the palace was the *culprit*.

Steeled, Dickie made his way from clue to clue.

Moonbeam pools picked them out. A dagger with the very tip sheared away, a half-burned page of cipher, a cigarette end with three distinctive bands, a cameo brooch that opened to a picture of a hairy-faced little girl, an empty blue glass bottle marked with skull and crossbones, a bloodied grape stem, a dish of butter with a sprig of parsley sunk into it, a dead canary bleached white, a worm unknown to science, a squat jade idol with its eyegems prised out, a necklace crushed to show its gems were paste, a false beard with cardboard nose attached.

Excellent clues, leading to his destination.

When he first glimpsed the palace through the trees, Dickie thought it a doll's house, much too small for him. When, at last, he found the front door, spires rose above him. It was clever, like one of Maeve's conjuring tricks.

Who *was* the culprit?

Mr. Satterthwaite Bulge (he had known the dead man best, and could have been blackmailed or have something to gain from a will) . . . Uncle Davey (surely not, though some said he was "touched"; he might have another person living in his head, not a nice one) . . . the clever gent and the Irish lady who had called this afternoon (Dickie had liked them straight off, which should not blind him to sorry possibilities) . . . Greedy Sid Silcock (too obvious and convenient, though he could well be in it as a minion of the true mastermind) . . . Miss MacAndrew (another vengeance plotter?) . . . Bitty, the rosy-cheeked maid (hmmmn, something was *stirring* about her complexion) . . . Ma and Da (*no!*) . . .

He would find out.

The palace disappointed. It was a wooden façade, propped up by rough timbers. There were no rooms, just hollow space. The exterior was painted to look like stone. Inside was bare board, nailed without much care.

He could not see much. Even through his magnifying glass.

"Hello," he called.

" 'lo?" came back at him, in his own voice.

Or something very like.

"You are found out."

"Out!"

The culprit was here.

But Dickie was still in the dark. He must remember to include a box of lucifers in his detective apparatus, with long tapers. Perhaps even a small lantern. Having left his candle with Maeve, so she wouldn't be lonely, he was at a disadvantage.

"The game is up," he announced, sounding braver than he felt.

"Up?"

"This palace is surrounded by *special detectives*. You are under arrest."

"Arrest?"

The culprit was an *echo*.

The dark in front of his face gathered, solidified into coherence. He made out human shape.

Dickie's hand fell on the culprit's shoulder.

"Ah hah!"

A hand gripped his own shoulder.

"Hah," came back, a gust of hot breath into his face.

He squeezed and was squeezed.

His shoulder hurt, his knees weakened. He was pushed down, as if shrinking.

The hand on his shoulder grew, fingers like hard twigs poking into him. His feet sank into earth, which swarmed around his ankles. His socks would get muddied, which would displease Ma.

Shapes moved all around.

The culprit was not alone. He had minions.

He imagined them—Greedy Sid, Miss MacAndrew, Uncle Satt, an ape, a mathematics tutor, a defrocked curate. The low folk who were part of the mystery.

"Who are you?"

"You!"

9: "two jumps behind"

There was light ahead. A candle flame.

Charles pointed it out.

The light moved, behind a tree, into hiding.

Charles played his lantern over the area, wobbling the beam to indicate where the others should look, then directing it elsewhere, hoping to fool the candle-holder into believing she was overlooked.

Charles was sure it was a *she*.

He handed his lantern to Kate, who took it smoothly and continued the "search."

Charles stepped off the track.

Whatever was passing itself off as snow was doing a good job. His shins were frozen as he waded. He crouched low and his bare hands sunk into the stuff.

He crept toward the tree where the light had been.

"Pretty princess," he breathed to himself, "sit tight . . ."

He had picked up night skills in warmer climes, crawling over rocky hills with his face stained, dressed like an untouchable. He could cross open country under a full moon without being seen. In this dark, with so many things to hide behind, it should be easy.

But it wasn't. The going was treacherous. The snow lay lightly over brambles that could snare like barbed wire.

Within a couple of yards of the tree, he saw the guarded, flickering spill of light. He flexed his fingers into the snow, numbing his joints. Sometimes, he had pains in his knuckles—which he had never mentioned to anyone. He stood, slowly.

He held his breath.

In a single, smooth movement, he stepped around the tree and laid a hand on . . .

. . . *bark!*

He summoned the others.

The candle perched in a nook, wax dribbling.

Clear little footprints radiated from a hollow in the roots. They spiraled and multiplied, haring off in all directions as if a dozen princesses had sprung into being and bolted.

Kate showed Charles a new-drawn picture of Maeve skipping away, tittering to herself.

"Have you noticed he never draws us?" he said.

"Maybe we're not in the story yet."

"We're here all right," said Mist. "Two jumps behind."

Mist supported Davey now. The lad was running out of paper. His pictures were smaller, crowded together—two or three to a page—and harder to make out.

"Let me try something," said Kate.

She laid her fingers on Davey's hand, halting his pencil. He shook, the beginnings of a fit. She took his chin and forced him to look at her.

"Davey, where's the palace?"

He was close to tears, frustrated at not being able to draw, to channel what he knew.

"Not in pictures," she said. "Words. Tell me in words."

Davey shook his head and shut his eyes. Squeaks came from the back of his throat.

". . . mother said . . . never should . . ."

"Dickie's in the woods," said Kate.

"With the gypsies?"

"Yes, the naughty, naughty gypsies. That bad girl is taking Dickie to them. We can help him, but you have to help us. Please, Davey. For Dickie. These are *your* woods. You mapped them and made them. Where in the woods . . ."

Davey opened his eyes.

He turned, breaking Kate's hold, and waded off, snow slushing around his feet. He pressed point to paper and made three strokes, then snapped the pencil and dropped the notebook.

"This way," he said.

Davey walked with some confidence toward a stand of trees. He reached up and touched a low-hanging branch, pushing a bird's nest, sending a ripple through branch, tree and sky. He took out his penknife, opened the blade and stuck it into the backdrop. With a tearing sound, the knife parted canvas and sank to the hilt. Davey drew his knife in a straight line, across the branch and into the air. He made a corner and cut downward, as if hacking a door into a tent. The fabric ripped, noisily.

Charles thought he could see for hundreds of yards, through the woods. Even as Davey cut his door, Charles could swear the lad stood in a real landscape.

Davey slashed the canvas, methodically.

There was a doorway in the wood.

Beyond was gloom but not dark. It looked like the quarter where backstage people worked, where Sir Boris had got dressed and prepared or took his infrequent meal and rest breaks.

"Through here," said Dickie.

They followed. Beyond the door, it wasn't cold any more. It was close, stifling.

Dickie cut a door in an opposite wall.

"I know where you're hiding," he said, to someone beyond.

A screech filled the passage. A small person with wild hair tore between their legs, launching a punch at Davey's chest, clawing at Kate's face, sinking a shoulder into Mist's stomach.

Charles blocked her.

The screech died. The girl's face was in shadow, but could no longer be mistaken. This was not—*had never been*—Maeve Harvill. This was Princess Cuckoo, of Pixieland. Rather, of the shadow realm Davey recreated in his pictures, which Satterthwaite Bulge had named Færie and built in the real world. That was what she had wanted all along.

"Where is he?" Charles asked. "Dickie?"

The little face shut tight, lip buttoned, chin and cheeks set. This close, she seemed a genuine child. No Thuggee strangler or Scots preacher could be as iron-willed as a little girl determined not to own up.

"I know," said Davey. "It's where she took me, where I got away from."

The girl shook her head, humming furiously.

"That's an endorsement," Charles commented. "Lead on, Davey."

10: "holes"

They descended into the ground. Brickwork tunnel walls gave way to shored earth and flagstones. She could not believe Regent's Park was only a few feet above their heads.

Kate squirreled through, following Davey. Charles dragged Maeve after him. Inspector Mist held the rear.

The place smelled of muck.

They emerged in the dynamo chamber, site of the sacrifice that had kept the throngs away from the Gift so Maeve could make her private exchange. Roots thick as a man's torso burst through, spilling bricks on the floor, entwining like angry prehistoric snakes. A canvas cover over the dynamos, stained with red mud, was partially lifted. Ivy grew like a plague, twining into ironwork, twisting around stilled pistons and bent valves. The weed grip had cracked one of the great wheels.

Green sparks nestled in nooks. Fairy lights, little burning pools which needed no dynamos.

Dickie sat in front of the machine, knees together, cap straight.

"There he is," said Maeve. "No harm done. Satisfied?"

Charles shone his lantern. Emerald light points danced in the boy's eyes. He raised a hand to shield his face.

"Princess," said the boy. "Is that you?"

They were here in time! Kate wanted to hug the errant special detective.

"Dickie," said Charles, offhandedly. "Tell me, what clue enabled you to solve the Baffling Business of the Cheating Governess?"

Dickie lowered his hand. His eyes were hard.

Ice brushed the untidy hair at the nape of her neck.

"Who was the Bun Bandit?" she asked.

No answer. The lightpoints in his eyes were fixed. Seven in each. In the shape of the constellation Ursa Major.

"That's not D-Dickie," said Davey. "That's . . ."

"I think we know who that is," said Charles.

Kate's insides plunged. She looked at the boy. He was like Maeve, but new-made. Clean and fresh and tidy, still slightly moist. He did not yet have the knack of passing among people.

Davey whirled about the chamber, tapping roots, tearing off covers.

Maeve and the boy exchanged gazes and kept quiet.

Kate knew Sarah Riddle would not be happy with a boy who merely *looked* like her son.

"So, it's another one," said Inspector Mist, walking around the boy.

He looked up at the policeman, unblinking, head rotating like an owl's.

"That's a good trick," she said.

The boy experimented with a smile of acknowledgment. It did not come off well.

Charles was with Davey, talking to him quietly, insistently.

"Think hard, Davey . . . this is that place, the place that was under Hill Wood . . ."

"Yes, I know. But this is London."

"The place where you were taken is *somewhere else*, Davey. Somewhere that travels. Somewhere with holes that match up to holes here. I don't know how the hole was made in Eye. Perhaps it was always there. But the hole here, in the Gift, you made."

Davey nodded, to himself.

"I thought I'd got away, but I brought it with me, in my head. The drawing, the dreams. That was it, pressing on me. I cheated *them*, by their lights. I owed them."

He felt his way around now, carefully. He began humming his rhyme—his long-lost sister's rhyme—then caught himself, and was quiet, chewing his lip like a Harvill.

"A hole," he said, at last. "There's a hole. Something like a hole."

Davey took out his penknife. He shook his head and threw it away.

"Would this be any use?" suggested Inspector Mist.

The policeman pulled a giant-sized spanner from the clutches of greenery and handed it over.

Davey took the length of iron, felt its heft, and nodded.

Charles stood back. Davey took a swing, as if with an axe. The spanner clanged against exposed root. The whole chamber rung with the blow. Kate's teeth rattled. Old bark sloughed, exposing bone-yellow woodflesh. Davey struck again, and the wood parted.

There was an exhalation of foul air, and a vast inpouring of soft, insect-inhabited earth. Almost liquid, it slurried around their ankles, then grew to a tidal wave that threatened to fill the chamber. Some of the lights winked out. She found herself clinging to Charles, who held onto a dangling chain to steady his footing. Mist hopped nimbly out of the way.

The sham children paid no mind.

In the dirt, something moved. Charles deftly shifted Kate's grip to the chain and weighed in, with Davey, shoveling earth with cupped hands.

A very dirty little boy was disclosed, spitting leaves.

Charles whispered in his ear.

"Jack of Hearts, with one corner bent off," Dickie shouted.

Davey hugged his nephew, who was a bit embarrassed.

The dirty boy looked at his clean mirror image. Dickie had a spasm of fear, but got over it.

"You'd better leave," Charles told the impostor.

The failed changeling stood, lifted his shoulders at the girl in a well-I-*tried* shrug, and stepped close to the fissure in the wall. The gap seemed too narrow. As the faux Dickie neared the hole, he seemed to fold thinner, and be sucked beyond, into deeper, frothing darkness. The stench settled, but remained fungoid and corpse-filthy.

Everyone looked at Maeve.

"So, Princess Cuckoo," said Charles, hands on hips, "what's to be done with you?"

She regarded him, blankly.

11: "you might not know what you get back"

The place was changing. The roots withdrew. The crack in the wall narrowed, as healing. A machine-oil tang cut through the peaty smell.

"The holes are closing," said Davey.

Charles considered the Princess. It had been important that there be *two* cuckoos, Prince and Princess. Davey's escape from the realm beyond the holes had stalled some design. If Dickie had been successfully supplanted, it would have started again, rumbling inexorably toward its end. Charles did not even want to guess what had just been thwarted. Plans laid in a contingent world were now abandoned—which should be enough for the Ruling Cabal.

That unknown place rubbed against thinning, permeable walls. Davey's drawings were not the first signs that barriers could be breached. Everywhere, he once said, has its stories. Many places also had their holes, natural or special-made. It was difficult, but travelers could pass through veils that separated there from here and here from there.

This girl-shaped person was one such.

"Princess, if I may call you that . . ."

She nodded. Her face was thinner now, cheekbones more apparent, pupils oval, skin a touch green in the lamplight.

". . . outside the Gift are two men dressed in black."

She knew the Undertaking

"They would like me to hand you over to them. You are a *specimen* of great interest. As you once had *plans* for us, they have plans for you. Which you might not care for."

"It doesn't matter," she said.

"You say that now. You're disappointed, of course. Your life for the past eight years—and I can imagine it has been utterly strange—was geared up to this moment. And it's proven a bust."

"No need to rub it in, Mr. Detective."

"I am just trying to make you realize this might not be the *worst* moment of your sojourn here."

The girl spat out a bitter little laugh.

She *was* like a child. Perhaps they all were. That childishness was evident in all the impressions that came through the holes, dressed up and painted in and cut about by Davey Harvill and Uncle Satt and Leslie Sackham and George MacDonald and Arthur Rackham and many, many others. They were the *little* people, small in their wonderments, prone to spasms of sunlit joy and long rainy afternoon sulks.

"Mr. Hay and Mr. Effe might tire of asking questions. It can be boring, not getting answers. In the end, the Undertaking might just *cut you up* in the name of science. To find wings folded inside your shoulder bones, then spread them on a board and pin you like a butterfly. There's a secret museum for creatures like you. It's possible you'd be under glass for a long time."

A thrill passed through her. A horror.

That was something to be proud of. He had terrified the Medusa.

"What do you want?" she said, quietly.

"His sister," he said, nodding at Davey.

She thought it over.

"There's a balance. She can't be here if I am. Not for long. You saw, with Dickie. Things bend."

"You're not going to *let her go*?" said Kate.

Charles sympathized with Kate's outrage. Mist, as well. This girl was responsible for at least one murder. Sackham, obviously—to keep the Gift shut, so her business could proceed. Almost certainly, she had contrived the death of Violet Harvill, who could not be fooled forever. (Did Davey know that? How could he not?) Charles was certain the Princess would answer for her failure to the powers she served or represented.

"It is for the best," he told Kate.

Mist gave him the nod. Good man.

"I should warn you," said the Princess, "you might not know what you get back. Time passes differently."

He understood. If thirty years fly past in a three days, what might not transpire in eight years?

The Princess stood by the fissure, which pulsed—almost like a mouth.

She looked at them all.

"Good-bye, Hawkshaw," she said. "The Dickie who was almost is less fun."

Dickie frowned. Kate had most of the dirt off his face.

"Auntie," he said. "I know you didn't mean it."

The Princess seemed sad but said nothing. Suddenly boneless and flimsy, she slid into the slit as if it were a post-box and she a letter. Long seconds passed. The fissure bulged and creaked. An arm flopped out.

Davey took hold of the hand and pulled.

Charles grabbed Davey's waist and hauled. Mist and Kate lent their strength. Even so, it was hard going. Davey's grip slipped on oily skin. Charles's forearm ached, as he felt the old bite.

A shoulder and head, coated with mud, emerged. Eyes opened in the mask of filth. Bright, alive eyes.

Then, in a long tangle, a whole body, slithered out. She drew breath, as if just born, and gave vent to a cry. Noise filled the dynamo chamber.

"Let's take the quickest way out," he said.

Kate went ahead with the lanterns. The three men carried the limp, adult length of the rescued girl between them. Dickie, magnifying glass held up, followed.

When they banged out of the waterfall door, Mist ordered a constable to fetch water from the horse trough in Regent's Crescent. The new-found girl lay on the ground, head in Davey's lap. A drapery wound around her, plastered to her body like a toga, but her bare, gnarled feet stuck out.

Kate held Dickie back.

Mr. Hay and Mr. Effe exchanged dark glances, unreadable. When Charles looked again, they were gone. A worry for another day.

Philip and Sarah Riddle got past the cordon and bustled around, too relieved at the return of Dickie to ask after the new arrival. They took their son, scolding and embracing him.

Mist had his men round up buckets of water, and had to stop P.C. Willoughby from dashing one in the woman's face.

"Looks like she's been buried alive, sir," said the constable.

"It's not so bad," said Dickie, bravely.

Charles requisitioned a flannel from a stray governess, soaked it, and cleaned the face of the woman who had come back.

A beautiful blank appeared with the first wash. She was exactly like the Princess. Then a few lines became apparent, and a white streak in her hair.

"Maeve," said Davey.

The woman looked up, recognizing her brother.

Charles would have taken her for a well-preserved forty or a hard-lived thirty. He stood back, and looked at the family reunion.

"How long's it been?" she said.

"Not but a moment," said Davey.

She closed her eyes and smiled, safe.

Charles found Kate was holding his elbow, face against his sleeve. He suspected a maneuver to conceal tears. A pricking in his eyes suggested discreet dabbing might be in order to repair his own composure.

A crowd began to assemble. There was still interest in the Gift. It occurred to Charles that it might even be safe to open the place, though Mist would have to write up the Sackham case carefully for the BQC files.

Maeve rolled in Davey's grasp and flung her arms around his neck.

Sarah Riddle noticed her sister, recognized her at once. She gasped, in wonder. Her husband, puzzled at first, caught on and began to dance a jig.

Charles slipped his own arm around Kate's waist. Her hands were hooked into his coat. They had been through a great deal together. Again. Pamela had been right about Katharine Reed; she was an extraordinarily promising girl. No, that was then. Now, she was an extraordinarily delivering woman.

He lifted her face from his arm and set her spectacles straight.

"What should a fairy tale have?" he asked.

Kate sniffed. "A happy ending," she ventured.

He kissed her nose, which set her crying again.

She arched up on tiptoes and kissed him on the lips, which should not have been the surprise it was.

Mist gave a nod to Willoughby.

The constable raised big hands to his belt, thumb tapping the handle of his truncheon.

"Move along, now," he told the gathering crowds. "There's nothing to see 'ere."

Honorable Mentions: 2005

Ackerson, Duane, "The Shadow's Friend," (poem) *The Magazine of Speculative Poetry*, Winter 2004–05.
——, "Wind Bones," (poem) *The Magazine of Speculative. Poetry*, Autumn.
Acord, David, "The Dispatcher," *All Hallows* 40.
Adams, Danny, "Village of One Thousand Cranes," *Revolution SF*, Mar.
Addison, Linda, "After the Tsunami," (poem) *Spiderwords*, Nov. 10.
——, "Between," (poem) Ibid.
——, "Nightshift," (poem) *World Horror Convention Program Bk*.
——, "Storm of Souls," (poem) *Fantastic*, Winter.
——, "Wet," (poem) *Spiderwords*, November 10.
Aegard, John, "The Court of the Beast Emperor," *Interzone* 198.
Albie, "Name this Film," *Bare Bone* #8.
Albrecht, Aaron, "The Evening Wolves," *All Hallows* 39.
Alexander, William, "The Birthday Rooms," *Zahir* 7.
Alexanders, Robyn, "Soul Stains," *Nemonymous* 5.
Alfar, Nikki, "Emberwild," *Philippine Speculative Fiction* Vol. 1.
Allan, Nina, "A Faust Overture," *Supernatural Tales* 9.
Allegretti, Joel, "Unimpressed with Offenbach, Weary of Rilke," (poem) *Chance of a Ghost*.
Allen, Mike, "Disturbing Muses," (poem) *Disturbing Muses*.
——, "Picasso's Rapture," (poem) *Strange Horizons/Disturbing Muses*.
——, "Pollock's Knives," (poem) *Disturbing Muses*.
——, "The Captive Pleads with the Memory Carver," (poem) *Tales of the Unanticipated* 26.
——, "The Clairvoyant, Between Dark & Dream," (poem) *Jabberwocky*.
——, "The Elders," (poem) *Star*Line*, March/April.
——, "The Golden Helmet (Casque d'Or)," (poem) *Disturbing Muses*.
——, "The Night Gardeners," (poem) *Star*Line*, Jan./Feb.
——, "The Unseelie Tree," (poem) *Space and Time*, Spring.
——, and Sng, Christina, "Asunder," (poem) *Star*Line*, Jan./Feb.
Allen, Nina, "Fleece," *Midnight Street*, Winter.
Allison, Nancy, "Counting on Phil," *Circles in the Hair*.
Anderson, Eric, "Zombies," (poem) *The Sun*, August.
Arnott, Marion, "Lest We Forget," *Nova Scotia*.
——, "When We Were Five," *The Elastic Book of Numbers*.
Arnzen, Michael A, "Those Who Landed, Surprised to Discover that Zombies Had Taken Over the Planet," (poem) *Dreams and Nightmares* 72.

Asher, Neal, "Acephalous Dreams," *Adventure! Vol. 1*.

Atkins, Peter, "The Cubist's Attorney," *Darkness Rising* chapbook.

Aulenback, Stephany "Grim Stories," *McSweeney's Internet Tendency*.

——, "More Grim Stories," *McSweeney's Internet Tendency*.

Ayres, Neil, "What's in the Box, Fox," *Whispers of Wickedness*, Autumn.

Baer, Will Christopher, "Deception of the Thrush," *San Francisco Noir*.

Bailly, Sharon, "The Witches of Cairn," *Space and Time*, Spring.

Baker, Kage, "The Two Old Women," *Asimov's*, Feb.

Baldry, Cherith, "The Avowing of Kay," *Paradox* 7.

Ballentine, Lee, "The Double," (poem) *Star*Line*, Nov./Dec.

Ballingrud, Nathan, "SS," *The 3rd Alternative* 41.

Bank, Sybil, "Brother," *Songs of Innocence (and Experience)* 5.

Barber, Peter, "Dust," *Aurealis* 33/34/35.

Barker, Clive, "Haeckel's Tale," *Dark Delicacies*.

Barron, Laird, "The Imago Sequence," (novella) *F&SF*, May.

Barrow, Stuart, "Like Clockwork," *Andromeda Spaceways Inflight Magazine* 18.

Barsotti, Kate, "Wild Roses," (poem) *Chance of a Ghost*.

Bartel, Paul, "Taste of Life," *On Spec*, Spring.

Barzak, Christopher, "The Language of Moths," *Realms of Fantasy*, August.

Bates, Paul, "The Town Crier," *Underworlds* 2.

Battersby, Lee, "Father Muerte and the Rain," *Aurealis* 33/34/35.

Baumer, Jennifer Rachel, "Stone, and Brass," *Not One of Us* 33.

——, "The Last Oracle," *Clarity*, February.

Bear, Elizabeth, "And the Deep Blue Sea," *SCI FICTION*, May 4.

——, "House of the Rising Sun," *The Third Alternative* 42.

——, "Long Cold Day," *SCI FICTION*, September 21.

——, "Wax," *Interzone* 4.

Beatty, Greg, "Doctor Jackman's Lens," *Poe's Progeny*.

Beeman, Michael, "Fifteen Minutes in Huntsville, Texas," *Midnight Street*, Winter.

Bell, Peter, "Only Sleeping," *Acquainted with the Night*.

Bennardo, M., "Nightmare," *Asimov's*, Oct./Nov.

Bennett, Nancy, "Mr. Frost," (poem) *There Is Something in the Autumn*.

——, "Yakshis," (poem) *Spellbound*, Fall.

Bernobich, Beth, "In Late December," (poem) *Lone Star Stories*, Aug.

Bertin, Eddy C., "Dunwich Dreams, Dunwich Screams," *Tales Out of Dunwich*.

Biffar, Donna, "Absent," (poem) *Chance of a Ghost*.

Bobet, Leah, "They Fight Crime," *Strange Horizons*, October 10.

Black, Terry, "Cold Fever," *Not One of us* 33.

Borneman, John & Moyer, Jaime Lee, "Minotaur," (poem) *Magazine of Speculative Poetry*, Spring.

Borneman, John, "Elwin's House," *Andromeda Spaceways Inflight Magazine* 21.

Boston, Bruce, "Bone People," (poem) *Inhuman* 3.

——, "Night Eyes," *Book of Dark Wisdom* 7.

——, "Puppet People," (poem) *Aeon Speculative Fiction* 4.

——, "The Glance of Mutant Eyes," (poem) *The Fifth Dimension*, Sept.

——, "When the Carnival Spills . . ." *Vestal Review*, October.

——, "White Whales," (poem) *Chizine* 25.

Bowen, Hanna Wolf, "Under the Bridge," *Chizine* 23.

——, "The Midnight Train, She'll Take You There," *Chizine* 25.

Bowen, Rhys, "The Wall," *Alfred Hitchcock's Mystery Magazine*, July/Aug.

Bowes, Richard, "Circle Dance," *Postscripts* 3.

——, "There's a Hole in the City," *SCI FICTION* June 15.

Bradley, Lisa M., "Healing Ritual" (poem), *Mythic Delirium* 13.

Brandt, Jonathan, "Dinner Shift," *Electric Velocipede* 8.

Braum, Daniel, "Ghost Dance," Ibid.

Braunbeck, Gary A., "Kiss of the Mudman," (novella) *Home Before Dark*.

——, *In the Midnight Museum*, (novella) chapbook.

——, "Need," *Corpse Blossoms*.

——, *We Now Pause for Station Identification*, chapbook.

Brenchley, Chaz, "Another Chart of the Silences," *Phantoms at the Phil*.

Brennan, Marie, "Shadow's Bride," *Shadow Box* CD-Rom.

Brennan, Tom, "Simon Says," *Brutarian* #45.

Brown, John, "Bright Waters," *Lady Churchill's Rosebud Wristlet* 17.

Brown, Simon, "Leviathan," *Eidolon* online.

Brown-Davidson, Terri, "Red Coat," *NFG Magazine* Issue 6 Volume 2.

Browne, Adam, "Heart of Saturday Night," *Lenox Avenue* 4.

Bryan, Eric, "The 'bility," *All Hallows* 39.

Budnitz, Judy, "Sales," *McSweeney's* 15, *Nice Big American Baby*.

——, "Where We Come From," *Nice Big American Baby*.

Burch, Michael, "Something," (poem) *There Is Something in the Autumn*.

Burke, John, "The Bite of the Tawse," *Don't Turn Out the Light*.

Burke, Kealan Patrick, "Empathy," *Corpse Blossoms*.

——, "The Grief Frequency," *Cemetery Dance* #52.

——, "Tonight the Moon is Ours," *Inhuman* 3.

Burleson, Donald R., "Papa Loaty," (novella) *Poe's Progeny*.

Burrage, Nathan, "Blurring," *Shadow Box* CD-Rom.

Burton, Jeffrey B., "The Acceptance," *Shadow Play*.

Byrne, Elena Karina, "Mask of Insomnia," (poem) *Chance of a Ghost*.

Cacek, P. D., "The Lingering Scent of Apples," *Taverns of the Dead*.

Cadnum, Michael, "Hazard," *Cemetery Dance* #53.

Campbell, Ramsey, "Breaking Up," *Acquainted with the Night*.

——, "Just Behind You," *Poe's Progeny*.

——, "Skeleton Woods," *Corpse Blossoms*.

——, "The Winner," *Taverns of the Dead*.

——, "Unblinking," *Lost on the Darkside*.

Campisi, Stephanie, "Gloves," *Borderlands* 4.

Cancilla, Dominick, "Josh's Collection," *Cemetery Dance* #53.

Canfie, Michael, "Flight to L.A.," *Flytrap* 4.

——, "Peas and Carrots," *Realms of Fantasy*, February.

——, "Wednesday," *Corpse Blossoms*.

Carl, William D., "Cunt," *Chimeraworld* #2.

Carr, Von, "East of the Sun, West of the Moon," *Son and Foe* 1.

Carroll, David, "The Grail," *Ticonderoga Online*, December.

Carroll, Jonathan, "Home on the Rain," *Conjunctions* 44.

Castle, Mort, "As Others See Us," World Horror Convention 2005 program book.

Castro, Adam-Troy, "Good for the Soul," *Cemetery Dance* #53.

Chan, David Marshall, "Memoirs of a Boy Detective," *Conjunctions* 45.

Chappell, Fred, "The Invading Spirit," *Weird Tales* #337.

Charles, Renée M., "The Twelve Nights of Callicantzaros," *Blood Surrender*.

——, "The Twelve Nights of Callicantzaros," Ibid.

Cheney, Matthew, "Variables," *Abyss & Apex* 13.

Chiaki, Konaka, "Terror Rate," *Inverted Kingdom*.

Cimo, Deborah, "Sacrifice," (poem) *Star*Line*, May/June.

Clark, Simon, "The House that Fell Backward," *Hotel Midnight*.

——, "Jack of Bones," Ibid.

——, "Langthwaite Road," (novella) *Fourbodings*.

——, "One Man Show," *Poe's Progeny*.

Clarke, Brock, "We Found Ourselves in Toronto," *Land-Grant College Review* 3.

Cleary, David Ira, "The Face of America," *Interzone* 196.

Clibborn, Benedict, "Hope End," *All Hallows*, 39.

Coates, Deborah, "Magic in a Certain Slant of Light," *Strange Horizons*, March 21.

Cockburn, D. J., "Summer Holidays," *Albedo One* Issue 29.

Cockle, Kevin, "Rat Patrol," *On Spec*, Summer.

Collier, Michael, "About the Moth," (poem) *New England Review*, Vol. 26, No. 4.

Colangelo, Michael R., "The God of Dust," *Fear of the Unknown: The Harrow Anthology*.

Collins, Merle, "The Wealth of Dreams," *Triquarterly* 120.

Condor, Jacques L., "Them," *Northwest Passages: A Cascadian Anthology*.

Constantine, Pamela, "Never Again," (poem) *There Is Something in the Autumn*.

Coombes, Mike, "Strange Love, Doctor," *NFG Mag.* Issue 6, Vol. 2.

Cooper, Brenda, "The Lingering Scent of Bacon," *Maiden, Matron, Crone*.

Cooper, Constance, "How the Sea People Mourn," (poem) *Mythic Delirium* 13.

Coover, Robert, "Grandmother's Nose," *A Child Again*.

——, "The Return of the Dark Children," Ibid.

Cowdrey, Albert E., "The Housewarming," *F&SF*, September.

Cox, Edward, "Nobody's Fool," *Shimmer* 1.

Crandall, Edward P., "Survivors," *Acquainted with the Night*.

Crawford, Dan, "Yellow Leaves," *AHMM*

Crisp, Quentin S., "Asking for It," *Chimeraworld* #2.

Crow, Jennifer, "Hedge Witch," (poem) *Magazine of Speculative Poetry*, Spring.

Crowther, Peter, "Thoughtful Breaths," *Subterranean* 1.

Cummings, Shane Jiraiya, "Cruel Summer (Sky)" *Shadow Box* CDR.

——, "Hear No Evil," *Borderlands* 4.

——, "Ian," *Ticonderoga Online*, September.

Cunningham, Michael, "In the Machine," (novella) *Specimen Days*.

Curran, Tim, "The Eyes of Howard Curlix," *Horrors Beyond*.

——, "Please Stand By," *Book of Dark Wisdom* 7.

Cythera, "White-Snow, A Tale With Elizabeth Bathory," (poem) *Dreams & Nightmares* 72.

D'Ammassa, Don, "Growing Old Together," *Inhuman* 2.

Daldorph, Brian, "The Augusta House," (poem) *Chance of a Ghost*.

Davidson, Craig, "The Apprentice's Guide to Modern Magic," *Rust and Bone*.

——, "A Mean Utility," Ibid.

Davidson, Rjurik, "The Interminable Suffering of Mysterious Mr. Wu," *Aurealis* 33/34/35.

De La Rosa, Becca, "The Fall of the Changes," *Strange Horizon*, Aug. 8.

de Lint, Charles, "The World in a Box," *Subterranean* 2.

Dedman, Stephen, "Watch," *Never Seen by Waking Eyes*.

DeLuca, Sandra and McCarty, Michael, "Mira," *Dark Duets*.

Di Filippo, Paul, "Eel Pie Stall," *Adventure, Volume 1*.

——, "The Emperor of Gondwanaland," *The Emperor of Gondwanaland and Other Stories*.

Dicks, Ainsley, "In Grandmother's House," *Jabberwocky* 1.

Dinniman, Matt, "Hurricane Bonnie," *Trailer Park Fairy Tales*.

Disch, Thomas M., "The Wall of America," *F&SF*, March.
Dodds, John, "The Anatomy of Seahorses," *The Horror Express* 4.
Donihe, Kevin, "Others," (poem) *Not One of Us* 33.
Dore, Deirdre, "A Glimmering," (poem) *Chance of a Ghost.*
Dornemann, Rudi, "The Sky Green Box," *Rabid Transit: Menagerie.*
———, "The Tenth Hat," *Spirits Unwrapped.*
Dorsey, Candas Jane, "Mom and Mother Theresa," *Tesseracts* 9.
Doyle, Christopher Kritwise, "The Missing Scroll," *Margin*, Autumn.
Duffy, Steve "Secrets of the Beehive," *Darkness Rising 2005.*
———, "Someone Across the Way," *Acquainted with the Night.*
Dugan, Grace, "The Devil Behind the Louvres," *The Devil in Brisbane.*
Dumars, Denise, "Remnants," (poem) *Star*Line*, Nov./Dec.
Dunbar, Robert, "Mal de Mer," *Bare Bone* 8.
Duncan, Hal, "The Chiaroscurist," *Electric Velocipede* 9.
———, "The Disappearance of James H___," *Strange Horizons*, June 13.
Dunlap, Kelli, "Victims," (poem) *Poe Little Thing* 3.
Duthie, Peg, "The Stepsister," (poem) *Magazine of Speculative Poetry*, Spring.
Eberhart, John Mark, "Just One Ghost," (poem) *Chance of a Ghost.*
Edwards, Graham, "Dead Wolf in a Hat," *Realms of Fantasy*, October.
———, "The Wooden Baby," *Realms of Fantasy*, April.
Edwards, Melanie, "Fragile: This Side Up," *Michigan Quarterly Review, Fall.*
Edwards, Paul, "Highways," *Midnight Street*, Spring.
Emerson, Efrem, "Grandmother's Body," *The Unauthorized Woman.*
Emshwiller, Carol, "I Live with You," *F&SF*, March.
Erpenbeck, Jenny, "The Old Child," (novella) *The Old Child.*
———, "The Sun-Flecked Shadows of my Skull," Ibid.
Esposito, Patricia J. "His Wounds," *Not One of Us* 34.
Evenson, Brian, "Mudder Tongue," *McSweeney's* 16.
———, "Younger," *Conjunctions* 45.
Everding, Kelly, "Beliefs Concerning Eggs," (poem) *Strappado for the Devil.*
Everson, John, "The Strong Will Survive," *Space and Time*, Spring.
Every, Gary, "Papago War Song," (poem) *Dreams & Nightmares* 71.
Ezzo, Joseph V., "Vado Mori," *Acquainted with the Night.*
Farris, John, "The Ransome Women," (novella) *Transgressions.*
Felps, Mark, "Harvest Girl," *Revenant.*
Ferguson, Andrew C., "Sophie and the Sacred Fluids," *Nova Scotia.*
Files, Gemma, "Song to the Selkie," (poem) *Jabberwocky.*
Finch, Paul, "The Belfries," *Acquainted with the Night.*
———, "The Black Wood of Sylburn," *Supernatural Tales* 9.
———, "Calibos," *Daikaiju!: Giant Monster Tales.*
———, "Down in the Dying-Rooms," *Dark Discoveries*, Summer.
———, "Evil Monsters," *Midnight Street*, Winter.
———, "The Gods of Green and Gray," *Paradox* 7.
———, "Hobhook," *Bernie Herrmann's Manic Sextet.*
Finlay, Charles Coleman, "The Nursemaid's Suitor," *Black Gate* 8.
———, Of Silence and the Man at Arms, *F&SF*, June.
Finley, Toiya Kristen, "7:33," *The Elastic Book of Numbers.*
———, "Juju Hoodoo Man Sangs the Blues," *TEL: Stories.*
Fletcher, Kay, "Next to Godliness," *All Hallows* 40.
Foley, Tim, "On the Pier at Midnight," *All Hallows* 39.

Forbes, Amy Beth, "A Bedtime Story for the Disenchanted, *Realms of Fantasy*, August.

Ford, Adam, "Seven Dates That Were Ruined by Giant Monsters," *Daikaiju!*.

Ford, Jeffrey, "A Man of Light," *SCI FICTION*, January 26.

——, "Giant Land," *Journal of Pulse-Pounding Narratives* 2.

Ford, John B., "A Box Full of Nightmares," *Penny Dreadful* 15.

Foster, Eugie, "The Bunny of Vengeance and the Bear of Death," *Fantasy Magazine* 1.

——, "Returning My Sister's Face," *Realms of Fantasy*, February.

——, "The Tiger Fortune Princess," *Paradox* 7.

Frances, Mary, "Aunt Concetta's Cat," *Invisible Pleasures*.

Francis, Diana Pharaoh, "Native Spinsters," *Lady Churchill's Rosebud Wristlet* 17.

Francis, Matthew, "The Vegetable Lamb," *The 3rd Alternative* 42.

Franklin, Bob, "The Snow Globe," *All Hallows* 40.

Frazier, Timalyne, "The Devil's Half-Brother," *TEL: Stories*.

Freeman, Brian, "Running Rain," *Corpse Blossoms*.

Fry, Gary, "0.05," *Bare Bone #7*.

——, "At Issue," *Midnight Street*, Summer.

Fry, Susan, "Twenty-Dollars," *Crimewave 8: Cold Harbors*.

Fulbright, Christopher, "A Twist of Hate," *The Blackest Death, Vol. II*.

Fumio, Tanaka, "Secrets of the Abyss," *Inverted Kingdom*.

Fuqua, C. S., "Contact is Everything," *Bare Bone #8*.

Gailey, Jeanine Hall, "The Haunting," (poem) *Female Comic Book Superheroes*.

——, "Instructions (in the Event of My Death)," (poem) Ibid.

——, "Okay, Ophelia," (poem) Ibid.

——, "Persephone and the Prince Meet over Drinks," (poem) Ibid.

Gaiman, Neil, "Sunbird," *Noisy Outlaws, Unfriendly Blobs*, etc.

Gallagher, John, "Ghost Children," (poem) *Southern Review*, Summer.

Garcia, Victoria Elizabeth, "Ask for Her Hand," *The Nine Muses*.

Garrott, Lila, "Old Storm Shadow," (poem) *Jabberwocky*.

Garton, Ray, "Glory Hole," *Where's Bobo?/Glory Hole* (chapbook).

Gates-Grimwood, Terry, "Soul Money," *Dark Animus #7*.

Gavin, Richard, "The Pale Lover," *Poe's Progeny*.

Gedge, Sue, "Never Speak Ill of the Dead," *All Hallows* 38.

Geiger, Barbara, "Little Black Boxes," *Apex*, Autumn.

Gerrold, David, "Chester," *F&SF*, June.

Gidney, Craig Laurance, "The Safety of Thorns," *Say . . . Have You Heard This One?*.

Goldbarth, Albert, "Why I Believe in Ghosts," (poem) *Chance of a Ghost*.

Golaski, Adam, "The Demon," *Supernatural Tales* 9.

——, "Weird Furka," *Acquainted with the Night*.

Goldbarth, Albert, "Why I Believe in Ghosts," (poem) *Chance of a Ghost*.

Goodfellow, Cody, "A Drop of Ruby." *The 3rd Alternative*, Spring.

Gorman, Ed, "Your World, and Welcome to It," *All Hell Breaking Loose*.

Goss, Theodora, "The Belt," *Flytrap* 4.

——, "Pip and the Fairies," *Strange Horizons*, October 3.

Gould, Steven and Harper, Rory, "Leonardo's Hands," *Revolution SF*, July.

Grabinski, Stefan, "Engine Driver Grot," *The Motion Demon*.

——, "Signals," *The Motion Demon*.

Graham, Seana, "The Pirate's True Love," *Lady Churchill's Rosebud Wristlet* 17.

Grant, Gavin J., "Heads Down, Thumbs Up," *SCI FICTION*, April 27.

Grant, Helen, "Nathair Dhubh," *All Hallows* 39.

Greenhut, Michael, "Son of Shadow," (poem) *Dreams and Nightmares* 71.

Grey, G.L., "Wonderful Spares," *Margin*, Autumn.

Grimes, Kate, "Whales," *Full Unit Hookup* 7.

Groome, Tim, J., "The Hollow Heart," *Darkness Rising 2005*.

Guill, Jane, "No One Marks My Passage," *Fantastical Visions III*.

Hand, Elizabeth, "Calypso In Berlin," *SCI FICTION*, July 13.

Hardy, K. S., "Land of Night," (poem) *Not One of Us* 33.

Harland, Richard, "The Greater Death of Saito Saku," *Daikaiju!*.

Harmon, Christopher, "Hill Shadows" *All Hallows* 40.

———, "The Listener," *Acquainted with the Night*.

Harper, Rory, "Tell," *Revolution SF*, November.

Harris, James, "Maternal Whispers," *Whispers of Wickedness*, Summer.

Haskell, Merrie, "Huntswoman," *Strange Horizons*, January 24.

Hatcher, Tim, "Maternal Instinct," *Circles in the Hair*.

Hayes, Sam, "Sixty Thousand Pieces of Glass," *The Elastic Book of Numbers*.

Henderson, C.J., "Nothing to Fear But Dust," (novella) *The Tales of Inspector Legrasse*.

———, "Patiently Waiting," Ibid.

———, "To Cast Out Fear," Ibid.

———, "Where Shadow Falls," (novella) Ibid.

Henderson, Mark P., "Rope Trick," *Acquainted with the Night*.

Henderson, Samantha, "Manuscript Found Written in the Paw Prints of a Stoat," *Lone Star Stories* 8.

———, The Passion (poem), *Neverary* 8.

Henricksen, Bruce, "Solitude," (poem) *Chance of a Ghost*.

Henry, Nancy A., "1742," (poem) *Penny Dreadful* 15.

Herter, David, "Black and Green and Gold," *Postscripts* 3.

Hill, Gregory, "Louisa/Louella," *Aurealis* #33/34/35.

Hill, Joe, "Best New Horror," *Postscripts* 3.

———, "The Cape," *Twentieth Century Ghosts*.

———, "In the Rundown," *Crime Wave* 8.

———, "Last Breath," *Subterranean* 2.

———, "My Father's Mask," *Twentieth Century Ghosts*.

———, "Voluntary Committal," (novella) Subterranean Press chapbook.

Hirshberg, Glen, "Safety Clowns," *Acquainted with the Night*.

Hobson, M.K., "Domovoi," *F&SF*, April.

———, "Hippocampus," *Chizine* 24.

Hoffmeister, Curtis, "Jade," *Thicker than Water*.

Hoing, Dave, "Kivam," *Interzone* 197.

Holder, Nancy, "Out Twelve-Steppin', Summer of AA," *Dark Delicacies*.

Holm, Catherine Dybiec, "Mau," *Spirits Unwrapped*.

Hood, Martha A., "See How She Dances," *Tales of the Unanticipated* 26.

Hook, Andrew, "The Honey Ward," *Beyond Each Blue Horizon*.

Houarner, Gerard, "The Blind," *Horrors Beyond*.

———, "The Crawl," *Lost on the Darkside*.

Howkins, Elizabeth, "Dead Blossoms," (poem) *Penny Dreadful* 15.

— — —, "The Devouring," (poem) Ibid.

———, "Fantôme," (poem) Ibid.

Hoyt, Sarah A., "Something Worse Hereafter," *All Hell Breaking Loose*.

Hughes, Matthew, "The Gist Hunter," *F&SF*, June.

Hughes, Rhys, "The Hydrothermal Reich," *Bernie Herrmann's Manic Sextet*.

Humphrey, Andrew, "Think of a Number," *Crimewave 8*.

Hunter, Rob, "Boys Night Out," *On Spec*, Summer.

Ireland, Davin, "The List," *Underworlds* 2.

Irvine, Alexander, "The Golems of Detroit," *F&SF*, May.

Jacob, Charlee, "Crave," (poem) *Sineater*.

——, "Eternity in the 9 Square Feet off the Upstairs Hallway," (poem) *Sineater*.

——, "Gein," (poem) *Bare Bone* #7.

——, "The Gulf," (poem) *Sineater*.

——, "Harbor," (poem) Ibid.

——, "Octave," (poem) Ibid.

——, "Pale Girl," (poem) *Chizine* 23.

——, "Rotkappchen," (poem) *Sineater*

——, "Sun Setting on a Thousand Hangings," (poem) Ibid.

Jacob, Charlee, "Wormwood Nights," (novella) chapbook.

Jacobstein, Roy, "Scariest Movie," (poem) *Prairie Schooner*, Fall.

Jamieson, Trent, "Downfall," *Shadow Box* CD-Rom.

Jasper, Michael, "An Outrider's Tale," *Gunning for the Buddha*.

——, "Black Angels," Ibid.

Jasper, Michael and van Eekhout, Greg, "California King," *Asimov's*, April/May.

Jasper, Michael & Pratt, Tim & van Eekhout, Greg, "*Gillian* Underground," *Polyphony* 5.

Jasso, Carmen, "Animal," *Triskaideka*.

Jennings, A. H., "Owasa," *FarThing*, July.

Jernigan, Amanda, "Lullaby," (poem) *Poetry*, December.

Jerome, Jennifer, "Tender," (poem) *Chizine* 23.

Johnson, Jaleigh, "The House Rules," *Darkness Rising 2005*.

Johnson, Jeremy Robert, "The Gravity of Benham Falls," *Ghosts at the Coast*.

——, "Precedents," *Angel Dust Apocalypse*.

Johnson, Sarah Brandywine, "Hanging the Glass," *Fantasy Magazine*.

Jones, Jaida, "Les Berceaux," (poem) *Mythic Delirium* 13.

Jones, William, "Rawhide and Bloody Bones," *Darkness Rising 2005*.

Justice, Faith L. "Better the Devil," *Circles in the Hair*.

Kasichke, Laura, "Miss Congeniality," (poem) *New England Review* Vol. 26, No. 4.

Katz, David Evans, "Forbidden Waters," *All Hallows* 40.

Kaysen, Daniel, "Torn," *Strange Horizons*, July 11.

Kayson, Daniel, "Four to the Floor," *Deathgrip*.

Kelly, Michael, "When Children Weep," *Book of Dark Wisdom* 6.

Kelly, Robert, "Walking to Auschwitz," (poem) *Conjunctions* 44.

Kemble, Gary, "The House," *Borderlands* 4.

Kennett, Rick, "Coming Home," *All Hallows* 38.

Kesey, Roy, "Asunción," *McSweeney's* 15.

Ketchum, Jack, "Monster," *Horror World*, November.

——, "Seascape," chapbook Shocklines Press.

Kidd, Chico, "Unfinished Business," *Poe's Progeny*.

Kiernan, Caitlín R., "Bradbury Weather," (novella) *Subterranean* 2.

——, "From Cabinet 34, Drawer 6," *Weird Shadows Over Innsmouth*.

——, "La Peau Verte," *To Charles Fort, With Love*.

Kilian, Monica, "Black-Winged Angels," *Margin*, Autumn.

Kilworth, Garry, "Phoenix Man," *Don't Turn Out the Light*.

Kimbrell, James, "Up Late Reading Whitman," (poem) *Kenyon Review*, Summer.

King, Stephen, "The Things They Left Behind," *Transgressions*.

Kirby, David, "Dogs Who Are Poets and Movie Stars," (poem) *Poetry*, July/August.

Kishbaugh, Greg, "Water Babies," *Cemetery Dance* # 52.

Klages, Ellen, "Guys Day Out," *SCI FICTION*, April 13.

Klavan, Andrew, "Her Lord and Master," *Dangerous Women*.

Koplik, Sarah, "The Mummy Speaks," (poem) *Jabberwocky*.

Kushner, Ellen, "Beauty Sleeping," *Parabola*, Spring.

Kwe, Francezka C., "Lovelore," *Philippine Speculative Fiction*, Vol. 1.

La Valley, Dustin, "A Taste for Deformity," *Chimeraworld* # 2.

Laden, Jonathan, "Braids of Glass," *Electric Velocipede* 9.

Laidlaw, Marc, "Jane," *SCI FICTION*, February 16.

——, "Sweetmeats," *F&SF*, June.

Laimo, Michael, " 'Til Death Do They Part," *Inhuman* 2.

——, "Comforts of Home," *Lost on the Darkside*.

Lain, Doug, "The Word 'Mermaid' Written on an Index Card," *The 3rd Alternative* 42.

Lake, Jay "Green," *Aeon SF* 3.

Lake, Jay & Carter, Scott William, "The Man Who Swallowed Mirrors," *Full Unit Hookup* 7.

Lambert, Charles, "The Scent of Cinnamon," *One Story* 64.

——, "The Zero Worm," *The Elastic Book of Numbers*.

Lamsley, Terry, "Sickhouse Hospitality," *Don't Turn Out the Lights*.

——, "So Long Gerry," (novella) *Fourbodings*.

Lane, Joel, "Among the Dead," *Cemetery Dance* # 52.

——, "Beyond the River," *Acquainted with the Night*.

——, "Black Dog," *Crimewave 8: Cold Harbors*.

——, "A Night on Fire," *Poe's Progeny*.

——, "Wake up in Moloch," *Pulp.net*.

Lanham, Carole "Don't Scratch," *Panic*, August

——, "The Good Part," *Trunk Stories #3*.

Lannes, Roberta, "Dès Lors," *Taverns of the Dead*.

——, "The Other Family," *Don't Turn Out the Light*.

Lansdale, Joe R., "The Shadows, Kith and Kin," *Outsiders*.

Le, Doan, "The Cemetery of Chua Village," *The Cemetery of Chua Village and Other Stories*.

Leary, John, "This Global Business," *NFG*, Issue 6 Volume 2.

Lebbon, Tim, "Casting Longer Shadows," *The Horror Express* 4.

——, "A Ripple in the Veil," *Poe's Progeny*.

Lecard, Marc, "Stuff," *All Hallows* 38.

Lee, Tanith, "En Forêt Noire," *Realms of Fantasy*, December.

——, "The Woman in Scarlet," *Lords of Swords*.

Lee, Yoon Ha, "Eating Hearts," *F&SF*, June.

Lees, Tim, "From the House Committee," *Midnight Street*, Summer.

——, "Jinner and the Shambly House," *The Life to Come*.

Leo, Teresa, "The World According to Narcissus," (poem) *Poetry*, June.

Levine, Jeremiah Job, "Skins and Scents," *Animal Magnetism*.

Lilly, Lisa, "The Merger," *Dispatch Litereview*, Issue One.

Lincoln, Natalia, "Expiation," *Circles in the Hair*.

Lindholm, Megan, "Grace Notes," *The Fair Folk*.

Lindy, Robin, "The Blue Room," *All Hallows* 40.

Ling, Samantha, "Waking Chang-er," *Asimov's*, July.

Link, Kelly, "Monster," *Noisy Outlaws, Unfriendly Blobs, and Some Other Things.* . . .

Lister, Sarah, "The Shimmering," *All Hallows* 39.

Little, Bentley, "Finding Father," *Corpse Blossoms*.

Llewellyn, Livia, "Brimstone Orange," *Chizine* 24.

Locascio, Phil, "And the Wind Cried Mary," *Potter's Field*
Lockley, Steve and Lewis, Paul, "Damp," *Chimeraworld # 2.*
Logan, Simon, "Closer to the Lung," *Fantasy Magazine* 1.
——, "Surgery," *Tempting Disaster.*
Long, Laird, "Return of the Warrior," *The Mammoth Book of New Comic Fantasy.*
Lopez III, Aurelio Rico, "Arise," (poem) *Mythic Delirium* 13.
Lovitt, Elaine, "Wire Down," *All Hallows* 38.
Lumley, Brian, "The Taint," (novella) *Weird Shadows Over Innsmouth*
Lundberg, Jason Eric, "Reality, Interrupted," *The 3rd Alternative* 42.
Lupoff, Richard A., "Brackish Waters," *Weird Shadows Over Innsmouth*
——, "The Golden Saint Meets the Scorpion Queen," *Terrors.*
——, "Streamliner," Ibid.
Lynch, Mark Patrick, "Breach of Contract, Clause 6A," *The Elastic Book of Numbers.*
——, "The Rapunzel Field," *Bare Bone* #8.
MacLeod, Catherine, "Assumption," *On Spec*, Winter 2004/2005.
Mamatas, Nick, "Quiet Types, Loners Mostly," darkfluidity.com, April–June.
——, "Real People Slash," *Son and Foe* volume 1, issue 1.
Mancina, Jill, "Iphigenia at Aulis," (poem) *The Maguffin*, Fall.
Marchand, Joy Remy, "Over the River," *Time for Bedlam: A Collection of Cautionary Tales.*
——, "The Sympathy of Five," *The Elastic Book of Numbers.*
Marr, Melissa, "Fighting the Tide," (poem) *Star*Line*, Nov./Dec.
——, "Pixie on a Pin," *Flytrap* 4.
Marshall, Helen, "Mist and Shadows," (poem) *Star*Line*, May/June.
Masahiko, Inoue, "Night Voices, Night Journeys," *Night Voices, Night Journeys.*
Massie, Elizabeth, "Pit Boy," *Outsiders.*
Masterton, Graham, "The Clock and the Cake," (poem) *The Horror Express* 5.
——, "The Press," *Wicked Karnival Halloween Horror.*
McAllister, Bruce, "Ombra," *Glimmer Train*, Winter.
——, "Spell," *F&SF*, August.
——, "Water Angel," *Asimov's* January.
McAuley, Paul, "Take Me to the River," *Weird Shadows Over Innsmouth*
McBride, Michael, "Zero," (novella) *Necessary Evil Books.*
McCarron, Meghan, "Close to You," *Strange Horizons*, April 18.
McDonald, Sandra, "Fir na Tine," *Realms of Fantasy*, February.
——, "The Writer's Orchard," *Fictitious Force* 1.
McFerren, Martha, "Notes of an Unrevealed Nature," (poem) *Chance of a Ghost.*
McKillip, Patricia A., "The Kelpie," *The Fair Folk.*
McMahon, Gary, "The Forgotten Prisoner," *Potter's Field.*
——, "Just Say You Love Me," *Bernie Herrmann's Manic Sextet.*
——, "New Science," *Nemonymous* 5.
——, "Out on a Limb," *Acquainted with the Night.*
McQuerry, Maureen, "Green Man," (poem) *The Magazine of Speculative Poetry*, Spring.
——, "Wolf Proof," (poem) Ibid.
McRae, Gordon C., "Spring in the Shadows," *On Spec* 60.
McRennary, Joel, "Sweet as This," *H. P. Lovecraft's Magazine of Horror*, Spring.
Melican, Sean, "Gears Grind Down," *Lady Churchill's Rosebud Wristlet* 16.
Melniczek, Paul, "That Magical Day," *Dark Animus* #7.
Melnis, M. P., "Now We Must Be Going," *Circles in the Hair.*
Meloy, Paul, "Dying in the Arms of Jean Harlow . . ." *The 3rd Alternative* 42.
Meynard, Yves, "Principles of Animal Eugenics," *Tesseracts* 9.

Menon, Anil, "Standard Deviation," *Chizine* 25.

Miéville, China, "Go Between," *Looking for Jake: Stories.*

Miles, Paul O., "Habe Ich Meinen Eigenen Tod Geseh'n (I Have Seen My Own Death)," *Polyphony 5.*

Miller, Deborah J., "Vanilla for the Lady," *Nova Scotia.*

Miller, Kevin James, "Biological," *Deathgrip.*

——, "Journey to an Island of Transformation," (poem) *Star*Line*, Jan./Feb.

Miller, Patricia Cleary, "Photographs of Ghosts," (poem) *Chance of a Ghost.*

Millhauser, Steven, "A Precursor of the Cinema," *McSweeney's* 15.

Mingin, William, "East and West of Nowhere," *Dark Notes From NJ.*

Minier, Samuel, "Fair Day," (poem) *Chizine* 25.

Mirai, Matsuo, "Inverted Kingdom," (novella) *Inverted Kingdom.*

Mitchell, Emily, "Five Serrated Dreams," *Agni Online*, January.

Mitchell, William, "His Wonders of the Deep," *Horrors Beyond.*

Monteleone, Thomas F., "A Fine and Private Place," *Taverns of the Dead.*

Moore, Lorrie, "The Juniper Tree," *The New Yorker*, January 17.

Moore, Nancy Jane, "Dusty Wings," *Polyphony 5.*

Morden, Simon, "Another War," (novella) Telos Publishing Ltd.

Morlan, A. R., "The Anabe Girls," *Challenging Destiny*, December.

Morrell, David, "Time Was," *Taverns of the Dead.*

Morris, James W., "The Mug House," *Zahir*, Issue 7.

Morris, Keith Lee, "The Culvert," *Southern Review*, Spring.

Morris, Neil, "The Last Blowoff," *Dark Notes From NJ.*

Morrish, Robert, "Do the Trains Still Run on Time?" *Cold Flesh.*

Morrissette, Micaela, "Ten O'Clock," *Conjunctions 45.*

Morton, Lisa, "Black Mill Cove," *Dark Delicacies.*

Moser, Elise, "Under the Skin of the Blade," *Descant*, Winter.

Motoi, Murata, "Sacrifice," *Night Voices, Night Journeys*

Murphy, Joe, "The Secret of the Broken Tickers," *Realms of Fantasy*, August.

Murphy, Jr. Robert Emmett, "Banshee," *Circles in the Hair.*

Muslim, Kristine Ong, "The Thin Men," (poem) *Not One of Us* 34.

Nagy, Steve, "A Paradigm of Coats," *Lenox Avenue* 7.

Nayman, Shira, "The House on Kronenstrasse" *The Atlantic Monthly*, 2005 fiction issue.

Nazerian, Vera, "The Slaying of Winter," *Lords of Swords.*

——, "Sun, in Its Copper Season," *Fantasy Magazine* 1.

Nestvold, Ruth, "A Debt to Collect," *Northwest Passages: A Cascadian Anthology.*

——, "Scraps of Eutopia," *The Nine Muses.*

Nevill, Adam L.G., "The Original Occupant," *Bernie Herrmann's Manic Sextet.*

Newman, Kim, "Another Fish Story," *Weird Shadows over Innsmouth*

——, "Richard Riddle, Boy Detective in 'The Case of the Boy Spy," *Adventure Volume 1.*

——, "The Serial Murders," (novella) *SCI FICTION*, October 19.

Newton, Kurt, "Beyond the Stone," (poem) *Life Among the Dream Merchants.*

——, "In Tangled Seines on Slumberous Seas," (poem) Ibid.

——, "The Waiting Room," (poem) Ibid.

Nezhukumatathil, Aimee, "Last Aerogramme to You, With Lizard," (poem), *New England Review*, Vol.26, No.1.

Nicholson, Geoff, "Some Language, Some Nudity," *Black Clock* No. 3.

Nicholson, Scott, "Watermelon," *Cemetery Dance* #51.

Nickels, Tim, "Nest," *The English Soil Society.*

Niles, Steve, "All My Bloody Things," *Dark Delicacies.*

Niven, Larry, "Rhinemaidens," *Asimov's*, January.
O'Connor, Michael, "Shadow of a Summer," *All Hallows* 39.
O'Driscoll, Mike, "The Hurting House," *Poe's Progeny*.
O'Keefe, Claudia, "Black Deer," *F&SF*, April.
——, "Maze of Trees," *F&SF*, August.
O'Leary, Patrick, "The Witch's Hand," *The Infinite Matrix*, February.
Oates, Joyce Carol, "*BD* 11 1 86," *The Atlantic Monthly*, 2005 fiction issue.
——, "The Corn Maiden," (novella) *Transgressions*.
Ochse, Weston W., "Blue Heeler," *IDW Comics*, October.
Ochsner, Gina, "Elegy in Water," *Black Warrior Review* V.31, N.2.
Oliver, Reggie, "The Babe of the Abyss," *The Complete Symphonies of Adolf Hitler*.
——, "Bloody Bill," *IDW Comics*, October.
——, "Difficult People," Ibid.
——, "Lapland Nights," Ibid.
——, "Magus Zoroaster," *All Hallows* 38.
——, "Parma Violets," *The Complete Symphonies of Adolf Hitler*.
——, "The Sermons of Dr. Hodnet," Ibid.
Osamu, Makino, "Necrophalus," *Night Voices, Night Journeys*.
Owens, Simon, "Burying in Eden," *Book of Dark Wisdom* 6.
Owton, Martin and Sebold, Gaie, "A Touch of Crystal," *Black Gate* 9.
Pal, Marie, "Another Door," (poem) *Chance of a Ghost*.
Palahniuk, Chuck, "Exodus," *Haunted*.
——, "Ritual," Ibid.
——, "The Nightmare Box," Ibid.
Paoletti, Marc, "Veils," *The Blackest Death, Volume II*.
Park, Carma Lynn, "Crow Eats Carrion," (poem) *Mythic Delirium* 13.
Parks, Richard, "Empty Places," *Realms of Fantasy*, December.
Parman, Sue, "Listen to the Trees," *Songs of Innocence and Experience*, Issue 5.
Partridge, Norman, "Second Chance," *Subterranean* 1.
Pearce, Edward, "Jenny Gray's House," *Acquainted with the Night*.
Pearson, Stefan, "The Bogle's Bargain," *Nova Scotia*.
Pelan, John, "Crazy Little Thing Called Love," *Acquainted with the Night*.
Pendragon, Michael, "As the Spirit Leads," *Songs of Innocence and Experience*, Issue 5.
——, "Ye Blodded Mone," (poem) *Penny Dreadful* 15.
Percy, Benjamin, "The Woods," *Amazing*, February.
Perry, K. Z., "Five Rivers of Mourning," *Chizine* 23.
——, "One Night, by the Baobob," *Lenox Avenue*, Jan./Feb.
Petty, J. T., "S& Man," *Cemetery Dance* #51.
Pflug, Ursula, "Black Lace," *On Spec* 59.
——, The Eyes of Horus, *The Nine Muses*.
Phillips, Holly, "By the Light of Tomorrow's Sun," *In the Palace of Repose*.
——, "The Lass of Loch Royal," *Jabberwocky*.
——, "One of the Hungry Ones," *In the Palace of Repose*.
——, "The Other Grace," Ibid.
——, Summer Ice, Ibid.
Pi, Tony, "An Enchantment, With Apples," (poem) *On Spec*, Spring.
Piccirilli, Tom, "An Average Insanity, A Common Agony," *Corpse Blossoms*.
——, "Two in the Eyes," *Taverns of the Dead*.
——, "Shadder," *Cemetery Dance* #52.
——, "With Eyes Averted," *All Hell Breaking Loose*.

Pollack, Gillian, "Impractical Magic," *Andromeda Spaceways Inflight Magazine* 17.

Poore, Michael, "The Wooden Mother," *Talebones* 30.

Popkes, Steve, "The Great Caruso," *F&SF*, May.

Porter, Karen R., "The Death," (poem) *Inside the Blood Museum*.

——, "Encounter," (poem) Ibid.

——, "Silk," (poem) *Star*Line*, Nov./Dec.

——, "Temptations," (poem) *Inside the Blood Museum*.

Pratt, Tim, "Bottom Feeding," *Asimov's*, August.

——, "Gulls," *TEL: Stories*.

——, "Lachrymose and the Golden Egg," *Journal of Pulse-Pounding Narratives* 2.

Pratt, Tim & van Eekhout, Greg, "Robots and Falling Hearts," *Realms of Fantasy*, Oct.

Prill, David, "Rocket Fall," *SCI FICTION*, April 6.

Prineas, Sarah, "Winged Victory," *Lone Star Stories* 7.

Prinzmetal, Donna, "What I Tell Myself at 3 A.M.," (poem) *Chance of a Ghost*.

Probert, John Llewellyn, "The Moving Image," *Supernatural Tales* 9.

——, "The Volkendorf Exhibition," *Poe's Progeny*.

Pulker, Donald, "Dial 1-800-2-to-Live," *The Elastic Book of Numbers*.

——, "Forced Perspective," *Bernie Herrmann's Manic Sextet*.

Rabe, Patrick G., "Cloverleaf," *The Wicked Karnival* #4.

Rainey, Stephen Mark, "The Transformer of Worlds," *Daikaiju!*.

Ralston, Jodi, "Duty Bound," *Triskaideka: Thirteen Tales from Midwest Authors*.

Rambo, Cat, "Grandmother's Road Trip," *Chizine* 26.

Rand, Ken, "The Henry and the Martha," *Eon SF* 3.

Rath, Tina, "A Chimaera in My Wardrobe 3: A Strong Look," *Supernatural Tales* 9.

Read, Bill and Jane, "According to Art," *All Hallows* 39.

Redwood, Steve, "Circe's Choice," *The Minotaur in Pamplona*.

——, "Epiphany in the Sun," *Darkness Rising 2005*.

Reed, Kit, "Getting it Back," *Dogs of Truth*.

——, "Song of the Black Dog," *SCI FICTION*, May 18

——, "Spies," *The Nine Muses*.

Reed, Robert, "The Cure," *F&SF*, December.

——, "Pure Vision," *F&SF*, August.

Reese, Jenn, "Tales of the Chinese Zodiac," *Strange Horizons*.

Reeves, Trish, "The Ghost of the Dove," (poem) *Chance of a Ghost*.

Richards, Tony, "Beyond the Western Walls," *Ghost Dance*.

——, "Under the Ice," (novella) Ibid.

——, "What Malcolm Did the Day Before Yesterday," *Midnight Street*, Winter.

Richardson, Robert Burke, "The Coming Years of Good," *On Spec* 62.

Richardson-Bryan, Michael, "Klingon Fairy Tales," *McSweeney's Internet Tendency*

Rickert, M., "Anyway," *SCI FICTION*, August 24.

——, "A Very Little Madness Goes a Long Way," *F&SF*, August.

Riedel, Kate, ". . . And a Pony," *On Spec*, Winter 2004/2005.

——, "Trying to Be kind," *Not One of Us* 33.

Ringler, Chris, "With Me," *Bare Bone* #7.

Rio, Matsudono, "Taste of Snake's Honey," (novella) *Inverted Kingdom*.

River, Uncle, "The Lizard," *Space and Time*, Spring.

Roberts, Andrew, "Lie-Down-Johnny," *Midnight Street*, Spring.

Roberts, Scott, "Blackberry Witch," *Writers of the Future XXI*.

Roden, Barbara, "The Appointed Time," *Supernatural Tales* 9.

Rogers, Stephen D., "Ice Sculptures," *The Meat Socket*, February.

Rosenman, John, "Going Away," *Space and Time*, Spring.

Rossi, Matthew, "Ghosts of Christmas," *Adventure! Volume 1*.

Rowan, Iain, "Driving in Circles," *Nemonymous 5*.

——, "The Turning of the Tiles," *Black Gate* 8.

Royle, Nicholas, "The Family Room," *Taverns of the Dead*.

——, "Sitting Tenant," *Poe's Progeny*.

Ruane, Deirdre, "Lost Things Saved in Boxes," *Interzone* 196.

Rudolph, Mark, "Alternate Ghosts," (poem) *The Magazine of Speculative Poetry* 25.

Rusch, Kristine Kathryn, "Worlds Enough . . . and Time," *Gateways*.

Russell, Karen, "Help Wanted," *Lady Churchill's Rosebud Wristlet*, 15.

——, "Haunting Olivia," *The New Yorker*, June 13 & 20.

Russo, Patricia, "Redemption," *Tales of the Unanticipated* 26.

Ryan, Kay, "Tar Babies," (poem) *Poetry*, April.

Sahu, Cathy, "You Should Have to Live With Yourself," *Acquainted with the Night*.

Salmonson, Jessica Amanda, "A Bottle of Egyptian Night," *Lost on the Darkside*.

Samerdyke, Michael, "After You Come Others," *The Dogtown Review* 2.

Samphire, Patrick, "Crab Apple," *Realms of Fantasy*, February.

——, "The Western Front," *The 3rd Alternative*, Spring.

Samuels, Mark, "Glyphotech," *Lost on the Darkside*.

SanGiovanni, Mary, "Goth and Crow," *Dark Notes From NJ*.

Santalucia, Jason, "The Truth," (poem) *Chance of a Ghost*.

Sarrantonio, Al, "Stars," *Hornets*.

Saunders, George, "ConComm," *The New Yorker*, August 1.

Savage, Ron, "Dating," *Crimewave 8*.

Scalise, Michelle, "The Beautiful Ones," Ibid.

Schaller, Eric, "The Five Cigars of Abu Ali," *SCI FICTION*, January 19.

Schoffstall, John, "Adventures in Dog-Walking in Downtown Philadelphia," *Strange Horizons*, Nov. 7.

Scholes, Ken, "Into the Blank Where Life Is Hurled," *Writers of the Future XXI*.

Schow, David J., "Expanding Your Capabilities Using Frame/Shift™ Mode," *Outsiders*.

——, "The Pyre and Others," *Dark Delicacies*.

Schutz, Aaron, "Moments of Grace," *Realms of Fantasy*, June.

Schwader, Ann K., "Not Fall, but Falling," (poem) *There is Something in the Autumn*.

——, "What Remains," (poem) *The Magazine of Speculative Poetry*, Winter 04–05.

Schwader, Ann K., "In this Season," (poem) *Penny Dreadful* 15.

Schwartz, David J., "A Whole Man," *Talebones* 30.

Schweitzer, Darrell, "The Emperor of the Ancient Word," *Space & Time*, Spring 2005.

Seamon, Tobias, "An Infernal Firmament," (poem) *Star*Line*, May/June.

Sedia, E., "Every Eight and Eleven," *The Elastic Book of Numbers*.

Sedia, Ekaterina, "Kikimora," *Jabberwocky* 1.

Sexton, John W., "Departure of the Seven Selves," (poem) *Vortex*.

Shapiro, Eric, "The Man in the Corner," *Corpse Blossoms*.

Shaw, Melissa Lee, "The Good Doctor," *Realms of Fantasy*, February.

Shawl, Nisi, "Wallamelon," *Eon SF* 3.

Shepard, Lucius, "Abimagique," (novella) *SCI FICTION*, August 3.

Shire, John, "Beneath the Black Tower," *Book of Dark Wisdom* 6.

Shope, Beth, "Dragon's Eye," *Lords of Swords*.

Silhol, Léa, "Under the Needle," *Outsiders*.

Simbulan, Vincent Michael, "In the Arms of Beishu," *Philippine Spec. Fiction* Vol. 1.

Simon, Marge, "A House with Many Openings," (poem) *Dreams and Nightmares* 70.

Simsa, Cyril, "Imbibing History," *Darkness Rising*, 2005.

Sinda, Petri, "The Quiet Agrarian," *Daikaiju!*.

Singleton, George, "Lickers," *Kenyon Review*, Summer.

Skillingstead, Jack, "The Tree," *On Spec*, Fall.

Smith, Michael Marshall, "Fair Exchange," *Weird Shadows Over Innsmouth*.

Smith, Sherwood, "The Hero and the Princess," *Lone Star Stories* 11.

Solomon, Mike, "Alice Blue Gown," *All Hallows* 39.

Somers, Jeff, "The Script," *Bare Bone #7*.

Speegle, Darren, "Hexerei," *Corpse Blossoms*.

——, "Illusions of Amber," *Underworlds* 2.

——, "Lago di Iniquità," *The 3rd Alternative* 42.

——, "Then the Snow Bled In," *Crimewave* 8.

Stallings, A.E., "Triolet on a Line Apocryphally Attributed to Martin Luther," (poem) *Poetry*, April.

Stanchfield, Justin, "Gypsy Wings," *Aeon SF* 5.

Steensland, Mark, "The Book Smeller," *Not One of Us* 34.

Sterling, Bruce, "The Blemmye's Strategem," *F&SF*, Jan.

Stewart, Don, "The Rest-House," *All Hallows* 40.

Straczynski, J. Michael, "The Darkness Between the Stars," *Book of Dark Wisdom* 7.

Strantzas, Simon, "A Chorus of Yesterdays," *All Hallows* 39.

——, "Fading Light," *Bernie Herrmann's Manic Sextet*.

Sullivan, Andrew, "Notes Concerning Events at the Ray Harryhausen Memorial Home for Retired Actors," *Daikaiju!*.

Sussex, Lucy, "Matricide," *SCI FICTION*, February 2.

Taafe, Sonya, "Asleep at Fortune's Wheel," *Zahir* 6.

——, "By Sunlight," *Clarity*, February.

——, "A Ceiling of Amber, a Pavement of Pearl," *Singing Innocence and Experience*.

——, "Doyna For August, and After," (poem) *Postcards from the Province of Hyphens*.

——, "Etemmu," (poem) *Magazine of Speculative Poetry*, Winter 2004–05.

——, "Gintaras," (poem) *Dreams and Nightmares* 70.

——, "Growing Season," (poem) *Magazine of Speculative Poetry*, Autumn.

——, "In Sight of the Seasons," (poem) *Not One of Us* 34.

——, "Little Fix of Friction," *Not One of Us* 33.

——, "Psyche, (poem) *Not One of Us* 33/ *Postcards from the Province of Hyphens*

——, "Salt and No Wounds," (poem) Ibid.

——, "Tarot in the Dungeon," (poem) *Mythic Delirium* 12.

——, "Time May Be," *Singing Innocence and Experience*.

——, "The White Swan," *TEL: Stories*.

Taku, Ashibe, "The Horror in the Kabuki Theater," (novella) *Inverted Kingdom*.

Tambour, Anna, "The Emperor's Backscratcher," *Infinity Plus*.

Tanner, Shei, "Elyssian Village," *Shadow Box* CD-Rom.

Taylor, Eleanor Ross, "In the Churchyard," (poem) *Chance of a Ghost*.

Taylor, Lucy, "A Hymn to Old Gods," *The Silence Between the Screams*.

——, "Into the Cage," Ibid.

——, "The Silence Between the Screams," Ibid.

Taylor, Mervyn, "Ghost Driver," (poem) *Chance of a Ghost*.

Tem, Melanie, "The Country of the Blind," *Outsiders*.

——, "Kristine's Kwiet Korner," *Taverns of the Dead*.

——, "Visits," *Acquainted with the Night*.

Tem, Steve Rasnic, "The Carving," *Argosy Quarterly*, Spring.

——, "The Company You Keep," *Outsiders*.

——, "Friday Nights," *Crimewave 8*.

——, "Inside William James," *Acquainted with the Night*.

——, "Invisible," *SCI FICTION*, March 3.

——, "Mysteries of the Colon," *Corpse Blossoms*.

——, "A Small Room," *Biting Dog Publications* chapbook.

Tennant, Peter, "Waiting for the Seasons to Change," *Darkness Rising 2005*.

Tessier, Suzan, "Neighborhood Watch," *On Spec*, Fall.

Theys, Lydia Fazio, "Elena's Seclusion," *Andromeda Spaceways Inflight Magazine*, 20.

Thomas, Jeffrey, "Behind the Masque," *Lost on the Darkside*.

——, "The Dance of Ugghiutu," *Dark Discoveries*. Spring.

——, "Pink Pills," *Punktown*.

Thomas, M., "Cicada," *Lone Star Stories 8*.

——, "Fire and Ash," *On Spec 62*.

——, "The Tinker's Child," *Aeon SF 4*.

Thomas, Scott, "Four Bronze Sisters," *Westermead*.

——, "Graves for Poems," *Songs of Innocence and Experience*, Issue 5.

Thompson, C. S., "At the Crossroads," *Strange Pleasures 3*.

—— ——, "The Night Wanderer," (poem) *Underworlds 2*.

Thornburg, Mary Patterson, "Darkness and Distance," *Zahir 8*.

Tidhar, Lavie, "The Dope Fiend," SCI FICTION, December 28.

——, "The Heist," *The Horror Express 5*.

——, "An Occupation of Angels," (novella) *Pendragon Press*.

Tierney, Brian, "A Child Born with Wings," *Ninth Letter* Vol. 2, No. 1.

Tobler, E. Catherine, "Vanishing Act," *SCI FICTION*, March 23.

Tomblin, Erik, "Before I Wake," *Darkness Rising 2005*.

——, "Riverside Blues," (novella) Earthling Publications.

Toten, Teresa, "Father's Day," *Secrets*.

Totten, Sarah, "The Pear Thief," *Fantastical Visions III*.

——, "The Teasewater Fire," *The Nine Muses*.

Tremblay, Mildred, "Picasso," (poem) *On Spec 62*.

Tucker, Diane, "I Know What I Know," (poem) Ibid.

Tumasonis, Don, "A Pace of Change," *Acquainted with the Night*.

Turgeon, Janelle, "An Eye for an Eye," *Son and Foe 1*.

Tyler, Kathleen, "At Port Mayaca Cemetery," (poem) *Chance of a Ghost*.

Underwood, Iris Lee, "Concentration Camp," (poem) *The Maguffin*, Fall.

——, "The Veil," (poem) Ibid.

Valente, Catherynne M., "Apocrypha," (poem) *Apocrypha*.

——, "Bones Like Black Sugar," *Fantasy Magazine 1*.

——, "Cardinales Virtutes," (poem) *Apocrypha*.

——, "The Ice Puzzle," *Jabberwocky 1*.

——, "Mother is a Machine," Ibid.

——, "The Oracle at Detroit," (poem) *Oracles: A Pilgrimage*.

——, "The Oracle at Miami," (poem) Ibid.

——, "The Oracle in Motion," (poem) Ibid.

——, "The Queen of Hearts," (poem) *Mythic Delirium 13*.

——, "Red Sevens," (poem) *Apocrypha*.

——, "Song for Three Voices and a Lyre," (poem) Ibid.

——, "Tokyo Transit Dream," (poem) Ibid.

——, "Z" (poem) Ibid.
Vanderhooft, JoSelle, "Helen," (poem), *Jabberwocky* 1.
——, "Joan," (poem) *Star*Line*, Nov./Dec.
VanderMeer, Jeff, "The Farmer's Cat," *Polyphony* 5.
——, "The Secret Life of Bob Scheffel," *Flytrap* 4.
Vaughn, Carrie, "Draw thy Breath in Pain," *Paradox* 8.
Vernon, Steve, "The Last Few Curls of Gut Rope," *Corpse Blossoms*.
Volk, Stephen, "The Good Unknown," *Poe's Progeny*.
——, "Three Fingers, One Thumb," *Acquainted with the Night*.
——, "Time Capsule," *Crimewave* 8.
Vukcevich, Ray, "Take the Stairs," *Talebones* 30.
——, "Tongues," *Polyphony* 5.
Wadholm, Rick, "The Hottest Night of the Summer," Ibid.
Waldrop, Howard, "The King of Where-I-Go," *SCI FICTION*, Dec. 7.
Wallace, Elsa, "The Amelie Boys," *All Hallows* 38.
Waltari, Satu, "The Monster," *The Dedalus Book of Finnish Fantasy*.
Warburton, Geoffrey, "Campion and the Demon Boy," *Albedo One*, Issue 30.
Ward, Kyla, "The Oracle of Brick and Bone," *Borderlands* 5.
Wardle, Susan, "Green Fingers," *Fables & Reflections* 7.
Warren, Kaaron, "Doll Money," Ibid.
——, "Fresh Young Widow," *The Grinding House*.
——, "The Grinding House," (novella) Ibid.
——, "The Smell of Mice," Ibid.
——, "Smoko," Ibid.
Wasserman, Jamie, "The Rainmaker," (poem) *Magazine of Speculative Poetry*, Spring.
Watkins, William John, "Senjin's Enlightenment," *Black Gate* 9.
Weatherford, Margaret, "East of the 5, South of the 10," *Zyzzyva*, Fall.
Weinberg, Robert, "Kiss Me Deadly," *The Occult Detective*.
Welles, Harvey and Raines, Philip, "Red Shoes," *Aurealis* #33/34/35.
Westwood, Kim, "Haberdashery," *The Devil in Brisbane*.
Wexler, Robert Freeman, "The Green Wall," *Polyphony* 5.
Whalley, Jo-Ann, "The Seasonal Collector," *Borderlands* 4.
What, Leslie, "Dead Men on Vacation," *Asimov's*, February.
——, "Nature Mort," *Polyphony* 5.
Whitbourn, John, "The Sunken Garden," *Acquainted with the Night*.
White, Wrath James, "Resurrection Day," *The Book of a Thousand Sins*.
Whitman, David, "Body Counting," *Body Counting*.
Williams, Conrad, "Once Seen," *Poe's Progeny*.
——, "The Return," *The 3rd Alternative*, Spring.
Williams, Liz, "Ikiryoh," *Asimov's SF*, December.
——, La Gran Muerte, *Asimov's SF*, April/May.
——, "La Malcontenta," *Strange Horizons*, March 7.
——, "Mortegarde," *Realms of Fantasy*, December.
Williamson, Chet, "The Smoke in Mooney's Pub," *Taverns of the Dead*.
Williamson, Neil, "Harrowfield," *Dark Horizons* 47.
——, "The One Millionth Smile," *The Elastic Book of Numbers*.
——, "Well Tempered," *Nemonymous* 5.
Willis, Connie, "Inside Job," *Asimov's*, January.
Wilner, Eleanor, "Establishment," (poem) *Kenyon Review*, Fall.

Wiloch, Thomas, "Dissection," (poem) *Stigmata Junction*.

Wilson, David Niall, "Burning Bridges," *All Hell Breaking Loose*.

———, "The Call of Farther Shores," *Lost on the Darkside*.

———, "Ennui," amazon shorts.

Wilson, Stephen M., "Dream Caused by the Flight of a Bee Around a Pomegranate," *Chizine* 26.

Witchey, Eric M., "The Fix in Mr. Giovelli's Bandit," *Ghosts at the Coast*.

Wittman, Jason D., "A Game of Knight Court," *Andromeda Spaceways Inflight Magazine*, 17.

Wolfe, Gene, "The Card," *Asimov's*, March.

———, "The Gunner's Mate," *F&SF*, Oct./Nov.

———, "The Vampire's Kiss," *Realms of Fantasy*, April.

Wood, Doug, "Lullabye," *Daikaiju!*.

Wood, Peter H., "The Labyrinth," *All Hallows* 40.

Wood, Simon, "Traffic School," *Horror World*, September.

Woodbury, Katherine, "Lodging," *Talebones* 31.

Woods, Sharon E., "Follow Me, Flood," *Spirits Unwrapped*.

———, "The Harps of the Titans," *Fictitious Force* 1.

Workman, Athena, "La Noche de Duelo," (poem) *Neverary*, April.

———, "Winter's Dark Memory," (novella) *Darkness Rising 2005*.

Worthen, Mark, "The Carrion Bird, the Angel of Death, and Me," *Thicker than Water*.

———, "The Minimart, the Ruger, and the Girl," Ibid.

Wrede, Patricia C., "Cruel Sisters," *Book of Enchantments*.

Wright, T. M., "The Eye of the Carp," (novella) Cemetery Dance Publications.

Yolen, Jane, "Black Dog Times," (poem) *Jabberwocky* 1.

———, "A Knot of Toads," *Nova Scotia/Realms of Fantasy*, December.

Youmans, Marly, "The Girl in the Fabrilon," *SCI FICTION*, May 11.

———, "Nesting Dolls," (poem) McSweeney's Internet Tendency.

Youn, Monica, "Ignatz in Pursuit," (poem) *Columbia* 41.

Young, Michael T., "A Haunted Landscape," (poem) *Chance of Ghost*.

Zambreno, Mary Frances, "Aunt Concetta's Cat," *Invisible Pleasures*.

Zeta, Marco, "Mary's Kiss," *Outer Darkness* Issue 31.

Zimmerman, Chanda K., "Perchance to Dream," *Triskaideka*.

Zivkovic, Zoran, "The Hospital Room," *Postscripts* 5.

Zwiker, Jason A., "Fairest," *All Hallows* 38.

———, Driving in Circles, *Nemonymous* 5.

The People Behind the Book

Kelly Link and **Gavin J. Grant** started Small Beer Press in 2000. They have published the zine *Lady Churchill's Rosebud Wristlet* ("tiny, but celebrated"—*Washington Post*) for eight years. With Ellen Datlow they won the Bram Stoker Award for editing *The Year's Best Fantasy and Horror: Seventeenth Annual Edition*.

Kelly Link is the author of two collections, *Stranger Things Happen*, and *Magic For Beginners* (one of TIME *Magazine's Best Books of the Year*). She edited the anthology *Trampoline*. Stories from her collections have won the Nebula, Hugo, World Fantasy, Tiptree, and Locus awards, and her work has recently appeared in *A Public Space*, *Firebirds Rising*, and *Best American Short Stories 2005*.

Originally from Scotland, Gavin J. Grant regularly reviews fantasy and science fiction. He cohosts the Fantastic Fiction Reading Series with Ellen Datlow at KGB Bar in New York City. Publications where his work has appeared include *Los Angeles Times*, *BookPage*, *SCI FICTION*, *Strange Horizons*, *Polyphony*, and *The 3rd Alternative*.

Horror Editor **Ellen Datlow** was the editor of the multi–award-winning website *SCI FICTION* for six years. She was fiction editor of *OMNI* magazine for seventeen years, and has nominated numerous anthologies, including *Vanishing Acts* and *The Dark*. She has also collaborated with Terri Windling on the first sixteen volumes of *The Year's Best Fantasy and Horror*, *Sirens*, the six volume *Snow White, Blood Red* adult fairy tale series, *A Wolf at the Door*, *Swan Sister*, *The Green Man*, and *The Faery Reel*. She has won many awards for her editing, including seven World Fantasy Awards, the International Horror Guild Award, two Bram Stoker Awards, three Locus Awards, and three Hugo Awards (one for the *SCI FICTION* Web site). She lives in New York City. Her Web site is www.datlow.com

Media critic **Edward Bryant** is an award-winning author of science fiction, fantasy, and horror, having published short fiction in countless anthologies and magazines. He's won the Nebula Award for his science fiction, and other works of his short fiction have been nominated for many other awards. He's also written for television. He lives in Denver, Colorado. His story collection *Flirting With Death* (Cemetery Dance Publications) will be published soon.

Comics critic **Charles Vess**'s art has graced the pages of numerous comic and illustrated books for over twenty-five years. His comicscwork has appeared in, among other publications, *Spider-man*, *The Sandman*, *The Books of Magic* and his own self-published *The Book of Ballads and Sagas* and have earned him two Will Eisner Comic Industry awards. In 1999, Charles received the World Fantasy Award for Best

Artist for his illustrations in *Neil Gaiman and Charles Vess's Stardust*. For current information, visit his Web site: www.greenmanpress.com. He lives amidst the Appalachian Mountains in southwest Virginia and enjoys his "simple" life very much.

Anime and manga critic **Joan D. Vinge** is the two-time Hugo Award–winning author of the *Snow Queen* cycle and the Cat books. Her most recent novel is *Tangled Up in Blue*, a novel in the Snow Queen universe. Her novels *Catspaw*, *The Summer Queen*, and *Dreamfall* have recently been reprinted by Tor Books. She's working on *LadySmith*, a "prehistorical" novel set in bronze-age Western Europe. She lives in Madison, Wisconsin.

Charles de Lint is a full-time writer and musician who presently makes his home in Ottawa, Canada, with his wife MaryAnn Harris, an artist and musician. His most recent novels are *The Blue Girl* and *Widdershins*. Other recent publications include the collections *Triskell Tales 2* and *The Hour Before Dawn*. For more information about his work, visit his website at <www.charlesdelint.com>.

Series jacket artist **Thomas Canty** has won the World Fantasy Award for Best Artist. He has painted and/or designed covers for many books, and has art-directed many other covers, in a career that spans more than twenty years. He lives outside Boston, Massachusetts.

Packager **James Frenkel**, a book editor since 1971, has been an editor for Tor Books since 1983, and is currently a Senior Editor. He has also edited various anthologies, including *True Names and the Opening of the Cyberspace Frontier*, *Technohorror*, and *Bangs and Whimpers*. He lives in Madison, Wisconsin.